a kiss
for you

K.A. LINDE • RACHEL VAN DYKEN
T.M. FRAZIER • STACI HART

the wright
brother

K.A. LINDE

To Rebecca Kimmerling,
for every wonderful book you've helped me with
and a million more to follow.

chapter
one

Emery

ROLLED MY SHOULDERS TWICE AND YAWNED. I HATED BEING AT THE OFFICE THIS early. It was mind-numbing, but at least I got to see Mitch. He didn't have class for another hour, and I figured we could use that time to get some coffee...or just occupy his office. I could think of a few things that I preferred to working.

My feet carried me straight down the hallway of the history building at the University of Texas, Austin. I was anxious for that uninterrupted hour alone with my boyfriend. It might be a bit taboo that he was also my professor and the advisor for my PhD, but it worked for me.

I reached his office and opened the door. "Mitch, I thought we could—" I stopped mid sentence and stared at what was before me.

Mitch was seated in the chair behind his desk—the very desk I had been fantasizing about. And a tiny blonde undergrad was sitting in his lap. Her skirt was hiked up; I could tell even from my vantage point.

My stomach dropped out of my body. *This could not be happening. I could not be this naive.*

"What the fuck is going on here?" I demanded.

The girl hopped up and straightened out her skirt. "Nothing," she squeaked.

"I was just helping her with some last-minute...assignments," Mitch said.

"You've got to be kidding me," I said, my voice low and menacing. My eyes snapped to the girl. "You should leave. Now."

"Emery," Mitch said consolingly.

"Now!" I yelled.

The girl grabbed her purse and rushed out of the room. I slammed the door shut behind her and glared down at the man I'd thought I loved for the last three years. But looking at him sitting there, adjusting himself, all I saw was a pathetic excuse for a man.

"God, this is embarrassing," I snapped. "I'm leaving. I'm leaving you, I'm leaving the program, and I'm leaving the university. I'm fucking done."

"You can't leave the program, Emery," he said, not acknowledging what else I had said.

"I can, and I will."

"That's ridiculous," he said, pushing back his messed up hair. "You only have a year left."

I shrugged. "Don't give a damn right now. You fucking cheated on me, Mitch."

"Come now, Emery. Do you really believe that?"

"Um…hello? I just walked in on you with Angela! She's an undergrad!"

"You don't know what you saw."

I snorted. "That's rich, coming from you. I'm well aware of what I saw. I doubt it was the first time, too. How many others are there?"

He stood and tried to reach for me, but I pulled away.

"We can make this work, Emery."

"God, do you think I'm an idiot?"

"Oh, Em," he said, straightening his black suit coat. "Don't act so childish."

I fumed at those repulsive words. "I am not acting childish by accusing the man I loved of sleeping with someone else. I'm standing up for what I think is right, and your bullshit routine is far from that. Are you sleeping with other students?"

"Honey, come on."

"You are, aren't you?" I shook my head and retreated. "Wow, I am an idiot. Not only do I really not want to be in academia, but I also really don't want to be with you."

"Emery," he called as I marched toward the door. "It's been three years. You can't do this."

I whipped around. "Tell me you're not fucking anyone else and that I'm the only girl for you."

He ran a shaky hand back through his long blond hair. He thought he was the cool professor, the one everyone could talk to about not just their research problems, but also their life problems. He'd reeled me in that way, and like a fool, I'd been blinded by the nice suits, fancy dinners, and finally finding a man on the same level as me. Turned out…he was a rat.

When he didn't respond, I scoffed at him. "That's what I thought."

Walking out of his office was one of the most liberating experiences of my life. He deserved to lose his job for what he had done all these years, but I didn't have it in me to go there yet. I walked into the history department and filled out the appropriate paperwork to withdraw from the program. Maybe, one day, I would want to go back and finish my PhD, but today, I knew that I had come to the end of the line. One too many panic attacks, my first ever prescription for Xanax, and a dissertation topic that seemed perpetually out of reach had done me in.

Screw academia.

I drove my Subaru Forester back to my one-bedroom studio, cursing

Austin traffic the whole way. *How was it possible for there to be bumper-to-bumper traffic at all times?*

Three years' worth of neglect had taken over my apartment, and my head ached from just imagining what to do with it all. At that moment, my life was completely open before me. No obligations. No job. No future.

I rolled my eyes at my own ridiculous thoughts and began to stuff half of my closet into the two suitcases I had. An hour later, I tucked my MacBook into my leather bag, remembered to grab my phone and computer charger, and kissed Austin good-bye. I'd eventually have to come back for the rest of my shit, but for now, I was going to forget all about Mitch, kick up the Christmas tunes, and drive the six hours home to Lubbock.

The weird thing about Lubbock was, most people had no idea where it was, and when you told them that it was actually not full of tumbleweeds or overrun by the desert, they'd seem surprised. As if that was all there was in west Texas. It was a city of three hundred thousand people, for Christ's sake!

The six years I had been in Norman at the University of Oklahoma, I'd gotten so good at responding to strangers' questions about where I was from that I still hadn't broken the habit of telling people I was from Texas, even when I'd moved *back* to Texas.

It would inevitably be followed up with a, "Where?"

And then I would have to explain, "Lubbock. It's west Texas. Stuff actually exists there. Texas Tech and Buddy Holly."

People would nod, but I didn't think anyone really believed me since they hadn't been to west Texas.

My sister, Kimber, was waiting for me outside when I pulled up to her brand-spanking-new house. She placed a hand on her swollen prego belly, and her four-year-old daughter, Lilyanne, ran around her ankles.

I put my car in park and jumped out in a hurry to scoop up my little niece. "Hey, Lily Bug," I said, twirling her in a circle before swinging her onto my hip.

"Lilies aren't bugs, Auntie Em. Lilies are flowers!"

"That, they are, smarty-pants."

"Hey, Em," Kimber said, pulling me in for a hug.

"Hey, Kimmy."

"Rough day?" she asked.

"You could say that."

I dropped Lilyanne back onto her feet and opened the trunk. Kimber hoisted the smaller suitcase out of the trunk, and I wheeled the larger one into her ginormous house.

"Em! Do you want to see my new dress? It has dinosaurs on it. Dinosaurs say *rawr!*" Lilyanne said.

"Not now, Lily. We have to get Emery into the guest room. Can you show her where to go?" Kimber asked.

Lilyanne's eyes lit up, and she raced for the stairs at lightning speed. "Come on, Auntie Em. I know the way."

Kimber sighed, exhausted. "I'm glad you're here."

"Me, too. She's a handful. But it's good to have her. How else would I be able to find my way around here?" I joked as we made our way up the stairs after Lilyanne. "Seriously, are we in *Beauty and the Beast*? Is there a west wing I should avoid?" I gasped.

Kimber snorted and rolled her eyes. "It's not *that* big."

"Never too big for a library with ladders, of course."

"Of course. We might have one of those."

"I knew it! Please tell me all the dirty romance novels we read in high school are proudly on display now."

Kimber dropped my suitcase in the guest bedroom, which was approximately the same size as my loft back in Austin. "Noah would kill me," she said with a roll of her eyes. "Most of those books are on my iPad now anyway. I've converted to e-books."

"Fancy," I said, fluttering my fingers at her. "I could use an iPad. Just throwing that out there in case Noah needs gift ideas for Christmas."

Kimber laughed. "God, I've missed you."

I grinned devilishly. Noah worked at the Texas Tech Medical Center. He worked long, long hours and made Scrooge McDuck–level dollar bills. He and Kimber were high school sweethearts and possibly the disgustingly cutest couple I'd ever encountered.

"Come on, Lilyanne," Kimber called. "We have cookies in the oven."

"Cookies?" I asked, my eyes lighting up. "Mom's recipe?"

"Of course. Are you going to go see her?" Kimber asked, as if she didn't care. But I saw her glance nervously in my direction.

It wasn't that I didn't get along with my mother. It was more like…we were the exact same person. So, when we were together, our stubborn heads butted, and everyone ran for the hills. But there weren't hills in Lubbock.

"Yeah…probably."

"Did you even let her know you were coming into town?"

Kimber picked Lilyanne up and dropped her down into a seat by the sprinkles. The timer dinged for the cookies, and Kimber pulled them out of the oven. Fluffy golden brown Christmas cookies, just the way we liked them.

I shot Kimber a sheepish look. "No, but…"

"Gah, Emery! She's going to kill me if you stay here without telling her you're in town. I do not want to deal with that while I'm pregnant."

"I'm going to tell her!" I said, reaching for a cookie.

Kimber slapped my fingers with the spatula. "Those are too hot. Wait for them to cool."

"You don't want a boo-boo," Lilyanne said.

I sucked my finger into my mouth and made a face at my sister. "Fine."

Kimber dropped the subject, and we spent the rest of the afternoon making cookies. Lilyanne and I got to cut out the shapes with Kimber's cookie cutters, and then she placed them on the tray and into the oven. Once they cooled, we iced and added Christmas sprinkles on top of them.

By the time Noah was home, earlier than usual for him, we were covered in flour with sugary-sweet hangovers. It was a welcome relief from the drama I'd endured with Mitch. It was a known fact that Kimber's cookies cured heartaches.

I pulled Noah in for a big hug. "Missed you."

"You, too, Em. I heard you were having some trouble."

My nose wrinkled. "Yeah. Thanks for letting me stay while I figure things out."

"You're always welcome here. It'll be good to have you around for Kimber, too. She's home a lot with this one, and I know she's ready to get back to work."

My sister owned a kick-ass bakery right off of campus called Death by Chocolate that made the best cookies, cupcakes, and doughnuts in town. But, with the new baby on the way, she'd taken a step back and turned more to management, so she could work from home. But her true passion was baking, and I knew she'd love to get back into the thick of things as soon as she could.

"Thanks Noah."

When it was Lilyanne's bedtime, I finally left their house and went to meet my best friend out for a drink.

When I pulled up to Flips, I was shaking from the bitter December cold that had sprung up out of nowhere. I rummaged through my backseat, extracted a black leather jacket, and then dashed across the parking lot.

I handed the bouncer my ID and then pushed through the hipster crowd to the back of the bar. As expected, I found Heidi leaning over a pool table and making eyes at a guy who thought he was going to make some easy money on a game against a chick. His friends stood around with smirks on their face, as they drank Bud Light. Lubbock was big enough that there were still enough idiots for Heidi to hustle, but the regulars steered clear.

"Em!" Heidi called, jumping up and down at my appearance.

"Hey, babe," I said with a wink.

"Guys, I'm going to have to finish this game early. My bestie is here."

The guy's brow furrowed in confusion. She leaned down and knocked the rest of her balls into the holes, hardly paying any attention. He and his friends' jaws dropped, and I just laughed. I'd seen it happen one too many times.

Heidi's dad had owned a pool hall when she was a kid, and her skills were legit. I was pretty sure pool was the start of her love affair with geometry. She'd gotten into civil engineering at Tech, and she now worked at Wright Construction, the largest construction company in the nation. I thought it was a waste of her talent, but she liked to be the only female in a male-dominated industry.

"You hustled us!" the guy yelled.

She fluttered her long eyelashes at him and grinned. "Pay up!"

He tossed a couple of twenties on the pool table and stormed away like a sore loser. Heidi counted them out and then stuffed them into the back pocket of her destroyed jeans.

"Emery, baby," Heidi said, flinging her arms around my neck. "I have missed your face."

"Missed you, too. You buying?"

She laughed, removed one of the guy's twenties from her pocket, and threw it on the table. "Peter, shots for me and Emery!"

Peter nodded his head at me. "Hey, prom queen."

"That was Kimber. Not me!"

"Oh, right," he said, as if vaguely remembering that had happened to my sister and not me. "You dated that Wright brother though, right?"

I breathed out heavily through my nose. Nine and a half years since Landon Wright had broken up with me on graduation day, and I was still recognized as the girl who'd dated a Wright brother. *Awesome.*

"Yeah," I grumbled, "a long time ago."

"Speaking of the Wright brothers," Heidi said, pushing a shot of tequila and lime toward me and adding salt to the space between her thumb and finger.

"Nope."

"Now that you're newly single after you kicked that jerk to the curb."

"Oh God, Heidi, can we not talk about Mitch?"

"I promise I won't talk about the skeezeball if you hear me out."

I sighed heavily. "All right. What about the Wrights?"

"Sutton Wright is getting married on Saturday."

"She is?" I asked in surprise. "Isn't she still at Tech?"

Heidi shrugged. "She found *the* one. It's kind of a rush job. They only got engaged on Halloween."

"Shotgun?" I asked.

The entire Wright family was riddled with scandal. With billions of dollars to throw around and no moral code, it was easy for anyone to get in trouble. But the five Wright siblings took it to a new level.

"No idea really, but I'd guess so. Either way, who cares? I am not missing a chance for an open bar and a swank party."

"Have fun with that," I said dryly.

"I'm taking you with me, bitch," Heidi said.

She raised her shot glass to me, and I warily eyed her before raising mine to meet hers.

After I downed the tequila and sucked on the lime, I finally responded, "You know I have a rule about Wright siblings, right?"

"I know you've been jaded against the lot of them after Landon, yes."

"Oh no, you *know* it's not just Landon."

"Yeah, so they're all a bag of dicks. Who cares? Let's go get drunk on their dime and make fun of them." Heidi seductively placed her hand on my thigh and raised her eyebrows up and down. "I'll put out."

I snorted and smacked her arm. "You're such a whore."

"You love me. I'll get you a new dress. We'll have fun."

I shrugged. *What could it hurt?* "Fine. Why not?"

chapter
two

Jensen

"MY WHORE SISTER IS PREGNANT AGAIN, AND THIS TIME, SHE WANTS TO keep it," I said to no one in particular as I expertly knotted the red bow tie at my neck.

"Yeah, that's kind of the point of the wedding today, Jensen," my brother Austin said. His bow tie still hung loose around his neck, and he was already on his third glass of whiskey. At twenty-nine years old, he was already shaping up to be the one who tarnished the Wright name. If he wasn't careful, he'd end up just like our father—a raving alcoholic up until the moment he was buried six feet under.

"Can't believe we're fucking doing this today."

"She's in love, man," Austin said.

He raised his glass to me, and I fought the urge to call him a sentimental dick.

"He's looking for a paycheck. A paycheck that I'm going to have to provide because there's no way he'll be able to take care of our little sister." I finally got the bow tie straight and turned back to Austin.

"Have a drink. You're being too uptight about the whole thing."

I glared at him. I *had* to be uptight about this shit. I was only thirty-two, and I was the one in charge of the business. I was the one who had been left with all the money and responsibilities to take care of my four younger siblings. If that made me uptight, then fuck him.

But I didn't say any of that. I just strode across the room and refilled his glass of whiskey. "Have another drink, Austin. You remind me so much of Dad."

"Fuck you, Jensen. Can't you just be happy for Sutton?"

"Yeah, Jensen," Morgan said. She stepped into the room in a floor-length red dress with her dark hair pulled up off her face. Her smile was magnetic, as usual.

Morgan was only twenty-five and the most normal one of my family. We all had our issues, but Morgan gave me the least amount of grief, which made her my favorite.

"Don't you start in on this, too," I told her.

"Sutton is her own person. She always has been. She does whatever she wants to do, no matter what anyone says," Morgan said. Taking the drink out of Austin's hand, she downed a large gulp. "Don't you remember that time she decided she was a princess superhero? Mom couldn't get her out of a tutu, cape, and crown for almost a year."

I laughed at the memory. Sutton had been a handful. *Fuck, she still was a handful.* Twenty-one and already getting married.

"Yeah, I remember. I'd be happier about the whole thing with what's his face if he wasn't such a completely incompetent dipshit," I told her.

"His name is Maverick," Austin cut in. "And you can't fucking talk, man. Your name is Jen*sen*," he drawled my name out, exaggerating the second syllable. "It's a fucking weird name, too."

"It's not a weird name. Maverick is a douche name, especially since he goes by Maverick and not Mav or Rick or something."

Morgan rolled the big brown eyes she'd inherited from our mother. "Let's drop it, shall we? Where is Landon anyway?"

As if on cue, my twenty-seven-year-old younger brother Landon schlepped into the room. His wife, Miranda, followed in his footsteps in the same dress as Morgan. My eyes slid over to Morgan. She returned the look, saying a million things in that one glance.

"Hey, Landon," Austin said when he realized neither of us were going to say shit since Miranda was here.

"Hey," Landon said, sinking into a seat next to Austin.

He looked beat.

Landon was the only one of us who didn't work for the company. Austin and Morgan both worked for me at Wright Construction, and Sutton would once she graduated—or that had been the plan before she got pregnant. Now, I'd probably have to hire *Maverick* in her place, so she could take care of that baby.

Landon had graduated from Stanford—unlike the rest of our family who had attended Texas Tech since the school's founding in the 1920s—but instead of putting his business degree to good use, he had joined the professional golf circuit. That was when he'd met Miranda. They'd dated for only six months before he proposed. Just like we were doing with Sutton, we'd all sworn that Miranda was pregnant and using him for his money. But when she hadn't had a baby nine months later, we had all been fucking baffled.

It was one thing to marry a girl like Miranda for a baby. You had to take care of the kid. That always fucking came first. No matter who the mother was. It was *another* thing to marry a girl like Miranda because you liked her—or, fuck, loved her.

"Well, what a happy reunion this is," Miranda said. She eyed us all like she was trying to figure out how to wiggle more money out of the Wright family. There might as well have been actual dollar signs in her eyes.

"Miranda," Austin said. He stood and gave her a quick hug. "Good to see you."

"Thanks, Austin," she said with a giggle.

Austin, the peacekeeper. That used to be Landon but not anymore. Not since the wicked bitch had sunk her claws into him.

As a man who had been through a brutal divorce already, I couldn't figure out why Landon hadn't handed over the paperwork. Being around Miranda for a solid five minutes was too much for me, and it made Morgan lose her shit. I hated that Landon always looked like someone had kicked his puppy.

I'd been there. I knew what that was like. I did not want him to have to go through the same thing I had. Or end up with the same consequences.

"Come on, Morgan," Miranda trilled. "I'm sure Sutton will need us with the other bridesmaids."

"I'm sure. Why don't you head over there and tell her I'll be just a minute?" Morgan said, using the slow voice she typically reserved for small children.

Miranda shot her an evil glare. Or maybe that was her face. I could never tell.

Then, she grabbed Landon's arm. "I'll see you at the ceremony, honey. Kiss?"

Landon turned his face up to her, and she latched on to his lips like a leech.

"I love you."

"I love you, too," he said automatically.

When she was gone, we all breathed a sigh of relief.

"Bless her heart," Morgan drawled.

"Y'all," Landon groaned, "don't."

Morgan started humming the theme song for the Wicked Witch of the West.

"Are you ever going to give it a break, Morgan?" Landon asked.

"No, probably not."

"We've been married for two years now."

"I can't believe you're staying at a hotel," I said.

Landon shrugged and reached for the bottle of whiskey, pouring himself a glass. "Miranda wanted to stay downtown."

"And, before we start World War III by bringing up Miranda," Austin cut in, "I feel like someone should grab Sutton. We're about to suffer through a couple of hours of pictures with eighteen of her closest friends. Might have some time, just the five of us."

"I limited her to nine bridesmaids," I said.

"That's a limit?" Morgan asked with a huff. "I don't think I even like nine people."

"You weren't in a sorority either," I reminded her.

"I don't like people. I certainly wouldn't like to pay for new sisters. Sutton is above and beyond."

Austin and Landon laughed, and that sound finally made me relax. It was nice to have all my siblings back in one place. With Sutton in school and Landon living on some beach in Florida where he could golf year-round, it just wasn't the same. Some people thought the Wright siblings were…odd. They thought we were too close, but we had to be. With both parents gone, we were all each other had.

"You want to go see if she's decent?" I asked Morgan.

She groaned. "This is what I get for being the only other girl."

I opened the door for her, and she hiked up her dress and stormed out. I knew she wasn't happy about having to spend the next twelve-plus hours with seven other girls she didn't know or like, plus Miranda, but there was nothing I could do about it. Trying to convince Sutton to do anything was like trying to move a mountain. She might be tiny, but she was a firecracker.

I grabbed the bottle of whiskey out of Landon's hands before he and Austin could finish it. Leaving the two of them alone with alcohol would guarantee a disaster. Then, I rummaged through my bag and found the group of shot glasses I'd brought with me. I was setting them up right when Sutton returned with Morgan.

"Hey, y'all!" Sutton said, flouncing into the room with a skip in her step. "Morgan said you needed me for something important."

I hefted the bottle of Four Roses Single Barrel whiskey at her. "Your brothers tried to drink the bottle before you got here, but I thought, a toast?"

She sagged in disappointment. "You know I can't have that."

I grinned devilishly and then grabbed a bottle of apple juice that I'd tucked away, knowing she couldn't drink. "How about this?"

"Yes! Make mine a double," she told me.

I laughed and poured out the shots. She was definitely part of the family. Addictive personalities ran in the Wright line. I had my fair share of vices, but I was lucky that alcohol wasn't one of them.

"Annnd," Sutton drawled out, "while I have you here, Jensen, I wanted to run one teensy little thing by you."

She widened her big blue eyes like she was about to ask me for a million dollars. She'd been giving me that same look for years. Once, it was a blowout sweet sixteen to rival that TV show *My Super Sweet 16*. Another time, it was for a trip to Europe with all her sorority sisters. I couldn't imagine what *more* she could want from me right now. We'd put together her wedding in six weeks, and she was flying first class to Cabo for two weeks. Still, she was upset that I wouldn't give her the jet.

"Oh no," I muttered. "What is it?"

"Look, I was talking to Maverick last night, and I *know* that he already signed the prenup, but—"

My face instantly hardened. "No."

"I didn't even ask anything!"

"I know what you're going to ask, and the answer is no."

"But it's silly, Jensen. Really! He's the love of my life. We're going to spend eternity together. A prenup is ridiculous. It's a bad way to enter a marriage. If you're thinking about how it's going to end before it even starts, then what does that say about a person?"

Morgan, Austin, and Landon had all gone still behind her. They could probably read the fury on my face. I didn't want to blow up on her on her wedding day, but I was dangerously close to doing so.

"You are worth a small fortune, Sutton. And I don't give a fuck who you're marrying. You get a prenup to protect yourself *in case* something happens. Thinking about the future is a way to ensure that you are not getting scammed. No matter how much somebody loves you."

"But, Jensen—" Sutton said, trying to reason with me.

"Sutton," Austin said, cutting in, "do you really want to do this right now? I mean, Jensen and Landon both had a prenup. No one marries a Wright without it."

"That's right," I said, silently thanking Austin for his backup.

"Plus, you're only twenty-one," Morgan said. "Who knows what could happen?"

"Oh, wow. Thanks, Morgan," Sutton grumbled.

"I didn't mean that Maverick isn't 'the one,'" she said with air quotes. "I just mean, Jensen didn't think he'd divorce Vanessa under any circumstances and look what happened."

I gritted my teeth at the mention of my ex-wife. Vanessa Hendricks wasn't a name that was usually brought up in polite conversation. But she certainly was a cautionary tale as to why a prenup was necessary.

"If Maverick really wants to throw out the prenup, I'd be happy to talk to him about it," I said to Sutton with raised eyebrows.

She rolled her eyes. "I'm not that stupid. You'd scare him half to death."

"Well, if he's trying to take you for your money, then he'd deserve it."

"Okay, fine. I get it. I just thought I'd ask. Maverick and I had a long talk about it."

"I bet," Landon muttered under his breath.

"Anyway, shots!" Sutton cried.

I passed out shots of whiskey to Austin, Landon, and Morgan and then handed Sutton the shot of apple juice.

I raised my glass high. "To Sutton, on the happiest day of her life and to many more amazing years to come."

We all tipped back our glasses. The whiskey burned all the way down my throat, but I just grinned at my siblings.

The world felt right when we were all together. No matter what challenges we might face, at least we had each other.

chapter
three

Emery

"HEIDI, WHAT ARE YOU DOING TO MY HAIR?" I ASKED.

Heidi laughed hysterically behind me. "I'm making you look presentable, Em. You just wait. It will come together at the end."

She threaded a few more strands of my hair into this crazy braid.

If Heidi and I hadn't been best friends since kindergarten and if I hadn't known all her deep, dark secrets, I was sure she would have dumped me for the cool crowd. Despite her obsession with geometry, her all black attire, and her pool-slinging skills, she had been a cheerleader and obsessed with popularity.

My sister, Kimber, had been the girlie girl—prom queen, homecoming queen, voted most attractive. The whole shebang.

But not me. Though I never had a problem with finding a date, I had not been the typical teenager. I had played varsity soccer my freshman year, I'd skateboarded circles around the dude-bros in town, and I had made up my mind that my dream job was to become a vampire slayer.

At the time, Landon Wright had tested my friendship with Heidi. *Why would the star quarterback have any interest in the loner tomboy?* I hadn't understood it any more than Heidi.

I closed my eyes and pushed the thoughts aside. I was only thinking about Landon because I knew he would be at the wedding this afternoon. He hadn't crossed my mind in a long time, and I hadn't seen him in longer.

"I swear, it's going to be cute," Heidi assured me.

"I know. I trust you," I said. "I cannot believe that you talked me into going to this wedding with you. Is it going to be like a high school reunion? I don't know if I'm prepared for that."

"It's not a high school reunion," Heidi said. "I got invited because I work for the Wrights and, like, half of the company was invited. It's going to be a big wedding. I doubt you'll even run into him."

"I am not worried about running into Landon. It's been almost ten years since we broke up," I told her.

"Didn't he get married anyway?" Heidi asked.

She yanked on my hair, and I winced.

"I don't follow him. You would know more than I would." I glared at Heidi in the mirror. "Stop giving me that look. Do you know how many guys

I've dated since Landon? No, you don't. Because I can't even remember, but it's a lot. And I'm currently sitting right here because of guy trouble."

"I just know you and Landon," Heidi said dreamily. "Perfect high school couple. That was, like, the only thing that you beat Kimber in. You and Landon got Best Couple in the yearbook."

I rolled my eyes. "Please stop reminiscing about high school, or I'll vomit."

"You were cute," Heidi added.

"If you think for a minute that something is going to happen with him at this wedding, you're out of your mind. Not only is he married, but he'll also be there *with* his wife. And, as of today, I'm officially swearing off men."

Heidi laughed. "Yeah, right, Em," she said. "You are boy crazy and always have been. Even when you were our little skater girl."

"Look, Mitch fooled me into thinking that he loved me. He was, like, fifteen years older than me and a total player. I'm almost certain he was sleeping with an undergrad," I told her. "I mean…how bad is my judgment skewed that I ended up with someone like that? I think I just need to be single for a while."

"All right," Heidi said with a shake of her head. Her blonde hair swayed back and forth down against the middle of her back in an amazing wave that she'd somehow created. "More for me tonight."

"All for you."

Heidi stepped back and observed her creation. She messed with my bangs and then added one more curl into the end. "There. What do you think?"

I looked in the mirror and hardly recognized myself. While I wasn't still a tomboy, when I felt down, I'd tend to fall back on old habits, as in no makeup and messy bun galore. But Heidi had practically digitally remastered my face. My makeup was flawless, and the shimmer shadow brought out the green in my eyes. My dark hair was braided into a crown atop my head that wove into a low side ponytail with curls.

"You have a gift," I told her. "You've made me look human again."

"Go put on your dress," Heidi said. "I can't wait to see it all together!"

"All right. All right. I'm going."

I shimmied into the dress that Heidi had picked out for me from a boutique downtown.

I stepped out of the closet. Heidi whistled.

"You're ridiculous."

But I liked the dress. Sutton's wedding was formal attire, and it was hard enough to find a dress I liked, let alone a full-length dress, but Heidi had done it. The dress was black with a gold shimmer layer underneath that accentuated my figure when I walked. Everything came together with cute peep-toes. Benefit of a winter wedding in Texas was that it would reach the seventies during the day if we were lucky. The weather was pretty erratic.

"You are so getting laid in that dress," Heidi said.

I dramatically rolled my eyes. "No boys. This is a no-fly zone."

"You won't be saying that tonight when you're getting fucked. All I'm saying," Heidi said. "Hopefully, it's Landon Wright. That would be so full circle."

"Don't even say that. If I see him, I will run in the opposite direction," I told her.

Heidi grinned, as if laughing at her own inside joke.

"All right, all right," Heidi said when she noticed my glare. "No boys. I got it. If Landon approaches you, I'll distract him. I still have some cheer moves."

She kicked her leg and nearly touched her nose. Then, she spun around in some intricate dance move. I wasn't even sure how it was possible that she was this flexible.

"Oh my God, if you do that in your dress, you are going to be more than a distraction for Landon. You are going to rip your dress in half for the entire party to see."

Heidi laughed and shrugged. "I'm going to get dressed, and then we can go."

A few minutes later, Heidi reappeared in a floor-length mermaid dress in the deepest, darkest purple. She shimmied over to me and winked. "Come on, sexy. You're my date tonight. Let's get Kimber to take a picture of us!"

We hurried into Kimber's bedroom, and Kimber agreed to take the shot. Heidi handed her phone to Kimber. Then, she threw one hand up in the air and placed the other on her hip while making a pouty face. I pointed my finger at the camera while kissing Heidi on the cheek. When we got a look at it, I just giggled with my girls. It was the most ridiculous and the most *us* picture in existence.

"This is so going on Instagram. Damn, it's good to have you back," Heidi said.

"Use a filter," I insisted.

"You just filtered your face," Kimber said, pointing out all the makeup on my face. "You don't need a filter."

"My life needs a filter," Heidi muttered.

Heidi posted the picture and then grabbed her clutch. She stuffed her phone and ID inside. I hated carrying a purse anytime, especially when I had to navigate a dress and heels. So, I gave Heidi my phone and ID, who rolled her eyes and added them to her bag.

"You really don't mind dropping us off, Kimber?" I asked.

"Not a problem. I want to hear all about the antics when y'all are done."

"I'll live tweet you," Heidi said.

"Oh my God, you are not going to be on your phone all night," Kimber said. "You should enjoy yourself. Get drunk and make a mistake or two."

"Done and done," Heidi said with a wink. "Let's get out of here."

We all piled into Kimber's car. The traffic around the Historic Baker Building, a venue in downtown Lubbock, was outrageous. And that was saying something because the only time traffic got this bad was on Texas Tech game days.

"How many people did Sutton invite?" I asked, craning my head out the window.

"It looks like everyone she's ever met," Heidi said.

"Or the whole freaking city," I grumbled.

"Maybe we should hop out here," Heidi suggested.

"Be safe," Kimber said. "Take some condoms for the kids."

Heidi rolled her eyes.

I laughed as I hopped out of the SUV. "Thanks, Kimber."

"Bye, babe!" Heidi called, following in my footsteps.

She slammed the door, and we darted through traffic and onto the sidewalk. The Baker Building was a block or two down the street, and already, I was cursing myself for wearing high heels. They had looked so adorable in the store. Now, they were little torture devices.

Who invented these?

Men.

Men invented these to torture us and make our butts look awesome.

Thank God my butt looked this awesome. Otherwise, I'd be taking these off so fast.

"Stop hobbling," Heidi said, strutting around in her heels like they had been made for her.

"I'm not hobbling. I just don't think I'll be able to wear these all night."

"We'll take them off once we get to the reception. But, right now, you need them to be able to see."

I smacked her arm. "I'm not that short. I can see fine. You're just super freaking tall."

"Well, we can't both be perfect, Em."

"Oh my God, why are you my best friend again?" I asked.

"Beats me," she said with a giggle. Then, she looped our arms together and strode up to the entrance of the Baker Building.

The place really was packed. At the entrance, a dozen ushers were escorting people to seats, and people milled about as they waited for their chance. I recognized about ten people in the span of a minute and slowly angled my body so as not to have to engage with anyone.

Eventually, it was our turn, and Heidi and I wrangled one usher for the both of us.

"Bride or groom?" the boy asked. He had ice-blue eyes and a real Southern drawl. He was probably in a fraternity at Tech and had gotten coaxed into this with the promise of free booze.

"Bride," Heidi said. "We're friends of the bride."

"Cool. How do you know Sutton?" he asked as he walked us, arm in arm, down the aisle.

"We grew up together," Heidi said.

When I raised my eyebrows, she shrugged.

"Family friend. Got it."

Then, he walked us right up to the third row. I felt myself panicking. *Why were we so close? Couldn't he have given us different seats? I did not want to be this near the Wright siblings. I was here for the booze and had been promised a good time.*

"Family friends up front," he said with a smile, gesturing for us to take our seats.

Heidi smiled brightly at him and then took the second seat inside.

"You're leaving me on the end?" I hissed at her.

"Yeah. Sit your ass down."

"This was not part of the deal, Martin," I spat at her as I sat down.

"Ohhh, using my last name. I'm real scared."

"You owe me big for this."

"Just enjoy it, Em. It'll be over in, like, fifteen minutes, and then we can drink for free all night."

"Right. Priorities," I muttered as the doors finally closed behind us.

As the remaining guests took their seats, my eyes traveled the room. It was elaborately decorated with flowers attached to every chair and shimmery curtains draped across the entire front of the room. White lights that twinkled down on the attendees were strung on the second-floor balcony.

Softly, a string quartet began playing classical music, and the lights dimmed. I looked back to the front as the pastor stepped out from a back room with the groom and a long line of groomsmen following in his wake.

My eyes scanned the length of the line. *Nine. He had nine groomsmen. Holy fuck!*

There were so many of them that they had to stand in two lines.

And the last three men in the line were very distinct and downright gorgeous.

The Wright brothers—Jensen, Austin, and finally, Landon.

The party had arrived.

chapter
four

Emery

I PURPOSELY TURNED MY ATTENTION AWAY FROM THE BROTHERS BEFORE ME. I really didn't want to look at any of them anyway. Luckily for me, the bridesmaids started walking down the aisle. Then, the traditional "Canon in D" began, we all stood, and Sutton walked down the aisle. I was pretty sure, the last time I'd seen Sutton in person, she was only about twelve years old. But it was shocking to me, now that she was all grown up, how much she looked like Landon.

All of them looked the same—dark hair, pouty lips, athletic figure. Though they had their differences, too. Just not enough noticeable differences. Anyone could see they were related.

Heidi leaned over to me to whisper into my ear, "Ten bucks, she's a crier."

"She's pregnant. She's definitely a crier," I muttered back.

I tried to hold my laughter in as Sutton finally reached the front of the room and immediately burst into tears. Her groom took her hands in his and grinned down at her.

The pastor raised his hands. "You may all be seated," he said.

I dropped into my seat and waited for this whole thing to be over.

"We are gathered here today to join Sutton Marie Wright to Maverick Wayne Johnson in holy matrimony."

My eyes rounded, and I glanced at Heidi. We had an entire conversation without saying a word.

Maverick Wayne.

Maverick?

That's his name?

Holy fuck.

Yeah.

Yeah.

She must be here for his Johnson.

I cracked up and had to cover it with a cough when a few people turned to glare at me. Heidi tried to hide her own laughter by reaching for her purse and digging around for her phone.

The rest of the ceremony progressed like any other I'd ever been to. If you'd been to one wedding, you'd been to them all.

Yada, yada, yada.

"I do."

Yada, yada, yada.

"Till death do us part."

Yada, yada, yada.

"You may kiss the bride."

I applauded methodically with the rest of the crowd and silently prayed for some really good champagne to make up for this. Champagne cured everything.

The music started up again. The end of their fifteen minutes was up. On to bigger and better things. Like an open bar and a dessert table.

Maverick took Sutton's hand in his, and they strode down the aisle, beaming like streetlamps. Each bridesmaid walked forward in her long, silky red dress, latched on to the arm of one of the groomsmen. With nine people on each side of the bridal party, it was taking forever. One after the other after the other.

The only bridesmaid I recognized was Morgan, who was the maid of honor. She was only two years younger than me and Heidi and had run in the popular crowd, of course. She was easy to figure out because she looked exactly the same as she had in high school. Unfortunately for her, she was on the arm of some leering frat boy. The other girls, I gathered, were Sutton's sorority sisters.

Then, finally, it was on to the Wright brothers.

Jensen moved forward first. He held his arm out for the girl who was blushing as bright as a cherry tomato. She looped her arm in his, and I was trying so hard not to roll my eyes. I had been that girl once. I knew what that was like. Back in the day, Landon had made me feel that swoony, over-the-top, oh-my-God feeling from having the attention of a Wright brother. And I wasn't that type of girl either. Now, it felt ridiculous. Money couldn't buy happiness, and it sure didn't fix shit when the guy broke your heart.

I was so deeply entrenched in my own thoughts that I didn't realize I was staring. At Jensen Wright. And he was staring right back at me.

Why? Why, oh God, did Heidi put me on the end? And why is he looking at me like that?

He hadn't even moved yet. He was just standing there, staring at me with those dark brown eyes. And I didn't know what he was thinking or what he was doing. Except for making a complete fool of himself because, surely, he needed to start walking right now. Like right fucking now.

Synapses must have fired in his brain again because he gradually moved the girl forward. And, when I thought I'd gotten past that look and away from his penetrating gaze, he turned around. He did a motherfucking double take. Right there in front of everyone at his own sister's wedding, he turned around and looked at me.

What world am I living in?

I didn't think I breathed normally again until he looked away and proceeded down the aisle. By then, Austin had already passed me, and I didn't even get a chance to see Landon and his wife. And that was the only thing I'd been interested in.

So what? I was an ex-girlfriend. I had every right to stalk his wife to see if she was prettier than me.

Heidi shook my shoulder, jarring me back to reality. "Did you just get eye-fucked by Jensen Wright?" she gasped.

An older woman sitting in front of us glared at her for the language. She hadn't exactly been quiet.

"No. Nope. No, I did not," I told her. I was still trying to figure out what had happened. Because nothing I could conjure up was making any sense.

"You so did. You so, so did!" Heidi said.

The two aisles in front of us left first, and then Heidi was pushing me out of the aisle, all while whispering in my ear about how excited she was. "Do you remember mooning over him in high school? He was, like, this hottie college guy, a totally unattainable god. Like Zeus on Mount Olympus. Or maybe we just wanted to get on his lightning bolt, if you know what I mean."

"Heidi, God, you're so embarrassing."

"Em, just think about Jensen when we were in high school. He belonged in a magazine."

"I was dating his brother."

"But *before* that," she insisted.

"Okay. I *might* remember staying at your house a time or two…"

"Or ten."

"Where we talked about him being hot."

"Yes. And he has gone from hot to one damn fine wine. The bottle gets better with age, honey," Heidi said, knocking her hip into mine.

"Are you really suggesting I hook up with Jensen Wright at his sister's wedding when I *dated* his brother?" I asked with wide eyes.

Heidi laughed. "Getting ahead of yourself, aren't you? I didn't say hook up with him. You said that. Are you thinking about that?"

"No," I spat.

Because, no. Seriously. That would never happen.

I was sworn off of the Wright brothers. None of that was going to happen. No fucking way. Jensen had probably just…seen a bug on my shoulder or something. That was all it had been because his interest would be illogical.

I was his brother's ex-girlfriend.

I was…*me.*

We made it to the reception space a few minutes later. The room was teeming with waiters in pressed tuxedos, handling silver trays topped with hors d'oeuvres. I plucked a fancy crab cake from a passing waiter and headed straight to the bar.

"Champagne, please," Heidi said, flashing the bartender a smile.

I held up two fingers as I took a bite out of the crab cake. *Holy fuck, this was delicious. Wow. Who the hell was the caterer?* I glanced around and found my answer. *West Table. Of course. Only the Wrights would hire catering from the most expensive restaurant in town.*

"We need more of these," I told Heidi when she handed me two glasses of champagne.

I had no shame as I double-fisted the drinks.

Heidi laughed and nodded toward the tables. "Let's find where we're sitting."

We wandered over to the table with the list of names elaborately tacked up on a rustic window.

Heidi plucked her name off the distressed clothespin. "We're table twelve. My lucky number."

"That's because Brandon McCain wore that number on the football team all through high school."

"Okay, fine," Heidi said with a shrug. "It's my get-lucky number."

I snorted. "That's rich."

"Here we are." She dropped her purse down right in front of her name. "Heidi Martin and guest. That's you."

"Who else are we with?" I asked.

Heidi and I scanned the names.

I shrugged. "I don't know any of these people."

"Work people," she said. "But at least we have Julia. Julia Banner. She's cool. You'll like her."

"I've never heard you mention her before."

"She's new. You know how it goes with the newbies," she said with a wry expression before downing half of her glass of champagne. "I like to make sure they're going to stick around Lubbock for more than a year. So many burned friendships with people who move here and then relocate immediately. We'll see if she survives, and then I'll decide if we bring her in."

"You act like we're in a gang," I told her with a shake of my head.

Heidi leaned over and conspiratorially whispered, "We are."

I laughed despite myself. God, I had missed her so much. My life had not been the same without her. No matter that I'd spent all those years in Oklahoma and then Austin, I never found a friendship to rival Heidi's. I was certain I never would.

We spent the next forty-five minutes downing glasses of champagne and eating as many of those little crab cakes as we could get our hands on. By the time the family and bridal party were announced into the room and Sutton and Maverick made their big appearance, Heidi and I were each one drink away from wasted. It was good that we immediately launched into dinner so that I could pad my drinking belly with carbs to survive the rest of the night.

By the time they were finished with the regular bouts of wedding festivities, including—*God help us all*—a choreographed dance with the bride and her sorority-sister bridesmaids *for* the groom before launching into a rehearsed first dance, I was ready to hit the bar again. If I ever had to sit through something like that again without another drink, I was sure I would drop dead.

"Bleach." Heidi giggled into my ear. "I need bleach for my eyes."

I laughed hysterically, probably louder than necessary, as we walked back to the bar. Other people had gotten up to join in on the dancing, and that meant one thing—more champagne. I was going to have a killer headache in the morning, but whatever. It would be worth it.

Heidi meandered us back over to her work crowd, and I stood with my back to the dancing catastrophe going on behind me. Julia did seem pretty chill. She was almost as tall as Heidi with mahogany-brown hair to her shoulders, and she had on a pretty green dress. I was figuring out more about her job as the head of HR when Heidi's face broke into a smile in front of me.

Not good.

"Landon!" Heidi called.

She waved at him, and I wanted to bury my face in my hands and disappear. Sometimes, my best friend was the worst.

"Hey Heidi," Landon said, appearing at my side. He leaned forward and pulled her into a hug. "Good to see you as always."

"Congratulations on your latest PGA win," Heidi said with a smile.

"Thanks. I appreciate that. I've had a pretty good year."

And there I stood as they talked about his normal year, as if I didn't exist. I was less than a foot away from him, and he hadn't said a word to me. He was engrossed in his conversation with Heidi.

With a deep breath, I chanced a glance at him. He looked...exactly the same. Except not.

Same tall body with chiseled features. Same clean-cut look with the dark hair and puppy-dog eyes. But he looked drained and downtrodden. The last time I'd seen him was at the stupid five-year high school reunion party that Heidi had forced me into going to because she had been the student body vice president. I'd gone in protest and reverted to my Vans skate shoes and oversize T-shirt. Heidi had hated it. But Landon had looked as sharp as ever. He hadn't lost his luster then. I wondered what had happened.

I seemed to have missed part of the conversation while staring at him… or maybe it was due to my buzz. But Landon was now holding his hand out to me. I furrowed my brows and stared at it.

"Sorry. I don't believe we've met," he said with his classic nonchalant attitude.

Heidi laughed next to me, but I couldn't even turn to look at her. *Is this happening?*

"Seriously, Landon?" I drawled with disdain.

Landon's eyes widened, and he instantly dropped his hand. "Emery?"

"In the flesh."

He opened his mouth like a fish out of water. It was nice to see a flustered Wright brother. "I didn't even recognize you."

"Um…thanks?" I couldn't decide if that was an insult.

My ex-boyfriend couldn't even recognize me. *Awesome.*

I finally turned to face Heidi. She looked like she was about to combust.

"How much makeup am I wearing?"

"No, I'm sorry. That was rude," Landon said, reeling it back in. "I recognized your voice right away. At least, the way you said my name. I just…wasn't expecting you to be here, is all."

"Yeah, I showed up with Heidi at the last minute."

Landon nodded, but he was still staring at me, as if I were a strange lab rat he was about to dissect. "Are you back in town for the holidays?"

"Maybe permanently."

"Permanently?" he said with raised eyebrows.

I shrugged. "We'll see. I'm back from college at the moment."

"Huh. Who would have guessed you would come back to Lubbock?"

And, right then and there, I remembered why I'd wanted to punch him in his pretty face. He was the one who had left me and made me feel like a pariah in my own hometown. He couldn't turn the tables around on me, as if I were the one who had left on my own.

But, instead, I giggled through the champagne buzz.

"I'm pretty sure, no one. Ever," I said dryly.

"There you are, honey," a woman said, walking up behind Landon and latching on to his arm. She was taller than me in heels with a bleach-blonde bob and glamorous makeup. She was good-looking in an overdone sort of way. "I've been looking for you."

"Oh, Miranda," Landon said, his face falling. "I was just talking to some old friends from high school."

"Well, introduce me, lover boy. Your friends are my friends, of course."

I caught Landon's grimace, and suddenly, his downtrodden expression made sense if he had to deal with her every day.

"Y'all, this is my wife, Miranda. Miranda, this is Heidi and"—he cleared his throat and apologetically glanced at me—"Emery."

Miranda eyed me up and down, as if she were sizing me up for a Miss America competition. "Emery. Like...Emery?"

"The one and only," I muttered.

"Your ex-girlfriend is here, and you didn't even tell me?" Miranda hissed.

"He didn't know I would be here," I said, stepping in for him for a reason I couldn't fathom. "I came with a friend."

Miranda didn't seem to hear me, or she didn't care. She turned on her heel and fled in the opposite direction.

Landon rolled his eyes and then scowled. "Sorry, y'all. I've got to..." He nodded his head after Miranda and then jogged to catch up with her.

My eyes widened with shock. Heidi's mouth was hanging open.

"Wow, what a bitch!" Heidi said.

"You're telling me."

"At least we know one thing."

"What's that?"

"You're way prettier!" Heidi said, holding up her glass for a toast.

chapter five

Jensen

THE HARDEST PART OF THE NIGHT WAS OVER, AND NOW, I COULD FINALLY HAVE another drink. Dealing with Sutton had been harder than I'd anticipated, and the whiskey bottle was calling to me stronger than normal.

Or maybe it was that woman who had been seated in the third row. I didn't know where the hell she had come from, but damn! Long dark hair, perfect legs spilling out of the slit in her dress, gorgeous mouth that had been begging me to kiss her. I had decided within three seconds that she was the hottest person in the room, and it had taken everything in me not to ditch the bridesmaid on my arm. I'd wanted to escort her straight out of the room and into my bed.

It had been a while…a long while…since I had that kind of reaction to anyone in Lubbock. Dating here was impossible, and since I did business all over the country, it was easier to meet people on the road. So, maybe she didn't even live in Lubbock. I sure hoped not. Made it much more difficult to date when everyone knew the precise dollar amount you were worth and the dirty business with my ex.

Here was to hoping she wasn't a local I'd somehow missed in my thirty-something years here.

I kept a stash of good liquor with me and poured myself a double out of a whiskey bottle that Austin had almost handled all on his own. He was out in the center of all those sorority girls, probably deciding which one or two or three he should bring home with him. But my eyes were searching out the brunette.

I nodded my head at Morgan, who was talking to Austin's best friend, Patrick.

"Hey, man!" Patrick said.

We shook hands and clapped each other on the back. I'd known Patrick forever. He was practically family. And, if Morgan didn't stop mooning over him, he'd end up as family for real.

"Hey, Pat. What did you think of the ceremony?" I asked.

Patrick cracked a grin. "Typical Sutton."

"That is the damn truth."

"She seems happy at least," Morgan interjected. Her eyes were glued on our younger sister, who was at the center of the dance party.

"She always looks like that," I said.

"Fact," Patrick agreed.

"Oh, shit," Morgan groaned.

I followed her gaze and saw Miranda storming across the room with Landon on her tail. Pretty common occurrence honestly. That was what their relationship always fucking looked like. I still did not understand how that idiot had ended up with her. And I hated that my failed marriage wasn't warning enough for him.

"I'm going to go check on him," Morgan said with a sigh.

"Just leave them," I insisted. "Your hatred of Miranda will only make it worse."

Morgan grinned wickedly. "Will it? Well then, I'll just be a minute."

I shook my head at my evil sister and watched her stalk out of the room toward Landon and Miranda. I wouldn't wish Miranda upon my worst enemy, let alone my brother. But, for a while now, Morgan and I had been on Operation Miranda, which consisted of seeing how far we could push Landon into divorcing her.

But, despite my brother's issues, my mind was still on that girl. There were hundreds of people in attendance for Sutton's wedding. *She* could be anywhere. I just needed to find her.

"Oh no," Patrick said.

I raised an eyebrow in question.

"You've got that look on your face."

"What look?" I asked.

"The one you get in the boardroom. It's the same one you get chasing pussy."

I grunted at Patrick. He wasn't wrong. "I hope she's as big of a challenge as the Tarman merger I'm working on right now."

Patrick laughed in that unabashed way of his. "I doubt it. You're a fucking Wright, man. Girls are not a challenge."

My grin returned at that. "We'll see."

That was when I saw her. Her body was turned, facing the exit. She had an empty glass of champagne in her hand, and fuck, did she look gorgeous. A tightly fitted dress showed off every single curve on her body. Her hair was tugged off to one side, and I almost licked my lips at the thought of kissing down her throat. I couldn't wait to hear her moan my name into the night.

I picked up a tray of champagne on the way over to meet the brunette. I was glad that she was standing with two of my employees so I had an easy in for the conversation.

I knew all of my employees' names who worked at the corporate headquarters for Wright Construction. I personally welcomed every employee and made sure they knew their value. No one was going to work at my company and not feel appreciated. I knew how I had gotten to where I was. I never planned to take it for granted.

"Ladies," I said with a charming grin. I offered the tray to the group of women standing with the brunette. "You looked like you could use a refill."

"Oh, look at that service," Heidi said, winking at the other girl.

"Not every day you get champagne from the boss," Julia said. She took a glass herself.

"Thanks," the other girl said. She exchanged her empty glass with one from the tray.

A waiter immediately snaked over and removed the tray from my hands.

"Are y'all enjoying the party?" I asked.

"It's nice," Julia said.

"Your sister sure likes to dance," Heidi said.

The brunette girl's lips thinned, and she stared down into her champagne.

Okay, different tactic.

"Well, I'm glad you could make it. Who is your friend?" I asked pointedly, turning my attention to the brunette.

She glanced up from her champagne. Her eyes were wide open and as vivid green as I had ever seen. Her mouth opened slightly, and that vision was more intoxicating than my whiskey.

"Heidi," she groaned, "what did you do to my face?"

"This is…Em," Heidi said over Em's widened eyes of disapproval.

I wasn't sure what that was all about. She seemed particularly affronted that I was asking about her. I was sure I'd never seen her before. I definitely would have remembered.

"Well, it's nice to meet you. I'm Jensen," I said, trying to smooth over her concerns.

"Uh-huh," Em murmured. She took a long sip of her champagne, as if she were looking for liquid courage.

I couldn't get a read on her. I didn't know if she was actually uncomfortable around me or if she was just nervous. But she seemed like she wasn't sure how she was supposed to be acting right now.

"Head of Wright Construction, Em," Heidi said, nudging her with her hip.

Em shot her a withering stare. "I know who he is."

"I promise, whatever you've heard is a lie," I said with a laugh.

"I didn't say I'd heard anything bad," she countered. She downed the rest of the champagne in one quick drink and then winced. "Seriously…what is it with you Wright brothers?"

"Excuse me?" I asked with a furrowed brow.

"Ignore her," Heidi said. "She's an old friend, and she just needs another glass of champagne." Heidi leaned over and hissed in Em's ear, but I could still hear her say, "Give. Him. A. Chance."

Em sighed, as if resigning herself to the task. But, when she turned back to face me, she did have a half-smile on her face. It seemed a little forced, like she wasn't used to smiling for strangers.

"I'm just..." She held up her champagne glass and motioned to the bar.

"Mind if I join you?" I asked.

"Sure," she said.

We weren't that far from the bar, but even that short distance, I couldn't seem to take my eyes off of her. And she seemed to be looking everywhere but at me. She chanced one look at me, and a blush crept into her cheeks. So, she wasn't completely unaffected by me.

I'd said that I wanted a challenge after all. She was gorgeous and probably had guys hitting on her all the time, but I hadn't expected her not to even give me the time of day. Something about that only made me want to try harder.

Why is she so closed off?

She retrieved another glass of champagne, but I stopped her before letting her walk back to her friends. I was not relinquishing this opportunity.

"I noticed you at the ceremony," I said, my voice low and gravelly.

Her eyes widened as she looked up at me. And, fuck, that face. Those intense green eyes and bright red lips. The way her dark hair tumbled over her features, as if it were used to being unruly and was having trouble with staying tamed. Just like her. Something in her expression, in those sharp cheekbones and angled jawline, said she was wild and reckless. No amount of makeup and pretty clothes could remove the girl underneath.

"Yes. That was..." She trailed off. Her eyes darted to my mouth, as if she were distracted. Then, she sighed this short breathy thing that went straight to my dick. "I noticed."

"Are you in town, visiting?" I prompted.

She slowly shook her head and then glanced away from me, as if she needed a breather. "Look, whatever this is, it's not going to work."

I arched an eyebrow. "And what do you think this is?"

"Honestly, I don't know."

"I'm just talking to you," I said.

"I'm not fooled by that notion, Jensen."

The way she dragged out my name was the sexiest thing I'd ever heard. I was going to have to make her say it over and over again.

But I was so distracted by the way her mouth moved around the syllables of my name, I hadn't processed what she had said. She wasn't fooled by me. I wasn't trying to fool her. I thought my intentions were perfectly clear now that we were standing together. So very close together.

I wasn't even sure she realized that she had drawn closer toward me, the longer we talked. But, as I stared down at her, we were mere inches apart. I could feel the heat of her body, and it was turning my brain fuzzy.

Why didn't she want this? Her body was saying something else entirely. I could think of only one explanation.

"Do you have a boyfriend?"

She stepped back from me, as if my question were insulting. "I don't need a reason to say no to you."

She tried to brush past me, but I reached out and grabbed her hand. She didn't need a reason. Of course not. But her refusal made no sense with the way her body was responding to me.

"I know you don't need a reason. But it feels like you have one," I said, instinctively pulling her toward to me.

"Yes, I have a reason. And, when you figure it out, you'll no longer be interested in me."

"I highly doubt that," I said with blustering confidence.

"I swore off the Wright family a long time ago. So, you'll have better luck somewhere else."

She extracted her hand from mine, gave me one last sad smile, and then retreated back to Heidi and Julia. Both girls were frantically waving their hands, trying to figure out what had happened. And that was exactly what I wanted to know.

chapter
six

Jensen

I HAD JUST STRUCK OUT.

Majorly struck out.

I was sure that I'd had girls who weren't interested in me before but certainly not any like this.

I couldn't remember having this sort of visceral reaction to anyone in a long-ass time. But even women I had been mildly interested in were eager to get to know me.

Biblically.

Yet Em seemed unfazed. She wanted me. I could tell that from looking into her bright green eyes. She definitely wanted me. Still, she'd held back. And I had no idea why.

What could she know about the Wright family that would cause this reaction?

Sure, we had more baggage than most families, but nothing that made sense in this situation. Well...okay, that was a lie. There were plenty of reasons for her to stay away from me. My reputation with women, for one. And my ex-wife, for another. But she couldn't have known anything else beyond that.

Her reaction flabbergasted me.

She didn't seem the type to play hard to get either. She had actually walked away and not looked back.

Mostly, I wasn't used to getting rejected.

Actually, I couldn't think of a time when I had been rejected. Not that it mattered. First time for everything. But it only made me want her more. I wanted to go back over there, pull her aside, and kiss the breath out of her. I wished that I knew where it had all gone wrong.

Seriously, what the fuck?

With an unfamiliar feeling of rejection, I retreated back to where I'd stashed my whiskey. I poured myself another glass as I contemplated my next move.

She obviously knew me, but I didn't know how. Nothing popped into my head. I had no clue how I could know her. And, now, I wanted to get to know her. It was an interesting woman who could turn me down...no matter how egotistical that made me. Just a healthy dose of self-confidence.

Morgan stumbled over to me a few minutes later as I was contemplating the dilemma.

"Fuck!" she said. "Gimme that."

She took my glass of whiskey and downed it like a shot. I glared at her and poured another glass. I was going to need that.

"Trouble with Landon?" I asked, passing her a glass.

"With Miranda, of course." She eagerly grabbed for the glass and took a large gulp.

"What happened this time?"

"Get this," she said with a shake of her head. She glanced back over to where she had abandoned Landon. "Miranda was pissed because Landon's ex-girlfriend is here!"

"Why would she care if his ex was here? He's married to her, for Christ's sake."

"Well, that's Miranda." Morgan shrugged.

"Yes, it is," I grumbled. I took another sip of my drink. "She drives me batshit crazy. I don't know why they're together."

"Your guess is as good as mine."

I nodded, but my eyes had locked back on Em, who was laughing at something Heidi or Julia had said. They each grabbed her hand and practically dragged her out to the dance floor. She shook her head, but they gave her pleading looks and started dancing to the hip-hop music that Sutton had requested for the night. It was as if she thought we were in a club or something, not a wedding.

Heidi was dancing all over Em while Em just stood there. She was saying something to Heidi and Julia, but they ignored her. And, after a few minutes, Em relaxed, and they were all dancing like they were having the time of their lives. Or they had just had an exorbitant amount of alcohol. Either way, I loved watching her move.

Once she got into it, it was intoxicating. The way her hips slid from side to side. The way she tilted her head back and laughed unabashedly with her friends. The way she lifted her arms over her head and sank low and then came back up to her full height. The way she tossed her hair and swung her hips in mouthwatering circles. It was hypnotic.

I stood there for two dances before she finally dared to glance over at me. Her eyes lit up when she saw that I was watching, and then she blushed furiously. She turned away from my look, but a minute later, she was back to staring at me. She was giving me a come-hither look, and it was killing me not to go over there and move with her on the dance floor. I wanted to oblige that look, but I didn't want to be turned away again either. I was dying for her to ask. Not just with her body, but also with her eyes and her smile and her mouth.

She turned back to her friends, but her eyes kept coming back to mine.

Over and over again. It was as if we were the only two people in the room. Everything else tumbled away, and she was dancing just for me.

Yes, I was watching.

Yes, she wanted me to.

She wet her lips and then did a little dance next to her friends. My dick pulsed as I thought about all the things I could do with those hips and all the promises I would keep with those lips. I had to straighten myself out, because thinking about fucking her while watching her dance was making my dick respond all too temptingly. I adjusted my pants and then finished my whiskey. She slanted her eyes back to mine and then discreetly tilted her head to the left.

I sighed.

Finally. Let's play ball.

She spoke hurriedly to her friends on the dance floor and then pointed toward the restroom. They said something back to her, but I could see the secret smiles on their faces. They knew where she was going and what she was doing.

Em meandered away from the dance floor. She glanced over her shoulder only once to see if I was following, and I was. When she realized I had interpreted her gesture, she smiled and then tried to smother it. We meandered into the darkness, past the restroom, far enough away from the crowds.

When she turned back to face me, her cheeks were pink from dancing and being here in this moment. "You were watching me."

"Is that a crime?" I asked.

"Suppose not. Why were you watching me?"

"Because you're the most beautiful girl in the room, and I like the way you move."

"Jensen, this could *never* happen."

"You mentioned that," I said, sliding another step toward her.

Her back pressed up against the exposed brick wall.

"Do you know who I am?" she pleaded.

"Em. And that's all I need to know."

I trailed a loose lock of her dark hair between my fingers. Her eyes were open and raw, showing me all the thoughts roaming through her head. She wanted me. I wasn't wrong in that regard. She might have rebuffed me, but she hadn't been able to walk away.

"Fuck," she whispered.

Her hand ran down the front of my suit, and I leaned into her.

"Yes," I agreed. "You tell me to go away yet ask me to come here. What exactly do you want?"

Even though she wanted me, her head was warring with her body.

Tension and desire mingled in the space between us. I could move in and take her lips with my own. I wanted to. But I didn't want to take. I wanted her to offer. Like she had offered to come back here with me.

"I don't know. This is a bad idea," she whispered.

"Seems like a good idea to me."

She released a breath. "I've had a lot to drink."

"Me, too," I said, taking a step closer.

"And, now, I really want to kiss you."

I chuckled. I liked her blunt honesty a lot more when it was directed toward me positively rather than negatively.

She practically glowed at my laugh, and her eyes darted down to my lips. "But we can't."

"Can't?"

She shook her head a miniscule amount and then tugged me a little closer. "Nope."

"You want to kiss me," I said, stepping into her personal space and glancing down at her lips. "But you can't. Or won't?"

"Oh, I will," she breathed. "But I shouldn't."

Then, she dragged me against her, and her lips landed on mine with a tenacity that was enthralling. Our lips touched, and the world ceased.

I ran my hands around her waist and pulled her flush against my body. My tongue licked along her lips, begging for entrance. She opened up to me at once, and our tongues met as we flat-out made out in the back of the building.

And she was a fucking amazing kisser. I could do this all day. Even though my dick was telling me to move faster, my brain was saying that this was incredible. Her body against mine. Her lips on mine. Her heartbeat ratcheting up to meet mine in tempo.

It was a life-shifting kiss. One of those that came only once in a lifetime. The kind that you didn't want to mean more. You wanted it to be a lust-induced kiss in the dark, but you couldn't even fool yourself. This one was everything.

I didn't know how long we stayed there, kissing. It could have been hours or days. My brain could not function beyond that moment.

But, eventually, she was pulling away, stepping back, shaking her head. And I had no idea what any of those motions meant.

Hadn't she just had the same kiss I had?

She touched her lips. They were swollen and red. "Jensen...I...we..."

"Em," I whispered, reaching out for her.

But she slipped through my fingers and disappeared into the night. I tried to follow after her, but one minute, she was there, and the next minute, she was gone.

My own fucking Cinderella. Great.

chapter
seven

Jensen

MY HEAD POUNDED THE NEXT MORNING AS MY PHONE BLARED ON THE nightstand. I grabbed it and pressed Accept without looking at who it was. *Fuck, how much had I had to drink last night?*

"Hello?" I said.

"Hello, Mr. Wright," my receptionist Margaret said. "I hope this is a good time. I got the paperwork in that you need to look over, and you told me to contact you as soon as it arrived."

"Yes. Thank you," I said as I tried to crawl out of bed.

Work. Of course, it's work.

I listened for a few minutes more as Margaret continued to discuss the paperwork.

I stumbled into the bathroom and downed a pair of Tylenol. I appreciated Margaret's enthusiasm for the merger, but I knew I wouldn't be able to concentrate on the logistics of the paperwork until I got rid of this headache.

"Do you need me to come into the office today to go over this with you, sir?" she asked.

"No, thank you, Margaret. I'll look at it in my home office and get back with you about it on Monday."

She hesitated on the other line. "I think they're going to want an answer today, sir."

"They've kept me on the line for five days about this. And I'll have to fly there to finish off the negotiations with Tarman. We have another day to wait. Plus, if I can lower their offer, we'll all have bigger bonuses this Christmas."

"Make them wait all you like then, sir."

"Thank you, Margaret," I said.

I hung up and then looked at myself in the mirror. I'd had way too much to drink last night. With a wince, I hopped into a scalding hot shower to try not to think about Em any longer. I'd tortured myself enough with it last night. Patrick, Austin, Morgan, and I had finished another bottle of whiskey while I was thinking.

By the time I completed my daily routine, I felt like a new man. Still a fucking confused man, but more like myself at least.

I checked the time as I changed into a pair of jeans and a button-up. It was still early. The alarm I had set for this morning hadn't even gone off yet. I could probably still get in at least an hour of work before I needed to meet everyone for church—Sunday morning tradition for as long as I could remember.

With the added time on my schedule, my office beckoned. I walked into the first-floor office and took a seat at my mahogany desk. The sun was just rising through the giant floor-to-ceiling windows overlooking the swimming pool that was closed for the season. I booted up my iMac and drowned myself in legalese that I would have to go over again with my lawyer. My eyes felt like sandpaper, and my throat was raw from all the alcohol and the sleepless night.

I thought my body would at least be used to not getting any sleep. Insomnia usually did that to someone. I couldn't remember the last time I'd had a full night's sleep. It was one of the reasons the company was flourishing. If you never had to sleep, then you could do double the amount of work.

My thoughts were so focused on the project at hand, I didn't even notice Landon standing in my doorway until he cleared his throat.

"Bad time?" Landon asked with a wry grin.

I finished typing up the memo I'd been working on and then stood from my desk. "Of course not. Just got bogged down in work."

"On Sunday, Jensen?" Landon said with a shake of his head. He entered the office and crashed back into one of the leather seats in front of the desk.

"Every day. Someone has to run the company. Not everyone gets to play golf on the weekends."

Landon laughed. "Every day. Not just the weekends."

"How's your back anyway?" I walked around to the front of the desk, leaned back against it, and crossed my arms.

The light left Landon's face. "It's fine. Better anyway. The physical therapist thinks I shouldn't be pushing it as much as I have this year, but none of the Wrights know how to slow down."

That's for damn sure.

"As long as you're taking care of it, then you'll be fine. People can have a professional golf career forever."

"Yeah, I'm on it." Landon shifted and stood. "Actually, I came over here so early because Miranda and I are going to head out."

"What?" I asked in confusion. "I thought you were staying through the holidays."

Landon grimaced. "Miranda wants to go back to Florida until Christmas. We'll be back."

"You're staying for church today though, right?" I prompted.

"I...no," he said.

I sighed heavily. "Not even for Mom?"

"I know," he said softly. "I want to, but Miranda..."

I wanted to make some wisecrack about Landon being whipped, but it didn't seem to be the time. Something was going on with him and Miranda. Their relationship was looking all too familiar. He knew better than this.

"Speaking of Miranda, I heard she freaked out last night."

Landon blew out a grateful breath at the change of subject. "Yeah, bro, my ex-girlfriend Emery Robinson was there. You remember her?"

My body stilled, and everything narrowed down to that name. "Emery Robinson," I whispered.

"Yeah. You know, my high school girlfriend. I didn't even recognize her, and Miranda was pissed that she hadn't been informed she'd be there."

"You didn't recognize her?" I whispered as horror and realization began to dawn on me.

"Nope. How fucked up is that?"

I ran a hand back through my short hair and closed my eyes. "Fuck."

"What?" Landon asked in confusion.

I shook my head. This could not be happening. Em—my mysterious Em, my fucking Cinderella—was Emery Robinson. Of course, she would recognize me. But I hadn't seen her in…God, ten years. No wonder she had ran away from me. I'd just tried to pick up my brother's ex-girlfriend.

"Jensen, what's up?"

I couldn't tell him. There was no way I could tell him that I'd had the best kiss of my life with Emery Robinson. I hadn't known it was her. And I knew Landon too well to drop that on him.

"Nothing. Hangover headache," I lied. "Tell me more about Emery. I remember her…only vaguely."

Understatement of the century. I remembered the taste of her lips and the feel of her skin and the way she kissed *very* well. Intimately. Everything else that came to mind about Emery was like a bridge over water on a foggy night. I knew it was there, but I couldn't see it.

"We dated in high school for two years, but we broke up on graduation. The last time I saw her was our five-year high school reunion, and we didn't talk then, and I had no idea she'd be at Sutton's wedding. I guess Heidi invited her." He shook his head. "I mean, I didn't even recognize her!" he repeated.

"How could you not have recognized her?"

"When we dated, she was the captain of the soccer team, who liked to skateboard on the weekends," Landon said in his defense. "Even at prom, she wore her hair up and no makeup. I don't know what she's been up to in the past decade. We're not even Facebook friends."

"And Miranda was pissed?"

Landon shrugged. "I don't know why. I'm not interested in the girl I dated in high school, who I haven't seen in years. I married Miranda."

Oh, I knew why Miranda was pissed off. Emery looked hot as fuck.

Whatever she had looked like and acted like in high school, she was a woman now. One I would very much like to get intimately acquainted with. Too bad I would probably never see or talk to her again.

"Is that the real reason you're leaving this morning?"

Landon groaned and glanced back toward the door. "I don't know, man. Probably. She's super jealous of all my exes."

I opened my mouth to say something to Landon about last night with Emery. It wasn't that I wanted to keep it a secret, but what would really come of telling him? I wasn't the dating type. I was the fuck-'em-and-leave-'em type. Even if I had done more than make out with Emery, it would have just been a hot-as-fuck one-night stand. It wouldn't have fucking mattered who had dated whom a decade ago.

"Are you sure you can't stay for church?" I asked instead.

At that exact moment, the front door crashed open. Landon sighed heavily and seemed to retreat into himself at the very thought of the person at the door.

"Miranda?" I hazarded a guess.

"The one and only," he agreed. "I should probably head out."

"Landon! Let's go! We have to get on the road!" Miranda yelled from the foyer.

Landon's eyes traveled through the open doorway. "I should probably go. I certainly don't want to stand between the two of you in another confrontation."

"Morgan's the instigator; I assure you."

Landon glanced back at me and rolled his eyes. "You don't fool as many people as you think you do."

I sure hoped I did in that moment.

I held my hand out to my brother. Landon clasped it tight.

"I just want you to be happy. Tell me Miranda makes you happy."

"Landon!" she shrieked. Her heels clomped across the hardwood floor, drawing ever nearer, like a dragon ready to breathe flames.

"You're a good brother," Landon said with a smile and shook my hand.

Miranda stomped into the room. "Would you hurry up, or would you rather me leave you behind so that you could be with your ex-girlfriend instead?"

Landon winced. "Come on, Miranda. I've told you a hundred times that I didn't even know she was going to be here."

"Well, I'm sure you'll know when we're back for Christmas so that you can sneak away and see her," she accused.

"Seriously, she's just back from college for a few days, visiting a friend. She'll be gone before we get back. Calm down," Landon said with a sigh.

"Whatever. Don't make me late for the flight," she said, turning on her heel and storming away.

"I'll see you in a couple of weeks," Landon said.

We hugged, and then he hurried down the hall toward his tyrant wife. And, while I was sad to see my brother go, I feared even more for the things he hadn't said. One day, I would figure out the disaster that Miranda had created in our family but not today. Today, I had to go to church.

chapter
eight

Emery

"I CANNOT BELIEVE YOU'RE MAKING ME DO THIS," I SAID TO KIMBER AS WE stood outside of our mother, Autumn's, house.

It was the house we'd grown up in. Small and squat with red clay bricks and dark roofing. Like everything in Lubbock, it had a monstrous fence for the entire backyard. A tree her mother had planted when she moved in towered over the property. The house was in one of those timeless parts of town. Nothing had changed, not even the people. They'd just settled here like dust.

"You were never going to come over here unless I made you," Kimber said.

She mashed the old, smashed-in doorbell, and I could hear it hollering through the house, announcing our presence.

"Don't act like you know me."

Kimber snorted. "Okay. Done," she said with a sarcastic bite.

The door popped open, and my mother's face appeared in the doorway. She was gorgeous. Even at her age, she was still a knockout. It was a bit unfair to think that Kimber had gotten all of my mother's beauty-queen looks, and I had only gotten her snarky wit and unbearable attitude.

"Well, look what the cat dragged in," she said.

"Funny, Mom. I've never heard that one before," I said with a grin.

"You're not too old to have your ass paddled, young lady."

Kimber nudged me forward, and I laughed. My mother had never paddled me in my life. Believe it or not, Kimber was the troublemaker.

The three of us wandered into the living room, and my mother closed the door behind us. Everything was exactly how it had always been—same brown fabric furniture with our initials scrawled into the wooden paneling on the side, my great-grandmother's china cabinet full to the brim with my mother's Precious Moments collection, and a sea of pictures on the mantel. At least some of those were new, the pictures with Noah and Lilyanne as additions.

But not a trace of my father. He had been swept clean out of the house since he walked out on my mom when I was a kid. Only a forgotten old military medal and a box of photographs in the attic crawl space remained.

We all took seats around the living room, suffocating from our past.

"If I'm not too old for a paddling, that means you're not too old either, Mom," I told her, searching for levity.

"Oh, I know, honey." Then, she winked at me. "You know, I've been talking to Harry Stevenson across the way, and he used to be a police officer."

"Oh God, Mom!" I said, covering my ears.

My mother cackled with glee at my embarrassment. "Now, where is my granddaughter? You can't make me feel old by popping out babies, Kimber Leigh," she said, patting my sister's very pregnant belly, "and then not bring them around when you come visit."

"Lilyanne is with Noah. We're going to meet up with them at the church."

"I suppose that will be fine," Autumn said with a sigh of dejection. "How am I supposed to spoil her rotten?"

"You're doing just fine at that," Kimber said.

My mother's eyes returned to me, assessing me in that uncanny way only she could do, and then she smiled softly. Light wrinkles crinkled around her eyes. Happy wrinkles. The ones I adored.

"I've missed you, Emery," my mother said. "But, girl, what have you been eating in Austin? Is anyone feeding you? You're skin and bones."

I glanced over at Kimber, whose eyes were wide with amusement.

Out of Kimber's closet, I'd chosen a plain black dress for church this morning. She couldn't wear it and had insisted that I should since we all knew I didn't have church-appropriate attire in the bags I'd brought from Austin.

"I'm eating fine. And...I left Austin," I blurted out. "I dropped out of the program."

"Oh. I was really looking forward to having another doctor in the family," Autumn said with a mischievous grin.

"Ah, if only I had been guaranteed Noah's salary."

"If only we all were," Kimber agreed.

"Are you sad about it? You don't seem sad," my mother asked.

Strangely, I wasn't. I thought I should have been. But, even though I'd dedicated three years to this endeavor, *sad* was not the word. I was relieved.

"Nope. I think it's the right choice. Just have to get a job and clean out my apartment. I know someone who will sublet it for next semester. At least that's covered."

"Maybe you'll change your mind," my mother said with a nonchalant shrug. "Let me put on my Sunday best, and then we can go."

As soon as my mom exited the room, I breathed out heavily.

Kimber swatted at my knee. "It was not that bad," she whispered.

"You're right. It wasn't. Probably because you're here."

"You're so dramatic. She's happy you're home."

"Yeah," I said, looking around the room again. "Maybe so."

"Okay, all ready to go," Autumn said, strolling back into the room. She was in a red dress with a black shawl, and she was wearing her signature red lipstick. "Think Harry Stevenson will be able to resist me?"

I groaned as I stood. "If we talk about your sex life one more time, I will vomit on your floor."

"We could talk about yours," my mother said.

"Let's not," I said with a sigh.

She followed Kimber out to her enormous SUV and took the front seat. Kimber pulled out of the driveway and headed toward the church down the street.

"I heard that you saw the Wright family yesterday," Autumn said.

"Good news does travel fast," I said dryly.

At the mention of the Wright family, my head spun...but not from Landon. It was because of Jensen. Seeing Landon had been...awkward, like seeing an old friend from high school you'd rather avoid. But Jensen...that was a different story. I hated to admit how much he had affected me. So much for swearing off men. It had been a total of one day, and already, I'd made out with Jensen fucking Wright.

"If you had told me that you were in town, I wouldn't have had to hear it from Barbara," my mother said. She peered at me in the backseat, and I blankly looked back at her. "Tina was there, too. She said you looked very pretty, and all the boys were staring at you."

Sometimes, I forgot that, my mother knew *everyone*. Born and raised and never left. She was a total extrovert and made instant friends with everyone she met. Another thing I had not inherited.

"Heidi did my hair and makeup. Only reason anyone looked at me all night. You know, Landon didn't even recognize me."

"What?" Kimber gasped. "You didn't tell me that."

"So, funny story, Landon didn't recognize me, and then his *wife* showed up and flipped her shit."

"Language, Emery," my mother said.

I rolled my eyes. Yeah, I did need to watch my language since we were about to walk into a church.

Kimber drove into the parking lot that was already more than half full. I knew Kimber and Noah only still went to this church because my mother had been going since she was a kid. Otherwise, they would find one a bit more... contemporary.

Lubbock was the kind of city that had a church on every street corner. Huge whitewashed buildings and old brick edifices dotted the brick-lined roads downtown. Giant pickup trucks with metal Texas Tech decals on the bumpers filled the parking lots. Jeans and cowboy boots were acceptable attire. The preachers were just as likely to give a sermon as spout political drivel. And, every week, there was a fifteen-minute interlude, mid sermon, for people to shake hands and greet their friends who lived down the street from them. In a town where crosses on walls in the living room were an interior design state- ment, church was practically mandatory.

We piled out of Kimber's SUV and meandered over to the entrance. I left my mother behind as she chatted with every Tom, Dick, and Harry—*gross!*— who stood in the entranceway. I trailed Kimber past the ladies handing out pamphlets, and I took one with a half-smile before going into the sanctuary.

The ceiling was mile high with stained glass windows over the chancel. The choir was already seated off to the right, and the pastor's wife was playing the piano nearby. A large wooden pulpit was rigged with a microphone, and there was a semicircle of cushioned prayer benches to be used for communion.

This wasn't exactly where I'd thought I'd be this early in the morning after drinking a couple bottles of champagne last night with Heidi. Mercifully, I didn't have a hangover. I'd had a bottle of Gatorade and some Tylenol before bed, and Kimber had babied me in the morning. But that still didn't mean I was prepared for this.

"Kimber," Noah said.

He waved from his spot near the front of the room. Lilyanne was seated in the pew, tapping away on her iPad.

We moved up the aisle, and Kimber kissed the top of Lily's head. "Hey, baby girl. Are you excited to see Grandma Autumn?"

"It's not autumn, Mommy," Lilyanne said, looking up very seriously. "It's winter."

"Actually," I interjected, "the winter solstice isn't until the twenty-first. So, it still *is* autumn."

"But it's cold," Lily said.

"Sound logic."

Noah cracked up and scooted Lilyanne down so that we could take our seats on the end of the row.

"So, tell me about seeing Landon," Kimber said, elbowing me in the side.

"Shh, Kim, we shouldn't gossip in church."

Kimber rolled her eyes. "It's not gossip if it comes from the source. Aren't you all about firsthand accounts in history?"

"Meh. Let's not talk about history right now. I've thought of next to noth- ing else for nine years. I need a break."

"A break like Landon Wright?" she whispered.

"Uh, no. Landon is married, remember?"

"Oh, right," Kimber said, sounding disappointed. "Well, there are a lot of other hot guys in town."

Noah's head swiveled around so fast, and Kimber's cheeks turned pink.

"What was that?" he asked.

"Oh, shush, you!" she said, flustered.

Kimber and Noah were a year older than Austin, the middle brother, so they never had a Wright in their grade. Though they knew the family, of course. Everyone knew the Wrights.

"I'm just asking if you are looking for some fun while you're here," Kimber said with a wink.

"Speaking of hook-ups in church?" I said, crossing myself in mock horror.

Kimber laughed and shook her head. "You're horrible."

"Lilyanne!" my mother said.

She burst onto the scene, as if she owned the place. But Lily adored her. She jumped from her seat, iPad abandoned, and threw herself into Autumn's arms. She twirled Lily around and then placed her on the ground before claiming the seat beside her.

"She sure loves your little girl," I said.

"She does. I couldn't have asked for a better grandma," Kimber agreed.

"Who would have guessed?"

"Everyone," Kimber said. Then she grinned. "Look who just walked in the building."

I swiveled in my seat just in time to watch the entire Wright family stride into the building. My eyes first latched on to Jensen in a crisp black suit, white button-up, and burgundy tie. He looked...sexy as hell. In fact, I would not mind so much seeing what was underneath that suit. My cheeks burned with the thoughts running through my head. I was in church, for Christ's sake.

My eyes darted down the line of people—Austin, Morgan, Sutton, and Maverick. *Huh, I guess not all the Wrights were here.* I couldn't help but feel grateful that Landon wasn't here with his wife. Then, I didn't feel as bad about checking out Jensen.

As Jensen passed my row, he turned all his attention to me. A smile dimpled his cheeks, and I stopped breathing. *Fuck, I had made out with that face.*

Then, he and the rest of his family took their seats in the front row. I distantly remembered that they came to church every Sunday after their mother died. They did it to honor her memory since she had been such a devoted churchgoer. It was pretty amazing that they still did it. Even the morning after Sutton's wedding.

Maybe I had judged them all a bit too harshly after Landon.

Maybe it wasn't the worst thing to fantasize about those dimples.

Maybe...just not in church.

chapter
nine

Emery

I'D SAY THAT THE SERVICE WAS INTERESTING, BUT I WAS A HORRIBLE PERSON AND didn't pay attention. Not that I was *not* religious. Not exactly. But, when the most eligible bachelor in the city was sitting three rows in front of you and you knew he'd wanted nothing more than to get into your pants the night before, it was a bit hard to concentrate.

Especially at the halfway mark when everyone was allowed to get up to greet their neighbors, and he turned to look right at me. I probably should go up to him to apologize for running away yesterday and just fucking explain who I was. I still couldn't believe that I hadn't just told him.

How hard was it to say I dated your brother?

Apparently, really difficult. Really, really difficult. Especially with his tongue down my throat.

I'd known what Heidi was doing by only giving him my nickname, Em. Emery was not common at all, and the light bulb would have registered immediately. Still, I hadn't corrected her, and I hadn't told him why I'd run away. Because I hadn't wanted to walk away. Maybe a part of me was still thinking about that unattainable, hot college guy that Heidi and I had dreamed about in high school.

Now, he was an even hotter billionaire CEO who was looking a whole hell of a lot more attainable.

If only I hadn't dated his brother.

My mother, of all people, saved me from humiliating myself in front of Jensen. She latched on to my arm and dragged me over to Betty, a woman I used to work for at the Buddy Holly Center when I was in high school. They had an opening after their latest hire quit, and she was more than excited to have me back on staff.

So, at least something positive came out of the whole church experience.

When the service ended, my mother milled around, chatting with all her friends. I knew that we wouldn't be going anywhere for a while unless I hitched a ride with Noah. And, by the look on Kimber's face, she was already getting ready to tell me off for considering it.

I stood and stretched, all the while wondering whether or not I should wait for everyone outside...or if I should say something to Jensen.

Before I could decide on what to do, Jensen left his family behind in the front row and then walked casually over to where I was leaning against the edge of the pew.

"Hey. Surprised to find you here," he said with that same charming smile.

God, did he have another smile? Oh my God, I had made out with those lips.

"Hey. Yeah," I said back, glancing away.

Smooth.

Let's just take awkward to a whole new level.

"I didn't realize your family went to church here," he said.

His eyes wandered past me to Kimber, Noah, and Lilyanne and then traveled to my mother.

"Yeah. My mom has been going here since…forever."

"Right. I didn't put two and two together." He smiled. "Well, I really came over to apologize about last night."

My eyebrow quirked, and I shot him a dubious look. "What exactly are you apologizing for?"

Last I checked, that kiss was the hottest thing I'd ever experienced, and he had no need to apologize.

"Everything apparently," he said. "I realized that my advances must have been…unwanted. I think I might have pushed you and made you feel…uncomfortable, which was not my intention."

Ha! Uncomfortable was not the right word. I'd felt like my body had a different brain. One that was screaming *yes* when I knew *no* was the right answer.

"You didn't push your luck. It's fine," I said with a wave of my hand.

What I wanted to say was, *Kiss me again. God, please, kiss me again. I won't run this time.*

And the look in his eye said he knew.

"I assume you've figured out who I am."

"Emery Robinson," he drawled. "Yes, I know who you are."

"And see, *now*, you're not interested," I said before tacking on a shaky laugh.

"Oh," he said, his eyes intense and commanding, "but I am."

My mouth popped open into a tiny little O of surprise. *Jensen knew I'd dated Landon, and he was still interested in me? No way. He must be mistaken.*

His eyes dropped to my mouth, and he swallowed. We both seemed to be having the same damning thoughts.

He took a step toward me, entering my personal space, and leaned in near my ear. "Perhaps we should take this conversation outside. I try to avoid impure thoughts in church."

A small gasp escaped my lips, and then I covered my mouth with my hand. My eyes slid from his to survey the church as I was slammed back into reality.

Jensen Wright was having dirty thoughts about me in church.

Oh, hell yes!

"Okay," I found myself saying.

He even seemed surprised that I had agreed. Last night, I'd dashed away from him and into oblivion. Found Heidi and disappeared entirely. Now, I was saying yes to talking to him again.

"Okay then."

"Hey, Kimber," I said, turning to face my sister.

Her eyes were as wide as plates when she looked at me.

"I'm...I'm just going to go outside, all right?"

"Sure," she said.

"Just, um, come find me when Mom is done."

"Will do. But...if you get another ride home, that's okay, too," Kimber said boldly.

I rounded my eyes in exasperation, but Kimber stifled a laugh behind her hand. Between Kimber and Heidi, they were determined to set me up by Christmas. As if I hadn't just gotten out of a sort of three-year relationship with Mitch. God, thinking about that made my head hurt. *What a huge mistake.*

"Good to go," I said, snatching up my cell phone.

Kimber had my wallet in her purse since I hated carrying one.

"That's it?" he asked.

"What? Oh, my phone? Yeah. Purses are annoying."

He laughed and cocked his head to the side. "Interesting. Why do you think that? I thought most women loved purses."

I fell into step beside him. "Yeah, well, I'm not most women. I think they're pretty, but why would I want to lug something around full of junk that I probably won't need, only to hurt myself by carrying the weight around?"

"Fair point," he said with an amused smile on his face.

We passed through the narthex and went out into the Texas sunshine. I stripped off my cardigan since the weather was in the seventies. It never stopped amazing me, how bizarre the weather patterns were here. But I would take it if I got to wear a short-sleeved dress in December.

"This is a little strange," I said.

"Why?"

I chewed on my lip and shrugged. "I don't know...because I dated your brother?"

Jensen shifted his feet and then stared down at me like I was his next meal. "That was a long time ago, right?"

"Yeah," I admitted. "You're right. It was forever ago."

"And you're away at school right now?"

I narrowed my eyes, wondering where he had gotten his information. Not that I wanted to tell him that I'd just quit pursuing my degree. Only my mother, Kimber, and Heidi knew that.

"*Away* is kind of a loose phrase for someone who hasn't lived in Lubbock in almost ten years," I said nonchalantly.

"That's true, I suppose. It's not like many people move back once they've seen the big wide world," he said with a grin.

"Yeah. There's a reason for that."

"What would that be?" he asked, genuinely curious.

But he had to know. Lubbock was suffocating. Big enough to have an airport, small enough for the airport to have to reroute you everywhere you really wanted to go. It had improved in every way since I left in high school. Better restaurants, better shopping, better amenities. But it was still Lubbock—dry, dusty, and flat as hell.

"Because not everyone has a private jet that can fly them wherever they want," I said. Then, I covered my mouth in horror. "Oh God, you know what? That was really rude. Definitely rude. I don't even know if you have a private jet."

"I do," he said with blatant amusement as I tried to cover up my mishap.

"Okay. Well, even if you didn't...still rude."

"Do you want to go out with me?" Jensen asked point-blank.

"What?" I gasped. "I was just rude to you. Why would you want to?"

"You're refreshing. You don't have to apologize to me. I've been in your presence for fifteen minutes, and I'm already certain that I want to continue to do so."

His eyes slid to my lips with the unsaid words hanging between us.

I'd like another one of those kisses. Please, and thank you.

"But...but you don't even know me," I said. I had no idea why I was arguing with him.

"That's true. However, I would very much like to get to know you, if you'd let me, Emery."

I was pretty sure that it was the way he said my name that made me realize he was serious.

It made no sense to me. I couldn't be like the other girls he had dated. I remembered a tall blonde girlfriend he'd had in college who was around the house when I dated Landon. Smart, beautiful, legs for days with a body that belonged in a Victoria's Secret ad and a smile that belonged on a Crest commercial. She was the kind of girl someone like Jensen Wright picked up. Not me.

Yet, in some strange twist of the universe, this was happening. To me!

I wanted to ask why. Perhaps the glamorous look from last night had won him over, but today, I was once again makeup-free. My hair still held the curls from last night, so they looked all right. But I still didn't understand it.

I was an average girl, and he was a gorgeous Texas billionaire. He could have anyone he wanted, but he'd picked me.

"All right," I said finally.

"Great. Let me get your number."

He handed me his phone, so I could add my number into his cell. Then, I texted myself from his phone.

"I was thinking tomorrow night. Does that work for you?"

"Tomorrow?" I squeaked.

"Fine, you've convinced me," he said with a grin. "How about tonight?"

"Tonight?"

"We could just go now," he suggested. "I don't have a free day, but I can rearrange."

My mouth was slightly hanging open in disbelief. "You want to see me right now?"

"I am seeing you right now." He passed me back my phone. "And I like what I see."

I laughed at the comment and felt a blush creeping up my neck. "Well, I think maybe tonight would be good. Where do you want to go?"

"I have an idea," he said with a grin. "Bring a big coat, and wear something comfortable."

My brows furrowed. "You don't strike me as a wear-something-comfortable sort of date."

"It's the suit, isn't it?" he asked.

"I suppose so."

"I have a question. How do you like sleeping?"

"What does that even mean?" I asked with a laugh. "I love sleeping. Doesn't everyone? Though I didn't get much of it in grad school."

"Okay, good. Don't plan on getting any tonight," he told me.

"That's awfully presumptuous," I said softly, averting my eyes again. The blush was full-blown now.

He pressed his finger under my chin and tilted my head up to look at him. His eyes were warm and inviting. I suddenly felt as if I could drown in them. My body responded to his touch like a struck match, and I was sure he knew it.

"Big coat and something comfortable. We'll see if I'm presumptuous tonight." He smiled and looked like he wanted to kiss me again. "I can't wait until then."

Then, he released me and disappeared into the parking lot.

My body was humming. I couldn't believe what had just happened. I had a date with Jensen Wright tonight. And he had already promised that I would be out all night. Even though my logical brain was saying not to lose my heart to someone like him, my body was screaming to lose everything else.

chapter
ten

Emery

"I SHOULD CALL AND CANCEL," I TOLD HEIDI A FEW HOURS LATER. She was crashed back on the guest bed at Kimber's and staring at me with raised eyebrows. "Why the hell would you do that?"

"Because he's Landon's brother!"

"So?" she asked, exasperated. "He's smoking hot! You've already made out with his face. You should so fuck him."

I rolled my eyes and flung a sweater at her face. "Shut up! We're not going to have sex."

"Sure. Then, why are you wearing that?"

I was standing in a skimpy black lace bra and a thong that I'd thankfully brought with me from Austin, and it looked sexy on my curvy frame.

"What?" I asked defensively. "I have nothing in my closet. I need to get the rest of my stuff from Austin."

"Yeah, okay," she said sarcastically.

I swung around to face her. "Isn't it just a little...weird?"

"You are the only one making it weird."

"I think maybe I'd feel better if I talked to Landon."

Heidi snorted. "Now, that's something I never thought I'd hear you say."

"Oh, shut it," I said, flipping her the bird.

"You've talked to Landon twice in over nine years since the breakup, including this weekend! Other than the sad, sappy messages you left on his voice mail in college."

"Don't," I hissed. My cheeks flamed.

I hated to think about the heartbroken girl I'd been when Landon dumped me. But, at eighteen, he had been my first serious boyfriend. I'd gone on to forget all about him with a long line of mistakes. And, now, I was going on a date with his brother.

"Come on, Em. This will be fine. You thought Jensen Wright was sexy as hell since before you had any interest in Landon. Cut loose."

I sighed. Sure, I'd had an unhealthy obsession with Jensen, just like every other girl my age, but I was a totally different person now than I'd been ten years ago—physically and emotionally. Plus, I'd gotten through three years of a PhD program. I could handle one night out with Jensen Wright and not make a fool of myself. Hopefully.

"All right. I won't cancel."

"Excellent. I'd go with this." She plucked a black V-neck sweater off the floor and passed it to me.

I tugged it over my head and paired it with my classic black skinny jeans and boots. Swishing my dark hair over to one side of my head, I held my hands out. "What do you think?"

"I still think a little black dress would be better. Are you sure he said warm and comfortable?"

"Definitely."

The doorbell rang downstairs, and my eyes widened to saucers.

I heard Lilyanne screaming, "I'll get it. I'll get it. I'll get it!"

"He's early," I groaned, glancing at the clock.

"Well, hurry up. Go and intercept the minion, or he's going to be taking Lily," Heidi said.

I snatched my phone off of the nightstand, slid it into my back pocket, and dashed out of the room. I could see Noah and Kimber moving toward the front door, and Heidi was on my heels. With my luck, this would turn into one big family affair. *Ugh!*

"And who are you?" I heard Jensen ask from the front door.

I hopped the last two steps and turned to find him bending down, eye-level with my niece. He had a big smile on his face and a bouquet of gorgeous flowers in white, deep dark reds, and plum purples.

"I'm Lilyanne. Who are you?" she asked.

"So nice to meet you, Lilyanne. My name is Jensen."

"Are those for me?" she asked, stretching her hands out toward the flowers.

He laughed. "They most certainly are. Do you have a vase to put them in? I can show you how to keep them pretty for a long time."

Lilyanne squealed and clutched the flowers to her chest. "Mommy! Daddy!" she shrieked. "I have flowers!"

"How nice," Kimber said.

"I think I have a boyfriend!"

Everyone laughed at that comment. But Lilyanne just twirled around in a circle and dashed to her parents.

Noah scooped her up in his arms. "You're a little young for a boyfriend, I think. Right?"

"Yep," Kimber agreed. "Much too young."

Lilyanne stuck out her bottom lip and hugged her flowers.

"Let's go with Mom to find something to put them in," Noah said, carrying her out of the room.

Jensen stood from where he'd been crouching, and his eyes found me across the distance of the living room. His eyes seared into me like a brand. I immediately felt flushed. I watched him peruse my outfit, starting at the tips of my toes and agonizingly dragging his eyes up to my face. My cheeks burned like a torch as a smile bloomed on his face, dimpling his cheeks, and it reminded me that not only was he drop-dead gorgeous, but he was also somehow *amazing* with kids.

Fuck, what am I getting myself into?

Heidi nudged me forward into the charged space and then disappeared into the kitchen.

"Hey," I said, feeling the weight of our distance and moving toward him like a magnet. *How did he have this kind of effect on me? Did all women feel like their bodies were on fire when Jensen Wright settled his gaze on them?*

"Hey, Emery," he said, taking another step toward me so that we were nearly touching.

He held out his empty hand and brushed my arm. My skin crackled, and I had to control my emotions not to show it.

"I had flowers for you."

I cleared my throat and smiled up into his deep dark eyes. "That's okay. You just made Lily's day. She's going to be talking about you forever now."

"Ah, good. She's adorable. How old is she? Four?"

I nodded and used the opportunity to glance back at Lily, who I could just see in the kitchen. "Yeah."

"That's a great age."

"She's the best," I agreed. I swiveled back to face him and was met with a molten gaze that brought back all of the dirty thoughts I'd had in church earlier today. Yeah, there was no way I could end this date tonight. Not with him looking like *that*.

A heavy black Arc'teryx jacket molded to his body over a T-shirt. Dark jeans ran down his powerful thighs, revealing dark boots that were definitely worn and loved. I was a lost cause.

"I know I'm early," he said. "I saw that a cold front would be moving through tonight. That was not in the plan, especially with how the wind is now."

"Only in Texas," I said with a laugh. "The weather is crazy unpredictable. With my luck, we'll have a dust storm blow through."

"Let's hope not."

"I'll get my coat." I dashed to the closet and grabbed my winter coat, sliding it over my sweater.

Heidi waved at me from the kitchen and mouthed, *Have fun.* I winked at her and then returned to Jensen.

"Ready."

Jensen raised his hand at my family, who were staring at the pair of us from the kitchen. I hurried out the door in embarrassment and put getting my own place on the ever-growing list of things that I needed to do. He pulled the door closed behind us and veered me toward a lifted black truck. It was huge and masculine and looked like I was going to need a step up to ride it. Just like Jensen.

I shook my head to get my mind out of the gutter and let Jensen open the door for me. I brushed past him. The contact sent shivers up my arm that I knew I couldn't blame on the weather. I sank into the passenger side, and then Jensen shut my door and climbed into the driver's side. I checked out the kick-ass interior and reworked my Jensen framework around this truck. I definitely hadn't pictured him for a big-truck guy. For some reason, I'd assumed he'd have a shiny little sports car. I really needed to get over my prejudices about this guy.

Jensen backed out of Kimber's driveway, and then we started heading toward town.

His eyes peeked over at me in interest, like I was a puzzle he wanted to put together. "So, what are you in school for?"

Okay, play it cool. I wasn't hiding why I was here, but I hadn't really talked about it with anyone outside of my family and Heidi. And we'd been friends long enough that she knew which questions not to ask.

"Um…PhD in history at UT Austin."

Both eyebrows rose at that, and I realized that I liked surprising him.

"A PhD? That's incredible."

"Thanks," I said. Even though I knew that I had made the right decision in leaving, I knew earning my PhD had made me stand out and given me focus. Without it, I didn't really know who I was or what I was doing.

"What kind of history?"

"Oh. European female figures with some interest in European monarchy mistresses. Well, I was writing my dissertation on Madame de Pompadour, who was the renowned mistress of King Louis XV of France."

"Mistresses," he said with a shake of his head. "There's a lot of research on that?"

"A surprising amount honestly," I told him.

"Interesting. I always wanted to go back and get another degree," he admitted.

"Pretty hard to do while you're running your own business, I would guess."

He nodded, resting his hand on the gearshift between us. I got distracted by his long, masculine fingers and the way they wrapped around the head of the stick. *Wow, he had big hands.*

My eyes shot back up to his as my thoughts strayed all over again. Damn, it hadn't been that long since I'd gotten laid. I felt like a dog in heat.

Jensen didn't say anything about the look on my face, but I could tell in the barely suppressed grin and cocky tilt of his head that he knew I'd been checking him out. "That would be the main reason. Just too busy to go back to school."

"Aren't you in charge though? Why would you need another degree?" I asked, keeping to safer territories.

"I wouldn't." His face went disturbingly blank for a second. His bright and shining eyes turned flat and empty. His smile disappeared.

It was like all the joy had been sucked out of the air from that one little question. And I didn't even know why.

I chewed on my lip and faced front again as we pulled off of the main road and into a parking lot. With my mind swirling with possibilities as to why that had upset him, I hadn't put much thought into where we were going to eat or what we were going to do on this date. I'd been too preoccupied by the warm clothing aspect.

But, now that we were standing outside of Torchy's Tacos, I burst out laughing. "You're taking me for tacos?" I asked when I met him by the bed of the truck.

All the seriousness of the last bit of our conversation had disappeared, and no tension remained in his shoulders.

"What? Do you not like tacos?" He apprehensively assessed me. "Tacos are a deal-breaker."

I gently shoved him as we angled toward the front of the restaurant. "Of course I like tacos. Do people not like tacos?"

He shrugged. "Traitors maybe."

"You're ridiculous," I said with a laugh. "I just didn't expect...tacos."

"What were you expecting?"

His body angled toward me, and once again, I felt that crushing inescapable force vibrate between us. There was something that made it so that I couldn't seem to get my bearings with him.

"I don't know. I guess I'm just realizing that you're not what I thought."

"Good. You aren't what I was expecting either."

"Oh, yeah? What were you expecting?"

"After meeting you yesterday? A girlie girl who likes makeup and hair and designer clothes."

I couldn't seem to help myself at that image and abruptly laughed out loud.

"Yes, well, I realize that's not who you are."

"Not even close." I straightened but kept my smile firmly in place.

He leaned forward, so our bodies were nearly touching and brushed a lock of hair off my face. My head tilted up, and I stared into those deep eyes, hanging on to every word with bated breath.

"Let's suspend all preconceived notions about each other then. What do you think?"

I nodded. "I'd like that."

chapter
eleven

Jensen

EMERY WASN'T WHAT I'D EXPECTED.

I knew that I had told her to put preconceived notions behind us, but she was turning me on my head. I had thought she was just a hot piece of ass. Patrick wasn't lying when he'd said I got a look in my eye when I was chasing women.

But Emery didn't seem to be the kind of girl who just fucked around. She was smart. Another quality I was not used to in the women I dated. She was clearly driven and seemed to have her shit together. It was actually refreshing.

I hadn't really known what to expect, walking into this. When I'd seen her at church, I couldn't help myself. Landon had said she was going to be here for only a few days. *What would he care about me going on a date with his ex?* It wasn't like we were going to get married or anything. No, I'd definitely sworn that off after Vanessa.

But, if this was a quick trip for her, then it wouldn't be any different than hooking up with someone I met when I was away on business. We happened to meet in Lubbock and not when she was in Austin.

Emery's phone buzzed noisily while we waited in line at Torchy's. Her laugh was effortless, and I enjoyed the flush that followed. Whoever had just messaged her certainly made my night easier.

I raised my eyebrows as she shoved her phone into the back pocket of her jeans. "What was that about?"

"Heidi," she said, as if that explained it.

Heidi. Right. They had been together at the wedding. I liked Heidi. She was a bossy, hard-working, and energetic woman and an HR nightmare. Not for me, mind you, since I didn't mix business with pleasure, but half of the men on my staff were head over heels for her.

"Heidi's great. I don't know what we would do without her. Though you'd never guess that from talking to her about it. How long have you known each other?"

We scooted forward in line, and she edged closer to me. I was glad that I'd gone for casual. I did enough fancy dinners to know when a girl was into it. As soon as she'd said that she didn't carry a purse, I knew a fifty-dollar steak wasn't going to do the trick. Plus, even though this never happened, I really did prefer this. Tacos were my favorite.

"That sounds like Heidi. Always the hard worker who acts as if she couldn't care less," she said, flipping her hair off her shoulder. "We've been best friends basically forever."

"Well, she's lucky then."

She shook her head and nudged me. "Nah, I'm the lucky one. She keeps me on the straight and narrow." She mischievously grinned up at me. "Well... mostly."

I decided right then and there that I liked that look and would do a whole lot to make her keep looking at me like that.

"No one wants to be too straight and narrow." I leaned down and whispered into her ear, "I color outside of the lines."

She burst out laughing as we reached the front of the line, and I held out my hand so that she could order first. I left her to fill up her drink and then grinned at the woman behind the counter.

A few minutes later, we had our tacos in a bag, and I hefted them up to eye-level. "Ready?"

She tilted her head in confusion. "Tacos on the go?"

"We have places to be," I told her.

Her eyes flickered between me and the bag of tacos. I couldn't read what was going on behind those eyes. *Is she enjoying this, or am I going too far?* I did have things planned for the night, but they could change if she wasn't interested. She looked adventurous, and I wanted to see if I was right.

"All right," she said after a minute, "lead the way."

We moved back out to my truck, and I passed her the bag of tacos after she hoisted herself up into the passenger seat. I didn't always drive my truck either, but where we were going, it was always better to have four-wheel drive.

I sped us out of town, and Emery handed me my tacos. She suspiciously eyed me while we ate.

"Where the hell are you taking me?" she asked halfway through her second taco.

"You haven't guessed?"

She seemed to consider it. "I mean...I know what's out this way, but I have no idea why you would be taking me into the middle of nowhere on a first date."

"Lubbock, by definition, *is* the middle of nowhere."

"That is a fair point," she agreed.

Her leg was bouncing in place, and I could see she was curious but trying not to be.

"You don't like surprises?"

She shrugged and then grimaced. Then, she shook her head. "I mean... sometimes. Like, surprise, my sister is pregnant, that's awesome. But I'm kind of horrible at this waiting thing. I was that kid who would sneak into my mom's closet and peek at my Christmas presents. I called Oklahoma before they announced scholarship letters and convinced the person in administration to tell me whether or not I'd made it."

I couldn't help it; I laughed. She sounded just like me. If someone had planned something like this for me, I would be losing my mind, having to know what was going on.

"Don't laugh at me," she said, swatting at my sleeve. "I'm impatient."

"I don't fault you. I am the same way."

"So…where are we going?"

"It's a surprise."

Then, she slumped back down. "Ugh! Okay. I'll wait."

Luckily, she didn't have to wait for long. Before she knew it, we pulled into the small town of Ransom Canyon. It was only about twenty minutes outside of Lubbock and generally considered a sort of suburb of Lubbock. Not that Lubbock actually had suburbs. It was just one of the closest towns.

"Ransom Canyon?" Emery asked, staring at the flat lake that took up the center of the canyon.

Unknown to most people, west Texas had a series of canyons that studded the land, like holes in Swiss cheese. Palo Duro Canyon, an hour and a half north of town and just outside of Amarillo, was the second largest canyon, after the Grand Canyon, in the United States. It was one of the many things that made this side of Texas interesting if you knew where to look.

"Have you seen their Christmas lights before?"

"Nope. I've been here a million times before. We used to go to the lake as kids. I've spent many a summer weekends on boats here. But I didn't know about the Christmas lights. When did they start to do that?"

"A couple of years ago. They even have a radio station tuned in so that you can listen to Christmas music as you circle the neighborhood and the lake."

"Festive." Her tone instantly changed. She had gone from skeptical to excited. She leaned forward in her seat, wondering where we were going to start first. "Are we going to see them all?"

"Of course," I told her. Even though I'd had something else in mind, I was not going to miss a minute of that smile.

I switched the station over to AM radio and drove around town. It was a small area of only about a thousand people, but the people who had chosen to move out on the lake rather than live in town generally had considerable wealth. The mansions were decked out in Christmas lights, which had all likely been done by the same company. It was like the modern version of *How the Grinch Stole Christmas* when the two Whos were fighting over who had the best lights. That was the entire town.

Our drive was punctuated by Emery's oohs and aahs and the occasional, "Slow down; you're going too fast."

I had to say, that was something I'd never heard before.

Emery lit up brighter than any of the houses that we'd passed. Halfway through, she must have begun to relax around me because she started singing along with the Christmas music. She was a little off-key, but I found that it didn't even matter. And, eventually, we were both belting out the chorus to Mariah Carey's "All I Want for Christmas Is You."

Emery was laughing so hard that a few tears rolled down her face. "Oh my God, if I had thought for one second in high school that I would be singing Mariah Carey with Jensen Wright on a real date, I think I would have dropped dead."

"Hey, don't dis Mariah," I said. "She's an icon."

"She can't even *sing* anymore!"

"I'm going to pretend like you didn't say that."

She snorted and then covered her face. "Oh my God, what is my life?"

"Seems pretty awesome," I said with a grin. "Even if you don't like Mariah."

"I do like Mariah!" she cried. "Stop twisting my words, you!"

"I'm not twisting anything."

Her smile was magnetic, and I just wanted to kiss her. I mean...I'd wanted to kiss her all night. But sitting there, in front of the last lit house, with Christmas music playing in the background and her smile radiating joy, there was nowhere else I'd rather be. That thought hit me so suddenly and I didn't even know why.

I put my truck into park, leaned over to her side of the car, and pushed my hand up into her dark hair. She froze, silhouetted by the light display behind her. Her eyes locked with mine, green meeting brown, and her eyes widened with surprise. She breathed out softly, and I could feel her pulse ratchet up at my touch.

This was the girl who had pulled me across the room at Sutton's wedding, like a magnet finding its pair. This was the tension that I'd felt when we first spoke. Here was the world of desire and lust that had clouded both of our minds ever since our first kiss.

My face was only inches from hers. I wanted to take what was mine. I wanted to claim her mouth and then her body right here in the cab of my truck, like we were young, wild, and carefree.

But, instead, I couldn't seem to stop staring at her.

She laughed lightly to try to defuse the tension. But it wasn't possible, and it was a feeble effort.

"Are you going to kiss me?" she whispered boldly.

I didn't need any further prodding. I crushed my lips against hers. It was like striking a match. Our lips moved against each other, desperate with the need to get closer, to have more. She opened her mouth for me, and I brushed my tongue against hers. The groan that emanated from deep in the back of her throat made my dick twitch. Our tongues volleyed for position. She was just as aching for attention as I was.

I heard the click of her belt buckle, and soon, she was pushing her body closer, moving over the divide of my truck. My hands fell to her ass, and I effortlessly hoisted her up and into my seat. She squeaked in shock but didn't break contact. Instead, she straddled me and let her hands wander across my chest.

My hands never left her ass because, damn, did that woman have an ass. She was grinding up against me, and I moved into a full-blown hard-on at her ministrations. She must have realized what she was doing to me because, when she swiveled her hips in place, she moaned against the feel of my dick.

In that moment, I didn't give a shit that we were acting like teenagers, parked outside of a stranger's house, bucking against each other for just an ounce of satisfaction. I was ready to strip her bare and fuck her until she forgot every word to every Christmas song and only remembered my name.

That was, until she rocked back just a little too hard, and a loud honk erupted from the hood of the truck.

chapter
twelve

Emery

I BROKE AWAY LIGHTNING FAST, AND MY HEAD WHIPPED TO THE SIDE. I STARED OUT at the house we were parked in front of. All the lights were lit, and surely, anyone who was inside had a front-row view to what we had just been doing.

"Fuck! I didn't mean to do that."

"It's fine. You should kiss me again," Jensen said.

He hadn't moved his hands from my ass, and I couldn't deny that I liked it.

Fuck, I had just had the most amazing make-out session in my life and ruined it.

Jensen nipped my lower lip, basically deciding for me. I leaned into his kiss again with a low moan.

Forget common decency. I just wanted Jensen Wright. Right here. Right now.

Then, I heard the sound of a door crashing open. I reared back and found an old woman rushing out of the front door in her nightgown. She had to be in her eighties with her white hair in curlers. She was shaking her fist at the truck as she wandered out into the frigid night.

"Fuck. Fuck. Fuck!" My eyes widened in horror.

No sweet talk from Jensen was going to change my mind this time. There was an old woman *shaking her fist* at us. Comically, I suddenly felt like I was in an old movie, and I was dying of humiliation.

I scrambled off of Jensen's lap and landed with a thud back into the passenger seat. I frantically waved my arms at Jensen. "Come on. We have to get out of here."

He laughed at me. There wasn't an ounce of shame on his face.

"Jensen," I spat like a curse, "get your cute ass moving."

"All right, all right," he said with a grin. He languidly adjusted his pants, which was a nice distraction from the woman approaching us from her front porch. "So long as you think my ass is cute."

I buried my face in my hands. Not only had we been caught making out by a woman, but I had also just admitted to checking out Jensen's ass. I was out of my damn mind. That had to be the only explanation.

Jensen put the truck into drive and pulled away without another word. He seemed to find the whole thing amusing. I thought he might have even found my own humiliation funnier than the woman rushing out at us. Just my luck.

"I cannot believe that just happened."

"It wasn't that bad," he said, slipping his hand across the seat and taking mine.

I let out a groan. "What is your definition of *wasn't that bad?*"

"You don't know that woman, and you'll never have to see her again."

"Not with my luck!"

Jensen reassuringly trailed his thumb down my knuckles. "Emery, look at me."

My gaze shifted to his from where I was bent over. "What?"

"Don't be embarrassed. I thought it was sexy as hell."

"Getting caught?" I asked.

He tilted his head and arched an eyebrow. "The way you rode me," he said in a husky deep voice.

I blushed at his words, but that got me to sit up. I shouldn't be so embarrassed. We weren't kids anymore. I was an adult...sort of. I wasn't that great at adulting. I didn't even really know what was considered adulting. But, if it involved riding Jensen like a bucking bronco, then I'd be on board with trying to be more of an adult.

"You liked that?" I asked, finally finding my voice.

"I'd like to do more than let you ride me in my truck," he admitted.

He took a left and then headed back up the canyon. His eyes slid to mine in the darkness, and the intensity of them shot heat straight between my thighs. I squeezed them together in anticipation.

"I'd love to get you to make those moaning noises all night."

I choked on my own saliva at those words. My mouth dropped open.

"I wouldn't mind *this* either," he said, untwining our hands to rub his thumb across my bottom lip.

"Oh, dear God," I whispered.

My tongue darted out and caressed his thumb, and we both shivered.

"Is that what you want?"

"For you to fuck me?" I countered.

He grinned, dimpling his cheeks and sending me swooning all over again. "I'd like nothing more than to fuck you, Emery."

My head nodded in agreement, as if without my body even realizing it. Because, hell yes, I wanted to get fucked by Jensen Wright.

Normally, I wouldn't talk about sex like that. It was Heidi who had messaged me at Torchy's to ask if we were fucking already. I hadn't thought for a split second that it was even a possibility that we were going to get hot and heavy. I had thought that maybe he'd kiss me on my doorstep when he dropped me off.

I wasn't naive. I'd gone through my one-night-stand phase in college. I'd meaninglessly dated a guy in college who I fucked every day until I realized I hated that he smoked. I'd dated my own PhD advisor for going on three years. We never commented on our sex life. We'd had long debates about seventeenth century monarchs, drunk French wine over philosophical commentaries, and made love in the dark under the covers on days when he didn't have to teach in the morning. But none of those relationships or pseudo relationships had ever had a guy who wanted to talk about what he wanted to do to me. To count the ways that he wanted to fuck me and then follow through.

Jensen Wright wanted to fuck me.

He wanted to use my mouth and body all night.

And I was perfectly fine with letting him.

A couple of minutes later, we pulled up to a one-story cabin overlooking the canyon and the flat lake in the middle. It wasn't as enormous as some of the ones inside the canyon walls, but it held its own. At least what I could see of it.

"Whose house is this?" I asked as Jensen pulled into the driveway.

He cut the engine, and he looked over at me, almost apologetically. "Mine."

"Oh," I said as realization dawned on me.

He had planned this. That much was clear. He had wanted to bring me back here for sex the whole time. Part of me wanted to be flattered, but I suddenly had a bad taste in my mouth, and I felt frozen in my seat.

"I originally planned to bring you here," he said. At my appalled face, he shook his head. "Not like that. I planned to use the fire pit and make s'mores. I have the supplies in the back. I figured it'd be about fifty degrees, and if the weather permitted, we could night hike. Hence the warm clothes…" He trailed off when I didn't move.

My brain was trying to catch up to his statement. I turned around and found a paper Sprouts bag in the back, and marshmallows were on the top. Okay, so I had overreacted. He hadn't brought me out here just to fuck me. He wasn't using me.

God, why had I automatically thought the worst of him? I was sure it was latent prejudice against the Wright family. Not to mention, my not-so-stellar luck with guys.

"We could still do that," he offered. "Though it has dropped down to twenty with a wind chill of eleven. So…we might freeze."

"You turned the car off, so I'm already freezing," I told him. My hands were shaking. I'd stupidly forgotten my gloves. I stuffed them into the pockets of my jacket.

"Let's get you inside and warm you up then."

I hopped out of the truck and followed him to the front door. He had the bag of groceries in his arm and unlocked the door with his other hand. He kicked the door open with his foot and let me in first. I still felt cautious after my suspicions returned to me. I had been having the best time with Jensen, and I didn't want to think things like that.

Having sex with him on the first date to get his hot body out of my system might be the best thing I could ever do. There was no future here. I didn't even want to date right now. And it didn't matter how much fun we'd had while Christmas caroling. Jensen Wright was Landon Wright's older brother. And Landon wouldn't disappear if this continued.

So, I might as well have my fun now.

"Brr," Jensen said. He flipped on the lights, and the cabin was illuminated. "I'm going to build a fire. If you want to look in that crate right there, there's a bunch of blankets. Make yourself at home while I get some firewood."

I took a few tentative steps inside as Jensen got to work. The cabin was even more spectacular on the inside with high vaulted ceilings and dark wood beams bisecting the room. The hardwood floors were a dark glossy finish, and a bricked fireplace took up half of one wall in the living room. It had clearly been professionally decorated, and it was the first time tonight that I remembered that Jensen owned and ran Wright Construction and had more money than God.

The wooden crate was behind the brown leather couch, and I fished out a half-dozen blankets. I still wasn't sure if that was going to be enough to keep me warm in the meantime, but it was a start.

I burrowed into the blankets, trying to warm up my extremities. Jensen appeared with a bag of twigs and an armful of firewood. The kindling took a while to ignite, but once it started going, he was able to add logs to it pretty easily. Jensen cut the overhead light and let the flames bathe the living room in a soft glow and easy warmth.

"Why don't you come get closer to the fire?" he suggested.

A sheepskin rug lay in front of the fireplace. I couldn't tell if it was real or fake, and I shuddered. "Did that thing used to be alive?"

"Synthetic," he told me. "Just as warm."

I relaxed, grabbed the blankets, and carried them over to the rug. Jensen grabbed a pair of red pillows from the couch and tossed them to me. Then, he disappeared into the kitchen. After the sound of a loud pop, he came out a few minutes later with a tray in his hands.

He offered me a glass of red wine with a smile. "I hope you like red."

"Red or champagne." I took a sip and nearly groaned again. This was the good stuff.

"And since we didn't get to do s'mores"—he placed the tray off to the side, pointing at the bars of Hershey's chocolate, graham crackers, and marshmallows in bowls atop it—"I thought this would have to do."

"This had better be a dessert wine," I joked.

He grinned and took the seat next to me, throwing a blanket over his lap. I reached for a marshmallow and popped it into my mouth. Jensen's eyes caught on my lips, and I almost forgot that I was still holding a full glass of wine. I took a good long sip to steel my nerves, and then I placed the glass to the side.

"If I didn't know better, I'd think you were seducing me," I teased.

"I think I made my intentions pretty clear in the truck." His hand slid up the leg of my jeans under the blanket and then across the top of my thigh.

My breath hitched, and for the first time, I realized that I was nervous. Not of the situation. This seemed magical. But of Jensen. I'd spent much of my life thinking he was entirely out of my league, and even when I despised their family, I never thought I was above them but certainly not on level footing either.

"But," he said, stopping his hand and then moving back to my knee, "I would be okay if you just wanted a nice fire, some good wine, and deconstructed s'mores. I could get you home at a semi decent hour even."

I swallowed all the apprehension I'd been feeling.

Who said I couldn't be on a level playing field with a Wright? Just because they had money and prestige didn't mean shit. Jensen wanted me, and I definitely fucking wanted him. Stopping myself from having the hottest rebound of my life sounded ludicrous.

"What happened to, *don't plan on getting any sleep tonight?*" I whispered huskily. I leaned forward, sliding his hand back up my leg.

My own hands moved to the hem of his T-shirt and ran along the exposed skin just north of his jeans. He inhaled deeply at my bold move. Whatever hesitation I'd had from my discomfort or the sudden change of plans disappeared at that touch.

He shoved one of his hands up into my hair and kissed me like a dying man begging for his last breath. Our bodies were perfectly in sync. One moving against the other in harmony, unbroken by any of the million little thoughts that had flitted through my mind before coming to this moment. There was only me and Jensen. And I couldn't think of anything else I wanted or needed.

Heat suffused us from the warmth of the roaring fire in the grate and the friction we were creating with our bodies. Jensen's mouth on mine pulled the pin on a grenade, and as his hands dragged my shirt over my head and slipped me out of my jeans, the tension exploded between us.

I forgot that I had once been cold and just marveled in everything that was Jensen Wright. I kissed my way down every inch of his six-pack abs. Then,

I unbuckled his belt and shoved his pants to his ankles. He bulged out of his boxer briefs, and I licked my lips. I was one of those freaks of nature who loved giving blow jobs. I loved making a man squirm underneath my ministrations. And Jensen certainly didn't object when I removed him from his pants and dropped my mouth over the head of his dick.

I licked all around the head and then down the shaft. His hand buried itself into my hair as I took him fully in my mouth. And his gasp made it all worth it. I bobbed up and down on his dick like I was deep-throating a Popsicle. His eyes were hazy and unfocused as I worked my magic. I could feel him getting close, and he grunted.

"Emery," he murmured to warn me. Proper etiquette and all.

But I had no intentions of stopping.

I sucked him off until hot liquid filled my mouth, and he was shuddering in ecstasy. I pulled back from his cock, braced myself, and then swallowed his cum like a champ. His smile was infectious.

"Holy fuck, woman," he growled.

He didn't even wait for a response. He pushed me back onto the fur rug, opened my legs wide, and buried his face between them. I cried out as he lapped at my clit while his fingers dug into my inner thighs. My back rose off the rug as trembles ran through my body. He slowly inched one hand down to the lips of my pussy and tenderly stroked my opening.

"Oh God," I cried out when he inserted two fingers at once inside me.

He didn't pump in and out like I'd thought he would, but instead, he strummed the inside of me like he was playing a guitar. My body responded like a harmony.

I tried to close my legs as pleasure hit me from head to toe, but he just forced my legs further apart. Then, he reached out with his free hand and tweaked my nipple. I nearly came right there. My nipples were unbelievably sensitive. And, since I responded so well, he left his hand there, playing with my nipple, until I cried out, and my orgasm hit me full-on.

My legs seemed to have a mind of their own, shaking like I'd just run a marathon.

"I take it back," he said, kissing up my orgasm-flushed stomach and then to my nipples. He lavished each one with his tongue as I writhed beneath him. "I like your screams as you come better than your groans as you ride me. I wonder if I would like your screams as you rode me the best."

"Do you want to find out?" I breathed suggestively.

"I want to find all the ways to make you scream." He nipped at my nipple, and I cried out all over again. "Fuck, woman. Fuck."

I could feel his dick against my leg, already hard again. I lazily stroked my hand up and down his cock, and it was his turn to twitch at the movement.

"Please," I pleaded.

"Oh, I do like when you ask nicely," he said with a grin.

"Then, let me try again," I said, bringing his lips down to mine. "Please, oh, please, Jensen Wright, fuck me. Fuck me right now."

He located a condom in his jacket pocket and slid it on before positioning himself at my opening. He positioned himself on his forearms so that he could kiss my lips one more time. My hands rested on his biceps.

God, I want this. I want him.

"I'd like to give you what you want, Miss Robinson," Jensen said, teasing his dick against my pussy. "I might have to hear you ask one more time."

I hooked my legs around his back and tried to tug him forward. I even lifted my hips off the ground, but he easily held me at bay.

"I want you inside me. All of you. Until you have me screaming again from your cock and not just your mouth."

"Fuck," he whispered and then slid inside me.

I rocked my head back and moaned at the feel of him stretching and filling me. It was perfect. Utter bliss. This was even better than I'd thought it would be. He started moving in and out of me, and I used my leverage to meet his practiced thrusts. He was controlled and methodical, and I was aching for more.

He was devilishly grinning at me, as if he knew how much I wanted him to fuck me senseless. But he held back as he worked me into an uncontrollable frenzy. Until I was right on the brink of the biggest orgasm of my life. Until I was ready to beg him to let me release.

"Jensen, God, please. Harder."

He picked me up off the rug, and let our naked bodies be silhouetted by the firelight. He held me up in his arms with his hands on my hips. Then, he moved me up and down on his dick as hard and as rough as I had just pleaded with him for. My tits bounced in his face, and his cock drove into me. And, as our slicked bodies were hitting the peak, I screamed out his name into the cold night air. He grunted and came inside me a few thrusts later.

We both sat perfectly still, collapsing in on each other.

"Wow," I whispered. "Holy fucking wow."

"You can say that again."

"We're...we're going to need to do that again."

"A few times."

Jensen was right. As we spent the rest of the night in each other's arms, we found that he did like my screams best when I rode him.

chapter
thirteen

Jensen

I CAME TO, HOLDING A BEAUTIFUL, NAKED WOMAN IN MY ARMS. MY EYES JOLTED awake, as I was unable to believe the turn of events. Not because I'd had the most amazing sex of my life. Or that the person I'd had it with was Emery Robinson. Or even that I was enjoying having her in my arms the next morning.

It was because I had slept.

I had *really* slept.

My eyes darted to the red alarm clock on the nightstand next to the bed we had migrated into at some ungodly hour last night. But, right now, it read nine o'clock.

Nine o'clock.

I had slept for seven blissful hours. I didn't even care that I was late for work for the first time in my life or that I probably had a thousand emails and just as many texts and calls to find out if I was alive. I hadn't slept seven straight hours since my father died nearly a decade ago.

"Mmm," Emery groaned, rolling over to face me.

In the light of day, she was even more gorgeous than lit by candlelight, and I hadn't thought that was possible. I'd been a fool to think she was beautiful as she could get coated in makeup with her hair done. Here she was with traces of last night's mascara on her eyelashes and her hair down and messy in a freshly fucked way, and I was done. I was…totally fucked.

"What time is it?" she asked.

"Nine."

"That early?" She stretched her arm out.

"Mmhmm," I said, suddenly realizing how utterly fucked I was. Utterly and completely fucked. I needed to get out of here and stop this now.

I couldn't have had fucking incredible sex and slept through a whole night with a woman who was so wrong for me on every level. Attachments were overrated, and I had prided myself on being emotionally unavailable. I needed to find that in me now.

Emery Robinson had belonged to Landon. She was living in Austin. She'd grown up here. And I could think of a hundred other strikes against her.

I flung the covers off my naked body and moved to get out of bed.

Emery reached for me with her delicate little fingers, and I careened away from her. I avoided her gaze. I didn't want to see if she was hurt. I wasn't an asshole. I just…couldn't do this. I couldn't feel anything for her.

I searched in the closet for clean clothes. Ours were still strewed across the living room.

"I'll just…get your things, so we can go," I said, stomping out of the room before she could say anything.

I found my cell phone first and glanced at the influx of messages. I texted my secretary, Margaret, to let her know I would be coming in late. Something had come up unexpectedly.

My phone dinged with a message from Vanessa, and I nearly threw the thing across the room. Just what I wanted to deal with my ex-wife after the night that I had and the morning that only reminded me why this was all a bad idea. Instead, I returned the message, because I knew she would hound me if I didn't, but I made sure that my impatience was blatantly clear.

I ignored everything else and scooped up Emery's clothes from the floor.

She was sitting up with the charcoal-gray sheet wrapped around her body. She seemed off-balance, as if last night had been a dream and she was waking up and realizing it hadn't happened. She had been so comfortable with her body last night that it seemed a damn shame that she was covering it up.

"Just late for work," I told her. "We have to get going."

"Right. Of course," she said.

She took her clothes out of my hand, and I gave her privacy to change. The notion was absurd, but between being late for work, how content I had felt the moment I woke up, and the text from my bitch of an ex, this morning itself felt absurd.

Emery appeared a minute later, dressed in the clothes she'd worn last night, with her dark hair up in a high ponytail. "All ready."

"Great."

We hustled back into my truck. The drive across town was quiet, punctuated only by the Christmas songs that were still playing on the radio. I didn't have it in me to turn it off even though they reminded me of our night together. I pulled up in front of her sister's house twenty minutes later.

She smiled weakly at me. "Have fun at work," she choked out.

I wanted to kick myself. But I'd known that this wasn't a smart idea. I didn't date girls in town—whether or not they were here for a weekend—for a damn good reason. It made things…complicated. And complicated was not something I could afford outside of the boardroom.

"Thanks. Have fun with your sister."

"My sister," she repeated numbly. "Okay. Well, um…bye."

She hopped out of the truck, gave me a half-wave, and then darted for the confines of the house. She didn't look back before disappearing into the house, and I had the distinct feeling that I had just made her feel cheap.

"Shit," I whispered in the still-freezing air.

I hurried back to my house, took a much-needed shower, and then changed into a crisp black Tom Ford suit that I'd had custom-made at Malouf's in town. It was like the Nordstrom of Lubbock. Family-owned, the store provided and tailored designer and custom-fit clothes by appointment only. I had a standing appointment. I looked like a million bucks. I should feel like a million bucks after last night. Instead, I felt like something had gone horribly wrong when it should have been much simpler.

An hour later, I tramped into my office and was ready for lunch since I'd foregone breakfast in my haste to get into work. Margaret was hot on my heels when I entered Wright Construction.

"Good morning, Mr. Wright," she said, shuffling along with a notebook, iPad, and a pad of sticky notes. "Mr. McCoy called this morning, said it was urgent about the merger, sir. You also had a call from Vanessa. Well, two calls, but I let one go to voice mail. Nick Brown left a message about canceling his appointment because he's going out of town. Alex Langley called out sick. Personally, it sounded like he was out late and hungover. Elizabeth Copeland had an important update on the Lakeridge complex, sir. Sounded rather urgent as well."

"Margaret," I said with a sigh as I reached the door to my office.

"Yes, sir?" She was bright-eyed and bushy-tailed this early in the morning.

"I feel a bit under the weather. Cancel all of my appointments for the day and let Mr. McCoy know that I'll handle the merger in the morning."

"But, sir—" she said again.

"Margaret, let me run my company."

"Of course," she said in a daze, handing me the iPad with my daily notes on it. "Also, Morgan is waiting in your office."

I sighed heavily. "Thank you, Margaret. That will be all."

When I entered my office, Morgan was sitting on the top of my desk, fiddling with the Newton's Cradle kinetic pendulum that swished back and forth. Her dark eyes met mine across the room. "Late night?" she asked with a sardonic tone.

"Indeed."

I set the iPad down on my desk and flipped through the list of things for the day. Margaret would cancel all the extraneous items, but I had a lot to catch up on.

"What's with the late start, bro?" She hopped off the desk, landing on her sky-high heels, and grinned down at me.

"I slept in."

Morgan's eyes widened in disbelief. "Yeah, right! You don't sleep. You're a vampire."

I shrugged. I had no response to that because, up until last night, that had been true. "Don't know what to tell you."

"How about who you were fucking when you *slept in* this morning?" she asked with a mischievous light in her eyes.

I stared back at her with a blank expression on my face and then nodded at the iPad.

"Wait…do I even want to know?"

"Probably not," I told her.

That was a lie. Morgan would love the juicy details. She adored gossip. She read all those trash magazines just to laugh at the absurdity of it all.

"Okay, whatever. Landon called this morning," she said.

My head snapped back up to her. "What for?"

She tilted her head. "Miranda, of course. Why? Why do you look so scared?"

I painted my face back into a mask of indifference. "What did Miranda do now?"

"She wants to keep him in Tampa for Christmas," Morgan said with a wave of her hand.

"He's not considering it, is he?" I asked.

She sighed. "I guess he is."

I grabbed my office phone off the desk. "I'll call him right now and set him straight. He can't stay there because of Miranda. It's Christmas, for Christ's sake."

"I know, Jensen. Miranda has it in her head that Emery Robinson is here to win Landon back," Morgan said with a roll of her eyes.

"That seems very unlikely," I said. I made sure to keep the edge out of my voice. "She's leaving in a few days."

"What?" Morgan asked. "No, she's not. Landon said she was staying here for a while."

"He…what?" I asked, my mouth going dry.

"He tried to tell Miranda that she'd be leaving soon to get her off his case. But she didn't believe him, and it turned out, she had a reason. Emery told Landon at Sutton's wedding that she was staying here indefinitely. But I mean…I don't know why Emery is back in town, but it sure isn't for Landon. He doesn't even live here. Miranda is out of her mind."

I was completely silent. My head was spinning. Landon had said that Emery was leaving only to appease Miranda. I'd never brought it up with Emery because I thought I already had all my cards in order. She was supposed to be leaving in a few days to head back to Austin. She was supposed to be finishing her PhD. She was *not* supposed to stay in town after we fucked all night.

"Shit," I hissed.

"Right? So, you have to call and convince Landon to bring Miranda here for Christmas. Do whatever you have to, all right? I mean…I can even call Emery or whatever and ask her to stay away from Landon if that helps…" Morgan trailed off when I said nothing. "Why have you gone pale."

"Morg," I said, meeting her worried gaze, "I fucked up."

Emery

"AND HE JUST THREW MY CLOTHES AT ME AND THEN DROVE ME HOME!" I recounted to Heidi over lunch.

"Bastard!" Heidi said on cue. "What a bastard!"

"Right? I mean…we had sex for hours last night, and then this morning, it was like a light switch had been flipped. Walking into this, I just *knew* it was a bad idea. He totally used me."

"And it sucked, using him back, right?" Heidi asked, digging into her pad thai—our requisite best friend meal—at the downtown Thai Pepper.

"Dude, the sex was phenomenal," I told her for the hundredth time. "The *turning into a jerk in the morning and dumping me at Kimber's, like a dorm-level walk of shame,* not so much."

I twirled my own extra-spicy pad thai noodles on my fork and dug in. I was famished after my late-night sexcapades. I'd only had two tacos, half of a bag of marshmallows, and some Hershey's chocolate in the last eighteen hours, and I was starving.

"Yeah, well, at least you had some fun," Heidi said. "That was good for you after Professor McJerkface."

I snorted into my food and then hacked and coughed to clear my airway. "Professor McJerkface?"

Heidi shrugged and winked at me. "Pretty much."

"Well, it was a good time. But, you know…it was more than that." Thoughtfully, I set my fork down and sipped on my water. "I kind of like him."

"A Wright brother?" Heidi asked with wide eyes. "Aren't you President of the Anti-Wright Family Fan Club?"

"Something like that," I agreed. "But he was different."

"Oh, boy! Here it goes," Heidi said.

"What?" I demanded.

"You're doing that thing."

"What thing?"

"You know," Heidi said. "The whole *the guy is a jerk, but he's different with me.* News flash, Robinson, he's not different. He just wanted to fuck you."

I flinched. "Thanks for that cheery message."

"Gah, I'm sorry. I had a weird night, and I worry about you. What happened with Landon was bad enough."

"You were the one pushing me into Jensen's arms."

"Yeah, but that was before you got all doe-eyed and decided he was different. I like Jensen just fine. He's a great boss. He cares about his employees. He knows what he's doing, and he makes us all a lot of money. But I can't pretend that he's this perfect person either. I've heard that he sleeps around when he's at business meetings out of town."

"Ugh! I don't want to think about it. We've all done stupid things. I don't want to judge him. Maybe he's just a manwhore, and that's what last night was about. But you should have warned me!"

"I thought you'd fuck around with him as a nice rebound, Em. I didn't think it'd be anything."

"Well, it's not," I said instantly. "It's definitely not. Remember the whole *dropped me off at Kim's like he was taking out the trash*? Because I'm pretty sure, no matter how different he was with me, that asshole sure shone through."

"Good. That's good. I don't want to see you get hurt again."

"I'm not going to get hurt. Now, what was this about a weird night?" I asked her.

She brushed her hand in front of her face and laughed. "Nothing honestly. I had a strange phone call, and I ended up talking to the person all night. It was unexpected."

My eyebrows rose in question, but Heidi was already moving on to another topic.

"Do you want to go shopping with me and Julia sometime this week?"

"Two weeks before Christmas. Your favorite time to shop."

"All the crowds and sales and screaming—it makes for a great horror flick."

"Sure, I'm in. I can never resist a good bit of horror."

Right then, my phone pinged noisily.

"Fuck," I groaned, digging it out of my pocket.

I'd forgotten to turn the ringer off this morning. I'd taken a good long shower and an even longer nap once I got home and left the ringer on, so I could get Heidi's text when she got out of her morning meeting.

I clicked the button, and my screen lit up. I had a text message from Jensen. My stomach dropped, and I glanced up at Heidi.

"Let me guess…lover boy?"

"Yeah."

I swiped to open and read the message.

Emery, are you free this afternoon? I canceled my meetings for the day and wanted to see if you would be interested in getting coffee. I know this little place over by campus; it's my favorite—Death by Chocolate. I don't know if you've ever been since it's pretty new. I could meet you. Say two o'clock?

"What does he have to say?"

I passed the phone over to Heidi. "I'm way more confused now."

"He wants to meet you at Kimber's bakery?" Heidi asked with a chuckle.

"I'm sure he doesn't know that she owns it."

"True, but damn. I wonder what happened in his head. Besides the fact that canceling meetings is so not like him. I've never heard of him willfully canceling a meeting. He must have realized how much he fucked up."

"Maybe."

"Or he wants round two."

I snatched my phone out of Heidi's hand. "There's no way."

"Well, are you going to meet him?"

"Did curiosity kill the cat?" I asked her.

"Yeah, but it had nine lives and shit."

Death by Chocolate was the love child of my sister's bachelors in food science and her achievements in culinary school. The sugary-sweet smell was what I always associated with Kimber. When we were younger, I used to jokingly sing the Bagel Bites commercial jingle to her with new words about all the baking she did.

"*Cupcakes in the morning, cookies in the evening, chocolate at suppertime. When Kimber's in the kitchen, you can eat baked goods anytime,*" I hummed to myself as the bell dinged overhead.

It was a quaint and totally adorable coffee shop and bakery. The floors were black-and-white tiles, and the walls were iced in mint glaze. The countertops were powdered-sugar white granite, and the cabinetry was a buttery lemon bar. Each table was a different-flavored French macaron with cushioned fruit-tart chairs. Elaborate wedding cakes in glass boxes decorated the room. The best part was the bar filled with row after row of sweets hiding behind glass, just waiting to be enjoyed.

"Can I help you?" a girl asked. She wore a Death by Chocolate apron and looked to be a Tech student.

"I'll take a snickerdoodle cookie and two of the strawberry macarons, please."

"And a slice of death by chocolate cake," Jensen said from behind me.

I nearly jumped out of my skin and whirled around. "Jesus, you scared me."

"I didn't mean to sneak up on you. I thought you'd have heard the bell chime," he said.

My eyes traveled the length of him, and I enjoyed every single moment, as if I were looking at my last sunrise. He had on a midnight-black suit that had to have been custom-fitted for his body. His button-up was white and crisp with a herringbone texture that had always been my favorite, and his Texas Tech Red Raiders red tie. And, even though he was dressed as sharp as ever, it was his eyes that caught me. Dark as Kimber's famous chocolate cake and looking at me like most of the customers did when the cake was presented to them.

"It's fine," I said, turning my back on him.

Because it didn't matter how hot he looked or how much he looked like he was ready to devour me again, he had reminded me all too well why I had sworn off the Wright family.

"Anything else for you two?" the woman asked. She placed our treats on the counter.

"I'll take a cup of coffee," I said.

"Make that two."

I pulled out my wallet to pay. I did not want him to think this was a date.

He shooed me aside. "I've got it."

"I can pay for my own things," I said irritably.

"I know you can, but I invited you here. So, I'm paying." His face was stern, and I realized he had switched into business mode or something. Because he was not brokering any arguments.

I raised my hands in defeat and grabbed my plate of sweets. "I'll get us a table."

A table was open in the back corner, and I plopped down into the open seat that faced the rest of the store. I was maddeningly curious about what Jensen wanted to talk about mere hours after ditching me. Part of me wanted to have a plan for whatever was going to come out of his mouth, but I felt woefully unprepared.

Jensen set our coffees along with his slice of cake on the table. I added cream and sugar while I avoided eye contact.

"Emery," he began, "I..."

I glanced up at him over the rim of my coffee. I blew on it a little and then took a sip. "What?"

"I think I've made a horrible mistake."

"And what would that be?"

"Going on a date with you," he answered.

I was out of my seat before I could even process what had been said. "Well, that's just...that's wonderful, Jensen."

"Emery, sit down. Come on, just sit."

"And why should I?" I set my mug of coffee down but didn't sit. "We had an awesome time last night, and then poof, you turned into an asshole. Then, you invited me here, only to tell me you regret last night?"

"Emery, please," he said. His body was still, perfectly in control. He didn't even glance around at the people who were looking at me funny. "Let me explain."

I sank back into my seat. "Explain what?"

"I thought you were getting your PhD. I thought you said you were still at school in Austin, studying history and European mistresses. That's what you told me. That's what I thought. But you're not doing that," he accused.

My blood ran cold. "What do you mean?"

"You're staying in town, aren't you?" he asked. The idea seemed to distress him.

"How could you possibly know that? I've told only a handful of people, and even my mom doesn't believe me," I told him.

"Because you told Landon," he said with raised eyebrows.

"You talked to Landon?" I gasped. "About me?"

"Not...exactly."

"You didn't tell him what happened, did you?" I asked with wild, wide eyes.

"Look, I didn't talk to him. Morgan did. His wife is still pissed that you're here. Morgan didn't know about what happened with us. So, no, he doesn't know. And I'd like to keep it that way."

"You said...*didn't* know. Morgan didn't know, but she does now?"

Jensen shifted uncomfortably. "It was kind of an accident."

"Oh, for the love of..." I cried, trailing off. "You don't want Landon to find out about your big mistake, but you told Morgan? Are you out of your mind?"

"Starting to feel like it," he grumbled.

"Great. You brought me all the way here to tell me what a big mistake I was and that Landon is probably going to find out." I grabbed my snickerdoodle cookie and took a giant bite out of it. Then, I gave him a thumbs-up and mockingly nodded my head.

"It's not like that. It's more a matter of principle, Emery. I had a great time, but I don't date girls in town. And, if I had known you were staying, I never would have asked you out."

I swallowed back the choked words that wanted to come out at that statement. I was wrong. Jensen Wright was not different. He was just like every other guy on the planet. He'd used me for sex, and then he'd ditched me. And, even worse, he was making it a point to cement that knowledge with me in person.

"I guessed that when you dropped me off this morning. You didn't need to come here to tell me that to my face," I told him with venom in my voice. I pushed the plate of macarons toward him. "Have a macaron. They're my sister's favorite. She owns this bakery. She'd want you to have one."

I stood and walked away from Jensen.

"Emery," he called.

And then I heard him curse loudly. He jogged to keep up with me as I walked to my Forester waiting on the street.

He grabbed my elbow and tried to pull me to a stop. "Emery. Hey, stop."

"Why?" I asked. "We had one night together. What am I to you?"

"I don't know!" he said, frazzled. "I don't know, all right? It's like some goddamn self-preservation kicked in, and I had to stop this before it got out of hand."

"How could it *possibly* get out of hand?" I demanded.

"Because being with you breaks all the rules!"

"Rules are meant to be broken."

"Not these rules."

I shrugged. "I have rules, too. I swore, I'd never look at another person from the Wright family. I decided Wright *isn't* right," I said, mocking the Wright Construction motto. "Yet here we are."

Then, suddenly, Jensen's fingers pushed up into my loose ponytail. His palms cupped my cheeks. His dark eyes gazed down into mine, and I didn't move a muscle to stop him. The energy felt charged, heating the air between us and dragging me into his downward spiral. I could see our breaths mingling in the frigid air. His lips met mine, soft and tender, searching to make sure this was allowed. I was frozen for a second before I met his touch. He pulled me against him, crushing our mouths together. And it didn't seem to matter in this moment that we were in broad daylight on one of the busiest streets in Lubbock.

I couldn't get enough of his mouth, his body. The feel of him through the layers of clothing. The taste of him. He was everywhere.

Slowly, my brain came back to my body, and I shoved him away from me.

"How dare you!" I spat. "You cannot send me mixed signals like this, Jensen. Either you want more or you don't. I won't play games with you. I'm tired of being jerked around by men who think that they can do whatever they want."

"Emery, that's not—"

"Save it," I said, raising my hand to silence him. "I've heard enough."

chapter
fifteen

Emery

I LEANED BACK AGAINST THE GIANT GLASSES SCULPTURE OUTSIDE OF THE BUDDY Holly Center. They were iconic to the legend who had been born here and gone on to such fame. I'd worked here on and off throughout most of high school, and being back felt just as surreal as everything else that had been happening in my life. I felt like I was reliving high school, only with a different Wright brother.

Betty hit the curb in her old red Buick LaCrosse and then parked in front of the center. She waved at me from the driver's side. I could only laugh. She had always been out there.

"Hi, Emery, dear. How are you?" Betty said. She hurried over to where I was standing and then gestured for me to follow her.

"Doing all right. How about yourself?" I asked.

Betty jingled the keys and then hit the door with her hip to let us inside. "I'm just fine. This way. Oh, you know the way."

I did, but I didn't say anything.

"I'm dreadfully sorry that we're closed today. We had to do some maintenance and decided to shut down during the holidays."

"Maintenance?" I asked.

"Replace the floors, new roof—that sort of thing. Wright Construction offered to do the whole thing at a discount since we're a historic museum. Isn't that wonderful?" Betty asked. She finally reached her office and let me inside.

"Just wonderful," I agreed, unable to escape the Wrights for even one day.

"That Jensen Wright came over to tell me himself."

"That was nice of him," I said through gritted teeth.

"Here we are," Betty said. "Thank you for being able to meet with me today. I'm going to Florida to visit my grandbabies for Christmas, and I won't be back until after the New Year. It would have delayed everything for you."

"This is great. I appreciate you coming in early for me. Who is going to be here to let people in for the construction crew?" I took the stack of paperwork from Betty and hastily filled out the sections to get my job back and be on payroll.

"We have a few people who will be here for the holidays. They have keys and can alternate days. But we're closed up from Christmas to New Years."

"Well, if you need someone, let me know. I will be around."

"I'm sure they would love to work you into the schedule. Let me get you a copy of the key while we're at it," she said.

A few minutes later, I had successfully filled out the paperwork, gotten ahold of the keys to the Center, and was on the schedule for the construction crew. That also meant I was going to be getting some money in for the holidays.

I left Betty, feeling more accomplished. Even though this wasn't my dream job, it was at least *a* job. Something tangible to hold me in Lubbock that wasn't just family and old memories.

When I hopped back into my Forester, I realized that had taken a lot longer than I'd thought. It had only felt like a few minutes, being inside there, but I was definitely going to be late for my shopping date with Heidi and Julia. They seemed intent on me going, and I did need a pick-me-up.

I had been trying not to think about Jensen and what had happened. But I was just so confused and upset, something I didn't really like admitting. I hated him thinking that what we had done was a mistake. I wanted more of his kisses. I wanted more of the guy who had unapologetically sang Mariah Carey with me. And, even worse, I knew that he was right. I hadn't thought this was a real thing to begin with. I'd wanted to get a piece of him without thinking about what would come next. I wanted to think it was better this way, but it didn't feel like that. I was hoping retail therapy would help.

Malouf's was swamped for the holidays, and it wouldn't have been my first choice. Mostly because I couldn't afford anything in the store. Everything was designer and custom-made. Kate Spade, Kendra Scott, Tom Ford. Oh, my! But Heidi and Julia each had well-paying Wright Construction jobs, and I was sure I could find *something*. Maybe on the sale rack.

I hurried across the parking lot to get out of the frigid, windy weather. Screw Lubbock and its freezing air the day after it was seventy. I barreled through the front door and found Heidi talking animatedly to Julia, who was holding up a black dress with a plunging neckline.

"I'm here. I made it. Sorry I'm late," I said to the girls.

"Em! Just in time," Heidi said. "Tell Julia that she would look smoking hot in this dress."

"It's black. I like it." That had been my motto since junior high. My closet was filled up with black jeans, black sweaters, black tank tops, and black sneakers. All black everything.

"I knew you would say that," Heidi said with a grin.

Contemplatively, Julia held the dress at arm's length. Black was a good choice with her hair that had all the burgundy undertones that she'd highlighted. Plus, it was slimming, which was good for everyone, except for Heidi, who was built like a Barbie doll. And, while Heidi had the enviable prom-queen looks, Julia just had something about her. Between her mahogany hair and studded ears and tattoos peeking out from under her edgy leather-detailed dress, she was the mysterious girl you didn't bring home to Mom. I liked her for that. Kind of felt like she and I could gang up on Heidi together...and maybe even win. But probably not.

"It's so not me, but I'll try it on."

"Nothing in this store is ever me either," I told Julia. "But, if you don't try on everything Heidi wants you to wear, then you won't make it out of here alive."

"Damn straight," Heidi said with a sharp nod of her head. "Now, let me play dress-up!"

We wandered around the store together with Heidi randomly throwing things into our arms. Julia and I exchanged looks full of sympathy for each other. I had something hot pink in my pile. Julia had a pastel. Heidi herself had all the best pieces that only worked on someone who was five foot nine or above.

The manager came over and procured dressing rooms for all of us, offering us assistance if we needed different sizes. I shimmied into the hot-pink dress first just to get it over with, and Heidi hysterically laughed at me until I went back into the dressing room for something else.

"Okay, I know it's a touchy subject," Heidi called over the dressing room wall, "but can we talk about Jensen?"

I stepped out of the dressing room and crossed my arms until she came out of her room. "No."

"What about Jensen?" Julia asked.

She appeared in a stunning olive-green dress that complemented her style perfectly. I was sure it would be a winner.

"Can I tell?" Heidi asked.

"Fine, but I'm not trying on that weird patterned thing you gave me," I told her.

"Ugh! Fine! I'm just trying to brighten up your wardrobe."

"You've been trying for twenty years. It's not going to work."

She laughed and flipped me off. "Anyway, Emery went on a date with Jensen."

"Oh, wow! Was it hot?" Julia asked.

"So hot," Heidi said.

"Heidi, can you not?" I demanded.

"Sorry!" she squeaked. "Anyway, he was a total ass to her afterward, and then he was an even bigger ass by asking her to coffee to tell her the whole thing was a mistake."

"That sucks. Sorry, Emery," Julia said.

"It's fine," I told them. "Really, it was one date. And then…another kiss that meant nothing. He kissed me after telling me how much of a mistake our date was because he doesn't date in town and how it never should have happened because I moved back home. Oh! And he fucking told Morgan. Now, Landon is totally going to find out."

"And Landon doesn't know you went on a date with his brother?" Julia asked.

I shook my head. "I'd like to keep it that way."

Okay, so I wasn't fine. I was still frustrated. Even more so because Jensen hadn't left me alone. He'd messaged me a handful of times to try to talk to me again. I couldn't figure out why he thought I would see him again. After our last conversation and how it had ended, I didn't think that was a good idea.

"Yeah, but he's still messaging you," Heidi said.

"Then, he must like you," Julia said. "Maybe he's just…bad at communication."

"Just what I want in a guy. A bad communicator."

"That's not what I meant," Julia said. "I mean, what if he is scared of how he feels for you? You said he didn't date in town. Maybe it freaked him out when he realized that you were going to live here, and he said things all wrong."

I slid my gaze over to Julia. "Jensen Wright does not say things wrong. He is a businessman. He says what he means and takes what he wants. I feel that I have to take him at face value."

"That seems fair," Julia said. "But the real question is it worth always having that what-if with him?"

I shrugged. That I didn't know. It was too much to think about.

"Just go into it with your eyes wide open," Heidi said. "You know he has baggage and shit. He's a Wright. He's filthy rich and sleeps with supermodels and all that. You know his deal. If you can live with him flying to New York every holiday, then who am I to stop you from having some fun? I just want you to be happy."

"Also, that dress is fucking hot," Julia said to change the subject.

I glanced at my dress in the trifold mirror and smiled. It did look fucking hot. Actually, it was perfect. It was a skintight black dress with a lace front neckline that went down to almost my navel and had an open back. Paired with some stiletto heels out of Kimber's closet, and I could even pass for a girlie girl.

"You need it," Heidi said at once. "I mean, you really, really need it."

I checked the price tag, and my eyes doubled in size. "It's three hundred dollars. I don't need it that bad."

"Oh, but you do! And…I haven't gotten you a Christmas present yet. So, that can be my present!" Heidi said.

"Psht! Are you insane? I'm not letting you get me a three-hundred-dollar dress for Christmas."

"Why not?"

"Because I could never repay you for a present like that. Anyway, where would I even wear this? I live in jeans and T-shirts. I would get no use out of it."

"Actually," Heidi said with innocent eyes.

"Oh no," I said with a sigh. "You're about to tell me the real reason we're shopping, aren't you?"

"There's a Christmas party I want you to come to with me and Julia on Friday night. And I thought we could all get our dresses for the party here!"

My eyes slid to Julia. "Where's the party? I know she won't tell me."

"Uh…"

"Come on, Em. It's just one party."

"Yeah, and it was just one wedding. Look how well that worked out for me," I told her.

"I think it worked out pretty well. You're not thinking about Professor McJerkface, and you had a lot of sex."

Julia snort-laughed and then covered her mouth. "Professor McJerkface?"

"It's a long story," I told her.

"Okay, picture this," Heidi said. "You wear that dress. I do your hair and makeup. You borrow Kimber's stilettos, the really fancy Louboutins that crush your pinkie toes. But how can you resist the red-lacquered bottoms?" It was as if she were reading my mind. "You walk into the party. All eyes fall on you. You're like fucking Cinderella for a moment. And then, poof, your Prince Charming shows up, and voilà, the night has endless possibilities."

"Oh God," I said in horror. "You're talking about your office Christmas party."

Heidi bit her bottom lip. "Um…yes."

"And, when you say endless possibilities, you mean, I trip over my feet in front of Jensen, and he's the same jerk he was and laughs at me or something."

"Don't be ridiculous."

"Yeah, really, I don't think Jensen would ever laugh at someone like that," Julia added. "Plus, it won't suck because, it's open bar, and we can all get wasted on champagne."

"Oh, I like you," I told her.

"See, Em?! Please, please, please," Heidi said.

"I'll think about it."

"Yes!" Heidi said, as if I had relented.

"While we're at it," Julia said, her cheeks turning a soft shade of pink, "want to find me something that sexy? There's a Wright brother I wouldn't mind looking at me twice in something like that."

"Landon?" Heidi asked at the same time as I said, "Austin?"

I glanced over at Heidi with an arched eyebrow. "Landon doesn't even *work* for Wright Construction."

"Process of elimination," she said quickly. "So, Austin?"

"I think he's scared of me because I work in HR. But he's not technically my boss; Jensen is. I don't think we could get in trouble. And I'm head of HR anyway."

"Oh, I can find you something," Heidi said. "Each of my girls with a Wright brother will be my New Year's resolution."

"You kill me," I said with a shake of my head. "I'm not letting you buy the dress."

I changed out of the dress and shimmied into a few of the other outfits. But none of them came close to the other one. I hung the dress back up, and Heidi snatched it back. We went back and forth until I finally gave up. In the end, I got the dress. And, secretly...I couldn't wait to see Jensen's face when he saw me in it.

chapter
sixteen

Jensen

PATRICK HADN'T STOPPED LAUGHING AT ME FOR A SOLID TEN MINUTES. IF I were a violent man, I would have put my fist through his face a long while ago. Instead, I waited patiently for him to chill the fuck out. Austin would be here in about twenty minutes, and Patrick needed to get his shit together before then.

It was bad enough that Morgan knew about what had happened with Emery. I didn't want Austin to know anything. Morgan and I, at least, were on the same page. We always had been; it didn't matter that she was seven years younger than me. For a long time, everyone had thought she and Landon were twins, but they couldn't have been further apart as far as personalities went. And, sometimes, I thought it was scary how much she and I were on the same wavelength.

So, at least I knew she wasn't going to run to Landon to try to make things right. I just had to figure out what I was going to do. Because texting Emery all week and getting radio silence had clearly not been working out well for me.

And I should have just left her alone. That was what I'd said I wanted even if it was a lie. It just wasn't smart to bring her into all of my baggage. Yet I couldn't stop thinking about her. And texting her. And I was considering showing up at her sister's house with a boom box and waiting until she came outside.

No, I probably wouldn't do that last one. That only worked in the movies.

"Tell me again that the girl from the wedding is Landon's ex-girlfriend. It's funnier every time you say it," Patrick said.

I stared back at him with a look of deep disinterest. "How about we skip that part?"

"Okay, okay," Patrick said. He straightened up and wiped a tear from his eye. "I'm just imagining you striking out now. I've seen you pick up more girls than most famous athletes."

"I didn't strike out," I told him through gritted teeth.

"Yeah, y'all fucked, and then she straight fucked with your head. What were you thinking, man?"

"I was thinking that things were too complicated with Emery already," I told him honestly. I leaned back against the door to my office with a weary expression. Things *were* too complicated. Much too complicated. Yet part of me didn't give two fucks. We'd had an amazing night, and then I'd slept through the night. Both things were nothing short of a miracle in my world.

"Complicated?" Patrick asked. He poured out two shots of top-shelf bourbon. The liquid made a *glub, glub, glub* sound as it flowed out of the crystal decanter. "Shit's not complicated, Jensen. You like her. That's why you're freaking out."

"That would be a problem," I told him.

Patrick shook his head and passed me a shot. He held his up in the air. "The problem is with your head, man. Get in good while you can. You don't know if things will go south, and stressing about it will only ruin it. Enjoy it while it lasts."

We each tipped back the shot of bourbon, and Patrick stood from the desk. He grinned with a boyish look. He never thought too hard or long on his own problems. It was why he and Austin were still bachelors and hadn't had serious girlfriends since college.

I hated to tell him that I *did* know that things would go south. It was a guarantee with me considering my past. I hated thinking that I liked Emery because I didn't want to hurt her. And, if she actually got to know me, it would be inevitable.

"Y'all ready?" Morgan asked, appearing from around the corner of my office.

She was decked out in a shimmery red cocktail dress with her dark hair curled, nearly reaching to her waist. Her eyes shot to Patrick. We were both sporting the standard-issue tuxedo. Her look said one thing and one thing only. And I wished she and Patrick would fuck it out or move on already.

Not that I was one to talk right at this moment.

"Yeah. Austin?" I asked.

Austin walked into the office a second later, carrying another bottle of bourbon. It was half-empty, and in his eyes, I could see that he was already drunk. All-too familiar at this point. As much as I needled him about it, I did fucking worry about him becoming the alcoholic that our father had been.

"Good to go, bro," Austin said. He held up the bottle, as if in a toast.

"Let's get upstairs then," I told them.

We all walked out of my office and down the hall to the elevator that led to the top floor of the Wright Construction building. It was a massive high-rise downtown that overlooked the Texas Tech campus. The restaurant at the top had a panoramic view of the skyline and some of the best food in town. We held business dinners up here and hosted parties, and every year, it was the spot for the annual Wright Construction office Christmas party.

Already, the room was full of the corporate staff who worked in the business below. People were dressed in their best cocktail attire, leaving behind their business suits for dress clothes. It was like seeing the office come to life once every year. Even Mick in accounting had dressed up, and he was acting like he was having a good time. He was the most curmudgeonly old man I'd ever encountered.

The line at the bar was the biggest attraction, and soon, the buffet would open up. We had the food catered every year as a thank-you that went with the year-end bonuses.

I shook hands and said my fair share of hellos as we moved through the crowd, heading toward the DJ that was currently playing Christmas music. It was my mission to make sure I knew each person on the team. Ever since my father had died and I'd taken over the company, my life had been almost entirely about work. The few exceptions still lived in New York and hadn't exactly worked out as I'd expected. Work was always reliable.

As I greeted people, my eyes sought out one person. Heidi. She was Emery's best friend. She would know what to make of the whole situation. And, though I had never had a conversation with Heidi that wasn't about work, considering the array of men falling at her feet, I thought maybe she would understand where I was coming from on this one.

But I never found her.

And then I was quickly ushered up to the DJ and handed a microphone.

Here goes nothing.

"Ladies and gentlemen, may I have your attention?" I said.

Slowly, the voices died down, and faces turned to stare up at me at the front of the room. My eyes roamed the room, trying to pick out Heidi in the crowd.

"I don't want to take up too much of your time. I just wanted to say thank you so much for all that you do for this company. Every single person in this room is integral to the development and continual progress of Wright Construction."

A few people in the back clapped, and then everyone joined in, applauding their own accomplishments.

"Additionally, I wanted to make you all aware that, as of next week, Wright Construction will merge with the Tarman Corporation headquartered in Austin."

There were loud whispers all around as everyone tried to figure out what that would mean for them.

"Wright Construction is purchasing the company to continue to grow and expand in and out of Texas."

I was about to say something else when a figure appeared at the back of the room. It was as if a spotlight were being held over Emery's body, revealing her to me. She looked stunning in a tightfitting black dress. And, for a moment, I was completely frozen in place. All thoughts of letting her leave for her own good disappeared. I was *not* going to let that woman walk away from me.

I could feel her eyes on me from across the room. She smirked like she fucking knew what she was doing to me. And it only made me want her more.

"Jensen," Morgan muttered, nudging me.

"Um...yes. Right. More details regarding that will follow," I said into the microphone. I'd completely lost my train of thought. "Now, more booze! Enjoy!"

I handed the microphone back to the DJ and turned to go find Emery, but Morgan blocked my way.

"More booze? Enjoy?" she asked in dismay. "What the hell is wrong with you?"

"Something else is on my mind."

"Jensen, you didn't even tell them that we weren't downsizing here. You didn't tell them what the merger meant or that we'd be getting new employees from Tarman."

"Then, you tell them, Morgan," I told her.

My eyes drifted over her head to try to find Emery again, but she was gone. It was as if she had come to me like a vision in that moment and had since disappeared.

"What?" Morgan asked, staggered. "You want *me* to address the crowd?"

"You're a Wright, are you not? You know just as much about the merger as I do."

"But, Jensen..." she whispered.

I smiled and bumped her shoulder. "I have faith in you."

"Wait, where are you going?" she asked as I moved away from her.

"To make another mistake," I told her before melting into the crowd.

chapter
seventeen

Emery

O KAY, SO I'D MADE MY GRAND APPEARANCE.

I'd felt like Drew Barrymore in *Ever After*, whispering to myself, "Just breathe," when I entered the room. I'd caught Jensen's eye. He'd stared at me, momentarily in shock. I'd basked in the glow of that attention. And then I'd promptly and completely lost my nerve, disappearing into the crowd by the bar with Heidi.

What am I even doing here?

He'd pushed me away. Twice.

It was no matter that he'd been texting me all week. His text messages had been nonsensical. Half-trying to convince me that leaving me was for the best and half-trying to convince me to give him another chance. I didn't know which half he wanted me to believe. So, I just hadn't responded. I was still hurt from the conversation we'd had at Death by Chocolate. I should have just stayed home. Actually, I should have probably already left.

What am I trying to prove by being here? That I can get his attention? Check.

I knew that I couldn't ignore him if he approached me. That was why I had moved out of the spotlight as soon as I had. I might have had the strength to push him away that day after our date, but after a week of his messages, I was too curious to step back now. I wanted to know why he had been acting like this and whether or not the guy I'd had that first date with still existed somewhere in there.

A hand on my elbow made me jump. I whirled around and came face-to-face with Jensen Wright himself.

"Oh," I said, feeling like an idiot.

"Oh?" he asked.

And then I stared at him because seeing him across the room had not done him justice. I never thought I would be the kind of girl who swooned at a guy in a tuxedo, but hot damn. Jensen Wright wore a tux like a second skin. It molded to him, and all the long, straight lines did things to his body that just weren't possible in other clothing. Or maybe I was biased.

"It's you," I finally managed to get out.

"You do realize that this is an office party, right?" he asked. He arched an eyebrow, as if asking, *What the hell are you doing here?*

"I might have heard that somewhere." I sank into my hip and let him get a good look at the black dress I'd gotten earlier this week.

"Last I checked, you didn't work for me, Miss Robinson."

"True," I agreed, fluttering my eyelashes. "Are you going to kick me out?"

"I might let you stay…if you tell me what you're doing here."

I swallowed. I had no answer to that one. I'd come at Heidi's request, but I knew that wasn't the answer he was looking for, and it wasn't even half of the real reason.

"I came to listen to your inspirational speech. More booze, Mr. Wright. Very motivational."

He laughed unabashedly. It was deep and masculine and sincere.

"Thank you. Probably not my best speech, but I got a little distracted."

"Oh, yeah?" I asked innocently. "What distracted you?"

"A beautiful woman walked in the door."

"Oh," I said with a shrug. "You must get distracted a lot then."

Jensen ran his hand down my bare arm and firmly shook his head once. "Never."

Where he touched me on my arm seemed to be radiating with heat. In fact, my entire body was aching to get closer to him. To let him run his hands all over my body again. Being with him was supposed to be something light and fun. I wasn't supposed to want more. I'd thought I could get him out of my system. Yet here I was, at his office Christmas party. It was now crystal clear that I was not going to get Jensen Wright out of my system with a one-night stand. But I was sure that I wouldn't mind trying it again and again until it worked out.

"I think I should escort you out, Emery," Jensen said, drawing me nearer to himself.

"Right now?" I asked, confused.

"Yes. Would you like to see my office on the way out?"

My mouth opened slightly, and I watched the way his gaze drift to my lips.

Was he thinking about how I'd sucked him? Was he thinking about much more?

It was all there in his eyes, and I was sure it was reflected in mine.

"I'd love to."

Jensen and I walked out of the party without a backward glance. I thought for sure that someone would stop us as we exited the top-floor restaurant. But it seemed that everyone was too engrossed in the end of Morgan's speech, the open bar, and the buffet. No one paid us any mind as we disappeared into the elevator and to the darkened floor below.

The elevator doors opened, and Jensen took my hand to guide me down to his office. We reached the end of the hall, and Jensen flicked the switch to turn on the lights. It was a massive corner office with a giant mahogany desk taking up the center of the room and an all-glass wall facing campus. It was modern and sleek and undeniably powerful. I could feel the energy from the room. It was the same power and control that I felt from Jensen.

He stood directly behind me and ran his hands down my arms. His mouth came down to my shoulder and placed a soft, possessive kiss there. "You've been ignoring me," he muttered.

I shivered at his touch. It was amazing, how moving from a crowded party and into his office had given him so much authority. We were on his turf. This was his domain. And he knew it.

"You told me you made a horrible mistake," I whispered into the room.

"Emery." His hands moved to my waist and trailed down the curves of my body.

The back of my dress was open, and I could feel the heat coming off of him through his tux.

"You have principles, Jensen," I teased.

That was what he had said. Though I still had no idea what it meant. It seemed to be an odd rule that he refused to date girls in town.

He spun me around, and I nearly stumbled into him. I wasn't used to Kimber's Louboutin high heels, and Jensen made me feel off-balance. Like I was teetering between fantasy and reality.

"Fuck principles," he said.

Shock registered on my face before I hastily concealed it. "Why? Why would you say that about the very principles that pushed me away?"

Jensen cupped my chin and forced me to look up at him. I hadn't even realized that I'd been staring down at his bowtie, trying to hide my emotions. But they were plain on my face. Confusion, desire, hope, disbelief.

My shoulders were up, as if to guard me from the oncoming disappointment. I could see it coming.

"Because I had the best night with you, the best *sex* with you," he added, pushing me back into his desk and making my imagination spiral away with all the things we could do on it, "and I slept seven whole hours with you in my arms. I'm an insomniac, and I cannot tell you the last time I slept that long. I said those things because I like you, and I didn't know how to react to that."

"So, you pushed me away?"

"I did, and I'm not proud of it." His lips nearly brushed mine when he said, "But I can't get you out of my head. You've taken over my thoughts, my daydreams, my every last desire, and I haven't slept since that night."

"How do I know you're not going to change your mind again?" I whispered. Though I was sure my voice betrayed the fact that I had already made up my mind. I would do unspeakable things with him and not think twice.

"You don't, but I'm willing to see where this goes if you are."

I nodded. "Yes."

"Good. One question, how much do you like this dress?" he asked, speculatively eyeing it.

"It's a Christmas present actually."

"God bless whoever gave it to you," he said with a grin, "but I'd like it on the floor."

I released a deep throaty laugh and reached for the side zipper. The dress slid down my body, all the way to my hips, and then it dropped into a heap on the floor. Since the dress was backless, I had to go braless. Now, I was dressed in nothing but a black lace thong and Louboutin heels.

I slowly stepped out of the dress and kicked it out of the way. *Thanks for the present, Heidi!*

"That's better," he said.

His hands slid behind my legs and lifted me off the ground. I squeaked at the sudden movement as he roughly placed me on the edge of his desk. He swept his hand over the top of it, letting half of the contents clatter to the ground, leaving a space for my body. He laid me back on the desk and raised my legs.

I tried to kick off the shoes, but he stopped me.

"Oh no," he said. "If you're going to wear designer shoes around me, then it'd be a shame not to fuck you in them."

The way he observed me made my core clench, and I could feel my body responding to him...and he hadn't even kissed me yet.

Then, I forgot all about the damn shoes as he kissed his way, achingly slow and tender, up my right leg. He reached the upper limit of my inner thigh, and I was writhing under him, practically begging for more. But he didn't give me what I wanted. Instead, he moved to my other leg and started kissing all the way up that leg. It was torture of the best variety. And different than the last time we had been together.

We might have been at his house, but we had been on equal footing there. Here, he had the power, and I was his to guide. And, for once in my life, I let myself be ravaged. I didn't care what would come after this and how we would move forward. I let him tease me until I could hardly take it anymore. His hands splayed my legs further apart, and then he blew hot against my damp underwear.

"Please," I whimpered.

He hooked his fingers under my thong and slipped it off my body. I was completely naked now, save for the high heels. He propped my feet up on the desk and stared down at me, as if he were taking a picture for safekeeping.

Then, his hands went to the button of his tuxedo pants. He slipped the zipper down to the base and then dropped his pants. His dick was bulging under his boxer briefs, and I ached to run my hand down it, to take it in my mouth, and to hear him make all those delicious noises all over again. But I could see in his eyes that he had other things on his mind.

He palmed his cock in his hand, found a condom, and slipped it on. Then, he strode back toward me. I hadn't moved a muscle the whole time. My breathing was shallow as I imagined what was to come. But I couldn't have prepared myself.

Without comment, he slid into me to the hilt in one thrust. I was practically dripping on his desk, but I still gasped in shock as he stretched me to the fullest.

My body felt alive.

Alive and euphoric.

He gripped my hips so tight that he left little indents in the skin, and I worried there might be bruising tomorrow. Yet I didn't care one bit. Just a sexy-as-fuck mark to show that he had claimed me. And claimed me, he did.

He pulled out of me and then slammed back in harder than the last time. My body rocked back toward the end of his desk, but he held on, rocking into me over and over again. Keeping up a jarring, uneven, intensely erotic pace that I couldn't hope to match. So, I let him take complete control and tried to keep from screaming so loud that the people one story up could hear me.

We didn't last like last time. We didn't stand a chance. We were both heated up from our time apart and desperate for another round. I wasn't trying to take my time, and he had no intentions of allowing it. It was clear that rough, hard, and fast were the only options in this scenario.

My mind disconnected from my body as I came violently and blissfully. I soared away into the abyss of pleasure. Relegating myself to base emotions only. Allowing myself to relish in how perfect every moment had been. To feel so extravagantly, so intentionally, and so unabatedly that all else fell away.

I realized Jensen was resting forward over me as I came back to myself. My legs were trembling like a newborn lamb, and a light sheen of sweat caressed my skin. Jensen's eyes glimmered with passion and elation. I knew that he could go again soon, but for now, there was only immense satisfaction.

He slid out of me and offered me the bathroom attached to his office. When I finished cleaning up, I came back to see that Jensen looked immaculate again. His tux was perfectly in place, and if I hadn't just seen the raw and wild man beneath, I'd never have known that he'd just fucked my brains out.

"Do you have to go back to the party?" I asked, unable to keep the caution out of my voice. I reached for my dress and slid it back on, securing the zipper in place.

"I seem to be otherwise occupied," he said.

He drew me into him, and for the first time all night, he planted an affectionate kiss on my lips. I fell into it, wanting nothing less than a thousand more of them.

"I like that," I said.

"I think I'm going to have to take you out now."

"Oh? Tacos?" I only half-joked.

"Probably something nicer than tacos after the week I've put you through," he said.

"You don't have to do that. I don't need a fancy dinner as an apology. I liked our first date," I told him truthfully. "It felt...real."

He smiled down at me and captured another kiss. "It was."

chapter
eighteen

Emery

"EMERY!" KIMBER YELLED.

"Just a second," I called back. I was putting the finishing touches on my hair, trying to make it do what Heidi had gotten it to do and failing miserably. I put the curling wand down and shrugged. It was better to go as myself than to try to be someone I wasn't. And a girl who fixed her hair on the regular was definitely not me.

"Emery, now!" Kimber screamed.

My eyebrows rose, and I hurried out of the bathroom. "What is it? What's going on?"

I found Kimber curled in the fetal position on the floor of her bedroom. She was breathing deeply and winced in pain.

"Oh my God!" I cried. "Are you having contractions? Are you in labor?"

"I don't"—she cried out and then clenched down, as if bracing herself—"know. It could just be Braxton Hicks contractions."

"You're speaking another language to me," I said. I hurried to her side and helped her back up onto the bed. "I don't know what that means. What can I do? Where's Lily?"

"Nothing. Just—oh God!" she said, clenching up again. "Just stay here a minute. Lily is playing in her room."

"Okay. Should I check on her? Should I just stand here?"

"Em, really not the time. Just hold my"—she viciously squeezed down on my hand—"hand."

"Got it. Hand-holding."

"Braxton Hicks contractions are prep for actual labor. They usually go away all on their own, but if they don't, then I'll have to go to the hospital."

"Should I call Noah?" I asked.

She nodded her head. "You'd better, just in case. I know he'd want to be here."

I dialed Noah's number and filled him in on what was going on. He promised he'd be on his way in a matter of minutes. When I hung up, Kimber was in the middle of another contraction. I didn't know anything about Braxton Hicks contractions, but she looked like she was in a lot of pain. Even if she wasn't going into labor, I wanted her to be seen by a doctor. Noah should be able to tell if something was wrong, but I'd be happier if we got her to the hospital.

Noah arrived from the medical center in record time. He took a quick look at his wife. "Looks like things are progressing quickly. Better safe than sorry, my love."

"Get the bag," Kimber said with a sigh. "I hoped that she'd wait until after Christmas. This is early."

"She's as stubborn as her mother. Comes and goes whenever she wants without consulting anyone at all," I joked.

Kimber gave me a grim smile. "Can you watch Lilyanne for us? I hate to ask. I know that you have a date tonight."

"Of course I can watch Lily. Don't even think twice about it. Just make sure everything is all right with you and know that I have things under control here."

Kimber kissed my cheek. "You're a lifesaver."

"Text me if you need me!" I called as I watched them go.

I traipsed back into my room and dialed Jensen's number. I knew he'd been planning our official date for a few days. He'd had a lot of business to catch up on, and I hadn't seen him, except at church on Sunday morning. But we'd talked every night, and I thought it was progress, on our way to something normal.

"Hey, Emery," he said when he answered the phone. "I was just about to leave my house."

"Actually..."

"Oh no, are you canceling?"

"Not on purpose," I assured him. "My sister went into labor, or maybe pseudo labor, and they're heading to the hospital. I promised her I'd watch my niece. So, I guess we'll have to cancel."

"Hmm," he said. "How about I come over there and help you babysit?"

"You...what? You want to help watch Lily?" I asked, confused.

"I'd still like to see you, and I like kids."

"But it's not our fancy dinner date..."

"Yes. But I haven't seen you in days, and I'm not giving up the opportunity. Unless you don't want me to be around your niece?"

"No, it's not that. I'd love for you to come over. I bet Lilyanne would, too."

"Great. Then, it's a date."

I pocketed my cell phone and hurried to Lily's room. She was still playing peacefully when I entered. Kimber didn't want Lily to know anything was wrong until they were sure she was in labor. She was certain that it would keep Lily up all night. So, it was up to me to entertain the munchkin until I had more substantial news.

"Hey, Lily Bug," I said. "What are you up to?"

"Playing with Barbies." She had a collection of them in various stages of dress on the floor.

"Well, I wanted to let you know that your mommy and daddy went to the doctor for a checkup, and I get to watch you tonight."

"Is my new baby sister coming?" she asked with big excited eyes.

"Not yet. Just a checkup, but that means you get to hang out with Auntie Em tonight. You know what that means?"

Lily jumped up to her feet. "Ice cream and sprinkles and Disney movies!"

"That's right, missy!"

I lifted her into my arms and carried her downstairs. We raided the freezer. I knew where Noah tried to hide all the good flavors of ice cream, and we took out every last carton to decide on what we wanted. I liked to make her a bowl of ice cream about the size of the one in *Home Alone* and then hand her off to my sister. Tonight, I'd have to deal with putting her to sleep, so I knew that a mountain of ice cream might not be the best bet.

I placed a couple of scoops of chocolate ice cream in her bowl and a mix of strawberry, vanilla, and strawberry cheesecake into mine. We fished through the toppings, drizzling chocolate fudge and sprinkles on our desserts, and then we carried our bowls out to the living room.

Lily was busy with perusing the movies when the doorbell rang. "I'll get it!" she cried. "Mommy, Daddy, is my new sister here?"

I laughed and followed her to the front door. "You know it's not time yet. I have another surprise for you instead."

Turning the doorknob, I opened it to reveal Jensen standing at the front door. My breath caught at the sight of him in jeans and a casual button-up. It had only been a few days, but I'd missed seeing that grin.

"My boyfriend!" Lily cried.

Jensen laughed. "Hey, Lilyanne. I heard you had a pretty awesome babysitter and thought I would drop by to hang out, too. How does that sound?"

"Yes! Where are my flowers?" Lilyanne asked.

I snorted. "Oh, boy!"

"Guess I should have seen that one coming," Jensen said.

I stepped back to let him come in out of the cold. Lilyanne took his hand and guided him into the living room. She babbled the entire time about our ice cream creations and asked him what movie he wanted to watch and if she could paint his nails. I tried to conceal the laugh that was bubbling up, but it was there anyway. Yet Jensen didn't seem in the least bit perturbed by her questions.

"I think I need my own ice cream before we start the movie," Jensen told her.

"I can help!" Lilyanne cried. "I'm great with sprinkles."

"I bet you are." He lifted her up and onto his shoulders, and he carried her into the kitchen.

Lilyanne screamed in pure joy at being so high in the air, and I just followed in awe.

Jensen scooped out his own ice cream and let Lily add the sprinkles. Then, he took the bowl back into the living room with Lily back on his shoulders. He easily dropped her in front of the shelf of Disney movies and then leaned over and pulled me tight against him.

"I missed you," he said. He planted a firm but quick kiss on my lips.

"I missed you, too. Are you sure you don't mind this?"

"Do I look like I mind?"

I shook my head. He definitely didn't.

"Who could pass up a big bowl of ice cream and Disney movies?" he asked.

"I'm certain, no one."

"Found it!" Lilyanne cried.

"Let me guess," I said.

"No! It's a surprise."

"Okay. I won't look," I told her. I took the Blu-ray from her and popped it into the player.

Lilyanne took the spot next to Jensen and instructed me that I had to sit on the other side of her. With Lily in the middle, Jensen draped his arm across the back of the couch and kept his hand on my shoulder. I smiled at him as the opening credits to *Frozen* began. It was only a matter of minutes before the entire thing became a sing-along. By the time "Let It Go" came on, Jensen and I were swinging Lily between us as we all led into the chorus.

We finished *Frozen*, and we were halfway through *Tangled* when Lily began to crash. To my amazement, it was already well past her bedtime. She lay stretched out between us with her head on a pillow in my lap. Her eyes kept fluttering closed as her sugar high dissipated. I waited until she was sound asleep before moving out from under her.

I reached for my phone and saw that I had a text from Kimber.

Everything is all right here. It was Braxton Hicks contractions, but they last a long time, so the doctor just wanted to check me out. I've been told I need to rest, but I might die since I haven't even finished Christmas shopping! Be home soon!

As long as you and the baby are okay, that's all that matters. We can shop on Amazon and have all the presents delivered!

"All right. Everything is okay with Kimber. They're leaving the hospital soon."

"Good. I'm glad that the baby didn't come early," Jensen said. "Want me to take this one up to her room?"

"You don't mind?"

Jensen didn't even reply. He just lifted Lilyanne into his arms like a baby doll and effortlessly carried her up the stairs. I followed, directing him along the way. He gently placed her on her bed and tucked the covers all around her. She let out a satisfied sigh, and Jensen just smiled at her.

Jensen eased the door closed behind us. He took my hand, and we walked back downstairs. I curled into his side on the couch as *Tangled* continued to play in the background.

"You're really great with her," I told him.

"I like kids."

"I like kids who are raised right. Lilyanne is an angel compared to some other kids her age."

"That is true," he agreed. His eyes slid down to me, and he smiled. "She's full of possibilities. I love that about her. She has so much joy and is full of life. I think she reminds us all that we need to live a little more. Be a bit more carefree."

I nodded. "That's definitely Lily." I sighed and thought about all the things in my life that hadn't been full of joy. All of those things that had led me to this moment. "It's part of the reason I left my PhD program."

"What do you mean? You didn't feel carefree anymore?"

"I didn't have any joy. I just wish I'd figured it out sooner. I wish I hadn't needed to be hit over the head to know the program wasn't right. I mean…I'd already completed my comprehensive exams. All I had to do was finish my dissertation and defend it to my committee to pass."

"How could you quit if you were so close?" he asked curiously.

I bit my lip and looked away from him. "I really didn't love it. I think I was doing it because one thread kept pulling me back to it. The stress got out of control. I couldn't handle it, and I had to get on anxiety medication. Plus, well, I found out my advisor was sleeping with an undergrad."

"Jesus," he said. "What a prick! Did he get fired?"

"I didn't turn him in. I just broke up with him and quit the department."

I wasn't sure I could have shocked him more. Jensen's mouth was actually hanging open.

"You were dating your professor?" he asked.

"Yeah, for almost three years. Welcome to my life," I said with a stiff laugh.

"How long ago did you find out about him cheating on you?" he asked.

His knuckles were white where he had bunched them into fists, and I noticed he looked pissed. No, livid. Like, if he could, he would murder Mitch right then and there for hurting me. Sometimes, I wanted to murder Mitch for what he had done to me. And, other times, I thought that the whole thing was a big joke. An easy, convenient joke. But I didn't think it was love or even lust anymore.

"I don't know. Two weeks?" I shrugged nonchalantly.

"Fuck. I'm sorry about that. And only two weeks ago? No wonder you didn't want to go on a date." He had released his fists, and his gaze returned to mine. "Is all of this too soon?"

"No," I said immediately. I reached out and ran my hand down his shirt. I didn't want him to think that I was still in love with Mitch or pining over him. "It had been over with Mitch long before I ended it. I just hadn't had the nerve to realize what I really wanted."

"And what do you really want?" he asked, sliding his hand across my back and pulling me toward him.

"Something I'm really passionate about."

"And what is that?"

"I'm really not sure. I think I'd just like time to decide."

"You have all the time in the world."

He brushed his lips against mine. I leaned into him with a sigh. I liked the idea that I had time to figure out what I really wanted in life. Because, besides Jensen kissing me right now, I really didn't know.

"What are you doing next week?" he asked against my mouth.

"Seeing you, I hope."

"I have to be in Austin for a few days to sign some paperwork. How would you like to show me around?"

I tilted my head to the side and looked at him in surprise. "Really? But it's only a few days before Christmas."

"Business calls," he said cynically. "But I'd love to have you with me if you could come."

"I'll have to check my schedule at the Buddy Holly Center, but I should be able to do it. Plus, it might be pretty awesome if we drove out there because I need to get the rest of my stuff from my apartment before someone comes to sublet the place in January."

Jensen smiled a devious smile. "We can definitely stop to get your things while we're there, but, Emery…"

His hands threaded through my hair, and I got lost in his touch and his gentle kisses down my jaw.

"Hmm?"

"We're not driving, love."

chapter
nineteen

Emery

N O, WE DEFINITELY WERE *NOT* DRIVING.

I stared at the Wright private jet with equal parts shock and awe. It was a gorgeous, sleek machine that would get us to Austin in just over an hour. And we had it all to ourselves. I'd joked about him having a private jet only a couple of weeks ago, and here I was, about to be on the damn thing. It felt beyond surreal.

"Allow me to get your bags, Ms. Robinson," a man said. He was decked out in a suit and looked proper as fuck.

"Oh, um…okay," I said, relinquishing my bags.

"Thank you, Robbie," Jensen said. He took my hand in his and smiled down at my stunned face. "Why do you seem so surprised? You knew we were flying."

"Sure. Just…crazy." I closed my mouth and tucked my other hand into my back pocket to try to cover my discomfort at the display of wealth. "Is this how you try to impress all the girls?"

"No." He used our linked hands to draw me into his body, and he gazed down at me with intense interest. "Just you."

I didn't believe him, but it didn't matter. I was sure he had used his private plane to woo many girls. But he was mine right now, and I wouldn't cloud our time together by thinking of something like that. I would enjoy the once-in-a-lifetime experience. Texas was a state that judged distance by hours, not miles. It was a luxury to skip the drive time that I had become so accustomed to.

We walked up the steps and into the luxury cabin. It was outfitted in cream leather with a full wet bar and mounted flat screen TVs. A door was closed in the back, and I could only imagine what it held. I was going to go with either a king-size bed or a Jacuzzi. I laughed at my own wandering thoughts.

Jensen came up behind me and put his arms around my waist. "What is so funny?"

"Nothing."

"Are you sure?" he asked, kissing my earlobe.

"I just suspect that you have a hidden Jacuzzi or something back there," I said with a shrug.

He kissed me again and laughed softly. "Not quite. It's used for business."

"Much more boring."

He drew me into him, and we took a seat on the couch. Robbie returned and offered us drinks before takeoff. Robbie brought me a mimosa and Jensen a Bloody Mary.

I raised my glass to his. "Cheers."

"It's five o'clock somewhere," Jensen said.

He clinked his glass against mine and took a long sip. Then, he rested an arm back across the seat as we taxied down the runway.

"So, what's the big plan for your paperwork thing?" I asked.

"I officially sign the paperback for the Tarman Corporation merger this afternoon. So, we'll have the morning to ourselves today and all day tomorrow."

"Oh, good. I like that. Is there anything you want to see while we are in town?"

"Whatever you want to show me. You're the one who lived there after all."

"True. I have a few things in mind."

"Good. Me, too," he said, dropping his mouth on mine.

We made out through most of the flight. Jensen disappointed me by showing me that the back of the plane was just for business. But I was excited enough being here with him, drinking, and eating gourmet sandwiches a mile up in the air. Soon enough, Robbie announced out descent and we buckled back into our seats.

Our flight landed seamlessly at the Austin-Bergstrom International Airport. Robbie retrieved our bags and placed them in the back of the waiting town car.

I could hardly wrap my mind around the fact that this was the Jensen that I was dating. When we were together, he was not the CEO of Wright Construction. He drove his truck and ate tacos and wore jeans. It lulled me into forgetting about his money, which I appreciated. I didn't find him ostentatious in any way, but I was sure he had to be at times with his business contacts. Appearances were everything.

"Apartment first?" he asked, opening the door to the town car for me.

"I suppose so." I slipped into the backseat, and he took the seat next to me.

I watched the city I had lived in for the past three years zoom by me. Despite having gone to college in Oklahoma, I adored Austin. Maybe not their football team but definitely the town. It had its own vibrancy that was impossible to find many other places. Between the food trucks, hipster living, and overall weirdness, it was a dream local if you could ignore what felt like eternal bumper-to-bumper traffic.

My apartment looked much the same as I'd left it. A mess.

I cringed when I opened the front door. A tornado had come through here for sure. That was the only explanation for what it looked like—besides the fact that I had been neglectful of the one bedroom for close to three years and then torn through it when I moved out.

"Um…maybe you should wait in the car," I said, barring him from entering the room.

"What? Why?"

"Well, because it's a hot mess. And I need a few minutes…or hours to tidy up."

Jensen arched an eyebrow. "We're not wasting hours here. Why don't we just get the things you need? Then, I can have a cleaning crew come through and box everything else up."

"No way! I can't let you pay to clean my apartment!"

"Fine. Then, let me inside," he countered.

I glared at him. I should not try to negotiate with someone who did it for a living. "All right. Well, don't judge me."

"I'll judge you for the incredible woman that you are, Emery. Not for anything else."

I swooned at his words and let him inside. "You've been warned."

He stepped inside and then laughed. "I spoke too soon."

I smacked him in the chest. "Jerk."

"I'm kidding. I'm kidding. Come on, let's get started."

We spent about forty-five minutes going through my bedroom before I eventually relented. He was right. This was way too much work for one morning. I'd be here for a couple of days, going through my stuff. It would be better if I just packed it all up and shipped it home where I could go through it later. Luckily, the furniture was staying for this semester for the person who would be subletting.

Jensen and I brought out the boxes to the town car and then checked into the suite he'd reserved. I hadn't even seen him pick up his phone to call for someone to come to the loft, but he told me on the way to campus that someone would be there tomorrow.

I might have dated a Wright in high school, but I hadn't had *this*. At that time, their father had been wealthy. But I hadn't understood money then. I hadn't realized what it meant the same way that I did now when I didn't have any. With Jensen, it was clear, the power and prestige that came with that kind of wealth. He made things happen. And he didn't even bat an eyelash.

The town car dropped us off in front of campus, and I was ready to show him around, but I could already feel myself crashing. Early mornings were not my thing.

"Coffee first?" I suggested.

"Definitely."

We traipsed across the street to my favorite local coffee shop. I'd been there about a million times since it was such a short walk from Garrison Hall where the history department was held. The next closest shop was a Starbucks, but in Austin, local was king. Especially when it came to coffee… and tacos.

My heart felt giddy as we approached the building with sleek black tables on the outside, already half-abandoned since school was out. Only a few people were still hanging out. We breezed in through the front door, and I breathed in the scent of the coffee brewing. I could already taste my favorite latte on my tongue.

Then, it all turned to ash.

My feet stopped moving.

Jensen took two steps ahead of me before realizing I had stopped entirely.

But I couldn't look away from what was in front of my face.

It hadn't occurred to me at all that Mitch might be here.

"What's wrong?" Jensen asked. He took one giant stride to appear before me. "Hey, tell me what's going on."

"Emery," Mitch said over Jensen's shoulder.

Jensen whipped around and took stock of the man standing before him. Mitch was about average height with slicked back long blond hair. He wore a black suit jacket with jeans. I had always thought he looked so sharp, and knowing the intelligence under the persona was even more appealing. But, seeing him now next to Jensen, I realized that Mitch looked cheap and grungy.

Cool professor, he might be.

Sexy CEO of a Fortune 500, he was not.

Jensen seemed to put the pieces together almost instantly. He bristled with barely concealed anger and tried to shield me from Mitch. "Let's just go somewhere else."

"It's okay," I said, finding my voice. I put my hand on his sleeve. "This is my favorite coffee shop."

"Are you sure?" he asked.

I nodded, and Jensen instantly backed off. But he was still tense and looked ready to pounce if Mitch came any closer.

"I'm so glad you're back. I knew you would be," Mitch said with a confident smile.

He took a couple of more steps and then tried to pull me in for a hug. I stumbled backward in shock and revulsion.

How could he think I would want to touch him after what he had done?

Before I even had a chance to speak, Jensen crushed his hand on Mitch's shoulder to keep him from getting near me again. He was boiling over.

"Don't lay a hand on her," Jensen growled. He gave a little shove and then released Mitch.

Mitch looked him over, as if he hadn't noticed him. Jensen stretched even taller and broader than normal. He was all testosterone and aggression. Mitch had his classic sly grin in place. He was assessing the situation but not to size Jensen up…just to belittle him with his eyes.

"Always nice to meet a friend of Emery's," Mitch said, sliding a hand back through his hair. "I'm her dissertation adviser, Dr. Mitch Campbell." As if Jensen hadn't just pushed him away from me, he held out his hand.

Jensen coldly stared down at it. "I know who you are."

"And you're not my dissertation adviser," I cut in. "I quit the program."

Mitch laughed and waved his hand like he was brandishing a magic wand that could make it all better. "You were just upset that day. I told the department to dismiss the withdrawal paperwork, and I had you reinstated. I knew you'd want to finish up. You only have another year."

My jaw nearly hit the floor when the words tumbled out of his mouth. "You did *what*?"

"The department seemed confused that you would up and leave out of nowhere. As was I, Emery," Mitch said. "I don't know what you think happened or what you think you were doing by leaving, but it's over now. You don't have to be so irrational about it all. I've fixed it for you."

"What I *think* happened?" I sneered.

"Gaslighting," Jensen said under his breath. "Priceless."

"I don't even have time to listen to this," I said with fury in my voice. "I know what happened. I know what you did to me. And I *am* leaving the program. I cannot believe you went behind my back to toss out the paperwork I'd filed."

"Emery," he said, stepping toward me again.

"Stop."

"You heard her," Jensen said. He moved in between us. "The last thing you want to do right now is make a scene. The last thing you want is for me to take this up with the president or the provost. I happen to be on a first-name basis with both."

"Are you threatening me?" Mitch asked.

"Depends on whether or not you walk out of here right now."

"Who is this guy, Emery?"

"He's my…" I began and then trailed off.

What was Jensen?

"Boyfriend," Jensen filled in.

My eyebrows rose dramatically. *Boyfriend? Whoa! Whoa! Where had that come from?* My mouth was open slightly, and I wanted to say something, but I didn't know what to say. Not that I didn't like the phrase rolling off his tongue, but I hadn't even known what we were doing. I hadn't known where this was going.

Now, he was claiming me.

Jensen Wright was claiming me.

"Boyfriend," Mitch said. He seemed to weigh his options. He faced me, but I narrowed my eyes in warning. "Well, that was fast."

"Not fast enough," I muttered.

"Why am I not surprised?" Mitch said, reaching for his trendy leather messenger bag. "You always did like to be a kept woman."

I winced at his assessment as he brushed past Jensen and out the door. Shots had been fired. And I'd let him have the last word. *Ass.*

"Emery..."

"Let's just get some coffee," I whispered. My head was spinning. Between the confrontation with Mitch and Jensen claiming he was my boyfriend, I needed a second to think.

"I didn't mean to spring that on you," he said. He sounded sheepish.

I glanced up at him and saw that he actually did look sheepish.

"I meant for the whole thing to be romantic. To take you out to dinner and ask you over candlelight if you'd be my girlfriend. Then, it just kind of slipped out."

"Oh," I said softly. "Wow."

"I know it's fast and that I have a lot to tell you, but I want you to be mine." He reached out and brushed a stray strand of hair out of my face. "I can't get you out of my head, and I don't want you out. So, do you want to be my girlfriend?"

I laughed abruptly, and then it suddenly poured out of me. This was so formal. So controlled. So purposeful.

"What?" Jensen asked. His body became guarded, as if preparing for the fallout.

"You really aren't like any other guy, are you?"

He arched an eyebrow in question.

"Most guys are too busy trying to keep girls dangling on the line, but you just come right out and say you want a relationship."

"I'm a businessman. I say what I want, I negotiate for it, and then I take it. I don't want to lead you on."

"I like that."

He beamed.

"And I like that you said you were my boyfriend."

"Good," he said, drawing me in for a kiss. "Does that make you my girlfriend?"

"I guess it does."

chapter
twenty

Jensen

I LEFT EMERY AT THE UNIVERSITY TO HANDLE THE REMAINDER OF HER SCHOOL issues. I hadn't wanted to abandon her when that prick was nearby, but she'd promised she would be fine. She'd claimed that Mitch was more bark than he was bite. After getting a good look at him, I had to agree. Though it didn't make me feel any better.

Time and time again, I had claimed that I wasn't a violent man. I'd been tested on that twice before.

One time, I'd failed.

One time, I'd succeeded.

This time, I had come so close to losing it and beating the ever-loving shit out of the skeezy, conniving bastard. My hands had fisted, aching to blacken his eyes and rearrange his face.

But I knew that wasn't what Emery wanted. Also, I had a company to think about, and assault charges never looked good in the media. In the end though, threatening him with administration interference had been enough to send him packing. Couldn't even stand up to me like a man. Even without knowing who I was, he had known, if I put some weight behind it, I could get him fired for what he had done to Emery and the handful of other girls he'd seduced in his time as a professor. With my blood boiling as it was, I had half a mind to make the call.

Luckily for him, I had a business meeting that I had to get to. I would have to deal with him later.

I stormed into the Tarman Corporation headquarters like a thundercloud.

A bunch of hurried receptionists teetered out of my way with a squeaked, "Hello, Mr. Wright."

All I had to do was shake hands, sign some paperwork, and then dismantle the Austin-based corporation I'd been trying to get my hands on for years. They were Wright Construction's biggest competitor, and now was the time for it to all get finalized. As our motto said, *What's Wright Is Right.*

"Gentlemen, lady," I said with a brief acknowledgment to Abigail Tarman, the only woman in the room, "let's begin."

I settled in for the long haul. I knew they wouldn't let this go easily. The owner was the son of my father's biggest adversary. We were about the same age and had attended Texas Tech at the same time. Then, we had each thought we would outgrow our respective father's ambitions. We'd both be architects and reshape the industry. It hadn't worked out that way. It had been way more fucked up than that.

"Marc," I said, holding my hand out to the current Mr. Tarman himself.

"Jensen," he said blandly.

He shook my hand, and we each squeezed tighter than we had to.

"Shall we?" Marc asked, gesturing to the long rectangular table in the center of the room.

"I believe we shall."

I stalked to the front of the room and took my seat across from Marc. The negotiations had been over weeks ago, but I knew that he wouldn't let me off this easily. I had been slowly eroding his company over the course of the last five years. I'd have loved to see it burn to the ground already, but it was better this way. Sweeter.

It was hours before I officially signed. I had known Marc would take me through the wringer, and I hadn't been disappointed. But I signed the last piece of paper with a flourish. Watching Marc hand over the company to me was perfection. I passed the paperwork to my lawyer to review one last time and then to file.

"Good doing business with you," I said with a smirk.

"I wish I could say the same to you," Marc said with barely concealed animosity.

"Now, now, Marcus," his younger sister, Abigail, said. "Would you care to join us for dinner, Jensen?"

"I have to decline. But thank you, Abby."

"Jensen, come on. I insist. We've known each other too long for it to all end this way."

My eyes cut to Marc's. "I have my...girlfriend with me."

Marc seemed to perk up with both shock and confusion at that statement. "Girlfriend? That's a new one."

"Marcus," Abigail snapped. "Your girlfriend is welcome to come, Jensen. I can't wait to meet her."

"All right. Let me let her know. She's at the hotel."

"Why don't we pick her up on the way?" Abigail suggested.

Marc looked like it was quite literally the last thing he wanted to do. I couldn't agree more. But, if it made Marc uncomfortable, then I was in for it.

I took out my phone and clicked over to Messages, only to realize I'd missed two in the midst of the negotiations. I gritted my teeth.

Vanessa. Goddamn woman had the worst fucking timing.

Don't do this.

You don't have to sign that paperwork today. Your father wouldn't have wanted this.

I clenched my jaw, willing myself not to show any emotions in front of the Tarmans. They fed on it. Vanessa bringing up my father was a low blow, and she knew it.

I responded shortly.

Signed, sealed, delivered.

Then, I erased her messages and pulled up Emery's number, letting her know that I would be picking her up at the hotel for dinner with the Tarmans.

We're going to dinner with the people who owned the company you just purchased? What should I wear?

Something sexy as hell. See you in fifteen.

I retreated to the lobby with Marc and Abigail. Marc was on his phone in deep conversation with someone who he probably cared very little about. Any excuse not to have to talk to me any longer. And I was grateful.

Abigail could field the tension like a professional.

"Who is the new girl, Jensen?" she asked.

"She's recently moved to town. Was a PhD student here at UT before coming back to Lubbock."

Abigail's eyebrows rose. She knew my policy as well as anyone. "An in-town girl? Why, you never fail to surprise me."

I shrugged. "She's worth it."

"And does she know?"

My eyes shot to her hazel ones. They were searching and curious. Abigail knew too much about me and my family. I suddenly had a bad feeling about bringing Emery to this dinner.

"She doesn't," Abigail said as a matter of fact. "God help you with Marc here."

I ignored Abigail's comment and slid into the limousine that the Tarmans had waiting. It was a bit ostentatious for the circumstances, but I had just paid them a small fortune for the company. They could afford it for now.

We pulled up in front of the hotel a short while later, and Emery was standing there, dressed to kill. I didn't know how she had managed it in the short time I'd given her, but she was in a stunning red cocktail dress and pumps. Her hair was swept off her face, and she had on cherry-red lipstick. A color that had me thinking a million dirty thoughts at once. Like what that color would taste like. And how nice it would look around my dick.

I stepped out of the back to open the door for her, and she practically glowed when she saw me.

"A limo?" she asked.

"A bit much?"

"Or just enough," she countered.

"You seem like you're in a better mood than when I left you."

"Well, I got all that nasty business resolved, and now, I'm with you again."

I slid my arm around her waist and placed a deep kiss on her lips. She leaned into me, both of us forgetting all about her red lipstick. She laughed when she leaned back and smudged a spot off my mouth.

"Come on, Jensen," Abigail called from the door.

"We have to talk," I whispered into Emery's ear as she moved to pass me into the limo. Her eyes shot to mine in confusion. "I just have to...tell you some things. Ignore Marc."

"I don't understand."

"I know. I'm sorry. I'll explain."

Emery slid into the limo, and I cursed, wishing I'd had more time to clarify everything. I hoped Marc could keep a lid on his anger for a whole dinner without ruining it for everyone.

Emery was already introducing herself to Abigail and Marc as I hopped back into the limo, and it zoomed away.

"Ah," Marc said, looking Emery up and down, "you don't seem the type."

Emery's lips pursed. "What does that mean?"

"Nothing," Abigail interjected. "Ignore my brother. He's in a foul mood."

I knew that Emery was frustrated when her eyes slid to me. I hated that look. She was wary and had her guard up again. I didn't want to blindside her, but I had to say something about Marc.

"I just mean that you're the girl of the weekend, right?" Marc asked. His eyes were mirthless. He seemed happy to taunt her, even before we made it to the restaurant.

"Marc!" Abigail cried.

"Just let it be, Marc," I growled.

"What exactly does that mean?" Emery asked.

He chose to respond only to her, "You know...the fling he has when he's out of town. You must realize that you're it."

"I'll have you know," she spat, "I know all about his reputation, and I don't appreciate your insinuation that I'm that kind of girl. Jensen and I are together. This isn't a one-time thing. And who the hell are you to even say something like that to me?"

I nearly choked on my own laughter at Marc's bewildered face.

"Just an old family friend," Marc said. "Tell me everything about yourself. How did you manage to catch Jensen's eye and keep it? I thought only one person was capable of that."

Emery frowned as she mulled over what Marc had said, and I realized it was an absolutely horrid idea to have brought her along. Marc was a snake, and I had released her into the viper's den.

"Blow jobs," she said quite calmly.

Marc sputtered and then started laughing. "You surprise me."

I couldn't help myself; I laughed with him. *Man, this girl. She is...perfect.*

"Also, I'm completely irresistible," Emery continued.

"I have no doubt," Marc agreed. His eyes swept up her bare legs and then back to her face. "No doubt at all."

I possessively wrapped an arm around her tense shoulders and leaned her back into me. As far away from Marc as possible. He shot me a look full of questions that I was all too aware of. I just wanted to enjoy this night, and somehow, I'd been left with this.

We all piled out of the limousine when it pulled up to the restaurant entrance. Abigail dragged Marc inside for their table, but Emery drew me aside before we entered the room.

"What the hell is going on?" she demanded.

I sighed and ran my hand back through my hair. "A lot."

"I can see that, Jensen. Who are these people? Why did you tell me to ignore Marc?"

"Marc is an old family friend. Sort of. He and Abigail are Tarmans, who, up until a few minutes ago, were the Wrights' biggest rivals."

"You were friends with your rivals?"

"Money talks to money," I explained.

"Okay," she said uncertainly. "But all of that other stuff?"

"I have a reputation."

"I know that much."

I hated that she knew. I hated that she seemed to fear my reputation. I could see it in her eyes. I could see it in the set of her shoulders and the stiffness of her body. I wanted to make it go away.

"But I'm not doing that anymore. That's why I brought you. That's why I asked you to be my girlfriend."

"So...you wouldn't be tempted to shop around?" she asked as quiet as a mouse. "God, I'm sorry. I shouldn't have asked that."

I held up my hand. "It's a fair question, considering my background, but no," I said through gritted teeth, "I would never do that. I am a one-woman kind of man."

"One woman being me...or that other girl Marc mentioned?"

"The woman he was talking about is my ex-wife, Vanessa."

"Okay. So, you've been married," she said. "I don't follow the Wright family drama."

"Any of it?" I asked with raised eyebrows.

"Nope. Kind of swore off the whole bunch. Are you still in love with her? Is that it?"

"No. Vanessa is *not* the woman for me. If she were, I never would have divorced her."

"Okay."

I reached out and cupped her cheeks. I hated this far-away, distant look on her face. The one that she used when she was bracing herself. The last thing I wanted was for her to be afraid of me. Afraid of what I would do to her. I would never be Mitch. That fucking bastard. I would never hurt her like that.

"Emery, I want you and only you. I would never cheat on you. Never, ever."

"How could you know that?"

I hated seeing her so hurt and vulnerable. Seeing what Mitch had done to her. But, at the same time, I was glad she was showing those vulnerabilities to me so that I could prove to her how I felt.

"Because Vanessa cheated on me, and I divorced her for it."

And that wasn't even the half of it.

Emery made a small, almost inaudible gasp. "Oh God."

"It was nasty, and I'd never put another human being through something like that."

"It feels insurmountable."

"It was," I admitted. "And I'm not perfect by any means, Emery. I have trust issues. After what Vanessa did, I never thought that I would be open to another person again, but you're different. I want to open up to you. It's all going to take time."

"No," she said, waving her hand. "I was just cheated on. I'm the one with major trust issues. I just freaked out, and then Marc—"

"Marc is a jackass."

"I've realized."

"Look, I don't want you to doubt me. This is the reason I reacted the way I did the first night we were together. I have enough baggage as it is. Though I may not be a hundred percent since the divorce, I know that I'm better when I'm with you. You make me a better man."

She beamed. The tension and chaos of that brief interaction with Marc Tarman evaporated. Just like that, she was my Emery again. And I knew, right then and there…I was lost.

chapter
twenty-one

Emery

I BRACED MYSELF FOR IMPACT AND FOLLOWED JENSEN THROUGH THE RESTAURANT. What he had revealed about his past explained so much about his behavior. It was as if I had been chipping away at the ice and I was finally finding the man beneath. When I'd decided to hate all the Wrights a long time ago, I had never once imagined that there would be so much more to who Jensen was or that he had been hurt like I had. He was so charming and gorgeous and everything.

How could someone do something like that to him?

And why did he even bother with Marc? Why go to dinner with someone he thought was a jackass and after just buying his corporation?

Seemed insane to me, but I wouldn't abandon Jensen, leaving him to deal with Marc alone.

"Sorry about that," I said when I took my seat.

"Of course," Marc said, staring at me with his all-knowing sharp gaze. "I took the liberty of ordering you a vodka tonic. You do like vodka tonics, don't you?"

His eyes slipped to Jensen's, and I noticed the slight tension in his jaw. This was going to be a problem.

"I'm more of a champagne drinker myself." I shrugged. "Or tequila shots. Whatever you're into."

"No vodka tonic? I'm shocked. A girl like you?" Marc leaned back in his chair. "Soon, you're going to tell me you've never modeled with that pretty face."

"Marc," Abigail and Jensen snapped at the same time.

I held my hand up. "Look, it's fine. Whatever you're doing is fine. Take shots at me all you want. I get you might be upset with Jensen, and you're petty enough to try to take it out on me, but I'm not a vodka tonic–drinking, pretty-faced model. I'm not anything you think I am. So, keep hurling insults and layered jabs. I can take it. It's not going to make a damn difference to me."

Marc closed his mouth on whatever he had wanted to say next. Abigail gave me an appraising look, as if I had passed some unknown test, while Jensen looked like he wanted to kiss me. Instead, my insides were roiling because I had acted so bold. But I couldn't ignore the effectiveness of it.

I flagged down the waitress. "Can you replace that vodka tonic order with a glass of champagne? Veuve Brut preferably."

"Of course."

My point being made now, the rest of the dinner went much smoother. Marc seemed to reel his claws back in, and I found I actually really liked Abigail. She seemed to be a genuine person. I had to assume those were few and far between in this industry.

And, once Marc stopped egging Jensen on, they settled into some kind of routine. Just over dinner, it was obvious that they had known each other for a long time. I had to guess they had even been friends. I knew from experience that only close friends could speak without saying a word and laugh at implied jokes. Jensen and Marc had that levity—underneath all the animosity at least.

Despite how good things had been going the rest of the night, I was glad when dinner ended. We said good-bye to Marc and Abigail and headed back to the hotel. Our fancy suite was waiting for us—something I found extremely strange. I had lived in this city for three years in a shoebox apartment. We could have stayed at my place, despite the disaster, but Jensen had insisted on this. And I enjoyed the luxury of it. Who wouldn't want a Jacuzzi to fit a party of ten and a full living room with a balcony? But it was also…strange.

"Glad I grabbed this dress from my place before we left or else I would have had to miss that really fun time," I said with dry sarcasm, slinging my jacket on the couch.

Jensen ran his hands down my bare arms. He pressed a kiss into my shoulder. "I'm sorry about that. I should have realized it would be a mistake."

"A mistake," I said softly. He was trailing kisses up my neck, and it was hard for me to concentrate. "Are you going to tell me what crawled up Marc's butt?"

Jensen laughed against my neck and then nipped me. "Besides the fact that I just bought his company?"

I swung around to face him. "It was more than that. I'm not blind."

He nodded with a sigh. "You're right. It's a long story. You already know part of it."

"We have all night," I reminded him.

"Indeed we do," he said, his hands landing on my hips and then moving to my ass.

"Tell me about it. I want to know you. I want to understand."

"All right." He took a step back and composed himself.

He gestured for me to take a seat, and I tucked my legs underneath myself on the couch. Jensen took the spot next to me.

"Marc and I have known each other a long time. We were always thinly veiled enemies but hopeful friends. Against his father's wishes, he ended up at

Texas Tech because of their architecture program. We were in the program at the same time."

"You went to school for architecture?" I asked in confusion. "I thought you majored in business."

"Yes. My father required I major in business, but I took architecture classes on the side. I believed, as did Marc, that business destroyed the soul, as we had seen it happen with our families. It didn't build anything. It only tore things down. It never made things better. We were visionaries. We wanted more."

"Yet you each run your respective father's business," I whispered.

"I knew I would always have a job at Wright Construction whenever I wanted it. So, post-graduation, I took an internship at an architectural company in New York for a year. Vanessa and I were engaged. My father was furious about the internship, but I had a whole plan. I was going to change the world."

His eyes cut to me, and then he shook his head. He clearly hadn't told this story in a while. "Anyway, long story short, my father died. Left with nothing but his disappointment, I took over the company and moved back to Lubbock. There wasn't another option since Austin was still in college. Landon, as you know, was about to graduate high school. The board needed someone they could trust. They got me. Vanessa stayed in New York. She was...modeling part-time, and things were looking up. We got married that summer. She started modeling full-time, and Marc got my full-time job at the architectural company."

I covered my mouth. I felt like I was watching a train wreck without knowing how to stop it.

"Wright did as much business in New York as I wanted. I could have flown there every weekend to see Vanessa, but I didn't. I was engrossed in work and still grieving."

"But it wasn't enough for Vanessa," I whispered.

His eyes were far away. "Never could have been. Then she ended up in Marc's bed."

I sighed heavily and leaned into him, wrapping my arms around him. "That's not your fault."

"No, it's not. It took many years of therapy to realize that it was entirely her fault. She was the one who found solace with Marc. She was the one who could have stopped the whole thing, but she hadn't. She'd wanted the visionary she had fallen in love with...but I wasn't that man anymore. So, she'd settled for Marc in the meantime. Second best."

"Everyone is second best to you."

Jensen had a sad, lost look on his face. "Thanks."

"So...why is Marc so bitter when he was the one who did wrong?"

"To him, I ruined his life."

"That's ridiculous."

"It is. I understand it from his perspective though. He was always in love or obsessed with Vanessa. Whatever the case was, he finally had her, and then she left him again for me. I got the girl. He ended up having to take over his father's company. And, now, I've taken that, too. He's bitter. But I don't, no, I can't sympathize with him. He might find it convenient to blame me, but he's the bastard who did this."

"And you shouldn't sympathize with him. I didn't, and I didn't even know the circumstances. I'm glad I snapped at him."

"God, you're amazing," Jensen said. "The way you handled dinner, it was brilliant."

His hands were back on my legs and moving up to my hips. He crawled forward over me, and I fell back onto the sofa. A smile teased at my lips. I loved the way he adored me like this. When his eyes were only on me and all those skeletons were shoved back in his closet, he was just a sexy, confident man, unhindered by his past and ready to devour me.

"You think so?" I whispered.

"Know so, love."

He pressed his lips to mine, and I forgot all about our night and deep discussions. I kissed him harder, held him more possessively. I wanted and needed more. This was our first time together since we'd become official, and in the past day, so much had happened to move our relationship forward that I couldn't seem to get enough of him.

We stood up, and I tore his suit jacket off and removed the rest of his layers in a hurry. I cared so little about the expensive designer suit he was wearing, only wanting the birthday suit underneath. My dress was hastily discarded.

He shoved me up against the wall and then fell to his knees to drag my thong off with his teeth.

I groaned and dropped my head back as he kissed and licked his way back up until he was between my legs. My body was on fire. I couldn't fathom how I had ever said no. All I wanted to do was scream *yes* over and over again.

Jensen obliged.

He hooked one leg over his shoulder and then sucked on my clit until I was dripping wet. Only then did he finger-fuck my pussy until I came on his face. My legs were shaking from exertion, but Jensen didn't even hesitate. He stood, hoisted my legs up around his waist, and then thrust into me in one easy swoop. He braced himself against the wall, and bounced me up and down on his dick at a bruising, rough pace that I matched stroke for stroke. It was only minutes before my legs were trembling again, and my entire body exploded.

Jensen lifted me off the wall, and we both tumbled down onto the floor.

He pounded into me a few more times with my hands raised over my head. My breath was coming out in pants. I didn't think it was possible that I could come again. But Jensen was so close, and feverish desire in his eyes practically pushed me over the edge a third time. His body sleek and rippled, he came with me, toppling onto me.

We lay there, heaving, for endless seconds before Jensen slid out of me and rolled over onto the floor.

"I can feel my heartbeat," I whispered. "Feel it." I took his hand and pressed it against my lower abdomen.

"You're welcome," he said throatily.

I laughed and then leaned over and kissed him. "Now, he has manners."

"Didn't seem like you minded."

"Not one bit."

"Good. Then, maybe you'll be up for round two?" he asked with an arched eyebrow.

"Oh God," I said with a laugh. "Let me recover first."

He leaned up on his elbow as I stood up to pad to the bathroom. He smacked my ass as I passed him. "How about we use that Jacuzzi for recovery?"

I glanced back at him from under my thick black lashes. "Why do I have a feeling that you'll make that sexual, too, Mr. Wright?"

"Everything about you is sexual, Miss Robinson." He grinned devilishly, flashing me those irresistible dimples. "And I intend to take full advantage of you being naked in my hotel room."

I seductively shook my hips as I walked away. "Guess I'll turn the jets on and get started myself then."

His gaze told me that he was thinking every dirty thought in the book. And I did not regret it one bit when he joined me in the tub and used those jets in all the best ways.

We rose late the next day, and I finally got to give Jensen the tour of Austin I'd wanted all along. It wasn't as spectacular as I would have wanted since we were short on time. But he didn't seem to mind when I dragged him back to the hotel, before and after dinner, to use that Jacuzzi again. The feel of those jets combined with his fingers sent me over the edge faster than I'd thought possible. It was even better when he bent me over the side. I could have stayed in that bathtub all day and night.

With all the revelations that had been shared and meeting the people who had been deeply involved in our lives, I felt closer to Jensen than ever. I'd walked into this whole thing, imagining one night of hot sex. Maybe a date after that. Then, our connection had been off the charts. Now, I couldn't get enough of him—physically, mentally, and emotionally. Spending three days with him, almost one hundred percent of the time, had not irritated me once.

If we didn't have to get back to town for work, I would have encouraged him to stay longer. I was reluctant to go home.

Jensen could sense it in me, but I thought he must have felt it, too, because he never commented on it.

After our short plane ride, Jensen drove us back to his place.

I wanted to get back to Kimber and see how she was doing with the pregnancy. She was getting pretty close now. Plus, I definitely needed some Heidi time to fill her in on my weekend. But I also wasn't ready to say good-bye to Jensen yet. I wanted to discover if he had a Jacuzzi as well. I just wanted…to spend more time with him.

As soon as we parked, I hopped out of the car and raced around to his side. He pulled me into his arms and ducked down to give me a firm kiss.

"God, I'm going to miss you," I whispered.

"Don't miss me. Stay here."

I rolled my eyes. "I can't stay here."

"Stay here every night you like. I sleep better when I'm with you."

"We have not been sleeping at night," I countered.

"Exactly."

He slid a hand around my waist and drew me toward the front door. We breached the entrance, my laughter filling the foyer. My gaze was still locked on Jensen's face when he stilled completely. His smile disappeared.

My head snapped to the side, and my stomach dropped. "Landon…"

Jensen

"WHAT THE FUCK IS GOING ON?" LANDON ASKED.
Oh, fuck!
Fuck!

"Landon, man"—I casually disentangled myself from Emery as she was hastily doing the same, looking shell-shocked—"you're back."

I'd been meaning to tell Landon about Emery so he wouldn't hear it from someone else first. I had known he was coming back for Christmas. But I'd thought I still had a few days. I'd wanted to make sure things were official with Emery before bringing it up with Landon. Now…he was here.

"Cut the shit, Jensen. Just answer the question. What is happening right here?"

Landon pointed between the two of us, but neither of us said a word. We just stared forward at Landon, as if he might be an apparition that would disappear at any moment.

"I meant to tell you—"

"Tell me what?" His posture was stiff. His eyes kept shifting between the pair of us, as if he were trying to decipher a particularly difficult code. "Are you two…together?"

"Yes," Emery said, regaining her voice, "we're together."

Landon's eyes moved, as if he were watching tennis. "I was only gone a couple of weeks. I don't understand how this could have happened…and why I was never informed that this was fucking happening." He shook his head and then glanced away from us.

"Where's Miranda?" I asked him to try to move the discussion into safer territory. "Did she come in with you?"

"Are you kidding me? After the *fit* she had when she found out that Emery was still here, you think she'd have let me fly back alone?" he ground out.

"So…she's here?" I asked warily. I did not want Emery to be here if Miranda was at my house. That was a recipe for disaster.

"She's out shopping. Fuck, could you imagine if she was here?" Landon ran a hand back through his hair and then glared at me. "Could you fucking imagine? I came back at your request, and you didn't even tell me about Emery? Is this what you wanted?"

"No," I said. It had been my request. I hadn't wanted Landon to miss Christmas with his family. I'd wanted him here because he was my brother, and I loved him. Now, he was pissed off, and I didn't know how to fix this. But I would have to. "I wanted to tell you in advance about Emery so we could talk about this like men and not just get pissed off at each other."

Landon looked like he wanted to tell me to fuck off.

"You know, I should go," Emery said. She took a step back toward the door. "It's been a long weekend."

I turned to face her and wondered what she must be feeling. We'd both been anxious about telling Landon that we were dating, because the whole situation felt out of our hands. I didn't want to piss off Landon. He and Emery might have dated almost a decade ago, but it was tricky dealing with someone else's past relationship.

"Are you sure?" I asked.

"Yeah. Um...I should go see my sister. Check in, you know."

"All right. I'll call you later."

"Yeah, sure." She didn't even lean in for a kiss. Just gave a half-wave and then was gone, out the front door, leaving me all alone with my pissed off brother.

"So, you're fucking my ex-girlfriend now?" Landon asked. There was fury in his voice. It was something I hadn't heard from Landon in a long time. Not since Dad had died.

"It's not like that."

"What is it like exactly? Gave up on messing around with every girl you came across when you were out of town and decided to dick around with all those in town, too?"

I ground my teeth and felt the hair rise on the back of my neck. Landon was looking for a fight, but I wouldn't oblige him.

"I don't want to fight with you," I said finally.

"Well, you don't get to make that choice, Jensen. You walked in here with Emery Robinson. We'd dated for two years. You *knew* her when we were in high school, Jensen."

"I didn't know her then, and like you, I didn't even recognize her at first."

"Like me?"

"At the wedding," I bit out.

Landon's face ignited, and he rushed toward me, shoving me backward. "You met her at Sutton's wedding? You've known who she is this whole time and didn't say anything?"

"Yes, all right? Yes. I've known who she was since that next morning. You were the one who told me that she was leaving town after a couple of days."

"That wasn't an invitation to go and fuck her!"

"I didn't take it as one!" I yelled back. "I was going to leave her alone, but then we kept running into each other. I've fallen for her, Landon. I have."

"For now," Landon said under his breath. "What happens when you're tired of her? We all know you bore easily. You can fool her with whatever you're doing, but I know your reputation."

"Emery does not compare to any other girl I've been with," I growled. "Comparing Emery to any of my flings is an insult to her."

"Or is it just an insult to you?"

There were a million things I could throw back at him—namely, his horrible wife—but I knew that wouldn't get me anywhere. I needed him to understand.

"I should have told you."

"You said that already."

"I was planning to tell you before Christmas. But I wanted to make sure this was a real thing. I didn't want you to find out this way."

"Whatever, Jensen. Just admit it. It's not that you didn't want me to find out this way. It's that you didn't want me to find out at all. Everyone else in the family can fuck up, and you solve *their* problems, but you can't solve your own." Landon sneered at me and crossed his arms. "You just hide them."

"That's not what I was going to do. I care for Emery. I wanted to make things right. This isn't a joke to me. And why are you so pissed off anyway? You're married." I reminded him. "By the way you're acting, I'd think you still had feelings for Emery."

"Fuck off, Jensen," Landon said. He turned away from me and paced toward the door.

He twitched his hand toward the handle but stopped when I began to speak, "The breakup was ten years ago, Landon. This is all harsh for someone you've barely spoken to since high school."

He whipped around to glare at me. "You don't know anything."

I bit out a laugh, harsh and low. "You went to different colleges. You were going different directions. A lot of couples break up for those reasons."

"If you believe that is what happened, then you don't know Emery."

I tilted my head in confusion. Ten years ago, that was *exactly* what Landon had said about Emery. I remembered it because he had told me after our father's funeral. They'd broken up shortly after that. I hadn't ever suspected there was more to the story.

"And you're smarter than this, Jensen," Landon said. "You know that you don't want to bring her into your mess."

"She already knows."

"Everything?" Landon prodded.

"Not everything," I said slowly. "It's only been a couple weeks. I'm trying to ease her into my life."

"You better tell her, Jensen or I will."

"Don't threaten me, Landon."

"Fuck! You know I won't tell her. Though I should," he said with a glare. "Emery is a good, kind, and genuine person. She's too good for you."

With that, Landon wrenched open the door, leaving me standing there in shock. I stared at his retreating form until he disappeared completely.

How had that all gone so completely fucking wrong?

chapter
twenty-three

Emery

A FTER CHECKING ON MY SISTER, I HURRIED OVER TO FLIPS TO MEET HEIDI. Peter was working the bar when I entered. He waved distractedly as he poured out beers for a few guys.

"Heidi here?" I asked.

"Pool table."

"Of course. Should have known."

I grabbed two tequila shots from Peter and then brought them to the back. Heidi was running the table, but it was a slow night, so she wasn't hustling anyone…yet.

"Shot?" I asked.

"God, yes," Heidi said.

We tossed back the alcohol, letting it course through our veins and make our minds all fuzzy. I needed a good fuzzy mind after the day I'd had.

"Good to have you back, baby," she said, winking at me. "Now, tell me all about your Wright brother. Is he the right brother?" Heidi cackled, as if her joke were hilarious.

"How many drinks did you have before this?"

Heidi innocently fluttered her eyelashes at me. "More than one."

"Whore."

"I didn't know you were back yet! And Julia is in Ohio or wherever she's from. Somewhere cold and snowy."

"It's cold and snowy here."

"Yeah, sometimes. But not today!"

"No, not today. But snow is on the forecast for forty-eight of the fifty states next week. Everywhere is cold, except for Florida and Hawaii."

Heidi sighed. "If only. Now, tell me about your sexy weekend. There were sexy times, right?"

"Yes," I conceded. "We ran into my ex-boyfriend, and Jensen bought a million-dollar company from a man who his ex-wife cheated on him with. Then, when we came home, *Landon* was waiting for us at Jensen's house."

Heidi blinked twice and then burst into laughter. She dropped the pool cue onto the table and then doubled over. "Oh my God," she cried. "Oh, phew! Wow!"

"What the hell are you laughing about?"

"Did you not hear how ridiculous you sounded?" Heidi asked. She swiped at her eyes.

"I just told you what happened!"

"Yeah. Yeah, you did. Wow!"

Heidi chuckled some more, and I couldn't help it; I joined in.

"God, you're such a bitch."

"You love me anyway."

"True," I admitted.

"So…Landon is back in town?" Heidi asked. Her eyes met mine, and then she glanced away immediately.

I narrowed my eyes in confusion at her strange body language. "Yeah. He just got into town with his wife. Not so great timing."

"Did you see Miranda? Was she there?"

"Nah. Lucky for us. Sort of, I guess."

"Yeah. She's a nutjob."

I nodded. "That's true. But Landon got upset when he saw Jensen and I together."

"Landon is a big boy. He's a grown-up and married and living halfway across the country. He shouldn't be upset."

"Yeah," I agreed. "But you didn't see his face when he saw us together. I know I haven't talked to him in forever, but I feel bad for Jensen that we didn't tell him. After all, he's his brother and, we probably should have said something when we realized things were getting serious."

"Serious?"

"I guess we're official now," I told her with a grin.

The idea that Jensen was my boyfriend was too exciting to contain.

Heidi screamed and jumped up and down. "Okay. Well, we definitely need to toast to that."

We hurried over to the bar, and Peter poured us some fancy shots that promised to knock us both on our asses. I tipped back mine and could already feel the ramifications of that drink coming on strong. I excused myself to use the restroom, and when I returned, I told Heidi the full details of my weekend with Jensen. I still felt rotten about leaving Landon and Jensen together like that, but it was good to be with my girlfriend. To not have to worry about it at all.

I was on my third round, and I was unsure of where that put Heidi. If we kept this up, both of us were going to have to cab it back home. I was just debating whether or not to nurse this one for the rest of the night when Heidi perked up in her seat.

"What?" I asked. I was more attuned to my friend's behavior than anyone else I'd ever known.

"Don't hate me."

"Oh God, I already do." I glanced over my shoulder and saw none other than Landon Wright walking into the bar.

He looked the same as I'd left him back with Jensen. Dressed down in a polo and jeans, he shrugged out of his jacket to reveal his perpetually sun-kissed skin from hours of golfing outdoors in Florida.

"Did you invite him here?" I accused.

"Well, he texted me to find out where you were…and ta-da."

"You're right. I do hate you."

Landon's gaze caught mine from across the room, and his mouth ticked up into a smile. He strode toward us with a purpose that I recognized from my recent, vivid acquaintance with his brother. It was a swagger that I was very familiar with. Strange, considering I didn't really compare Jensen to Landon when we were together. But it felt impossible not to compare Landon to Jensen.

"Hey," he said, slinging his jacket onto the back of the seat next to mine.

"Hi."

"Hey, Landon!" Heidi said with a big grin.

His eyes moved to Heidi's and softened briefly. "Hey, Heidi. Thanks for the info."

"For sure. Why don't you two just…" She trailed off, swallowed, and then darted back to the pool table.

"Do you mind?" Landon asked, gesturing to the empty seat.

I shook my head and concentrated on my drink.

"Emery, I didn't mean to ambush you," he said at once.

"Why not? I kind of ambushed you."

He breathed out heavily. "Not on purpose."

"True."

"I just wanted to apologize."

I turned my head to look at him again. *What was with these Wrights that I always got apologies out of them?* They were the kind of men who probably didn't use the word much.

"*You* want to apologize to *me?*"

"Yeah, I just saw you there…with him…and I kind of blew a gasket."

"I noticed that."

"Which I had no right to do."

I would have freaked out if I had hypothetically found out he was dating Kimber. Jensen and I should have fixed this long before it got here. I knew that. I'd just been too blissful to consider what would happen and where things were going. I hadn't wanted to do anything that could hurt something so fragile. And our relationship was fragile.

THE WRIGHT BROTHER | 125

"How are you and Jensen?" I asked carefully.

Landon ground his teeth and motioned for Peter to give him a beer. "I needed some time to cool off."

"So, you came to me?" I arched an eyebrow. "Don't think we were ever the cool-off type. I think we argued most of the time."

"Only so we could make up," he said with a grin.

I shrugged, unable to deny it. "You know, Jensen and I didn't mean for it to happen."

"I don't really want to know," he said, holding up a hand. "It might have been ten years, Emery, but it's still weird to me."

"It's weird to me, too."

"Just...be careful," Landon said. He dropped his hand onto my shoulder and looked me deep in the eyes. "I love my brother. But he's an asshole, and he's bad with women. Plus, he has more baggage than the rest of our family combined, and I think one Wright has hurt you enough for a lifetime. I wouldn't want to see you like that again."

I pulled back and let his hand drop off my shoulder. "I know about Jensen's reputation and his past. I know that he hasn't always made the right decisions with women. But that doesn't necessarily mean that he's going to fuck this up, too. If I thought he was playing me, I wouldn't be in his life. This is *me* we're talking about, Landon."

"I know," he whispered. "That's what I'm afraid of."

I sighed and shook my head. "You know what? I've had enough crap for one weekend. I apologized for not telling you about Jensen, but I'm not leaving him because of it. And I'm not being naive about our relationship."

"I don't think you know him."

"You're right," I conceded. "I definitely do not know him like you do. How could I? But that doesn't mean I don't care for him and want to get to know him."

"I just don't want to see you get hurt."

I stood from my seat and reached for my drink. "It's about ten years too late for that, Landon."

Landon winced, and I could see that my jab had cut deep. We both knew it. This was why he'd ignored all my messages after graduation. This was why we hadn't really spoken since.

"That's fair. I deserve that," he said.

"Let me take care of myself. I've been doing it long enough without your help. So, why don't we go and play some pool with Heidi and hang out for a while? I'd love to see Heidi hustle you like old times."

Landon glanced down at his phone. He grimaced, and I had to gather his wife was messaging him.

"Okay, but I don't have that long. Miranda is almost finished shopping. It would be bad for both of our health if she found us in the same place, let alone at a bar."

"She seems a bit...controlling," I ventured as we joined Heidi at the pool table.

"I really do not want to talk about her."

I held my hands up. "Okay."

"What don't we want to talk about?" Heidi asked. Her eyes darted back and forth between me and Landon. She had this little worried tilt to her mouth.

She was seriously confusing me.

Was she...vibing on Landon?

No way. That couldn't be it.

It had to be that she was just concerned about me and Landon being in the same vicinity after everything that had happened with Jensen.

"Miranda," Landon said gently.

"Is she coming here?" Heidi asked, her voice rising an octave.

"God, no."

"We're trying to make sure everyone makes it out of this alive. I mostly want to see you kick Landon's ass in pool. So, hop to. Make this happen for me," I said to Heidi.

Heidi grinned devilishly. Her eyes swept to Landon. "You rack, and I'll break."

"I'd expect nothing less," he said as he got to work.

And, suddenly, the three of us were back in high school. We'd spent countless nights at Heidi's dad's bar playing pool and having a good time. Half of the time, one of Heidi's boyfriends would show up. There was a lot of making out in back booths and trying to convince someone to get us drinks and a whole lot less actual pool.

So, this felt normal and comfortable.

I never thought I'd feel like this around Landon Wright again.

And it was nice.

chapter
twenty-four

Jensen

ONE MORE CALL COULDN'T HURT.

I'd told myself that after the last five calls.

But Emery still hadn't picked up.

After Landon had stormed out of my house, I'd called Morgan, and she came over. She hadn't known that Landon was coming in early either. So, she hadn't been able to warn me. Though she thought the whole thing was poetic justice.

I thought she was full of shit. I *had* been planning to tell Landon. That wasn't bullshit, as Morgan kept insinuating. But a part of me had known he would freak out. I'd told myself that I never would have gone after her if I'd known who she was. I'd told myself I never would have touched her if I'd thought she was staying in town. I'd told myself I'd stay away from her when I knew she was here for good.

With Emery, I couldn't seem to keep my promises to myself. And I didn't want to.

I didn't believe in coincidences. If I kept running into her, it was for a reason. Not on accident. And I wasn't about to walk away from someone just because of what might be.

But I hadn't wanted to face Landon. That much was for sure. And it had gone much worse than I had anticipated.

I didn't know what he was doing. I didn't know what Emery was doing. And I just wanted to make this all right.

Landon was wrong about me hiding my problems. I'd fixed one problem this weekend when I bought Tarman Corporation out from under Marc's nose. I could fix this one with Landon a lot quicker if I could talk to my girlfriend.

Except she wasn't answering her phone.

Morgan gave me a worried look. "Maybe you should let it go."

I wanted to throw my phone across the room. "I can't just let it go. Landon is out there, pissed off at me. Emery isn't answering my calls. What the fuck am I supposed to do, Morgan?"

"I don't know. You made this mess."

"Well aware of that. Thanks."

"Look, I'm not patronizing you. But you knew this was going to happen. You knew that you would have to tell Landon."

"And I planned to," I told her for what felt like the hundredth time.

"Then, you should have just done it."

"You're right," I said with a sigh. "Do you have Heidi's number?"

Morgan frowned. "I might."

"I need it."

"No."

"Why not?" I asked tersely.

"Emery is not answering your calls for a reason, Jensen. Give her some time. I'm sure that she is freaking out about all of this. No one likes to be ambushed."

"So, I should let her walk?"

"That's not what I'm saying. I'm saying, give her space. If you were the one freaking out, would you want her to bombard you?"

I closed my eyes and sighed. That was how I had reacted with every other woman post-Vanessa. I hadn't liked to be bothered. I'd wanted my space. I hadn't slept. I'd just worked. That had been my life. I didn't know what it was like anymore.

"Normally, no, but right now, I'm considering going to her house to see if she's there."

Morgan rolled her eyes. "You men, so dramatic."

"What if this were Patrick?" I countered.

"This also has *nothing* to do with me or Patrick. Stop projecting. I cannot believe I'm even having this conversation with you. With Austin, sure. He's the one who fucks everything up. He even fucked up whatever was going on with that girl in HR."

"Julia?" I asked. "They were together?"

Morgan shrugged. "They're not anymore. But I thought you were always the one who had your shit together. Austin always has trouble with women. Landon has Miranda." She scoffed. "Enough said. But your life is put together, even with everything going on with Vanessa. Why are you acting crazy over one girl?"

"I care about her. And I care about Landon. I don't want to see either of them hurt. Not knowing is making me feel insane. I have to go out there and do something."

I reached for my jacket and pocketed the keys to my car.

"What exactly are you going to go do?" Morgan demanded, following me into the garage.

"I don't know. I'll make it up as I go along."

I hurried past the empty space where my black Mercedes always rested and hopped into my truck. Morgan stood, watching, as if she wanted to jump into the passenger seat or talk some sense into me. I noticed the exact moment when she decided it wouldn't matter. She sighed and looked resigned.

"Will you let me know how it goes?" Morgan asked.

I nodded briskly and then pulled out of the garage. Before I had a second thought, I was already barreling across town. The logical explanation was that Emery was at home. She'd wanted to check on Kimber to make sure everything was all right. They were probably up late, talking, or maybe they had gone to sleep.

Except I didn't believe that.

I didn't know *why*.

But I just had this feeling. A gut instinct.

I wanted to shake it, but I wouldn't until I saw for myself that she was there. I careened down Milwaukee Avenue, out toward her sister's house. Pent-up tension and energy coursed through me. I felt on edge about her lack of response to my messages.

I parked my truck across the street and killed the engine. Shoving my hands in my pockets against the cold, I dashed across the street and up to the front door. I went to ring the doorbell and then shook my head. I couldn't ring the doorbell because Lilyanne could be asleep. That would be a real dick move. I didn't want to wake her up. They probably had a crazy routine to even get her to sleep in the first place. Instead, I knocked on the door and hoped someone was up to hear it.

After about a minute, the door cracked open, and Kimber's face appeared. "Jensen?" she asked in surprise.

"Hey, Kimber. I didn't mean to wake you up."

"Oh, you didn't. It's almost time, and it makes it kind of hard to sleep." She placed her hand on her belly and gave me a genuine smile. "Can I help you?"

"I was hoping to talk to Emery."

Kimber frowned. "She went out hours ago to meet Heidi. She hasn't come home yet."

"Oh," I said slowly. "I see."

"Have you tried her cell?"

"A couple of times."

"Heidi is a bit of a bad influence. Love the girl to death and back, but they're trouble together. I can't even tell you what they went through in high school."

"I believe it."

"Do you want me to give her a call and see where she is? I didn't even check before she left."

"Uh, no. That's all right."

"Just come on inside. It will only be a minute," Kimber said with a kind smile.

I ducked inside without another protest.

She shuffled over to her phone and then smiled. "I have a text here. Looks like Emery is on her way home. She should be here soon, I guess."

I clenched my jaw and then released it. *Emery was responding to Kimber's messages but not mine? What the fuck?*

Something was wrong here. I could feel it. I could sense it. But I didn't know what was happening.

"You can stay and wait if you want?" Kimber offered.

"Oh no," I said immediately, backing away. "Uh, no. I'll check in with her tomorrow. If she's safe, then that's fine by me."

Kimber tilted her head in worry. "Are you sure?"

"Completely," I said.

Then, I exited the house and hurried back to my truck. The reasonable and rational thing to do would be to wait until Emery got home. I wanted to talk to her about Landon—the things that had been said and the things that I suspected about Landon. I needed to clear the air. I needed to figure out why they had broken up and what Landon had meant about me not knowing her.

But maybe tonight really *wasn't* the best night for it. Maybe we should have that conversation when I was in a better headspace.

I shook my head at my own frustrations and then put the truck into gear. I touched the accelerator and hurried down the road. I was almost out of the neighborhood when my eyes cut to the car that was passing me—a black Mercedes.

There was nothing special about it. Nothing to draw my eye at all. It was a plain, standard black Mercedes. It should have been completely unidentifiable. Any number of people could have the same car in this neighborhood where wealth was on display.

But my instincts told me it didn't belong to just anyone.

My instincts told me that it belonged to *me*.

I waited until the car passed me before making my decision. I did a U-turn in the middle of the street and slowly drove back to Emery's house. When I turned onto her street, I cut my lights and parked two houses down the street. My stomach cramped, and tension bottled in my shoulders. My hands were white on the steering wheel. Of all the scenarios I had concocted in my head, *this* had never been one of them.

The Mercedes was parked at Emery's house. The Mercedes that Landon had driven off in earlier that day. He always had access to my cars when he was in town. I'd never cared what he drove or when. Getting a rental when I had a garage full of cars seemed ridiculous. Now, I couldn't believe that he was using my car to come here.

The passenger door opened. My gaze darted to it in surprise. Then, Emery stepped out, and my hands shook in disbelief.

Emery had been with Landon all night?

Kimber had said she was with Heidi. But it was right in front of my face. Landon was stepping out of the driver's side. He sprinted around to Emery's side and wrapped an arm around her waist. She turned her body into his and held on to his shoulder.

I felt like I was going to be sick. I didn't think I could watch any more of this. If I had thought half-hearted that Landon still had feelings for Emery before, it was now confirmed. He'd run out on me to go see my girlfriend. And here they were, together.

They walked arm in arm up to the front door.

As much as I wanted to look away, I couldn't seem to. Landon definitely still had feelings for Emery. And the way Emery was acting—leaning against him, holding on to him, practically gluing herself to his body—showed that not everything was gone from her either.

Emery rested back against the brick wall next to the door that I had walked out of only minutes before. She was staring up at Landon's face, and I didn't even need to hear what they were saying. The picture was clear enough to me.

I put the truck into drive and zoomed away from the sight before me. I couldn't watch any more.

I'd thought that there was nothing that would keep me from Emery.

But I would not compete with Landon.

Not in this lifetime.

Not in any lifetime.

chapter
twenty-five

Emery

M Y BACK WAS AGAINST THE BRICK WALL TO KIMBER'S PLACE, AND MY HEAD felt like I'd blown up a balloon inside it. Landon was hovering. *Little hoverer.* But I should be thankful because I wouldn't have made it to the front door without his help.

Somehow, I'd gone from a three-drink max to, like, ten drinks. I didn't even know how it had happened. At one point, I had been standing, and the next, I had proclaimed to the bar that I was definitely not drunk before suddenly wanting to make out with Heidi. Sure signs that I was a drunky-drunk face.

"Are you going to be okay? You look like you might throw up," Landon said.

"Just go check on Heidi. If she vomits in that Mercedes, Jensen is going to be *sooooo* pissed."

Landon grinned and shook his head. "Man, you're so fucked up."

"This is all. Your. Fault," I said, punctuating each word with a smack to his chest. It might have been some stupid girlie hit, but I felt fierce while doing it.

"Where is your key? Do you still not carry a purse?"

"As if the key would magically appear in a purse," I said, patting down my pockets in a half-assed effort. "It'd be full of other junk I didn't need. I'd never find it."

"You can't find it now, and it's in your pocket."

"Judgy McJudgerson doesn't find pockets acceptable. You only have pockets," I slurred, poking at his pocket and giggling.

"Do not make me look through your pockets for you," Landon said with a sigh. "God, if my wife saw me right now."

"Her head would explode," I crooned. Then, I made the boom sound for an explosion.

"Something like that," he conceded. "So, hurry up, so I can get home and incur her wrath."

I giggled again and then finally dug out the missing key.

Landon plucked it out of my hand and unlocked the door for me. He shoved the door open. "Here you go. Inside with you," he said, helping me blunder inside.

A light flickered on, and Kimber appeared around the corner. She stopped short, her mouth hanging open and her eyes darting between the two of us.

"Hey, Kimmy," I said happily.

"Landon?" Kimber asked softly.

"Hey, Kimber," he said with a short wave.

"That is not the Wright brother I was expecting," she confessed.

Landon's cheeks turned pink, and I giggled at his embarrassment. *Man, I am loaded.*

"Just wanted to make sure she got home safe. Caught her at Flips with Heidi, and they needed a ride home," he told her.

"I see." She crossed her arms over the top of her pregnant belly. "Don't you have a wife to get home to?"

She was using her mom voice, and I wanted to tell her to stop. But Landon seemed to take a cue from her and backed off. I stumbled onto the couch and watched the ceiling spin.

"Good seeing you again, Kimber. Good night," Landon said.

"Good night," she said, closing the door behind him. She turned back to face me with a sigh. "What have you gotten yourself into?"

"Clouds."

"Clouds?"

"They're twirling on the ceiling."

"Oh God, you're so drunk. Why didn't you answer Jensen's calls?"

"He didn't call," I said, trying to sit up. I pulled my phone out of my pocket and tried three times to light up the screen before realizing it was dead. I sheepishly glanced up at her. "Um…it's dead."

Kimber sighed heavily again. "Well, charge it, and give him a call. He was here earlier, looking for you."

"He was?" I asked, sobering up a bit at that revelation. "Why?"

"He wouldn't say, but he seemed concerned. And, since I just saw you with his brother and your ex-boyfriend, I could see his concern."

"Whoa! Wait a second, Kimmy. Reel that mom voice back in. There's so nothing going on with me and Landon. He just apologized to me for blowing up on me when he found out about Jensen. He played pool with Heidi. We had a few drinks. He drove us both home. No big."

"All right. What do I know? Just happily married with no drama in my life."

I giggled. "I love you."

"I love you, too. Now, go. Charge. Now."

I nodded at her and gave her a quick salute. Then, I meandered the way to the stairs like I was walking through a hedge maze, and I more or less crawled up the stairs. I found my charger resting on the nightstand and plugged it in, waiting for the signature *beep, beep* to let me know it was ready to use again.

Then, it beeped and beeped and beeped.

Kimber had *not* been joking. Jensen had definitely texted me. And called. And texted some more.

Holy text messages!

They were very blurry though and kind of all melded together. I didn't know what he was so desperate to tell me, knowing that he'd shown up here after I didn't answer, but I might as well call him. Probably not the *best* idea I'd ever had, considering the amount of alcohol I'd consumed.

Imbibed. Drank. Drunk.

I flopped back onto my bed and stared at the spinny ceiling, contemplating which word was the best. Probably drowned in. Because I felt like I was on a boat adrift in the water, bouncing up and down and up and down on the waves.

Oh God, I was going to be sick.

I sat up in a hurry and tried not to think about vomiting. That was better. Now, I could call Jensen.

I dialed his number and let it ring about a million times before it got to his voice mail.

Then, I tried again. No luck.

I stared down at it in confusion. *Why would he call and message me so many times and then not answer my phone calls?*

I tried one more time and then gave up. I was too drunk for this.

Maybe he'd call me back tomorrow morning. He was probably already asleep or something. And I clearly needed to do the same.

Stripping out of my clothes, I crawled into bed naked and promptly blacked out into oblivion.

After puking my guts out all night, I remembered that I had to open the Buddy Holly Center today. I'd switched my schedule around so that I could get away to Austin for the weekend and had given myself the morning shift. I felt like shit and looked even worse. My face was pasty, and my hair was limp. I brushed my teeth three times to get the taste of throw up out of my mouth.

And then I checked my phone.

Again.

Still nothing from Jensen.

I'd called him in between bouts of vomiting and texted him before I hopped into the shower. I double-checked that I'd contacted him as I put on clothes for the day.

I was royally confused. Beyond confused. And sick as a dog.

Why call and text and show up, only to ignore me when I tried to get in touch with him again? Is he trying to punish me or something for not answering?

That didn't sound like Jensen. That sounded petty.

With a heavy sigh, I grabbed my keys and cell, which was fully charged, and left the house.

The Buddy Holly Center was empty. The construction crew from Wright Construction wouldn't show up for another ten minutes, which meant I had a few extra minutes to try to recuperate and not to throw up again. I didn't have anything left in my stomach. I'd packed a few snacks that would be easy on the stomach, but the thought of doing anything but sipping on water made me feel nauseated.

A knock on the door broke me away from staring aimlessly at my phone, hoping for a text message. I couldn't think that Jensen was sleeping. He didn't sleep unless we were together. The insomniac would rear its ugly head when we were apart. I couldn't imagine that he was ignoring me.

I unlocked the door and allowed the crew to come inside. Once they were all inside, I could go back to the office and dick around until someone else came to take over at lunch. We really didn't have to stay the whole time, but some of the artifacts were pretty priceless, and no one liked to leave the place empty. Even if we'd hired the people.

I lay back down on the couch in Betty's office and took another sip of my water. Feeling slightly up to par, I found the number for Jensen's office and pressed Call.

"Mr. Wright's office," his receptionist said. "How can I help you?"

"Hi. Um…this is Emery. I was wondering if Jensen was in."

"Unfortunately, Mr. Wright is out of the office today, but I would be happy to take a message."

I furrowed my brow. *Jensen isn't at work? That seems…wrong.*

"Do you know when he's going to be back in?" I pressed.

"Mr. Wright is away on business right now."

"Away on business?" I asked in confusion.

"Yes. He had to go to New York at the last minute to take care of some business. I'm not sure when he will be back in the office, but I could get him a message if you like."

New York.

My brain stalled on the word.

What is in New York?

The only thing I could think that was in New York was what he had told me. Vanessa had lived there. He and Vanessa had been together in New York. *Did she still live there? Was he on his way to see her?*

No, that didn't make any sense. He had said that he divorced her for cheating on him. That definitely could not be it.

I was just trying to freak myself out.

Or I was just freaking out, period.

Why wasn't he returning my calls?

What kind of business could he possibly have in New York the week of Christmas right after he had gotten back from purchasing Tarman? And what kind of business would he have where he had to disappear so quickly without telling me...or responding to any of my messages?

By the time lunch rolled around and I was off my shift, I felt like I was going insane. Jensen and I had had an awesome weekend. I'd left him alone with Landon to clear my head. Jensen had called and texted, and then when I'd responded, he'd gone radio silent.

What the hell had Landon said to him?

Before I could second-guess my train of thought, I canceled my standing lunch date with Heidi and swung by Jensen's house. I rang the doorbell and impatiently tapped my toe.

When no one answered, I rang the bell again and again.

Finally, a bleach-blonde appeared at the door. Miranda's gaze dropped to mine, and then she pursed her Barbie pink lips. "What the hell are you doing here?"

Fuck. I hadn't counted for on seeing Miranda. I hadn't even thought about her. I just wanted to talk to Landon about Jensen.

"Um...hi," I said. *This is not going to be fun.* "Is Jensen here?"

"You can't fool me," Miranda said.

She eased the door open more, and I could see she was in some kind of tennis getup. But I didn't know if she had been playing or what because her hair and makeup were still perfect.

"I know why you're really here, and if you get near my husband, I'll file a restraining order."

I held my hands up. "No interest in your husband. Just trying to find Jensen."

Right then, Landon's face appeared. He looked green when he saw that I was talking to Miranda. "Emery? What are you doing here?"

"Came looking for Jensen. I haven't seen him since last night. He's not answering my messages, and his receptionist said that he was away on business."

"Landon!" Miranda cried. "Why the fuck are you talking to her right now? I thought we discussed this before we left Tampa. I would come if you didn't go anywhere near her!"

"Hello? Standing right here," I muttered. "I'm not interested in Landon. I'm dating Jensen."

"I'm not an idiot."

Beg to differ, was what I wanted to throw back at her. But, instead, I just turned back to Landon. "Help? Thoughts? Anything?"

"Landon!" Miranda whined.

"Just give me a minute, honey, okay?" He kissed her forehead as he crossed the threshold. "Just one minute."

"I cannot believe this. You are so going to owe me for this."

"Just one minute. Don't you have a tennis lesson?" he asked.

"Don't you dare try to get rid of me."

"I'll be right back," he said. I could hear the exasperation in his voice as he shut the door in her face. But he looked livid when he turned around. "What the fuck are you doing here, Emery? Miranda is going to murder me in my sleep."

"Jensen is gone and not returning my messages. What did you say to him last night?"

"I don't know. I was pissed last night. Said some dumb things."

"What dumb things?" I demanded.

"It was just me overreacting. I was going to talk to him this morning to try to clear the air, but when I woke up, he was gone."

"What did you say?" I said, my voice low and deadly.

"I might have said you were too good for him."

"Ugh!" I groaned. "Great. I don't know what he's thinking, but he's gone. He went to New York. Why would he be in New York?"

Landon's face dropped, and he was utterly silent. When he glanced away, that was when I knew it was bad.

"What? Tell me!" I said, pushing him.

"Nothing."

"Landon! Is it Vanessa?"

"I know Vanessa has a place in New York, but that doesn't mean he went to see her. He's probably working. That's all he normally does anyway."

"Landon, *why* would he go see his ex-wife? Why would he do that?" I didn't really want him to answer. I didn't want to consider why Jensen would go see Vanessa in New York after being upset last night. He'd promised he'd never cheat on me, and I had to believe that. I had to latch on to that with everything I was, or I might fall apart entirely.

"It's complicated."

I winced. "Then, make it uncomplicated."

"I can't. You should just…talk to Jensen about this."

"I can't!" I cried in frustration. "He won't return my messages."

"I'm sorry, Emery. I can't talk about it."

"Can't talk about what?"

"Nothing," he said quickly. "Don't jump to any conclusions. It's not Vanessa. This is normal Jensen behavior. He'll come back soon and then all will be back to normal."

I shook my head in disbelief. I couldn't believe what Landon was saying. Things were complicated? Things were always complicated.

But Jensen running away from his problems was not solving anything. Whether this had anything to do with Vanessa or not...Jensen was purposely ignoring me. And that alone infuriated me.

chapter
twenty-six

Emery

J ENSEN DIDN'T RETURN A SINGLE MESSAGE FOR FIVE WHOLE DAYS. By then, I'd thought of every worst-case scenario—from him being with his ex-wife to his death. My imagination was ripe, but it had no reprieve. I knew that I hadn't done anything wrong. Not a damn thing. And, at this point, he was ignoring me on purpose. We *definitely* needed a good long talk, and maybe he needed a sharp kick in the ass.

By Christmas Eve, I was even agreeing to go to church with my mother of all people just to see if he showed up. That way, we could get all of this out in the open.

Kimber, Noah, and Lilyanne decided to stay in since Kimber was due soon, and the days had gotten harder. She wanted to conserve all of her energy for Christmas morning when she would get to see Lilyanne open her mound of presents from Santa.

So, I drove myself over to my mother's place to pick her up.

"Look what the cat dragged in," my mother said when she answered the door in a chic black dress.

"Ha, Mom. Never heard that one before." It was our normal routine and slightly comforting, considering the week I'd had.

"Well, I *was* going to let Gary Lupton drive me to church, but I suppose you're a worthy substitute."

I cringed. "What about Harry Stevenson?"

"A girl has to have options, Emery."

"Oh God, Mom!"

She cackled and walked out to my Forester. "Don't be such a prude. I know you're seeing Jensen Wright. Everyone knows that he isn't a prude."

I ground my teeth as I turned over the ignition. "I really, really don't want to talk about my love life. Thanks, but no thanks."

"Why do you have to be like this? I thought we were bonding."

"I can't bond with you over who you're having sex with. It grosses me out," I told her as I pulled out of her driveway.

"Well, you refuse to come by and see me. You aren't getting married. You aren't getting your degree anymore. You hate shopping and pedicures and makeovers. What exactly *am* I supposed to bond with you over?"

"Hey, I like pedicures!" I said. "But just because I'm not…Kimber doesn't mean that I don't have my own qualities or whatever."

"I only needle you because I love you. I just want to make sure you're happy. I don't want to see you waste your life away at the Buddy Holly Center again."

"You set me up to work there!" I accused.

"Temporarily. I thought you'd be going back to school."

"Well, I'm not," I said. My mind was still locked on Jensen, and here was my mother, trying to plan my career. As if I wanted to add to the list of things that I had to deal with right now.

"You used to be so full of love for things. Things I hated but you loved them. Soccer and that horrendous skateboard and coaching and tutoring after school and honors society and—"

"Yes, I get it. But, now, I'm adrift, and I need something of my own."

"Exactly."

I rolled my eyes. "I'll figure it out."

My mother put her hand on my arm and sighed. "Maybe you should consider working at the high school. You have the degrees. You'd need to be certified, but I know you could do it."

"High school students?" I shuddered.

"You'd make a difference."

I brushed her hand off my arm.

I didn't want to admit that she was right. I probably could get a job teaching history at the local high school, and maybe I'd even get to help coach the soccer team. I'd played on the intramural team at Oklahoma and at an adult rec league for two years at UT. I just didn't know if that was *it*.

I'd loved teaching when I was in graduate school. That was the best part. The least stressful part honestly. It was the research and papers and endless criticism that had done me in. Some people were made for that and loved it but not me. I could take some critiques, but eventually, my head had exploded, and I'd felt like it was doing more harm than good.

"Just think about it," my mom said as we pulled into the church parking lot.

"Okay," I said, "I'll think about it."

"Good, or else I'd have to start talking about Jensen Wright again."

I groaned and parked in a spot. "You kill me."

"I love you, too," she said. Then, she hurried toward a cluster of her friends standing at the entrance.

I scanned the parking lot for Jensen, but it was impossible. The church was huge, and I would never find him out here like that. I killed the ignition and then checked inside the church to see if the Wrights had arrived yet. No luck.

Then, I planted myself at the front of the church with my arms crossed.

I felt like I was staking the place out as I waited, but if Jensen was here, then I needed to talk to him. I needed to figure out what the fuck was happening… or end it. Because I was not going to be toyed with.

Just when I had that thought, a bleach-blonde bob appeared before me.

"Ugh! Are you literally following me everywhere?" Miranda asked.

She was in a skintight blue dress that barely hit her at mid thigh and had a low-cut neckline. She looked good in it, but it wouldn't have been my first choice for a relatively conservative church service.

"I go to church here," I responded with a sigh.

"Uh-huh. Oh, I'm sure."

"Miranda," Landon said, hurrying to catch up, "let's just go inside."

"You *knew* she was going to be here."

"We've gone to the same church since we were kids, Miranda. I can't help that."

"And I get no warning?" she asked.

"You don't need a warning," I said, "because there's nothing going on here, and you're worrying for nothing."

"Don't tell me how I feel. Just stay away from us."

Then, she sauntered inside, as if she owned the place, and Landon gave me a sympathetic look before following her. I shook my head at her ridiculousness and then looked to see if the rest of the Wrights were following. I wasn't disappointed.

Little Sutton Wright and her new husband, Maverick, had finally come back from their honeymoon in Cabo. She was a deep olive tan, and his nose was a bit red, but they both looked happy. After them, I saw Morgan and Austin enter. She looked to be scolding him, pointing at his pocket. I narrowed my eyes to try to figure out what she was saying. Then, I noticed the top of a flask peeking out of his pocket.

Oh, eesh!

Then, I couldn't be bothered. Because walking straight toward me was none other than Jensen Wright himself. He looked…unbelievable. I might be mad at him, but he was undeniably attractive. He was in a tailored charcoal suit that fit him like a glove. He had on a red patterned shirt and a dark tie. His cheekbones were sharp, and his eyes were even fiercer. But I could see underneath it. He looked like he'd lost weight…and definitely sleep. There were dark circles under his eyes, like he'd been living off of caffeine and power naps.

He caught my eye, and I stopped breathing for a second. In that second, I just wanted to forget the last week. I wanted everything to be right. I wanted Wright to be right even though it felt so wrong.

But then that moment passed, and I knew what I had to do.

I marched straight over to Jensen and blocked his path before he could get inside. "Where the hell have you been?"

"Language, Emery," he said, his voice clipped.

"Don't do that," I ground out. "Just answer the damn question."

"I've been in New York."

"Why haven't you answered any of my calls or messages?"

"I've been busy," he said simply.

I grabbed his sleeve and pulled him out of the way of the entrance. "I'm missing something here. What the hell happened? Is it because I didn't answer your calls that night? My phone died, and I didn't see you'd called until I got home. I called you back as soon as I charged it," I rambled on.

"Not *as soon as*."

"What the hell does that mean?" I asked, not following him.

"I really don't want to get into this with you, Emery."

He moved to brush past me, but I latched on to his arm. "Was it Vanessa?"

Jensen turned back to face me with confusion. "What do you mean?"

"Do you still love her? Is that why you were in New York?" I knew I sounded desperate and jealous, but I cared very little at this point. If it was going to end, then I just wanted him to do it.

"You ask me that after last week?"

"Why shouldn't I?" I demanded. He wasn't making any sense.

He took a step toward me, towering over me. "I saw you with Landon. I saw the way you were all over him that night. Landon is still in love with you, and it sure looked like you felt the same."

Landon was in love with me? Ha! That was a riot. And Jensen thought I was still in love with Landon? That was equally laughable.

"That is not what you saw!" I told him.

"Save it, Emery."

Then, he turned and walked into the church, leaving me sputtering in shock. He thought I loved Landon. He thought that I had somehow chosen Landon over him. And I didn't even know how he could think that.

Where had he seen me with Landon? At Flips? I definitely had not been all over him then. I'd never even touched him, except when he'd helped me to the door so that I wouldn't fall over.

I stumbled back a step. *Oh, shit.*

Kimber had said Jensen had come by. Maybe he'd seen Landon help me. Maybe he thought something had been there that wasn't. Because *nothing* was there. And it was preposterous to presume something like that. It was even worse to assume it, not have a conversation about it, and then run.

chapter
twenty-seven

Jensen

E MERY'S GAZE BURNED ME LIKE A BRAND THROUGHOUT THE SERVICE. Luckily, the Christmas Eve service was almost entirely comprised of singing, and there was never a point where she could talk to me.

I'd been prepared for her to be here tonight. I'd figured, after the way I'd left things—or hadn't left things—that she would want a confrontation. She was that kind of girl. But she'd made her choice that night, and then I'd made mine when I hopped on that plane and flew to New York.

What I did regret was that things were still tense with Landon. I should have fixed things with him before leaving. He was my brother. He would always be in my life, and if I had to endure his love for Emery, then I should at least let him know that I would stand down. I knew he was married to Miranda. But I always thought that was a temporary thing and that he'd find someone better in the end.

It had been impossible to get near him when I got back this morning. Miranda never left his side, and I couldn't be in her vicinity for more than a few minutes before wanting my eardrums to burst.

But I would fix it tonight.

When the service ended, I reached down for my jacket, and when I stood back up, there was Emery, looking pissed as all hell. She was looking up at me with fire in her eyes, and it was impossible not to stare back. She was...stunning. Breathtaking. My chest tightened when I looked at her.

Avoiding her had seemed like the best option. I'd thought that telling her what I had seen would send her careening away from me. Yet, here she was, gazing up at me, as if she couldn't decide whether she wanted to kiss me or punch me. *What a quandary, this woman.*

"You're an idiot," she snapped.

"Not now," I muttered.

"Yes! Right now. I've waited all week for this. Why wait another minute?"

I could see in her eyes that she was in no way going to let this go. "Fine. Let's do this somewhere else."

"Fine," she spat. "Outside then."

I made my excuses to my family and then followed Emery outside. Emery nodded her head to the left, and we started walking in the bitter cold weather. She was in a warm jacket and scarf, and already, her cheeks and nose were pink from the cold. Temperatures were dropping rapidly, and we were actually expecting a white Christmas.

"All right, we're outside," I said. "What is it that you have to say to me?"

"You're being such an incredible idiot right now."

"You mentioned that."

She glared in my direction. "I can't do this, Jensen."

"Can't do what?" I asked, knowing full well what she meant.

"You don't trust me. You don't value my opinion. You couldn't even bother to talk to me. You ran at the first sign of trouble. Then, when things got tough, you went to see your ex-wife."

"This has nothing to do with Vanessa. You know that."

"How?" she demanded. "How could I know that? Do I know anything at all about what the hell this is about? You're pissed about Landon. Then, you ran to your ex, and you expect me to not care about that? Look at how you reacted when you *thought* something had happened with Landon. I have every right to be upset."

"You do," I conceded.

None of what she was saying was wrong. But that didn't mean I was going to stand here and let her yell at me. I knew Landon. I knew what he was feeling and thinking. She must just be blind to it.

"But it doesn't change what I saw or how you feel about Landon or how Landon feels about you."

"Oh my God, give it a rest! I do *not* love Landon, and Landon does *not* love me," she hissed.

"I know what I saw."

"No, you don't. You really don't. You have never given me a chance to explain what you *think* you saw. I can't sit around and let you walk all over my heart, Jensen. I put myself out there after I'd been hurt. And then, at the first sign of trouble, you ditched me. And all of it could have been fixed with one little conversation that you *refused* to have with me."

"If you think that one conversation will magically change everything, then tell me what I saw. Tell me what really happened."

"Look, the night you saw me with Landon was in no way romantic. He came to apologize to me for being a dick when he found us together. Then, Heidi and I got drunk, and he offered both of us a ride home. I was too drunk to walk to the front door, so he helped me. I got inside and immediately called you. The end. That's the whole story."

"And you were all over him because…"

"One, I was not all over him. Two, I was drunk, and I'm not a good drunk. I'm a face-plant-into-the-concrete-and-bust-my-nose-and-get-two-black-eyes kind of drunk. Trust me, I've been there."

I snorted, just imagining her falling over like that.

"That's really all that happened?" I asked.

I suddenly felt panicked, like maybe Landon hadn't been the one who overreacted...that I had been the one to overreact. If what she was saying was true, then I had hurt her this week for no good reason.

"Yes!" she cried, exasperated. "And you would know that if you had bothered to pick up the phone. Go ask Landon. Go ask Heidi! She was in the car that night. If anything, I think that Heidi might be into Landon. Not me! I don't understand what I did to make you not trust me, but I hate this."

"Emery," I said slowly. I was an idiot.

"Save it," she said in frustration, throwing my words back at me.

"You're right," I said automatically.

She gave me a wary look. "I am?"

"Yes. I am an idiot."

"Well, that's very obvious at this point."

"What I'm trying to say is, I was so afraid of losing you that I pushed you away. I made assumptions. It didn't help that Landon had said that, if I didn't know what had really happened in your breakup, then I didn't know you at all."

Her eyes ignited in fury. "He said what?" she cried. "Oh, I'm going to kill him, I swear."

"What I'm saying is that I want a second chance," I said, reaching for her hand. "I don't want to argue with you, and I don't want to run. I was an idiot. A complete idiot."

"I don't know," she whispered, turning her face away from mine. "How do I know that this won't happen again?"

"You don't. But I don't know how else to make this right. We both have pasts. We both have issues. Trust is mine. After what happened in my past, I have a hard time taking anyone at face value. But I'd really like to try to handle everything together. To start over."

She sighed. "Jensen..."

"Give me a chance, Emery. Please."

Snow slowly started to fall around us. She looked up at me through snowy lashes with fluffy flakes tumbling into her dark hair and blanketing her jacket. I knew she was hurting, and I had done almost irreparable damage. But I wanted to make this right...if she would just let me.

"Okay," she said finally. "One chance, Jensen. That's it."

Then, I tilted my face down toward hers, and our lips met, gently and nurturing. It was a kiss I'd missed all week. A kiss I'd remember forever.

"You won't regret it," I whispered against her lips.

She sighed into me and wrapped her arms around my waist. "I hated the last week."

"Me, too. I hated being away from you."

"Why are you such an ass?"

I laughed. "Can't seem to help it."

"God, we're so fucked up."

"Emery?"

"Hmm?"

"What really happened with your breakup with Landon?"

She sighed again, heavier, and took a step back from me. "You really want to know?"

I nodded. "Yes. I would like to be on equal footing. Figure things out together. That way, maybe neither of us will be blindsided again."

"All right." She dropped her head forward, swallowed, and then nodded. "Landon and I had dated nearly two years when he got into Stanford on a golf scholarship, and I got into Oklahoma as a National Merit Scholar, but both of us wanted to stay home and go to Texas Tech, so we could be together. We had this whole plan. Then...as far as I know, your father told him to go to Stanford."

"No way," I argued. "My father wanted nothing more than for all of us to go to Texas Tech, just like him and all our relatives."

She shrugged. "I was there. This is what happened. He thought Landon should be more serious about school and about sports. He wanted Landon to go to Stanford and try to walk onto the football team, which Landon didn't want to do."

"That at least sounds like my father."

"Yeah. Landon was a good football player, but he always preferred golf. He got into a huge argument with your dad one night right before the deadline where we both had to decide where we were going to school. His dad said that he needed to break up with me or something like, if I was so important, then we could make it work long distance. As you know, your dad died shortly after that."

I nodded. That part, I was well aware of.

"Landon felt...responsible for what happened. As if that argument had pushed him over the edge."

"He wasn't and it didn't."

"I knew that; I still know that. But the last thing that he ever said to your dad was something mean, and he couldn't cope. He accepted the full ride to Stanford because that's what your dad had wanted, and I took the Oklahoma spot. Then, Landon was just...gone."

"Gone?"

"Adrift. I tried to bring him back and to help, but he disappeared those next couple of weeks before graduation. We were still together. I knew he still loved me, but he was broken. So, he broke up with me the day of graduation. He told me that he'd talked it over with his family—with you—and you'd all agreed it was best."

"We never talked about this. He told me that you were going to different colleges, and you'd grown apart."

"Well, I see *now* that you didn't know." She swallowed hard. "But, as you can imagine, as an eighteen-year-old, I was heartbroken. He still loved me. I still loved him. I knew he was only doing this because of what happened to your father. I tried calling him and messaging him and emailing him. No answer. He just disappeared off the face of the planet. I know he got my messages. He never blocked me. He knew how much I was hurting and ignored it. Sound familiar?"

I winced. It did. I'd seen her messages and how desperate she was. I'd put her in the same spot Landon had ten years ago, and I hadn't even known it. And I'd done it for no good reason.

"I'm sorry."

"I know," she whispered. "But, as you can see, history repeating itself wasn't so good on my psyche. Landon made his choice all those years ago. I know he did what he thought was right. I just hated all of you for a long time because of him."

We walked on in the snow in silence for another minute. I didn't know what to say to all of that. I hadn't realized how hurt Landon had been. When he'd disappeared to Stanford, I'd thought he'd been fine. Boy, was I wrong.

"So, since we're being all open and honest now," Emery said, glancing over at me. "Did you see Vanessa when you were in New York?"

"I did," I answered slowly.

I weighed my options. How much could I tell her right now. There were still things that she didn't know. Things that I knew I should tell her. But she looked so tense and ready to run. I worried one more thing would push her over the edge. I promised myself that I would tell her though when the time was right.

"But I didn't go there to see her, and absolutely nothing happened. I was there for business."

"Landon said it was complicated between the two of you."

"It is. Vanessa is complicated," I confirmed.

She crossed her arms over her chest, as if she were trying to keep her insides from squirming at the thought.

"But it's not like that," I rushed on. "I told you once that I could never be with her after what had happened, and that hasn't changed."

"Then, why did you see her?"

"We're divorced, but not…disentangled. It's complicated."

"Disentangled?"

God, I didn't know how to explain this. "I'm working on the disentangling, part of the reason I went up there. Plus, I was selling off a part of Tarman. I bought the company to dismantle it," I confessed.

She frowned and pursed her lips. She looked like she was considering everything else I had just said and finding it unsatisfactory.

"That's not really an answer," she said finally. "Why did you see her?"

"She still lives in my apartment in New York."

"Why the hell would you let her live there?"

"This is part of the disentangling," I admitted. Soon. I would tell her soon.

"And nothing happened?"

"Emery, no," I said softly.

"I know, I know," she said, shaking her head. "I should trust you in return. If you said it's not like that, then it's not like that."

God, I had fucked up. She was so wary now. It was so clear to me, what an idiot I'd been.

Staring down into her beautiful face as snow slowly fell from the sky, I knew.

I'd tried to run.

I'd tried to hide.

I'd tried to say fuck it all.

But there was no turning back.

Emery Robinson was it for me.

And I would do anything to keep her.

"I'm sorry," I finally said, pulling her to a stop again. I ran my hands down her arms. "I knew, even while I was doing it, that what I was doing was wrong. I just...fuck, I was just so angry. I felt like I was going through the same shit again. But, this time, I would not just be hurting the woman I love but my brother, too."

"Love?" she whispered. Her mouth opened slightly in shock. "You love me?"

"Oh, Emery," I said, threading my fingers through her hair and pushing it behind her ear. I stepped toward her, feeling all my walls crumbling down. "Of course I love you."

chapter
twenty-eight

Emery

H AVING JENSEN WRIGHT LOVE ME WAS LIKE WALKING IN THE SUN.

But, while I played in the sunlight, I feared the darkness.

I wouldn't forget the week Jensen and I'd spent apart. The shadow that he cast when the sun disappeared. I wasn't crazy enough to believe that love would conquer everything, and I wasn't naive enough to think that running was out of the question for him. He had proven that he would do it, and now, he had to prove to me that he wouldn't.

Things hadn't been perfect since I agreed to give him a chance. I was guarding my time and my heart, wary of what was to come. I'd seen him on Christmas after his time with his family and had been mostly welcomed, Miranda aside. Landon had been uncomfortable around the two of us, but there were no more outbursts from him. It would take everyone a while to adjust. Our time post-Christmas had almost been too perfect. Maybe I was gun shy, but I worried that everything wasn't what it seemed.

Still I'd agreed to go with him to a New Year's Eve party at the Overton Hotel downtown. I wanted things to be right. I wanted to bask in his love and affection. But I also didn't want to get hurt. And my heart was warring with my head.

"Why do you look so nervous?" Heidi asked. She was fussing with my hair, having already done my makeup for the event.

"I'm not nervous," I lied.

"Yes, you are," Julia said, leaning back against the chair.

We had all convened at my house to get ready. Julia already looked stunning with her recently dyed burgundy hair piled on the top of her head and dressed in a rocking black dress.

"Things are rocky, and you have turtle head now," Heidi insisted.

"Turtle head?" I asked with a laugh.

"Yeah, you're crawling back into your shell because you're worried he'll fuck up again," Heidi said.

"I'm not worried. I'm cautious."

Heidi nodded her head. "Yep. Turtle head."

"Wouldn't you be cautious?" I demanded.

"I don't know," Heidi said with a shrug.

"He abandoned me for a week. I'm trying to take it easy."

"Just try to have fun, okay?" Heidi asked.

I nodded. That was the plan. I was just going to have fun tonight. We were going to be back in a good place again. I *wanted* us to be back in a good place.

"Good," Julia said. "Now we need to find someone for me to kiss at midnight."

"Oh, me too!" Heidi said.

"Landon?" I coughed under my breath.

Heidi's eyes were round as saucers. "What? No! He's married!"

"What if he wasn't?"

"Then he'd be *your* ex-boyfriend."

"I'm dating his brother, Heidi."

"Nuh-uh. No way. This is girl code we're talking about! Sacred shit here, Em."

I laughed at her vehemence. I knew something was up even if she wouldn't admit to it, but I decided to let it slide. "Well, you know I'm good for that kiss at midnight for the both you."

Heidi snort-laughed. "Oh my God, yes, my love. Take me away!"

"Lesbian threesome. I'm in," Julia said with a laugh.

Heidi threw herself into my arms and made ridiculous kissy noises. We laughed like we were back in school together, when the world was a lot easier to deal with.

Julia stared at us and shook her head. "You two are so hot for each other."

Heidi laughed again and kissed my cheek. "Always."

The doorbell rang, and I had déjà vu, back to the first time Jensen and I had gone on a date. I dashed downstairs with my friends following behind me. Lilyanne rushed to the door, and there was Jensen holding out flowers for her. She beamed up at him.

"Mom! My boyfriend is here!" Lilyanne called to Kimber.

Kimber groaned. "We are going to need to break that habit."

Jensen ruffled Lily's hair. "How are you doing, munchkin?"

"Fine. Thank you for asking," she said politely. "We should have another ice cream date."

"We should," he said, grinning from ear to ear.

"Good. I know how to fix the flowers," Lilyanne announced before hurrying off to her mom and dad.

Jensen stood up, and I got a full view of him in a tuxedo. I heard the other girls scurry back upstairs. They would follow us to the party later.

"Wow," he said when his gaze found mine. "You look amazing."

I smiled, grabbed my jacket, and strode toward him. If I was going to give him a chance, then I needed to give him a chance. Be the confident, sexy woman he claimed to love.

"You look pretty good yourself."

"That dress though." He ran his hands down the silky material of the emerald-green dress, which matched my eyes, that I'd borrowed from Kimber's closet.

I blushed at the way his eyes devoured me. "Thanks."

He seemed to get himself together and then gestured to the door. "After you."

When I stepped outside, I gasped. A black stretch limo was waiting on the street.

"What? Are we going to prom?" I joked.

Jensen arched an eyebrow. "Didn't you go with Landon?"

"Oh, yeah. Twice."

"Then, nope. No prom for you."

"Fair enough."

Jensen opened the door to the stretch limo, and I sank into the leather seat. He followed behind me. It was jet-black and swanky on the inside. A bottle of my favorite champagne was chilling in a bucket of ice. Soft music filtered in through the speakers, and I laughed when I realized it was Mariah Carey.

"Mariah Carey?" I asked. "You're playing Mariah Carey?"

"Look, I know she made a fool of herself, but she is our singer now."

"Oh my God, it's 'Always Be My Baby.'"

"And?"

"This is a good choice."

He had clearly put some thought into all of this. He was taking this whole business of making things right serious. Between the limo, champagne, and a nod to our first date…we were off to a good start.

He reached over to pour me a glass of champagne.

I downed it before he had finished pouring his and handed my glass back to him. "More, please."

He grinned, flashing me those irresistible dimples. "Don't get face-plant-on-the-concrete drunk on me."

"I'm a good girl," I crooned.

"Don't bet on it."

Jensen took a sip of his champagne and then set it down. "Now, before we get there, I do have your Christmas present."

"My what? But it's New Year's and I thought we weren't exchanging gifts." We had decided on Christmas Eve since our relationship had been on the rocks that we would hold off on presents.

"Yes. Then, fine, your New Year's present."

"But I don't have anything for you."

Jensen leveled me with a flat look. "I absolutely do not need anything."

He procured a black velvet box from his jacket, and I stared at it in awe. When he tried to hand it to me, I just continued to look at it. I'd never gotten anything like this in my life, and I didn't even *know* what it was. He was taking this making-up thing to a new level.

"Go on. Open it," he instructed.

I gently took the box in my hand and popped the cover open. Inside was a simple chain with a round diamond encased in a halo of diamonds. It was soft, elegant, and probably cost a fortune. It looked as if it cost more than my Forester.

"I can't…"

"It's a present. You can."

"Wow. Okay," I whispered. "Will you put it on me?"

I slipped the necklace out of the box, pulled my hair up, and then let him clasp it into place. It felt like a weight sitting in the middle of my sternum, but it didn't overpower the dress. It was as if he had known. Or the man just had amazing taste in diamonds.

"Thank you. It's really too much though."

"Emery, for you, it's never going to be enough."

I leaned toward him, letting the necklace dangle between us, and then kissed him deeply. "A girl could get used to this if you're not careful."

"I'm not planning on being careful. Kid gloves are off. You might have to endure fancy dinners and random presents and unplanned trips on my private jet. This is the man I am, Emery, as much as the man I am when I'm with you. I'd like to have you in both worlds."

I nodded, suddenly speechless. Jensen was offering me his world. I'd be a fool not to take it.

The limo stopped in front of the Overton, and we were whisked out and down the breezy walkway inside. The room was already packed with people, but I could see that much of his family was already there. We meandered over to their table, and Jensen left me with Morgan before he went off to get us drinks. Apparently, our table had bottle service, but champagne wouldn't be passed out to the room until right before midnight.

"Oh!" Morgan gasped. "He gave you the necklace."

I reflexively touched the diamond. "Yes."

"It looks great on you."

"Thank you."

"I'm so glad things are going well again. Jensen gets so cranky when he's being a total idiot and refuses to admit it."

I laughed and covered my mouth.

"I'm glad things are going well too," I admitted with a smile.

"Also, I'm so happy that you're here. Seriously. The whole family is."

I smiled, unable to convey how much that meant to me. "I think I'm just going to slip to the restroom while Jensen waits in that outrageous line."

"All right," Morgan said. "Do you want me to come with you?"

"Nah, I'm okay. I'll just be back in a minute."

Then, I disappeared into the crowd to locate the restroom in this huge ballroom. It was off some hallway, and luckily, since it was so early in the night, it wasn't full with a line. I did my business, washed my hands, and then exited, only to almost run into someone.

"Oh! Sorry," I said, trying to sidestep the woman.

"Just the person I was looking for," she said.

I glanced up at her and finally took her in. My stomach dropped. This could not be who I thought it was. "Have we met?"

"We haven't had the pleasure. I'm glad to rectify that. I'm Vanessa."

She stuck her hand out, but I just stared down at it in shock. When I didn't say anything, she dropped her hand, looked down at my necklace, and then back up at me.

"Vanessa, as in…"

"Yes, Jensen's Vanessa." The way she said it was soft and seductive, as if she belonged to him and he belonged to her.

She was stunning, like drop-dead gorgeous. Her hair was a soft blonde color, and it came down nearly to her waist in supermodel waves. She had a good four or five inches in height on me, and she was in a black dress that accentuated her rail-thin figure. But it was her face and the honey color of her eyes that had clearly gotten her modeling jobs. She was exotic but familiar, striking but down-to-earth. She confused the senses.

And I hated her on sight.

"What are you doing here?" I demanded.

"Well, I came here to be with Jensen."

"Too bad. He's here with me," I said, getting territorial on instinct.

"Ah, yes," she said, eyeing me up and down like I was a piece of trash and she was considering how to dispose of me. "Are you the flavor of the week?"

"Nope. I'm his girlfriend. So, you should probably just leave. I don't want to have to deal with you when we're having a perfectly good night together."

"Girlfriend," Vanessa said, breaking into this little musical laugh.

No one laughs like that! No one!

I shrugged. "Believe what you want to believe. I really don't care."

"But how could you be his girlfriend when he stayed with me all last week?"

My heart stuttered. I'd known that Jensen had seen her last week, but I hadn't known he'd *stayed* with her.

"I knew he was in New York and that he saw you. I doubt he stayed with you."

"I saw you walk in here with him, but he never even mentioned you once," she said, digging the knife in deeper.

"Jensen told me he saw you and that there was *nothing* there. I know that you cheated on him. I know that he divorced you for it. If you came here for a catfight, consider me tapped out."

I turned and strutted away, back down the deserted hallway. I felt fierce. I felt like I was on fire. I was in control. I didn't know why Vanessa was here, but I had handled her like a champ. I'd go tell Jensen, and he'd tell her to get the fuck out. The end.

"But did he tell you about Colton?"

My feet stalled. *Who the hell is Colton? And why did he matter?*

"Of course he didn't," Vanessa said with a staged sigh. "Because you're clearly just a fling."

I turned slowly and faced her. I wanted to ask her the question, but it was stuck on my tongue. Something was telling me that I didn't even want to know. I didn't want to deal with this.

"Just face it. You could never compare to me," Vanessa said with a sweet tilt to her head. "How could you compare to the mother of his son?"

chapter
twenty-nine

Jensen

"SHE SHOULD BE BACK ALREADY," I SAID TO AUSTIN.

I'd left Morgan flirting with Patrick when I found out where Emery had gone off to. But that had been a while ago. I'd had enough time to get our drinks from the crazy line and return.

Austin shrugged. He'd been drinking nonstop, and I just wanted to slap the drink out of his hand. He had a problem. He'd brought a flask with him to church. I needed to send him to rehab or something. He needed to be sober, or he'd end up choking on his own vomit, like our father after an overdose. I didn't want that for him. And I'd been so lost in my own mess to see it. New year and all that, and I'd get him help.

Right after I found Emery.

"What could be taking her this long?" I asked.

Austin shrugged again. "Don't know, man. There's probably just a line. You know how the girls' restroom is."

"Right, line," I murmured but didn't believe it.

I didn't know why exactly. Maybe I was paranoid. After the week we'd gone through, I'd been trying to be on my best behavior. I had a big surprise for her. I was finally going to tell her everything. It would be such a relief when it all came out.

I was about to go find the restrooms and make sure everything was all right when Emery appeared out of the crowd. She looked…shaken. Visibly shaken. As if she had seen a ghost.

She had her hands clenched in low at her sides, and her eyes were wide, darting here and there and everywhere. Her stride was fierce, like she was anxious to be away. Her shoulders were tight. Something had happened. Something had definitely happened.

"Hey," I said, instantly stepping toward her.

Whatever had hurt her…I would destroy it. This was supposed to be our night.

"I want to leave," she said immediately. She wouldn't even look at me.

"Emery, what happened?"

"I said I want to leave," she said, raising her voice.

"Okay, okay. I'll get your coat."

I reached for her jacket without a word and ignored the concerned looks on my friends' and family's faces. They knew what had been going on with me and Emery. They knew not to interfere.

I handed her, her coat, and she snatched it out of my hand.

"Let's go."

"Emery, what happened?" I asked. I followed behind her as she hurried from the room. I reached out and grabbed her elbow to stop her. "Please, talk to me."

She jolted away, as if I had burned her. "Why don't you ask Vanessa?"

I furrowed my brow in confusion. "Vanessa?"

"Yes, your ex-wife. She can help you out."

My mouth opened and then closed. "She's here?"

"What do you think?" she asked before storming back toward the door.

I followed, but my gaze was wandering around the room as I tried to figure out how my life had crumbled to ashes in a matter of minutes.

Why is Vanessa here today? What did she hope to accomplish?

I hadn't even mentioned Emery the week that I was in New York. She couldn't know that I had a new girlfriend, because I knew she'd try to wreck our relationship. Whatever her motive, I was not going to let her win.

We were almost to the door when Vanessa seemed to materialize out of thin air. I could see that she had made an effort. She was here for a reason, and the look on her face said that reason was me.

Emery noticed her presence, and her hackles rose. "I'm leaving with or without you."

"With me," I said automatically.

"Fine," she said, passing into the foyer.

Vanessa reached me just before I followed Emery. "Hey, where are you going?"

"What are you doing here?"

"I came to see you, baby."

"Colt was supposed to come tomorrow with the nanny. That is what we agreed on. Not that you would come here and bombard my girlfriend at a party that I never invited you to!"

"Well, you forgot to mention this *fling* to me, so I thought I would come spend time with you," she said, placing her hand on my sleeve.

"Vanessa, just fucking stop. You know I don't want to spend time with you, and you've clearly offended my girlfriend. I love her, and I choose her. Just her. Only her." I snatched my arm back, feeling extra disgusted with her at the moment. It wasn't enough that she had cheated on me with my own friend, but now, she was trying to ruin everything else, and I wouldn't stand for it. "I think you're scum on the bottom of my shoe. I wish you would stop trying to ruin my fucking life."

"Jensen," she murmured, her voice dipping an octave.

"You're in my life for one reason, Vanessa. One." I held up my finger. "Colton. That's it. Otherwise, you can go to hell."

I turned on my heel and walked away from her. The last thing I wanted was for Emery to think that I wanted to talk to Vanessa or that I had more interest in what she had to say than Emery hurting. Because that was the furthest thing from the truth. I sprinted out of the building and found Emery hovering by the valet stand.

She dismissively waved her hand at me. "I already called for a cab."

"No. We have the limo." I gestured to the valet to have the limo come around for us.

"I can't—"

"Emery, please. I don't know what Vanessa said, but she is just trying to get between us. There is nothing between me and Vanessa. Nothing."

"She said you have a son," she said in a deadly whisper.

Her eyes were bullets targeted on my face. She was waiting for a reaction. She was waiting for me to deny it. My heart sank. This was not how I'd wanted her to find out. I'd wanted to tell her tomorrow the best way that I knew how. Fuck, Vanessa ruined everything.

"I do," I said, dropping my hands. "I do have a son."

She shook her head and glanced away from me. "I cannot believe this. You knew that I didn't know! That I stay out of your family's drama. I gave you a million opportunities to tell me. This whole second-chance business, and you didn't think I should know?"

"It's not that, Emery. I was going to tell you. I'd been planning to tell you tomorrow."

Fuck, this was why I didn't date in town. I liked to be able to control when I was able to tell someone about my son. Then when I found out she didn't know, I thought I'd finally have that opportunity to make it right, and Vanessa had fucked it all up.

"Well, you blew it. Vanessa is here. She's in Lubbock. She found me and cornered me and tried to make me feel worthless. And you know what? She didn't succeed. She said some horrible things, but I knew where you and I were, and I was giving us a chance. But then I found out...nope, *you* weren't giving us a chance."

The limo pulled up in front of the stand at that time. The driver jumped out and opened the door for Emery.

She shook her head. "You take it."

"Please," I begged. "Please just let me explain. I gave you the opportunity to explain. Give me that same chance. We said we'd try this together. I want to do this together. After we talk, if you think I've relinquished our second chance, then I'll just…drop you off at home. But I won't let you go. I'll keep fighting for us because you are the only woman I have ever met who has made me feel like this."

She swallowed and looked away from me. Tears glistened in her eyes, but she wouldn't meet mine. She was torn. I could see it. She was willing to hear me out, but she didn't think I deserved another chance. I would have to prove her wrong. Because this was all a mistake. A misunderstanding. We could get through this. I would make sure of it.

Without another word, she sank into the limo. That was her answer. Yes. Yes, she would try.

I deflated in relief. I knew that this needed to happen. I'd just thought I'd have more time. I also…hadn't anticipated her being on the defensive when I finally told her.

It felt like control was slipping out of my fingertips, and I wanted to be able to hold on tight. It just seemed, with Emery, I was never in control. A feeling I was unaccustomed to. But I was beginning to realize, this wasn't a power struggle; it was just two people in love. And I needed to stop trying to hold on to my past and move forward with my future.

I took the seat next to her in the limo.

She scooted over so that she could face me. "Why didn't you tell me that you had a son?"

"We've only been dating a couple weeks, and I'm a very private person. I wanted to make sure that this was the real deal. I don't introduce people to my son who are going to leave his life. I don't think it's fair to him. Since he lives in New York with Vanessa, that's where his life is. I fly to New York all the time actually. Nearly every single holiday and at least once a month so I don't have to uproot his life. I'm fortunate enough to be able to do that."

"So…you thought that I would leave your life?" she asked.

"Honestly, until this week, I didn't know." I ran a hand back through my hair and tried to ignore the death glare she was sending me. "But I changed my mind this week and wanted to make it right. Colton was supposed to fly in tomorrow with the nanny so that you could meet him. I had no clue that Vanessa was going to show up unannounced or why she decided to come a day early."

"I think she made it perfectly clear to me," she grumbled.

"I promise there is nothing going on with me and Vanessa. Our relationship centers entirely around our son."

"I just hate that I found out from someone else."

"I was planning on telling you tomorrow," I repeated with a sigh.

"Too little, too late," she whispered.

"Honestly, Emery, I was going to tell you *tomorrow*. I wanted to get through our date and have an amazing time with you. I even gave you my mother's necklace."

Her hand dashed to the diamond hanging around her throat, and her eyes shot to mine. "You gave me your mother's necklace?"

"Yes. Morgan and Sutton have most of her pieces, but she left me a few. She wanted them to go to the woman I loved, and I gave one to you. I'm sure that's why Vanessa freaked the fuck out. She's seen it before."

Emery retracted her hand from the necklace at the mention of Vanessa. "And you really didn't know that she would be here?"

"No. Fuck, no. I don't want her here. She obviously just wanted to fuck with me." I cleared my throat. "You told me that you wanted to do these things together. I was going to give you that opportunity."

"I think it's sweet that you wanted me to meet him," she said softly, "but I don't know why you wouldn't tell me before I met him, like…I don't know… the day you said you saw Vanessa in New York. You were clearly there to see Colton, not her, right?"

I nodded. "I was."

"Yet you didn't tell me. You told me the whole story about Vanessa cheating on you with Marc, how your ex-wife and Cheaterpants horribly ruined your life, but you left out the part where you had a son in the mix of it all. It's like I know only half of your story. I got the abridged version of the book. You could have told me at anytime, and you didn't. Did you think that I wouldn't be understanding?"

"No," I said immediately. "Emery, that's not it."

She wrapped her arms around herself and shook her head. "I think I just need to cope tonight, Jensen. I don't fault you for having a son. I love Lilyanne, and now, I understand why you're so good with her. But I just fear that you'll never really trust me. Maybe you'll never trust anyone again."

Her words lingered between us.

Half an accusation, half a prayer.

I didn't know what to say to that. *Had I not trusted her? Had I really been trying to push her away?* I'd been planning to tell her, yet that hadn't been enough. Landon had known that when he had confronted me two weeks ago. Even if I had told her tomorrow, she would have been upset. I could see that now. Falling in love with someone and leaving out the most important thing in your life was showing no trust at all.

I could see the hurt and despair in her eyes. That I had claimed to love her, yet I had fed her lies about my life.

She turned her face away from me, and I was struggling to find words when her phone started ringing from the pocket of her coat.

"Kimber," she whispered when she checked the screen. Her mouth opened slightly in worry. She picked up the phone right away. "Hey! What's going on? Is everything okay?" There was silence as I waited for an answer. "Yes. Yes. I'll be right there. Do you need anything? Okay. Don't worry about it."

She hung up, and I knew what had happened.

"She's gone into labor?" I asked.

"Yes. I need to get home, so I can drive over to the hospital."

"What about Lilyanne?"

"My mom is watching her."

"Then, I'll have the limo drop you off."

"No—"

"We're going straight there," I insisted.

"Okay," she said.

She didn't argue at all, which was a sure sign of how worried and excited she was for Kimber.

I told the limo driver where to go, and we sped off to the hospital. The rest of the ride was silent. She was brimming with nerves about her sister, and I couldn't bear to bring up what had happened with us and what we were going to do next.

The driver stopped in front of the entrance to the hospital wing where the maternity ward was.

"Thank you for dropping me off," she whispered.

"You're welcome. Tell Kimber good luck."

"I will."

She reached behind her, unclasped the necklace, and held it out to me. "You should keep this."

"It was a gift."

"It's your mother's. I only want you to give it to me if this works out. And, right now…"

She dropped the necklace into my palm, and I suddenly felt cold.

"Right now what?"

She started to slide away from me, but I reached out and pulled her in close.

"What does this mean for us?"

She shook her head. "I don't know. I can't think right now. I just need to be with my sister."

"I understand. That's what's important." I placed a soft kiss on her forehead. "We'll figure the rest of this out another time."

"Yeah," she said, sad and distracted. "Another time."

With a weight on my chest, I watched her disappear. I'd thought tonight would be the start of everything new. I'd thought, tomorrow, she would meet Colton and see why I loved him so much. And, now, I was left wondering if we were even going to make it to tomorrow.

chapter
thirty

Emery

TEARS STREAMED DOWN MY FACE AS I STOOD IN FRONT OF THE ELEVATORS. THE hospital ward was empty. I was sure the ER was packed with drunken accidents, but here, in this part of the hospital, it was deserted. And I was grateful.

I couldn't seem to stop crying. My breaths were coming out in short spurts, and my chest constricted. I felt like I was hyperventilating, unable to get enough air in and hiccuping to try to recover.

My heart ached. My chest ached. My head ached.

Everything hurt.

Walking away from Jensen hurt.

I hadn't wanted to do it. But I'd meant every word that I said. He didn't trust, period. And I couldn't be with him if he didn't trust me. That left us at an impasse.

After the mess back in Austin, I'd thought moving home and trying to figure out what I wanted in my life would be easy. I'd spend time with Kimber and Heidi. I'd find a real job. I'd discover what I wanted.

Instead, my heart, mind, body, and soul belonged to Jensen Wright.

I should have stayed sworn off of men.

I should have stayed far away from the Wrights.

Then, I wouldn't be standing here with a heart threatening to shatter.

"Fuck," I whispered, jamming the button to go upstairs. I scrubbed at my face.

No more tears.

No more.

Kimber would notice. I was sure of it. But I was here for her now, and that was what was important. Meeting my new niece.

I took the elevator up to the fourth floor and was directed to my sister's room.

"Knock, knock," I said, entering the room.

Kimber was lying in the bed with Noah hovering next to her, holding a cup of ice chips.

"Hey!" she said with a genuine smile. "You made it."

"I made it."

"Are you okay?"

"Totally. I'm so excited to finally meet the little one!" I put on a big smile and pushed the last couple of hours out of my mind.

"Well, it's still going to be a while," Noah said. "Water hasn't even broken, but she's dilated and having contractions at a regular interval. Same as last time."

"I'm here for an all-nighter then."

"You look like you came straight from a party. Did you give up your midnight kiss for me?" Kimber asked.

I glanced up at the clock and realized it was only ten thirty. We'd totally missed our New Year's kiss. Not that I was exactly up for a steamy kiss right now.

"Meh. Don't worry about it. I know you brought a couple of extra outfits. I'll just steal your clothes and send Mom back with more when I take over for Lily."

"You are going to send Mom here?" Kimber asked hysterically.

I cackled, finally feeling an ounce of buoyancy. "Now, you admit your true feelings! She's crazy, right?"

"I don't need coaching! I already have two doctors. Sorry, Noah."

"No offense taken."

"Ohhh!" Kimber yelled. She doubled over as a contraction hit her full force.

And then I went into full-on sister mode. Kimber gave me something to focus on. I was able to be helpful and be there to make her smile and laugh through the worst of it.

Right after midnight, my phone started ringing and I saw that it was Heidi. "Is it okay if I take this?"

"We're going to be here a while," Kimber said. "Go ahead."

I walked out of the room and found a quiet place to answer. "Hey Heidi."

"Em! Where are you?" Heidi asked. "I found the hottest guy for my New Year's kiss, and I want you to meet him."

"I actually left."

"Oh, you and Jensen left early for some sex," Heidi said. I could tell she was drunk.

"Actually, no. Kimber went into labor, and Jensen and I got into a huge fight."

"Kimber went into labor!" Heidi cried, sobering up. "Should I leave? And wait, what fight? What happened?"

"No, don't leave. We're going to be here all night. I can text you when the baby comes."

"Okay. But what happened with Jensen?"

"His ex-wife Vanessa showed up at the party and told me that Jensen had a son."

"Well, of course he has a son," Heidi said. "Duh."

I froze in place. "What do you mean of course he has a son, Heidi! You knew? Why wouldn't you tell me something like that?"

"Jesus Christ, I didn't know that you didn't know, Emery. Everyone knows he has a kid. He's like this absentee father, who spends all his money on child support and only sees his kid for the holidays. What did you think I meant when I said that he flies to New York every holiday?"

That conversation all those weeks ago when Heidi had said that came back to me. God, I hadn't even known what she had meant, but now that I did, I felt like an idiot.

"Fuck. Really everyone knows?" I asked.

"I mean it's not a secret that he had a kid. I swear I thought you knew before you even hooked up with him."

"I didn't."

"Shit, I'm sorry. I would have said something, but I figured you knew and thought it was no big deal. It's not like this is his first hook up post-child."

"Yeah," I said softly. It sure wasn't. "It just…I don't think he's an absentee father, Heidi. I think he's really involved in his son's life. He said he's very protective of people meeting him. He wants me to meet him, and I don't know if I want that. I don't think he really trusts me."

"Maybe he thought you already knew about his son like I did."

I shook my head. "I don't think he did. We would have talked about it."

"Well, now I feel even shittier. What are you going to do?"

I leaned my head back against the wall and closed my eyes. "I have no idea."

"Look, when you and Jensen started this, it was supposed to be a fling. It's only been a few weeks since you've been together."

"Yeah. That's true. Why would he share crucial information with a fling?" she asked miserably. God, I knew that I wasn't a fling to him, but this whole trust thing was taking me to a bad place.

"You're not a fling anymore. So, if he wants you to meet his kid, then this is a good sign, Em," Heidi said. "Just because you didn't find out the way that you wanted doesn't mean that he doesn't trust you."

"Maybe."

"Okay. Worry about Kimber right now and deal with Jensen tomorrow. Maybe you'll have a clear head then. We can talk more if you need to work through it."

"Thank, Heidi."

"You're the best."

"Don't forget it."

We ended the call, and I took my time getting back to the hospital room.

I couldn't believe that Heidi had known…that everyone had known. I knew I was out of the loop on Lubbock gossip, but I thought I would have heard something like this. But no, I had closed myself off from the Wright family so much that I didn't even know this one piece of information. And Jensen hadn't trusted me with it.

I sure hoped Heidi was right and that by tomorrow I would know what to do. Because right now, I had a long night ahead of me. A long, tiring night.

chapter
thirty-one

Jensen

LEAVING EMERY AT THE HOSPITAL WAS MUCH HARDER THAN I'D THOUGHT possible. Her words had put my entire life in perspective. I was the one letting Vanessa continue to ruin my life. And I wouldn't do it any longer. I wouldn't be ruled by her dictatorship in our relationship. I didn't care what she wanted or what she thought she could threaten me with. Colton wasn't a game piece in an adult battle. And I refused to let her use him in such a manner.

He was a six-year-old boy. Vanessa using me and our past as weapons only hurt him. And the last thing in the whole world that I wanted was to hurt my son.

I spent the rest of the night fighting with myself to go to sleep. Even for a half hour. But it never came. When it was finally time that normal humans would be awake, I stumbled out of bed and decided to do something about it. I texted Vanessa to find out where she was staying and then drove the Mercedes over to the hotel downtown.

I parked the car out front and took the elevator to the top floor. I knocked on the door and the nanny, Jennifer, answered the door. She was a twenty-something live-in that Vanessa had hired last year full-time.

"Hey, Jensen!" Jennifer said. "Oh, Colton has been talking about you nonstop!"

"Hey Jennifer. Good to see you too."

I stepped inside, but before I even fully entered the living room, I heard the familiar ring of, "Daddy!"

Colton launched himself from the couch in the living room and straight into my arms. I picked him up off the ground and swung him around in a circle.

"Hey, champ," I said, squeezing him tight.

I could never get enough of this. I could never have enough hugs or enough of these moments. Him living in New York was a vise on my chest at all times. I hated it. The week I'd seen him before Christmas wasn't long enough by far. He'd been in Paris with Vanessa for the two weeks before that, and it had been so hard to let him out of the country. Even if he had done it before, I still worried. Having him here with me always made me less nervous.

Most days, I still couldn't believe that I had moved back to Lubbock. I'd had to admit that the two years I'd lived in New York were bad for the company. It had been a devastating decision, one I could never take lightly. But I also couldn't take Colton out of New York. I wanted what was best for him, and even if Lubbock had good schools, I'd be stripping his known environment from him and taking him away from better schools.

On days like today, I wanted to not care.

"God, I missed you so much," I told him as I moved him to one hip and carried him into the living room.

"I missed you, too! Are you coming home with me and Mommy and Nanny Jenn?" Colton asked. He was an adorable kid with unruly dark hair and big brown eyes that got him anything he ever wanted.

"Home?" I asked, setting him on his feet on the couch. My eyes jumped to Jennifer's. She shrugged helplessly and the nodded her head to the bedroom as if to say leaving was Vanessa's idea.

"Yeah, Daddy. Mommy said that we're going back to New York today. I want you to come with us. You can meet my new art teacher when I start school again."

I grinned down at him. Colton loved art. Vanessa had sent me pictures of the dinosaurs he had drawn after I'd taken him to the American Museum of Natural History. I wanted to take him all over the world and feed his addiction. But I definitely did not want him to leave today.

"Going to have to talk to your mom about that," I told him.

Just then, Vanessa walked into the room. She leaned her hip against the wall to the kitchen and crossed her arms. Her eyes were guarded and wary. It was a look I was used to getting from people today. Vanessa's was warranted after the way I'd spoken to her at the New Year's Eve party. She'd deserved it, but I didn't like to argue with her. It wasn't good for Colt to see us angry even if simply being in her presence pissed me off.

"You're leaving?" I asked. "I thought you were staying for a couple of days."

She shrugged. "Changed my mind."

"Hey, Daddy!" Colton said, still holding my hand. "Look at my new drawings."

I gave Vanessa a look that said this was not over and then sat down on the couch next to Colton.

"This one is a pterodactyl," he said, showing me a flying green dinosaur. Then, he showed me another one with horns. "This is a triceratops."

"Wow. These are really good, champ."

I inspected the one he was working on now. They were good for his age. It made me proud, how much he loved this. He was excelling in school, but I never wanted to suffocate my kid's love like my father had.

"Are you going to be an artist when you grow up?"

"No, Daddy, I'm going to be just like you."

I laughed, and then life flashed before my eyes of Colton being just like I was with my father. I shuddered at the very idea. God, I hoped I wouldn't ruin him.

"You can be and do whatever you want."

"I'll fly on planes then!"

"Like a pilot?"

"No. I'll run my business in the air."

I chuckled again. There was no deterring him. Perhaps, it was normal for your child to want to grow up to be like you. At least at this age. I knew he'd grow up to have huge dreams, and I wanted to be there to encourage every one of them.

"You know, little man, I have someone very special that I want you to meet when you're ready. Would you like a new friend?"

"Yeah!" Colton agreed. "I love friends. Do you think he'd color with me?"

"Jensen!" Vanessa snapped from the kitchen.

Vanessa clearly was unhappy with the idea that I was going to introduce him to anyone. And I was sure she was pissed that it was coming on the heels of meeting Emery.

"I'm sure she would color with you," I said. "But I'm going to go talk to your mom for a minute, okay?"

"Okay, Daddy."

I kissed him on the cheek and then left him to his drawings. Jennifer moved into to play with him while I stepped up to Vanessa.

"We need to talk." She strode into the bedroom of the suite without another glance.

I took my time, following her inside and closing the door. I took over the space, stretching in height and crossing my arms over the bulk of my chest. She might want to have this conversation, but I wasn't going to give her any concessions.

She whirled around on me and then took a step back. I knew that look on her face. I'd made my point. I wasn't going to give an inch to the woman who frequently took a mile.

"You are not introducing your latest fling to Colton."

"She's my girlfriend, Vanessa. I can, and I will introduce her to my son."

"Jensen, absolutely not! You don't even know if she's going to be in your life past tomorrow! I won't allow you to disrupt his life like that."

"Let's get to the bottom of this, Vanessa. You don't like that someone new is in my life, and you don't want it to disrupt your delusions. This has nothing to do with Colt."

"I don't like that you're going to introduce him to someone that might leave. That's selfish."

I ran a hand back through my hair and sighed. "You're right, Vanessa. Under any other circumstance, it would be selfish. But it has been four years since we divorced. It's not unreasonable for me to meet someone new in that time."

Vanessa rolled her eyes. "She's not someone new in your life. She's another fling. I know you have them all the time. I know the signs."

"Emery is different."

"Really? How did you meet?" she asked, crossing her arms.

"At Sutton's wedding."

"Let me get this straight. You met her a month ago, probably banged her that night, didn't tell her about Colton, and now think you're ready to introduce her to him? I don't think so."

"What I do in my free time is none of your business. Emery is my girlfriend. You may not like that Vanessa, but that's not about to change. Good try showing up last night and trying to break us up though."

"I was just trying to tell her the truth. You're the one who was a raving jackass," Vanessa spat.

"The truth. Right," I said sarcastically. "You were trying to break us up. Even though you were, I am sorry that I spoke to you the way that I did." I had been harsh in the moment. Normally I never would have spoken to her that way, but after seeing Emery's reaction, I'd lost it. "I didn't come here to argue with you about last night. I wanted you to understand where I'm coming from."

"Oh, I understand where you're coming from," she spat. "You're thinking with your dick."

"I can't handle this Vanessa. I'm tired of arguing. I apologized for how I treated you, but you can't dictate who Colton meets. Emery is in my life, and Colton is my life."

I turned and opened the door to go back out to see my son. I knew that I needed to talk to Emery about again. I wanted to make things right and get us on the same page.

"I'll tell Marc," Vanessa spat.

I shook my head. I'd heard that one before. "Empty threats, Vanessa."

"They're not empty threats," she spat. "I will tell him."

"I don't believe you. If you think meeting Emery isn't in his best interest, then I have no idea how you could think Marc would be either."

Then I strode away from her. After kissing Colton good-bye and promising to come back later, I left the hotel and went to go see Emery. We had some catching up to do.

chapter
thirty-two

Emery

K IMBER'S CONTRACTIONS WENT ON FOREVER WITH NO END IN SIGHT. BY THE next morning, I was worn out and had barely slept. I couldn't even imagine what Kimber was feeling.

Luckily, she had finally managed to get some sleep, which was my chance to find the Starbucks downstairs and drink the entire store dry. I let Noah go first though. He'd been there longer than me, and I knew he needed to eat something even if he claimed he wasn't hungry. As a doctor, he was used to the weird hours, but he needed to be Kimber's rock. I'd take care of him for her.

While Noah was gone, my phone pinged. Heidi and I had been texting on and off all night. I swiped my phone and checked the screen, expecting another text from Heidi about the guy she had hit on all last night. But, instead, it was a message from Jensen.

Coffee and doughnuts?

It was as if he had read my mind. I wanted those things so bad. My stomach grumbled. *But did I want the added struggle of Jensen right now when I was sleep-deprived?*

He texted me again.

It's just coffee and doughnuts. We don't have to talk if you don't want, but I thought you could use some sustenance.

Noah walked back in the door at that time with his own cup of coffee. "Hey, I saw Jensen downstairs. I think he's waiting for you. So, you can go ahead. I'll take watch."

I ground my teeth. Of course he had presumed to show up without checking with me first.

You're already here?

Guilty.

Fine. I'll be down. But I'm not a person right now.

I left Noah to watch over Kimber and then headed back down to the first floor. My stomach noisily growled again. I couldn't remember what I'd last had to eat. A candy bar or something in the middle of the night. I'd been so shaken, and I hadn't even realized it until I'd gone to find something to help me power through the wee hours of the night.

Jensen was waiting in the lobby, holding two coffees and a bag of doughnuts. He looked…beat. He probably hadn't slept all night either. And this was the first time I'd ever seen him with stubble. Jensen and clean-shaven went hand in hand. But, fuck, it was definitely sexy on him. Like I wouldn't mind finding out exactly how he could use that in the bedroom. I was sure it would leave a trail of wonderful marks up my inner thighs.

Damn sleep-deprived brain was yelling at me, *Sex, sex, sex.*

I shook my head and tried to put everything back in perspective. I was standing on quicksand. If I kept struggling, I'd be swallowed up even faster. But, if I stayed still, maybe, just maybe Jensen could pull me back out.

"Rough night?" I asked when I approached him.

He grimaced slightly at the comment. "You could say that."

"Yeah. Me, too."

Jensen passed me the coffee, and we moved to a table inside Starbucks, which was blissfully quiet at such an early hour.

"Noah said that you're going to be here for a while longer."

"Looks like it."

I reached into the bag and smiled when I saw an apple fritter and a cinnamon twist inside. My two favorite doughnuts.

"Thanks for these."

"I thought that you might be hungry."

I nodded. For the first time ever, there was awkwardness between us. We had one foot in the water and one foot on solid ground. Not knowing where we stood or what would come next seemed to be killing both of us.

"I know I said that we didn't have to talk," Jensen said, breaking the silence.

"Too much to ask for, I guess," I mumbled.

"And we don't have to if it's too much, but I stayed up all night, thinking about what you said."

"Which part?"

"Me not trusting you…or anyone," he clarified. His eyes darted up to mine, and I could see the hours of anguish and self-deprecation that radiated from him. "I don't think that I ever realized until last night that I absolutely do not trust anyone other than myself. Not one person. Not even my family."

I nodded, having found out firsthand the truth of that statement.

"I wish I could say that I don't know how that happened to me, but I do." He sighed and glanced away, as if he didn't want to continue, as if the next words would rip through him. "Colton isn't my son."

I opened my mouth, stuttered incoherently, and then closed it again. I shook my head in confusion, trying to understand how his own son couldn't be his. "What do you mean?"

"I mean, Colt is Marc's son," he said so calmly that I knew it must have been killing him to admit it. "I've never told anyone this. Not even my family. The only people who know are me and Vanessa."

"Not even Marc?"

"Especially not Marc," he growled low. "I'm a better dad than he could have ever been. I'd spent two years with Colt. He was my son, and I couldn't lose him. Not to anyone."

My heart ached for him. *How could he possibly live with the fact that his son wasn't really his? How had he kept that secret locked up for all of these years?*

"What happened?" I asked, suddenly desperate for him to tell me the story. To finally have an explanation for why he was so guarded.

"Vanessa and I had been married for almost two years when she found out that she was pregnant. I had been living in Lubbock, taking over the company for my father after his death. I'd barely been in New York. We weren't even trying. I was still too devastated by his death to think about that. When she called and told me she was pregnant, I was ecstatic. Maybe I should have been more cautious." He shrugged, as if he had played this over and over again in his head before.

"But you weren't."

"No. I never suspected once that she and Marc were together. I was too grief-stricken and dealing with the company to consider what was going on with her when I was away."

"You were dealing with all of that, and she was banging someone else on the side," I said, furious. "What a bitch."

Jensen looked off in the distance, the memory hitting him fresh once more. "As I told you, I moved back to New York. As far as I know, their relationship stopped after that. I don't know if I believe it for sure, but I think Marc was worried Colton was his kid and cleared out. His dad wasn't doing that well, so he moved back to Austin around the same time that I got to New York." He took a long sip of his coffee and leaned back in his chair.

"What a creep," I grumbled. "So, how did you find out?"

"I was there when Colton was born. I took him home from the hospital. I changed diapers. I fed him when Vanessa was sleeping. I was there every single second that I wasn't working. Colton *is* my son in every way that matters."

I smiled at that statement. I loved the thought that Jensen had never treated his son any differently.

"Marc was in town on business for Colt's second birthday. We all went out to dinner together."

"And you had no idea?"

"None."

"How could Vanessa go out to dinner with him?" I gasped.

"I think she thought it would be fine. I really don't know. The next day,

I found her sitting in Colt's bedroom, crying. I asked her why she was crying, and she said she couldn't keep lying to me. Then, she told me about her affair with Marc. It must have been weighing on her for a long time for her to actually break down and tell me." He set his cup down and sighed heavily. "We probably could have survived that. It would have taken a long time, but we could have made it. But then she told me that Colt was Marc's, and I lost it."

"I don't blame you."

"No, I mean, I *actually* lost it, Emery. I rampaged throughout the apartment. I broke furniture. I found Marc and beat him to a bloody pulp." Jensen clenched and unclenched his fist, remembering the bloodlust. "I never told him it was because of Colt though. He thought it was because of Vanessa, which is probably why he didn't press charges."

"Still…I don't blame you, Jensen."

And I meant every word. *How could I possibly blame him for what happened?* Vanessa and Marc were to blame. They had taken everything from him. Even his son. A son he had raised for two years, thinking Colt was his. No wonder he never told anyone. *How could he bear the shame? The sense of loss?*

I reached out and took his hand. He glanced up at me with surprise in his dark eyes. He must have thought that I would turn on him, like everyone else had in his life.

He deflated before my eyes. As if he had been so pent-up over the whole thing that finally telling someone else the truth had drained him. He tightened his fingers around my hand, and we stayed like that for a few minutes in silence.

"So, that's the whole story," he finally said, drawing back. "I know that you're upset with me, and you have every right to be, but I do trust you. Or I want to. I want you in my life, but I know that we have a ways to go. But, now, you know the whole story. I feel like our train got off the rails somewhere or took a wrong turn, but I want this to work. I wouldn't be here, and I wouldn't have given you my mother's necklace if I didn't want that."

He pulled the diamond necklace out of his pocket and let it dangle between us.

"This belongs to you."

"Jensen," I whispered.

He took my hand and gently laid the necklace into my palm. "It's a promise. I'm going to make this right. One way or another."

This was a lot to absorb.

He wanted to prove to me that he trusted me. That he *could* trust.

It didn't make up for what we had gone through, but it was a start.

I closed my hand around the necklace. He smiled brilliantly, the hours of anxiety from the past day falling off of his shoulder. He leaned forward and brushed his lips to my forehead. Slowly, I let a smile stretch across my face as I put the necklace back around my neck and tucked it under my shirt.

I'd given him hope…and now, I had some, too.

He stood up to leave and give me space when his phone started ringing. He gave me a sheepish look and then glanced at the screen. His face paled.

"Who is it?" I asked. I did not like that look on his face.

"Marc."

"Why would he be calling?"

Jensen shook his head as if he didn't know, but I could see on his face that he did. And it was bad.

He sank back into his chair and answered. "Hello?"

Marc's response was so loud that I could hear it through the other line. "You son of a bitch!"

"What do you want, Marc?"

Marc responded, but I couldn't hear what he said, then Jensen said, "Are you out of your fucking mind?"

"I have a right to know!" Marc shouted back.

"It's been almost seven years, Marc. This is fucked."

"What's fucked up is you lying to me for that long! I'm getting on a plane right the fuck now. I'll be in Lubbock tonight, you motherfucker."

"Marc, you cannot get near my son."

"He's not even yours!" Marc screamed.

"I am his father!" Jensen said, raising his voice in fury.

"We'll fucking see about that."

"Colton is my son, and I'll be damned if I let you fuck with his head by walking into his life. What you're going to do is irresponsible and reckless. And there's no way I will let you near him."

"Well, you don't get to decide that!"

"Like hell I don't."

Jensen slammed his phone down on the table and fumed. "Fuck," he muttered. He put both of his hands into his hair and pulled. His teeth were gritted. His body tense. He looked as if he were ready to erupt.

"What's just happened?" I asked softly, though I feared I already knew the answer from that conversation.

"Vanessa told Marc."

My heart stopped beating for a split second. I couldn't believe that Vanessa would go to such extremes.

"Fuck, I should have known. I went to see Colton this morning, and we argued. She threatened me by saying she would tell Marc, but she has said that a million times before. I told her it was an empty threat. Apparently, she took that to heart. I guess, she was so upset that I was going to introduce Colton to you that she decided that the best route was to inform his *real* father and get me out of the picture."

"You cannot stand for that! You have to do something!"

"I'll get my lawyers on the situation. They knew this was a possibility and we're prepared for it," he told me. But he sounded like he'd been hit by a truck when he said it. "I just…I have to meet with Marc tomorrow when he comes into town. Before he can see Colton, he'll have to get permission. My lawyers will file paperwork so that neither of us can go near Colton until this is resolved."

"Oh, Jensen," I said, my heart breaking for him. "You won't be able to see him at all?"

It took him a full minute before he could respond, "No."

"What do you need from me?"

"I can't ask…"

"You can."

"I just…I can handle this, Emery. I can stand up to Marc again. I can face down Vanessa for the hundredth time. I can fight for Colton, like I have been doing since he was born. I need…want…"

"Jensen," I whispered, reaching out for him, "I'm here for you if you need me."

"I hate to ask it of you when your sister is about to have her baby."

"The baby will come soon, and then they're going to need their space. Kimber will understand. I want to help."

"I need you," he told me.

"Okay. What's the plan?"

chapter
thirty-three

Emery

I STAYED AT THE HOSPITAL THE REST OF THE AFTERNOON AT JENSEN'S INSISTENCE. I wanted to be there for when the baby was delivered, and I know that he had to deal with his lawyers in the meantime.

Later that day, I finally got to hold my new niece in my arms. She was as light as a feather and adorable to boot. Little Bethany Ilsa Thompson came in at seven pounds and three ounces and nineteen inches. She slept, swaddled up to her chin, with her eyes firmly shut, and everyone in the room was huddled around her.

I wasn't ready to relinquish her. I knew I was going to spoil her to death as she got older. But I also knew that her mom and dad and older sister wanted a turn. Not to mention, her grandmother kept trying to take her out of everyone's arms.

But it didn't matter. This was perfect.

Forget the last couple of weeks of madness in my life. Bethany was too perfect for drama.

Reluctantly, I handed her back to Kimber, who was setting Lilyanne up to hold her. A nurse knocked on the door just as we got Bethany into Lily's arms.

"Hey, hey, everyone!" she said with a bright smile. "Coming to check on y'all and see how you're doing. I'm going to need to take Bethany for a little while for some tests if that's all right."

Lilyanne looked like she was about to cry, but she nodded and handed Bethany to the nurse.

"I promise I'll bring her right back to you, big sister."

Lily beamed at that. She was loving the idea of being a big sister.

"All right, it's that time," Kimber said with a sigh. "I'm taking a shower."

"About time, you mean," I joked.

"Such a kidder."

"I think I'm actually going to head out and go see Jensen. I'll be back in the morning!"

"That's cool. We're going to be sleeping," Kimber said. "And probably eating and showering."

I laughed. "All right. Don't let her do anything cute without me."

"Promise."

I smiled at Kimber as she grabbed some fresh clothes to take into the bathroom. I knew she'd be in there for a long time after the night she'd endured. Hours and hours of labor with no respite. It had been tough, but I knew she thought it was worth the effort. We all did.

I was excited to see Jensen again. I hated what was happening to him because of Vanessa. After we had just sat down for our big talk at that. I appreciated that he had recognized that he couldn't trust and that he was working to fix it. I still wanted that man who had gone out of his way to drive me through Christmas lights, who couldn't resist asking me out—in church, no less—and who had hired someone to pack up my apartment so we could spend the afternoon together. But I wanted him with all his skeletons out of the closet and our pasts firmly in the past. Hopefully, after this week, that would be the case.

I left the hospital and went straight to Jensen's place. The door was unlocked, and I entered the house.

"Hello?" I called into the foyer.

Jensen appeared then at the top of the stairs in dark-wash jeans and a plain T-shirt. His muscles rippled from the tightly fitted shirt, and I practically salivated at the sight of him. I knew I was here to be emotional support and help him make it through the next twelve hours, but my mind apparently had other plans.

He smiled, and those dimples did me in. "Emery," he said with a deeply relieved sigh.

"Hey," I said climbing the stairs. "We have a new baby girl in the family."

"Congratulations. I'm so happy for Kimber and Noah. What did they name her?"

"Bethany Ilsa. And she's adorable. I can't wait for you to meet her. Though Lilyanne might be worried about her boyfriend coming to see her sister."

Jensen grinned. "She shouldn't worry. Her real competition is standing in front of me."

I grinned and willed my mind to get myself under control. It had been too long since we slept together. And, now that I could see him clearly again, all I wanted to do was jump his bones. Except that I knew he needed something more than sex tonight. Sex might make him forget, but it wouldn't heal anything.

When I came eye-to-eye with him, I noticed how ragged he looked. Still sexy as hell but beaten down. Vanessa was trying to undo him. And, while he stood tall and had the presence of the brilliant CEO that he was, I knew him well enough to know that he was lost and crumbling into that dark place in his chest. A place from which I feared he would not return.

"Have you slept at all?" I asked.

He cocked his head to the side and stared off into space. "Sleep doesn't get anything done. There's too much work, too much to deal with for sleeping."

I sighed. I was sure that, in his head, that was true. But I also knew that his body would start to shut down, and he had to be cognizant tomorrow. To be able to face Marc and not lose control again around him, not like the time he'd beaten his face in after Vanessa had told him about the affair. He needed to be sharp.

Wordlessly, I took his hand.

He stared down at it with a mixture of awe and concern. "You don't have to do this."

"Do what?" I asked, bringing his hand up to my lips and kissing it.

"Be here."

"Don't I?"

"No."

"You're wrong."

"All too often."

"You need me," I whispered, drawing him closer to me. "So, I'm here."

"Good," he said, his voice deep and guttural. A feral sound that bordered on hysteria.

"And I know what you need."

"That so?" he asked.

I could see in his eyes that he thought I meant everything sexual. A thought that had obviously crossed my mind. I wanted that to make him feel better, but I knew he needed so much more.

I held on to his hand and pulled him down the hallway without another word.

Our relationship might have been a bumpy ride. We had secrets. We'd traded lies. We'd tried to find ways to fit the other into the mess that we'd been living in. But, at the end of the day, I knew Jensen Wright. I'd chosen him, and I'd be here for him through the worst of it.

When we entered his bedroom, I languidly tugged his shirt over his head. Lust swirled in his eyes as I did it, and I knew, if I gave in, *neither* of us would sleep ever again. We'd stay in bed all night. Lost in our own desires.

He reached for my shirt, but I stopped him.

"Uh-uh. Look but no touch," I warned him.

He fumed but dropped his hands. I flicked the button on his jeans, dragged them down his legs, and watched as he kicked them off, leaving him in his tight boxer briefs. He was rock hard for me, and it took everything in my power not to lick my lips.

I directed him into bed, and he went willingly. *What man wouldn't?*

Then, I stripped out of my jeans and T-shirt. Jensen looked ready to launch himself across the room when he saw the black lace set I'd been wearing for him on New Year's Eve. But I hastily threw on his T-shirt, which was way too big for me.

Then, I turned out all the lights and crawled into bed. He reached for me as soon as I was under the covers, pressing his dick firmly against my ass and squeezing me tight to his chest.

"You're killing me," he breathed into my neck.

"I just came here to help," I whispered.

"This is helping." He thrust against my ass, and I squeezed my legs together.

"You need to sleep."

"You think I'm going to sleep after seeing you in lingerie?" he asked, as if I were insane.

With effort, I turned to face him and saw his dark eyes filled with lust. I wanted this. He wanted this. But I didn't trust myself to stop.

With Jensen Wright, there were only two speeds—more and, God, more.

I gently placed my hand on his chest and slightly pushed him away. "You need to sleep. You're a walking zombie. I came over to help you. I don't think marathon sex is going to help."

"It's not going to hurt," he groaned.

He slid his hand up and down my side, fisting his shirt and exposing my stomach and lace thong. His hand snagged on the material, and he flicked it with his thumb. It snapped against my skin, causing my whole body to clench up.

"Jensen," I moaned. My walls were weakening.

He pushed into the space I'd put between us and ran the stubble of his chin across my shoulder and up my neck.

His voice rasped into my earlobe as he tugged on it. "Let me make you come, Emery. I want your taste on my lips."

"Fuck," I whispered.

He took that as a yes and slipped the rest of my clothes off of me with aching slowness. First, the T-shirt went over my head. Then, he snapped my bra off and tossed it off the bed. Finally, he dragged my thong down my knees and over my feet. I shivered the whole way down. He removed his own boxer briefs next with much less care, and just when I thought he was going to give me what I wanted, he flipped me over on top of him.

His dick nudged at my wet opening, and it took everything in me not to rock back onto him. I eased down, savoring the feel of him. Just the head…just the tip…just an inch…maybe two. My body tightened around him, wanting to feel him fill me up.

But then he stopped me and pulled me off of his dick. I groaned with dissatisfaction.

"Jensen…"

"Sit on my face," he demanded.

My eyes found his in shock. "Seriously?"

"I said I wanted to taste you. This is *how* I want to taste you."

I hesitantly edged forward until my pussy was directly over his lips. Then, he clamped his hands down on my ass cheeks and ground his face up into my body. I cried out as he ravaged me from below. My hands jerked out and landed on the headboard, bracing myself as my body abandoned my control.

He licked and sucked and got the taste of me on more than just his tongue. My whole body convulsed, and I tried to pull up from his incredible assault, but he wasn't having it. He tightened his grip on me and brought my pussy closer to him. I writhed in ecstasy until I exploded from the most amazing orgasm. Then, I sat there, trembling, with him still licking me past the point of my release…prolonging my pleasure.

When I was finally sated, he flipped me backward and fell on top of me. I was so wet, he slid into me with ease. I arched my back off the bed, purring like a kitten as he took me balls deep.

Nothing else mattered in that moment. All my fears and worries stripped away. There was only here and now. There was only sex and lust and passion. We could ride the wave. We could survive the current. We could fucking rein it in with a lasso and make it our own.

He drove into me with relentless force. Meeting him stroke for stroke and falling into oblivion for the second time, I actually thought I might pass out from pure pleasure. He followed right after me, and his heavy weight collapsing over me was the best feeling in the world.

He nipped at my neck. "This is the best sleep I've ever gotten."

I laughed, low and raspy. I'd used my vocal cords properly as I came. "Me, too."

We didn't have to say anything else. Words were beyond us at this point. We had a world to face tomorrow, but for tonight, he was mine, and I was his.

chapter
thirty-four

Jensen

WHEN I FINALLY WOKE UP, IT FELT LIKE I'D SLEPT FOR DAYS. IT HAD BEEN so long since I got a full night sleep and days since I slept at all, period, I was shocked that I had even been functioning. The only good sleep I ever got anymore was when Emery was in my arms. Like she was right at this moment—naked and completely satisfied.

We probably should have gone to sleep like she had said last night. But, once she'd stripped me down and put me in bed, I had known there was no way that was happening. I'd been thinking about this girl nonstop—up until Marc had uttered those unbelievable words.

"Vanessa told me."

I still couldn't believe she'd done it. She had been hanging it over my head for so long that I'd become complacent to the threat. I never thought she'd actually break down and do it. Then again…it had taken her years to admit to cheating on me with Marc. Maybe I shouldn't have been surprised that it'd taken her this long to tell him the truth.

The girl was a snake. I didn't know how I had never seen it all those years we had been together. Or maybe New York had poisoned her. Maybe she hadn't actually been cut out for the big city and modeling, and her way of coping had been to become worse than the city itself. But these were just excuses. They didn't justify her behavior. Lots of people moved to New York and didn't cheat on their husbands…didn't have a child with someone else.

I closed my eyes, wishing that I could disappear back into last night. Feel Emery's warm body against mine and pretend not to have a care in the world. But reality was crashing back down. I had to face Marc and Vanessa today. I had to claim my son. Last night had been a dream, but it was time to wake up.

Kissing Emery's forehead, I washed last night's events off of my body and changed into a crisp black Tom Ford suit. Everything about the ensemble screamed power and money. Both things I wanted to exert to the two people who had ruined my life. Marc had stolen my wife. He wasn't going to steal my son, too. It wasn't enough that I had bought out his company and was in the process of selling it off for parts like a used car. I would bury him before letting him have access to Colton. My lawyers had been working on a case against Vanessa since the day I left New York. We could handle her if need be.

"You're up early," Emery mumbled from the bed when I appeared once more.

"Six hours of sleep is plenty for me. You can go back to sleep."

"Mmm," she said, letting the sheet slip down her naked body.

"If you keep that up, you're never going to leave that bed."

She blushed a soft pink that I adored. After all our sex, she still blushed at my comments.

"I should probably check on Kimber. When do you meet Marc?"

"This afternoon. He had to fly commercial," I said with a twitch in my lips. *Oh, how the mighty have fallen.*

"Oh, the horror," she joked.

"So, I can pick you up from the hospital later if that works for you."

"Yes, as long as you think you'll be all right."

I nodded. "I have some work to do and a meeting with my lawyer before that. I'll be occupied. Plus, you helped me last night. I can face another day with you at my side."

She smiled lazily at me. "Good. I'm glad."

It was hours before I would get to see that smile again. Work was torture. I hadn't wanted to worry her, but the hours waiting, even when I was busy, didn't help. She dampened the pain. Only her.

By the time I finally got to pick her up again, it was like a balm. I didn't show nerves or stress. Only a few people—primarily Morgan—even noticed, but Emery seemed to have a radar for it. She put her hand on mine as soon as she sat down in the Mercedes and kissed my cheek.

"I've been thinking about you," she said with such candor.

"How are Kimber and Bethany?" I asked as I pulled away from the hospital and drove across town.

"They're great. All of them are. Ready to go home."

"I bet."

"They're getting discharged within the hour. So, they get to take the little cutie home with them."

"I remember what that's like," I said softly.

I rarely talked about what it had been like in those first two years with Colton. The facade that Vanessa had created was so great that, when she took it all away, even the happy memories were tainted with her lies.

Emery squeezed my hand and nodded. "We'll work it out."

"You're right. We will," I said, going back to that cold, detached place that fought my battles and won my wars. I would damn sure win this one.

We parked out front of the lawyer's office. I recognized Vanessa's father's car, which meant she must have left Colton with him for this meeting. Good. I didn't want Colton anywhere near this. It was going to get ugly. I didn't know what Marc was driving, but I didn't see anything pretentious enough for him.

Emery hurried around to the other side of the car and took my hand. She held it, as if we were a united front against the enemy. And I couldn't have been more thankful to have her there. She made me a better man. And, with her, I had the added benefit of putting Vanessa on edge.

As expected, when we walked into the lobby, Vanessa whipped around and glared at our entwined fingers. Her lawyer was talking on a cell phone in a corner.

"You've got to be joking," she spat. "She can't be here."

I shrugged and gave her a cool smile. No reason to give in to her antics. We were only here because of her bullshit. We would end it here, too.

We waited another five minutes in tense silence before Marc finally showed. I was surprised Abigail wasn't with him. She went everywhere with him to temper his anger. I wondered if he'd even told her what was happening before disappearing. Instead, he only had his lawyer present with him. I shouldn't be surprised that he'd gotten someone on his own to represent his interests instead of relying on Vanessa.

Marc's eyes landed on me first. "You fucking douche," Marc spat. "You spent all this time taking everything away from me, and now, you took more than six years away from me and my son."

"We'll see," I said.

Marc stalked right over to me and got in my face. Emery squeezed my hand.

"I'm here to take my son back."

"You can try," I told him. *And fail.*

Just then, the door to the lawyer's office opened, and my lawyer, Jake McCarty, appeared. He was a short, stocky man, who had been my father's lawyer before me. He knew his shit, and he knew how to get his clients what they wanted.

"You can all come in now."

We moved into a large conference room with Marc and Vanessa on one side and me and Emery on the other.

"Does she have to be here for this?" Vanessa asked. "She's not even involved!"

"She stays," I told her crisply.

"She's fine by me," Jake said with a nod at Emery. "Considering my client has made it clear that he wants Miss Robinson in his life and eventually in Colton's life, I think her presence makes sense for this."

"Never happening," Vanessa hissed.

"We'll see," I said calmly.

"After going over everything in the last twenty-four hours, I got a judge to approve my request that no new people could be introduced into Colton's life until we have this all sorted out. That includes you, Miss Robinson, and Mr. Tarman. Unfortunately, due to the nature of the concern over who is the father to Colton Wright, I've also asked my client, Mr. Wright, not to have contact with Colton until we have this all resolved. All of this is, of course, temporary, barring no complications in the proceedings. Is that all understood and acceptable?"

The other lawyers agreed with the terms even though Marc looked ready to explode that he had come all this way and had no access to Colton. I was pleased with that even though I was pissed that I couldn't see my own son.

"Additionally, I've requested a paternity test be taken immediately to determine who is Colton's biological father. That test should be administered at this location," he said, passing paperwork to both me, Marc, and Vanessa, "within forty-eight hours."

"My client disagrees that a paternity test is necessary," Marc's lawyer said. "He was the only one sleeping with Ms. Hendricks at the time in which Colton was conceived. There is no doubt in his mind that Colton is his."

"If there is no doubt, then he won't have any problem with the test," Jake said dryly. "And, furthermore, if he is so certain, why is he just now coming forward?"

Marc's lawyer glanced at Marc, as if to say, *Want to go to bat?* "When Ms. Hendricks told my client she was pregnant, she said the child belonged to Mr. Wright, and she was going to stop seeing my client. He chose to believe her, but it appears that she has been lying to both of them this whole time."

Vanessa gasped, as if Marc's lawyer had slapped her. Either way, she was the villain. I approved.

"Regardless of Ms. Hendricks's actions or comments during or after the pregnancy, a paternity test is mandatory to determine the custody situation for Colton. Our first priority is his continued health, especially his mental health. The last thing we want to do is introduce new people to him without first being sure that what we are doing is legal. If your client wishes to have any contact with Colton, then he must submit to a paternity test."

"I'll do it," Marc said, cutting his own lawyer off.

"Good. Then, we will reconvene after the results have come in, and then we can determine what will happen next."

Marc and Vanessa glared at me before filing out of the room and leaving the three of us alone.

"That went as well as expected," I told Jake.

He shook my hand and nodded. "The test takes a few days, Jensen. Don't do anything foolish in the meantime."

"Foolish?" I countered.

"Like kidnapping your son."

I couldn't deny that I'd thought about it. I wanted to steal Colton away and never have anyone interfere in our lives again. But I wouldn't. I would be a mess and in a total panic if Vanessa ever did such a thing. I could never do that to her, no matter what she had done to me. And I could never hurt Colton like that.

"I won't."

"Good. I might recommend that you take some time off. Just get away for a few days. I can handle the heavy lifting from here, and you should try to take your mind off of this until we get the results in. If you stay here, I suspect you'll do something else foolish…like assault Marc Tarman," Jake said with a measured look. "Again."

"I think, this time, he wouldn't be so generous," I said, thinking about how he hadn't pressed charges all those years ago.

"No, he wouldn't," Jake said flatly.

Emery's hand went into mine again. I hadn't realized I'd been clenching my fists.

"I'll take care of him," she said.

My solid rock.

God, I believed her.

chapter
thirty-five

Emery

"THERE'S ONE THING I DON'T UNDERSTAND," I SAID AS WE LEFT THE lawyer's office behind.

"Just one?" Jensen asked.

"Well, probably a lot of things but one in particular."

"What's that?"

"Why didn't you ever get a paternity test done?"

"You mean…if I thought that Colton was Marc's all along, why didn't I confirm it?"

"Yes."

That had been bugging me from the start. He had just let that stand without confirmation. It would have driven me crazy.

"For a couple reasons. Proof could have only hurt me. Proof could have taken him away. Proof could have shattered our reality. If I got a paternity test, and it said, as I suspect it will in a couple days, that Colton is Marc's son, then I could lose him. But if I never got one done, then Vanessa only had the threat to hang over my head, and nothing else.

"That makes sense. You didn't want her to take him away. So, you never gave her the proof she needed to do it."

"Right, but the other reason is because I didn't need a paternity test to tell me that Colton is my son. I didn't need the confirmation. Colton *is* my son. Regardless of biology or anything else. He's mine. I love him."

My eyes widened, and a smile stretched my face.

"I didn't need proof when I held him in my arms every day and watched him grow up. I had all the proof I needed when he kissed me good night and called me Daddy."

A tear glimmered in my eye, and I wrapped my arms around his waist, drawing him into a hug. He held me tight and placed a kiss on the top of my head.

"You're a good dad, Jensen Wright."

"It is what I have always endeavored to be."

I released Jensen and wiped my eyes. "Don't ever let them take that away from you. No matter what."

He warily stared down at me. "If they take my son from me, I will no longer be a good person. There'll be little hope for anything else."

He moved past me and took the driver's seat in the Mercedes. It took me a couple of seconds to get composed. I couldn't imagine what he was feeling or how he was handling this right now. My heart went out to him, and I truly feared that, if all went as I suspected it would, with Marc's test coming back as Colton's father, that Marc and Vanessa would wreck him.

With a gulp, I followed Jensen into the car. We drove across town to the lab specified on the form. I told Jensen I would wait in the lobby while he got his test done. It took forever. I wasn't sure why since all he had to do was a normal cotton swab or a blood test. But that was a doctor's office for you.

I flipped through my phone and read a few magazines while I waited. By the time he finally came out, I had a full plan of action for the few days we'd have to wait until the tests came back.

"Painless?" I asked as we exited.

"Yeah. Now, the waiting begins."

"I have an idea about that."

"Hmm?" he asked, distracted.

"I thought we might disappear for a bit. Not too long but just to get your mind off of things."

"Are you really sure I should leave?"

"I think it would be good. Plus, your lawyer agrees."

"Yeah, but what if Vanessa does something crazy or Marc interferes? What if I'm not here?" he asked.

"We won't go far. I promise."

He sighed, knowing I was right. "All right."

"You could come meet Bethany when I stop by my place to get clothes."

"I'd like that."

Jensen drove us to Kimber's place in a hurry. He took corners so fast, I thought we were going to go flying. But I didn't tell him to stop or slow down. I knew what had kindled this aggression.

Heidi's car was in the driveway when we showed up. And she greeted us at the door with baby Bethany.

"Hey, cutie," I said, accepting her like a present.

"About time you showed up!" Heidi said with a grin. "Hey, Jensen."

"Heidi," he said with a smile.

She gave me a strange look, as if she couldn't figure out what was up with us. How could I blame her? I was sure she was wondering what the hell was happening with us. Last she had heard, we'd gotten in a fight on New Year's Eve, and now, he was showing up to see the baby. There was a lot I needed to explain, and there was no time like the present to do it.

"She's so cute," I said with a grin.

"Isn't she?" Kimber said from the couch. "Noah's at work, and Lily is upstairs, napping."

"Beautiful," I confirmed. I turned my attention to Jensen, who was looking down at Bethany like she was the most exquisite thing. "Do you want to hold her?"

"If that's all right?"

"Of course," Kimber said. "You're great with Lilyanne."

He nodded, and then I passed him the little bundle of joy. He immediately softened. I knew he was thinking about Colton at this age. He couldn't see his son right now, but it must have felt nice to hold a baby regardless.

"I'm going to go pack."

"Pack?" Kimber asked.

"I thought y'all might like some space with Bethany home and all. I'm going to go stay with Jensen for a few days."

"That's sweet, Em," Kimber said, "but not necessary. I don't mind you staying."

"I know, but I don't want to be in the way when you want to bond. I'll be right back."

Heidi followed me upstairs and leaned against the doorframe as I stuffed clothes into my overnight bag. "Your shit is still in boxes from Austin. Are you ever going to unpack?"

"Not until I move in with you," I told her with a grin.

"Seriously? You think I want you in my apartment?"

"Of course you do. I'm awesome."

"Move in whenever you want, whore. But give me the deets on you and Jensen. Fighting. Not fighting. What gives?"

I shrugged. "Things were put into perspective. He went out on a limb for me, and I want to trust him and see this through."

"Way to vaguebook. Give me the down and dirty."

"I can't," I told her, facing her. "I love you—you know that—but this isn't my secret to tell. Until Jensen is ready to tell it, I don't want to mess up his trust. We're kind of on new ground here…and I like him too much to lose that."

Heidi held her hands up. "That's fair. I'm not trying to pry. Okay, I am. But I don't want to fuck up your relationship. Everything okay?"

"Honestly…we'll find out in a few days."

"Seems grim."

"You've no idea."

"Okay, okay. Well, fill me in when you can, and let's set up a plan for you to actually move in. You'd better not be that girl who moves in with her bestie and then sleeps at her boyfriend's house the whole time."

"You know I've got time for you in my bed."

Heidi snorted. "I love you. So, where are you going?"

"Surprise. Will you check on Kimber the next couple of days? I really don't want to smother them, but I'll miss my niece."

"You know it."

I finished filling up my bag, slung it over my shoulder, and then retreated downstairs. I hugged Kimber, who was cooing over Bethany asleep in Jensen's arms. It was almost comical really. He was such a big guy, and she was so tiny. Yet he held her as if she were the most precious cargo.

"She's gorgeous, Kimber," Jensen said before passing her back. "Congratulations to you both."

"Thank you," she said, smiling down at her daughter.

"I'll see you in a couple of days. Call me if you need me," I said to Kimber.

"Okay," Kimber said, giving me a hug. "Love you."

Jensen and I retreated back to his Mercedes.

"You going to fill me in on where we're going?"

I grinned as we drove to his place. "You haven't guessed?"

"Coming up blank."

"Back to our first date."

He smiled the first real smile all afternoon, and his eyes raked over my body. "The cabin."

Jensen's cabin in Ransom Canyon was exactly the way I remembered it. Chic furniture and hardwood floors. Sheepskin rugs and modern appliances. A roaring fireplace with soft music filtering in through a surround sound stereo system. It was everything I could want in a place that was both somehow high-end and old school.

It brought back memories of camping when I'd been in school yet exuded a realm of luxury I'd never understood until Jensen.

Here was where we had first had sex, giving into desire and never thinking forward from that moment. If I had known then where we would be standing now, I probably would have thought I was insane. No way would I be Jensen Wright's girlfriend. He'd been out of my league. I'd merely been a conquest… and happy to oblige for a night. Yet…here we were.

"Maybe we should go back," Jensen said doubtfully.

"Look, I know you're worried," I told him, divesting myself of my jacket and tossing it on the back of the couch. "I'm worried, too. But you need to get your mind off of things just until we know the test results. If not, all you'll do is worry yourself to death…and probably do something stupid."

He ran a hand back through his hair. His eyes were haunted. "You're probably right."

"I'm definitely right."

His eyes slid back to me. "And how exactly are you going to get my mind off of things?"

"I had a few ideas."

"Does the first start with you stripping in front of the fire again?"

I smirked. "That's like the third idea."

His hands slid up my sides. "We should move it up the list."

Then, he wrapped his arms around my thighs and hoisted me up into the air. I latched on to his neck, holding myself in place. He effortlessly carried me to the sheepskin rug where we had first had sex.

"Help me forget," he breathed against my neck as he lay me back on the rug.

He didn't have to tell me twice. If he wanted sex, I was there, but I knew he wouldn't really forget like this. It would dampen but not change how he felt. I knew that talking was the only thing that would get us there. However, I was all for talking after.

I slipped my shirt over my head and reached for the button on his jeans. Pushing myself into a sitting position, I stripped off his jeans and then ran my hand over the edge of his boxer briefs. He groaned, even before I slipped under the material and took the length of him in my hand. He grew in size at my careful ministrations. Then, I leaned forward, removed his boxers, and licked him from base to head. He definitely was not thinking about anything else now.

I brought him almost to climax with my mouth before he wrestled me to the ground, removed my clothes, and rammed into me. His eyes were full of emotions now. Lust, desire, heat. He wanted me, and I wanted him.

My hand reached up and brushed his cheek. "I love you," I murmured.

His pacing slowed, and he eased forward onto his elbows, so he could look directly into my face. "I will always love you."

He kissed me, slow and purposeful, matching our lips to his strokes. I twined my legs around his body, reveling in the sensation. Before I knew it, my whole body convulsed, and I was coming with him deep inside me. He tipped his head back and followed on the heels of my orgasm.

It felt like more than just sex.

More than just fucking.

It was deep and personal.

He had touched my soul.

Devoured my heart.

And brought us both back to life.

Jensen Wright had rewritten my world.

We both lay back on the rug, spent...for now. My breathing was irregular, and my heartbeat was skyrocketing. Yet all I wanted was to start up again. I was insatiable for this man. And it terrified me that we had come so close to stepping away…to saying that this was too much.

Love was hard.

It shook you to your core.

It remade you into a different person.

But that was what made it beautiful. Knowing that no one else in the world could ever make you feel like you did in that moment. Accepting the pain and really experiencing what it meant to be together.

It moved mountains.

It certainly moved me.

"How are you doing?" Jensen asked, kissing my shoulder.

"Never been better."

"Mmm," he agreed.

"I think I want to teach," I told him out of nowhere.

"I bet you'd be amazing at it."

"My mother, of all people, suggested I do it, and now, I think it sounds like the right choice."

"Is that what you want then?"

"It was the only thing that really made me happy in grad school. I thought it would get easier. All the research and papers and such, but it was the class-room that made me happy. I just…thought that was normal."

"Maybe it was telling you something," he said, twining my dark hair around his finger.

"Maybe it was," I whispered. "I've never really told anyone that. It was anathema to what everyone thought I should be focusing on in grad school. No one talked about loving the teaching side."

"Well, I think you should stop caring what they think and follow your heart."

I glanced over at him. Naked and satisfied on a sheepskin rug with noth-ing but Jensen Wright in my sight.

"I think I have."

"You are my heart," he said. He took my hand up to his lips and kissed each individual knuckle. "And I can't thank you enough for being here right now through all of this. I know that things haven't been easy. You could have left at anytime. Yet you are here with me through the hardest moment of my life. No matter what happens, Emery, when I walk out on the other side of this…I want you to be with me. I want you to be mine."

I touched his face and drew his lips to mine. "I am."

chapter
thirty-six

Jensen

E MERY AND I HAD SPENT THE LAST FOUR DAYS IN MY CABIN, LOCKED AWAY FROM the outside world. As stressed as I was about what was to come, Emery was right. I'd needed to get away and to try not to think about anything for a while. I couldn't do anything to change the situation while we waited for the test results to come back in. All I could do was stress. So, here we had been, just far enough away for me to relax some.

I was still on edge, but Emery wouldn't let me stay there. At least not for long.

We were coming down from our morning sex on the fifth day when I got the call.

"Tests are in," Jake said. "Showtime."

"Do you know what they say?"

"They're sealed. We'll find out at the same time as everyone else. But be prepared."

I nodded and then hung up the phone. "Time to go."

Emery stretched out in bed and yawned. Her tits looked amazing in the morning right after I fucked her brains out. "Right now?"

"Test results are in."

"Fuck," she said, jolting up. "Let's go."

"We have to get everyone together at once before we can go through the sealed paperwork. But we should get over there as soon as possible."

She jumped out of bed and hurried to clean up the mess that we had made while we were here. Clothes were scattered all across the room, hastily discarded in our den of iniquity. Neither of us had minded. It was easier to let everything go and enjoy how much we fucked than to consider what was coming next.

But, now, that time had come.

We put the place back together in record time and were out of the cabin. It was a quick drive back to Lubbock and to reality.

After this moment, I would definitely know that Colton was Marc's son. I didn't know what I would do with that information. It would be up to Vanessa if she wanted to try to change the custody agreement. But this was a day I had been dreading for a long time. A day I'd hoped would never come.

We made it back to my lawyer's office in good time. He had already spoken to both Vanessa's and Marc's lawyers, and we would be reconvening within the hour. I chose to wait. I couldn't leave, knowing that we had the results waiting. I'd spent years waiting for this moment. I could wait another hour.

Vanessa and Marc showed up separately and warily looked at each other. I wondered what they had done in my time away with Emery. I hoped it had driven them both as crazy as it had me. But they hadn't had the benefit of amazing sex to forget about it. The way they were looking at each other, I was sure they hadn't indulged, which made me grin.

"What?" Vanessa snapped.

"Nothing," I said, purposely glancing between them. "Just had an amusing thought."

"Your thought was so clear on your face. Maybe turn off the broadcast."

I shrugged. Of course she could read me. I'd wanted her to.

Jake reappeared a few minutes later with the information in his hands, and everyone took their seats. Marc was jittery. I could tell by the way he kept fiddling with his hands. He'd done that in school, too. Vanessa looked stoic, as if her relationship with her son didn't depend on this moment. Emery squeezed my leg under the table, and I met her gaze only briefly. I was glad she was here to ground me. I didn't know what I would look like otherwise.

Rattled and a mess.

Neither of which I ever showed to anyone else anymore.

"Thank you for joining us again on such short notice," Jake said, beginning the meeting. "We just received the paperwork from the laboratory that did the paternity test. This is the first time any of us will be seeing it.

"As stated before, Ms. Hendricks has claimed that Colton's father is not her ex-husband, Mr. Wright, but Mr. Tarman instead. This allegation, if true, will begin a change in the custody agreement to potentially allow Mr. Tarman rights to see his son. If the allegation is false, the custody agreement will remain the same unless Mr. Wright or Ms. Hendricks wants to return to court to renegotiate. Is that clear?"

Everyone but Emery said, "Yes," around the table, anxiously staring at the paperwork.

He bent back the metal brackets holding the envelope secured and then opened it. A stack of papers came out, and on the top, were the results. I held my breath as Jake read through the document. You could have heard a pin drop in the room.

"The paternity test came back positive for…Mr. Wright." Jake turned to face me with a giant smile on his face. "Jensen, you're the father. Colton *is* your son."

Vanessa exclaimed from across the room, and I heard Marc cuss. But it was all background noise to me. It was like being sealed in a vacuum.

Colton was my son.

He was mine.

My boy.

I nearly broke down at the very thought that, after all this time, all this worrying, all the arguments and debates and complications…Colton had been mine all along. I'd been so sure that Vanessa was telling the truth. She had been so sure of the truth. I had let her hang it over my head for years. Years!

But she was wrong. Or she had lied. She had lied to my face all those times. Told me countless times that I hadn't even been in New York the month that she got pregnant. My schedule hadn't always overlapped with hers, but I'd believed her. She'd had no reason to say otherwise. Colton had been two years old before I even knew about it. By then, the exact travel dates had been lost on me. I could see them on my work schedule and the flight schedules, but we hadn't always had sex every time I was there. It had been impossible to determine if I was Colt's father.

Now, I knew that I was.

Colton was mine.

Emery's arms were around me, and I stood, lifting her into the air.

"I'm so happy for you," she whispered through the vacuum.

"God, I love you," I murmured back, forgetting everyone else in the room.

I set her back down on her feet, cupped her face in my hands, and kissed the breath out of her. This was the moment I had been born for. The knowledge that I had the woman I loved here with me now and that I would never have to worry about my son again. It was euphoric.

"What the fuck, Vanessa?" Marc cried, jarring me out of my moment. "Why would you drag me into this?"

Marc's and Vanessa's lawyers were looking at the document, but it was clear from their faces that they agreed with Jake.

"I swear, it was you, Marc. I swear," Vanessa said. "Jensen wasn't even in town that month. We weren't together. You know that."

"You just wanted the drama. Fuck!"

"I really believed it was you," she whispered. Tears brimmed in her eyes. "I did."

"You lied to all of us, Vanessa," I said, drawing her attention to me. "You lied to me, to Marc, to everyone. But even worse was that you deluded yourself into believing it. You're never holding this over my head again. I'm free. Free of you."

At those words, Vanessa completely lost it. She broke down into tears and covered her face in her hands. Vanessa had been holding onto this fact for so long, thinking it was a way to keep me. As if she had thought for a second that I would still hold a flame for her after all she had done.

But it was over. There was nothing left. And she had no more control.

"If this satisfies everyone, we'll leave the custody agreement as it stands and deny Mr. Tarman's request for access to Colton," Jake said. "If we want to take this further, then we'll see you in court, Ms. Hendricks."

Vanessa shook her head, blubbering about how she'd sworn she knew. She'd thought this would fix it all.

"Sounds good to me," I said to Jake.

Sure, I would love to get custody of Colton and have him live here in Lubbock with me. But I didn't want to go to court with Vanessa over it, and I wasn't willing to disrupt Colt's life. He was happy in New York, and he had a great school there. I wasn't the type of person to do something like that just to make someone else miserable. That was all Vanessa.

We filed out of the office and stood in the foyer. Vanessa was shaking, talking to her lawyer.

Marc approached us. "I see you've taken everything from me now. Vanessa, Colton, the company."

"Interesting how you put that," I said. "All I see is that you were trying to take things from me that never belonged to you. And the company was just for fun."

Marc glared and looked ready to throw a punch. Instead, he turned to Emery and grinned. "When he gets tired of you, give me a call."

Emery arched an eyebrow in disgust. "Not even in your dreams."

He laughed. "Oh, be sure, he'll tire of you. He bores easily."

"Unless you want a repeat of that time I found out you had an affair with my wife, I would step away," I growled. "Now."

"Don't even waste your breath on him, Jensen," Emery said. "He's trying to provoke you because he's jealous. You have the world at your feet."

I turned to face my girl and smiled. She was right. Of course she was right. "I want you to meet my son."

"I'd love to meet him."

I took Emery's hand then and left the lawyer's office. I knew there was more to take care of, and I definitely had to get back to the office. But first things first. I needed to set all of this straight. Vanessa might be upset about it. Frankly, I didn't care for Vanessa's opinions any longer. Emery was in my life, and she was here to stay.

We showed up at the hotel right after our meeting, and I took Emery up to the top floor. I knocked on the door and Nanny Jennifer answer.

"Jensen! I'm surprised to see you here," she said. "I thought Vanessa said that you couldn't see Colton for right now."

"Change of plans. Just got it approved by the judge that I have full access back."

"Oh, that's wonderful." Jennifer smiled at Emery. "And you must be Emery."

"Hi, nice to meet you," Emery said, holding out her hand.

"Let me go check on Colt for you two."

I turned to Emery. "Can you stay here for a minute. I want to talk to him first."

"Of course," she agreed.

"Colton, your dad is here!" Nanny Jennifer called.

I walked into the suite just as Colton came running. "Daddy!"

He launched himself into my arms, and I hugged him tighter than I'd ever squeezed him before. *My son. Mine!* No one could ever take him away again.

"Hey, champ," I said. I set him back down. "Remember how I told you that I wanted you to meet a friend of mine?"

"Yes. A *girrrl*," Colton singsonged.

I laughed. "Yes. A girl. She's my girlfriend, and her name is Emery."

"You have a girlfriend?"

"Yep, and I want you to meet her. I think you'll like her. Are you ready?"

Colton looked down at himself and gave me a thumbs up.

God, I loved him.

I took his hand, and we walked together to the front of the suite where Emery was waiting.

"All right, champ, this is my girlfriend, Emery," I said to Colton.

Colton stood very still and smiled up at Emery with the brilliance that only a child could have.

Then, I looked up in Emery's big green eyes. "Emery, this is *my* son."

"You're very pretty," he said with a Wright grin.

Emery laughed. "Why, thank you. It's so nice to meet you. I've heard so much about you."

"Dad said that you were going to be my new friend."

"I would like that very much."

"Are you going to come visit me at home?"

Emery smiled and looked up at me with a question in her eyes.

"Yes," I answered for her. "She will most definitely be visiting you in New York. I'm going to bring her as often as I come to visit."

"I'd like that," Emery said as much to me as to Colton. "I'd like to spend all my time in your lives."

We moved back into the living space and took a seat. I picked Colton up and planted him on my knee. Emery sat next to me, and I wrapped my other arm around her.

This was our life. It wasn't perfect. It was far from easy. But it was ours. And I loved them both more than words for being a part of it.

epilogue

Emery
Eight Months Later

"HEIDI, HAVE YOU SEEN MY BLACK PUMPS?" I CALLED INTO THE LIVING room.

"Which ones?"

"The closed-toe ones. Roundish."

She appeared in my bedroom a minute later, holding a pair of shoes in her hand. Curse of living with someone who could pretty much wear all the same sizes as me. Except jeans, because she was a giant compared to me.

"Gimme those."

I put them on my feet and looked in the mirror at the knee-length black skirt and black top I was wearing with the heels. "How do I look?"

"I'd fuck you," she said with a laugh.

"Oh God, I hope all the high school boys aren't going to think that."

"Um…hell yes, they are."

At that moment, a knock came from the front door, and I groaned, trying not to think about high school boys wanting to fuck me. I'd had enough torture for one lifetime on that front. Before I even reached the front door, Jensen popped open the door with his key to the place.

"Hey, babe," he said, giving me a kiss. "Are you really wearing that on your first day?"

"Why? Do I look like shit?" I asked, concerned.

"No, you look hot as fuck. Every kid in the place is going to want to bang their teacher."

I groaned. "Ew. Should I go for flats?"

"Only if you change into the heels for me later." He winked.

I plucked the shoes off my feet and shoved them into his hands. Then, I dashed back into my bedroom and slipped on a sensible pair of black flats. I grabbed the official-looking teacher bag that Jensen had gotten for me as a congratulations for landing my first high school teaching job.

I'd spent all last semester substitute teaching to build up hours for the certification that I needed to be able to be in the classroom. Then, I'd applied to what felt like a million jobs all over Lubbock, and somehow, against all odds, I had gotten a job teaching European history at my old high school. My life could not be more ironic.

"Come on, before you're late to class," Jensen joked, smacking my ass on the way out the door.

"See you later, Heidi!" I called.

"Have a good first day at school, darling!" she yelled back.

Jensen had the truck, which calmed my nerves. I couldn't imagine driving the Mercedes or the flashier sports car he had recently purchased to Lubbock High School. Sure, there was some oil money at the school...and there had always been the Wright family, but I wasn't part of that elite inner circle—or, at least, I kept telling myself that.

Because, when the billionaire CEO himself dropped me off in front of the school, I felt pretty inner circle.

Things with Jensen had been much smoother sailing since the post-holidays madness. I spent a couple of nights a week at his house. We flew to New York once a month to see Colton, and he started spending a weekend here every month. I knew Jensen wanted more time with him, but he also didn't want to interfere with Colton's schooling. Vanessa had mellowed out. I wasn't sure if it was the large quantities of Xanax she was taking or what, but she stopped fighting us when we came into town. After eight months, she must have finally decided I wasn't going anywhere. And I wasn't.

"Thanks for dropping me off," I said.

I was trying not to be nervous even though it was really my first official day teaching high school students. I'd been a TA in college and taught my own introductory history class, but for some reason, high school had felt more daunting than college. Maybe because I'd found out who I was in college, and I had been so scared of high school.

"Have a good first day," he told me, leaning in and giving me a lingering kiss.

"Is anyone actually ready for their first day of high school?"

"You survived once before. You can probably make it a second time."

"And with the right brother this time."

"Ha-ha!" he said with a roll of his eyes. "I'd better be the right brother."

"The one and only," I whispered against his lips.

"Good. Now, get in there, and then later, we can enact all my naughty teacher fantasies."

I blushed despite myself. It didn't matter how much sex we'd had. I couldn't seem to keep it together.

"God, I love you," he said.

"I love you, too."

I kissed him once more and then hopped out of the truck.

I adjusted my skirt and took in the world I was about to enter. I never thought that I'd be back. It was kind of cool to think that I could start over here. I entered the building with more optimism than I'd thought possible.

The day went by lightning fast. Way faster than I remembered high school going when I had been there. But, before I knew it, my first day was over. I had over a hundred and fifty names to remember that had completely flitted out of my brain. But I'd survived.

There was Jensen, waiting for me, when I left. Of course, he was in the flashy Corvette. Bright red and low to the ground with the top down. I shook my head and laughed as I approached the car that all the students were staring at.

"Miss me?" he asked with a grin.

"Every moment."

"Good." He popped open the passenger door, and I dropped inside. "So, where do you want to go to celebrate your birthday?"

I dropped my head into my hands and groaned. "Oh my God, how did you find out?"

"Heidi." He sat down in the driver's seat and then obnoxiously revved the engine.

"Bitch." I shook my head in disbelief. "I don't know. Let's stay in and work on those fantasies."

He grinned. "Thought you'd say that."

The drive back to his house was unbelievably short in his new car. It blew my hair all around my face, but it was exhilarating. I could see why he loved the thing, and he was already talking about getting something sleek and distinctly European. He was addicted.

He parked in the garage and took my hand as I stepped out of the car.

"I am so *not* a birthday person," I informed him with a sigh. "I do like cake though."

"I was made aware of this. But I don't care. You'll celebrate with me if I want you to."

"Just be warned, I will retaliate!"

He laughed and drew me in for a kiss. "I'll take all the punishment you're willing to offer."

We stepped in through the garage and straight into the kitchen.

Jensen flipped the lights, and suddenly, a whole group of people jumped up and screamed, "Surprise!"

I put my hand over my mouth. "Oh my God!"

There were party streamers all over his kitchen and out through the foyer. A giant party cake that read *Happy Birthday, Emery* with a bunch of lit candles sat in the middle of the island. And all around it were my friends and family and Jensen's family.

My heart expanded enough to hold them all. I might not have been a birthday person before, but today changed that. I'd never had good birthdays growing up. They'd always been filled with disappointment—kids missing parties, no one showing up, and all that. But right here was exactly what I'd always wanted.

Heidi was jumping up and down next to Landon. They both looked ecstatic that they had been able to surprise me. Austin was across the room from Julia but kept glancing her way. She was making a point not to look at him so much that it was clear she wanted to look over. Instead, she beamed extra hard at me. Morgan was leaning into Patrick, and Sutton was holding her new baby boy, Jason, in her arms. Maverick was at her side, indulging her. Then, there was Kimber, Noah, Lilyanne, and Bethany all standing to one side with my mother, of all people.

But it was the one other little face who nudged Lilyanne and smiled back at me that surprised me the most. Jensen must have gone to great lengths for this entire thing because Colton was even here.

Jensen wrapped an arm around me as Heidi pushed me toward the cake.

"Make a wish," Jensen said.

I stared down at the cake and realized that I already had everything I wanted.

What I had always been searching for.

Home.

I took a mental snapshot of the beauty before me, at my new reality, and then I leaned forward and made my wish.

the end

acknowledgments

The Wright Brother came out of the idea from a total stranger, who I can now call a friend. Thank you, Kristina, for telling that random story to my husband.

And, of course, the long list of incredible people who helped me make this book what it is today: Rebecca Kimmerling, Anjee Sapp, Katie Miller, Polly Matthews, Anjee Sapp, Diana Peterfreund, Lori Francis, Rebecca Gibson, Sarah Hansen for the amazingly hot cover, Sara Eirew for the sexy photograph, Jovana Shirley for the incredible editing and formatting, Danielle Sanchez for keeping me sane plus your marketing guru genius, Alyssa Garcia for beautiful graphics, and my wonderful agent, Kimberly Brower, for all her amazing work.

Additionally, the much-needed love from authors who kept me up late at night writing and supported me along the way: A.L. Jackson, Lauren Blakely, Kristy Bromberg, Corinne Michaels, Tijan, Rachel Brookes, Rebecca Yarros, Sloane Howell, Jessica Hawkins, Staci Hart, Belle Aurora, Kendall Ryan, Meghan March, Jillian Dodd, Jenn Sterling, S.C. Stephens, Laurelin Paige, Kandi Steiner, Claire Contreras, and many more!

All the incredible bloggers who worked tirelessly day in and day out to get content to readers just because you love books so much, I see you. I appreciate you.

As always, thank you so much to my husband for dealing with me being sick, wanting to write three books at once, late nights, and deciding to take up piano and working out in the same month. I love you and the puppies to the moon and back.

Finally, and most importantly, YOU! That's right. You, as the reader! Thank you for reading this book. I hope you loved it, and I can't wait to give you more amazing books to follow.

also by
K.A. LINDE

WRIGHTS
The Wright Brother | *The Wright Boss*
The Wright Mistake | *The Wright Secret*
The Wright Love | *The Wright One*
A Wright Christmas

CRUEL
One Cruel Night | *Cruel Money*
Cruel Fortune | *Cruel Legacy*

SEASONS
His for a Season | *The Lying Season*
The Hating Season | *The Breaking Season*

RECORD SERIES
Off the Record | *On the Record* | *For the Record*
Struck from the Record | *Broken Record*

AVOIDING SERIES
Avoiding Commitment | *Avoiding Responsibility*
Avoiding Temptation | *Avoiding Extras*
DIAMOND GIRLS SERIES
Rock Hard | *A Girl's Best Friend*
In the Rough | *Shine Bright*
Under Pressure

TAKE ME DUET
Take Me for Granted | *Take Me with You*

STAND ALONE
Following Me

Paranormal Romance

BLOOD TYPE SERIES
Blood Type | Blood Match | Blood Cure

Young Adult Fantasy

ASCENSION SERIES
*The Affiliate | The Bound | The Consort
The Society | The Domina*

ROYAL HOUSES
House of Dragons

about the author

K.A. Linde is the *USA Today* bestselling author of the Avoiding Series, Wrights, and more than thirty other novels. She has a Masters degree in political science from the University of Georgia, was the head campaign worker for the 2012 presidential campaign at the University of North Carolina at Chapel Hill, and served as the head coach of the Duke University dance team. She loves reading fantasy novels, traveling, and dancing in her spare time.

She currently lives in Lubbock, Texas, with her husband and two super-adorable puppies.

Visit her online at Facebook, Twitter, and Instagram @authorkalinde.

Join her newsletter for exclusive content, free books, and giveaways every month. www.kalinde.com/subscribe

The Dark Ones Saga Book 1

RACHEL VAN DYKEN

To my AMAZING fan group Rachel's New Rocking Readers!
I LOVE having you guys do group beta reads of my books.
Thanks for helping me out with this one
and being a part of the creative process; you are amazing!

chapter
one

Genesis

I WAS NEVER ONE TO BE ACCUSED OF BEING PATIENT. THEN AGAIN, I'D NEVER understood the need for patience. To me, patience meant that I was either in the process of getting lectured or about to get lectured. I chewed the edge of my thumbnail and waited in the darkness.

"Ugly." My mother shook her head in my direction. "Remember that… you will always be ugly to them."

Them.

The very word dripped with hatred. You'd think after centuries of working together, we'd have found a happy medium. My mother had her own reasons for hating them, and up until this point, I'd had exactly none.

I'd spent my entire existence balancing my normal school life with my folklore studies, something I'd always hated but it had been necessary, just in case my number was called.

My entire family had a bad reputation for going against the rules, against the calling that had been given them, so I'd never been really concerned about being called in.

Until now.

I'd been eating soggy cereal, staring into the Corn Chex, when my mother's scream erupted through the house, followed by her passing out and my dad needing to call the paramedics.

Her heart had stopped. Literally. Stopped.

All because of a phone call.

Naturally, my parents had lied and said she'd been having chest pain, but I knew the truth.

It was fear.

Fear had stopped her heart, almost resulting in her death.

And fear was about to stop mine.

"Stop," Mother hissed at my side. "Do you want them to think you're a barbarian?"

To them? I already was, so I didn't really see the point in pretending to be anything else. To those individuals, I would always be the dirt beneath their feet, the little plaything they had to put up with.

I knew their history.

Probably better than most of them.

I'd been studying them for most of my life, pouring over books and research with constant dread that, one day, my number would be called, and my life would be played out for me in absolute horror.

Humans were like little insects that they allowed to survive only because it was necessary for their own survival. We die. They die. Therefore, we live.

The darkness lifted for a few brief minutes as the door creaked open.

"Genesis?" a seductive male voice spoke into the darkness. "They will see you now."

My mom, with her long dark hair and bright green eyes, gave me one more look and shook her head. "Remember, you are nothing, you are ugly, you are humble, you are stupid, you aren't brave, you are nothing. You. Are. Nothing."

I nodded and repeated the mantra in my head.

The same one she'd pounded into my skull since my birth. She'd had her reasons, not that it made hearing those words any easier. Several times during my upbringing, I'd locked myself in my room and just stared at myself in the mirror. I'd focused on each feature and wondered what was so horrible about my eyes, my lips, my face—even my cheeks—that I had to repeat those ugly words until I was blue in the face.

The one time I'd asked her, she'd snorted and said something about our bloodlines being wicked and selfish, and how the females in our family were not known for our humility.

Basically, my own mother believed that if my number was called…

I would be killed.

My sarcastic nature didn't help things, and if my number was called, I figured it would get my tongue cut out.

And even though it was 2015, and I thought we'd come a long way with equality and human rights…

I was still nothing. In their eyes I was both nothing and everything, all wrapped up into one.

Human.

Special.

But unable to grasp my own uniqueness because of my imperfect creation.

"Nothing," I chanted under my breath. "I am nothing."

My black, over-the-knee boots clicked against the concrete as I made my way toward the light, the only light in the room, peeking out from the grand doorway.

I'd chosen to wear black leggings with a wraparound cream sweater, hoping that if I covered enough of myself, it would look humble, but not so humble that I didn't at least try to look nice for my meeting.

I'd never been the most secure girl in the world. Then again, how could I have confidence when every day of my life my mom had repeated that same mantra in my head? *"You are nothing."*

I sensed a sudden presence at my back. A hand, I realized. The contact made me gasp. A slight warm tingle ran through and somehow down my neck.

"Sorry," a man said to my right. I couldn't see him yet, but his voice sounded like a soothing melody, causing me to almost sway on my feet. "I forget how fragile humans can be."

I nodded. "It's okay."

"This way." The pressure from his hand wasn't necessarily painful, but it wasn't pleasant either, almost like an electric current was passing from his body into mine. I'd heard that it was nearly impossible to turn off certain powers—it would be like me trying to tell my heart to stop beating.

Once I was through the door, I looked around.

It was magnificent.

The floor was a dark black marble; the walls had sconces that I'm sure at one point had held torches—before electricity.

Two large doors stood in my way. I could feel the power on the other side; the room practically sang with it.

"Do not speak," the man on my right said. Finally, I glanced up and closed my mouth immediately.

What would a perfectly healthy twenty-five-year-old say to someone who had no eyes? Only dark spots where eyes once were?

Not to mention, his mouth wasn't moving, yet he was speaking.

I knew what he was.

"Fear isn't welcome here." He spoke again, this time rubbing my back as if to comfort me. But his mouth still didn't move. Regardless of the knowledge in my head about this type of creature, I was still having trouble breathing.

This was really happening.

My number had been called.

I was at the ceremony.

My life was going to change forever.

To run away would mean death.

To take a few more steps—well, it meant the same thing. Especially if I didn't please them.

I tugged at my sweater, my palms sweating.

"You look lovely, just remember. No fear. You are nothing. You are everything. You are simply... you." He nodded again and the two oak doors opened.

A gasp escaped between my lips before I could stop it.

"They have that effect on everything," he whispered.

And then the lights brightened.

All the schooling in the world couldn't have prepared me for what I saw. All the pictures, all the movies, all the preparation.

And suddenly, I wanted very much to fall to my knees and cry.

chapter
two

Genesis

"GO ON," THE MAN URGED.

I took another step forward.

And suddenly he was gone. The doors shut behind me. I was completely and utterly alone.

Facing *them*.

Was I allowed to look directly at them? Was I supposed to speak? I had no idea what the protocol was, only that if I broke it, I wouldn't even feel pain before they sliced me up and tossed my parts back to where I'd come from.

I held my head high and waited, all the while repeating the same mantra in my head. *"I'm nothing, I'm nothing. I'm everything."*

"Genesis." A smooth voice called my name. It was so beautiful on his lips I wanted to cry again, and I'd never thought myself an overly emotional person, one of the only things my mom had applauded me for.

Slowly, I turned to the left. A man dressed in dark jeans and a white T-shirt stood from a silver throne. His hair was impossibly light, almost white, his eyes a glowing blue.

He was smiling.

It looked painful on him.

Only because it was so beautiful.

"Fear isn't welcome here." He repeated the same thing the first man had said.

"Apologies... sir." Or was it my lord? I couldn't remember and hoped it wouldn't be the last thing I uttered. How bad would that suck? Not that I'd be alive to actually care.

"Ah..." A blindingly white smile flashed in my direction as heat from his body flew at me in waves, nearly sending me to my knees. From my fingers all the way down to my toes, I wanted to touch him. I wanted to taste him. It was more than just being near him—I wanted everything about him to consume me until I wasn't even me anymore.

Don't you though? His voice sounded in my mind.

I blinked, trying to stay strong as the pieces fell together. He was a male siren, someone so sensual, so strong in his sexuality that he couldn't help but give off pheromones by merely breathing. Our books hadn't mentioned male sirens, but I couldn't imagine him being anything but that. He was too perfect, too strong, too warm. My body hummed with awareness.

"Beautiful, isn't she?" he said, the waves getting hotter and hotter, making me want to whimper aloud. I wanted to touch him, any part of him, even his feet. How stupid was that? I would literally sell my soul if I could touch his big toe.

He threw his head back and laughed. "This should be fun."

"Alex, stop it," a woman said to his right. "She's shaking."

"So am I." He winked.

Something flew by his head, barely missing his chin.

"Damn it, Stephanie, let me have my fun."

"You have fun," the woman rolled her eyes, "every day. Now sit down before you give her a heart attack."

Alex sat, the waves slowly dissipated, and I was able to focus on the woman next to him. They could have been twins, except she wasn't just beautiful, but absolutely flawless—her eyes were the same bright blue, and she was wearing one of the dresses I'd seen at Nordstrom the week before... the price tag had been too high, and I'd been convinced that even if I'd put it on, it would look dumpy on me.

Because my mother's voice chimed in my head, *"You are nothing."*

I clenched my fists tighter and managed a head nod in her direction.

When my eyes fell to the third person in the room, I took a step back.

"Fear is not welcome here," the man barked, his eyes black and cold.

"Right," I whispered. "I'm—I'm sorry."

His lips twitched. Where the others were bright and pretty, he had shaggy brown hair that hung past his shoulders and black eyes that seemed to see right through me; his smile was attractive but predatory, and I was pretty sure that if he wanted to break me in half just to prove he could, he'd only need to use two fingers.

"You're different from the others."

I wasn't sure if different was good or bad; it was on the tip of my tongue to ask, but I thought better of it when he leaned forward, causing my heartbeat to sky rocket.

He was a beast or werewolf. I'd studied his kind, even though it had terrified me to go over those chapters in class. They were unpredictable, angry, scary hunters that thought emotions were for the weak.

It was believed they lacked the ability to empathize with others, making them one of the most dangerous creatures to humans.

He was proving the text hadn't lied. No smile. No light behind his eyes, just emptiness.

"You really are a pretty one, aren't you?" another voice chimed in, this one deep, smooth, soothing… like a stream where the water trickled over the rocks.

Giving my head a shake, I turned to the man next to the werewolf and barely managed to hold in a gasp.

He was gorgeous.

Light green eyes glowed in my direction, beamed and twinkled with each blink, almost like I was staring at stars. His skin was smooth and light. Dark brown hair was pulled back into a low ponytail, and he had a leather bomber jacket on.

He was the epitome of every girl's fantasy come to life.

I quickly averted my eyes, aware I was blatantly staring at him.

"What?" His warm chuckle made my body tingle. "Are you afraid to look at me, human?"

"No." I found my voice, "Not at all." Slowly I lifted my gaze to his and waited.

His smile was blinding. "Good, that's good, as we'll be spending many hours together in the near future." His smile suddenly dropped as if the idea saddened him, or maybe just made him want to kill me and get it over with.

Yeah, that was what I was afraid of.

Maybe I was better off with the werewolf.

Or the siren.

"Enough." A booming voice sounded throughout the room, shaking me out of my stare-down with the man. Only vampires had green eyes, so I imagined that was what he was, though he looked nothing like I imagined a vampire would look.

I glanced around for the location of the voice but saw nothing.

The smile froze on the vampire's face. He shared a look with the others and leaned back in his chair, while the other three seemed to stiffen in theirs, as if they were afraid. What could they possibly have to fear? They were immortal.

I looked around the room again. The lights flickered.

That couldn't be a good sign.

Up until now, I'd had no idea what immortals I'd be meeting with, and I wracked my brain trying to think of who else would be there—who else I should be afraid of… when suddenly the room went black.

It was only three seconds.

But it was enough for my brain and survival instincts to kick in.

I had to force my feet to stay planted.

I had to force the scream to stay in my throat.

And when I felt a hand reach out and touch my shoulder, the pain I felt at that touch was so life-altering that I fell to my knees, my body giving out.

"That's better," the voice said. "Don't you know you are to kneel in front of those you serve?"

"S-sorry," I said through clenched teeth. "It won't happen again."

"No," he said, "it won't. Because if it does, you'll be dead. Understand?"

"Yes."

The ice from his touch wouldn't let up; it continued to flow through my body like he was trying to freeze every vein I had.

The lights flickered again, and then he was standing in front of me.

All seven feet of him.

It hurt to stare.

But not as much as it would have if I hadn't—I, at least, had paid attention to that part of my studies. To look away was like experiencing the greatest pain imaginable because, as a human, I was drawn to his beauty, drawn to his essence in a way that had been programmed since the beginning of time.

He was a Dark One.

A fallen.

Half angel. Half human.

And he was the leader of the immortals. His punishment, along with the others of his kind had been to watch over both races, keeping them as separate as possible while still making sure both thrived. Requiring him to live with humans and play police with the immortals was a punishment.

They were called Dark Ones because both light and dark fought for them, making it impossible for lights to stay on or the dark to stay dark for too long a time span.

They commanded the dark.

But were forced to live in the light.

They were equal parts good and bad, which made them the most dangerous as they had no moral compass.

"Interesting..." His head tilted in a cat-like stance. "...that you know so much about me. Pray tell, are you going to give us a history lesson? You may stand."

Crap. I stood on shaky feet.

They could also read thoughts if they wanted to.

Though most weren't powerful enough to do so.

"I am."

Those two words devastated me. If he was that powerful, he wasn't just any Dark One. He was—

"Cassius." He finished my thought, his lips tilting up in a seductive smile. White teeth flashed, and then he turned on his heel, slowly walking up the stairs to where everyone else was seated. "But to you..." He turned slightly, his eyes flashing white before going back to a normal blue. "...I am Master.

chapter
three

Genesis

CASSIUS. THE NAME BURNED ON MY LIPS THOUGH I HADN'T SPOKEN IT OUT loud—was too afraid to. I knew the power behind his name, behind who he was.

He was like a god to the immortals.

And to me?

Well, he was more than that. He could kill me with a simple snap of his fingers. He could make me see my worst nightmares by simply willing it to happen. But worst of all? He could own me. It was said that Dark Ones treated humans as pets, playthings—an amusement. But because Dark Ones had such heightened emotions, when they abandoned a human out of boredom or something else trivial, it killed the human.

Instantly shattering their hearts in their chests.

Once the Dark Ones were finished with you—you didn't survive it. No one could survive the emotional break that came when someone like Cassius left.

It was emptiness.

It was death.

I needed to stay far, far away from him if I wanted to live.

The only happy thought that occurred to me was that someone as old as Cassius most likely despised humans enough not to toy with them. Unlike the vampire and siren, who found it amusing and harmless.

"Do you know your duties?" Cassius barked. "Or am I to go over them with you? From the looks of Alex, it seems he's been too preoccupied to do much of anything except fill the air with his arousal."

Alex's nostrils flared, but he said nothing.

"And, Stephanie, what's your excuse?"

She dropped her head and gave a little shudder. "Sorry, Cassius."

"Mason?" He turned to the werewolf. "Your looks don't betray you, but your rapid heartbeat does. Tell me, does she set your blood on fire?"

The werewolf rolled his eyes. "Only in irritation, my lord."

"Ethan…" Cassius barked. "You've been quiet."

"I've been watching." Ethan tilted his head, making himself look more vampire than before. The way his eyes glowed in my direction sent shivers all the way down my spine. "I think I'll keep her."

Stephanie jumped up from her seat. "Ethan—!"

"Please." Ethan waved her off. "He owes me, don't you, Cassius?"

The temperature in the room dropped at least thirty degrees while Cassius stood and, with little effort, threw Ethan across the room. He slammed into one of the rock walls.

Pieces of dust flew into the air. I gasped, covering my mouth with my hands.

"Dramatic," Ethan huffed beneath an array of rubble and rock. "Then again, you've always been dramatic, haven't you, Dark One?"

Cassius released Ethan and turned to face me. "You will go with Ethan. You will do your... duty." The way he said it made me feel dirty, like I was being whored out.

"I don't need to explain the rules, but I will, for your sake, explain them once. You're hired to do a specific job for us. You are not here to try to land yourself an immortal husband, so leave those hopes and dreams at the door. Physical contact between you and an immortal is forbidden, and if you are on the receiving end of it, outside of your duties, *you* will be the one punished, not the immortal.

Yeah, that was what I was afraid of.

"They may touch you, may do whatever the hell they want with you. But if you seek them out, touch them without proper invitation..." His voice trailed off, his nostrils flared. "Do you understand?"

Not at all. But I had no choice. I gave a quick nod, wringing my hands together. "Yes."

"Ethan," Cassius turned, "consider my debt paid."

Ethan's smile grew to gigantic proportions. "Oh, it's been paid," he licked his lips, "in full."

I knew that look.

I was going to die.

Because there was no way that vampire wasn't putting his hands or his fangs on me—and it would be my fault because I was the human.

To them, we weren't victims. Just nuisances they put up with.

"Well then..." Ethan held out his hand in my direction. "Shall we?"

Fear kept me rooted to my spot.

Then suddenly warmth spread throughout the room. I quickly glanced to the siren; Alex had his hand raised in the air, and I could almost see the heat radiating from his hand toward my body.

Be calm, he whispered in my head. *Ethan will not harm you.*

And you?

None of us mean you harm.

My gaze flickered to Cassius.

Alex gave a slight shake of his head. *Yes, human. He means you harm. You are never to be alone with him. Ever. If you are, I cannot help you. I cannot shield you from his power. If he touches you, if he claims you, it will be the last time you own your own body, soul, and mind. He will destroy you. If you must... run.*

My hands shook at my sides, but I managed a nod in his direction.

Ethan held out his hand again. "Come."

I followed him, careful not to touch his hand lest he have the same effect on me a Dark One would, and followed him through a side door.

He moved silently next to me, opening door after door, finally leading me into a dark parking garage where a black unmarked town car was waiting.

"Hurry, get in."

"What?"

He shoved me in the car and ran to the other side, faster than my eyes could follow, then sped off as if we were being chased.

"We don't have much time." He looked behind him. "Damn it, we have less than that much time."

"What are you talking about?"

"He will *hunt* you."

"What?" I gasped. "Who?"

"Cassius..." He spat. "He wants you. I could feel it. Could see it in his mind's eye as if I was living it myself. The reason you're here isn't for the immortals. It's for him."

"But, my mom said that—"

Ethan barked out a laugh. "Yes please tell me what your human mother told you about what your job is to the immortals?"

I swallowed the dryness in my throat. "I'm to educate you about the ways of the humans so you don't have to interact with us. Teach any of the immortal children how to use the Internet, cell phones—technology—and at the end of the day, I—"

He roared with laughter, interrupting what I thought was a pretty good speech.

"So that's what they tell you now?"

"Wh-what?" I looked behind me only because he kept looking behind us. For Cassius to fly overhead? Or what? We were in the middle of Seattle. It's not like the immortal would want to be seen.

"Immortals cannot have children with one another, Genesis."

"What?" I gasped. "But that's impossible. That would mean—"

Ethan's eyes flashed. "Do you really think that with all the money we have, all the resources, we would need a tiny pitiful ugly little human to tell us how to use a damn computer?"

Well, when he put it that way...

It didn't make sense. I mean, I'd studied their history, studied everything about each race. I'd studied my butt off so I could be useful for them, to them. And when all of that was finished, I'd even had to take classes on proper etiquette—how to serve at an immortal feast, how to dress when I was presented, how to—

"Oh, my gosh," I gasped, reaching for the seatbelt.

Ethan's hands went to mine. "Stop. It will pass. You're just scared."

"But—"

"Shhh." Something shifted in the car, maybe it was the temperature, maybe it was just Ethan trying to calm me down, but my heartbeat slowed way down.

"Did you just…" My words felt funny. "…slow down my heart?"

"I'm a vampire, love. What did you expect me to do? Bite you into silence?"

Yeah, that's exactly what I expected; it's what the books had said.

"Don't believe everything you read. Besides, I'm not the least bit hungry." He winked and took the next exit toward Lake Washington.

"So…" He drove the car like a maniac. Turns weren't just turns. It was like he was jerking the car so hard the steering wheel was about to come off. "Tell me you believe me."

"Believe you?"

"About your purpose?"

"What is my purpose?" I asked. "I mean, sir, or… um…" Crap, I'd drawn a blank on how I was supposed to address him. He was above me; I needed to show him respect.

"Ethan." He sighed heavily. "Damn, do they brainwash you that much these days?"

"These days?"

"We haven't called a number up in fifty years." Ethan shook his head. "Pity that Cassius would do it now. Then again, after looking at you…" He licked his lips. "…I'd probably do the same damn thing."

"What?"

"Home!" Ethan screeched the car to a halt in front of a gigantic, fenced-in mansion overlooking the lake. A few men stood outside the gates. When they magically swung open, Ethan sped inside then turned off the car. "Come on."

With no other option but to follow, I quickly got out of the car and followed him to the door.

Two men with the same-colored eyes but darker hair glanced from me to Ethan and back again.

The first spoke. "Apologies, my lord, but she… you cannot bring a breeder into the house! Not if you want to live through the night." He leaned forward and sniffed. "She's marked!"

"Stay out of it, Ben." Ethan gripped my hand and jerked me into the house.

"Breeder?" I repeated. "What did he mean by that?"

"Silence, human." Ethan continued pulling me through the house until finally stopping in a gourmet kitchen. "I don't know what to do with you yet. I don't suppose you'll take kindly to the doghouse out back or the nice water bowl with the name *Scratch* on it?"

My mouth dropped open. "A dog? You're going to treat me like your dog?"

"Joke." He smirked. "But good to know you're opposed to sleeping outside."

My knees threatened to give out. He must have noticed; in an instant I was in his arms being carried to the nearest chair.

"Humans," he whispered into my hair. "So fragile."

It didn't register I was in a vampire's arms. In fact, nothing was registering. Nothing was making sense, and I wasn't sure if I was even allowed to ask questions. It wasn't my place. My mom had made that clear.

I was terrified of doing the wrong thing—and suffering for it.

The room felt warm again. Warm and familiar. I looked up just as Stephanie and Alex rushed in the room.

"Your scent is all over the thing." Alex shook his head. "It's not enough."

Ethan hissed. "I've had her for fifteen minutes. He freaking marked her. What do you expect me to do?"

"Try harder," Alex clipped then turned his cold blue eyes toward me. "Sorry, little one, but this day's going to get a hell of a lot worse before it gets better."

"I'll do it," a third gruff voice said.

"Mason…" Ethan nodded. "…do your worst."

Mason grunted then held out his hand to me.

I didn't take it.

"Hell, Ethan, what did you do to her?" Mason rolled his eyes. "She's petrified."

"She's human," Stephanie pointed out.

"S-sorry." I shook my head. "I'm sorry that I'm scared."

They all stopped glaring at one another and instead turned their full focus on me.

"Fear attracts immortals," Mason said plainly. "It would be good of you to stop shaking."

"Slow her heart." Stephanie slapped Ethan in the chest. "Hurry."

Rolling his eyes, Ethan focused in on me, and slowly my racing heart went back to normal.

"Mason," Alex barked, "hurry."

"Right." Mason took a step forward. "*We* won't hurt you... but it will hurt."

"What?"

"Just..." Ethan cursed and looked away. "...stay as still as possible, human."

"She has a name," Alex grumbled, earning a fiery look from both Ethan and Mason.

My breath hitched when Mason leaned down, gripping my shoulders, and softly nibbled on my neck. It felt good—until a slicing pain followed the nibbling.

I shrieked.

He didn't let go.

When I was about ready to pass out, he pulled back, his eyes completely black. "It didn't work."

"Shit." Ethan ran his hands through his hair.

"You have to do something." Stephanie looked toward Ethan. "He'll find her if you don't."

"What the hell do you expect me to do?" Ethan roared. "Bite her?"

The room fell silent. Didn't vampires bite?

Isn't that what the text had said?

Alex exhaled loudly. "I'll try, just don't get all pissed off when she melts into a puddle on the floor."

"Oh please." Stephanie rolled her eyes.

"Focus." Alex snapped his fingers in front of my face. "Let me try to at least smother his scent with mine."

His lips descended.

And I was being kissed—by a siren. Something the texts described as indescribable ecstasy.

I was too afraid to feel anything except for heat and desire.

My heartbeat picked up again. My body went damp and hot as his mouth moved against mine.

When he pulled back, it wasn't with a satisfied smirk but one of hopelessness. "I'm so sorry, little human."

"He'll come for her," Stephanie whispered, her eyes flickering to Ethan. "If he takes her—"

"I know," Ethan barked. "Don't you think I'm well aware of our own prophesy?"

"Yet we play right into it... every century," Alex muttered. "I thought... for a second, I thought this one would be different. It felt different, right?"

The room fell silent again.

"What..." My voice was hoarse. "...what am I really doing with you? Why was my number called?"

THE DARK ONES | 223

"Oh dear..." Stephanie plopped down into a seat. "Ethan didn't explain that?"

"Again, fifteen minutes," Ethan muttered under his breath. "And she's human. It's not like her capacity for learning new information has evolved."

I glared at him.

Mason chuckled.

"Honey..." Stephanie reached her hand across the table and placed it on mine. "Whatever your family has taught you is a lie. You aren't here to teach us or do anything of the sort. You're... you're a breeder."

"A breeder," I repeated. "Like a horse?"

Mason laughed harder. Well, at least I knew werewolves weren't out to kill me.

Ethan swore and sat down on the other side of me.

"We call numbers every fifty years to breed. Immortals cannot procreate with other immortals," he explained. "Humans are chosen based on their scent, strength..." He coughed and looked away. "Physical appeal."

"But I'm ugly," I blurted. "To you I'm ugly. We're ugly, we're nothing, we're—"

Ethan shook his head slowly. "And that's the greatest deception of all." His hands moved to my chin. "To us you're not ugly. You are absolute perfection."

"To a Dark One," Mason continued, "you're life itself."

chapter
four

Genesis

MY BREATH HITCHED IN MY CHEST AS I STARED AT THE STRANGERS AROUND me. What did that even mean? Life itself? I was nothing. Why would I be taught humility and self-hate my whole life only to be told by the very ones I was supposed to fear that I was life itself?

"Jealousy," Ethan said softly, "quickly turns to envy. Envy is a dangerous thing because you end up wanting so desperately what you'd never been given in the first place. The greatest sin an immortal can commit is to laugh in the face of what we are… and want." His eyes were sad. "He wants you."

"To kill me?" I whispered hoarsely.

"No." Ethan cupped my chin with his smooth fingers. "He wants to possess you, and believe me when I say you'll like every part of that possession—until he leaves you. Dark Ones always leave, and you'll die."

"Maybe she's different," Stephanie said in a quiet voice.

"You'd be willing to sacrifice another?" Mason roared, slamming his fists onto the table. It split down the middle right in front of me.

Gasping, I slid my chair back and nearly fell out of it.

"How many times have we said we'd stop testing the prophecy?"

Stephanie looked down at her hands. "It's the only hope we have."

"Hope," Alex muttered. "What a sad, pathetic little word."

"We aren't letting Cassius have her." Ethan's green eyes flashed as he released my chin. "We won't repeat what happened last time."

"What happened last time?" I asked, knowing I'd probably regret the answer.

Mason's entire face crumpled with pain as he let out a howl and ran out of the room.

"Shit." Alex stared after him. "It's going to take hours to get him to come out of his state now."

"I'm so sorry." I held up my hands. "I had no idea—"

"Of course you don't," Ethan snapped. "You know nothing."

I am nothing.

I hung my head.

"Be easy on her," Stephanie said in a calm voice. "She's been brainwashed for quite a while."

"Will he be okay?" I asked in a small voice. "The wer—" I was about to say *werewolf* and had to stop myself. "Mason? Will he be okay?"

"After he runs." Ethan hung his head. "Maybe if he eats something other than berries and the damn pinecones I keep finding in the upstairs bedroom."

Stephanie's lips pressed together in a small smile. "He finds comfort in the outside."

"Yeah, well, he's ruining my wood floors," Ethan grumbled.

"You live together?" I blurted.

All eyes fell to me. "All immortals live together in one sense or another." It was Ethan who kept answering my questions. "And you didn't offend Mason as much as remind him of what should have been... what could have been."

"Oh." I swallowed against the dryness in my throat. Shock must have been wearing off as I could at least feel my body again, though what I felt was shaky and weak.

"Ethan..." Stephanie glanced between us. "I know you don't like the idea, but it's really the only way."

He chewed his lower lip; fangs descended from the top of his mouth. "I know."

"It's the only thing we haven't tried." Alex put his arm around Stephanie. "It won't be so bad, will it?"

What were they talking about?

And why was I suddenly feeling rejected all over again?

"It won't be so bad," Ethan repeated. "It will be absolute torture... hell rising to earth... and you ask me to do this still? Knowing what you know?"

The two of them hung their heads but said nothing.

It was on the tip of my tongue to ask when the entire temperature in the room dropped.

I saw my own breath.

"He's close." Alex cursed. "Do it now!"

Ethan's green eyes met mine; they flashed then went completely black before he said in a low gravelly voice, "I'm so sorry."

All I felt was pain.

As black overtook everything.

"I love you so much." The woman danced in the field, throwing her hands up into the air in excitement. "Say you love me."

"I love you." Ethan grinned. "Always, you know this."

"Say it again!" She laughed and threw herself into his arms.

I felt everything he felt, like it was me. He wasn't just elated, he was... perfect. Life was perfect. The universe was at one with him and his mate.

"The hour grows late," he whispered against her temple. "Shall we go back to the castle?"

She pulled away and pouted. Her dark hair fell in loose waves all the way down to her waist. "Catch me first."

"Too easy."

"Do it!" She laughed than took off ridiculously fast.

Laughing, Ethan chased her into the forest.

It was impossible not to laugh with them, not to experience the love firsthand. It was so beautiful I wanted to weep, but I couldn't feel my face or any part of my body. Maybe I was dead. But at least I'd seen true love once. It was something I'd never forget—the way he held her, the way their hearts beat the same rhythm.

The scene changed.

She was in a large bed. The curtains were pulled back from the window, letting in the moonlight.

"A daughter." She held the baby up in her arms and grinned. "Ethan, we have a daughter!"

Ethan's face was pure awe as he took the small bundle in his hands and whispered against the baby's head. "So perfect."

"She is."

"We did it," Ethan said with tears in his eyes. "I cannot believe after all these years—"

The temperature in the room dropped.

"Quickly…" Her eyes were fearful. "Take her away from here."

"He would never harm a child." Ethan shook his head. "We can trust him."

"We can't!" she cried. "You've seen what they are capable of."

"Leave it!" he roared. "I will protect us."

The door to the room burst open as Cassius casually walked in, his eyes scanning the room with a cold detachment that caused me to shiver.

"So…" Cassius tilted his head; it looked animalistic. "You defy me?"

"She's half human," Ethan said. "You know the rules."

"The rules…" Cassius grinned. "…and you've broken them."

"No." Ethan shook his head. "That's impossible."

The woman in the bed started to cry softly in her hands.

"Maybe you should ask your wife where her loyalty lies."

"Ethan…" she sobbed. "I'm so sorry! It was the only way! It was the only way!"

Realization dawned in Ethan's eyes as he fell to his knees. "Tell me you didn't do this, my love… tell me!"

No more words were spoken.

I felt like my heart was breaking right along with his.

Cold green eyes met mine as if he truly knew I was there, in that heaven or hell, in the dream.

"Awake!" he screamed.

I jolted up from the bed in a cold sweat and confused, who carried me there? Ethan hovered over me, Stephanie rocked in the corner, and Alex paced the floor.

"It worked." Alex paused his walking, still not looking at me. "Thank God, it worked."

"Of course it did," Stephanie agreed; her eyes held such a deep sadness, my heart clenched in my chest. "Ethan..."

He shoved away from the bedside and walked out of the room, slamming the door behind him.

"He won't hurt you." Alex gave me a sympathetic smile. "Just... give him time."

"Time?"

Stephanie nodded. "To get used to the idea."

"The idea of what?"

"You're his new mate." Stephanie stood, just as the sound of a man screaming in agony pierced my ears. "We'll leave you now."

chapter
five

Genesis

THE DOOR CLICKED SHUT, LEAVING ME COMPLETELY AND UTTERLY ALONE. I pulled the blanket up to my chin and gave another jolt when another guttural roar came from somewhere in the house.

Ethan.

The minute I thought his name, I reached to my neck to see if he'd bitten me like Mason. Nothing but smooth skin met my fingertips, though my entire body still felt frozen—as if Cassius had marked me with a frigid temperature or something. But that was crazy.

In fact, the whole scenario was crazy.

I'd left every belonging I'd had with my mother, thinking I'd probably see her after I met with the immortals—she hadn't given me reason to believe otherwise.

I had no cell phone.

No money.

Absolutely no identification.

And, up until this point, I'd thought I'd been chosen to work for some secret society that hated me—but needed me desperately.

Instead, I'd been scared within an inch of my life.

And bitten twice—or at least I assumed twice.

My fingers grazed my neck again.

Nothing.

Another yell, this one hoarser than the ones before, as if Ethan was losing his voice.

I shivered and watched the flames flicker in the fireplace. The room they'd put me in was extravagant. I was lying in a king-sized bed with sheets that felt like silk against my fingers. A flat screen TV was positioned next to the fireplace, and pieces of artfully chosen furniture in tans and brown were scattered around, making everything look like I'd just stepped into Pottery Barn.

You know, if Pottery Barn included screaming as their background music.

Was I just supposed to wait until Ethan was done having a nervous breakdown? I mean, what was the protocol? My stomach growled on cue, reminding me that I hadn't eaten anything all morning.

Well, maybe if I starved to death, they wouldn't have to worry about me anymore. It seemed I was causing more trouble than anything.

My teeth chattered.

Why couldn't I get warm?

With a huff, I moved away from the bed and went to stand in front of the fireplace just as the door to my bedroom jerked open, nearly coming off the hinges.

Ethan stood in the doorway, blanketed in the warmth of the fire's glow. My breath hitched in my chest, even though I tried to stop my physical response. It was impossible—and embarrassing—knowing he probably heard my racing heart.

His hair was loose from the ponytail, falling around his sharp cheekbones and jaw.

His nostrils were flared as if he smelled something horrific.

And when I opened my mouth to speak, he held up his hand and hissed at me.

Freaking hissed.

Like a cat.

I held my tongue and stared at the fire, thinking that was probably the best option for me at that point.

Get warm.

Funny, my entire life had been about rules, memorization, planning, and now I had one goal in life—to get warm and stay that way.

It was all I could allow myself to focus on. I was pretty sure if I let myself fully think about what had just happened to me, I'd have a nervous breakdown. After all, I was only human, something that was impossible to ignore with someone like Ethan standing next to me.

His fluid movement from the door to the fireplace was quick. I blinked, and he was standing next to me, holding his hands out.

I knew he could feel the heat, so I wasn't going to insult him by asking, even though it seemed like some of my studies had been clearly lacking. After all, I'd always thought vampires bit, but I had no bite marks, no recollection, nothing except blackness and the idea that his touch had been so painful I'd wanted to die.

"You are safe," he whispered in a hoarse voice. "Cassius won't be coming for you. He'd have to track you first."

"Am I untraceable now?" Now that I was his. Now that I didn't belong to myself anymore.

Ethan pulled his hand back from the air, clenching his fingertips into a tight fist. "To everyone but your mate."

"You." I closed my eyes and willed the tears to stay in. What was happening?

"Me," he confirmed.

My heart continued to race. I tried to glance at him out of the corner of my eye, but when I did, those eyes—once green—were black and still trained on me. I didn't know vampires had black eyes, didn't know any part of their physiology—outside of their fangs—changed.

"The cold will pass," he said, still staring at me.

Finally, I turned to give him my full attention, hoping it wouldn't be the last thing I did. "Why am I so cold?" My teeth chattered as if to prove a point. I hugged my arms closer to my body and got closer to the fire.

"You'll be cold until he leaves you completely," Ethan said slowly. "I marked over him... took away what I could." His hand reached out cupping my face. "Soon you'll be warm again."

"B-because you're warm?"

He dropped his hand and smirked. "Scorching."

I was swaying toward him, not even realizing it, but his hands came out and steadied me then stayed. When he touched me, I could feel his heartbeat through his fingertips; it was addicting, fascinating. I moved closer. He didn't release me. His black eyes changed to more of a gray and then finally changed back to a flashing green as I moved into his arms. It was like I had no control over my body—I just wanted to be close.

And he was so warm.

And alive.

Very much alive.

His eyes hooded.

Inches apart—our lips were almost touching. My mind screamed at me to back away, but my body told me it was exactly where I needed to be.

"You're hungry." He twirled a piece of my hair with his fingertip then sniffed it. "I'll bring you food. Under no circumstances are you to leave this room until the marking is complete."

He released my hair. His other hand fell from my arm.

And the loss was heartbreaking.

"How will I know when it's complete?" I croaked out, like any terrified prisoner would.

His face cracked into a seductive smile before he looked away and his jaw clenched. "You'll know... because you'll be so on fire for me, you'll think of nothing else. Not food, water, safety—not anything. Your only need will be me."

I gulped. "Then what happens?"

He turned and walked to the door at a normal pace, pausing only to call over his shoulder, "I give you exactly what you need."

That's what I was afraid of.

chapter
six

Genesis

I T WAS AN HOUR LATER BEFORE ANY FOOD WAS BROUGHT TO ME. I'D FOOLISHLY assumed it would be Ethan bringing food; instead, it was Alex.

I breathed a sigh of relief when he came into the room, tray of food in hand, and offered a shy smile—without the noticeable waves of seduction. Apparently, he could turn it off and on.

"Actually…" He sat the tray down on the bed and took a seat in the nearby chair. "…now that you're his mate, I could try my damnedest to seduce you, and you wouldn't feel a thing."

"Great," I croaked, reaching for a piece of toast.

"Mason cooked." Alex offered an apologetic yet radiant smile. "Word of warning, the man's been surviving on tree branches for the past twenty years, so if he's a little rusty in the kitchen, I apologize."

"Tree branches?" The toast was a bit dry, but it satisfied the hunger. I kept chewing, waiting for Alex to elaborate. Maybe he'd give me the answers I needed.

Alex propped his feet up on the bed. "His way of punishing himself, I suppose—ridiculous if you ask me. Then again, he's a werewolf, more beast than man. Who am I to judge?" His blue eyes twinkled briefly before he reached for the teakettle on my tray and poured some into one of the mugs. "Ethan didn't specify what to make for you. Sorry if we made a terrible mess out of things, but we mostly eat out every day, so there wasn't much food in the house—not to mention a vampire lives here so…"

I leaned forward, my eyes narrowing. "So he doesn't eat?"

Alex burst out laughing. "Just adorable. I may love you."

I scowled.

"Humans are funny," he said to himself more than to me. "I'd keep you if you weren't already being fought over and owned."

"I'm not a pet."

"Believe me when I say I treat my pets very well," he said in a low voice. "No complaints. Ever."

"Good for you." Arrogant much?

"Feeling the effects yet?" he asked, once I finished the toast and had moved on to the small slices of cheese and fruit. Crackers were on one side of the plate. Alex leaned forward, folding his massive hands in front of him. "A vampire's mark isn't something to be taken lightly."

"Well," I sighed, "I don't even know what the mark is, let alone what it should feel like. Apparently, I've been wrong about what I've been studying my entire life so, really, I don't know what to expect." I snorted. "You know, other than certain death if I disrespect any of you."

"That's still true," he said quickly. "With us four? Not so much. With the rest of them… keep your head down and try to say please and thank you."

"Noted."

"Fast learner."

"Survivor," I fired back.

He sighed, his smile slowly fading as did the light behind his blue eyes. "It's fifty-fifty."

"What?" I was just popping a piece of cheese into my mouth. Why did the food taste so bland? I was hungry—ravenous—so I didn't care, but it was like eating sandpaper.

"The survival rate, of course." Alex examined his fingernails then clicked his tongue. "Most humans are able to survive it, the strong ones."

"Survive what?" I clenched my teeth together as another chill wracked my body.

"The marking." His eyes narrowed. "It's made easier when your mate actually holds your damn hand through the process." I could have sworn he said ass under his breath, but it was too low to hear.

"He didn't…" I licked my lips and reached for a cracker. "He didn't want to do it though."

"Tough shit," Alex said in a louder voice, repositioning himself on the chair, dangling his legs off the side. "We've all had to make sacrifices for the greater good—this is his."

"Okay…" Feeling full and a bit sick, I put the cracker back on the plate. "And when this marking is all over… when I survive it—and believe me I will—"

Alex grinned, making me all the more irritated that he'd doubted my strength—that any of them would.

"What happens then? I'm Ethan's mate? I live to serve him, then I die? Only if Cassius doesn't ever find me?"

Alex went deathly still. "It's sad… tragic, actually… how little they tell you these days. About us. About the world and about your place in it."

"So tell me!" I pounded my fist into the pillow next to me, scaring the crap out of myself. I'd always been controlled—it had been bred into me from birth. And I'd just yelled at an immortal like he was a petulant child.

Alex grinned. "I think you'll do just fine, Genesis. Just fine." He chuckled warmly. "Try not to be too hard on us. We've been waiting for a chance to change things for a very long time… and you just may be exactly what we've been waiting for."

"I can't do anything if you don't tell me what I'm supposed to be doing!" Tears threatened, the confusion and fear back full force. "I don't know what to do. Just tell me what I'm supposed to do."

"And that's the problem right there." Alex leaned forward, sadness etched in his every feature. "Your whole life, choices have been taken from you, rather than given to you." He hung his head. "I'll do this once and only once... I'll throw you a bone, isn't that what it's called? Do you a solid? A favor? And give you one goal this evening, one thing to set your small misinformed mind toward."

I waited in anticipation.

"Survive," he said softly. "Just survive. And when the flames threaten to take you higher and higher, give in. When the heat scorches you from the inside out, when tears no longer come, when the need is all you can contemplate... you survive."

He stood and shrugged, as if he hadn't just scared the crap out of me.

"Oh, and also? It would probably be good to call for your mate..." He offered a haphazard shrug. "When it's time."

"When I'm dying?"

"Only when your need is so great for him that you've forgotten yourself completely. That's when you whisper his name. Pray to God he answers—because he still has a choice in this, and if he doesn't choose you, survival will be pointless. You. Will. Die."

A lone tear fell down my cheek before I could wipe it away

Alex reached out and captured it with his thumb. "It's been years since I've seen real tears. I hope you keep yours. I hope the gift of feeling such strong emotions remains—then again—for your sake, at the same time, I hope they don't."

He left me.

Just like that.

With shaky hands, I put the tray on the nearby table and went back to lie on the bed, freaking out, wondering when the heat was going to come, when the pain would arrive, and when I would be out of my mind for a mate who clearly didn't want me.

A mate.

Like a husband.

Rejection washed over me.

I would never get *normal*.

Never have a family.

And most likely never have the type of love I'd always secretly wanted—it had all been stripped away from me the day I'd walked into that room. And a part of me hated my family for not telling me the truth about what I was about to do.

My mom had smiled.

And she'd probably known it was a death sentence.

I tried not to dwell on it—tried to stay positive—so I focused on what Alex said.

Survival.

I counted the seconds, the minutes as they turned into hours, and when the clock struck midnight out in the hall, I thought that maybe I would be different, maybe whatever was happening to me wasn't going to be as bad as both Alex and Ethan had warned.

Then the heat started in my toes.

I welcomed it because I'd been so cold all day.

It spread from my toes up my legs, warming me up like a blanket; by the time it reached my thighs, it was uncomfortable. I started throwing covers off me, but it didn't help.

Fire reached my chest, making it hard to breathe.

And when it touched my lips, it was like someone had placed coal in my mouth.

I cried out.

But no sound came.

I pounded my chest; the motion made the heat worse. I didn't think it could get more painful.

But it did. I glanced at the clock again.

It was two minutes past midnight.

And I already wanted to die.

The pain skyrocketed; I reared back, hitting my head on the headboard. Another surge of scorching heat flared.

The door opened, but my vision was blurred. It was hard to see who had come in.

It wasn't until he lay down on the bed next to me and grabbed my hand that I could focus on the form.

Mason.

As a werewolf.

Or a very large dog.

His eyes were sad.

And when I cried out again, he pulled me into his arms and squeezed while my body convulsed.

chapter
seven

Genesis

HE WAS BEAUTIFUL. LONG BROWN HAIR CASCADED PAST HIS SHOULDERS—PART OF IT was braided. Pieces fell by his perfectly sculpted face.

He smiled. His green eyes illuminated my whole world.

I reached for him, but each time my hands lifted, the burning was worse, so I learned to keep them behind me.

A sword was clasped in his right hand. He slid the blade across his left hand and held it in the air as blood dripped in slow motion onto the ground.

It was red until it touched the ground, turning into the same green I saw in his eyes. The green liquid seeped into the ground, nourishing it, causing grass and flowers to take root.

I gasped, reaching again.

The pain was too much.

He closed his eyes and cut again.

No! I tried yelling, but my voice simply didn't exist.

He continued, letting his blood spill around his feet. Hours went by, or maybe it was minutes. Soon an entire forest grew around us. I sighed in relief as the shield of the trees shaded me from the sun. The heat dissipated.

Only to return when Ethan looked at me again.

He turned and, in an instant, was in front of me, his black shirt open midway to his muscled chest.

We were in our own forest.

It started to rain.

I turned my face up, welcoming the cold.

But the raindrops weren't cold.

They were hot—searing hot.

The trees weren't protecting me anymore. I reached for Ethan, but he moved back. My need for shelter outweighed my need for him.

The scene changed. And suddenly I was standing near a river; he was on the other side.

I wanted him—I wanted the water more.

I tried jumping in, but each time I made a movement toward the water instead of him, the pain was unbearable.

With a silent sob, I fell to my knees.

When I looked up, Ethan was standing over me; he'd somehow made it past the river.

"When it's me you cry for—the pain ends."

I shook my head, fighting his words.

Because they meant the end of me. I knew it in my soul. If I gave in to the heat, if I gave in to him, if I ignored my basic human needs—I wouldn't be human anymore.

I would be fully reliant on a strange being who didn't want me to begin with.

"Stop fighting it!" he roared.

I shook my head as heat consumed my body.

We were back in the throne room.

Cassius stood over me, his cold stare haunting. "And you still choose him? When I could give you relief?"

"Genesis, NO!" Ethan roared, but I couldn't see him.

All I could see, all I could feel was relief in Cassius's presence.

My body shook.

Cassius grinned, moving closer and closer to me.

The lesser of two evils.

Ethan.

I reared back; the heat got worse. I continued stepping backward until I was falling.

I landed in his arms.

His body was warm, not too hot, just warm enough to make me feel more comfortable.

"Genesis," Ethan whispered, his mouth near my ear. "Don't fight it."

"Don't…" I fought to get the words out. "Want. Me."

His eyes flashed green, and then his mouth was on mine.

It was like ice.

And all I saw was him.

All I wanted was him.

All I could think about was him.

As our heartbeats and breathing synced in perfect cadence with one another. I tugged his head harder toward mine—greedy for his lips, needing so desperately to taste him I thought I'd die.

With a cry I jolted awake from the dream.

To find myself not in Mason's arms—but Ethan's.

Completely.

Naked.

chapter
eight

Genesis

I IMMEDIATELY TRIED TO RECOIL, ASHAMED, EMBARRASSED, AND HORRIFIED THAT I was in his arms without any clothes on. As if sensing my thoughts, Ethan looked away, jaw clenched. "You were taking them off."

"I was hot!" I yelled, happy that my voice was back but still shaking from the pain. It was still there—the searing heat—but it was bearable.

"I had it under control," a voice said from the corner.

I pulled the blankets and covered myself as Mason stepped out of the shadows, now looking like his normal self.

"You didn't need to interfere, Ethan."

"She's. Not. Yours." Ethan hissed.

"Now you claim me," I mumbled.

His jaw popped, as if he'd been trying to clench his teeth but had overdone it and nearly dislocated his entire face. "If you would have given in right away, your clothing wouldn't have been an issue!"

"So it's my fault." My lower lip trembled. "Is that what you're saying?"

"Damn it, Ethan." Mason made his way to the bed and threw another blanket over my body. I'd completely forgotten I was still naked—and arguing—probably because I was still so hot. "Just leave."

"She's my mate." Ethan released me but didn't leave his position next to me on the bed.

Mason hung his head. Dark circles framed his eyes. "Then do what's best for her. Just leave her be."

"If I leave, the marking won't be complete."

"She's been through enough this evening. Let her rest before the final stage. I think it's the least you can do... considering."

Ethan hung his head and whispered, "For my sacrifice... I'm the bad one in this scenario?"

"You became the bad one in this scenario the minute you heard your mate's screams and didn't come running. Now get out." Mason growled the last part so loud my ears started to ring.

Ethan cursed and stomped toward the door, leaving me.

I learned something in that instant.

He was a jerk.

No, he was a selfish ass.

But I missed him.

And I hated both him and myself because he'd turned away, and I needed him to be close.

My body yearned for him.

And the heat returned full force; I threw off the blanket then panicked and grabbed it again.

"I'm not going to seduce another immortal's mate." Mason rolled his eyes, "Just... try to stay still."

"If I close my eyes," I whispered. "Will I keep dreaming... things?"

Mason nodded slowly. "It's part of the process. The pain will come and go three times in the next twelve hours. You survived the first. Now you have two more."

"And Ethan?" My body shook with fear.

"Is an ass." Mason shrugged. "But I'll be here. I've seen worse, believe me. When my..." His voice died, and with it, his eyes closed. "Never mind. Just know, it will pass, and when you open your eyes, I'll be here. With water."

"And a margarita," I added, thinking that next to Ethan it sounded like the best thing in the world.

Mason burst out laughing. "I'll see what I can do." His eyes flickered to the clock by the bed. "You have five more minutes."

"You'll be here?" I asked in a weak voice.

He studied me, frowning before giving a firm nod. "I swear it."

"Thank you." I closed my eyes and lay back against the pillows, waiting for the next wave.

I expected Mason to stay put.

Instead, he lay down next to me and grabbed my hand. "You won't break me."

The last thing he whispered, "Sweet dreams," was funny because I knew that the next few hours would be nothing but nightmares and wanting something I knew I could never have.

chapter
nine

Ethan

THE PAIN WAS UNBEARABLE—BECAUSE IT WAS A REMINDER OF WHY I HATED MY entire existence—why I had a reason to hate.

Cassius.

Didn't it always come back to him? After all, it had started with him. Or maybe it had just started with Ara.

Another shudder wracked my body. Bones felt like they were twisting around one another before suddenly resetting themselves over and over again.

I felt her pain.

Because she was a part of me now.

So her pain was my pain.

Only for me, it was worse.

Because it was the second time in my existence I'd experienced it—when it was only supposed to be experienced once. Immortals mated for life. That was, unless someone or something intervened.

Hands shaking, I took another drink of blood. It did nothing, or maybe it did, and I was just too bitter to allow it to heal me.

She'd been naked, inconsolable, and I'd left her.

With Mason, of all creatures. My best friend, the only being other than Alex that I trusted.

My body convulsed. Falling to my knees in front of the fireplace in my room, I lifted my head to the ceiling and listened for her cries.

It was going to be a long evening.

Made longer because I'd refused to give her what she needed to make it better. I'd thought I could do it when I walked out of that room, smug as shit. I had thought I could do it.

But the pain had been too much.

The reminder.

And then the visions I'd shared with her—too personal. She'd seen Ara. She knew the shame that consumed me—or would soon know. There would be no secrets between us, and in order for the mating to continue, I had to make sure that I completely marked her, possessed her, made her mine.

It was the last thing I'd expected this morning when the number had been called.

It had been a normal day.

As normal as my life had been for the past century.

And then Cassius had breathed her name… *Genesis*. And my world stopped.

His eyes had gone completely white, and then the bastard had smirked at me, like he knew the future before the present had even happened.

It was impossible to describe the need I'd felt when I walked into that throne room. I'd heard her heartbeat on the other side of the door and had given a shaky nod to Alex, who'd seemed more amused than upset at our new circumstances.

Let Cassius have another one—and fail.

Or steal her.

Fifty years ago, I had given up my request for a breeder, as had Mason. The bond hadn't lasted like it was supposed to, and even though the bliss we'd felt at the hands of the humans we bonded with was incomparable, they'd always died.

Every. Single. Time.

And we'd been the ones left to bury them.

I could bite her and hope that she'd be the one human to finally change things.

The last one had lived past one hundred and fifty—Mason's mate. We'd thought it had worked—had thanked God.

Until he'd awoken with a corpse.

I'd already lived through enough death and betrayal, and now it seemed my existence was on repeat.

"Damn it, Ethan!" Alex stomped into the room. "Could you at least hold her hand?"

"And what? Squeeze it so hard I break every fragile bone in her pathetic body?" I hissed. "Is that what you want?"

He hung his head. "She's stronger than that."

"Is she?" I snorted out a laugh. "That's what we said about the last one."

"Who lived longer than the rest," Alex pointed out. "Look, all I'm saying is there's something very wrong about having Mason up there consoling the human when she's not even his mate, when… he may have to kill her before it's complete. I can't watch him go through loss again. He's known her for less than a day, and already he's like a kicked puppy."

"Tell him that…" I stared into the fire. "…and you'll get your throat ripped out—again."

"Once. He did that once." Alex elbowed me and took a position in front of the fire. "You did what you had to do."

"Right." My voice sounded hollow, funny, because I felt hollow, like an empty shell. "And now I'm bonded—to someone I don't love. Tell me, how does that work out in all those romance novels Stephanie likes to read?"

Alex ignored me as another one of Genesis's screams rocked the mansion. She was transitioning, meaning, for a human, she would be going into an absolute frenzy to be with me. I should be pleased.

I wasn't.

I wasn't that type of vampire.

One who feasted on the lust of others.

It was a trick—like magic. The mating caused her physical body to want me in ways that were indescribable, but she still had full control over her mind. And wasn't that the horrible part?

I could own her body.

I had to earn her heart.

"You're the only being alive who's pissed about having meaningless sex," Alex said in a low voice.

"Siren," I hissed, "you base your life on meaningless sex."

"And my blood pressure's way lower," he joked.

"Not laughing."

"It was kind of funny," he mumbled. "Look, just… hold her again. Maybe it will help things along. You'll sure as hell feel better. I'll sleep better. Mason won't have to kill her because she doesn't make it through, and Cassius won't end up finding her. We win."

"But do we?" I spoke the question we'd been asking ourselves for years upon years. "How long do we repeat the process? How long does the madness continue?"

Alex was silent.

Another scream.

I winced and braced myself against the mantel, nearly prying it from its place on the wall.

Alex shook his head. "If it's this bad for you—imagine how bad it is for her. She's human, Ethan. She could die. Or is that what you want? To take it all back? Would you… let her die? Just because you're afraid of what happens if she lives?"

"Take it back!" I roared; my hand crumpled the wood and tossed it into the fire.

"Fear isn't welcome here," he mocked.

I punched him in the jaw.

He went flying across the room, slamming into the wall, before chuckling and regaining his balance. "That all you got?"

"Don't tempt me to end you."

"Like you could," he spat. "Now do your job, Ethan. Go to her."

A piercing scream had me catching my breath, holding my hand to my chest.

Alex looked heavenward and swore.

"Fine," I barked. "I'll hold her—again. But you know what you ask, if that much physical contact is made? I'll be lost to her."

Alex's smile fell from his face. "You've been lost to her from the minute Cassius uttered her name. Don't for one second think otherwise. Now go to her, before you give her to Cassius like before."

"Leave," I barked. "And never speak of that again."

Alex held up his hands and stomped out of the room.

While my heart decided to ram against my ribs so hard I had to fight to catch a breath again.

Slowly, I made my way up to her room. The screams were getting louder and louder, but the closer my body was the less the pain.

Finally, when I entered the room, it was to see Mason pacing a hole through the damn floor and pulling at his overly long hair.

"Leave us," I whispered in a hoarse voice.

Mason paused, tilted his head, and smirked, "Careful, humans do break."

"I can be gentle."

He barked out a laugh. "You drove your fist into a granite countertop when we ran out of wine last week."

I rolled my eyes and pointed to the door.

chapter
ten

Genesis

OOL WATER TOUCHED MY LIPS. GREEDILY, I REACHED OUT, MY HANDS coming into contact with the glass and something else warm. I drank as much as I could and then slowly opened my eyes.

Ethan.

My heart clenched in my chest. Was he back to make fun of me? Watch me suffer only to leave again? I recoiled, the pain started to subside enough that I didn't want to actually kill myself.

Apparently, I'd asked Mason to do just that a few times.

"Sorry..." Ethan mumbled, setting the glass down on the table. "If I stay, it will be... easier."

It didn't feel easier.

It felt hot.

Not exactly painful, but hot to the point that my body kept telling me if I only scooted a little bit closer to him, I'd be okay. If only he'd tilt his head a fraction of an inch and kiss me—the pain would dissipate completely. I was at war with my own body, and I hated him for causing it—for bonding with me without even asking if it was okay first.

Not that I'd had a lot of options once my number had been called.

And once Cassius had marked me.

I'd dreamt of him again.

Of his cool lips. I'd reached out, but the minute my hands had come into contact with his body, I'd been jolted awake by Mason.

His words had been clear. *"Never, under any circumstances touch Cassius."* Even in my dreams.

Weird.

A shudder wracked my body. Ethan let out a curse then wrapped his arm around me. His skin was hot to the touch, but it still comforted me. I ducked my head under his arm and let out a heavy sigh as another wave of pain shot from my toes all the way up to my head, causing a splitting headache.

I turned into his body—not really in control of my own actions—just knowing that he would make it better.

He shifted next to me, pulling me closer.

"So..." His voice was hoarse. "Tell me about... school."

"What?" I gasped, my voice sounded like I'd spent the night screaming at a concert. "School?"

"Yeah, your studies… about immortals. Tell me about it."

"Immortals suck." I sighed. "If I disrespect you enough, will you kill me?"

His lips twitched as if he was fighting a smile. "Not now, no. It would be like killing myself."

"And that's supposed to deter me from wanting certain death?"

This time he did smile. "What did you learn about mating?"

"There was no mating chapter." My hand pressed against his chest. What was I doing? My fingers ducked into the V of his white shirt, pressing against his warm skin. I wanted to taste him. Why?

"Hmm…" His free hand moved to cover mine and slowly peel it from his body. "That's unfortunate."

"Yeah." I jerked my hand away from his and placed it against his skin again. It felt too good, and I was so sick and tired of feeling pain.

He hissed out a breath and closed his eyes, leaning his head back against the headboard. "You have one more transition before the bond is complete. Your body will crave mine… but it doesn't have to mean anything."

"Huh?" I was too distracted by the curve of his full mouth to hear all the words coming out of it. His lips were so full and inviting. I leaned forward.

Ethan kept my body pinned so I couldn't move. The more I squirmed against him the more irritated he looked. His eyes were so green and captivating it seemed like they were glowing.

"Not this way," he whispered. "When you come to me… fully as yourself. When your love for me and only me blots out any sort of physical need you have—that's when I'll give in."

"And if that never happens?" I fought against him; I just wanted a taste, and I didn't even like him. It made no sense.

He shrugged. "Wouldn't be the first time."

I closed my eyes and tried to focus on the pain rather than on him… because when I focused on him, I hated myself a little bit more.

"Questions—" he choked out. "I know you have questions… so ask."

"Can't…" I shook my head. His voice was so pretty, so deep. What would it feel like to be with him? Just once. He'd make the pain go away; he'd make everything better. If I could just touch him more, taste him. My body strained toward his. "I can't stop thinking about you."

"Flattered," he said dryly. "Try."

"But—"

"Favorite color."

"What?" My eyes jerked open. "Did you just ask me my favorite color?"

He smirked. "Tell me it's green."

I rolled my eyes, some of the need dying a bit at his arrogance. "White."

His nostrils flared. "Cassius would be pleased."

"Not because of Cassius," I said in a soft voice. "Because white's like a blank slate. It means starting over."

"You wish…" He swallowed, his head tilting to the side, pieces of dark hair falling across his sculpted face. "…to start over?"

"I wish I would have run…" My body trembled as more heat invaded my stomach. "…when they called my number."

His smile made my stomach clench. "You can't run from destiny."

"I could have tried."

"You would have failed," he said in an amused tone. "And you would have most likely died at Cassius's hand for trying."

"Why did he mark me? How did he mark me?"

Ethan sighed. "His touch… if he touches any part of you, it marks you. He has to will it to happen, so it's a switch he can turn on and off. All of the Dark Ones can. He touched your shoulder, infused your body. It never takes much from a Dark One. They're… powerful."

I nodded my head, remembering the sting of cold that hit me when Cassius had touched my shoulder. "And the only way to take the marking away?"

"Is to cover it up." Ethan clenched his teeth. "Or in this case… infuse you with my essence."

"Your essence is strong enough to do that?" My teeth clenched together in pain. The heat from my stomach had traveled to my mouth. I eyed the water greedily.

Ethan lifted it to my lips. "Only if I'm without a mate…"

I sipped the liquid and took a breath. "You had a mate."

"Had," Ethan repeated.

I didn't push him; if there was one thing I'd learned, it was that when his eyes glowed, it wasn't because he was in a particularly happy mood. Water dripped from my chin; he caught it with his fingertip and brought it to his lips.

"You taste…" He closed his eyes. "…heavenly."

"Did you bite me?" I blurted.

He dropped his finger from his mouth and smirked. "You'd know if I bit you."

"So what did you do?"

"Shared my blood with you… the old fashioned way. With a knife."

"But wouldn't it have been easier to—"

"Biting is too personal," he finished, "intimate… not something shared with strangers."

"Or humans?" I asked.

"Or that."

"But Mason bit me."

"Mason has a different way of doing things, and, not that it matters, but his bite wasn't one of mating. It was done to try to cover up Cassius's mark, nothing more."

"So…" I pulled myself away from him; I was starting to get too hot again. "You've saved me… to what end?"

Ethan's eyes turned very serious as he whispered, "Hopefully, one day… you'll be able to return the favor. And save us."

chapter
e l e v e n

Ethan

HER EYEBROWS DREW TOGETHER IN WHAT I COULD ONLY ASSUME WAS frustration. Her heart started to race, and then her eyes dilated as she glanced at my mouth again. If she did that one more time, I was going to lose my mind. I was already trying desperately to keep her from touching me too much. Because it affected me, as much as I wanted to deny it, to deny her.

Her physical contact was everything I'd been craving.

Giving in would be easy.

Staying away would be hard.

But traveling down that road again—knowing how it was likely to end— well, I wasn't so sure I would survive it. I was immortal, but my heart was still fragile.

And when it broke…

As an immortal, I suffered with unimaginable pain. Pain I never wanted to experience again, thus the reason for keeping myself firmly tucked away from the weak little human with the pretty smile.

I liked her hair.

It was gold, not really brown, not blond—just gold. The firelight made certain pieces glow. It was tempting to grab it, to sniff it, to wrap it around my fingers and imagine what she'd be like in the throes of passion.

"Ethan…" My name on her lips was ecstasy. I shook the thought away and tried to appear indifferent.

"Yes?"

"I can't save anyone… I can't even save myself."

"You're stronger than you think," I encouraged. "Trust me."

"That's just it." She tugged her lower lip into her mouth and chewed, her dark blue eyes sad. "You've given me no reason to."

"You're alive," I pointed out. "That's reason enough."

"He's not the best at comforting humans," came Alex's voice from the door. I could hear the amusement in his tone.

I rolled my eyes and turned, ready to bark at him to leave.

"Cassius called," Alex said in a bored tone. "Wanted to know if I know where the human is."

"And?"

"I lied." Alex rolled his eyes. "Of course."

"And he didn't believe you?"

"Naturally." Alex examined his fingernails and shrugged. "So I told him you'd trapped her in your lair and were having your way with her."

Genesis let out a little whimper and ran her hands down my chest again.

I clenched my teeth and hissed out a breath. "Could we not discuss this now?"

Alex held up his hands. "Just thought you should know… he isn't pleased that you've bonded with her. I lied and said it was complete."

"He'll still try to take her, regardless." I licked my lips and tried to focus on Alex rather than the fact that Genesis was drawing circles on my chest, making me want to lean into her, capture her lips and suck.

"Yup." Alex grinned as he watched the scene in front of him like it was some hilarious movie and not my life. "So, this looks cozy."

"Was there anything else?" I barked.

"Complete the mating." He nodded. "At least then her eyes will be opened fully… and we can see if this was all worth it."

Genesis let out a moan. Heat shot through my body, slicing me nearly in half. She was transitioning into the final phase.

Alex had the good sense to look like he felt sorry for her before nodding his head again and shutting the door.

"Please!" Genesis begged, gripping my shirt with both of her hands. Her eyes rolled to the back of her head. "Make it stop, please! It's so hot."

It was about to get worse.

The final stage always was.

Like taking knives from a fire and slicing up your body. I'd always been told that during this stage, humans dreamt of Death.

And because of that fact, Death visited them, beckoned them, and many, took his outstretched hand and never woke up.

"Listen…" I cupped her face with my hands. "…focus on me… not the pain. It's almost over."

"And you'll be here?" Her body started to convulse as my blood merged with hers. The same blood I'd shared with her when I'd marked her. "P-promise?"

"Yes."

Her eyes flashed green, mimicking mine.

"I won't leave your side."

"My mouth…" She shook her head violently, her lips swollen from the heat. "…hurts."

I pressed my mouth to hers gently and then pierced the skin of her upper lip, relieving the pressure of the blood in her system—my blood fighting hers as it should, her blood refusing to give up as it should.

Humans always tasted the same—like life—like earth mixed with sugar. It was addicting. I'd always thought it was too sweet.

But she tasted perfect.

"More..." She tugged at my shirt again.

I kissed her again, this time slanting my mouth over where my fangs had dug into her tender skin.

I was old.

Able to control myself.

At least that was what I said when I kissed her a third time, this time more passionately. And when she clung to me like I was her only chance at survival, I wanted to roar with excitement. It was the bond.

Nothing more.

I kissed her harder.

Her nails dug into my skin.

"Fight it, Genesis." I was speaking to myself as much as I was to her. I needed to fight it too... because I knew firsthand there was nothing worse than mating with someone, wanting someone so badly, and thinking it was love.

And realizing it was nothing but a very pretty lie.

Her head dropped back, exposing her full neck.

Sweat dripped from her face down her neck as another stab of pain hit me and her in the chest.

She was fighting it.

But she was also fighting me.

She had spirit.

I only hoped that when death visited her in her dreams, she wouldn't take his cold lifeless hand.

Because maybe I could never love her. Maybe she could never love me. But I respected her strength.

And in all my years—I was beginning to think maybe it was time to have a friend I could at least share the loneliness with.

A real mate.

She screamed.

And blacked out.

I pulled her into my lap and kissed her forehead. She moved against me and then stopped.

Her body went ice cold.

Death was visiting.

All I could do was wait.

chapter
twelve

Genesis

I FELT ETHAN NEXT TO ME. I WANTED TO ASK HIM WHAT WAS HAPPENING NEXT, why my body was suddenly cold—why everything felt numb—but I couldn't open my eyes.

I was trapped in darkness.

"So," a low whispery voice spoke into the darkness, "will you stay or will you go?"

"What?" I spoke into the darkness, unable to see anything around me. White smoke suddenly appeared in front of me, and then a hand reached out through the smoke.

"Will you come with me? Allow me to ease all your pain? Or will you stay?"

The hand looked so welcoming.

The closer it came to my body the more I wanted to take it.

But I could still feel Ethan, and leaving him… felt so wrong. My body shuddered at the thought.

"Choose," the voice commanded.

I didn't want to choose. I just wanted to go back to my normal existence, where I went to Starbucks in the mornings and did homework in the afternoons.

Those days were long gone.

"Choose," it said, louder this time.

I swayed toward the hand.

But something held me back.

The pain flared again—unbearable—as if someone had stabbed me in the heart.

"I can take it all away," the voice soothed. "Just take my hand."

Was I crazy? To choose the pain over this man's hand? Over what I was sure would be complete and total peace?

Ethan meant pain.

And as much as I hated him in that instant—I needed him… even if it meant pain.

It was his eyes.

They reflected what I felt in my own body—in my soul.

He was suffering, just like me, only it was a different kind of suffering, one that I'm sure had to do with the vision I'd seen of him and the woman.

"Choose!" the voice boomed.

I stepped backward and wrapped my hands around my body. "Him. I choose him."

The cloud disappeared, revealing a man who looked a lot like Cassius. I wasn't sure if he was a Dark One, but the air around him seemed to freeze in place. I shivered.

His eyes flashed white.

So he was a Dark One.

His teeth were shaped like tiny knives.

"It won't be easy," *he spoke softly,* "choosing life."

"It shouldn't be easy…" *I found my voice.* "…to choose death."

He smiled, bowed his head, and disappeared.

The pain in my chest spread to my back. I arched, and then everything stopped. The pain, the heat, my heart slowed.

And I blinked my eyes open.

Ethan hovered over me in a shielding stance, almost like he was protecting me from someone coming into the room and knifing me in my sleep. His eyes were black.

"I…" My voice sounded groggy, foreign to my ears. "I think it's done."

His eyes slowly faded to gray and then green. "You chose me." His voice cracked.

"Well…" I licked my lips, just looking at his mouth at my body, yearning for his touch. "It was either you or the guy with the creepy voice."

Ethan's delicious mouth broke out into a smile. "Does that mean you don't find me creepy?"

I examined the fangs protruding over his plump lips. "You're a different kind of creepy."

He leaned back on his knees and pulled me up so I was in a sitting position. "Didn't think you'd wake up spouting compliments and poetry." He sighed. "It's almost complete."

"Almost?" I croaked. "I have to go through more pain?"

"No…" His eyes flashed. "…just pleasure."

"Wha—"

His mouth was on my neck before I had a chance to utter any more words. His tongue twisted and pushed against the base of my throat.

I bucked off the bed as a sweet sensation of euphoria washed over me.

When he pulled back, his eyes were so bright green it hurt to stare directly at him. "Now that… was me biting you."

"Yeah…" I managed to push the word past my stunned lips. "It was."

He moved off the bed at epic speed and was already at the door when I blinked for a second time. "Stephanie will be in to help you shower and dress. We'll discuss your… duties… when you've regained some of your strength."

"Wait!" I blurted.

He paused at the door, his hands digging into the wood. "Yes?"

"Am I still human?"

He burst out laughing and turned. "Of course... still weak, still fragile, still very much... human."

"Oh..." I nodded, my studies of vampires were clearly lacking since I'd learned that a bite could turn you or worse, kill you. "...that's good, right?"

"Depends on who you ask, I suppose." He shrugged and shut the door softly behind him.

I was too tired to focus on what that cryptic sentence may have meant and didn't have time to mull it over like I typically would because Stephanie burst through that same door two minutes later yelling, "You lived!"

Did that mean she'd thought I would die?

"Good for you." She nodded. "Things are finally looking up!" She clapped her hands and dropped a set of clothes onto the nearby chair. "Let's get you showered and looking your best so you can start producing little vampire babies."

I felt my stomach drop. "Wh-what?"

"It was a joke." She winked. "Well, the vampire babies part. Now, let's get you feeling better. I'll have Alex in here a bit later to stabilize you and—"

"Stabilize me?" I repeated. "What?"

"It's what he does." She nodded. "He's a siren—makes girls feel calm when all they want to do is pull their hair out and scream. I'd do it, but it only works on men... thus the need for him to do it. Don't worry though. It's like taking a Xanax, only it feels way better."

"I don't want to feel drugged," I mumbled, my body aching in places I didn't know even existed. "I think right now I just want a shower."

Stephanie shifted on her feet. "He didn't hurt you... did he?"

Well, my physical body was intact, but my heart was really confused. Did it hurt? No, but something felt wrong. Like I should be happy, elated even, rather than depressed and rejected.

"No," I finally answered. "I'm great."

"Good." She exhaled. "Now, about that shower."

chapter
thirteen

Ethan

I STILL TASTED HER BLOOD ON MY LIPS, WAS EMBARRASSED FOR THE FIRST TIME IN A century when Alex glanced up from his spot at the kitchen table to see me licking my lips like I'd just devoured the poor girl.

He shook his head. "Been that long, huh?"

"Alex..." I closed my eyes and prayed for patience. "...remind me why I let you live here?"

"I'm good-looking," he answered simply. "Besides, I'm a hell of a fighter—scrappy, I think is how you define my kind. You need me."

"Stop." I pressed my fingertips to my temples and rubbed. The ache to have her had consumed me so much that I'd run down the stairs moving so fast I'd nearly collided with a wall, and grabbed blood from the fridge.

I didn't need it.

But I craved it.

And if I didn't drink the donated blood, I sure as hell was going to drain her and enjoyed very last drop.

"I wonder..." Alex's voice pierced my thoughts. "What's it like?" He leaned forward. "Having to learn self-control all over again... being as ancient as you are?"

I ignored him.

He kept talking.

"Blood-free for a century and now..." He grinned and licked his lips. "Kind of like falling off the wagon, yeah?"

"You're giving me a headache." I threw the empty bag of blood at his face. He moved to the side and snickered. "And I'm fine. Everything is just—"

Her smell was intoxicating. She was walking down the stairs, so her heart picked up speed, her body giving off a scent of burnt vanilla and oranges with a hint of sugar. My mouth literally watered.

"Fine?" Alex said in a mocking voice. "Was that what you were going to say? Damn, man show a little decorum, you look... starved."

"I am," I whispered and fought the urge to rock back and forth. That was the problem with mating—with bonding. Nothing tasted like her, nothing ever would, and typically, having her as my mate gave me full access.

But the more I took...

The stronger the bond.

And the more I wanted…

It was a vicious overwhelming cycle. It would lead me to become emotionally invested while she, as a human, could simply pretend.

It wasn't fair.

Immortals, in essence, were cursed with a deep desire to be like a human—to possess them, to bond with them forever—while humans only felt the same draw to us if they actually loved us.

Ridiculous.

"Oh, there you are." Stephanie pushed Genesis forward and pulled out a chair.

Slowly, Genesis took a seat and glared at each one of us. "Where's Mason?"

It shouldn't have pissed me off.

But it had.

"He's none of your concern," I spat.

"Easy!" Alex chuckled. "Rule number one, don't ask your mate where the other dude is. Just… don't."

Genesis blinked at Alex then back at me. "Because you guys have the capacity for jealousy."

Alex whistled while Stephanie laughed.

Immortals were the most jealous beings on the planet. Had her school taught her nothing?

Was I to be her tutor as well?

"So…" Alex trained his eyes on her, putting her at as much ease as he could without stopping her poor heart. "Now that the mating is complete, you get to learn all about us and service your man here." He slapped my back.

Really. Really. Poor choice of words.

Genesis paled.

I rolled my eyes. "He's kidding."

Alex laughed. "I think it needs to be said that having a human at the house has already helped my mood immensely."

"That makes one of you," Genesis said under her breath.

Alex leaned forward and whispered, "Ethan, try not to be so grouchy. Keep the fangs in and all."

I extended them just to prove a point.

Genesis recoiled.

I instantly felt guilty.

Damn it.

"You won't…" I licked my lips. "You won't have to service me, as Alex so delicately put it."

"Is that what mates do?" Genesis asked, her eyes searching mine. "They…" She lifted her hands into the air and dropped them.

"If that's what you think they do, we have a very big problem." Alex mimicked her movements and winked.

She blushed.

I hissed at him and returned my attention to her. "It's like a human relationship, only stronger. You'll attend functions with me, be by my side, at my beck and call for as long as you live."

I didn't want to say until one day she just didn't wake up. It sounded too cruel.

"And when I'm bored out of my mind… I do what?" She crossed her arms. "I mean, what could you possibly need from me?"

"Adorable." Alex sighed happily. "I'm so glad we kept her."

"Alex…" I was two seconds away from slamming him into the nearest wall. "Make yourself useful and find our human a snack."

"I'm not a pet!" Genesis yelled. "And I'm not your human!"

"You are," I yelled right back, "mine!"

"Kids." Stephanie stepped between us.

I didn't even realize I'd gotten out of the chair and was towering over her, fangs out, hands raised. She'd turned me into a monster. And still, my eyes found her erratic pulse. One more taste…

"Ethan—" Stephanie pushed against my chest. I didn't move. "Ethan!"

"Friend…" Mason walked into the room. "Sit your ass down before she hands it to you."

"Like she could!" I roared.

"Like I have!" Stephanie pushed me again. "Don't tempt me… again."

I sat, while Mason made his way over to Genesis and offered an easy smile. The man had nothing to smile about, yet he was smiling—at my mate.

I growled.

Mason gave me the finger and kept his attention trained on Genesis. "How do you feel?"

"Better." She returned his smile and squeezed his outstretched hand. "Thanks for not… killing me when I asked."

"Damn…" Alex said from the kitchen.

"You were in pain." Mason shrugged. "And I'm glad you're alright."

"She's fine. We're fine. Everything's fine," I said through clenched teeth. "Now it's probably time to give her answers before she thinks she can run off and actually survive in the real world without being hunted by a Dark One, or worse, found by Cassius."

"He isn't all bad," Stephanie said defensively.

We all glared at her.

"What?" She lifted her hands into the air. "I'm just saying he's been trying as hard as we have. So what if he's gotten a bit possessive over the last few numbers that have been called."

Alex slammed his fist onto the table. "He stole Ethan's—"

"Enough." I held up my hand. The pain in my chest grew until it was hard to breathe. I knew what would take that pain away.

Genesis.

But I was too angry to ask for it. Too ashamed to fall to my knees in front of a mere mortal and beg for her to end the pain by allowing me one solitary drop of her blood.

As if on cue, another bag of blood hit me in the head.

Alex must have sensed my mood.

I bit into it and looked away from Genesis's horrified expression.

"Lesson time." Alex placed some fruit and cheese in front of Genesis and clapped his hands. "Who goes first?"

Nobody said anything.

Genesis cleared her throat. "Maybe if you'll start by telling me what our real job is... as human breeders. All my life I've been taught a lie and now... well, now I'd really like to know how this all started and what my place is."

Overwhelming her with information just might kill her. It would be like telling a child that her existence was simply for the pleasure of the parent, that she meant nothing in the grand scheme of things.

"The numbers," Mason cleared his throat, "have been called for centuries. It used to be every year, then it went to every two years, every decade—you know the trend. The last human number called was fifty years ago." His face contorted like he was going to change shape, but he gained control over himself. "Immortals, as we've said before, cannot simply procreate. They need humans in order for the process to be complete. Basically, human men and women help immortals continue to populate the planet. If the balance is somehow... broken, then chaos erupts, thus the need for humans. The balance is very important for both our races."

"Okay." Genesis, nodded her head slowly. "So why wait fifty years?"

You could hear a pin drop in that room.

I didn't want to answer.

Mason kicked me under the table. I glowered in his direction then said as gently as I could, "Because immortals become attached to their humans in a very... possessive way. They mate for life... it's a beautiful thing, but the human always has the choice to reject their mate." *Even after they've bonded*, but I wasn't going to say that aloud lest she reject me. "If the mating is completed, both parties happy, babies are born into the world, and everyone lives happily ever after—that's fantastic, but recently, humans started... dying."

"That's what we generally do." Genesis's eyes narrowed. "We don't live forever."

"After giving birth to an immortal, you should. You used to." Mason explained. "It's life's final gift... immortality for your sacrifice to us. But somehow, along the way, it stopped working."

"Oh." Genesis glanced at me.

I looked away. Not wanting her to see my pain.

"And how does Cassius fit into all of this?" she asked.

"The Dark Ones don't mate. They don't bond in the way we do. When they infuse a human mate, it's too strong for the humans to handle it, but he was... or we were... for a while, experimenting with the idea. Thinking we were possibly losing our powers. He's been taking humans... to see if he can reverse it, but along the way he became..." I sighed. "...addicted."

"What?" Genesis shook her head. "To what exactly?"

"He's part angel... part human," Mason said in a low voice. "His human counterpart wants desperately to join with humanity again—but his angelic essence won't let him. He's stuck in hell. But when a Dark One infuses a human, for those blissful weeks they last, life is perfect. Cassius is convinced if he only found the right human, he could bond eternally."

"And that was me?" Genesis croaked. "Or he thought it was me?"

Because of her marking.

Because of her name.

The beginning. Her name meant the beginning. And our prophecies specifically stated that a woman's number would be called who represented a fresh start.

A new beginning.

Cassius wanted her for his own selfish reasons.

The rest of the immortals wanted her so mates would stop dying, children would no longer be motherless or fatherless.

I kept my groan inside. It was even harder for the men. The minute they bonded with an immortal woman their original chemical makeup ceased to exist, relying solely on their immortal wives for nutrients, their organs simply started shutting down only days after the bond was complete.

I wanted to believe my own reasons weren't selfish.

But with each breath she took, each beat of her heart, I realized I was more selfish than Cassius, because, as of right now, I wouldn't give her up—even if it meant war. Even if it meant the end of my own people—my existence.

For being as old as I was, retraining myself wasn't going to be easy. Keeping emotional barriers between us would be necessary because my body screamed for her.

chapter
fourteen

Genesis

WORDS DIDN'T HAVE POWER, RIGHT? THEY WERE JUST WORDS, STRUNG together in sentences, big scary sentences that had me shaking. I wondered when or if the fear would ever leave.

I stared at the fruit on the table, not in the least bit hungry.

"I can't just..." I found my voice and glanced up at Ethan. "I can't just sit around trapped in this house away from the world. It would be like prison."

"A beautiful prison." Ethan smiled.

I chose not to smile back. I didn't want to encourage him or encourage my body to lean any closer to his. His body was like a magnet, even if I fought against the pull—I still couldn't help it. I found myself inching my chair closer. When it scraped against the floor, everyone smirked but Ethan.

He seemed angry.

Angry, yet he'd been the one to do that to me.

"I don't care," I said, ignoring the thumping of my heart in my chest and the fact that the closer I got to him the more it raced. "I can't just sit around here being worthless."

"You won't," Stephanie piped up. "Your life will be relatively normal. Ethan can even get you a job if you want... close by... so he can keep an eye on you, of course."

"A job?"

"Work," Ethan said slowly. "Isn't that what humans live for? A divine purpose? Though, if you'd rather stay here and cook and clean, you won't get any complaints."

"A job would be nice." Anything to get me out of the house or compound.

"Fantastic," Ethan said, his teeth snapping together.

I had a sinking feeling it was anything but fantastic, but I wasn't about to bend over backward and let him make yet another decision for me—regardless of how much I wanted to launch myself at him and never let go.

It was the bond.

Nothing more.

And that really sucked if you asked me, because someone like Ethan... well, he was the type of man, person, being that you wanted to want you. Not just because he had no choice, but because he couldn't imagine existing any other way.

Ashamed of my thoughts—or maybe just embarrassed—I returned to my stare-down with the kitchen table.

"Drystan owns a book shop," Stephanie suggested. "When Genesis isn't with us fighting crime, she can go there. God knows she'll need to get away from Ethan in order to have some breathing room."

Ethan rolled his eyes.

"Drystan?" I repeated. "He's immortal too?"

"Ancient." Mason nodded. "Another werewolf obsessed with books. It should be a good arrangement."

"Arrangement," I tested the word. "And when I'm not at the book shop?"

The others fell silent while Ethan reached across the table and grabbed my hand. My skin buzzed to life at his touch. "I teach you everything you need to know about us... about your job, about the humans' place with us... and I take you to your first Gathering."

"Like a party?" I gripped his hand tighter, pulling strength from him that I didn't know I needed but lusted for, nonetheless.

"Yes." He shrugged. "In fact, if you're up to it, we can introduce you this evening."

"Oh." Waves of pleasure washed over me as he released my hand; his fingertips dancing along the pulse in my wrist. "I think I can probably manage that."

"The others will love to meet you," Stephanie encouraged, placing her hands on my shoulders.

"How many others are we talking here?" I squinted. "In my studies it said that the oldest leaders... you guys..."

Alex choked on his laugh.

"...only number in the hundreds."

The laughter died, amusement gone from Alex's eyes.

"Four of us," Ethan answered. "There are four Elders left, and Cassius makes five. The rest are relatively younger, but they number in the thousands."

"For just Seattle?" I squeaked out.

"Of course." Ethan rolled his eyes and released my hand. The temperature in the room dipped. My hand itched to reach back and grasp his. "Immortals are able to live in society, you know. Most of us either have a job in the real world or have had in the past until it began to bore us."

"Weird, I was always told you kept to yourselves."

"We aren't good at keeping to ourselves, just like we aren't good with sharing." Alex grinned. "Isn't that right, Ethan?"

Ethan growled while Alex walked around the table and held out his hand. "Has anyone ever told you how beautiful you truly are? It's extraordinary... the color of your hair, the light of your eyes, the—"

Ethan kicked Alex in the back of the legs, sending him colliding into

Stephanie. His laughter was the only thing that made me think that Ethan wasn't going to kill him, since his eyes had gone completely black.

"Need more blood?" Alex asked in a soothing tone. "Don't want you accidentally attacking your mate tonight in front of God and everyone."

My gut clenched. "Do you, um, take my blood?"

"Please." Alex laughed. "Like Ethan would... he's been celibate from blood for over a hundred years."

"Until now," I whispered.

Ethan looked away, his eyes getting blacker, if that was even possible. "Until I tasted you."

A small part of me hoped I tasted good to him.

Oh you do, came Alex's voice in my head. *Like pure sin.*

I felt my cheeks heat.

Ethan's eyes narrowed. "Stephanie, help Genesis get ready for this evening... keep her occupied while I go meet with Cassius."

"What?" I yelled. "You're going to meet with him? After what happened? After going to all this trouble to protect me?"

"Hear that?" Alex cupped his ear. "Her blood roars for you, Ethan."

Ethan seemed to focus on my mouth as his fangs descended over his bottom lip. Holy crap, was he going to bite me again? My breathing slowed.

His eyes went from black to green then back to black again as he cupped the back of my head and brought me close, his teeth grazing my neck.

With a hiss, he pushed me away, almost hard enough for my chair to topple backward if Stephanie hadn't caught it with her hands.

"Go," he said in a hoarse voice, "before I drain her."

I didn't need to be told twice that it was dangerous just being next to him. I bolted from my seat, ready to protect myself, if need be, when Mason moved to stand in front of me, bumping against Ethan's chest. "Not necessary to scare her shitless, vampire."

Ethan looked over Mason's shoulder, his body calling to mine, singing, beckoning, even though he was dangerous, even though he'd just threatened me, I wanted to push Mason out of the way more than I wanted air.

"Take care of her," Ethan barked. "I won't be long."

"Stay alive," Alex said in a cheerful voice. "And do tell Cassius hello."

Stephanie put a protective arm around me and whispered in my ear. "It will get better, you know. He's just angry and confused."

"And I'm not?" I wrapped my arms around myself. "This morning I woke up, and the only thing on my mind was if I wanted eggs for breakfast or a protein shake."

"And now," Alex offered with a slight shrug, "you get to worry about two immortals wanting your blood. No big, right?"

"Is that you trying to make me feel better?"

"No…" He smiled. "But this is." His blue eyes lit up just as Mason shoved him out of the way and Stephanie began tugging me back up the stairs.

"He's insane, but I love him." She shook her head. "Now, let's get you ready for this evening. I think I'll put you in red. Won't that drive Ethan absolutely wild?"

"I'm thinking Ethan needs no encouragement to end me," I grumbled.

Stephanie pushed open the door to another room, one I hadn't seen before. "He doesn't want to end you. He wants to drink from you—so much, in fact, that I'm pretty sure if he doesn't regain some focus, he's going to punch Cassius in the face."

"That can't end well."

"They fight." She shrugged. "Quite often."

"Isn't Cassius your… king?" I was going to try to find a better word, but that was the only one that seemed to fit.

"Somewhat." She looked down at the ground. "Or at least at one point, he was supposed to lead us—but it's hard, for an imperfect being, pulled between two mortal planes, to do that without losing himself in the process."

"What do you mean?"

"He's both human and immortal. He has two different types of chemical makeup fighting for dominance. Sometimes his human side wins. Other times, the angel side. It's frustrating to follow someone who doesn't even know himself."

"Hmm." I thought about that for a while; they'd made me believe Cassius was like Satan himself, but now I was starting to wonder if he was just misunderstood.

"When you close your eyes," she whispered under her breath, "he'll explain himself better."

"Who?"

"Cassius."

"What? Did I miss an important part of this conversation?"

"You'll see." She smiled. "And then you can make your own judgment, yes?"

"Um, sure?"

"Yes, this!" She moved to a large closet and opened the doors. "I think the dress is in here."

I was still mulling over the fact that Cassius would somehow explain himself to me when a shoe flew by my head, missing my cheek by mere inches. I flinched.

"Sorry! I forget you're breakable."

"Very." I paid special attention to flying objects and went over to the closet. "Will Cassius be there tonight?"

"If Ethan allows it."

"And he won't try to take me."

"Not with us there, no."

"But he'll still try."

Stephanie's hand hovered over the other shoe. "Every day. Until you no longer exist."

chapter
fifteen

Ethan

I SHOULD HAVE KNOWN SOMETHING WAS WRONG THE MINUTE I GOT INTO MY NEW Lexus LFA and drove like hell down the winding road.

I'd become accustomed to nice things in life. Living as long as I had, I'd learned to take pleasure from hobbies. My interests ranged from collecting fine art to archery. Had I not done something with my time I would have gone absolutely insane.

My most recent pleasure? Cars. The leather felt smooth against my hot skin; the smell tantalized me. And the speed? Well, the speed was just a bonus. But not now… it seemed everything absolutely paled in comparison to the taste of her.

Maybe it had been too long—the effects of bloodlust could drive a vampire insane—but it wasn't mindless lust I was feeling for her, just intense desire to be near her, to drink from her, to share my soul with her for no other reason than I'd bonded with her.

But if I shared more of my blood, if I took more from her, giving her mine in exchange, she'd continue to be able to see my memories, my dreams—everything I'd been keeping close for the past hundred years.

And the horrible part? She wasn't invested, at least not emotionally, and the last thing I wanted was for her to pity me. The idea made me snort out loud, a human pitying an immortal. The idea was laughable, if it wasn't so damn tragic.

She'd want to make the pain go away…

When really I just wanted to start over.

Cassius wasn't at his usual spot, opting for a more public arena. I hadn't wanted to argue with him yet again over what his presence did to mere mortals. I'd simply sent him a text and agreed to meet in the U District for coffee.

Cassius hated coffee.

But he drank it because it made him feel normal.

I drank it because it took the edge off wanting to rip someone's throat out.

The car squealed into a nearby parking spot. I hit the alarm and made my way toward Starbucks.

People stared.

They couldn't help it.

Just like they couldn't help but ask for autographs, even though they had no idea who I was—just assumed, by my looks, that I was famous or about to be.

Years ago, it had been flattering—when I still possessed a heart and didn't think the world was going to come crashing down around me at any second. Years ago, I had been naïve.

No more.

Cassius was sitting outside, though it was drizzling. He was covered by the umbrella, sipping at his cappuccino and reading the freaking newspaper, like he didn't already know everything there was to know.

I dropped my keys onto the table loudly.

He didn't look up. "Got you a caramel-macchiato thing that tastes like hell. You're welcome."

Rolling my eyes, I took the cup into my hands and sat down, bringing the hot liquid to my mouth.

It was bitter.

It tasted nothing like her.

I couldn't even pretend that I was enjoying myself. Would nothing take the edge off?

"So…" Cassius set down the paper, and gazed at me from behind his sunglasses, which kept people from asking why the hell his eyes kept turning white. "That was clever of you."

"Vampires… we're known for it," I said in a dry tone, leaning back in my chair. "Besides, you owed me, and you know it."

"I saved your life." Cassius snorted. "I hardly think that puts me in your debt."

"You had no proof, no right, no—"

He held up his hand. "Enough. I don't wish to discuss the past."

He never did.

I cursed and took another sip of coffee. "What's done is done. Now we wait."

Cassius looked so out of place sitting in a small chair, appearing to fit in. His body was too large, his countenance too dangerous. He tilted his head as if listening to the wind. "Her scent is on you."

"Caught that, did you?"

"A hundred years."

"People really need to stop reminding me," I grumbled, no longer interested in my coffee or the conversation we were having. Why the hell I'd agreed to meet with someone I used to call brother was beyond me.

"You aren't as strong as I am, Ethan. You cannot hope to keep me from her, not when so much is at stake."

And there it was.

I hissed out a breath. "I'm afraid your hands are tied."

"Are they?"

I stood, placing my palms on the table, towering over everyone. "You'd repeat history for your own selfish reasons? Is that what this is? I'm trying to save lives, Cassius! This has nothing to do with her!"

"Which is why your eyes," he said calmly, "continue to go black, why your blood boils beneath the skin that covers it, why your heart is in perfect cadence with hers. Yes, I can hear it, even from this far away, though I can't directly find her. Know this... I will."

"Unless you get her alone, you have no chance." I sat, half-tempted to toss my coffee in his face and tear his throat out for good measure.

"She'll come to me of her own accord. When you fail—and fail you will—she'll come to me. They always do."

My body shuddered with the onslaught of past memories. "You brainwashed her."

"I offered her a solution."

"You gave her death."

"I didn't say it was a good solution." Cassius shrugged. "Remember this, I've been damned to earth to help your cause—to help the immortals and humans keep balance. When you fail, it's my head—not yours."

I rolled my eyes. "It's been over five-hundred years since we've had a visit from one of the archangels. I highly doubt they're going to do it now. There's nothing special about her." That was a lie.

"I smell your doubt, vampire." Cassius growled my name pushed back the chair and stood. "Have your fun, try to win her affection, but know in the end, it will be me who has to save everyone."

"Has anyone ever told you that you have a god-complex?"

"I come by that quite naturally, I assure you." He nodded and walked off, calling behind him, "Do your worst, Ethan, or maybe I should say... try your best?"

"Ah, so may the best man win and all of that." I laughed. "Yet you forget. Your very essence will kill her."

"We don't know that for sure." He raised one hand and lifted the opposite shoulder in a seemingly casual shrug. "And I'm willing to take that risk. In order to save us all, I would take that risk every time. I wonder... would you?"

I swallowed and looked away, knowing he'd hit me at my weakness. Because I'd seen the signs with Ara and had ignored them because I'd thought I loved her, and in the end, I'd still refused to give her up, forcing his hand. Humiliation ate away, pinching my chest.

"This evening? She'll be in attendance then? Since the mating is… complete?" he asked, toying with his keys.

"She'll be there."

His grin was menacing. "Lovely."

Right.

He walked off.

And I stayed, planted in my seat, wondering if history truly was repeating itself, and if she wouldn't have been better off dying by Cassius's hands—dying in a blissful state—than living with someone who apparently had no capacity for love… or who, for some reason or another, was unlovable.

And that was the crux of the matter.

Regardless of what I'd done, my mate had never loved me back. Had never looked at me with the same adoration as I'd looked at her.

My love had destroyed her.

And in the end, I truly had no one to blame but myself, for being selfish enough to have hidden the truth from Cassius until it had been too late—selfish enough to have wanted to keep the child who hadn't even been mine.

Love, in all my experience, was just that—selfishness wrapped up in a pretty little bow.

I took one last drink of coffee and stood, just as a few giggling girls walked out of the coffee shop. They stopped. Their hearts, however, picked up speed as they glanced at me and blushed.

I didn't have time to placate them. Instead, I growled and stomped off in the other direction.

Stay alert.

Keep to the plan.

And above all—don't allow Genesis in. Because I wouldn't survive it a second time.

chapter
sixteen

Genesis

I DIDN'T SEE ETHAN THE REST OF THE DAY. STEPHANIE TRIED TO DISTRACT ME with reality TV. It worked for a while, and then I'd gotten restless again. It wasn't that I was worried about him or anything. I just wanted to know that Cassius hadn't removed Ethan's head from his body. When I'd asked Alex about them fighting, he'd simply rolled his eyes and started talking about the Gathering that evening.

The women.

The lights.

The dancing.

But mostly the women.

It was time to go, and Ethan still wasn't there. I fidgeted with my dress, hoping it would please him and hating myself that it was even an issue. Why would I care? He'd rejected me over and over again only to offer me comfort and then reject me again. He made absolutely no sense, and in my current emotional state, I really desperately needed something to make sense.

Next to Stephanie, I felt like the ugly friend. The one you took with you and forced your brother or cousin to dance with. As if on cue, Alex stepped forward and offered his arm.

It's not that I needed compliments—I'd lasted my entire life without them. I'd turned them away, knowing that if my number was ever called, I would never feel pretty again, because I'd be in the constant company of immortals.

Though I'd foolishly thought I'd be a type of teacher.

It was what I'd lived for, to either live to teach them or continue on with my boring life and find a career I was passionate about.

"Hey now," Alex whispered in my ear, "hold your head high. They'll smell your fear from a mile away."

"Fear isn't welcome," I repeated under my breath.

"Good girl." He patted my hand. "And you look gorgeous."

"Don't," I snapped. "Just... don't lie, please."

His eyebrows drew together; he opened his mouth but earned a slap on the shoulder from Mason.

I hadn't noticed his arrival. Mason was wearing dress pants and a shirt that left absolutely nothing to the imagination. Every muscle was outlined—it was hard not to stare. The man was huge. Had he not shown me compassion, I would be afraid of his size.

"She rides with me." He started prying my arm away from Alex.

Alex rolled his eyes. "Why not me?"

"She's safer with me, and those were Ethan's instructions. Check your phone."

Alex pulled out his iPhone. "Damn, how am I supposed to make an entrance without little human on my arm?"

"Name." Mason barked.

"Calling her human is my term of endearment, like sweetheart or babycakes."

"Call me babycakes, and I'll scratch your eyes out," my mouth fired off before I could stop it. Closing my eyes in embarrassment, I shook my head. "I'm sorry, I mean."

Alex barked out a laugh. "You're allowed to have opinions, babycakes."

I groaned.

"It's staying," he announced, "because it makes her turn red. Look."

He was pointing at my cheeks. I was sure they matched my dress. I'd just yelled at an immortal, threatened bodily harm, and he was laughing.

Mason removed Alex's hand from mine and took my arm. "Let's go, beautiful."

The attention, the compliments, the nicknames—they were too much. It was the opposite of what I'd expected, meaning, it was like being made fun of. Like I was naked for the class picture. It was embarrassing, being told I was beautiful when I knew, without a shadow of a doubt, that I paled in comparison to the ugliest of immortals.

"Did I say something wrong?" Mason asked once we were in his truck driving toward downtown. "You seem… upset."

My fingers slowly caressed the rich leather seats. I don't know what I expected him to drive, but a brand new GMC truck didn't really fit the image I'd had of werewolves.

"Um, no…" I lied. "It's nothing."

"You seem sad."

"Just… in shock, still."

"It will fade," Mason said in a calm voice. "It always does. My own mate, well, she…" His voice cracked. "She had a hard time at first."

"Was her number called?"

His eyes were black; it was hard to see where his pupils started and ended as he gazed at me then back at the road. "Yes."

"And you loved her?"

"Of course." He said it so quickly I didn't doubt him for one second. "With my entire life, my soul, my existence, I loved her."

"Loved."

"She simply…" His voice was hoarse. "She simply didn't wake up one morning. The evening before we'd been talking about children. The next morning she was cold."

"Mason…" I reached across the seat and grabbed his hand. "I'm so sorry."

He clenched my hand in his and brought it to his lips; his rough kiss across my knuckles warmed me from the inside out.

"It's not your fault."

"But…" My mind whirled. "I could change that? I could make it so that doesn't happen anymore?"

He was quiet for a while. "Possibly, but there's no way to know."

"So I live past a certain year, and what? We're home free?"

The truck pulled up to one of the hotels in downtown Seattle. It was newer, a boutique hotel right on the water. "Ethan wouldn't like me discussing such things with you. I'll allow him to explain."

"But—"

"That's all I'll say," he growled. "Now, let's go show you off to your mate."

The mate who hadn't even driven me to the Gathering?

The mate who hadn't spoken to me all day?

The same mate who'd looked like he wanted to shake me to death earlier that morning?

Great.

I choked back the fear at being in a room with possibly hundreds of immortals —in a room with Cassius himself—and followed Mason out of the truck.

He grabbed my hand again. I ducked against him, allowing his body to shield me.

He handed his keys to the valet, who eyed me up and down like I was a piece of candy.

Mason growled at the valet, who jolted out of his stare-down and ran toward the truck. "Idiots, all of the demons."

"Wh-what?"

"Demons." He shrugged. "Even hell won't take 'em, so they toil here for us until it's time for judgment."

"And then?"

"Hell welcomes them back with open arms."

I shivered.

"Are you cold?"

No, just completely freaked out. My studies had said nothing about demons. Nothing.

What other immortals hadn't I been told about?

I was almost afraid to ask.

Mason walked me through the doors of the hotel. Music sounded from somewhere in the lobby, or maybe it was the restaurant. The music grew louder as we walked toward it in silence.

When we stopped, it was in front of a black door.

Mason nodded to a tall man wearing head-to-toe black. He had an earpiece in his ear and examined the iPad in his hands. He turned the iPad toward Mason, who placed his hand on the screen.

It flashed green.

And the door opened.

I think, in my head I'd built the Gathering up to be something like I'd seen in horror movies—an orgy, blood-drinking, people in little to no clothing.

Instead... it was like I'd just walked onto a Hollywood movie set. Heads turned, both male and female, and they were flawless. My fingers dug into Mason's arm.

It wasn't fear.

More like awe. It had been hard enough to keep my jaw tight when I'd entered the throne room. This was a bazillion times worse.

Every woman in that room was perfectly proportioned—tall, exotic, beautiful. There was no imperfection—at all.

The men, if I could call them that, since most of them were most likely immortal, were all pretty large in size and seemed more curious than anything. I noticed a few smiles in my direction.

A few sneers—from the women.

And in the far, far corner of the room, there were a group of people who looked like me, who looked normal, not like they belonged on the cover of a magazine.

"Humans," Mason whispered. "Over in the corner, most likely gossiping about their mates."

"What?"

On closer inspection, the humans looked... different. I couldn't really put my finger on it, but their skin was brighter than mine. Their eyes too. They just appeared extremely healthy.

There were both men and women, which I hadn't expected. Not that men's numbers had never been called. I just hadn't really thought about it much.

The room was decorated in blacks and silvers; long tables lined the walls, piled high with food and champagne.

The curious stares continued, so I clung to Mason like he was my lifeline; that was, until Alex came up beside me and offered a glass of champagne. "They stare because they're curious."

"They always stare at new humans?" I took a sip of the champagne, but it tasted off. I couldn't put my finger on it, but it seemed almost bitter on my tongue.

"No." Alex grinned. "Only you. Because of you who are, and well... you know… the fact that Ethan's your mate and Cassius started a pissing contest over you."

"Alex…" Mason rolled his eyes. "Stop."

"What?" Alex shrugged, and then his blue eyes brightened. "I think I see my conquest for the night."

A wave of heat washed over me; I didn't feel lust this time or anything close to it, just heat. He winked, and then he was moving through the crowd to a tall, dark-haired lady with a black dress slinked around her body.

"Another siren?" I asked.

"Human." Mason nodded. "One of Alex's favorites."

"What?" I stopped him from walking. "Aren't all humans mated?"

"Er…" Mason scratched his head and looked around. "…Ethan really should explain that to you."

"Screw Ethan!" I stomped my foot. "He isn't here. You are."

The air around me crackled with warmth. Ethan.

"Hmm…" Ethan's smooth voice danced across the back of my neck. "Miss me that much, Genesis?"

Slowly, I turned and came face to face with sheer beauty. I couldn't look away even if I tried. His green eyes glowed against his smooth skin; long dark eyelashes fanned across his chiseled cheekbones. He was wearing all black—it should have looked ridiculous—a vampire in all black?

It didn't.

Look ridiculous, that was.

He looked edible.

I stepped away from Mason, not because I wanted to, but because my body couldn't help itself.

"Not every human mates… of course that's been the goal… but we do, at times, make exceptions for some. They want so desperately to be a part of our world that they're willing to do anything to be in it—even if it means they don't mate with an immortal. Getting screwed by one is enough."

"Harsh." Mason coughed.

"You've done your duty, Mason." Ethan looked over my shoulder. "Leave us."

Mason rolled his eyes and walked off.

"His duty?" I repeated.

"Take my arm," Ethan commanded.

"You've ignored me for an entire day, and you want me to take your arm?"

"You're my mate." He said it so simply, so matter-of-factly, that I wanted to punch him across his perfect mouth. "Take my arm, Genesis. You know you want to."

Every cell in my body screamed for me to take his arm and just be done with it, but I didn't want to give in, didn't want to give him the satisfaction.

"How was Cassius?" I asked, ignoring his outstretched arm and glancing away from him so I could gather myself.

"Cranky," Ethan hissed. "Like I'm about to be if you don't follow orders."

"Maybe if you said please," I whispered under my breath, "I'd be more likely to do your bidding."

"I could just kiss you into submission... bend you backward over the buffet table and have my way with you."

Lust surged through me. "I think that's the last thing you want to do."

His lips were suddenly grazing my ear. "Then you clearly don't know me very well."

"Whose fault is that?" My fingers clenched the champagne glass harder as I fought for control over my own body.

"Let's blame Alex." Ethan wrapped his muscled arm around my shoulders. "Now I'm sure in your studies you were told to respect immortals, that you were... *nothing* compared to us."

"Yes," I croaked.

"Good. So your first lesson is this... humans don't disrespect their mates, regardless of the circumstances. If I asked you to bend over and tie my shoe, I'd expect you to do it with a damn smile on your face."

"You're a jackass," I hissed, trying to pull away from him.

"I'm not actually asking you to tie my shoe, Genesis. I'm just telling you how it is. At a Gathering, there is a certain expectation. We talk, we show off our shiny treasures, and at the end of the night, we part ways, each of us comparing ourselves to one another. Every type of immortal is in attendance tonight. It would be good of you to stay by me, lest one of them trap you in a corner and try to take advantage."

"They'd do that? To you? Someone so old?"

His mouth pressed into a firm line. "I'm not that old."

"You are."

His arm tightened around my shoulder. "Great, then that makes you a child?"

"No, but—"

"They'd challenge me still, yes. And if Cassius approaches, try not to touch him, any part of him."

"What about breathing?" I tilted my head mockingly. "Am I allowed to do that?"

"Ethan!" Gushed a high pitched female voice from my right.

I turned and had the sudden urge to hide behind a potted plant, or maybe just Mason, wherever he'd gone. The woman was at least six feet tall, had long ebony hair, crystal green eyes, and a smile that seemed completely unreal.

"Where have you been?" She pushed me slightly out of the way, as if I didn't exist, and kissed him on both cheeks then pulled back.

"Busy," Ethan answered, tugging me yet again close to himself.

The woman's eyes squinted in my direction. "Oh…" She smirked. "Sorry. I didn't see you there."

Right.

Because I was ugly.

Nonexistent.

Worthless.

I tried to appear meek, but it seemed the longer I was in the immortal world the more anger issues I was developing. A week ago, I would have blushed and shrugged it off.

Now? I wanted to find a fork and stab her with it.

I clenched my fists together and offered a pathetic smile.

"She's the one then?" The woman kept talking. "I don't see it. I really don't. I heard Cassius is on a rampage."

"Cassius is always on a rampage." Ethan shrugged. "Delora, this is my mate, Genesis."

"Already?" Delora gasped. "Ethan, I thought—"

"It was great seeing you." Ethan dismissed her as if she were nothing but a tiny bug beneath his shoe. "I promised my love a dance though. Excuse us."

I fought the urge to snort. His love? Right.

Without asking me, Ethan set the champagne glass down on a nearby table and pulled me onto a small dance floor.

"She was lovely," I said once the music started.

A smile teased the corners of Ethan's mouth. "She's horrible, but at least you didn't throw your champagne in her face."

"I was tempted."

"Me too." His voice caressed my body. I tried to keep my distance from him, but he wasn't having it. Instead, he pulled me as close as physically possible so we were chest to chest. "I like your dress."

"It's red." *Lame. Someone, put me out of my misery.*

His warm chuckle had my knees shaking together. "Like blood."

"Yeah."

"About as damn tempting too."

I was desperate to hear him say it wasn't just the dress that was tempting, but me, even though I knew it was stupid, and I was just setting myself up to get hurt all over again.

"You look… nice."

Nice. He said I looked nice. Not pretty, not even cute, or beautiful, just nice. Like a dog.

Or a plant.

"Thanks." I swallowed the lump in my throat.

chapter
seventeen

Ethan

EVERY DAMN WOMAN IN THAT ROOM PALED IN COMPARISON, AND THAT WAS THE truth. It was like fighting a war with myself—not telling her how I really felt, like dragging her away from the watchful eyes of people who'd do her harm and kissing her senseless then promising her forever.

It was instinctual.

Nothing more.

If I pushed her away, I wouldn't attach myself more emotionally—at least, that was what I told myself—then she'd gone and gotten cranky, which, frankly, was adorable.

She crossed her arms.

I half-expected her to stomp her foot or at least claw my eyes out. Damn, I would have been gone if she'd done any of those things.

She still had control.

I wondered if she noticed how her personality was slightly changing. Vampires weren't known for being calm and collected. Perhaps on the outside… but on the inside? Blood boiled; it always boiled. And I knew it was just a matter of time before she snapped.

Because my blood flowed through her veins, and if that didn't make me want to shout at the top of my lungs.

Her scent was covered up with perfume.

I didn't like it.

I sniffed her neck harder.

She flinched.

I licked.

And she froze in my arms.

I hadn't meant to actually lick her, or maybe I had, and I just hadn't fully thought through the ramifications of my actions.

"Sorry…" Since when did I apologize? "I was… curious."

"So you licked me?" Her body trembled in my arms.

I held her tighter. "Yeah." That's all I had.

The song was ending.

"What do I taste like?"

"Heaven," I said before I could lie. Being honest with her about her own taste was the least I could do, right?

But just admitting it out loud made me want more.

"What's heaven taste like?"

"Genesis." My mouth curved into a small smile at her swift intake of breath. Her heart picked up speed, like a horse getting ready to race. Her palms began to sweat against mine.

"Care to know how I taste?" I asked, dipping her low in my arms.

She blinked up at me. "Yes."

I almost dropped her on her ass. I'd been taunting her, teasing. I wasn't serious.

Slowly, I brought her back up to standing position. "Then take a bite."

"What?" she gasped.

"Just a small one…" I teased. "It's perfectly natural."

"But I'm a human."

Her cheeks were completely flushed; her heart beat faster and faster. It was like a drug, listening to the physical effect I had on her body.

I raised her hand and twirled her twice, fast, and bit into my wrist on the third twirl. Three drops of blood met her lower lip.

She licked. Her eyes flashed green—my green.

And I lost complete control.

My mouth met hers in a frenzy; the perfect mixture of my blood and her taste was devastating to my senses.

What was worse?

Her hands had moved to my shoulders and were now fisting in my hair, tugging me closer, her body arching, trying to gain better access.

Her lips suddenly turned cold.

I pulled back and met Cassius's gaze across the room. He was smirking, the bastard.

Genesis shivered, her eyes confused. "What just happened?"

"I kissed you."

"Yeah, got that part." Her cheeks were still flushed. "But then it was cold… like before."

"A trick…" I turned her slowly.

Cassius nodded from his spot across the room.

Genesis leaned back against me, her knees buckling. "I want to go home now."

"You can't."

"What?" She turned in my arms, grabbing my jacket with her hands. "You mean we have to stay here all night?"

"Wait, what?" I shook my head. "Home as in… back to your mother?"

Her cheeks went bright red. "No, I mean… back to the house. Your house."

Home. She'd called my house her home. Male pride roared in my chest. Barely keeping it together, I nodded my head and pressed a kiss to her forehead.

"Yes, but first you must acknowledge Cassius."

"Why?" She dug her heels into the floor.

"Because he's as close to a king as we get, and every immortal, regardless of their feelings toward him, has to pay his respects."

Genesis reached for my hand, squeezing the life out of it. "But he won't hurt me, right?"

Pieces of her golden hair clung to her ruby red lipstick. I tugged them away and cupped her face. "He can't touch you—not with me here. I swear."

Nodding, she kept her tight grip on my hand as I led her through the crowd. The closer we got to Cassius the quieter it became. By now, it was no secret that I'd stolen Genesis from him—marked her, claimed her, and then had had the nerve to show up with her at the Gathering.

People knew our history.

But that didn't make what I'd done acceptable.

In fact, had I not been an Elder, I was pretty sure he would have ripped my heart from my chest and crushed it in his hand.

Cassius leaned against one of the tables, his arms crossed. He wore a smile that would make anyone—mortal or immortal—sell his soul for just one more.

I hated him in that moment, all over again, because I'd known an immortal once who'd been willing to do anything for one of Cassius's smiles or touches.

Feeling sick, I held Genesis tighter. Not her. Please not her. Cassius had taken everything from me. Would he take her too? Was she weak like Ara had been?

A lie.

It had all been a lie.

Just like my bond with Genesis was a lie.

I bit into my lip, drawing blood as Cassius's grin grew with each step we took toward him.

He was wearing a white button-up shirt, revealing half his chest. I rolled my eyes. Dark Ones were vain, nice to look at, but they knew it.

At least vampires tried to appear humble.

Cassius knew he commanded the world and lived for that power.

"Genesis." Her name on his lips had me hissing aloud.

He grinned wider.

I imagined myself strangling him then removing his head from his body.

"Cassius," Genesis whispered.

The room was completely silent.

Cassius held out his hand.

Genesis looked at me, refusing to take his hand.

"Ah, he's taught you well." Cassius drew his hand back. "Apparently, your mate doubts your ability to stay true. If you really loved him… if the bond has truly worked… you'd be able to touch me and feel nothing. Did he tell you that?"

"Yes," she lied.

I could kiss her. I hadn't told her the truth—was afraid to—because of my own insecurities.

"I just don't want to disrespect Ethan."

Cassius's eyes narrowed in on Genesis. "Interesting."

Stephanie appeared by Cassius's side; he pulled her close to his body, his eyes going from blue to white then back again after releasing her. I didn't understand their special type of friendship, and a part of me didn't want to.

Sirens could become just as addicted to Dark Ones, and I hated to think that Stephanie had fallen into his trap like so many others before her.

Though her eyes stayed blue, and she didn't give off the normal chill a woman claimed would.

"Tell me, is the party to your liking, Genesis?" Cassius asked.

"It's beautiful." She wrapped her arm around my body, placing her head on my chest. "But Ethan promised me we'd spend some time alone tonight, so we're actually leaving."

Brave girl.

Cassius's eyebrows shot up.

"And does Ethan speak for himself these days, or do you do that for him?"

"Cassius," I warned. "Perhaps I like hearing her voice. I've been alive so long I've tired of hearing my own."

People around us laughed.

Genesis looked up at me adoringly.

So I did what any male would do in my position. I kissed her—hard. Our mouths fused together, our tongues tangled, and I forgot completely that I was in front of Cassius—or anyone. I lifted her against my body, my hands digging into her hair as she let out a little moan.

"Enough!" Cassius grunted out. "This isn't a brothel."

I released her, though it was hard, considering all I could focus on was the pulse of her heart through her swollen lips. I wanted to bite—again.

"Control yourself, Ethan," Cassius sneered. "Her blood will still be there when you get home. Then again, you're probably not going to be taking her blood, will you?"

Genesis hung her head.

"You know…" Cassius shrugged. "I wonder if it would be considered fair or loyal to your old mate? Taking a new one and destroying her as well?"

I released Genesis and pushed against Cassius's chest. "Take it back!"

He grinned and held up his hands. "My mistake."

Shaking my head, I stepped back and grabbed Genesis's hand. It killed me, absolutely killed me to bow my head to Cassius, to give him the respect he was due, when all I wanted to do was end his life. But I managed it, a slight bow.

He returned the sentiment.

And in a flash I was outside with Genesis.

When the demon threw me my keys, I almost threw them back at his head, needing some sort of violent act to soothe me.

"Sorry." Genesis voice was weak, afraid. "I hope I didn't make things worse, I was just—"

"You," I turned and cupped her face, "did beautifully."

I kissed her again.

Because I could.

Because she calmed me.

Because I knew I couldn't claim her again in public, and I knew that once we got to the house, I'd have to leave her, lest I lose complete and utter control of myself.

When her arms snaked around my neck, I let out a pitiful growl and took a taste… just a few drops… directly from her tongue.

She gasped into my mouth, driving me into a frenzy to have her body closer.

Without thinking of her being as fragile as she was, I pushed her against the waiting car.

She let out a little grunt.

"Shit." I stepped back and pinched the bridge of my nose. "I'm sorry. I forget how fragile you are."

"Do I look broken?" Her eyes were shadowed, hazy, lustful. Damn, it was a beautiful look on her.

"No." I smirked. "You don't."

She reached for me.

I stepped back again, my breath coming out in gasps. "We should go."

The look on her face nearly brought me to my knees. I couldn't keep it up, kissing her and pushing her away, wanting her yet lying to myself about it.

"Okay." Again I was struck by how small her voice sounded.

I opened the door and ushered her in…

Then contemplated lying down in front of the car and asking the demon to hit the accelerator.

chapter
eighteen

Genesis

H E KISSED ME LIKE A MAN DYING OF THIRST—AND MAYBE HE WAS, MAYBE IT was my blood. Was it wrong to hope it was my smile? Maybe even my dress?

I played with the beautiful silk fabric, waiting for Ethan to acknowledge the kissing—or at least part of what Cassius had alluded to.

When the silence stretched the entire ride home, disappointment stabbed me in the chest.

We reached the house.

He pulled the car up to the massive gate; it opened.

Still nothing.

He turned off the car and reached for the door when I blurted, "Do you hate me?"

His hand froze on the car door; in fact, his entire body froze. My heart picked up speed. I knew he could hear it, but there was nothing I could do about the effect he had on me.

"No…" His voice was low, almost a growl. "I could never hate you."

"I'm sorry…" Tears stung the back of my eyes. "…for whatever I did. I'm sorry you were forced to protect me when you didn't want to."

"You're apologizing?" His voice rose. "To me?"

My throat got tighter. "Yes."

He looked over his shoulder at me, his green eyes glowing in the darkness of the car. "You're tired."

"Yeah, but—

"We can talk tomorrow. I'll show you to your room."

So that was it.

My fingers clenched the silk dress tighter. I didn't trust myself to speak. The warmth I'd felt in his presence was long gone, replaced with nothingness.

He didn't even place his hand on my back as he led me into the dark house.

I walked mindlessly through the kitchen and up the stairs, not sure if I was even going in the right direction. A slight tap on my back to the left had me turning the corner at the end of the massive hallway.

Double doors.

Huge double doors.

They were at least twelve feet tall; two metal dragons twisted around the large doorknobs.

Ethan reached around me and opened them.

A roaring fireplace was the first thing I saw. It was see-through, and on the other side of the wall, I noted what looked like the bathroom. Extravagance dripped from every corner of the room—from the crystal chandelier suspended overhead to the sitting area with leather couches and fur throw pillows.

A matching fur rug lay in front of the fireplace.

The king-sized bed could fit at least five people. The down comforter was black and looked so plush that I was afraid I was going to get lost in it if I sunk too deep.

"Bathroom," Ethan whispered over my shoulder, "is to your right. I'll have Stephanie take you shopping later this week after you've grown accustomed to your new environment."

I nodded and turned to thank him, but he was already gone; the door shut in finality behind him.

Tears filled my eyes.

I wasn't sure why I was acting so emotional… other than being rejected. I'd been built for tougher situations, right? Hadn't I been prepared for the worst when I'd awakened—was it only twenty-four hours ago?

At least I wasn't dead.

There was that.

But I wasn't accepted, and I think a small part of me had hoped that maybe I would fit in this world better than my own.

I was smart enough to fit in.

I'd studied hard enough to make it a possibility.

But everything I'd studied had been a lie—or close enough.

My own mother hadn't given me the attention I'd craved—too afraid that if by chance my number was called, the separation would destroy me.

And now… I had the most beautiful man in the world kissing me—because he couldn't help himself.

Like a chocolate addict.

I was covered in his addiction; it flowed through my veins, but it wasn't me.

Slowly, I made my way into the bathroom. Expensive soaps lined one side of the tub. I started the hot water and began peeling my clothes away.

When the tub was full, I stepped in.

I'd just closed my eyes when I heard the doors open to the bedroom.

Ethan walked around the corner of the bathroom—like it was the most normal thing in the world—and held out a glass of wine.

I was too stunned to do anything but stare at the glass in his hand; it shook slightly. "I figured this would help you relax."

With a gulp, I reached out, and took the wine glass. Our fingers grazed each other, causing a jolt of awareness to wash over my body. I imagined he felt it too, if the elongating of his fangs was any indication. Quickly, he looked away and walked out of the bathroom.

Slamming the door behind him.

⁙

An hour later, and I was in bed, too exhausted to sleep. The door to the room opened again.

I could make the outline of a body.

Then the person moved into the firelight.

"Ethan?"

His eyes started to glow in the darkness as he removed his shirt, followed by his pants, and every other article of clothing on his body.

Was he? Did he think something was going to happen?

I tensed beneath the covers.

"Relax..." His voice was both soothing and commanding. "...and try to sleep, Genesis."

With him. Naked. Next to me?

Right.

I was lucky I was still breathing. The man's body was made for sin. Muscle packed around his midsection so tightly it didn't look real. I blinked, thinking it was some sort of trick, because men really shouldn't be that good-looking.

Then again...

His eyes continued to glow.

He wasn't really a man, was he?

The bed dipped.

My erratic breathing increased. I closed my eyes and focused on calming down my own heart.

"I'm going to lose every ounce of control I have if your heart keeps beating that wildly whenever I take off my shirt." Ethan's voice held amusement, but I couldn't see his face, so I wasn't sure if he was smiling.

His warm hand touched my chest; his palm pressed against my skin. "Sleep, Genesis. Tonight... we sleep."

His words were like a drug, his hand was warm, and soon my entire body calmed down, sinking further and further into darkness.

"That's it..." His lips touched my ear. "Sleep."

My body was still fighting the sleep even though it sounded like a good idea.

Something warm trickled against my lips.

"Sleep," he commanded more forcefully this time.

My body immediately obeyed as I swallowed what I'd later discovered was his blood.

"*So we meet again.*" *Cassius grinned, holding out his hand.*

I frowned. "Is this a dream?"

"*I love dreams.*" *He shoved his hands in his pockets. "So vivid, colorful—tell me, do you like the rainbow?" He pointed to the sky where the band of colors arched over us. We were on a boat on some sort of lake. "I created it just for you.*"

"*Is this real?*"

"*As real as you allow it.*" *His massive shoulders seemed to broaden as he inhaled deeply and motioned around him "Wonderful, isn't it? You share his bed, yet I can share your dreams.*"

"*That seems incredibly invasive.*"

"*Don't forget unfair.*" *He winked.*

"*You're bad.*"

"*Am I?*" *His deep laugh echoed through my body. "Or do you just wish I was bad in order to make yourself feel better about the choice that was forced upon you?*"

"*It was the only way.*"

He threw his head back and laughed. "Oh, believe me, it wasn't."

"*You?*" *I bit down on my lip until it hurt. "Forgive me for not wanting to be taken by a Dark One... I've heard stories.*"

"*Books lie.*" *He shrugged. "Perhaps you would have survived me.*"

"*Perhaps?*" *I repeated. "You're kidding, right?*"

His eyes flashed. "Better."

I looked down. I was in a white bikini. I quickly tried to cover myself up; his laughter made me want to drown him. "May I have more clothing... please?"

His eyes flashed again, leaving me in a sarong. "Better?"

"*No.*"

"*Too bad.*" *He leaned back on his elbows. "Ethan can't give you what I can.*"

"*I'm not with Ethan because of what he can give me.*"

Cassius went still. "So they told you?"

"*About the prophecy?*"

He nodded.

"*Yes.*"

"*Did they tell you all of it?*"

"*Yes,*" *I lied.*

"*I can smell the lie on your tongue.*" *His eyes blazed white. "Never lie to me or any of my kind. It's infuriating and insulting to think you could get away with it in the first place.*"

Great, that meant he knew I'd been lying at the Gathering.

"Yes," his voice was smug, his smile matching it.

"Please... don't," I whispered.

"Don't?"

"Read me like that... I don't like it."

He studied me for a minute then gave a firm nod. "Fine. I won't pull the strings of your mind in an effort to give you exactly what you want before you even know you want it."

I clenched my teeth together. "What's the rest of the prophecy?"

"Why don't you ask your mate?"

"Because my mate is sleeping."

"Believe me..." Cassius laughed, the sound of it washed over me like he'd just stripped me naked. "The minute I invaded your dreams, he's been trying to wake you up. Sleep? He won't sleep until he knows you haven't touched me."

"If I touch you?"

Cassius's grin turned deadly. "Then I own you. Even in your dreams... you'd be mine regardless of the mating. Though, because you're bonded with Ethan, the desire to touch me lessens considerably, and there is that whole ridiculous issue with stealing you away from him since I can no longer smell you."

"Yet you can invade my thoughts? My dreams when I'm sleeping?"

"Only because I marked you first..." His eyes went white. A soft wind picked up, causing his black-as-night hair to blow across his face. "You think you've already made your choice—but you haven't, not yet."

"You or him." I nodded. "In the end, does it really matter?"

"Of course it does." Cassius said quickly. "Because there was once a human just like you... a human we thought was the one to fix everything and she failed. Care to know why?"

I didn't know how to answer. I wasn't sure if I could trust anything he said.

"She pretended... you see, Genesis. The prophecy specifically says a human will be called—she'll be the beginning of the end, she'll have golden hair..."

I touched my hair self-consciously.

"...eyes so beautiful an immortal could get lost in them."

I hung my head; I wasn't beautiful.

"You are breathtaking, more so than she could have ever hoped to be."

I looked up. "What happened?"

"She wanted too much," Cassius said in a sad voice. "And my hand was forced."

"I don't understand."

A soft rain started to fall. I held out my hands; the raindrops were blazing hot and turned to blood the minute they touched my fingertips.

"His blood calls to you." Cassius nodded in understanding. "Better return to him before he takes a bite."

"But you didn't tell me—"

I jolted awake to see Ethan hovering over me, his eyes completely black. "Tell me you didn't touch him. Tell me!" he roared.

I shook my head, my heart slamming against my chest. "I didn't touch him."

Ethan closed his eyes and swore. "I can't protect you in your dreams."

I reached for his face, shocked that he let me touch him now that the transition was over. "Then you'll have to trust me."

"Trust is earned."

"So let me try to earn it." I fought back angry tears.

He turned his head in my hand and kissed my palm. "I feel like I've already failed you. And that's the truth."

His breath was hot against my skin. I was afraid to move my hand, afraid it would shatter the moment. "Then stop failing."

"Not that simple," he whispered.

"Make it."

Black soulless eyes met mine. "Give me time."

"Do we have that? Time?"

He shuddered then leaned over me; his muscular body coming into contact with mine had me trembling with need. "I honestly hope so."

His lips grazed my neck.

I stopped breathing altogether.

"You taste like rain."

"I was on a lake."

"Dark Ones love water."

"Why?" I loved the feel of his lips against my neck as he talked.

"Because they love their own reflections."

I burst out laughing. It felt good.

Soon Ethan joined me and pulled my body on top of his. "Sleep, Genesis."

"No more dreams?"

"He can only invade once in a night."

"Oh... good." I yawned and stretched my arms above my head.

"Do that again, and I won't be held responsible for my own actions," he said in a husky voice.

"S-sorry."

"Don't be." He tugged my body against his.

It should have been uncomfortable, lying against his chest, but it was better than the bed.

"Now sleep."

chapter

nineteen

Ethan

"S o..." Alex grinned over his cup of coffee. "How was your evening?"

"It's too early," I growled. My body was still on fire. Sleep had been hell—or maybe heaven? Vampires still needed sleep, regardless of what silly books and movies said, and I'd gotten absolutely none.

Every breath she took I took with her, soaking her in, feeling her body move against mine. It was pure torture.

The human moaned.

She moaned! In her sleep! And clung to me like I was her lifeline. I hadn't felt that complete in a long time and didn't realize how hungry I was for that sort of affection until she freely gave it. Then again, she had been sleeping while I watched her.

"You're eyes are glowing," Alex mused.

"Why are you up? Didn't you take a woman home last night?" I desperately needed a subject change if I was going to make it through the rest of the morning with Genesis, teaching her, rubbing against her, smelling her. I nearly broke the mug in my hand just thinking about it.

"Kicked her out of bed after I was finished." Alex shrugged and examined his fingernails. "I bore easily."

"She wasn't entertaining enough?"

Alex let out a long snort. "It was only too easy. I asked her to strip—she stripped. I asked her to lie down on the bed—she lay down on the bed. Hell, I even asked the woman to purr—"

"Enough." I held up my hand.

"What?" Alex reached for his coffee and took another sip. "Boring. All of them. I need a challenge. Now Genesis—"

I hissed.

"Easy." He grinned. "I was only joking."

"Joke elsewhere."

Stephanie and Mason walked into the room, both of them wearing knowing smiles. Did everyone know of my hellish night?

"Ask him how he slept." Alex winked.

I threw a fork at his face. He moved his head out of the way, and the fork impaled itself into the wall.

"He's gotten quicker in his old age," Mason mused.

"It's all the women who throw things at him," Stephanie agreed. "Makes him quick."

"Oh please." Alex rolled his eyes. "They throw their bodies at me, would probably sell their souls if they could, and—" He coughed. "Hey, Genesis, you look well-rested. Happy. Content. Beautiful—"

"Alex." I stood, almost slicing my fingers through the table at his amused expression.

Genesis did look good.

Too good.

Gorgeous.

Flushed cheeks, red lips, gold hair.

I let out a groan, gaining everyone's attention, hers included. "Er, sorry... coffee got caught in my throat."

"You weren't drinking coffee," Alex pointed out.

"So..." Stephanie held out her hands to Genesis. "The jeans fit? I'm so glad. We'll go shopping later this week for more clothes, so you don't have to keep borrowing my stuff."

She looked perfect.

In jeans and a T-shirt.

My mouth watered the longer I stared.

Mason coughed.

I continued staring.

"Hungry?" Mason moved around the kitchen; pots started banging together. Genesis's eyes locked onto mine.

I smiled.

She blushed harder.

One. Small. Lick.

I moved closer, only to be intercepted by Mason. "Let her at least eat before you... do anything."

I shook myself out of my stupor and gave a firm nod. "Food, right. Eggs?"

Genesis flashed me a smile then turned her attention to Mason. "Eggs would be great, but I can cook."

"Nope." Mason shook his head fiercely. "A woman's place is not the kitchen."

"Really?" Genesis looked dumbfounded.

"Course not," Alex joined in cheerfully. "It's the bedroom."

I groaned.

Genesis let out a small laugh and shook her head. At least she could pick up on when they were joking and didn't stomp back up the stairs in frustration at our backward ways.

Mason cooked while Alex stole every single ounce of Genesis's attention.

Stephanie shared a pitiful look with me. Right, something's wrong in the world when a female siren feels sorry for a vampire.

I cleared my throat.

Genesis looked up.

"Would you like to take a tour of the house while Mason finishes up?"

"Sure."

I held out my hand.

"Careful." Alex stood and placed his hands on her shoulders. "If he gets you alone, you may not get breakfast…"

"Hilarious." I rolled my eyes.

"If he's hungry, I don't mind feeding him." Genesis's smoldering gaze met mine.

I swayed a bit on my feet as my fangs dug into my lower lip. I could actually feel my blood soar from my chest out to my fingertips as I anticipated her taste. Hell, I was in deep. My hands started to shake.

"Careful with your promises, human." Alex's lips curved into a smile. "He may just take you up on it."

Genesis took my hand, ignoring Alex, thank God, and squeezed.

We made it as far as the hallway.

I'd like to think I had enough self-control to make it further than that. I was old, controlled—but I'd never had her before.

And she made all the difference.

My fingers dug into the skin on her wrist as I tried to think of a sentence—any sentence—that would make sense, that I could say.

All I had was "Look, a hallway."

It was Genesis, the meek, brave little human, who stopped, lifted her head and said, "I don't mind."

Three words.

I don't mind.

Three words. They weren't romantic. They held no lust, no desire, nothing—but to me it was trust. It was her trying.

So I gently pushed her against the wall and took her mouth with all the slowness she deserved.

Blood soared through her veins.

I'd only taken small amounts, enough to satisfy, enough to taste, enough to complete the bond.

I'd only planned on taking another few drops.

But she turned her head, causing my fangs to graze down her neck.

Blood dripped.

So I licked, savoring the feel of her warmth on my tongue.

And when I accidentally grazed her again…

I bit.

chapter
twenty

Genesis

THE MINUTE HE BIT DOWN—I KNEW-I'D JUST DONE SOMETHING I COULDN'T undo… experienced something I would never, in all my days, be able to forget.

He said I'd know when he bit.

What he'd meant was I'd know when he finally gave into his instincts. It wasn't fast, like I'd expected, where he greedily sucked, pulled from my life source until I was drained.

Instead, the minute his teeth slid into my neck…

The world stopped.

Time stopped.

I closed my eyes, only to open them again and watch the world go by me in slow motion. Dust flicked in front of my face. The clock on the far side of the hallway moved… slower. Everything was slowed, even my heartbeat, and for those brief seconds or maybe even minutes…

I felt every single part of him.

Every stretch of muscle.

Every breath.

His pleasure was mine. It was almost hard to breathe because my senses were so overwhelmed with not only him, but with the world around me. The world I'd always known to be normal… was anything but normal.

The color of the wall had been blue.

Now it was electric blue.

Even Ethan's skin looked different, almost transparent as he clung to my body, his fingers digging into my flesh.

It was indescribable, and I was failing at trying to soak everything in.

His tongue swirled across my neck, and then I felt him draw a little bit more; this time the feeling changed, and suddenly all I could smell was burnt sugar—like Christmas, only better.

My body felt heavy; it pulsed in perfect cadence with him.

Ethan sighed against my neck, and the world returned to normal bland colors. The clock finally made it to the next minute.

And I had to fight to keep myself from crying out for him to keep going.

"I'm sorry." His voice was so low, so hoarse it was almost hard to understand his words. "I—you—" He cursed and pulled back.

His eyes were so green that I looked away. I had to because I was afraid if I kept staring, they would somehow burn my irises, blinding me.

"Don't be," I whispered. "I offered. Besides, you pulled me from my dream last night. It was the least I could do, right?"

"You have no idea," his lips lingered in front of mine, grazing my mouth with each word he spoke, "how good you feel—how wonderful you taste."

I leaned forward; the temptation to kiss him was too much.

A throat cleared. "Uh, do you still want eggs?"

I pushed against Ethan's chest, taking a step back, and glanced at Mason. His eyes betrayed nothing, so I wasn't sure if he'd seen us, or if he'd just assumed I'd been offering up myself as Ethan's breakfast.

"Yes," Ethan answered for me. "She's lacking protein."

"Huh?" I asked, dumbfounded. "How would you know…?"

He smirked.

"How's my iron?"

"Perfectly balanced."

We shared a smile. It felt good to talk to him like he didn't hate me, yet I still felt like I had no choice but to keep my guard up. It was a tie between wanting to open up to him, yet knowing that if I did and he rejected me again, I'd have no one to blame but myself.

I needed to remember he was still an immortal.

School really hadn't prepared me for what I was up against.

"Eat," Ethan urged. "I'll wait for you in the study. We can go over your horrible education after Mason's convinced you've eaten enough."

Mason held up the pan of eggs again in his hand.

Ethan kissed my head and left, leaving me and Mason alone in the hallway.

"So…" Mason moved out of the way so I could step by him. "Good morning so far?"

I fought to hide my grin. "The best."

"Wait until you eat my eggs."

"You mean it gets better?" I joked, elbowing him in the side.

"Yes, but be warned, I made the whole carton on account I'm used to cooking for more than one person. You'll insult me if you don't eat. Besides, according to your mate, you're lacking in protein."

I rolled my eyes and sat at the table while Mason served me an ungodly amount of eggs.

Both Stephanie and Alex were nowhere to be found.

I shoveled some eggs into my mouth and fought back a moan. The man could cook. They might tease him about eating berries and pinecones, but his eggs were fluffy. "So what do you guys do during the day?"

"As opposed to during the night?" Mason laughed. "Tell me, are you under the impression I go outside and howl at the moon when night falls?"

I felt my cheeks heat.

He barked out a laugh. "I may sit in on your studies this afternoon just so I can watch you blush the entire time."

I poked a few more eggs. "So?"

"The four of us are Immortal Elders, not only do we each have business holdings all over the world—ones we're still very much involved in—but we keep the peace."

I frowned. "Like the police?"

"Sort of." Mason shrugged. "I guess, in a way, I'm pack leader. I check in on the different families of werewolves in the Greater Seattle area and keep in constant communication with them. Some of the families like to live outside of the city and, naturally, outside of the country, so I get reports on them on a daily basis."

"Alex and Stephanie? What about them?"

"Sirens," Mason leaned back in his chair and lifted a mug of coffee to his lips, "tend to focus on play more than work."

"Meaning?"

"Curious little thing, aren't you?"

"Well…" I put down my fork. "I'm curious because, to be honest, when I was in school, I was taught you guys kept to yourselves. Nothing ever mentioned jobs or hobbies. I guess I assumed you just sat around and thought about your own immortality."

"How boring…" Mason's eyebrows lifted. "To sit around and only think about yourself. Sounds more like a Dark One than a werewolf."

"Is that what they do?"

"I'll let Ethan explain exactly what Dark Ones do, other than rule with an iron fist and petition archangels."

My ears perked up. "Real archangels?"

"No, fake ones… we just like the name because it sounds cool." He smirked. "Yes, real ones."

"You've seen them?"

"Once, a very long, long time ago. As long as we keep the peace between all species, they don't interfere. They have no reason to."

"And if war breaks out?"

Mason glanced over my shoulder, his eyes drawn to the hallway. "Ethan's irritated with me for keeping you so long. Two more bites then go back down the hall, first door on your left."

"But—"

"Two bites." Mason held up two fingers. "And then you get to go to school with a vampire."

I felt myself blush again because all I could think about was Ethan, in all his sexiness, trying to teach me something—anything—in that deep seductive voice of his. Yeah, it was going to be a really long day.

chapter
twenty-one

Ethan

I PACED IN THE STUDY LIKE SOMEONE WHO'D JUST DRUNK AN ENTIRE POT OF COFFEE and needed to work it out of his system.

All I tasted was her.

Her blood was still on my tongue—on my lips—and her memories, the ones that came with her blood—the ones that came at the price of me sharing my own—were so horrific I'd checked my watch at least five times to see if I'd make it across town and back without her knowing.

I wanted to murder her mother.

And the rest of the humans she'd been studying with.

Yes, secrecy was necessary, but to force the humans to think so little about themselves—especially Genesis—was criminal.

She was nearing. I could smell her.

Two footsteps and she'd be in the room.

And I'd probably lose my mind with the madness that always came with her scent.

"Nice study." Her voice was husky, dripping with seduction without even trying.

I broke the pencil in my hand and dropped it to the ground, turning on my heel, knowing that just staring at her would cause my heart to pound.

"Thank you." I managed the words between my lips, but they sounded more like a hiss— or possibly a choked whisper.

She pointed at one of the chairs. "Are we sitting?"

The damn chair taunted me. What I wouldn't do to have a king-sized bed in that room I could toss her onto.

I coughed into my hand. "Yes, the chair is fine."

Genesis tucked her golden hair behind her ears and sat, folding her arms across her chest. "So, school's in session?"

And you've been a very bad, bad, girl.

I groaned and turned back around, focusing on the dusty textbooks lining the walls. "Yes... why don't we start with what you know. Or at least what you've been learning up until now."

She took a deep breath.

I waited.

Still not turning back to face her because I was having a hell of a time keeping my body under control.

"I'm ugly."

Not what I expected.

"What?" I hissed, nearly knocking over the table in front of me to get to her. "What did you say?"

Her face paled. "The first phrase I remember as a child."

"Explain." Murder was definitely going to be on the agenda. Exquisite, painful, spectacular, satisfying murder.

Experiencing her memories of indoctrination by humans who were supposed to love her, provide for her, protect her, was one thing. But hearing the testament of the ugliness she was forced to endure—it was hell. It was heartbreaking, to still have her taste on my lips—to know the purity of her soul—and hear the firsthand account of a mother who basically spat in her face.

"I think most normal children imagine their first Christmas or their first birthday. All I can remember from my childhood is my mom telling me that I was ugly. She even wrote it on a piece of paper and put it on the bathroom mirror so I wouldn't become vain."

"Why would she do that?"

"It may sound cruel." Genesis nibbled her lower lip as tears filled her eyes. "But it's what we've been taught all our lives. We'll never live up to immortal standards, never be loveable, never be beautiful. We're mere objects. We study as hard as we can so that if our number is called, we can do a good job and bring honor to our families. My family has a sort of black mark on it for reasons my mother never told me. I never expected my number to be called, but in case it was, that's the only phrase she kept repeating to me. 'You are nothing. You are ugly.'"

"It's a lie," I whispered fiercely, taking her chin in my hands so she couldn't look away. "It's an absolute falsehood. You aren't ugly."

"It's okay if I am." Genesis's eyes were glassy with tears. "I mean, compared to immortals I'm—"

"Perfect," I finished for her. "And if I ever hear you say that about yourself again, you'll be punished."

"Punished?"

I released her chin. "Yes… I'll force you to eat pinecones instead of Mason's eggs."

She let out a laugh.

"You're beautiful, Genesis." I swallowed, placing my hands on the table in front of her. "Immortals would fight wars over you, and not just your face or your hair or the way your smile penetrates to someone's very soul—but because you're good."

"You don't know that. I could be a horrible person…"

"Your blood would taste bitter," I said honestly, "because the emotional manifests into the physical. Your blood would be repugnant to me, and other immortals would shy away from you because the last thing any immortal wants is to mate with a human who is pure evil."

"Oh…" Her breathing picked up speed. "They didn't teach us that."

"They wouldn't. It's a secret." I winked.

Her smile brightened considerably. "Thank you… for saying that. But it's hard to believe you after everything I've already seen and the way I seem to repel you and—"

I burst out laughing. "Oh, Genesis, if only you did repel me, things would be so much easier."

Her eyebrows squeezed together; I could read the frustration on her face.

"What else?" I sat down on the table in front of her. "What did they teach you?"

"They taught us that you scorned technology, that you didn't have time to teach your children what was necessary to survive, so as humans, it would be our job to educate your children as well as the families we were placed with."

"A glorified nanny."

"Yes." She nodded. "Exactly. And if we served the family well, then word would spread and more immortals would want me or my bloodline specifically."

"I wonder…" I tapped my chin. "Why they would lie?"

"Maybe because telling us our only job as a human was to become a mate to an immortal would terrify some people?"

"Possibly…" My mind reeled. None of it made sense. Sure, we'd kept our secrets over the years to protect ourselves, to protect the humans from getting greedy. "A hundred years ago, the schools taught respect for immortals and gave you knowledge about our world, about your place in it, about the balance. Why would they suddenly change that?"

Genesis shrugged. "If I had to guess, it may be because humans started dying. You said so yourself."

"There is that." I gritted my teeth together, suddenly worried that I wasn't doing enough to nourish her, to take care of her. It was my job, damn it!

"Ethan?" She licked her lips and leaned forward. "Your eyes are turning black again."

"Yes, they do that."

"Why?"

"Because they can."

"Seriously?"

I smiled. "No, because sometimes I can't control myself. They lose color when I'm feeling something extreme. The green simply fades into black. A lack of color doesn't mean I'm soulless or anything ridiculous. It just means the vampire blood has spread to other parts of my body, readying me for a fight."

"Hmm…"

"Your eyes turn green too, you know."

"What?" Her eyes widened. "What do you mean?"

"I've shared blood with you. When you're feeling something extreme, your eyes will turn green like mine. They match your mate's. You'll also notice that you don't need as much sleep as usual. Your skin will become softer. Think of it as having a very nice beauty regimen." I laughed at her excited expression. "You're welcome?"

"Wow."

"Not that you need it," I added quickly. "The last thing you need is to offer more temptation for me and my kind."

She didn't say anything.

"I'm curious to learn more about you," I said honestly. "But I don't want to keep you cooped up in the study all day. You don't seem like the type who enjoys studying."

She sighed. "What gave me away?"

"Your emotions easily betray you—and if they didn't, your blood surely would."

Red stained her cheeks, causing all of my blood to once again whoosh from my face to my lower extremities—only this time I wasn't bracing for a fight, but for a few hours tangled in bed with her.

"Why don't I take you to that bookstore we told you about? You can meet Drystan and see if it's something that you'd enjoy doing while I work."

"You work?"

"I'd like to think so."

"Like Mason?"

"Like Mason. Unlike Stephanie and Alex, however." I held out my hand. "I'll show you after the bookstore. Would you like that?"

"Yeah." She took my hand then squinted down at it.

"Something wrong?"

"I'm just trying to figure out what a vampire does for a job."

I barked out a laugh and wrapped my arm around her shoulders. "Yes, well, I think I may keep you in suspense until later."

She leaned into me.

I inhaled her scent, and my body shuddered with awareness.

It was horrible knowing that my reaction to her was so strong, yet she had no idea the war that raged inside of me, the desire I had to tell her everything,

296 | RACHEL VAN DYKEN

to cut myself open and show her my pain, my shame, and ask her to take it all away.

I was balancing with my life—possibly hers.

And yet, I couldn't find myself to regret anything.

Not anymore.

Not after talking with her.

Not after truly tasting her.

"Hungry again?" she asked.

"What?"

"You were licking me."

"Uh…" Damn it, I really needed to stay focused. I moved away from her, enough to evade the temptation of her neck. "Sorry."

She glanced up at me through hooded eyes. "It's okay."

I growled.

She bit her lower lip.

And again, we were in the damn hallway. What was it about the hallway that destroyed every shred of sense I possessed?

"Ethan?" Mason called from the kitchen. "You going out?"

"Yeah…" I called, never taking my eyes from Genesis. "The bookstore."

"Get me berries!" he yelled. "We're out."

I shook my head, the spell broken. "Eat meat, for God's sakes, wolf."

"Berries," he repeated.

Genesis laughed softly.

"Damn berries." I led her to the door. "Shall we?"

"Should we ask him if he needs pinecones too?"

A pinecone flew by my head. "Clearly, he still has some left if he's using them as ammo."

chapter
twenty-two

Genesis

"I'VE BEEN HERE BEFORE," I BLURTED WHEN ETHAN PULLED UP TO A downtown book shop around fifteen minutes from his house. It was one of my favorites. It had the best scones in the world, and the coffee was well-known in the area. "It's called Wolf's."

"Funny, right?" Ethan smirked.

I rolled my eyes and got out of the car. Did that mean I'd met the owner before? The bookstore wasn't huge like a Barnes and Noble, but it was big enough that it had two levels and multiple employees.

The bell on the door chimed as Ethan opened it and ushered me in. The smell of books was so familiar my knees almost gave way.

"Ethan." A man who looked like he was around my age smiled in our direction and made his way toward us. He seemed younger than Mason even; he had the same shaggy hair and really dark brown eyes—almost black. "So this is… Genesis."

"Hi." I waved awkwardly, unsure of how I was supposed to address him since, technically, nobody knew what he was.

He grinned. "You're cute."

Ethan growled.

"I meant it in an innocent way." Drystan held up his hands. "Easy…" He turned his attention back to me. "You've got the job."

"Just like that?"

"Just like that."

"But what if I'm horrible at it?" I blurted.

Drystan laughed. "If an Elder vouches for you—well, it's as good as done. Now, why don't I go over the schedule with you while Ethan makes himself scarce. Are you okay with starting work tomorrow? I had to fire someone yesterday for stealing, so I'm a bit shorthanded."

"Sure."

I was about to follow him when Ethan tugged me back and whispered in my ear, "Be careful."

A cold chill settled over me. I wasn't sure why I needed to be careful, considering he was going to be leaving me alone with this guy for hours on end, but I decided to listen to him regardless.

"Schedule…" Drystan moved toward a workstation located in the middle of the store. "…is always kept on the computer. And we do all our sales through Square, so we don't really have a typical cash register. Are you familiar with it?"

Technology. Yes. I was the one who was supposed to be teaching them— at least at one point. I nodded.

"Good." He clapped his hands together. "We get new books every Tuesday. You'll have to sign for them, and if we aren't busy, you're free to stock the shelves." He pointed behind him. "Books that are left out need to be reshelved at the end of the day and, luckily, you don't have to make coffee or scones. My wife does all that."

"Wife?"

He grinned. "We work together. It's a mate thing."

"Do all mates work together?"

His eyes darted behind me as if looking for Ethan. "Well, it's different for each of us."

"Oh."

"I'll pay you fifteen an hour. Though it's not like you need it, considering who you're with."

I blushed. I didn't like the idea of owing Ethan anything; somehow it felt wrong. I didn't deserve it, didn't earn it, and regardless of how well things were going that day, I had no idea if one minute he was going to get tired of me, and I'd need money for some reason.

"Great." I found myself shaking his hand, excited that I wouldn't be stuck at the house and would be able to actually contribute to society.

Drystan squeezed my hand, then flinched and jerked it back, like I'd hurt him.

"Is everything okay?" Ethan asked, approaching us.

Drystan shared a look with him. "Ethan, a moment?"

Ethan's smile was forced. "Sure. Genesis, why don't you pick out some books?"

I nodded and watched them walk off.

Had I done something to offend the werewolf? Everything had seemed fine until I'd touched him.

He'd flinched.

Why would he flinch?

I started mindlessly walking the aisles of books, when I heard Ethan's growl.

Slowly, I moved closer until I could hear his voice.

"I can't protect her if he comes." Drystan's voice was frantic. "I have a family, Ethan."

"He won't."

"He could bring them down on me and my family. You know he could, and I don't know how much time I have left with her—before she dies like the others. I don't want to spend that time worrying that a Dark One's going to kill me."

Ethan sighed heavily. "Trust me."

"I do. You know I do. It's her I don't trust."

What? That made no sense! I was a mere human!

"She's trustworthy," Ethan barked. "You dare insult my mate?"

"You dare bring in a marked one?"

"We've bonded—it's done."

"But it's not," Drystan argued. "Not unless she fully gives herself to you—you know that."

"She will."

Drystan swore. "How long do you have?"

Ethan's breathing picked up. "We have time."

"How much?"

"This is ridiculous. I'm an Elder."

"Ethan—"

"She's already chosen."

"No." Drystan's voice was distant. "She hasn't. Ice still flows through her veins. She may have said the words, but she isn't there, not yet, and until she is, he will continue to come for her."

I was listening so intently that I almost let out a yelp when Ethan called for me.

I grabbed the first two books I saw and ran around the corner to find him. He didn't seem on edge, but I knew he was. I could feel the distance building around his body again.

"What books did you choose?"

I looked down at the books in my hands and almost choked. "Um, you know what? I don't need any books today."

He rolled his eyes. "Give me the books, Genesis."

"I think I've changed my mind. I'm just going to go—"

He snatched them out of my hands and looked down. I knew the exact moment he'd read the titles.

Because he started shaking.

His eyes flashed black then green then black again as he looked at me, his fangs elongating.

I took a step back.

Drystan pretended to ignore us.

And my heart picked up speed as Ethan's gaze devoured me.

"We'll take these." He set them on the table, his smile indulgent. "It seems my human likes to… study."

Drystan gave nothing away as he scanned the books, took Ethan's change, and handed him the bag.

"See you tomorrow, Genesis."

I waved with my free hand while Ethan placed a death grip on my other. Yeah, things were about to get embarrassing really fast.

The minute we were outside, he pushed me into the car.

The silence was thick. Tense.

"So," Ethan spoke in a gravelly voice, "'Three Hundred and Sixty-five Positions for Three Hundred and Sixty-Five Days.'"

My body flamed.

"And what was the other?" He scratched his head. "'Kama Sutra for the Advanced'?"

I banged my head against the car's window. "In my defense, I was distracted."

"Mmm, care to share what had you so distracted?"

"No."

"I feel very much distracted," Ethan mused. "In fact, I may need you to distract me from the distractions."

My heart picked up speed. "Oh?"

"Yes."

He said it like a mere whisper, but I felt it in my chest. I felt the yes everywhere. I gripped the leather seat with my hands to keep from reaching for him.

"Work," I blurted. "You said you'd show me what you do."

"I'm not thinking about work right now."

I trembled.

"Care to know my fixation?"

I turned, slowly making eye contact with him. "Books?"

"Genesis." He said my name like a vow.

I reached for him at the same time he reached for me. Our mouths collided; warmth spread from my chest down to my toes as he lifted me from my seat.

And then a sudden chill filled the air.

Abruptly, he let me go and cursed. "He's close. Let's go."

Freaked out, I buckled my seatbelt and almost hit my head on the dash as Ethan peeled out of the parking spot. When I glanced at the rearview mirror, it was to see Cassius standing on the curb, blowing an ice-filled kiss in my direction.

※

"Fish," I repeated in disbelief. "That's your job?"

"What?" Ethan shrugged.

After our *almost*-run-in with Cassius, Ethan had decided it was best to confuse the Dark One and get my scent all over Seattle.

We'd gone to at least three bakeries, two Starbucks, bought flowers, berries, and finally ended up by the pier.

The building said *Immortal Industries*.

Talk about blatant.

"You ship fish?" I still couldn't believe it.

"Worldwide." Ethan grinned. "Disappointed?"

"The name needs work."

"Yes, well, I decided that sometimes the best way to hide is to do the opposite of hiding." He frowned. "You're cold?"

I shivered. "A bit."

He wrapped his arms around me. "It's Cassius."

"You lied to me."

His breathing slowed. "Eavesdropping is frowned upon—always."

"What aren't you telling me?"

"A lot."

"At least you're honest about that much."

Ethan went very still. My back was to him; his arms wrapped around my body, warming me from the inside out. "I'd have to show you—talking about it is too difficult."

"Is it scary?"

"No." His lips touched my neck. "Just very sad, embarrassing, a lot of other unfortunate emotions."

"Show me."

"Not here."

"Yes, here." I turned in his arms. "Eventually, you're going to need my help, right? You can't just keep information from me then expect the bond— or whatever we have—to make up for everything else. We're at least friends, right?"

His eyes widened. "Yes."

"And friends share."

"They do."

"And you drink from me."

"Shhh…" He pulled me closer. "Yes."

"So, you owe me this. Honesty, you owe me."

"You raised your voice." He sounded amused.

"Yeah, well… you make me angry."

Another heavy sigh. "If I show you, you may leave me."

"I'd have a choice?"

"We always have a choice, Genesis."

"So trust me to stay."

He was still again; his heartbeat slowed—I could feel it like it was my own. Finally, he answered with a brisk, "Alright."

We walked in silence back to the car.

"It's safer at the house," he whispered. His gaze no longer had light in it; it was like the conversation sucked all the energy, all the spark from his body, leaving him haunted.

When we walked hand in hand through the door, Mason was waiting. Ethan chucked the berries at Mason's head and dragged me down the hall and up the stairs.

Once we were blanketed in the silence of the bedroom, the doors locked behind us, Ethan turned, his eyes black, his fangs elongated. "Promise me to wait ten minutes."

"What?"

"Ten minutes. When you wake up, wait ten minutes before you decide to leave or stay. At least give me that."

"Okay…" I swallowed the lump in my throat. His heart was breaking, I could feel it, and I had no idea why. "Ten minutes."

His teeth ripped into his wrist, and then that same wrist was pressed against my mouth. "Try to understand…" His last words before sleep overcame me.

Before a dream appeared in front of my eyes.

Before I came face to face with the most beautiful woman in the world. The same one from Ethan's dreams when the transition had occurred.

Her eyes danced with life.

Ethan adored her.

I adored her.

She danced around him.

He laughed and tugged her across his body. "I love you."

"I love you too, silly." She drank from him freely, yet she was human. She had fangs—just like Ethan. But I knew she was human. I could feel it.

"Make me immortal." She pouted, bracing herself over his body. "It's time already."

"After our child is born, it will happen. You know this."

"I'm tired of waiting."

Her pouting was getting on my nerves. Rage poured through me as she dragged her fingernails down his chest. That was my chest; those lips were my lips.

I clenched my fists at my sides and kept watching.

More scenes of them laughing, playing.

I tried to look away, but it was impossible.

Cassius appeared. I flinched, thinking it was a trick, but he was part of the dream.

"And how is my favorite girl?" He kissed her palm.

"Upset." She put her hands on her hips. "He refuses to make me immortal."

"Is that what you want? Your greatest desire?"

She nodded.

"Above Ethan, even? Your own mate?"

"He may be my mate…" Her hands trailed down Cassius's chest. "…but we both know I have a wide range of tastes."

"If you don't truly love him, the change will kill you." Cassius pushed her hand away. "You know this."

"I do love him!" She twirled around. "I love everything about this life. Is it so wrong to want more?"

"Sometimes…" Cassius's face fell. "…it really is."

The scene changed.

Cassius was walking with Ethan. "She's going mad."

"I know."

"It's the power—your power's drugging her, Ethan. You must let her go."

"No!" Ethan roared, pushing at Cassius. "I could no more cut out my own heart, you know that!"

"It's you or her," Cassius said.

"She's pregnant."

Cassius cursed and looked away. "Is it yours?"

"How dare you!" Ethan roared. "Of course it is!"

"And you know this for a fact? Because your mate is true?"

"I'd know if she weren't. I'd taste it in her blood."

"Unless you were too blinded by your own feelings… friend." Cassius shook his head again. "If the madness overtakes her, if you're wrong, you'll have to kill her yourself."

"I'm not wrong."

"So arrogant."

"Are we done here?"

I blinked away the tears. How could Cassius ask that of Ethan? I felt the love he had for her; it was powerful, like a star exploding in the sky.

"A daughter!" Ethan laughed and held up his daughter. "Ara! You've given me a daughter!"

She nodded.

The scene from the dream replayed, only slightly different than what I'd watched before.

Cassius entered the room.

Ara, Ethan's mate, looked away from both of them.

"I told you what would happen," Cassius said. "I warned you." He reached for the child.

"No!" Ethan screamed. "Don't. Cassius if you do this—"

"It's already been done." Cassius turned and pointed his hand at Ara. "Is this the daughter of a vampire?"

She trembled beneath the blankets then burst out laughing. "No, no, you know whose daughter she is."

Ethan paled. "Ara? My love?"

"He promised me immortality." Ara pointed at Cassius. "So give it! I birthed a daughter! The daughter of a Dark One! I will be queen!"

Her laughter hit a point where I needed to cover my ears.

"Cassius?" Ethan whispered. "Tell me you did not do this. Tell me, brother, that you did not—"

"She was tested. She failed," Cassius said simply, grabbing the child. "Now finish it."

"Cassius!" Ethan roared.

Ara continued to laugh. "I'm going to be queen. Finally, Ethan. I'm sorry I didn't tell you, but I was afraid you'd be angry. You know I love you, yes?"

Ethan's eyes turned black; the entire room shook.

"You bitch!" He clenched his fists so hard blood began trickling from his palms. And then, in an instant, he was on top of her.

One bite.

She struggled for two seconds.

Before I felt her life-force leave the room.

"It's done." Ethan swore, falling to his knees, blood dripping down his face.

"She would have died regardless," Cassius answered.

"My daughter."

"She's not your daughter, brother."

Ethan's eyes flashed. "Give me my child!"

"One day," Cassius started to fade into the darkness, "you'll thank me."

"One day... I will kill you."

Cassius disappeared from the room with the newborn, his voice a mere whisper. "You can't."

I woke up gasping for air.

I was lying in bed. Ethan was a statue next to me.

"Y-you killed her!"

Tears streamed down my face. I hated him. Hated us. I couldn't explain it, but the anger he'd felt—I felt; the shame—it was mine. I tasted revenge on my tongue. I wanted to scratch his eyes out, yet scratch my own out because it was like I was the one who had committed murder.

The darkness consumed me.

"Ten minutes," Ethan whispered.

"No."

"You promised."

He reached for my hand.

When I didn't take it, he straddled me and pinned my arms to the mattress. "Ten minutes. You promised. In ten minutes, I'll release you. Not a second sooner."

"Get. Off."

"He can still take you from me—like he took her."

"She chose herself, not him."

Ethan nodded sadly. "Yes."

I struggled against him, but he was too strong.

"Ten minutes, Genesis."

chapter
twenty-three

Ethan

HER EYES WERE GREEN.

Just like mine.

I felt her emotions like they were my own—relived the entire thing as if I was killing Ara all over again.

She'd done the unthinkable. She'd not only lied to her mate but cheated on him and produced a child with that lie. I knew Genesis wouldn't understand. But I also knew trying to get her to understand while she was still trembling from shock wouldn't do any good.

"You didn't have to kill her." Genesis's voice was hollow, her eyes still blazing green.

"I did." I touched my forehead to hers. "Because if I didn't, Cassius would have."

"She slept with Cassius?"

"He never said." I sighed. "He never admitted it. The child was—not normal."

"Not normal?"

"She wasn't a vampire."

"What was she?"

"I don't know," I whispered. "Perhaps I'll never know—maybe that was Cassius's way of protecting me, of protecting my bloodline, my reputation, though it hardly mattered once everyone discovered my mate was suddenly dead."

"But…" The green of her eyes started to fade. "Is that what would happen to me if I left you?"

"No." My hands shook holding her down; from showing her the memory, my strength had been depleted. If I didn't feed, I was going to sleep for the next fifteen hours. "Humans are turned immortal after they produce a child, a gift we bestow upon them."

"So she should have lived."

"I killed her before she could accept the gift because Cassius was right. She was going mad with a lust for power. Had I given her immortality, I would have created a monster."

"You still killed her."

"I loved her too much to let Cassius do it—loved her too much to turn her into a monster. She wasn't made for it. She was one of the first humans to start... showing effects of the imbalance. A part of me believes it's my fault that the humans keep dying."

"What are you saying?"

"No human mate had died—until I killed my own mate."

"And then?"

"Every human after... has died—not right away. Most live past a hundred having not aged at all. We think the immortality takes, and they simply don't wake up."

"You did something," she whispered, "to the natural order."

"Possibly."

"So it's your fault."

Heaviness descended like a fog. "It was my fault... for loving her too much."

"Your love for her destroyed everything."

"So now you know." I moved away from Genesis and laid my head down on the pillow next to her. "Loving again will take everything I have left."

"You can't love again? Or you won't?"

"It's already too late..." I slurred my words, darkness overtaking me. I needed blood and sleep. "It's too late for me now... but not for you."

"What?" Genesis shook my body. "What do you mean?"

"If you don't love back, the final step never completes itself. You'll be free. I'm setting you free."

"Ethan." Her voice was distant. "Ethan, what's happening?"

"Exhausted." I barely got the word past my lips.

Something soft hit one of my fangs. And then blood was trickling into my mouth.

Memories flashed.

"Now it's your turn to dream," Genesis whispered. "Dream of me."

Blackness overcame me and then, in an instant, I was sitting in a desk with other humans listening to the instructor drone on and on about immortals.

"Never look an immortal in the eye!" the teacher snapped. "You are nothing. Remember that."

I cringed.

A bell rang in the distance. I watched as Genesis stood and walked out by herself.

Her mother was waiting for her at the end of the hallway, hands on hips. "Where's your backpack?"

"Oh..." Genesis covered her mouth. She couldn't have been older than seventeen. "I totally forgot. I'll go back to my locker and—"

"Do you really think any immortal will want you? If you can't even remember something as silly as a textbook?"

Genesis shook her head, tears welling in her eyes.

"Useless." Her mother gripped Genesis's arm and shoved her the rest of the way down the hall. "Good thing your number will never be called—you're too ugly."

"Yes, Mother."

I wanted to scream in outrage. She was gorgeous! Even in the dream, I could see the purity of the blood, taste the goodness on my lips.

A house appeared in the distance.

It was poorly lit. The shutters were falling from the windows, and the porch steps had seen better days. The foundation crumbled beneath the heaviness of the home, making it appear depressing.

I took the steps two at a time and found myself in Genesis's room.

She had books everywhere. Books about vampires, werewolves, and sirens. Then finally, Dark Ones.

"Are you studying?" Her mother's voice sounded from the other side of the house.

"Yes!" Genesis yelled, tugging a piece of licorice through her teeth. "Almost done for the night."

Her mother appeared at the door, took one look at Genesis, and scowled. "Candy makes you fat."

The licorice fell from her lips as tears welled in her eyes. "I thought you said I could have licorice if I skipped breakfast?"

"Ugly." Her mother sighed. "And now you'll be fat for them."

"But a number hasn't been called in years!" Genesis argued.

Her mother stilled. "Are you challenging my authority?"

"No." Genesis hung her head. "I'm sorry."

"I do this because I love you."

Bullshit!

Instead of staying in Genesis's room, I followed her mother to the other room where she sat down at a kitchen table and started pouring over bills.

Most of them were overdue.

"Stupid girl," she said under her breath. Her hands shook.

I glanced harder into the mother's eyes.

Jealousy stared right back.

"My number wasn't called." Her mother sniffed, still talking to herself. "Of course hers won't ever be called. It's all because of that stupid bitch."

She wasn't talking about Genesis.

Confused, I moved away from the mother and made my way down the hall again. Pictures lined the walls.

I smiled at the pictures of Genesis as a child.

Something about her struck me as familiar. Almost oddly so.

Her mother was in one picture.

And then another elderly woman. She had pretty, almond-shaped eyes.

The pictures went on, years and years of pictures. The color turned to black and white.

When I reached the end of the hallway, there was one final picture.

It was ancient. I leaned in.

My knees buckled as I braced myself against the wall.

"Ara," I breathed.

chapter
twenty-four

Genesis

HE SLEPT FOR HOURS. I STAYED. A PART OF ME WANTED TO LEAVE, BUT HE WAS right. After ten minutes, I'd calmed down enough to think about the situation logically, not that I still wasn't terrified he'd end up killing me. I no longer felt safe, but I didn't feel like Ethan was a threat.

I'd used his fangs to drop blood into his mouth, hoping it would have the same effect, since he was going to sleep. I wasn't sure if it would help him understand me better, but if it was a night for sharing, maybe he could at least pull information from my past.

I wasn't confident it would be helpful. He'd probably be bored out of his mind, but it was worth a try.

Two hours after giving him my blood, he jolted awake, nearly sending me off the bed in fear.

"Ara," he yelled.

I flinched. "Ethan? You were dreaming. It's okay." Clearly, my blood hadn't worked.

He turned, his eyes predatory. "Tell me you didn't know."

"Know what?" I brought my knees to my chest. "What are you talking about?"

"She's from your bloodline."

"Who?"

"Ara."

"The mate you killed?"

He growled.

"I—" Tears welled in my eyes. "Are you sure?"

"Her picture." His eyes went black. "I saw a picture. It was old—it was her."

"You have to believe me." I held up my hands. "I would never lie."

Ethan shook his head; dark circles appeared under his eyes. "Sorry…" He trembled. "I'm still exhausted. It was a shock. We need to visit your mother."

"She hates me."

"Shall I kill her for you? Once I've gained the information I need?"

"No," I blurted.

Ethan sighed against my neck. "Just give me the word if you change your mind. The woman's insane."

"Ara?"

"No. Your mother."

"I hope it doesn't run in the family."

"Your blood is pure." Ethan kissed my neck. "Believe that truth, and you'll be fine."

"Is that—" Insecurity wrapped itself around me. "Is that why you wanted to mate with me? Because I remind you of her?"

"No!" Ethan pounced on me, his eyes so black that I was afraid if I stared too long I'd fall into their depths and never come back to reality. "You're different—you feel different."

"Different," I repeated.

"Better," he soothed, nipping my lower lip. "The best."

"I don't want to be her."

"You aren't." His voice was commanding. "And I'm too exhausted to spend the night arguing with you."

"You can take more blood… if you need to." The thought sent a little thrill of excitement through me as his eyes faded back to green.

Ethan moved off me and stared up at the ceiling. "You don't want me to do that."

"Why?"

"Because," he growled, "it won't be a little blood, just like it won't be a little bite… just like I won't stop at the bite but will continue kissing you and possessing you until you can't breathe—until my body fills yours, until you scream for more just when you don't think you can take it."

I had no words.

"Scared you?"

"I'm not sure." Was I feeling fear? Or excitement?

"Your heart's racing."

"Yes."

"If I asked you for everything, would you give it freely, knowing what you know?"

"If I offered you everything, would you take it? Knowing the possibility of my bloodline?"

We lay in silence.

I thought Ethan had fallen asleep.

Until he moved, hovering over me, his lips grazing mine with the softest of kisses. "I don't think I can stop myself…"

"What?"

"I can't set you free. I know I said I could. I can't. I lied."

"A vampire who's a liar. Who would have thought?" I teased.

He didn't return my smile. "It's a death sentence."

"Then show me sweet death." I wrapped my arms around his neck. He let out a pitiful groan before his mouth touched mine again.

"You ask for death—yet you offer me life."

"I'm human. We're confusing like that."

His smile felt good against my lips.

"Kiss me harder," I begged, hooking my legs around his body.

"I'm old… go easy on me." He returned my frantic kiss with a slow torturous one of his own. He licked my lips then pierced the bottom, sucking away droplets of blood.

"You don't want easy." I sighed.

In a flash, I was on my back, my shirt completely gone. "You're right." He tongued the curve of my ear. "Mine."

"Yours."

My jeans went flying. "All. Mine."

Cold air bit at my skin. My heartbeat sped up as Ethan's body hovered over me, his lips hot on my neck. With a growl, he tugged my hair, forcing my head back, exposing my neck completely to his lips.

His fangs slid across my neck. "I'm going to mark you forever. You still have a choice, Genesis."

"No," I breathed, squeezing my eyes shut, "I really don't."

"You do," he urged. His body was scorching hot behind me. "Tell me no."

"I can't," I repeated, tilting my head back further, arching my back.

With a growl, he pierced my skin. I felt each drop of blood leave my body.

I reached for his shirt, but he slapped my hands away, pinning my wrists above my head as his mouth nipped my neck again. My body almost bucked off the bed when he drank more. It was different than before.

His tongue scalded me—in the best way—almost like he really was forever marking me, making it so anyone who looked at me knew whom I belonged to.

"Ethan—" I almost choked on his name, stunned I could even remember it after all the emotions swirling inside me—fear, excitement, lust, and something else, something bigger than me, bigger than him, having him pressed against me, his hot mouth on my skin. It was right, even though I couldn't explain anything beyond that.

He drank deeper.

The room exploded into a burst of light.

I gasped in response. His mouth left my neck and moved along my chin.

He released one of my hands. I immediately dug it into his hair and pulled his mouth to mine. Our mouths met with such aggression—almost violence—that I was sure more blood would be drawn.

He chuckled against my lips. "Is the need for me greater than anything else?"

"No," I lied, not wanting to admit to him that my need was so great I didn't even want to survive without him—couldn't.

His eyes darkened as his tongue slid across my mouth. "I can taste the lie on your lips."

"Really?"

"God, you're beautiful." His eyes were so black, so inviting.

I tugged his head again then moved my hand down his chest. He closed his eyes; a hiss escaped between his teeth.

He lifted the shirt over his head and grabbed my hand, holding it firm against his muscled stomach. "Touch me."

I really didn't need an invitation.

I don't know what possessed me to lean forward and lick his stomach—but that's what I did.

A guttural growl erupted from him as soon as my tongue licked along the thick lines of muscle along his stomach. "I said touch me. Don't kill me."

Laughing, I traded licks for kisses; he tasted sweet—scalding. Power surged through me with each tremble of his body, each moan. His hands dug into my hair, tugging me closer to his chest. I reached for the button of his pants, expecting him to slap me away or say something.

He went very still.

Too still.

Nervous, I pulled back and looked up at him.

His eyes were back to green. "There's no going back, Genesis."

I kept my gaze trained on him as I slowly undid the button and slid my hands inside.

Green turned to black as his fangs dug into his bottom lip. His head tilted back. He was like a god... in that moment more immortal than I'd ever acknowledged or realized.

chapter
twenty-five

Ethan

H ER HANDS STOPPED MOVING.
I'd killed her.
That was my first errant thought—because at that point, I'd stopped thinking rationally and had moved past logic, straight toward possessing Genesis and marking her beyond recognition.

With a groan, I touched my forehead to hers gently, so as to not scare her into realizing that she was, in fact, ready to give herself fully to something not human.

Her breathing picked up speed again.

I smirked and moved her hands down the side of my hips. When her fingers came into contact with my length, she let out a tiny gasp.

"Care to explore?" I taunted. "Or does the human not like playing with fire."

She gripped me—hard, almost painfully so—considering I was ready to impale the poor thing.

"I can handle it," she whispered in a husky voice.

"Prove it," I smirked, licking her lips again, needing that taste more than I needed anything else in my existence.

Her tight little fingers began to move. I enjoyed her innocence for about two seconds before I was ready to lose my mind.

"What?" she asked when I moved her hands away and quickly ripped off the remainder of my clothes. "I thought you wanted me to explore."

"We'll explore later," I said gruffly.

Her cheeks stained with delicious blood.

"I'm not patient," I blurted. "Not when it comes to you—your taste." I lunged for her. "Your essence."

With a predatory growl, I tugged her bra down and bit between her breasts then licked my way down toward her navel. Her body was made for exploring for hours on end—hours I didn't have—because selfishly, waiting seemed like a horrible idea.

Each lick had her muscles clenching.

Each kiss, her body damn near flying off the bed.

She was sensitive to my every touch. Possessiveness washed over me as I moved down her hips and bit the inside of her thigh, where her life source—her blood—ran purest.

I received a kick to the head. Dodging it, I chuckled and bit the other side of her thigh.

"That... feels... funny." She gripped the sheets in her hands.

"I believe, in this situation, the correct word is amazing... not funny, humorous, or any of the sort," I growled.

"S-sorry." She tried clenching her legs together.

"No." I pulled them apart and gazed upon every inch of her. "You're mine. I get to see every inch of you, I get to lick all of you, and when I'm done, I get to taste over and over again until you scream for me to stop."

"You think I'll want you to?"

I barked out a laugh. "You're only human."

"Don't break me."

"Wouldn't dream of it," I whispered against her inner thigh. "Now let the vampire play."

"I'm not sure I'm capable of handling that without passing out," Genesis whimpered when my mouth found her core. She let out another gasp while I steadied her hips exactly where I wanted them. She tasted so sweet I could have died.

"Ethan!"

I pulled back. "That was more of an irritated yell, not a scream." Sighing, I sucked harder, drinking her in. "Try again, human."

Tremors wracked her body.

She clenched her eyes shut. When they opened, they were bright green.

"Ethan." Now she said my name like a prayer.

"Yes?"

"What's happening?"

I was making sure she never left me—that's what was happening. "You're ready for me..."

"No." She shook her head. "I don't think I can take anymore of—"

I took possession of her mouth then lifted her into my arms. My lips moved to her neck, and I bit, knowing the effect it would have on her.

Our lovemaking wouldn't be fast.

Not if I drank.

I was going to extend every sensation... in slow motion.

One drop of my own blood lingered on my tongue. I shared it with her just as our bodies joined together.

Genesis's green eyes blinked in wonder as I lowered her down on me, inch by inch, sensation by sensation, each second sharing another drop of my blood, slowing down the process and making it so she would never forget what it felt like to be with her mate—to be possessed by me and only me.

Her body was made for mine—stretched around me so perfectly that even in my old age, with my experience, with my patience, I refused to share more drops of blood, refused to drink anymore. I just wanted her. Over and over again.

"You're mine," I demanded, thrusting faster and faster. "Say it!"

Her nails dug into my back.

I needed to hear the words.

Her green eyes flashed. "Ethan."

"Say it…" I slowed.

"Don't stop."

"Say it!"

"I'm yours."

The words washed over me as I thrust one last time, the walls of my carefully built world crashing down around me in shattered pieces.

She gave me her body.

In return, I gave her my soul.

chapter
twenty-six

Genesis

MY BODY WAS HEAVY—ON FIRE—AND THE ONLY WAY IT FELT BETTER WAS when I was pressed against Ethan. I had no idea how long we'd slept. He woke me up three times in the middle of the night. Each time, he'd drunk from me, never a lot, but enough to make it so my world stopped.

Each kiss was like a slow drug.

Each touch of his fingertips, each caress, went on for an eternity until I lost complete track of time.

I fell asleep with my face pressed against his solid chest and my legs wrapped halfway around his body.

"Genesis." His smooth voice was hypnotic. "Genesis, wake up."

"No." I pressed my face harder against his chest.

A warm chuckle erupted. "Yes, we have work to do. Well, you have work to do, and then after your so-called work, we're going to pay your mother a visit."

I didn't open my eyes. "No staying in bed all day?"

"About that…" Ethan sighed. "The good news is it will feel like we've been in bed for days when really it could have been mere hours."

"Hmm?" I perked up. "Well, that's a nice trick."

"I'm full of them." His eyes sparkled. "Care to know more?"

"Yes," I whispered, my mouth finding his.

With a groan, he pushed me back against the mattress and loomed over me, his naked body glorious-looking against the sunlight streaming through the window. "Perhaps we'll stay a bit longer."

"Yes." I nodded my head eagerly. "I'm your mate, after all. Don't you want me to be pleased?"

"You were pleased at least four times last night, possibly five, if we count the time I—"

"Shh." I put my hands over his mouth.

He smirked. "Afraid the dust will hear?"

I rolled my eyes.

"Ethan!" Alex's voice boomed on the other side of the door. "Feed her!"

"Ignore him," Ethan hissed.

The knock got louder. "For the love of God, she's human. Give her food."

"He's a siren. He knows nothing." Ethan continued kissing me.

"Mason will break down the door if he has to." Fighting broke out in the hall. "Ethan, I can smell the sex from here. One immortal to another, feed her before you can't feed from her anymore."

Ethan growled and pulled back from me. "They have no manners."

I was half-tempted to cover my face with my hands. Had they heard us? Of course they'd heard us, and they knew, and they could... Yeah, I wanted to crawl under the bed and hide for a few days. Instead, Ethan pounced from the bed, put on a pair of jeans, and jerked open the door while I tried to hide beneath the covers.

Alex peered over Ethan's shoulder and waved.

I had no choice but to wave back and hope that I wasn't as red as I felt.

"She's alive." Alex held up his hand for a high five. "No? Not funny? Too soon?"

"Horrible joke," Mason said next to him. "I made eggs. She's going to need food. Make her eat everything on the plate and—"

He was still talking when Ethan slammed the door in his face and brought a giant plate of food over to me.

"Forgive them." Ethan scowled. "There aren't typically secrets between us, and they're just concerned for you."

I pointed at the eggs, ten slices of bacon, and toast. "Clearly, they don't want me to starve."

"Wolves." Ethan looked heavenward. "He should be more concerned with his own diet, the ass."

"It does smell good." I moved up the bed so I could lean against the head-board. "Do you eat?"

Ethan's lips curved into a predatory smile. "I ate several times last night. Care for me to refresh your memory?"

My cheeks burned.

"So tempting." He reached for a piece of bacon and held it to his lips, taking a small bite that had my entire body clenching to keep from reaching out and attacking him. "And yes, I can eat. I typically do eat but haven't been because when we drink, we don't need normal food."

"But before me..." I grabbed a piece of toast. "You were eating normal food."

"I like you better." He winked. "But yes, I was."

"Good to know I'm better than bacon."

"Your taste..." His eyes brightened. "...is unlike anything I've ever had."

"Hmm..." I licked my lips.

"Stop it," he hissed and looked away. "Damn, I can't watch you eat. I'm going to shower while you eat your entire plate as per Mason's orders, and then I'll contemplate letting you leave this room so you can go to the bookstore."

"Ah!" I almost knocked over the food. "My job! Am I late? Will I get fired?"

Ethan burst out laughing. "It's eight in the morning. He's expecting you when I drop you off. No sooner, no later. You won't get fired. He wouldn't dream of it, and you really are adorable."

"And hot." I sighed.

"That too."

"No, I mean hot, as in, it's scorching in here."

Ethan winced. "You may be that way for a few days."

"Hot?"

He nodded.

"Why?"

"Too much vampire blood makes you overheat a bit." He shrugged. "It won't turn you— You're very much human, like I've said before, but sometimes the vampire blood causes a type of burn to take over in your bloodstream, not painful, just not exactly pleasant if it's a hundred degrees outside."

"Good thing it's Seattle." I bit into the toast.

"Yes, well, I imagine at this point, raindrops would simply turn to vapor if they landed on your skin."

I smiled.

"Shower." He nodded. "I'm going to turn around now and walk away."

"Narrating?"

"Apparently, that's what I do when I can think of nothing more than ripping that sheet from your body, slamming you into the nearest wall, and possessing you all over again."

I dropped the toast.

He growled, taking two steps toward me, then swore and turned back around.

"Have a good shower!" I called.

Another growl was his answer, and then his jeans went flying. I wasn't laughing anymore.

The ride to the bookstore was torturous. Ethan pulled over a half-dozen times just to kiss me. It was noon by the time we actually made it there, and even then, I almost refused to get out of the car.

"Four hours," Ethan repeated for the tenth time. "Do your work, contribute to society, enjoy yourself, and after… we'll make a visit to your mother."

My stomach dropped to my knees.

He gripped my chin between his fingers and kissed my mouth softly. "We need to know the truth, Genesis."

"Why?" My voice trembled.

"Because it may have something to do with the prophecy, or it could just be a rare coincidence. I swear, I won't let her hurt you."

I sighed, already drawing into myself.

"My offer still stands," Ethan whispered.

"What?" My head snapped up. "What offer?"

"I'll kill her," he said softly. "All you need to do is ask it—and it's done. She doesn't deserve life for the way she treated you, and it would make me happy to see you hold your head high around her."

"But she'd be dead."

"Perhaps I'll just toy with her a bit."

I giggled.

"Go." He kissed me again. "And if Cassius shows up—" Ethan swore. "Which he may, considering he's insane and has a death wish... try to ignore him."

"Done," I answered. "Besides, I could touch him all I wanted..."

Ethan growled.

"...and still crave you."

His face softened. "I wish that was true."

"It is."

His face was sad. "I'll see you in a while."

chapter
twenty-seven

Genesis

D RYSTAN'S EYEBROWS SHOT UP TO HIS HAIRLINE WHEN I WALKED INTO THE store. I wondered if all immortals could smell what I'd been doing—or where I'd been. Then again, Ethan had said he'd marked me.

So maybe it was just like walking around with his scent all over me.

"Genesis." Drystan pointed to a stack of boxes. "We just received another shipment. Why don't you put the books away to start off with, and then I'll have you help customers."

"Great." I reached for the boxes and was surprised when they didn't feel heavy at all, maybe it was compliments of the vampire blood which was currently making my veins feel like they were on fire.

Ethan had said it would wear off throughout the day, but my body still felt hot. I wasn't sweating, but I felt like I should be.

I carried the stack of boxes over to the corner and started pulling out books. Each one was in alphabetical order, making it easy to find a spot on the shelf for them.

I was halfway finished when I felt it—the chill in the air.

"Cassius," I breathed, "didn't take you for a reader." I knew I was safe from him as long as I didn't touch him. I was bonded with Ethan, meaning, at least part of Cassius's charm was going to be lost on me.

He chuckled darkly. "How'd you know it was me?"

I turned, welcoming the relief the cold of his body brought me. "You're chilly."

"I am that." He nodded, shoving his hands into his jean pockets. He looked almost human. His dark hair was pulled back from his face, tucked behind his ears. His eyes appeared more gray than white, and he was wearing a perfectly harmless combination of jeans and a white T-shirt.

He still looked huge.

And completely out of place in society.

Then again, people probably assumed he was an NFL player or something.

"Did I pass inspection?" He grinned.

I rolled my eyes and turned away. "Have any good dreams recently?"

"Are you saying you miss my invasion, sweet?"

"No." And I didn't. I was just curious, more curious about him than I cared to admit, especially after everything Ethan had shown me. My hand caressed the spine of the book I was placing on the shelf.

"Questions… Perhaps I should sit down." He pulled a chair from a nearby table and sat, folding his arms over his chest. "You may begin when you're ready."

"Arrogant," I snapped.

"Feisty." He sighed cheerfully. "Always happens when you have a bit of spice in your blood. Vampires aren't known for their calm demeanors."

I licked my lips. "What happened to Ethan's daughter?"

Cassius stilled, his breathing stopped altogether. "So he's shown you… That's brave of him, all things considering."

"Mates don't keep secrets."

"Oh?" His voice dripped with doubt. "I must have missed that lesson in the last two thousand years."

I couldn't hide my shock. "Two thousand years."

"Give or take a few days." He shrugged. "Ethan's daughter was not Ethan's daughter. I took care of the situation as I saw fit. Don't forget who I am, human. Or what I am and what that means for you and your pitiful fleeting little life."

I swallowed and backed away. "Are you threatening me?"

"Think of it as a reminder," Cassius whispered. "When all this is said and done… if you fail, if Ethan fails, you'll be just another blip on the immortal life. A mere… *memory*."

"Great pep talk," I muttered, reaching for another book.

"I didn't sleep with the human," Cassius offered. "I know that's what you're thinking. What type of friend… or brother… would do such a thing? Did I kiss her, try to win her affection? Naturally, because that's the order of things in our world. If she cannot stay strong for her mate, she doesn't deserve immortality."

"So you test all the humans?"

"Yes." His voice was final. "And if they fail…"

"They die."

"They're simply eliminated before the natural order of things happens. Eventually they die. Take Mason's mate, for example. Lovely girl, obsessed with the wolf—dead."

My eyes burned with unshed tears. "Ara…" I hated saying her name. "She didn't love Ethan."

"In her selfish heart, I believe she thought she was in love with him. She loved him in the best way she knew how. She loved herself more."

I nodded, sadness piercing my chest, making it hard to breathe.

"More questions, or shall I simply touch you and be done with it?"

Ignoring him, I shoved another book in its place. "Stephanie says you aren't bad."

He said nothing.

I thought he'd left, but when I glanced over. He was staring into the space above my head as if in a trance. "Stephanie." Her name sounded different on his lips. But as soon as he'd uttered it, he closed his eyes and shook his head as if he didn't want to talk about it anymore.

"I'm not bad." His eyes turned white. "But I'm not good either."

"What? So you just hang out in the middle?"

"When it suits me." He smiled then stood. "Tell me, do you believe yourself strong enough to resist a Dark One's touch?"

"I did before." I stepped back from him. "Before I was mated to Ethan."

"His blood makes you strong. His mark... stronger than before." Cassius tilted his head. "But the human heart is the strongest of all. It surpasses all immortal claims."

"My heart is my own."

Cassius sighed, his eyes sad. "And that is the problem with humans, is it not? They continuously lament not being able to find love, and when they do, they still refuse to relinquish their most prized possession. Oh, they give their bodies, their souls, but their hearts?" His chest almost grazed mine. "They keep for themselves."

"Why?" I blurted.

He stilled, tilting his head to the side, making himself look more predatory, like an animal ready to pounce. "Fear."

A gasp escaped my lips.

"Fear," he repeated, "is not welcome here."

And suddenly my world made sense.

"I wonder," Cassius whispered, his breath freezing the air in front of me, "when the time comes, will you also choose yourself? Give into fear, or finally sacrifice the one last shred of humanity you have in order to gain immortality?"

I opened my mouth to answer.

"About done?" Drystan called then appeared around the corner.

My lips were freezing, probably blue, but Cassius was nowhere to be seen.

"Genesis?" he repeated. "Are you alright?"

"Yes." I found my voice. "Fine. I'm almost done."

"Good."

He walked back around the corner. I lifted another book just as the barest of whispers flew past my ear.

"Until you sleep..."

chapter
twenty-eight

Ethan

I KNEW HE'D VISITED HER THE MINUTE HER EYES MET MINE. SHE SHOULD STILL BE on fire for me; instead, she felt—warm.

Yet her heart still pounded for me. That was all that mattered. That's what I told myself as I gripped the steering wheel and drove us toward her mother's residence.

"Cassius." I hated that she said his name with such familiarity. "You said he's like your king?"

"Mmm-hmm."

"Who does he report to?"

"The archangels." I sighed. "When they care enough to check in on us."

"Are they bad?"

"Humans—and please don't take offense to this—like to categorize things so they can better understand them. If something is bad, they stay away. If it's good, it must be safe. But is chocolate really good? Perhaps to you, but what if someone's allergic? What's worse, what if you gorge yourself? Then something that was once good in your eyes is suddenly very bad because it has the power to kill you. The same goes for immortals. Are all Dark Ones bad? No. But they aren't good. Are archangels bad? Yes. In a way they can be very bad, but they also have such goodness that it's blinding. What you should concern yourself with is not trying to understand, because you never will."

Genesis let out a frustrated sigh. "Easier said than done."

"If I told you he was bad," I reached for her hand, "you may stay away longer, but it may also cause fear to grow in your heart, and fear is not an emotion I want you to feed."

She nodded. "I'm afraid now."

"Of me?"

"My mother." Her eyes were distant, locked on the house I'd just pulled up to.

It looked better, as if someone had made repairs. The shutters no longer fell from the window, and the porch had been rebuilt.

"Say the word, and I end her life," I vowed. "Now hold your head high."

Genesis nodded wordlessly and followed me out of the car to the door.

Her mother was by herself; I picked up only her scent. I knocked.

Footsteps creaked against the wood floor. And a short woman with graying brown hair appeared in the door. Her eyes were bland, her skin wrinkled. Life had been hard on her, or maybe that was humanity's punishment for being such a horrible mother.

Her eyes met mine, widening briefly before settling on her daughter. Her smile was full of venom. "So, you're his whore now?"

With a hiss, I shoved the woman into the house and walked her backward until she was against the nearest wall. I gripped her throat with my hand, lifting her until her feet dangled beneath her.

"Say it again," I dared her.

Tears filled her eyes.

"What? Trouble breathing?" I tilted my head. "Care for me to end your miserable existence?"

She croaked out a *no*.

I released her then whispered in her ear, "Disrespect my mate one more time, and you won't even feel the slice of my teeth across your throat."

The woman paled.

Genesis's hand gripped mine, steadying my heartbeat, when all I wanted to do was rip her mother's throat out and laugh over her dead corpse.

"Mother." Genesis trembled next to me. "We won't be long. I just had a few questions."

"Knew you would." She snorted. "But I don't have answers for you, at least the ones you're looking for."

I moved away from Genesis, walked down the familiar hallway, and located the picture. I pulled it from the wall and tossed it to her mother. "This woman. Who is she?"

Her mother's face paled as she stared at the picture. "Dead."

"Caught that," Ethan hissed. "Who is she?"

"Ara was her name." Genesis's mother petted the picture as if she was reliving something. "Everyone hated her."

I tensed.

"She was beautiful, and she knew it... so vain that she made the family look bad. Her number was called, but of course it was. The rest of the families were jealous. And then she failed."

"Your great-grandmother?"

"Great-aunt." Her mother set the picture down on the table. "She's a stain upon the family name. We don't discuss her. This is the first time our number has been called since Ara's disgrace." She snorted. "And I knew it would happen the minute Genesis was born—that skin, that hair." She rolled her eyes. "So beautiful, just like Ara."

Genesis's heart thumped wildly, so loudly I had to concentrate on what her mother was saying in order to hear the words above the beating.

326 | RACHEL VAN DYKEN

"I made her strong." Her mother's eyes met mine. "Better she hate her own reflection than fall prey to it."

"How tragic," I whispered, "that you felt the need to shame a little girl for having golden hair and pretty eyes."

"It worked!" her mother screamed. "Look! Mated to an Elder! A vampire, no less!"

"It worked," I repeated, "because her blood is pure... because her soul is pure." Anger crashed over me at her mother's proud expression. In a flash, I moved behind her, biting a small mark on her shoulder and whispered, "For the rest of your days you, will see nothing but Ara's reflection when you look in the mirror. You will hate, and it will drive you mad. That is the gift I leave with you for bestowing such kindness upon the woman I love."

Her mother swayed and then fell to her knees. A tear fell down her cheek. "No, please no. Don't do this."

"It's done." I gripped Genesis hand. "We'll bother you no more."

Genesis didn't want to follow me; her feet dug into the ground, so I tossed her over my shoulder and carried her out of the house.

When she still didn't make a noise, I buckled her seatbelt and peeled out of the parking spot, driving like hell back toward our home—toward safety.

Ready to lose my mind, I opened my mouth to apologize when she blurted, "You love me."

"If that's what you wish to discuss..." I reached for her hand.

She squeezed mine. The heat from my blood took over, making her skin hot to the touch.

"And you won't leave me? Ever?"

"No," I vowed. "I don't think I'm capable of surviving such a loss."

She nodded, wiping a tear from her cheek. "Cassius visited today."

"I know."

She sighed. "He told me things... about you. About Ara."

"Did he touch you?"

"No," Genesis whispered. "But one day soon, he will. He touches all the human mates."

I scowled. "So he told you..."

"To test them."

"Yes."

"I'm going to pass."

"Alright."

"You don't believe me?" She pulled her hand away.

I sighed and focused on the road ahead of me. "I have no reason not to believe you."

Genesis let out a loud sigh. "Do you think the only reason you love me is because I'm related to Ara?"

"No." The entire idea was ridiculous. "Not only was she horribly self-ish—something I've finally come to terms with—but you're nothing like her. Besides, you don't stop and stare at yourself every time you see your own damn reflection."

"Thanks to my mother," Genesis mumbled.

"That's it." I pulled the car over, forced it into park, and reached for Genesis. With a growl, I tugged her body across the console and into my lap. "She did you no favors. That woman was no mother to you. A weaker female would have crippled beneath that type of emotional scarring. I should have killed her for what she put you through."

Genesis's eyes pooled with tears.

I cupped her chin. "Beautiful inside and out—the last thing you need to be is afraid of your own beauty. Embrace it, but don't let it overtake all sense of reality. You are beautiful. You are strong. You are pure. Those are simple facts. Outside of that, nothing else matters other than the way I feel about you."

"If being beautiful means I turn into Ara, I'd rather be ugly."

"You could never turn into her." I pressed an urgent kiss to her mouth. "You're... *you.*"

Genesis returned my kiss, biting down on my lips.

I flicked her tongue with mine then deepened the kiss. "Home."

"Bed."

"Yes," I growled, rubbing my body against her. "Now."

She let out a little gasp.

"Or here." I tugged her shirt over her shoulder, kissing the bare skin. "Vampires can be very... creative."

"Show me." Her eyes burned bright green.

I ripped the rest of her T-shirt with my teeth. "Never... challenge me."

Frenzied hands reached for my jeans while I reached for hers, both of us colliding with one another as we tried to peel clothing away.

Layer after layer went flying.

And then she was naked, straddling me.

"Mmm..." I took her fingers between my teeth. "...I've never tasted anything so incredible."

"My hands?"

"Your skin." I chuckled then placed myself near her entrance. "You know... we could always wait until we get home and—"

She welcomed me into her body.

But didn't move.

I let out a frustrated growl and gripped her hips. "You think to tease me?"

"I was told never to tease a vampire."

A mixture of laughter and ecstasy left my lips as our bodies began to move.

"No bite this time?" she asked.

"Sometimes," I growled, thrusting hard, then pulling out, "faster is better."

chapter
twenty-nine

Genesis

WE MADE IT HOME.

But I was without shirt, considering Ethan had ripped mine to shreds. So he handed me his while he walked into the house sporting a pair of jeans and a really big smile.

"Ethan." Alex was in the kitchen drinking wine and reading. "Is today no-shirt day? Should I remove mine as well?"

He reached for the edges of it but earned a growl from Ethan.

Mason was sitting in front of a bowl of berries; his hand paused midair as he looked between the two of us. "Damn, Ethan, at least feed her every once in a while."

"He's very concerned with food, always concerned with food." Alex nodded. "Hurry up, Mason, your berries are drying out."

A berry went flying by Alex's head.

I didn't notice Stephanie in the corner; she wasn't normally so quiet. When her eyes met mine, they lit up. "Hey, how about shopping tomorrow? Before your fun little human job?"

She looked like she'd been crying. "Are you okay?"

"She's fine," Alex snapped, his good humor completely gone. The room turned tense in an instant. He cleared his throat and forced a smile. "Sirens, very emotional."

Stephanie smiled. "Very."

"Ethan, a word?" Alex stood.

"Sure." Ethan kissed the top of my head and left the room while Mason started rummaging around the kitchen; pots and pans clanged together, and then he pulled out a giant piece of steak.

"I hope that's not for me." I pointed.

"Protein…" He threw the steak into the pan. "…feeds the blood, which feeds the mate, which, in turn, feeds you."

"You gonna start singing Circle of Life?" I joked.

"Circle of life?" he repeated.

"Lion King?"

"Cassius is king."

I looked helplessly to Stephanie, who was trying to hide her smile behind her hand.

"Have you seriously never watched *Lion King?*"

"Werewolves are scared of TV," Stephanie said with a soft laugh.

"And sirens are afraid of the dark," he fired back, while she shuddered. "I'm not afraid of the TV. I just don't see the point in sitting in front of a flat box and watching people make fools of themselves."

"He'd rather be the fool." Stephanie nodded and winked in my direction.

"Mason…" I walked over to him and put my head on his shoulder. "How about I eat the steak and we watch *Lion King?*"

"No."

"*Dances with Wolves?*"

Stephanie snickered loudly behind her hand.

"Wolves do not dance," Mason growled.

"Oh, we know." Stephanie nodded. "I've seen it once. Don't care to see it again."

"Too much whiskey." Mason kissed the top of my head. "Eat the whole steak, and then we'll talk about King Lion."

"*Lion King.*"

"Same thing."

I sighed helplessly and went to sit at the table while Mason cooked.

Stephanie gave me a side hug. "Eight tomorrow morning, alright?"

"Great."

"Bed." She shrugged. "It's been a long night." Her eyes misted again.

"Are you sure you're okay?"

"Yeah." Her voice cracked. "Like Alex said, we get emotional. Can't help it."

It felt like she was lying, but I was human, how would I know? I nodded and turned my attention back to Mason, who'd started searing the steak.

"So you cook meat but refuse to eat it?"

"I'm a vegetarian." He smiled. I'd never realized how pointy his teeth were on the sides. Maybe that's how he'd been able to bite into me before Ethan had mated with me.

"Your teeth say otherwise." I pointed. "Flat means vegetarian. Pointy means carnivore."

Mason rolled his eyes. "I didn't say it was natural for me to be a vegetarian."

"Okay… so why?"

He let out a heavy sigh. "Meat made my mate sick… for one reason or another. It gave her headaches. She only ate fruits, vegetables, nuts." He flipped the steak. "So I learned to like other foods."

"And now?"

He went very quiet, his eyes focusing in on the steak. "Now…" His voice was hoarse. "I honor her with my every meal."

My throat clogged with emotion.

The fact that he honored her at all—but with every single meal—killed me. How did he survive that? How did he live every day having known true love? And know he may never experience it again—living forever?

"Don't pity me." Mason let out a gruff growl. "It makes it harder."

"Sorry," I whispered. "So pinecones, huh?"

He laughed. "Yes, well, it's an acquired taste."

"I bet."

My heart picked up speed, and then I smelled him. Ethan entered the room, briskly walking by me, kissing my head. "Steak almost done?"

"I'm a perfectionist." Mason held up his hands. "Let the juices seal."

Ethan scrunched up his nose. "Her blood tastes better than that steak."

"Yes, well, her blood tastes good because she's living. She's living because I feed her."

"Werewolf has a point," I teased. "Besides, if I eat my whole steak, we're going to watch *Lion King!*"

"Whose king?" Ethan tilted his head. "What lion? Mason's a wolf."

And that's how I ended up spending my evening between a vampire and a werewolf, eating steak and watching a Disney movie while they argued over the animal kingdom, not to mention the lion's choice in song.

It felt right.

Like I'd finally found my place.

My home.

I had no idea that the security I felt was about to get ripped from me, from the very people I'd put my trust in.

chapter
thirty

Ethan

I TRIED TO WATCH THE CHILDISH MOVIE. I EVEN ENGAGED MASON IN AN ARGUMENT over the silly cartoon, but my thoughts were elsewhere.

On Alex and Stephanie.

On what he'd just revealed to me, betraying his own sister's confidence because he was so damn worried about what she would do—what she was capable of.

"She thinks she loves him," Alex muttered sourly. "Yet she doesn't wear his mark. It's as if he's refused to mark her, but she still… craves him."

"Sirens crave sex," I mumbled. "You know this."

"This is much different." Alex shook his head. "Something's shifted, I don't know what… but…"

I pinched the bridge of my nose. "He wouldn't dare mark her for death. Immortals don't mate with each other—not in that way. It's not natural."

"That's what I said."

"We can talk later." I sighed. "I'll try talking to her."

"Thank you." Alex's body slumped against the chair. "I worry more than I should."

But really, his worrying was merited because Stephanie wanted what was forbidden for her to want.

A Dark One.

Our king.

To want him was to invite death.

And I wasn't so sure she would listen to any of us, regardless of how wise our words, our warnings. The heart, I'd learned in all my years of living, wants what it wants, and damn the rest of the world for trying to tell it otherwise.

Genesis fell asleep in my lap. I carried her to bed then hovered protectively over her, instinct kicking in. I would die for that girl. I would do anything for her.

I wasn't sure she felt the same.

I doubted myself and hated that I doubted myself.

She stretched her arms above her head. She looked like a cat, all seductive and curvy. "Ethan?"

"Yes?"

"Why are you watching me sleep?"

"Because you fascinate me when you dream."

"I don't want to dream of him." She reached for my body, tugging me against her. "How do I keep him from getting in?"

"You don't." I sighed helplessly. "Just know you're safe in my arms. You'll always be safe."

"But in my dreams I'm in danger?"

"Remember what I said about good and bad… the same goes with danger. When all else fails, Genesis, you follow your heart."

"The heart can be evil."

"Not yours." I shook my head. "Never yours."

"I'm going shopping tomorrow."

"I know." I chuckled. She was so tired she wasn't making much sense. "Stephanie will charge whatever you want to my card."

"Too much money."

"I'm rich."

"Because of the fish."

I laughed. "Yes, the fish. They make me rich. Sleep, little human." I kissed her nose as she wrapped her body around mine and fell into a deeper slumber.

I waited, unable to sleep until I felt the cold seep from her body into mine.

Her breath staggered.

And then her skin went from hot to cold.

"Cassius," I whispered, "you take her from me, and I'll rip your heart from your chest."

"Trust her," he said back to me.

Agony washed over me as I waited for Genesis to return. Every second that went by was torture because I knew it was another second he was tempting her with forbidden fruit.

Just like he'd tempted Ara.

Only Ara had bitten.

And with that one bite, destroyed a part of myself I'd never been able to get back.

Until now.

chapter
thirty-one

Genesis

"IT'S SNOWING." I HELD MY HAND OUT AND CAUGHT A FEW SNOWFLAKES. "No lake today?"

Cassius shrugged. His mood was different, darker. "I wanted the comfort cold brings me."

"Normally it's heat."

"I'm the opposite of warmth." His eyes turned white. "Therefore, it's cold that comforts. It's my fire."

I pulled the fur blanket around me. We were sitting outside a cabin in front of a roaring fire. It was beautiful; snow-blanketed the forest, making it seem enchanted.

"More questions..." Cassius sighed. "I sense them."

I stared into the fire. "What was Ethan's daughter?"

"Different question," Cassius snapped.

"Can you mate?"

Cassius let out a slew of curses. "Our punishment or maybe our prize? Women die at our hands. Human women." He shrugged. "Vampire blood and human blood co-exist. Angel blood and human blood are an abomination."

My throat went completely dry. "So it can't mix."

"It can... for a time, and then the angel blood overwhelms what weakness the human has. It makes them evil, destroys them from the inside out."

"So you can't mate."

"We don't mate," Cassius snapped, "because there is no point, Genesis."

"That's lonely."

His eyes closed. "You have no idea."

"What about other immortals. Can you mate with them?"

"Why risk more lives?" Cassius threw a piece of wood into the fire. His eyes still hadn't returned to a normal color—they were void of color, void of emotion. "Is that it for this evening?"

"One more..." I held my hands out to the fire.

He nodded.

"Is there a way to test the prophecy? To make sure it works?"

"There is always a way," Cassius sneered, "but I highly doubt it is a road you want to travel—or one your mate would let you even step foot on."

"So I wait to live or die?"

"You pass all tests, you live—and hopefully restore balance. The prophecy says *a human will mate with an immortal. It will be the new beginning, and they'll have a child."*

I shuddered. "I don't want to die."

Cassius's eyes met mine. "Then don't."

"Wha—" He disappeared in front of my very eyes.

And then I jolted awake, shivering in Ethan's arms.

"What did he do? Meet you in a freezer?" Ethan swore, gathering me against him, wrapping blankets tightly around my body.

"S-sorry." I shivered. "I didn't realize how cold I was."

"He thrives on the cold." Ethan rubbed my shoulders. "And clearly forgets himself if he put you in the middle of a blizzard."

"It was a snowstorm... I think... but pretty."

"Oh well, as long as it was pretty," Ethan hissed.

I tucked my head against his chest, focusing on his warmth. "We need to have a child."

Ethan's hands stopped moving. "Cassius told you that?"

"It's part of the prophecy, right?"

"Yes, but—"

"So that will make it come true, right?"

"No," he said, sadness evident in his tone. "I wish that were true, but no, Genesis, we won't know until..."

"I no longer exist." I trembled. "He said there's another way—"

"No!" Ethan yelled. He gulped in a breath released it then said more softly, "No, it isn't an option."

"Maybe if you told me."

"It's forbidden."

I pretended to be satisfied with that—but I wasn't. If there was a way to fix the balance of things, I was going to find it. Not just for me, but for Ethan—for Mason, who'd lost the love of his life—for Cassius, who seemed lonelier than Death.

If I could save them—

I had to try.

chapter
thirty-two

Genesis

"READY?" STEPHANIE POPPED HER GUM AND HOOKED HER ARM IN MINE. "Ethan gave me his credit card with no limit, meaning we have damage to do."

I nodded, forcing myself to smile. Something felt... *wrong*. I'd spent the night in Ethan's arms, yet I felt like my balance was off, like I was straddling a line and was about to get pulled over to the wrong side.

Stephanie directed me toward a white Lexus hybrid and practically shooed me inside.

"So I'm thinking Downtown, since it's close to work."

She nodded. "Work? Why would you want to work anyway? I'm just curious."

I shrugged. "I need a purpose."

"But Ethan is your purpose."

"Right, but Ethan has a job too. It's not good to be idle, you know? Plus, I'm not really good at anything... other than reading... so why not work at a bookstore? It helps out Drystan, and so far I like it."

She snapped her gum and shrugged.

Her hair was pulled back into a ponytail, exposing her neck. I was about to glance away when I noticed a mark on her neck.

"Did someone bite you?"

"Lovers all bite..." She smiled. "If they're good."

"Oh."

"Hey, relax. We're shopping. This is fun. You get to spend your mate's money, and you get me as your personal shopper for the next few hours."

I forced myself to smile and embrace the moment. "You're right."

"Course I'm right." She turned up the music and started singing at the top of her lungs.

By the time we'd made it downtown, we only had a few hours until I had to be at work.

Shopping with Stephanie was like an Olympic sport. She took me from store to store, tossing clothes in my empty arms and ordering me to try them on before I'd even told her I liked them.

She knew my style well. Not fussy, comfortable—but cute. I tried on several pairs of jeans, bomber jackets, shirts, boots—the list went on and on.

I needed more coffee if I was going to make it through the rest of the day without passing out.

Or maybe I just needed Ethan.

He would be nice too.

"Hey!" Stephanie knocked on the door to the dressing room. "Hurry up in there. We only have a few more minutes."

I rolled my eyes and stared at my reflection. "Can I ask why you put me in a black evening gown?"

"Because!" She laughed. "Ethan will want to show you off."

"Fine." I pressed the heavily beaded fabric against my stomach. It was strapless and ridiculously heavy. Black with silver beading cascaded from floor to ceiling, it seemed.

I was like a walking pageant queen. "Stephanie, I don't think I like this."

No answer.

"Stephanie?"

With a sigh, I opened the door. Words died on my lips.

"Hello." His white eyes matched his long white hair. He tilted his head to the side as if examining me. "Come."

I stepped back and shook my head. "Where's Stephanie."

"Come." He held out his hand. His body was massive, bigger than Cassius and Ethan combined. He stood at least eight feet tall. Why was no one else running and screaming? He was beautiful, but it was a deadly type of beautiful. I don't know how, but I knew if I touched him, I'd die.

When he ducked into the dressing room, I gasped, covering my mouth.

Wings. He had wings.

Gold feathers that appeared then vanished right in front of me.

Ethan! My mind screamed.

Cassius... he could read my thoughts; he was powerful enough. I started yelling for him in my head, hoping he was tracking me, hoping in vain he would be able to find my scent. There was no way I was escaping the immortal in front of me.

"You're an archangel," I whispered.

"And you're the human."

Not *a* human. *The* human.

I gulped. "Please don't make me go with you."

His smile widened. "Are you afraid?"

It felt like a test.

I didn't know what to say.

I opened my mouth to yell no, but it was like he'd stolen the words from my lips. His head tilted back. "Come."

I shook my head, forcing myself to breathe, to not give into the fear that threatened to choke me.

"Come, or I kill your vampire. Your choice."

My throat released. "Don't!"

"So you'll come?" He seemed pleased.

"Just don't hurt him."

"You have my word. It won't be me who hurts your mate."

I nodded and reached out, touching my hand to his. And my world faded to white.

chapter
thirty-three

Ethan

"SO THINGS SEEM TO BE PROGRESSING NICELY." ALEX SMIRKED OVER HIS morning coffee.

Ignoring him, I rolled my eyes and continued reading the paper. I was just about to put it down and grab my keys so that I could finish what I needed to do for the day and find an excuse to stop at the bookstore, when pain sliced through my chest.

My knees buckled as I reached for the table to steady myself.

"Ethan?" Alex was immediately by my side.

My blood boiled, turning to acid beneath my skin as the room started to spin. "Something's wrong."

"Sit down."

I pushed him away.

Mason was soon at my other side.

The door to the house opened, and Stephanie appeared right in front of us. "Ethan, I tried to—"

Our eyes met.

Hers were white.

"What. Have. You. Done." I roared, the heat in my blood searing every rational thought in my body.

Stephanie held up her hands and took a step back. "Nothing. I did nothing. I woke up, and she was gone!"

Alex cursed. "Cassius."

"No," I repeated. "It isn't Cassius."

I would feel Cassius—I'd felt him before when he'd taken one of my mates, knew the way it felt when my blood turned to ice in my veins.

"Stephanie?" Alex's eyes narrowed. "Your neck."

Growling, I pushed away from both men and slammed her against the granite countertop, tilting her next to the side so severely I was surprised her head hadn't come off.

"No." Hands shaking, I stepped away. "No."

Stephanie rubbed her neck; tears streamed down her face. "What? What's happening?"

Her eyes were still white.

"Did you see… it?"

"See what?" She was nearing hysterics. "Something knocked me out, and when I woke up, she was gone!"

"The archangel," I said in a hushed tone. "You wear his mark."

Stephanie's horrified gaze met mine as she started vigorously rubbing the spot I'd just discovered. It was small, white, and had the appearance of a snow-flake tattoo. It would have been beautiful if it hadn't been a mark of death.

"No." She hugged her arms to herself. "I'm so sorry. I thought we were safe. We should have been safe."

"Can you track her?" Mason growled next to me, his body trembling with the need to change and tear something limb from limb.

"Yes," I said in a voice I didn't recognize. "But it may be too late. I'm strong enough to fight him, to distract him, not strong enough to defeat him alone."

The room fell silent.

Pride kept me from saying his name.

But my love for her trumped everything.

So in that moment at my kitchen table, I closed my eyes and uttered a plea—to my greatest enemy.

"Cassius," I whispered, "help."

chapter
thirty-four

Genesis

M Y TONGUE FELT LIKE SANDPAPER IN THE ROOF OF MY MOUTH. WHEN I tried to lick my lips, it was like someone had dehydrated me then handed me peanut butter.

I tried moving my lips. They were heavy, pressed together.

"You won't speak."

I blinked my eyes open. Having already thought they were open, I was surprised when I saw a blinding light appear in front of me then fade into the darkness surrounding my body.

"I allow you to speak after you've earned it." It was the same man or angel as before. His feathers were now fully visible; pieces of every color of the rainbow shimmered from the large wings, though his seemed to favor purples and blues. It seemed like that should be significant, the colors, but I couldn't talk, so instead I stared, knowing I probably wouldn't ever see anything like it in my entire life.

I wanted to be afraid.

And I was.

But I was also fascinated by the sheer beauty of the archangel in front of me. Long white hair, which should have looked stupid and old, created an ethereal effect around his sculpted face. His eyes were a bluish-white, more aqua than anything, and his mere presence filled up the entire room.

"Are you afraid?" He tilted his head to the side, his eyes studying me for a reaction.

I didn't nod.

I simply stared back.

"I'll take that as a no." His full lips curled into a smile. "I am Sariel. I've been watching you."

Creepy statement. I shivered. The last thing I wanted was a being like him watching me.

"It intrigues me…" His smile grew as the light faded around his body, making him look more human than immortal. "How they fight over something so insignificant."

I flinched.

"I don't mean you, little human." He moved around the room. Lights followed each footstep until I realized I was sitting in a large open room—a lot like a typical living room with couches and tables—facing the Puget Sound.

It would be normal...

If an archangel wasn't walking around in front of me, glowing all over the place.

"The situation—it's insignificant. Tell me, why should my brothers—why should *I* bother myself with the prophecy? It does not directly affect me."

He waved at my mouth.

My lips pulled apart. I inhaled then spoke. "It may not affect you, but it affects others. People are dying—what if I'm the answer?"

He turned his back to me. "Do you think that we would put the balance of immortal lives in the hands of a mere human?"

"Yes," I whispered, "because it's the only thing that makes sense."

"You speak to me as if you have the right to breathe in my presence without falling to your feet in terror."

"And you speak to me like you deserve to be worshipped, when you've done nothing but kidnap me and mock me."

His body stilled.

I blamed Ethan's blood. I'd spoken out of turn. And I was going to pay for it.

"Keep that heartbeat under control. Wouldn't want that vampire blood to boil you from the inside out... quite painful I've heard, the process of a human turning immortal."

"What?" My heart raced. "But I'm human."

"Yes." He turned back to face me. "For now you are human. Until the choice will be made by the immortals. You will stay that way, in my care."

"Why?" I gulped. "Why take me?"

His shoulders hunched; it was the only chink I'd seen in his armor the entire time we'd been talking. "Because once, a very long time ago, one of my sons made a great lapse in judgment, and the immortals have been paying for it ever since."

Sariel folded his hands in front of his large body, his wings going once again transparent. "Because of his sins, a darkness—a sickness—descended upon both races. I mean to rectify that in the only way I know how."

I was afraid to ask.

"Well?" he smirked. "Aren't you the least bit curious?"

"No."

"Lie." His eyes flashed white. "Blood will be spilled. They will come for you."

"And if they don't?" I whispered.

"Blood will spill either way."

Was it my imagination, or did his eyes hold a hint of sadness?

"Balance always needs to be restored, and you, Genesis, will be tested. I wonder, are you strong enough to do what needs to be done?"

I gulped. "What needs to be done?"

"Telling you defeats the purpose, now, doesn't it?"

"So I'm your prisoner... until blood is spilled?"

"Think of it as a vacation." He shrugged. "I've provided for all of your needs." He pointed to an open kitchen I hadn't noticed before. "You won't starve, you won't thirst—unless it's blood your body craves—and you have a view. What more could you want?"

"Is that a trick question?"

His grin blinded me. "I enjoy humans... so small."

My eyebrows knit together in frustration. "Thanks."

"...and interesting."

"You said you had sons." I tried changing the subject.

His face shadowed. "I have... sons, yes."

The conversation must have been over because he quickly walked out of the room.

I thought he'd left me alone...

Until someone or something walked in. I wasn't sure how I knew since I hadn't actually seen anything, but I felt something.

And then I heard chains.

I had a brief vision of watching *Christmas Carol* and shivered, sitting on the nearby couch and pulling my knees to my chest. "Hello?"

"Hello." The voice was smooth, like a caress against my face.

The couch sunk next to me.

A hand reached out of the air. I followed the fingertips up an arm; the body slowly came into focus.

It was a man. Not an angel.

A Dark One—or something else entirely.

He had chains around his feet, though clearly he'd still been able to walk, and his hands were chained together as well.

"I'm Aziel." He leaned back against the couch. "I hope you're stronger than the last human who visited."

"The last human?" I repeated.

"She looked like you." His eyes went cloudy as he stared out through the windows, his jaw set in a firm line. "The same blood flows through your veins."

"She died?" My mouth was like cotton. I wasn't sure how much more I could take.

"She was murdered." His teeth snapped. "I would have made her my queen."

I tried to scoot away, but he put his chained hands onto my legs, holding me in place.

"She was tested," he sighed in a cheerful voice, "and found lacking."

"Why was she tested?"

"Because she wanted too much—because it was within our capacity to give it to her—but we were too early. The prophecy never said when balance would be restored. And we are not perfect."

We?

"We are still flawed." His voice was hollow. "And we were wrong. I was blinded by her face... then again, I've always had a fascination with pretty things." He turned his head to me. "You remind me of her."

I flinched, trying to move my body to the side. His hands grew heavier and heavier on my lap.

"And you will probably die just like her."

chapter
thirty-five

Ethan

66 "THE LAST TIME YOU CALLED FOR ME WAS OVER A HUNDRED YEARS AGO," Cassius said from behind my spot in the kitchen. I'd been pacing for the past ten minutes, waiting for him to arrive.

Stephanie and Alex tried to get me to feed.

I didn't want blood from a bag.

If I couldn't have her—if I didn't have her—I wanted nothing. Death. I would welcome death.

"She's gone." I didn't recognize my own voice. It was hoarse, like I'd been choked and barely survived. "An archangel—"

Cassius moved by me and held up his hand, his eyes blazing white for a few seconds before he uttered a curse. "Sariel."

Mason whistled and fell down into a chair, hanging his head in his hands. "We should have kept better watch of her. We should have—"

"Mason..." I shook my head. "It wasn't your fault." I turned my attention to Stephanie. "Care to explain how you earned the angel's mark?"

Cassius's head craned to the side, his eyes so white they almost glowed. He stalked toward Stephanie then with one hand pushed her up against the wall, pulling her head to the side to glance at the mark. "Decided to whore yourself out?"

Stephanie's face paled. "I had—"

"Do not lie." Cassius dropped her to the ground. She crumpled against the floor, holding her head in her hands. "He didn't say he was going to hurt her."

I lunged for her.

Mason intercepted me.

"He said she needed to be tested. You all knew there was another way." Slowly, Stephanie inched to her feet. "If an archangel deems the human pure, he'll restore balance, regardless of the prophecy!"

"And that worked out so well last time," Cassius hissed.

Lost, I simply waited for someone to explain. When nothing happened, I pretended to lose my irritation. Mason's arms slackened. I lunged for Stephanie's throat, my fangs hovering over her artery. "What. Exactly. Did he promise you?"

Her heartbeat picked up.

"Worth dying for, siren?"

"Love always is," she whispered.

It wasn't a lie.

I stepped back. Tears filled her blue eyes. "He promised me Cassius."

Cassius went completely still next to me. The room temperature plummeted, causing a frost to cover the granite countertops. "So, you thought to enslave me?"

"No!" Stephanie sobbed. "You said we could never be together… immortals do not mate. I simply—"

Cassius held up his hand. It shook in the air, and pieces of frost fell from his fingertips. "You would betray a defenseless human—one for whom we have been waiting for over a hundred years—because you think yourself in love with me?"

The room began to freeze; pieces of ice formed along Cassius's face, shattering into the air the minute he opened his mouth to speak. "Dark Ones do not love."

A tear slid down Stephanie's cheek, freezing against her porcelain skin. "But we've spent nearly every night together."

"And every morning I spend with someone else," Cassius said in a flat voice. "I didn't think you were becoming so attached as to sell your soul to an archangel in order to align your destiny with mine."

"But—"

"Enough," Alex barked. "Stephanie, stop… you're making it worse."

Cassius hung his head. "You can track her blood?"

"Yes," I hissed. "But going up against Sariel…"

"He's old," Cassius stated in a bland voice. "Older than me."

"Not hard," Mason grumbled.

Cassius snapped his teeth together. "The only way to rescue her, to pull her away from the archangel's scent, would be…" He looked up, his eyes flashing once again. "…to mix the blood."

"Yes." My voice shook. "She needs angel blood."

"She won't take it." Cassius shook his head. "Believe me."

"She has no choice!" I yelled, pain searing my limbs, making them feel heavy. "She either drinks from you and makes the choice to leave, or he'll keep her forever. You know he will."

"He does like his toys." Cassius swore. "Unless he truly believes she's the human we've been waiting for, and then things are about to get a lot worse."

Alex pushed Stephanie into a chair and crossed his arms. "How can it get worse?"

"Death," I whispered. "We can distract him long enough to grab her, shield her from his scent. But if he truly believes what we do—then blood will be spilled."

"For balance to be restored." Cassius sighed. "Blood always needs to be spilled."

"Does it matter who?" Alex asked. "Because I vote Stephanie."

Her soft sobs were grating on my nerves. I should have watched her closer—should have seen the signs of her infatuation. Dark Ones did not mate for a reason. They were too addicted to those who fell for them, destroying the other half that should help make a whole.

"Track her," Cassius finally said. "We'll go when he's at his weakest."

Night.

Sariel taught the stars how to shine. At night his resources were depleted on account that his power was shared with the sky.

"Alex…" I nodded toward the siren. "Keep her locked up until we return. And Mason?"

He stood. "Let me go with you."

"You're not strong enough." I hated saying it, almost as much as I hated that I was right.

Mason let out a growl.

"Wolf…" Cassius put his hand on Mason's shoulder. "Your diet makes you weak. Therefore, it makes us vulnerable. You stay."

I knew it hurt Mason's pride.

His eyes went completely black as he slowly sank into the chair, his face completely tight with outrage. Berries and cones didn't make a werewolf strong—he knew that as much as we did.

"Ten miles away." I sniffed the air for traces of the woman I loved—the woman who was taken from me. Anger overtook all good reason as I started moving toward the door.

"Level head, Ethan." Cassius's cold grip stopped my blood from boiling over. "She'll need you at your strongest."

"I know."

"Drink."

I had to have heard him wrong.

"Drink." His teeth snapped. "Before I change my mind." He lifted his hand to my lips.

With a sneer, I pushed him away.

He slammed me against the wall. "You want to save your love? Stop being so damn prideful and drink."

With a hiss, I bit into his arm and sucked deep. His blood was like ice, cooling my veins, making my body so calm I was finally able to think clearly. I took a step back, the blue tint of his blood dripping from my fangs. "I won't thank you."

"And I won't expect it." He moved his fingers along the small indents. The skin slowly closed back together.

"If she touches you—" I whispered.

"When she touches me," he clarified, "you will finally see it."

"That you were right all along?" I growled.

"That you should have trusted her to begin with."

chapter
thirty-six

Genesis

AZIEL SAT WITH ME FOR WHAT FELT LIKE HOURS. SOMETIMES HE SPOKE, BUT mostly he rocked back and forth. It didn't make me feel better.

When I tried to get up and grab something to eat, he told me that the food was poisoned.

I didn't know if I should believe him or not.

I got up anyway because I couldn't handle just sitting and staring out the window, even though that seemed to be his own specialty.

I found a bottle of water in the fridge and drank, then made my way back over to the couch. Sariel hadn't returned. I wasn't sure if Aziel was supposed to be my guard or just a punishment.

"What's with the chains?" I asked, taking a seat next to him, careful to be out of his reach just in case he decided to put the same hands in chains on top of me, forcing my legs to go to sleep.

"A punishment." His eyes went white as snow. "For my sins."

"What did you do?"

"I wanted."

"What did you want?"

His hair became more visible. Pieces of black and white tendrils fell across his face. "I wanted."

"Okay…"

"Haven't you ever wanted so desperately you'd do anything to have it?"

That was how I wanted Ethan, but it wasn't just want. To say want almost seemed selfish—I needed him.

Just thinking about him had my heart racing. My entire body trembled with a need to just be in his arms.

"I wanted," Aziel continued, "so I took."

"And you were punished?"

"Very much so." Aziel nodded. "I can no longer fly." He shrugged. "I'm grounded with chains, and now I must watch history on repeat until the balance is restored."

"Until humans stop dying," I clarified.

"Yes."

"Is it me?" I was afraid to ask but needed to know. "Will I bring balance?"

"We could have waited to discover the truth." He ignored my question.

"Better this way—to get it over with. I pushed Sariel to pursue it, though he'd deny my involvement. I smelled her on you. And I knew we needed to try."

Great. So I had two people to blame for my captivity.

"Soon." Aziel faded into the air briefly before flickering back. "Very soon now."

The sun had already set, casting a pink glow across the sky.

Ethan was out there somewhere... I wished in that moment I could communicate with him, tell him not to come for me. I didn't think it was a trap, but something in my gut told me things wouldn't end well, and I'd rather sacrifice myself than see him hurt.

I swallowed the fear.

Cassius had made sense when we'd talked earlier.

Fear was selfish. It kept me thinking about me and not about others. It kept my heart safe, because if I stayed afraid, I wouldn't risk losing.

But for Ethan? I would risk it all.

My life.

My soul.

My heart.

"So the Vampire has decided to work with the Dark One." Aziel clapped his hands together, shooting me an amused grin. "Perhaps you *are* worth the trouble."

Sariel walked through the door, eying Aziel briefly before making his way toward me. "They're close. Shall we begin?"

I took a step back.

"Fear?" He smiled mockingly.

"Let's try excitement."

His mocking smile faded into a real smile. "Ah, that's better."

"What?"

"I can see why my son was so enraptured with you."

"Aziel?" I guessed.

Sariel glanced to the couch and shuddered, "No."

"Then I'm confused."

"My son..." His eyes went from blue to icy white. "Cassius."

chapter
thirty-seven

Ethan

CASSIUS WAS IRRITATED THAT WE HAD TO DRIVE, BUT NOT EVERYONE COULD simply appear out of thin air. Part of his angelic heritage made it so that he could, in essence, fly, though he preferred not to discuss it with anyone. Just another reason Dark Ones couldn't be trusted. There were parts, dark parts, they kept hidden that we would never understand.

His blood continued to ice my veins, taking away some of the pain at having Genesis ripped from me.

I'd only experienced this type of pain once before.

When I'd had to kill my own mate.

It had taken me fifty years to stop craving her.

Every evening when I went to bed, I'd dream of her only to wake up in a cold sweat, craving her taste, her smell—everything about her.

The only way to exorcise it from my system was to starve myself of blood, allow her blood to leave my body. It was a battle, possibly with my own bitterness at her betrayal.

"He will not kill her," Cassius said once we reached the Sound.

I snorted. "You think that's what I'm worried about right now?"

"Yes."

I looked away, clenching my teeth, unable to speak because I hated that he was with me, hated that I needed him at all.

"I never took your mate," Cassius said in a detached voice. "I tested her. I never stole her from you. Her betrayal was not my fault."

"You still touched her," I whispered.

"After she begged me," Cassius fired back. "You know I would never force myself on a human."

"You took my mate and my daughter."

"I will say this only once," Cassius growled. "You have no daughter."

"She was more mine than yours."

Cassius ignored me and continued driving. "When we arrive at the house, try your best not to charge the archangel."

I rolled my eyes. "You make it sound like I have no self-control."

"When it comes to Genesis, I believe self-control is something you seriously lack, brother."

"I love her."

Cassius sighed, a slight frown marring his face. "Yes, I know."

"What do you know of love?" I spat, clenching my hand into a tight fist, my knuckles cracking against each other as I fought to keep my rage at bay.

"I know," Cassius said in a hoarse voice. "Believe me when I say I know."

I didn't point out that Dark Ones didn't love—that love was just as forbidden as mating, just as ridiculous a notion. They felt no love because they gave themselves over to their angelic blood more than their humanity, and everyone knew angels didn't feel, didn't love.

They simply existed and ruled, but never by such human emotions. To feel such strong emotions was the reason the Dark Ones had been cursed in the first place.

"Are we close?" Cassius asked.

"You truly can't trace her?" I was curious, with all his strength, how he couldn't pick up her specific smell. From where I sat, I could even make out her heartbeat.

"No." Cassius sighed.

"There." I pointed at a large house facing the Sound. It was a two-storied beach house; intricate brickwork lined the front. A door big enough for two angels to fit through loomed in front of us.

"Well?" Cassius shut off the car. "Shall we?"

I grunted.

It would be impossible to catch Sariel unaware. He was an archangel, not necessarily all-knowing, but most likely expecting us. What mate wouldn't fight through hell to gain his love back?

We walked in silence toward the door.

I wasn't surprised when it opened.

My heart beat wildly in my chest as the scent of Genesis became stronger, her heartbeat more erratic.

"Easy," Cassius said under his breath.

I clenched my teeth together.

The solid oak door opened before our very eyes. A blast of humidity shot through the air making me hold my breath as the sting of sweet sugar invaded my nostrils. It smelled of angel—of the heavenlies. I wondered how Cassius dealt with it—when my own body was already shaking with the need to run in the other direction. Because that very smell was the one I'd always been warned about. *If it smells too good, it is too good—run.*

Suddenly the archangel appeared, his wings dripping with purples and blues as his feral face tilted to the side, a smirk lining the corners of his mouth.

"Sariel." Cassius smiled, of course he would. "I think you have something that belongs to the vampire."

"But of course." Sariel nodded. His wings fluttered as he looked me over with a calculating glare. His head tilted to the side. "Vampire, your love for her, is it pure?"

"Yes." It hurt to speak. I could feel her presence. I just wanted to see that she was all right, take the fear away, give her my blood, and get her the hell out.

"Mmm…" Sariel nodded to both of us. His eyes were blazing white. He wasn't just immortal, he wasn't human, wasn't man—more being or spirit than anything else. "After you."

Cassius stepped in the house first.

I followed, my nerves on edge as I pushed past the archangel, not caring that I was being disrespectful to someone who could end me if he willed it.

I didn't turn around.

And maybe that was where my instincts were off.

I always turned.

Always smelled.

Always sensed.

But this, this I didn't see coming, because the minute I moved away from the angel, my eyes locked on Genesis.

Blood. So much blood. I reached for her just as a jarring pain stabbed me in the back.

With a curse, I stumbled forward. Warm blood oozed down my back, mixing with the icy blood Cassius had given me.

"No!" Genesis screamed. "Ethan!"

Cassius turned, his eyes horrified as he reached for my back, and pulled out a single purple feather dripping with red.

"And now…" Sariel pushed me to my knees in front of Genesis. "…we begin."

chapter
thirty-eight

Genesis

I'D NEVER BLED SO MUCH IN MY ENTIRE LIFE. JUST WHEN I WAS ABOUT TO PASS OUT, Aziel appeared by my side and told me to drink. Whatever he brought me tasted funny. I tried to jerk away from him, but I was too weak from blood loss.

I heard Ethan's voice. My heart soared. He was there.

And then Sariel turned and offered a sad smile, almost as if he was apologizing for having made over a hundred different small cuts around my arms and neck.

It had happened so fast the pain didn't even register for the first minute, and then everything stung like a hundred fire ants had all bitten me at the same time.

"Genesis…"

Ethan had eyes for me and only me. I wanted to yell for him to stop because something wasn't right. Something felt very wrong. Cassius moved away from Ethan toward me, maybe to help, maybe to finish the job. When I saw Ethan stumble forward…

I knew.

Things were about to get a lot worse.

Cassius swore, pulling a feather from Ethan's back.

"Now we begin," Sariel said in a calm voice, picking up his pace as he stalked towards Cassius.

Confused, I watched as Ethan fell to his knees and reached for me, his face ashen, his eyes black.

"What did you do to him?" I yelled.

"Simply making him… a bit more human." Sariel shrugged, stopping directly in front of Cassius.

Cassius clenched his fists, his stance predatory. "It's been a while… Sariel."

"Father." Sariel shrugged, "And apparently I've been a horrible one… neglecting my children. Then again, you know all about being a father, don't you… son?"

In a flash, Cassius had his hands around the angel's neck. He threw him against the wall.

Sariel simply shook his body, his wings elongating to at least seven feet across. "I see I've touched a nerve."

"Ethan." Cassius growled. "Get her out of here."

Ethan shook his head then slowly stood and stumbled toward me. When his hand touched mine, it was slapped away by chains.

Aziel laughed. "No, no. The vampire watches. This concerns him, after all."

"Be silent." Sariel sneered, waving his hand at Aziel.

"Did you think you could bring the balance all on your own?" Sariel laughed mockingly, making my ears ring with its loudness. "Did you think that you were strong enough to shield all the immortals and humans alike from your sin?"

Ethan reached for my hand again, tugging me close to him.

My head slumped forward on his chest.

I didn't know if it was my blood getting all over him or his getting all over me. But I felt safe—finally.

Until Aziel lunged for me.

Ethan kicked him in the chest, causing a snarl to erupt between Aziel's lips. "If I were whole, I'd rip you limb from limb—then again, I've already taken everything from you. Do you know..." He stood to his full height, which I hadn't noticed until now, matched Sariel's. "She gave me her body—her very soul—before you killed her."

Ethan shook in my arms, his fangs grazing my neck.

"And when I took her over and over again," Aziel laughed, "I promised her I'd make her immortal. If she did one tiny, little thing for me."

"Ethan, don't listen to him." I gripped the sides of his face. "Focus on me."

"Birth me a son," Aziel yelled. "And you know what that bitch did?"

Sariel had Cassius by the throat. With a growl, he punched Sariel in the chest, sending the angel soaring through the air again. "No!"

He was running toward us.

My mind wasn't putting the pieces together fast enough.

Aziel leaned down and whispered in Ethan's ear. "She gave me a daughter."

Cassius fell to his knees.

Sariel walked around him, pulling a long sharp feather from his wings. "One should never have to kill his own offspring."

"Cassius! Behind you!" I yelled.

Cassius hung his head like he wanted to die.

In a flash, Ethan's fangs were in Aziel's neck. He hunched over him, blue blood dripping from his fangs as he completely drained the angel.

When he stood, his eyes were white just like Cassius's. In two strides, he had Cassius by the neck and tossed him against the wall.

A crack ran from the bottom to the top of the ceiling as plaster fell from overhead.

"This is my favorite part," Sariel sang, removing himself from the fight between Cassius and Ethan and coming to my side. "Where they are finally forced to finish what they started so long ago."

In my weakened state, I saw two of Sariel. I shook my head. "He can't die."

"Which one?" Sariel asked.

"Both." I forced the word out. "They'll kill each other."

"Ah, but balance must be restored."

"I don't understand," I whispered. "Ethan, stop!"

Cassius wasn't fighting anymore. It was like he wanted to die.

"Please!" I reached for Sariel, my fingers coming into contact with his soft velvet feathers. "Please."

"You know..." His eyes closed briefly. "That's the first time a human has dared touch me in... years."

"Sorry."

"It was warm." He sighed. "I've been cold for a very long time."

The air in the room shifted, turning to ice.

Ethan growled, his fangs nearly dipping into Cassius's neck when Cassius finally punched him in the jaw and stumbled backward. "I couldn't do it!"

"A daughter!"

"She wasn't yours!"

"You still killed her!"

Cassius fell to his knees. "No. No, I couldn't."

The room stilled as if someone had pressed pause on the TV.

"And so the truth reveals itself." Sariel put his arm around my shoulders. I was too weak to do anything but lean against his cold body.

"A daughter," Ethan hissed. "You would kill an innocent human."

"Abomination," Sariel said in a deadly tone. "Another Dark One. No Dark Ones have been born since Cassius—since *my* sin."

Cassius flinched.

I wanted to hug him.

His own father thought him an abomination.

"No more Dark Ones must live." Sariel sighed. "And now that Aziel is dead, I am almost appeased. You see, balance was shattered the minute Cassius allowed the Dark One to breathe."

"I couldn't." Cassius shook his head back and forth. "She was innocent."

"So one of you will take her place." Sariel nodded. "One of you will take her place, and balance will be restored. It's as simple as that." He turned his head to me. "Choose, human."

"Wh-what?"

"Your destiny. You must choose."

"I don't understand."

"Who lives? Who dies?"

chapter
thirty-nine

Ethan

ADRENALINE PULSED THROUGH MY BODY AS MADNESS OVERTOOK ME. ALL I knew was that I had to kill him—kill him for taking something important from me. But what?

"*Kill, kill, kill,*" the voice whispered in my head.

Cassius wasn't fighting back. His eyes were white, haunted. It didn't register that he was giving up. I just wanted him dead.

"*Dead, dead, dead,*" the voice continued to chant.

"Ethan, No!" Genesis screamed.

I wrapped my hands around Cassius's neck, ready to snap, ready to kill. When his eyes met mine, something had me pausing.

Why was I strangling him?

Why was I so upset?

I looked down at my hands, the same hands gripping his neck. Blue blood trickled from my fingertips.

"Damn it." I pulled back, chest heaving as my hands shook.

Aziel's blood was poison.

"*Kill, kill, kill,*" his voice whispered. "*He took from us.*"

"No." I fell to my knees, the blue blood continued to drip from my fingertips. I quickly bit into my wrist, letting more of the blood fall out of my system.

"Choose," Sariel said from behind me.

Cassius shook his head slowly. There was a piece I was missing, a piece of the puzzle that wasn't fitting together.

A daughter.

My mind replayed back the images. The baby was wrapped in a blanket—he or she wasn't human.

Half-angel?

A Dark One.

"*Mine,*" Aziel whispered in my head.

"No." I choked out a hoarse cry. "You destroyed her."

Aziel would live until the last of his blood left my body. Images flickered in front of my eyes as if I was watching a movie.

Aziel crooked his finger at Ara. She didn't need any more encouragement than a flick of his wrist, a smile in her direction. Ara had been lost to him before she even took the first step in his direction.

"Wanted her," the voice whispered in my head. *"So bad."*

"You killed her." I hung my head.

"You killed her."

"Because it had to be done." I was arguing with a dead angel, arguing with the last of his lifeblood.

Cassius reached for me.

I gripped his hand and helped him to his feet. His face was covered in bruises. His lower lip bled blue. Dark hair mixed with blood caked on his cheeks.

"You didn't kill her?" I asked.

"Well done," Sariel said from behind us. "Didn't think a vampire could control himself, and now I see him touching a Dark One. Impressed, but this is going a bit too slowly for my taste."

The room went black.

A chill filled the air.

The last thing I heard was Genesis scream before the room flashed again.

Everything was in black and white.

The house around us faded to an apple orchard.

A little girl with bright blue eyes was climbing a tree, giggling as she went faster and faster.

"Keep up!" she yelled. "You can't catch me!" She laughed harder.

Cassius was standing beneath the tree, his hands on his hips. "Get down! You'll hurt yourself."

"Nope!" She hung upside down, her long hair nearly sweeping the grass beneath her.

Cassius grinned and grabbed her, setting her on her feet. "Remember to take your medicine."

She crossed her arms. "It tastes funny."

"I know," Cassius said in a low voice. "But it won't always be this way."

"Promise." Her eyes filled with tears, the blue flashing with such ferocity that it turned white.

"Promise," he echoed.

The scene changed.

The girl looked to be around twelve. The apple orchard was the same, only this time it was fall. Leaves were scattered around the grass, and she was reading a book.

"Boo…" Cassius stepped around the tree. "I've come to say goodbye."

"No!" The girl threw her book onto the ground. "Why? Why would you leave me?"

Agony crossed over Cassius's face. "You hardly see me as it is."

The girl hung her head. "It's my favorite part of the year. When you visit."

Cassius sank to his knees so he was at eye-level. "It's for the best. Besides, you have a brother to take care of."

"Yeah." She wiped her nose with her sleeve. "He's cocky though."

"Heard that," a voice said from behind the tree.

Alex stepped into view and shared a serious look with Cassius.

"Please don't go." The girl wrapped her arms around Cassius's neck. "I'll miss you. You belong to me."

"I don't." Cassius choked out the words. "Now, run along and help your mother with dinner while I talk with your brother."

"Will I forget you?"

"No," Cassius whispered.

"You'll come back? One day?"

"Yes."

Satisfied, she ran off, leaving Cassius with Alex.

"You lied," Alex said, leaning against the tree.

"It's best this way." Cassius waved his hand into the air.

The girl staggered forward, scratched her head, and then kept running toward the house.

"The memories are removed. Just make sure she continues to donate blood and keep the glamour on her at all costs."

Alex shook his head. "I swear they'll never discover her true identity. On my life."

"Good." Cassius nodded. "That's good."

"Are you alright?"

"Of course!" Cassius pulled the hood over his head, covering his dark hair and white features, a pure giveaway to any of the townsfolk of what he was, what he was capable of. "Run along, Alex."

Alex rolled his eyes and left.

The girl stopped at the house, turned around, and lifted a hand in a cautious wave.

"Goodbye... Stephanie." Cassius cursed and walked in the other direction. Each step he took covered the grass with ice.

The scene faded.

And Ethan was back in the house with Cassius, Sariel, and Genesis.

Had they seen it too?

He turned to gauge Genesis's reaction. Tears streamed down her face as she shook her head in disbelief.

Cassius let out a pitiful moan.

"So you see..." Sariel rubbed his hands together. "...an abomination was allowed to live—still lives—for I've marked her, tasted her blood to be sure of it. Balance was wrecked the day she was born, and now we have someone from the same blood line living." He turned to Genesis. "Your great-great aunt should have made the call, should have paid for her sins. But she's dead, and soon Aziel's blood will leave your mate, and he will be gone from this world as well. So I tell you again, Genesis. You must choose who lives and who dies."

chapter
forty

Genesis

MY HEART WAS SHATTERING, BREAKING OVER AND OVER AGAIN IN MY CHEST. It was hard to breathe.

Watching Cassius with Stephanie—it was like I could feel his pain, his agony as he watched her skip off—knowing that she would never remember him.

And things suddenly made sense. Why Stephanie was drawn to him. Why she loved him.

Why he pushed her away.

When all he wanted was to hold her close.

Tears streamed down my face at Cassius's helplessness.

Ethan looked absolutely dejected, his eyes black as he swallowed and gripped Cassius's hand.

It seemed, in the end, peace had been made between them. But who was I to decide? I loved Ethan, but I wept for Cassius, for what he'd gone through. I'd always been told Dark Ones had no capacity to love.

I'd been taught wrong.

Sariel, on the other hand, clearly had no heart—to put his son through that, to watch that and still ask me to choose who lived and who died.

I knew balance had to be restored.

It was my bloodline that had ruined everything in the first place. Ara had been selfish, and her selfishness had caused a split between our races.

But her selfishness had also caused a Dark One to love. And I couldn't be mad at her for that.

"Time's wasting," Sariel said in an irritated voice. "If you don't tell me, I'll just assume you wish for me to eliminate both of them."

"I love Ethan," I whispered. "But does that mean Cassius doesn't also deserve to live?"

"This has nothing to do with what Cassius deserves or your feelings for Ethan." Sariel pushed me forward. His feathers brushed against my skin. "This is logic, pure and simple. Two plus two does not equal three. For humanity's sake... for the sake of the immortals and keeping both races thriving... a life must be taken."

I trembled.

"You think me evil." Sariel's voice was so cold, so detached. "But this isn't evil. This is life and death. This is the most simple fact about both worlds—something that unites us, despite our differences."

"What about yours?" I asked. "What if I spilled your blood?"

Sariel's eyebrows shot up. "Interesting. You'd spill my blood to save them?"

"Yes."

"Impossible. But brave."

"A girl has to try."

He held out the purple feather. "Take it and make your choice."

My hands shook as I took the feather between my fingertips. How could something so soft be so deadly? The tip was pointed, like a knife.

"I love you." My eyes filled with tears as I looked up to Ethan. "You know that. You hear my heart."

"Genesis..." His eyes flashed. "Whatever you're thinking—don't. I can't live without you, but you can live without me." His voice cracked. "Cassius will take care of you, Alex, Mason..." His eyes pleaded with mine as a red and blue tear slipped down his cheek. "I'll always be with you." His hands reached out toward the feather, but Cassius moved him out of the way.

"I was the one who did wrong," he said in a strong voice. "I deserve punishment." His face cracked into a smile. "And I cannot love." His nostrils flared. "Even if I want to."

"But you did," I argued.

"In the past." Cassius eyes turned black. "And now I feel nothing."

"Lie." My voice was hoarse.

His breath hitched as he reached for the feather, his fingertips grazing the edges of it. "Genesis, stay with your mate."

Sariel hissed out a breath next to me.

"Sometimes it's best," I held the feather out. "To love for a moment than to never experience it."

"Genesis!" Ethan moved toward me just as Cassius reached for the stem of the feather.

I stumbled backward.

And pointed the edge directly into my own chest.

"No!" Ethan roared.

Sariel turned his back to both men, covering me with his wings as I fell slowly back, my heartbeat slowing in my chest until I didn't feel a beat anymore.

Sariel's face broke out into a smile as his wings blanketed my fall to the ground. His forehead touched mine, and with a brief touch of his mouth against mine, he whispered, "Fear is not welcome here."

"Not afraid," I choked out.

"I know." His eyes blazed white. "There is no greater sacrifice than laying down one's life for the life of a friend."

The room flashed white.

And I knew I was dead.

chapter
forty-one

Ethan

I COULDN'T REACH HER IN TIME.

My body screamed and a part of my soul, perhaps the last piece I actually possessed, went dead in my chest as the sound of her heart slowing brought me to my knees.

Dead.

I knew what death sounded like—and I'd just received the final blow of my existence.

Sariel disappeared.

Leaving her body behind. Her lips were blue as if the angel had infused his blood into her mouth before leaving me behind to pick up the pieces.

I let out a guttural moan. Tears streamed down my face. I couldn't hear her heart. I couldn't feel the warmth.

Heat seared my limbs as my blood boiled, killing any of the angel's blood still left in my system.

Cassius slowly walked over to her body and shook his head. "Humans... are not supposed to die for darkness."

I couldn't speak.

It hurt too much.

"Kill me too," I whispered. "Please."

Cassius's eyes flashed. "She wouldn't want that."

"She's dead!" I roared, charging him. "Just kill me."

Cassius flung me across the room. I stumbled against the farthest wall and charged him again.

With a flick of his hand, my body stilled. He'd frozen me, the bastard.

Vampire blood boiled to the surface, heating the ice.

"You'd do anything to get her back, but you take a chance she isn't the same." Cassius sunk to his knees. "You take the chance that you may lose her."

"You mean to make her immortal."

"Only I can bring her back from death."

I turned my head. "You know what your touch would do to her."

"Not with certainty," Cassius whispered. "No."

"She may become immortal—but forever be tied to you."

"But she would live," Cassius said. "It's your choice, but her heart stopped beating two minutes ago. We are running out of time."

The ice completely melted around me. I rushed toward her lifeless body and shook my head in disbelief. "I'd rather she live—a full life—a life she deserves, even if it's apart from me—than survive one more second with her light extinguished from this world."

Cassius nodded. "Grab her hands."

They were cold, so cold that her fingertips nearly burnt me.

Cassius leaned forward, his lips hovering over hers. Eyes white as snow, his face began to immediately heal as his mouth grazed hers, and then he whispered, "Breathe."

She was still motionless.

Blue lines made their way from his temples and neck toward his lips as he blew across her lips and whispered again, "Breathe."

His hand moved to her chest, and with one more exhale, he pushed down and commanded, "Breathe, human."

Genesis choked and then inhaled. I gripped her hands as hard as I could as her fingertips began to warm against mine. Body taut, I waited for her eyes to open, waited to see if they would be white like Cassius's—or green like mine.

She was breathing.

Her heart stuttered.

And then began to take off.

"Why aren't her eyes opening?" I yelled, reaching for her shoulders. "She's alive, she's breathing but—"

"I don't know." Cassius rubbed his face. "It's been a while since I've actually given immortality to a human." His eyes were no longer white but bright blue, his skin pale.

"I'm sorry." I choked on the apology. "I know what it cost you to do that."

Cassius said nothing, rubbing his hands together as if to ward off the chill of his own blood.

He would be weak for days, possibly weeks. After all, he was still part human.

"What do we do?" Her heart still beat, but color wasn't returning to her face.

"We take her home," Cassius whispered, "and wait."

I rode home in the back seat, Genesis cradled in my arms. I kissed her neck—I even bit, hoping my blood would help infuse some of what Cassius had given her of himself.

I was desperate.

I loved her.

And I refused to believe that she would stay in that state, comatose, unable to react to the world around us.

When Cassius pulled up to the house, Alex and Mason were already outside, running toward the car.

Alex opened the door first. "What happened?"

I couldn't speak. I just shook my head, holding her closer to my body as Mason shoved Alex out of the way and let out a guttural howl before changing in front of my very eyes and running off into the darkness.

"It's still fresh, the death of his own mate," Alex whispered.

With a nod, I slowly lifted Genesis up and got out of the car. Alex shook his head and glanced at Cassius. "Stephanie's been asking for you."

"Stephanie is dead to me," Cassius said in a cold voice.

I froze and turned slowly, ready to rip his head from his body. "She better mean more to you than you say, Cassius. It's because Stephanie breathes that Genesis sacrificed herself. Go. Now. Apologize. Tell her the truth."

Alex cursed. "No." He shook his head. "No. It would destroy her. It's been over a hundred years. Just let her believe the lie. It's better for everyone."

"She has no idea what she is!" I roared. "And Cassius saved her pathetic life only to have her turn over Genesis to the very archangel who commanded her death!"

Alex hung his head. "She's my sister."

"Not by blood."

"In every way that matters." Alex clenched his teeth. "You're asking me to tell her I lied to her my entire life? About what she was? About who she was? You know the best part? I weakened myself purposefully to keep her strong, to keep the glamour in place, and now you want me to take that all away? All those years?"

"Alex." Cassius held up his hand. "I should have never asked it of you."

"You are king," Alex said in a deadly voice. "You speak. We do. Regardless of right and wrong."

"And I was..." Cassius seemed to trip over the words. "...very wrong to ask you to limit your own immortality in order to shield people from what she was—who she is."

As if hearing our discussion, Stephanie slowly walked out of the house, tears streaming down her face. "Is she dead?"

"No," I growled. "She's going to be fine."

"I'm so s-sorry," Stephanie sobbed. "It's my fault. I just wanted... I don't know why, I can't explain why. I just... something has always been missing."

Cassius swore while Alex held up his hands and walked off in the other direction. "I'm taking the car. Let me know what you decide. I can't watch this."

Stephanie wiped her cheeks. "I'll help you take her to the room. Maybe if she's in some place familiar, she'll wake up."

I grunted and pushed past Stephanie. "Maybe."

"Ethan..." Stephanie croaked. "You have to believe me. I'm so sorry."

"I know," I whispered hoarsely. "I know." With a curse, I turned to Cassius. "Tell her, or I will."

Stephanie sniffed. "Tell me what?"

Cassius seemed to pale in that instant, all at once, as he swayed on his feet, gripping the door with both hands. "Stephanie..."

"What?" She looked between us. "Cassius, what's wrong with you? Why do you look so weak?"

"He saved Genesis," I answered.

Realization dawned on Stephanie's face as she stumbled back from both of us. "When she wakes up... she'll belong to him."

I didn't say anything because I didn't know what would happen, and neither did Cassius.

"Possibly," Cassius finally said.

Stephanie choked out a sob and ran past both of us and up the stairs.

"Cassius," I growled. "Tell her."

"Yeah." He licked his lips. "Just let me catch my breath first."

"It won't get easier with time."

"I know." He hung his head. "Let me just... give me just..." He shook his head. "Something's wrong."

"Cassius?"

"Very wrong." His eyes narrowed until they were fully white then black, tiny pinpricks. "I think I'm dying."

The last sentence he uttered before falling to the ground.

chapter
forty-two

Genesis

S ARIEL WAS STANDING WITH ME, HOLDING MY HAND. IT FELT GOOD. HE WASN'T so cold anymore, mostly warm like me.

"His blood calls to you," Sariel whispered.

"Who?" I felt happy, complete, yet a part of me missed something, like I was staring at a really pretty picture, but it was missing something epic, something that would change my world.

"Cassius and Ethan, both of their blood fights for you right now. I'm afraid you must yet again make a choice."

I sighed, my heart remembering Ethan, my mate, my love. "He's so warm. Why is Cassius cold?"

"Opposites, I suppose." Sariel squeezed my hand. "It was never meant to be like this, Genesis."

"Like what?" I continued watching the waves crash in front of me. He'd brought me to the beach. It was calming, beautiful.

"This…" Sariel held out his hand. "Dark Ones were never meant to exist, but it seems a human is just like a siren in the sense that their blood sings to angels in a way immortals' does not."

"Was Cassius's mom beautiful like him?"

"Yes." Sariel hung his head. "And she died just like Ara."

"Because she loved you?"

Sariel was quiet then whispered, "Because I loved her—too much."

"How can you love someone too much?"

"When that love overcomes all sense of reality and logic—when the love once beautiful starts to create fear and jealousy. Just because something starts out good does not mean it ends good. Do you understand?"

I sighed and laid my head on his shoulder. "You aren't good, but you aren't bad either. You're simply both."

"That I am." Sariel sighed. "His blood still calls. When you return to them, you'll have to make a choice, Genesis, but it's yours. Not theirs. Cassius gave you his essence."

"Will he die because of it?"

Sariel closed his eyes; a blue tear slid down his cheek, hitting me in the shoulder. "That depends on the balance of things."

"But…" I frowned. "I thought balance was restored."

"Yours... Ethan's." Sariel rubbed my hand. "But Cassius is still very much unbalanced. That's what love does to a Dark One. It is also why it is forbidden."

My eyes welled with tears. "He loves Stephanie... in that way?"

"He stayed away from the girl for a very long time... pushed her so far out of his mind, out of his consciousness, that he simply rejected the idea of even knowing her. When a female was needed, as an Elder I put the suggestion in his mind, made him think it was his own... made him think he was powerful enough to face his past in hopes he could finally start living."

"Instead, he got worse." I sighed.

"Because every day her smile reminds him of what he can never have."

"There's always a way," I argued.

Sariel let out a laugh. "And this is why I like humans, always optimistic."

"What other choice do we have?"

His eyes met mine. "Exactly."

chapter
forty-three

Ethan

N OT HOW I EXPECTED TO START MY DAY OR END IT.

Cassius was in the room next door to mine.

Genesis still hadn't woken up, but her breathing had evened out. Her heartbeat sounded less erratic. I had faith she was just healing—taking her time.

"Have you tried kissing her?" Mason said from the doorway.

"What?"

"Kissing her." Mason walked into the room, his arms folded, eyes tense. "In those movies, the prince always kisses the princess."

"What the hell are you talking about?" I growled. "What movies?"

"Like the King Lion movie… there's tons of them. I had nothing else to do, so I went out and bought them because they made Genesis happy, and I was losing my mind with worry so I watched a few… or maybe… seven… and the prince always kisses the princess."

I fought hard for patience as my fangs elongated, wanting to take a bite out of his silly neck. "You watched cartoons. All day?"

"I made steak…" Mason fidgeted with his hands. "…for when she'd return. I thought maybe we could share it."

I glanced back at Genesis. "She would like that."

"I figured it would give her something to look forward to."

"Sharing meat with a wolf?" I smirked.

"And watching cartoons." Mason pulled a seat up to the bed. "And it's worth a shot. Maybe kiss her, then tell her about the steak."

Werewolves.

"Any change with Cassius?"

Mason shook his head. "His temperature drops for seconds before it sky-rockets again. It's like he doesn't have enough blood to self-heal."

"He gave it all to her." Tears filled my eyes. "To save my mate."

"There must be something we can do for him," Mason growled. "He's still king. He's still…"

"Our friend. Brother," I finished. "Watch her for me? I need to find Stephanie."

Mason's face was impassive, but I could hear his heart pick up speed. "So, you'll risk breaking her heart by telling her the truth?"

"Yes." I licked my lips.

"Good luck." Mason shook his head. "I think I'll stay here and talk to Genesis about steak."

I smiled—the first time in a few hours—and patted him on the back. "Don't leave out any juicy details, wolf."

"Wouldn't dream of it," he growled then leaned over the bed and grabbed Genesis's hand. "Listen, human, if you don't wake up soon, I'm going to eat all the meat, and we both know what that would do to my digestive system at this point."

I let out a chuckle and moved down the hallway, my ears sensitive to all the heartbeats in the house.

Cassius was weak, so weak. I'd never heard his heart flutter that way.

Another strong heartbeat joined the mix.

Picking up speed.

I waited as Stephanie reached the top of the stairs. Her hair was piled in a knot on her head, her blue eyes still blurred with tears.

"Remove it," I whispered.

Alex could hear my thoughts—could hear me in the house. He'd just walked in the door when I'd uttered the command. He cursed a blue streak.

"I said…" My voice edged with venom. "Remove it."

Alex's tortured heart slowed, and then the house trembled as Stephanie's hair went from light to dark, her lips from cherry to pale, her eyes—white.

She stumbled back and felt her face.

It would feel different, smoother, stronger.

Her hands shook in front of her. "What did you just do?"

"We need to talk." I held out my hand. "Trust me?"

She gulped, her white eyes blinking in confusion. "I feel different."

"Because you are."

"I don't understand."

"But you want to?"

She nodded.

"Take my hand."

The minute her fingers touched mine, she gasped. We'd always felt warm to one another, but the minute her skin came into contact with mine, frost formed across her fingertips.

"But—"

"Let's go visit Cassius. He may be sleeping right now, but I believe he'd want to be in the room."

"He hates me."

"No." I sighed. "That's where you're wrong."

"Dark Ones do not love," she whispered. "I know that now."

I tilted my head and smiled sadly. "Don't they?"

chapter
forty-four

Genesis

IT'S TIME." SARIEL RELEASED MY HAND.

"Will I see you again?"

He laughed, his feathers ruffling next to me. "Do you really want to?"

I shrugged. "You're not so bad."

"So many compliments my head may explode."

He wasn't. It was weird. He was dangerous; he had potential for both evil and good, but he was also in a position where he had no choice but to force the rules on people—and hope that in the end everything worked out. I felt sorry for him.

Sariel tilted my chin toward him. "Don't."

Tears filled my eyes. "Thank you… for staying with me."

"Always." He plucked a purple feather from his wings and placed it in my hands. "I'm only a thought away."

I clenched the feather in my hands and nodded. "Goodbye."

His lips touched my forehead as cold spilled through my body, followed by such intense heat that I started to convulse.

I saw Ethan's warm smile… the first time he'd bitten me, our shared kisses, our mouths fusing together as if we needed each other so desperately we would die without touch.

And then Cassius—his heart of ice—shattering, breaking, and transforming into something beautiful right before my very eyes as his lips met mine, and he whispered, "Breathe."

I wanted to breathe.

But not him, not Cassius.

I tried to yell for Ethan.

Clenching the feather tighter in my hands, I fought. Fought for the warmth like it was the only way I would see him again. The cold threatened; it also offered me peace.

While the heat reminded me of the mating, of the severe pain I'd had to go through in order to be his—

I would go through it all over again.

Through the fires of hell to be with Ethan.

I embraced the heat, holding out my hands as the fires singed my fingertips. I welcomed the pain—because would it really be worth it if it was easy? If loving him was that simple?

Fire exploded in my chest, pinching, trickling down my fingertips until my knees buckled beneath me.

There was no relief.

And I was okay with it—I welcomed it. Because soon—I would be with Ethan again.

"Steak," something whispered.

I cried out. Had I heard that right? Steak?

"Lots of steak and other meat. Hell, I'll get you your own butcher... I think Belle had a butcher? Or maybe that was another princess."

What?

The fire got hotter and hotter.

"I told him it was true love's kiss, but does he listen? No, just walks off and lets me talk about food. I have a confession. I hate berries."

Mason? I tried to speak his name, but my mouth was too hot; when I opened it, more heat entered, stealing my breath.

"And pinecones taste like shit, but hey, a wolf does what a wolf does. It's not like it will kill me. Do you think I'm grumpy like the beast?"

I smiled, focusing on Mason's voice as the pain increased. *Keep talking!* I wanted to yell. *Just keep saying something!*

"Don't expect me to sing—wolves do not sing."

I smiled.

"Aw, was that a twitch of your lips, human? Alright, I'll tell you something else... something you can never speak of again. When I was a pup, I had a pet caterpillar... cried when the damn thing turned into a butterfly. Circle of life... hey, that's King Lion's song!"

A laugh escaped between my lips as I tried to open my eyes. They felt like sandpaper.

"Come on," Mason urged. "You know you want the steak."

I shook my head back and forth, and then finally, with great effort, opened my eyes.

Mason grinned. "Green. Your eyes are very, very green."

chapter
forty-five

Ethan

I GRABBED STEPHANIE BY THE ARM AND GENTLY LED HER INTO THE ROOM WHERE Cassius was sleeping—resting—hopefully healing.

The minute we stepped inside the door, I could see my breath leave my lips. Frost lined his body; his lips were completely blue.

He shuddered in his sleep, reaching his hand up to the ceiling only to drop it down again by his side.

"What's wrong with him?" A tear froze on Stephanie's pale cheek.

I sighed, running my hand through my hair. "I have no idea."

"You mean, he's never been like this before? In all the years you've known him?" Her eyes were accusing. Then again, she was scared for him—she loved him.

"Just how old do you think I am?" I fired back. "And no." I released her hand. "I've never seen him like this. I can hear his heart... it's slow."

She slowly made her way to his side and reached for his hand. The minute she touched him, the temperature in the room rose a few degrees, I could taste it on my tongue, taste the heat of life building, boiling inside him.

"I can't explain it." Her eyes locked on him. I imagined she couldn't look away even if she wanted to. "The pull he has on me. Like I've known him my whole life—like I've waited for him—" She hung her head. "Or maybe like he's been waiting for me. It's stupid." Her laugh was hollow. "I know it's stupid, but I can't help it."

"Stephanie..." I took a seat across from her. "It's not stupid... because a very long time ago... there was an innocent little girl caught in the middle of a war that should have never been started. He saved her life and, in return, hid her true identity from herself."

"What?"

The easiest way was to show her, so I bit into my wrist and held the blood to her lips. "Drink and see."

"I've never drunk vampire blood."

"Yes, well, this is a day of firsts." I rolled my eyes. "Just know it's going to burn going down, always does for your kind."

"Sirens?"

My throat was thick with emotion. "No. Dark Ones."

Her mouth dropped open. I took advantage and shoved what I could of my wrist past her lips. The minute the blood entered her body, her head fell back, eyes white, mouth open.

I closed my own eyes and focused in on the exact memory I needed to pull.

Cassius in the Orchard with Stephanie.

Stephanie and Alex.

Him wiping her memories.

And finally, her waving goodbye.

It broke my heart all over again to feel his sadness—to experience his loss as if it was my own.

With a gasp, Stephanie opened her eyes and stared at Cassius. "He saved my life."

"He did."

"He..." Tears streamed down her cheeks. "He promised I would never forget him." Her lips trembled. "He lied."

"He had to protect you—at all costs. Dark Ones are no longer made, Stephanie. You know that. He's one of the oldest, one of ten who were allowed to live."

"But I'm alive," she whispered, touching her fingertips to her mouth. "I should be dead."

"Yes, well... Genesis made an offer Sariel couldn't refuse."

Stephanie covered her face with her hands. "Tell me she didn't sacrifice herself for everyone."

I didn't deny it. "And when she did Cassius offered her immortality—something that only he was strong enough to give—to bring her back from the brink of death."

"And now he's cold... dying."

"We don't know that," I said in a soft voice. "But I do know he needs you... he needs your blood."

Stephanie's gaze snapped to mine. "Would it work?"

"No idea." I licked my lips and stood. "But it's worth a try." I cringed at the thought of Mason's advice but offered it nonetheless. "The werewolf seems to think a kiss does the trick."

Stephanie's lips twitched. "He never let me kiss him."

"But I thought you spent the evenings with him and—"

"Talked." A rosy hue pinched her cheeks. "I just wanted to be by him. For some reason, his touch never affected me the same way it did others. It was comforting, familiar, so I've been pestering him every night for the past few years. At first he only let me visit once a year, after I'd come of age... and then it quickly turned into once a month, once a week, every night."

"He cares for you," I said. "I'm sure of it."

"I wish that was enough… caring." She gripped his hand tighter. "But maybe I can love him enough for both of us."

"Nobody deserves to live that way, Stephanie, regardless of what he did."

"He saved my life," she said simply. "How selfish of a person would I have to be to not offer him the same kindness, regardless of how I feel for him?"

"Dark Ones have never tried to bond to one another—ever."

"I know."

"You could die."

"I know."

"I didn't bring you in here to save him… but to give you the truth."

"Then thank you," Stephanie stood and kissed me on the cheek, "for giving me both."

In an instant she turned in my arms and lunged for Cassius. The room plummeted in a blanket of cold as she leaned over him.

"I'll need your teeth, Ethan." She held her arm behind her.

I bit deep.

Pain marred her features, and then she was in my arms. "On the lips."

"What?"

Before I could react, she turned her mouth against my fangs, slicing open her bottom lip.

The tinge of angel blood hit my tongue just as she once again leaned over Cassius and kissed his mouth, breathing out the word, "Live."

chapter
forty-six

Genesis

"G REEN?" I REPEATED. "LIKE ETHAN-GREEN OR MILKY GREEN?"

"What the hell does milky green mean?" Mason scowled. "And they're Ethan-green—almost creepy."

My face cracked into a wide smile. "Does that mean I'm a vampire now?"

"Does your face itch?"

"What?"

Mason shrugged. "Does it itch?"

"No."

"Do you smell berries?"

"Huh?"

"Just answer the question," he growled.

I sniffed the air. "No, I smell… wood burning."

He grinned. "Then you aren't a werewolf."

"Gee, thanks." I tried to get up, but he moved around me and tugged my body to a sitting position. "I was worried there for a second. Do werewolves really smell berries?"

"Sometimes." He chuckled, brushing a kiss across my forehead. "To vampires we smell like burning wood… outdoors, warm."

I nodded and leaned in. "I like the way you smell."

"Care to keep your paws to yourself, Mason?" Ethan said from the door, his grimace turning into a grin as he strode in and practically threw Mason off me and pulled me into his arms. "Your eyes are green."

"Why do people keep telling me what color my eyes are?"

"Because," Mason said from his spot behind Ethan, "it's a sign."

"Of what?"

"Greatness." Ethan's mouth found mine; his tongue tasted like sugar.

With a moan, I threw my arms around his neck and tugged him harder against me.

Mason coughed.

Ethan waved him away, moving onto the bed, pulling my body tightly against his.

Our mouths were fused together. I never wanted to let go—never wanted to breathe if it wasn't heavy with his taste, his scent.

I forgot about the feather in my hands, pushing it against his chest.

Ethan flinched and pulled back with a hiss. "Sariel?"

I nodded. "He was with me… when I closed my eyes."

"Well, I'll be damned," Mason muttered under his breath. "The archangels rarely visit immortals, and now you're saying you spent actual time with him?"

"After my kidnapping," I muttered.

"Doesn't matter." Mason's eyebrows shot up. "Time is their currency, to spend time with any being—when you're an angel—is a gift."

I lifted the feather to my face, the purple shining in the light of the room.

Ethan reached out and touched the edges of the feather. "When an angel gives one of his feathers, it's like wishing on a star. Tell me, what did Sariel say to you?"

"He said to choose," I whispered, and he gave me the feather.

"The desire of your heart." Ethan's eyes shone with green. "Cassius may have saved you—granted you immortality—but it was Sariel who let you choose how you'd return."

"I just…" I gripped Ethan by the shoulders. "I just wanted you."

"You have me," he vowed, kissing my mouth hard, "for an eternity."

Mason coughed again.

"Then leave!" Ethan growled over his shoulder. "Nobody's asking you to watch."

A loud male scream pierced the air.

"Cassius," Mason and Ethan said in unison.

In a flash, I was in Ethan's arms, being carried into the room next to us. He set me on my feet just as Cassius jerked up from the bed, his eyes white, veins in his neck pulsing blue.

Stephanie braced herself over him protectively.

He reached for her arms, gripping her shoulders so hard I wanted to flinch on her behalf. "What have you done?"

"What needed to be done," she whispered.

With a groan, he touched his forehead to hers gently, something that seemed odd for him to do. He was always so abrasive, big, looming, scary.

It was then I noticed that Stephanie didn't look the same. Her hair was black, her eyes matching Cassius's.

Alex entered the room.

The temperature rose a few degrees. I felt like a fight was about to break out. But instead of Alex lunging for anyone, he simply gripped the wall and watched as if fascinated by what was taking place.

"What did she do?" I whispered in Ethan's ear.

Ethan's eyes narrowed, searching.

I followed his gaze and nearly fell to my knees when I saw the blood drenching Stephanie's chest.

"She gave him... her heart." Ethan's hoarse voice pierced the silence in the room. "The only good a Dark One possesses."

"Wait? What does that mean?" I asked.

Right before my eyes, Stephanie's glow faded. Her eyes turned blue, her hair stayed black, but her skin was no longer glowing.

"It means," Cassius's voice rumbled, "she gave her essence, her immortality, to me."

Alex sighed from the door. "It means she's now human."

Stephanie nodded slowly and whispered, "It was worth it."

chapter
forty-seven

Ethan

I'D NEVER SEEN IT ACTUALLY DONE BEFORE—AN IMMORTAL GIVING ESSENCE TO another. Only Dark Ones were fully capable of doing it. They were the strongest, after all.

And now. She was nothing.

Stephanie swayed toward Cassius.

He caught her body with his hands, his eyes swirling white. "Why would you do this?"

Stephanie squinted as if she was having trouble focusing. "Because a long time ago, you saved a little girl who should have died. It was the least I could do."

I watched the scene unfold. Something was off. Stephanie wasn't dying, not that I thought she would, but Cassius was—

"Cassius!" I yelled. "Stop touching her!"

Cassius frowned and looked down at his hands. They were still touching her skin, but Stephanie wasn't acting like a typical human being touched by a Dark One. Usually they were filled with so much lust that they attacked, and their arousal was so evident you could smell it in the air.

I smelled absolutely nothing but my own mate and every other person in that room.

No lust.

"Well…" Alex chuckled from the door. "How's that for a fun twist to the story? The great Dark One has no effect on Stephanie as a human."

I was relieved.

Cassius looked irritated.

He moved his hands down her arms then back up again, his face twisting with curiosity until he finally cupped her chin. "You feel nothing?"

Stephanie shrugged. "You feel a bit cold, but other than that, it's nice to be touched."

"Nice…" Cassius repeated. "Nice?"

"Bad answer," Genesis said under her breath.

I wrapped my arm tighter around her, tugging the warmth of her body against mine.

Cassius continued inspecting Stephanie as if he couldn't understand why she wasn't affected by him.

"You would know if she was lying," I finally pointed out. "And Stephanie, you should rest."

She nodded, suppressing a yawn with her hand. When she rose, she leaned over and kissed Cassius on the cheek. "I'm glad you're okay."

Cassius's face was priceless.

Never in his existence had he ever had any creature not be affected by his presence. I imagined it was a humbling experience—one he didn't enjoy.

"Thank you." He released her, his arms falling to his sides as if they carried the weight of the world.

She stumbled toward us.

Alex moved quickly, lifting her into his arms. "You know, you're still my sister… in every way that matters."

"Ha." She yawned. "So you won't disown me?"

"Not unless you really piss me off—then again, you are a human. By the way, do I affect you? Feeling warm and tingly?"

She frowned. "First of all, gross… second, no."

"Fascinating." Mason rubbed his chin and shook his head. "It must be because she started out immortal."

Cassius was still staring at the door long after Alex had carried her out of it.

"I need to talk to him," I whispered into Genesis's hair.

She nodded and held out her hand to Mason. "I believe you promised we'd share a steak?"

"You heard that?" Mason growled.

"All of it." She grinned. "Come on, feed me, wolf."

He smiled and tucked her into his body. "I'll feed you, but I may need help with my own eating habits."

"Together." She patted his chest. "Alright?"

He kissed her forehead and walked out with her.

Typically, I would have ripped his lips off for daring to graze her skin, but I felt her heart beat for me, saw her green eyes, knew without a shadow of a doubt that she loved me—and only me.

"Controlling your emotions well, I see," Cassius said in a low gravelly voice.

"One of us should," I fired back.

He looked away and cursed. "I have no idea what you're talking about."

"Oh?" I moved toward the bed and sat on the edge. "No idea at all?"

Cassius stared at the blankets.

I laughed. "Lie."

Mumbling another curse, he crossed his arms. "Dirty vampire trick, tasting the air to see if I'm being honest."

"Well..." I shrugged. "At least be honest with yourself. You're disappointed."

"It's called shock. Hasn't happened in a great while... I imagine it will pass." He licked his lips only to have those same lips covered in frost again.

"You love her."

"Dark Ones don't love."

"I really wish people would stop saying that when all evidence points to the contrary." I arched my eyebrows. "She's human now."

"Thanks, caught that."

"You could mate with her."

Cassius went very still.

I kept talking. "She's immune. She wouldn't become addicted or obsessed."

"Right," he croaked.

"Fear..." I tilted my head. "Now I taste fear. Odd, since Dark Ones are afraid of nothing."

"It's a day of firsts. I should sleep."

"You rarely sleep."

Cassius pounded the mattress with his fist. "Damn it! Why didn't she just let me pass? Things would have been so much easier."

"Do you truly want easy?"

"No."

"Cassius—"

"No!" He pointed at the door. "That woman... that, that—" He bit down into his lip. "She'll ruin me."

"How do you figure?"

"Because I'll fail."

"I think you lost me."

Cassius pushed the dark hair from his face and swallowed. "I don't know the first thing about honestly pursuing someone or something without using every ounce of power I possess. To Stephanie, I may as well be human."

"And that's so bad?"

"It's horrible." His eyes met mine. "Because I'll be found wanting."

"So insecure."

"Honest," he said in a humorless laugh. "She couldn't possibly want me, darkness and all, and even if she did, I have no power to convince her of anything."

"So don't use your power."

His nostrils flared.

"Don't pursue her as a Dark One..." I whispered. "Pursue her as a man."

Cassius closed his eyes and leaned back against the headboard. "Or I simply don't do anything."

I burst out laughing at the way his heart picked up pace. "I'd really like to see you try."

"You don't think I'm strong enough?" he roared.

"No." I shrugged and got up. "I think you're tired of fighting what's been in front of you too damn long, but good luck with your plan. I'm sure that will work out really well, you miserable bastard."

"Since when do you talk to your king like this?"

"Since I realized he's more friend, more brother, than king."

Cassius's lips twitched. "Don't let that get around. Imagine what it would do to my horrible reputation."

Laughing, I turned on my heel and walked toward the door. "Cassius?"

"Hmm?" He lifted his head.

"You owe it to you, and you owe it to her to at least try."

"And fail?"

"Trying isn't near as fun when you already know you'll succeed."

"Go find your mate. I'm tired of you making sense, vampire."

Smirking, I waved him off and made my way downstairs, passing Stephanie's room on the way. Alex was just leaving, his expression amused.

"What?" My eyes narrowed.

"She's human."

"So?"

"I just find it funny." Alex slapped me on the back. "We gain a human a few days ago only to lose her and gain another."

I stopped walking. "Genesis is still human."

Alex tilted his head. "Her heart still beats, yes. But..." His smile grew. "Interesting. You didn't even notice."

"Notice?" I gripped him by the shirt and slammed him against the wall. "Notice what?"

"Holy shit!" Mason screamed from the kitchen.

Alex burst out laughing. "I think you're about to find out, poor Mason. I do hope he was able to get away in time."

chapter
forty-eight

Genesis

"MASON!" I COVERED MY MOUTH WITH MY HANDS—MY VERY SHARP mouth. "I'm so sorry! I don't know what came over me!"

His mouth was still open, maybe in shock, possibly a bit of horror as he looked from the raw steak back to me. "Blood."

I shook my head. "It just—I didn't—"

Mason roared with laughter then carefully set the knife down and made his way around the table. "Fangs look good on you."

I covered my mouth again. "But I'm human."

"Vampires get very protective when they feel threatened." He held up his hands then tilted his head. "May I?"

"What?"

He winked and leaned down, pressing his head against my stomach. Was he insane?

"Mason, please, tell me why the hell you have your head pressed against my mate before I rip your tongue out."

"Such violence," Alex said in an amused voice. "You'll have to learn to guard what you say when you have a little person running around."

"Little person?" Ethan repeated.

"Shh…" Alex held his finger to his lips. "…listen."

Ethan stared at me then at Mason then at Alex. "Three heartbeats, but—"

"But…" Alex nodded. "Do you hear that fourth one? Kind of sounds like a horse taking off, its hooves hitting the race track in rapid succession."

Mason grinned and looked up at me. "Healthy."

"Wh-what?" I was still covering my mouth.

"Vampire blood…" Mason laughed and slapped his knee as he sat down. "For one reason or another the mixture of the bloody steak and me holding a knife set your heart racing. Protective vampire blood took over, compliments of your mate and newfound immortality, and here we are…"

"I attacked you!" I wanted to crawl under the table and hide.

"To protect your little one." Mason winked. "It won't be the last time."

"Little one," Ethan repeated still as a statue.

Alex grinned between all of us. "I'd like to point out I knew first."

"How?" Ethan growled.

"I counted." Alex rolled his eyes. "The heartbeat was so faint at first. I thought it was because we were losing Cassius, and then when Genesis walked in, it was stronger. And we all know what happens when a mate is made immortal. They take on different... gifts... from their immortal partner. She's still human, but mama bear will most definitely fang a bitch or..." He smirked. "...a werewolf—my apologies—if she feels threatened."

Mason let out a low growl while Ethan moved around the table and gathered me into his arms. "You're pregnant."

"Um..." I gulped. "Apparently."

"Immortals move fast and all that." Alex yawned. "Oh, and here's some good news. Six months—not nine. Immortal blood develops faster."

I nodded my head, unsure if what I was hearing was actually happening. "I think... I think I need to sit."

"Yes, well, just keep your fangs in." Ethan grinned.

Horrified, I touched my mouth again only to find the fangs gone. "What happened?"

"Retracted." Alex winked. "Cool trick, right?"

"Alex, don't you have somewhere to be?" Ethan hissed.

"No." Alex pulled out a chair. "I really don't, and it's *Uncle* Alex."

Mason grinned.

"Does that make me a grandfather?" Cassius stumbled into the room. "Because as much as a new life excites me, I'm the oldest here, and the thought doesn't sit well with me." He winced and pulled out a seat.

"Hip bothering you again?" Alex joked.

Cassius tilted his head, white filling his eyes, while Alex jumped out of his chair and started scratching his arms violently. "Make it stop."

Cassius smirked. "I have no idea what you're talking about, siren."

Ethan rolled his eyes. "Cassius..."

"Fine," Cassius snapped, his eyes flashed, and Alex stopped itching.

"You know I hate ants," Alex grumbled, crossing his arms. "Making me see one of my fears isn't a good way to make friends."

"I have friends." Cassius shrugged.

I smiled and reached for him. Ethan's eyes were leery, but I knew it would be okay, knew that touching Cassius would do nothing to me.

He must have realized it too because the minute my hand snaked out, Cassius clenched it with his and kissed me on the knuckles. "I'm glad you're feeling better."

"Me too." I squeezed his hand back and then kissed his cheek.

Ethan growled.

"Settle." Cassius rolled his eyes. "She feels nothing for me. Her heart is pure green."

"Funny," Ethan hissed.

"Like her eyes." Cassius smiled.

"I only have four steaks." Mason interjected. "So, if you guys need more food, someone has to go to the store, and I vote Alex, since he's the most irritating of the group."

"I don't eat." Cassius frowned. "But…"

I laughed and pointed to the meat. "Maybe you should try to be more human."

"She has a point." Ethan pulled me into his lap. "It may help things along."

"Things?" Alex squinted. "What things?"

Cassius growled.

Alex's eyes narrowed. "Oh no. Hell, no."

Mason chuckled. "So, we get more steak."

"Am I the only one who thinks this is a really bad idea?" Alex shouted.

"What idea?" I played dumb, knowing exactly what was going to happen. Cassius was going to pursue Stephanie… as he should.

"I'll murder you," Alex said in a low voice.

"Any more fears, Alex?" Cassius taunted.

"Bastard."

"King." His eyes flashed. "And don't you forget it."

chapter
forty-nine

Ethan

THE MINUTE I'D DISCOVERED SHE WAS PREGNANT, IT WAS LIKE I'D CEASED TO exist, and every thought focused on the tiny life growing inside of her. I couldn't stop staring at her all throughout dinner. I didn't want to eat food. I wanted to taste her—taste and make sure the baby was healthy—and force my own blood down her throat even if I had to trick her. It would make the baby grow faster.

And I'd feel a hell of a lot better about protecting both their lives.

"Stop fidgeting," Alex said to my left. "You're worse than a woman."

"Don't call me a woman," I snarled, trying to pay attention to the card game, while Genesis and Mason attempted to bake a cake.

She wanted chocolate.

He had some extra berries for the toppings.

And now they deemed themselves professionals. Pans went flying, and I knew it was only a matter of time before my gourmet kitchen was going to have dings all over it from both Mason's inability to do anything gentle and Genesis's newfound strength.

A knife had impaled itself into Alex's thigh when she was cutting vegetables. Don't ask me how. One minute it had been in her hand; the next minute it had gone flying. Naturally, I'd gotten out of the way.

Alex, however, had been too busy daydreaming.

He'd bled for mere seconds before he healed.

But he was still irritated.

It was torture—waiting for the cake to bake. Waiting for everyone to stop talking.

Waiting, waiting, waiting.

Finally, Cassius cleared his throat and whispered something in Genesis's ear before giving me a fleeting look and walking out of the room.

She jumped to her feet, reached for my hand, and the next thing I knew, she was pulling me up the stairs toward our bedroom.

The doors slammed behind us.

And her mouth was on mine.

"You taste like chocolate," I growled, biting at her lips. "Sweet."

"Mmm…" She gripped my hair with her hands, jumped into my arms, and wrapped her legs around me. "…and you taste like sugar."

I chuckled and bit at her lips again. Tasting a bit of her blood mixed with her scent had my mind racing as I tossed her onto the bed and ripped at her clothes aggressively. "I've been wanting to do this for hours."

"Rip clothes?" she teased.

"Only yours."

"I didn't know." Genesis tilted her head back while my lips found her neck, trailing kisses all the way down until I came into contact with her bra—worthless piece of material. I ripped it off and made a mental note not to let her wear any undergarments—ever. Too many unnecessary layers.

She let out a moan when I licked between the valley of her breasts, my mouth making a wet trail down her stomach.

"Cassius said we needed alone time."

"Remind me to vote him into office." I swirled my tongue around her belly button and moved lower, tugging her leggings away. Damn, she wore a lot of clothes. Where the hell were all those dresses I told Stephanie to buy for her?

"You vote for king?"

"Stop talking," I hissed, licking her hipbone then biting the sensitive flesh above it.

"O-o-okay." Genesis gripped my head and forced it down.

I chuckled. "Demanding."

"Sorry, I was… distracted."

"Allow me to distract you more." I leaned up on my knees, still hovering over her and ripped off every stitch of clothing left on my body. "Also, remind me to lock you in the bedroom for the next few weeks."

She laughed, her hands dancing across my naked chest. "You're beautiful."

"Vampires are deadly. Not beautiful."

"Fine. You're deadly."

I smiled.

"Still pretty though."

"Dangerous," I corrected her.

Her eyebrows arched.

With a hiss, I flipped her onto her stomach and moved between her thighs. "Still think I'm pretty?"

"Very." She moved up to her knees and looked over her shoulder. "Is this you trying to prove me wrong?"

With a growl, I rocked her hips back, plunging into her. "Guess I'll have to try harder."

"Yes, harder." She closed her eyes and whimpered.

With a growl, I filled her and began slowly stroking, moving. I ducked my head down and bit the side of her hip, drawing blood between my lips as I went deeper, filling every inch of her.

Eternity.

Immortality.

I experienced it only with Genesis.

And I knew my life would never be the same. Because she lived… I was forever changed.

"Ethan!" she screamed.

I pulled out and flipped her onto her back, sinking my fangs into her neck as I thrust one last time, nearly taking us both off the bed. "I love you," I whispered hoarsely against her neck. "Forever."

epilogue

Cassius

I WANDERED THE STREETS, LETTING THE DARKNESS CONSUME THE LONELINESS inside my chest. The irritating little jab that continued to beat in a melodic rhythm, reminding me that I was alive.

That she'd almost died.

I muttered a curse and pulled the hood of my jacket over my head, moving through the shadows, watching, waiting.

"You called?" an amused voice cracked into the night sky.

I flinched at the way his every syllable made my body want to convulse with anger—rage. "Yes."

"And?"

"She gave me her immortality. Is it possible to give it back?"

He stepped out of the shadows, his white hair a stark contrast to the dark air swirling around us, protecting us from watchful eyes. "Why would you want to do that?"

I hated my father, hated Sariel for forcing me into the position of king over a people who, for the most part, feared me but despised me with a hateful rage that could never be fixed. "She's weak."

Sariel smiled, folding his large arms across his chest in a manner that reminded me what he was—and what I was in comparison. Small. "There is always a way to return what has been given, but things always come at a cost. You give back the gift—you earn the same fate."

I figured as much.

"Being human, is it so horrible?" Sariel held his hands out in front of him as the cloud of darkness disappeared and people walked around us, mindless of our presence. "Some of them are happy."

"But most of them are full of fear, anger, sadness." I shook my head. "The same emotions that would overtake me if I didn't have your blood."

Sariel's eyes flashed white. "Emotions are something we don't readily experience."

I licked my lips and nodded once. "Thank you."

His eyebrows shot up. "That's a first."

I ignored him and turned my back, walking in the other direction. It was a mistake to call for him, a mistake to meet with him—only to find out that I was in the same damn position I'd been in a few days ago.

In love.

Chasing after something so forbidden that I'd risked my life in order to follow my heart.

"Thirty days," Sariel called behind me.

I glanced over my shoulder. "Thirty days?"

"Thirty days of humanity—learn to love as a human does. If she loves you in return, truly loves you as you are and mates with you, I'll restore your immortality—and allow her hers."

My heart picked up speed in my chest. "And if I fail?"

Sariel grinned menacingly. "Then I kill you. Blood must always be shed for balance. You know that by now, son."

"Thirty days," I repeated.

"Thirty days, oh, and do try not to get shot or develop a sickness that's not yet found a cure."

"I haven't agreed."

"You agreed the minute the words fell upon your ears." Sariel raised his hands above his head.

A clap of thunder sounded.

Severe pain ripped through my legs as I fell to my knees onto the cold wet pavement.

Heart racing, I reached for my chest only to find that my skin was warm to the touch.

"Thirty days," he whispered and disappeared.

Shaking, I rose to my feet, stumbling past buildings. When I finally made it out of the alleyway and into the lit up street, I glanced at my reflection in the store window and almost got sick.

My skin had color.

And my eyes... were blue.

Want more Dark Ones?
Check out these books:

The Dark Ones (Ethan & Genesis's story)
Untouchable Darkness (Cassius & Stephanie's story)
Dark Surrender (Alex & Hope's story)
Darkest Temptation (Mason & Serenity's story)
Darkest Sinner (Timber & Kyra's story)
Darkest Power (Horus' story)

acknowledgements

I'm so thankful to the amazing editors who worked on this book with me! Laura Heritage, Paula Buckendorf, and Katherine Tate! You guys are AMAZING and always do such an incredible job!

Jill Sava, thank you for saving my life and making sure I NEVER put a book out before you read it and fix it, and then email me and go, um did you mean to use those commas the wrong way? You are awesome.

To my publicist Danielle Sanchez and the rest of the crew at Inkslinger, thank you for always having my back and making sure each release is incredible!

The Rockin' Readers fan group, wow, you guys seriously stepped it up and helped me with this book and didn't laugh when I said, hey I think I'm going to write a vampire novel. Thank you for hanging out with me on a daily basis and helping me with these fun projects!

ALL THE BLOGGERS, ah, you guys, seriously. I can't even express my gratitude for all that you do.

Erica, you're the best agent a girl could ask for!

Nate, thanks for not getting irritated when dinner burns because I'm busy finishing just one more chapter.

And last but not least, I thank God every day that I'm able to do what I love! He's everything.

about the author

Rachel Van Dyken is the #1 *New York Times*, *Wall Street Journal*, and *USA Today* bestselling author of over 90 books ranging from contemporary romance to paranormal. With over four million copies sold, she's been featured in Forbes, US Weekly, and USA Today. Her books have been translated in more than 15 countries. She was one of the first romance authors to have a Kindle in Motion book through Amazon publishing and continues to strive to be on the cutting edge of the reader experience. She keeps her home in the Pacific Northwest with her husband, adorable son, naked cat, and two dogs. For more information about her books and upcoming events, visit www.RachelVanDykenauthor. com.

also by
RACHEL VAN DYKEN

Kathy Ireland & Rachel Van Dyken
Fashion Jungle

Rachel Van Dyken & M. Robinson
Mafia Casanova (Romeo Sinacore's story)

Eagle Elite
Elite (Nixon & Trace's story)
Elect (Nixon & Trace's story)
Entice (Chase & Mil's story)
Elicit (Tex & Mo's story)
Bang Bang (Axel & Amy's story)
Enforce (Elite + from the boys POV)
Ember (Phoenix & Bee's story)
Elude (Sergio & Andi's story)
Empire (Sergio & Val's story)
Enrage (Dante & El's story)
Eulogy (Chase & Luciana's story)
Exposed (Dom & Tanit's story)
Envy (Vic & Renee's story)

Elite Bratva Brotherhood
RIP (Nikolai & Maya's story)
Debase (Andrei & Alice's story)
Dissolution (TBA)

Mafia Royals Romances
Royal Bully (Asher & Claire's story)
Ruthless Princess (Serena & Junior's story
Scandalous Prince (Breaker & Violet)
Destructive King (Asher & Annie)
Mafia King (TBA)
Fallen Dynasty (TBA)

Waltzing With The Wallflower—written with Leah Sanders

Waltzing with the Wallflower (Ambrose & Cordelia)
Beguiling Bridget (Anthony & Bridget's story)
Taming Wilde (Colin & Gemma's story)

London Fairy Tales

Upon a Midnight Dream (Stefan & Rosalind's story)
Whispered Music (Dominique & Isabelle's story)
The Wolf's Pursuit (Hunter & Gwendolyn's story)
When Ash Falls (Ashton & Sofia's story)

Renwick House

The Ugly Duckling Debutante (Nicholas & Sara's story)
The Seduction of Sebastian St. James (Sebastian & Emma's story)
The Redemption of Lord Rawlings (Phillip & Abigail's story)
An Unlikely Alliance (Royce & Evelyn's story)
The Devil Duke Takes a Bride (Benedict & Katherine's story)

Other Titles

A Crown for Christmas (Fitz & Phillipa's story)
Every Girl Does It (Preston & Amanda's story)
Compromising Kessen (Christian & Kessen's story)
Divine Uprising (Athena & Adonis's story)
The Parting Gift—written with Leah Sanders (Blaine and Mara's story)

king

T.M. FRAZIER

For Charley & Logan

prologue

King
Twelve years old

"COME ON YOU FUCKING FAG! YOU'RE SUCH A LITTLE FAG PUSSY!"

I'd seen some of the kids in my school bully other kids before, but I'd never felt like I should butt in. If a kid didn't have the balls to stand up for himself, then they deserved whatever they had coming to them.

But that morning I'd made the decision to leave home for good. Mom's current boyfriend had used her as a punching bag yet again. But this time, when I'd stepped in front of her, not only did she push me aside, but she defended the fucker.

She said she deserved it.

She even went as far as apologizing.

To *him.*

I hated her for that. For becoming weak. For letting him lay his hands on her like that. I wanted to wail on John's face so bad that I sat on the side of the school during recess clenching and unclenching my fists as I replayed that morning over and over again in my mind. I may not have been able to win in a fight against a grown man, but I was convinced I could have at least done some damage.

So when I heard those words shouted from across the playground it was like my anger had made the decision before I had a chance to really think about it. Before I knew it, I'd leapt across the sandbox and was on my way to a group of kids gathered in a circle on the far side of the yard next to the kickball field.

I towered over all the other kids in my grade and could easily see over their heads. In the center of the circle was a brute of a kid named Tyler, a dark-haired boy who always wore band logo t-shirts with the sleeves ripped off. He was holding this skinny kid by the collar of his shirt, punching him in the face over and over again with his closed fist. The littler kid grunted each time Tyler made contact. The boy's ripped shirt rose up over his pale stomach revealing bruises in varying shades of purple and yellow. His ribs were so visible I could count them. Blood dripped from his nose and fell to the ground. I pushed aside two little girls who were cheering on the beating.

Kids can be fucking cruel.

Adults can be crueler.

I jumped in front of Tyler and cocked back my fist. With one punch to the bully's pimpled jaw, I knocked him flat on his ass. The back of his head landed with a thunk against the pavement. Out cold.

I instantly felt better, although the need to inflict violence was always like a rat gnawing on my every thought and emotion, punching Tyler had temporarily dimmed the feeling from blaring spotlight to burning candle.

The skinny kid was on the ground holding his bloody nose. He moved his hands away from his face and looked up at me with the biggest most ridiculous smile, blood coating teeth that were too big for his mouth. Not what I expected from someone who'd just been beaten. "You didn't have to save me. I was just letting him get some punches in before I rained down the pain." His voice cracked on every other word of the lie. Tears ran out the sides of his eyes and down through the blood smeared across his lip. The circle of kids had broken up and gone back to their kickball game.

"I didn't save you," I said, stepping over him. I started walking away, but somewhere around the sandbox the kid had caught up with me.

"Of course you didn't. I could totally have taken him. But shit man, that fucking prick has a stick up his ass," the kid swore, throwing his hands up into the air as he jogged to try and keep up with my long strides.

"Oh yeah, and why is that?" I asked.

"Cause he wanted me to do his fucking math worksheet, and I'll tell you something. I'm no one's fucking bitch. So I told him to fuck off." His voice was muffled since he was still trying to stop the blood dripping from his nose by pinching his nostrils together.

"All you said to him was 'fuck no' and he started beating on you?" I asked, although I didn't find it hard to believe, aside from the bullshit with my mom and John it was mostly little things that had been making my fist ache for something to connect with.

The kid smirked.

"Well, there was that... and then there was how I told him how I thought it was cool that his dad didn't mind that his son was the spitting image of his mama's boss at the Price Mart." He brushed the dirt off the scrapes on his elbows, then dusted the palm of his hands off on his wrinkled khakis. "Name's Samuel Clearwater. What's yours?"

I stopped and turned to him. He extended his hand to me and I uncrossed my arms and shook it. For a gangly kid who was the same age as I was, he dressed and spoke like a foul-mouthed grandfather, someone too old to give a shit about filtering his words. And what eleven-year-old shook hands?

Samuel Clearwater, that's who.

"Brantley King," I answered.

"You got a lot of friends, Brantley King?" Samuel's unruly sandy blonde hair fell forward into his eyes, and he brushed it away with dirt caked fingernails.

"Nope." None of the kids in school were like me. I'd felt alone since my very first day in Kindergarten. While everyone else was learning the words to Old McDonald, I was worried about how long I was going to have to wait until after dark to go home. Too early and whatever guy my mom let move in that month would be ready to brawl.

Being on my own was natural to me. As time went on, it became something I liked. Although I was the biggest kid in school, I'd always managed to move around like a ghost.

Until I started getting in trouble.

Then WE started getting into trouble together. Preppy and I. Two peas in a juvenile delinquent pod.

"Me neither. Way more trouble than their fucking worth," Samuel said, almost convincingly. He re-tucked his too-large plaid shirt into his khaki pants, righting his suspenders that fell off his shoulders every few seconds. He straightened his yellow polka-dotted bow-tie.

"What's up with the bruises?" I asked, pointing to his ribs.

"You saw those, huh?" Sadness crossed over his face, but he fought back whatever he was thinking about and pursed his lips. "Step-daddy from hell with issues, ever since my mom died. Actually, he's got only two issues. Beer and me. Beer he likes though. Me? Not so much."

I could relate. Although I didn't have one stepdad, more like a constant parade of men. They all had different names, different faces, but essentially they were all the same.

"Well, kid, I don't think Tyler is going to bug you again." I started walking again, heading back to my spot on the side of the building where I could be alone. In the corner of my eye I saw Tyler hobbling up the steps into the school, clutching his jaw.

Pussy.

"That's it?" Samuel followed close behind me, knocking into my heels.

"What else is there?" I ducked under the branch of a low hanging tree. Samuel was easily a foot shorter than me and scooted under it without any problems. When we got far enough away from the other kids I lit the half-cigarette I'd been saving in my back pocket with the last match from the book I'd been hiding in my shoe.

"Can I try?" Samuel asked, startling me. I hadn't realized he was still there.

I passed him the cigarette, and he inhaled deeply. He then spent the next five minutes choking. I put the cigarette out on the sole of my sneaker while his face turned a weird shade of purple before going back to pale smeared with freckles and blood. "That's really fucking good, but I'm a menthol man myself."

A burst of laughter escaped me, and I bent over, hugging myself at the waist. Samuel ignored my outburst and continued talking. "Where do you live?"

"Here and there." Nowhere was the truth. I wasn't ever going back home again. School would now become just a place to go during the day so I could sneak into the locker room before class to shower and for the free breakfast program. Everything I owned was in my backpack.

And it was light.

"I'm over in Sunny Isles Park. It's a fucking shithole. When I grow up, I'm going to have one of those big places on the water on the other side of the causeway with the long legs that look like they're from Star Wars."

"Like one of them stilt homes?"

"Yeah man, a fucking Star Wars stilt home, right on the bay." This boy lived in a trailer park where he was beaten up by his stepdad, and here he was dreaming about his future. I couldn't see my way past next week, never mind to the next ten years. "What about you, man?"

"What about me?" I unhooked my pocket knife from the waistband of my jeans and used it to pick at the falling stucco on the side of the building.

"What are you gonna do when you grow up?"

The only thing I really knew was what I didn't want. "Not sure. I just know that I don't want to work for anyone. Never liked being told what to do all that much. I'd like to be my own boss, run my own shit."

"Yeah, man. That's fucking amazing. Yes, that. I'll help you. We can do it together. You run the shit. I'll help you run the shit. Then, we'll buy a big 'ole Star Wars stilt home and live there, and no one will be able tell us what to fucking do ever again!"

Samuel removed a composition notebook from his backpack and turned to a blank page. "Let's make a mother fucking plan."

The idea seemed silly, sitting down with a kid I didn't know and planning for a future I'd never thought of, but for some reason the thought of hurting his feelings made my chest feel stabby, a feeling I was very unfamiliar with. Unsure of what to do next I gave in. I sat down next to him in the grass and sighed. He smiled up at me like just me being there meant we were halfway there.

"We can't be pussies about this," he continued. "We aren't going to get the Star Wars house by getting jobs in a shitty hotel or factory, and I never been much of a fisherman. So this shit starts now. Pussies get pushed over and stepped on. My uncle, who's a total fucking asshole douche-bag, sells weed. We could steal some from him and sell it. Then, we can use that money to buy our own to sell."

Using a black marker from his bag, Samuel began to draw on the page.

The top read GOAL and he drew a house with legs underneath that did look like a stick figure version of the whatever-you-call-it-thing in Star Wars. I didn't know the name of it because I'd never seen the movies, just the previews. Then, he drew what looked like it was supposed to be us, him much smaller than me. With a green marker, he drew dollar bill signs all around us floating in the air.

"So what? We friends now, Preppy?"

I'd never had a friend before, but there was something about this boy with the foul mouth that got my attention. I plucked the marker from his hand and took over his drawing. I was never good at much in school, except for art. Just drawing really.

Drawing was my jam.

"Fuck yeah!" Preppy said, watching me add on to his stilt home. He'd also drawn a picture of what I assumed was his uncle because he'd written douche-bag over the top. "You're fucking good at that. Man, we've got to have you do that, too. Art shit. Write that down in the plan. We gotta have hobbies, too."

"Then what's your hobby?" I asked.

"My hobby?" He smiled and wiped his nose, which had just started dripping blood again, a single drop fell to the page and splattered on stick figure Preppy. He nodded slyly and purses his lips, hooking his thumbs under his suspenders. "Bitches."

I think I laughed more that day then I ever did in my whole life. I also learned that 'bitches' could be a hobby.

"So what happens if we get caught?" I asked, pausing the marker over the page.

"We won't. We're too fucking smart for that shit. We'll be careful. We'll make plans and stick to the plans. Nobody will get in our fucking way. Nobody. Not my step-dad, not my uncle, not teachers, and especially not bitch-ass bullies like Tyler. I ain't ever getting married. I ain't ever having a girlfriend. This is just about Preppy and King crawling out of the shit instead of rotting in it."

"But really, what if we get caught?" I asked. "I'm not talking about by the cops. I'm talking about by your uncle, or anyone else that does the kind of shit we're talking about doing here. These are rough people. Bad people. They don't like being messed with." I knew these kinds of people first hand. More than one dealer had come to our house armed with guns, demanding payment. Mom would settle her debt by taking them into her bedroom and closing the door.

This kid may have just been screwing around, but the more I thought about it the better it all sounded. Living a life without answering to anyone.

A life without fear of what someone could do to me or to this little preppy kid, who by the looks of it had enough bullying to last him his whole life.

The idea of growing up and being my own man, the kind of man people didn't mess with, the kind of man who didn't take shit from anyone, became more and more appealing as it rolled around in my brain and latched on, taking up residence where I was missing other things the guidance counselors said I was lacking, like a 'firm sense of right and wrong'. But they were the ones who were wrong. It's not that I didn't know the difference.

It's that I just didn't care.

Because that's what happens when you've never had anything to care about.

If I was going to take this kid seriously, I needed to know that he wasn't going to bitch out on me if it all went south. I needed to know he was as serious about the plan as I was getting, so I had to ask, "What really happens if someone gets in our way? In the way of our business? In the way of our plan?"

Preppy held the end of a marker to the corner of his mouth where blood had begun to dry and crust over. For a moment, he stared over my head, deep in thought. Then, he shrugged and locked his eyes onto mine.

"We kill them."

chapter
one

King

ON THE DAY I WAS RELEASED FROM PRISON I FOUND MYSELF TATTOOING A pussy on a pussy. The animal onto the female part.

A cat on a cunt.

Fucking ridiculous.

The walls of my makeshift tattoo shop pulsed with the heavy beat of the music coming from my homecoming party raging on the floor below. It shook the door as if someone were rhythmically trying to beat it down. Spray paint and posters covered the walls from floor to ceiling, casting a layer of false light over everything within.

The little dark-haired bitch I worked on was moaning like she was getting off. I'm sure she was rollin' because there was no way a tattoo directly above her clit could be anything other than fucking painful.

Back in the day, I could zone out for hours while tattooing, finding that little corner of my life that didn't involve all the bullshit I had to deal with on a daily basis.

In the past when I'd been locked up, albeit for much shorter periods of time, the first thing on my mind was pussy and a party. But this time the first thing I did when I walked through the door was pick up my tattoo gun, but it wasn't the same. I couldn't reach that place of temporary reprieve no matter how hard I tried. It didn't help that the tattoos people requested were getting dumber and fucking dumber.

Football team logos, quotes from books you know they've never read, and wannabe gangsters wanting teardrops on their faces. In prison, the teardrop tattoo represented taking a life. Some of the little bitches who wanted them looked like they couldn't step on a roach without cowering in the corner and crying for their mamas.

But since the majority of time my clients paid in favors and consisted mostly of bikers, strippers, and the occasional rich kid who found himself on the wrong side of the causeway, I should've lowered the bar on my expectations.

But then again it was good to be home. Actually, it was good to be anywhere that didn't smell like vomit and wasted lives.

My own life had been moving forward at nothing short of full fucking speed ahead ever since the day I'd met Preppy. I'd loved living outside the law.

I fed off the fear in the eyes of those who crossed me. The only thing I'd ever regretted was getting caught.

When I wasn't locked up, I'd spent almost every single day of the twenty-seven years I'd been on the earth in Logan's Beach, a little shit town on the gulf coast of Florida. A place where the residents on one side of the causeway lived solely to cater to the rich who lived on the other side, in high-rise beachfront condos and mansions. Trailer parks and run-down houses less than a mile from the kind of wealth it takes more than one generation to accumulate.

On my eighteenth birthday, I bought a run-down stilt home hidden behind a wall of thick trees, on three acres of land that practically sat under the bridge. In cash. And along with my best friend Preppy, we moved on up to the rich side of town like the white trash version of the motherfucking Jeffersons.

True to our words, we became our own men and answered to no one. We did what we wanted. I turned my drawing into tattooing.

Preppy got bitches.

I fucked. I fought. I partied. I got wasted. I stole. I fucked. I tattooed. I sold dope. I sold guns. I stole. I fucked. I made fucking money.

And I fucked.

There wasn't a party I didn't like or that didn't like me. There wasn't a chick who didn't give me the go-ahead move, lifting her hips so I could slide off her panties. I got that shit every single fucking time.

Life wasn't just good. Life was fucking great. I was on top of the fucking world and no one fucked with me or mine.

No one.

And then it all changed and I spent three years in a tiny windowless cell, studying the changing cracks in the concrete block walls.

When I was done with the purple cartoon cat, I applied salve, covered it with wrap, and disposed of my gloves. Did this girl think that guys would be turned on by this thing? It was good work, especially since I'd been out of commission for three years, but it was covering up my favorite part of a woman. If I undressed her and saw it, I would flip her over.

Which sounded like a good idea. Getting laid would help shake this post prison haze and I could get back to the things that used to be important to me without this lingering sense of dread looming in my conscious.

Instead of sending the girl back out to the party I roughly grabbed her and yanked her down the table toward me. I stood, flipping her over onto her stomach. With one hand on the back of her neck, I pushed her head down onto the table, releasing my belt buckle with the other. I grabbed a condom from the open drawer.

She knew beforehand that money wasn't the type of currency I was looking for, and I didn't do free. So I lined up the head of my cock and took her pussy as payment for her new tattoo. Of a pussy.

Fuck my life.

The girl had a great body, but after a few minutes of irritating over-the-top moaning, she wasn't doing anything for me. I could feel my cock going soft inside her. This wasn't supposed to be happening, especially not even after years of my right hand and my imagination being my only sexual partners.

What the fuck is wrong with me?

I grabbed her throat with both hands and squeezed, picking up my pace, taking out my frustrations with each rough thrust in rhythm with the heavy beat from the other room.

Nothing.

I was about to pull out and give up.

I almost didn't notice the door opening.

Almost.

Staring up from my doorway was a vacant pair of doll-like blue eyes framed by long icy-blonde hair, a small dimple in the middle of her chin, a frown on her full pink lips. A girl, no older than seventeen or eighteen, a bit skinny.

A bit haunted.

My cock stirred to life, dragging my attention back to the fact that I was still pumping into the brunette. My orgasm hit me hard, spiraling up my spine and taking me by complete surprise. I closed my eyes, blowing my load into pussy tattoo, collapsing onto her back.

What the fuck?

By the time I opened my eyes again, the door was closed and girl with the sad eyes was gone.

I'm fucking losing my mind.

I rolled out of and off the brunette who was luckily still breathing, although unconscious from either strangulation or the dope that had made her pupils as big as her fucking eye sockets.

I sat back on my rolling stool and dropped my head into my hands.

I had a massive fucking headache.

Preppy had organized this party for me, and the pre-prison me would've already been snorting blow off the tits of strippers. But post-prison me just wanted some food, a good night's sleep, and these fucking people to get the hell out of my house.

"You okay, boss-man?" Preppy asked, peeking his head into the room.

I pointed to the unconscious girl in the chair. "Come get this bitch out of here." I ran my hand through my hair, the pulsing of the music making the pounding in my head grow stronger. "And for fucks sake, turn that shit down!"

Preppy didn't deserve my rage, but I was too fucked up in the head to dial down my orders.

"You've got it," he said, without hesitation.

Preppy slid past me and didn't question the half-naked girl on the table. He hoisted her limp body over his shoulder in one easy movement. The unconscious girl's arms flailed around on his back, smacking against his back with each step. Before he could get too far, he turned back to me.

"You done with this?" he asked. I could barely hear him over the music. He gestured with his chin to the brunette on his shoulder, a childlike grin on his face.

I nodded, and Preppy smiled like I'd just told him he could have a puppy. *Sick fuck.*

I loved that kid.

I closed the door, grabbing my gun and knife from the bottom drawer of the tool box I kept my tattoo equipment in. I sheathed my knife in my boot, and my gun in the waistband of my jeans.

I shook my head from side to side to clear away the haze. Prison will do that to you. Three fucking years sleeping with one eye open in a prison full of people with whom I've made both friends and enemies.

It was time to keep some of those friends and call in some of those favors, because there was something more important than my own selfish shit that I needed to take care of.

Someone more important.

Sleep could wait. It was time to go down stairs and make nice with the bikers. I'd avoided doing business with them in any capacity for years even though their VP, Bear, is like a brother to me. Bear tried to get me to join his MC a hundred times, but I'd always said no. I was a criminal who liked my crimes straight up, without a side of organized. But now I needed connections the bikers could provide as well as access to shady politicians whose decisions and opinions could be swayed for a price.

I never cared about money before. It used to be something disposable for me, something I used to fund my *I don't give a fuck* lifestyle. But now?

Payoffs to politicians didn't come cheap, and I was going to need a lot of cash and very fucking soon.

Or I was never going to see Max again.

chapter
two

Doe

N IKKI WAS MY ONE AND ONLY FRIEND IN THE ENTIRE WORLD.
And I kind of fucking hated her.
Nikki was a hooker who'd found me sleeping under a bench. I'd
unsuccessfully avoided the previous night's downpour and had just shivered
and chattered myself to sleep. I'd already been living on the streets for several
weeks at that point and hadn't had a real meal since running away from Camp
Touchy-Feely, a nickname I gave the group home I'd been left to rot in. I'm
pretty sure Nikki was trying to rob me—or what she thought was a corpse—
when she just happened to have noticed I was still breathing.

Frankly, I'm surprised she even bothered with me after realizing I was
very much alive.

Not so much living, but alive.

Nikki snorted the last of her blow through a rolled up post-it-note off a
yellowed sink that was days away from falling free from the wall. The floor was
littered with toilet paper, and all three toilets were on the verge of overflowing
with brown sludge. The overwhelming scent of bleach singed my nose hairs
like someone doused the room with chemicals to lessen the smell but hadn't
bothered with any actual cleaning.

Nikki tilted her chin up toward the moldy ceiling tiles and pinched her
nostrils together. A single fluorescent light flickered and buzzed above us, casting a greenish hue over the gas station bathroom.

"Fuck, that's good shit," she said, tossing the empty baggie onto the floor.
Using the wand from an almost empty tube of lip-gloss, she fished out whatever was left and applied it to her thin cracked lips. She then smudged the thick
liner under her eyes with her pinky until she nodded in satisfaction into the
mirror at her racoon-esque smoky look.

I stretched my sleeve of my sweater down over the heel of my hand and
wiped the filth off the mirror in front of me, exposing two things: a spider web
crack in the corner and the reflection of a girl I didn't recognize.

Light blonde hair. Sunken cheeks. Bloodshot blue eyes. Dimple chin.

Nothing.

I knew the girl was me, but who the fuck was I?

Two months ago, a garbage man discovered me in an alley where I had
been literally thrown out with the trash, found lying in my own blood amongst

a heap of garbage bags beside a dumpster. When I woke in the hospital, with the biggest fucking headache in the history of headaches, the police and doctors dismissed me as a runaway. Or a hooker. Or some hybrid combo of the two. The policeman asking me questions at my bedside didn't bother to hide his disgust when he informed me that what probably happened was a simple case of a John getting rough with me. I'd opened my mouth to argue but stopped.

He could've been right.

Nothing else made any sort of sense.

No wallet. No ID. No money. No possessions of any kind.

No fucking memory.

When someone goes missing on the news, teams of people gather together and form a search party. Police reports are filed and sometimes candlelight vigils are held in hopes the missing would soon return home. What they don't ever show you is what happens when no one looks. When the *loved ones* either don't know, don't exist…or just don't care.

The police searched the missing persons reports throughout the state and then the country with no luck. My fingerprints didn't match any on record, and neither did my picture.

I learned then that being labeled a missing person didn't necessarily mean I was missed. At least not enough to require any of the theatrics. No newspaper articles. No channel-six news. No plea from family members for my safe return.

Maybe, it was my fault no one had bothered to look for me. Maybe, I was an asshole and people celebrated the day I went away.

Or ran away.

Or was shipped down river in a fucking Moses basket.

I don't fucking know. Anything was possible.

I don't know where I came from.

I don't know how old I am.

I don't know my real name.

All I had in the world was reflected back at me in the bathroom mirror of that gas station, and I had no fucking clue who she was.

Without knowing if I was a minor or not, I was sent to live at Camp Touchy-Feely, where I only lasted a couple of weeks among the serial masturbators and juvenile delinquents. On the night I woke up to find one of the older boys standing at the foot of my bed with his fly unzipped, his dick in his hand, I escaped through a bathroom window. The only thing I left with was the donated clothes on my back, and a nickname.

They called me Doe.

As in Jane Doe.

The only difference between me and a real Jane Doe was a toe-tag because what I was doing sure as shit wasn't living. Stealing to eat. Sleeping wherever I could find cover from the elements. Begging on the side of freeway off-ramps. Scrounging through restaurant dumpsters.

Nikki ran her chewed-off fingernails through her greasy red hair. "You ready?" she asked. Sniffling, she hopped on the balls of her feet like she was an athlete amping up for the big game.

Though it was the furthest thing from the truth, I nodded. I wasn't ready, never would be, but I'd run out of options. It wasn't safe on the streets, each night in the open was a literal gamble with my life. And not to mention that if I lost any more weight, I wouldn't have the strength to fight off any threats. Either way I needed protection from both the elements and the people who lurked around at night before I ended up a real Jane Doe.

I don't think Nikki was capable of registering the feeling of hunger. Given the option, she chose a quick high over a full stomach. Every single time. A sad fact made obvious by her sharp cheekbones and dark circles under her eyes. In the short time I'd known her, I'd never seen her ingest anything but coke.

I judge her and I feel shitty about it. But something inside me tells me that she's better than the thing she does. When I'm not extremely irritated with her I feel almost protective of her. I was fighting for my own survival and I wanted to fight for hers, but the problem was, she didn't want to fight for herself.

I opened my mouth to lecture her. I was about to tell her that she should lay off the dope and change her main priority to food and her overall health, when she turned toward me. There I was, my mouth agape, ready to rain down judgment on her regarding like I was better than her. The truth was that I could've been knee deep involved in the same shit before I lost my memory.

I closed my judgmental mouth.

Nikki eyed me up and down, appraising my appearance. "I guess you'll do," she said, blatant dissatisfaction in her tone. I refused to cake on makeup or pluck out all of my eyebrows just to draw a thin line in their place like she did. Instead, I'd washed my hair in the sink and used the hand dryer to speed along the drying process. My face was makeup free, but it would have to do, because if I was going to do this, I was determined to do it my way and without looking like Nikki.

Yep, I am a judgmental asshole.

"How is this going to work again?" I asked. She'd already told me ten times, but she could tell me ten thousand times and I still wouldn't feel comfortable.

Nikki fluffed out her limp hair. "Seriously, Doe, do you ever listen?" She sighed in annoyance but continued on. "When we get to the party all you have to do is cuddle up to one of the bikers. If he likes you there is a good chance he might want to take you in, keep you around for a while, and all you have to do is keep his bed warm and a smile on his face."

"I don't know if I can do it." I said meekly.

"You can do it, and you will do it. And don't be all shy like that around them, they won't like that. Besides, you're not the shy type, that's just your nerves talking. You're all rough edges, especially with that horrible case of foot-in-mouth syndrome."

"It's eerie how you have me pegged in the short time you've known me," I said.

Nikki shrugged. "I'm a people reader, and believe it or not, you are very easy to read. Like for example, right now you're super tense. I know this because your shoulders are all hunched over." She presses my shoulders back. "Better. Stick out your chest. You don't have much to work with up top but without a bra, if you keep your shoulders back, they can catch a glimpse of a little nip, and guys love the nips."

That was it. I could get a biker to like me, he would protect me, hopefully long enough for me to figure out plan B. "Worst case scenario is that he's only looking for a quick one-time thing and he'll throw you a few bucks and send you on your way." Nikki made it sound more like a vacation than prostitution.

I could fool myself into thinking that if I wasn't soliciting on the street then I wasn't like Nikki, but the truth was no matter which way I twisted the facts, this plan would turn me into a whore.

Judgey McJudgerpants.

When I wracked my brain for other options, I'd come up as empty as my stomach.

Nikki pushed open the door, and sunlight invaded the dark space as it swung back and forth. With one last glance at the plain-faced girl in the mirror, I whispered, "I'm sorry."

It was a comfort knowing that whoever I was before my slate was wiped clean didn't know what I was about to do.

Because I was about to sell her body.

And whatever soul I still had.

chapter
three

Doe

I SAT IN THE BACK SEAT OF SOME BALD GUY'S ANCIENT SUBARU, WILLING MYSELF TO become temporarily deaf so I wouldn't be forced to listen to Nikki suck off the driver. He was taking us to the party, which was in a house in Logan's Beach. When we finally came to a stop, I leapt out of the car like it was on fire.

"Bye, baby," Nikki said sweetly, wiping the corner of her mouth with one hand and waving with the other as our ride pulled away. When he was out of sight, she rolled her eyes and spit onto the ground.

"I think I'm going to be sick," I said, trying not to gag.

"Well, I didn't see you offering to suck his cock for a ride," Nikki snapped. "So shut the fuck up about it. Besides, I got us here didn't I?"

Here was on a dirt road at the edge of a property overgrown with trees and hedges. A small gap in the brush allowed room for a narrow driveway. It was dark and there were no street lights to guide our way up to the house, the path seemed to go on forever. A mild fish odor permeated the air. My empty stomach rolled, and I covered my mouth and nose with my hand to keep from getting sick.

Flickering lights appeared in the distance. As we approached the house I realized what we were seeing weren't lights at all, but plastic torches stuck into the ground at awkward angles, creating a makeshift path through the grass around to the back of the house.

The house itself was three stories and built on a foundation of pilings. The majority of the bottom floor under the house was open area, filled with shiny motorcycles and cars parked in every inch of available space. Two doors took up the far wall, one with a deadbolt and a metal bar across it and another a few feet off the ground with two concrete steps leading up to it. Wrap around balconies made up the second two stories and lights flashed through every window, revealing shadows of the people within. The music vibrated off the wet ground, shaking the water off the tall blades of grass onto my legs.

"Do the bikers live here?" I asked Nikki.

"No, this house belongs to the guy they're throwing the party for."

"And who is that?" I asked. Nikki shrugged.

"Beats me. All I know is that Skinny said it was a coming home party." Skinny was Nikki's sometime boyfriend, sometime pimp.

When we reached the back of the house, I got my first glimpse of the bikers and my stomach rolled again. I stopped dead in my tracks.

There they were, surrounding a fire pit in the center of the massive yard, flames and billowing smoke shot up as high as the house. I was so caught up in what I was going to have to do I'd forgotten to stop and think of who I was going to have to do it with. There were seven or eight men, some sitting in lawn chairs, some standing with a beer in their hands. They all wore leather vests with varying amounts of patches adorning them. Some wore long-sleeved button-down shirts under their vests; others wore nothing at all. Women who looked like they took their fashion cues from Nikki laughed and danced around the fire. One girl was on her knees, bobbing her head up and down on the lap of a man who casually talked on his phone while guiding her head with his hand.

This is just a means to an end.

I turned to tell Nikki that maybe we should reconsider the plan, but she was already gone. Scanning the yard, I spotted her with an arm already draped over a tall guy with a red braided beard. An American flag bandana tied around his forehead.

Strong arms wrapped around my waist from behind and hauled me hard against a wall of muscle. My immediate reaction was to shake him off, but when I struggled to break free he held me tighter. His hot breath smelled of garlic and liquor, assaulting my senses when he spoke with his lips pressed against my neck. "Hey, baby girl. I'm ready to party. How 'bout you?" Grabbing my wrist he forcefully wrenched it behind my back until I was sure my shoulder had dislocated. He shoved my hand down the front of his jeans, rubbing my clenched fist up and down the length of his erection. "Feels good, don't it, baby girl?"

I opened my fist and grabbed his balls, squeezing them with all the strength I could manage.

"You bitch!" he yelled out.

Releasing me, he dropped to his knees in the grass. Hands cupped over his privates, he fell onto his side and raised his thighs to his chest. I raced up the steps that led into the house.

"You fucking bitch! You're going to fucking pay for that!" he called as I disappeared into the house sliding past a ton of party-goers. I took the first set of stairs I came across and ran all the way up to the third story. I tried the handle of several closed doors down a narrow hallway, but they were all locked. It wasn't until I was almost to the end of the hall when one finally gave.

I hadn't even taken a step inside when I quickly realized the room may have been dark, but it wasn't empty.

A smattering of neon paint on the walls made the room look like as if it were glowing. I couldn't see much in the way of features, but I could make out two bodies in the center of the room. At first glance it looked as if someone was standing behind another person who was lying down. It took me a second to register it, but after I did, there was no mistaking what it was I'd walked in on.

Skin slapping against skin. Moaning. The smell of sweat and something else I couldn't quite place. It seemed like hours I'd been standing there, but in reality it wasn't more than a few seconds. I should've turned around and closed the door the instant I realized the room was occupied, but I couldn't tear myself away from the scene playing out in front of me.

A magnetic pair of eyes locked onto mine. Under the artificial lights, they glowed bright green. The man stared right through me and much to my surprise he didn't blink or look away. Faster and faster, his hips slammed against hers. His eyes bore into mine as he thrust over and over again. When he closed his eyes and threw back his head with a long throaty groan, our connection was severed.

The man collapsed onto the girl's back and released his grip from her throat. He'd been strangling her? She was moaning when I first walked in on them, and then she had fallen silent.

Dead silent.

I quickly remembered I had feet and closed the door, fleeing back down the stairs. I hid beside the water heater under the house, beside all the cars and bikes, where I sat for over an hour, running the gravel through my hands and hoping to come to terms with the shitty direction my life was heading in. As much as I wanted to take off into the night and run I couldn't go far, my overwhelming fear of the dark held me captive at the house where I may have just witnessed a murder, but at least I could find light.

Fear had seriously fucked with my priorities.

It was that fear, as well as my growling stomach and light-headedness that reminded me of why I was there in the first place.

Basic survival.

I am desperate, and desperate people don't have the luxury of options.

I sucked in a deep breath. I had to do what I had to do, even if I didn't exactly know what that was. I mean, I knew the mechanics of it. But my brain was like a car with the mileage turned back to zero. A clean slate that I was about to make filthy dirty.

I may have been homeless and starving, but I was determined to get myself off of the streets and into a real life someday. A life with a soft bed and clean sheets. Once I didn't have to worry about my safety or my stomach, I could focus on finding out the truth about who I really was.

I made a promise to push through the here and now and do what needed to be done, then I would never think about this time ever again. It would be a small spot on the radar of my life that I vowed I would never dwell on.

I stood up and brushed myself off and began my internal pep talk. I was going to do this. I was going to make it. I was going to have to fake like I knew what I was doing, like I wasn't afraid, but pretending like I wasn't scared shit-less wasn't something new for me, I'd done it every single day since I woke up with no idea of who I was.

I would be a biker whore because it was what I needed to be. I would be a tightrope walker if that's what it took to stay alive.

With newfound determination, I walked back around to the bonfire, grabbed a beer out of the cooler, and cracked it open. The cool liquid lubricated my dry scratchy throat. I darted around from biker to biker and the girls who had their attention. I found myself particularly interested in a girl straddling the lap of a biker who must have outweighed her by at least a hundred pounds.

It was the look on her face I was intrigued by. The smile she wore that said *your dick would feel great jammed down my throat.* I mimicked her demeanor, and hoped it was enough to get the attention of someone who would take an interest in me.

Someone who could help me survive.

"Hey there," a deep voice rumbled against my ear.

When I turned around, I was eye level with a wall of leather with white patches sewn into it. One read VICE PRESIDENT and the other, BEACH BASTARDS. The man wearing the vest had long blonde hair that draped over to one side of his head, revealing the shaved area beneath. He had a beard, not stubble, a full-on beard that was a few inches long and very well groomed. He stood well over six feet, his frame lean yet very cut and muscular. I couldn't tell what color his eyes were because his lids hung heavy and were slightly reddened. His entire neck was covered with colorful tattoos and when he went to light a cigarette I noticed that the backs of both of his hands and were covered in ink as well.

"Hey," I answered back, trying to assert my newly found false confidence.

He was beyond attractive. He was gorgeous. If I had to end up in someone's bed, I imagined that being in his wouldn't be half-bad. He sniffled, drawing attention to the light dusting of white powder trapped in his nostrils.

"They call me Bear. You belong to anyone?" he asked seductively, leaning in toward me.

"Maybe…you?" I winced at my choice of words. Of all the fucking things I could have said, THAT was what came to mind? Stupid fucking mouth. Nikki was right. I spoke first and thought second.

Bear chuckled. "I'd love that, beautiful, but I've got something else in mind."

"Oh, yeah? What would that be?" I asked, trying to keep my tone light although my mind and heart were racing.

"This party? It's for my buddy. And he was down here for a total of thirty minutes before he hightailed it upstairs to drown himself in a bottle of Jack. He's like a cat in a tree, can't seem to talk him down. It's understandable, seeing as he's been away a while, but I figure you can help me out."

He hooked his finger into the front of my skirt and slowly dragged me toward him until my nipples were flush up against his chest. He pressed his fingers into the skin right above my pubic bone and I resisted the urge to jump back by biting down on my bottom lip.

"The BBB's have never really been his thing." He paused when he saw the confused look on my face at his abbreviation. "Beach Bastard Bitches." He explained. "But you? You're new. You're different. You've got this cute little innocent thing going on, but I know you're not or you wouldn't be at this kind of party if that was your deal. I'm thinking he'll like you." Bear brushed his lips against the side of my neck. "So maybe you go up there. Make him happy for me. Make little him happy by wrapping those gorgeous lips around his cock for a while. Then when you're done, bring him back down here to civilization. And maybe later, if you're a good girl and do what you're told, we can go back to the clubhouse and have some real fun." He grazed his teeth along my earlobe. "Think you can you do that for me?"

"Yeah, yeah I can do that," I said. My skin prickling from his touch. And I could do it.

I think.

"What's your name anyway?" Bear's hand slowly traveled up the back of my leg, pushing up my skirt, it came to rest on my ass cheek, which was then exposed to anyone who might have been looking in our direction.

"Doe. My name is Doe," I breathed.

"Fitting," He said with a chuckle. "Well, my innocent looking little Doe." Bear leaned in close and surprised me by planting a soft kiss on the corner of my mouth. His lips were soft, and he smelled like laundry detergent mixed with liquor and cigarettes. I was just beginning to think that the kiss meant that he'd changed his mind and didn't want to send me away to his friend, but no such luck. He pulled away abruptly and turned me around by my shoulders so that I was facing the stairs. He swatted me on my ass, propelling me forward. "Up the stairs you go, sweetheart. Last room at the end of the hallway. Be good to my boy, and me and you will get to play later." He sealed his words with a wink and as I made my way up the stairs I turned back and flashed him a fake smile. I hoped the guy at the end of the hallway was like Bear, because then maybe it wouldn't be so bad.

Then a thought hit me that had me fighting back the tears that sprung from my eyes with a sudden force that almost took me to my knees.

I'd officially sold myself, and the price was far more than any dollar amount.

chapter
four

Doe

Boom. Boom. Boom. Ba-boom.

It was hard to tell where the bass ended and my pulse began.

I wiped my palms on the tattered skirt I'd lifted from the Goodwill donation bin and maneuvered through a sea of bodies rhythmically writhing up against one another. A thick layer of smoke lay trapped under the low ceiling. Hauntingly robotic party goers danced and gyrated under the flickering lights on every available inch of floor space.

In the dark, with only the pulsing of the lights to guide me, I made my way up the stairs, and as Bear instructed, to the door at the very end of the hallway.

The door to my salvation.

The door to my hell.

I turned the handle, and the hinges shrieked. The only light in the room was courtesy of the dim and muted TV on the far wall. The heavy scent of pot wafted from the room.

"Hello?" I squeaked into the darkness, trying as hard as I could to make my voice sound as sexy as possible, but failing miserably.

A voice, deep and rough, broke through the silence, his words vibrating through to my very core. "Shut the fucking door."

Snaking its way into every crevice of my already fragile mind and body, an entirely new feeling enveloped me, causing the hairs on the back of my neck to stand on end. I'd expected to feel hesitant, nervous, and even anxious.

But what I felt was far more than that.

It was fear.

Heart racing. Pulse pounding. Red alert. Fear.

The impulse to turn and run as fast as my trembling legs could carry me was overwhelming, but any thoughts of immediate escape were interrupted.

"Door," the voice commanded again. I hadn't moved an inch. As much as I wanted to run, my desperation propelled me forward.

I closed the door behind me and the chaos downstairs disappeared with a click of the latch, shutting out the noise as well as the possibility of anyone hearing my cries for help.

"Where are you?" I asked hesitantly.

"I'm here," the voice said, offering no indication of where *here* really was.

I took a deep, steadying breath and then a few steps toward the TV until I was close enough to make out the outline of a bed in the middle of the small room and a pair of long legs hanging over the edge.

"Ummm, welcome home? Bear sent me." Maybe, talking would give my heart time to get a grip inside my body. But the realization of what I was about to do struck me stupid and left me standing paralyzed in front of the shadow.

Ignoring my pitiful attempt at conversation, he shuffled to the edge of the bed. Although I couldn't make out his features, his shadowy frame was massive.

He sat up and reached out, I braced myself for his touch, but there was no contact. Instead, he grabbed a bottle off of the nightstand behind me. He tilted it up to his mouth, taking a long, slow pull. His swallows were loud in the silence of the little room.

Again, I wiped my palms on my skirt, hoping the darkness cloaked my nerves better than the perspiration on my hands.

"Do I make you nervous?" he asked, as if reading my mind. I could smell the fresh whiskey on his breath.

"No," I answered breathlessly, the lie getting caught in my throat. A large hand grabbed my waist roughly, tugging me into the space between his legs. His fingers dug into my hips and I squealed in surprise.

"Don't you lie to me, girl," he growled, without a hint of playfulness. My blood ran cold. My heart raced. He took another swig from the bottle, reaching behind me again to set it down. This time when he trailed back, he did it slowly, rubbing his cheek against mine, his facial hair not long enough to be considered a beard but longer than stubble. Unexpected tingles danced down my spine, and I fought the urge to touch his face. "Do you always ignore people when they ask you a question?"

Yes, yes he made me nervous. He made me so fucking nervous I couldn't find my tongue. I didn't expect this. I expected to spread my legs for some drunk horny asshole so he could have his way with me in a room that was too bright.

Instead, I stood in the dark, pressed between the thighs of a man I could barely see, but the feel of him alone sent shivers up my spine.

"I'll take your silence to mean you want to skip the small talk." He grabbed hold of my shoulders and shoved me down hard. I reached out to brace myself, my hands landing on rock hard thighs as my knees hit the carpet. "That's better."

You can do this. You can do this. You can do this.

"Suck me," he ordered, leaning back on the bed, propping himself up on his elbows.

I ran my trembling hands up his thighs until I found his belt. I slowly un-buckled it, my fingertips brushed the heated skin of his stomach. His ab mus-cles clenched under my touch and he sucked in a breath through his teeth. I shook out my trembling hands, trying to regain some control. When I reached for his zipper, I hesitated.

Desperate people.

Desperate things.

I steadied my hands as much as possible and slowly I dragged his zipper down. I closed my eyes in an effort to calm my erratic breathing, fearful that I was going to pass out and fall into his lap. I was hoping that closing my eyes was going to bring me some sort of comfort knowing I could remove myself from what I was about to do.

I'd just gotten his zipper down and was reaching into his jeans when his voice boomed over me like a cannon shot at close range. I jumped back in sur-prise, falling ass first onto the carpet.

"What the FUCK?" he roared. With my eyes closed, I hadn't seen him turn on the side lamp, but when I looked up from the floor, I found myself staring into a beautiful pair of hate-filled green eyes, boring into me like I was the reason for everything wrong with the world.

Familiar eyes.

He pushed my hands away from his fly and grabbed me by the wrists. He stood and yanked me up to my feet, his hard chest pressed up against mine. "I walked in on you earlier, you were having sex with some girl," I blurted, instantly regretting it. Fuck me and my speak-before-I-think disease.

His tight black wife-beater showcased the ripples of his impressive mus-cular frame. A myriad of colorful tattoos decorated one side of his neck, chest and shoulders, continuing all the way down both arms to the backs of his hands and knuckles. He wore bracelets that weren't actually bracelets at all, but leather belts with metal studs wrapped around his wrists and forearms. Dark hair cropped close to his head, a black stud in each ear. A white scar through his right eyebrow. Stubble on his square jaw that was more than a few days past needing a shave.

I thought he was large when he was relentlessly pounding into the girl on the table. Even when he was only a shadow I knew he was big, but in all reality I'd had no concept of the wall of man who stood before me.

This guy didn't look like he hung with the wrong crowd.

This guy was the wrong crowd.

"You?" he asked. His nostrils flaring as he glared down at me. I don't know what I did to make him so angry, but getting a look at him in the light made me more fearful than I ever was of him in the dark, and I wished I'd just listened to my instincts earlier and ran when I had the chance.

"Obviously you don't know shit because if you did you would know that what you saw wasn't sex."

"I know what I saw," I argued.

"No, you don't because you would know that I wasn't having sex with her. I was *fucking* her." The way he said the word fucking sent a flush of wetness into my panties.

You stupid girl. Your brain must really be damaged, because this is not someone who warrants that type of reaction. "Who are you?" he demanded.

"I'm no one," I answered, truthfully. My heart ached at hearing the words spoken out loud from my own mouth.

"You're no fucking biker whore," he stated flatly. He cocked his head to the side as he stared down at me. Running over my features as if he were trying to figure me out. His gaze lingering on my lips, his tongue darted out to wet his own.

"You don't know who I am," I spat. I tried to take a step back but he held me firmly in place.

"No, but biker whores typically don't tremble and practically hyperventilate when they're about to suck cock." He squeezed my wrists tightly and pain shot up my arms.

"Let me go!" I jerked my wrists unsuccessfully from his grip. I needed to get out of there, but he held me even tighter, forcing me backwards until the back of my head hit a wall.

"So you're saying you do this all the time then? That you know what a guy like me wants? That you know how to suck and fuck like a pro?" He ran his index finger down the side of my cheek and I tried to ignore the heat that lingered in their wake. "You think you can take care of me, little pup? Fine. We can start back up right where we left off." He guided one of my hands to the front of his pants and held my open palm to the bulging erection threatening to spring from his open jeans. The hairs on the back of my neck stood on end. "Aren't you going to show me how you can make me come?" he taunted, his words a warm whisper against my ear, although the words themselves were cold. Terrifying. I could hear my blood coursing through my veins as my heart beat faster and faster. "You already made me come once tonight." I looked at him and furrowed my brows.

"That's a lie. I barely touched you."

"No, not now. When you saw me earlier, with that girl. You stood in the doorway and you watched us. Did you like what you saw? Did you like watching me come for you?"

"You give yourself way too much credit. I didn't stay to watch you. I was just surprised. You were practically strangling her, why would I stay to watch that?"

He moved his hands to my throat and squeezed hard, leaving me with just enough airway so I could still breathe. "You mean like this?" He asked, looking into my eyes as I tried to hide the terror alarms going off in my body. He was feeding off my fear.

"Fuck you," I spat, mustering all the courage I could manage. He was toying with me, and I may have been afraid, but I was no fucking pushover.

"I know that you wanted to be that girl. You wanted it to be you who my cock was slamming into. I saw the way you looked at me and it made me explode. I see the way you look at me now and behind the fear you want me, maybe even because of it."

"You're wrong. That's not how I'm looking at you."

"No? Then tell me what you are really thinking when you look at me. Right now. What's going through that pretty head of yours?"

"I was thinking about what a shame it was that good looks are wasted on someone like you." He smiled out of the corner of his mouth and squeezed my throat tighter, leaning in so that his cheek was flush with mine and I could hear his words vibrate off my skin.

"How old are you, Pup?"

"What the hell is it to you?" I seethed through gritted teeth.

"I just want to know if you're illegal." He pulled back and his gaze roamed over my body with one long slow sweep. He released my throat and pinned both my wrists above my head with one hand. He dipped a calloused finger into the low neckline of my tank top, slowly tracing the rounded flesh of my breasts. Goosebumps rose on the flesh of my arms.

I inhaled sharply.

"I've seen all the shit going on out there," I said, tilting my head toward the door. "Like you really give a shit about illegal." My breaths shallow and quick.

"I don't give a shit," he said with a deep chuckle, "As a matter of fact, I'm hoping you *are* illegal." He pressed his forearms against the wall on both sides of my head, caging me in with his massive frame, pressing his erection up against my stomach. "Cause I do illegal real fucking well."

I gasped and my lungs felt heavy in my chest. I squirmed in his grip and couldn't decide if I wanted to rub up against him to find the friction I now craved or slap the living shit out of him. He must have sensed my indecision because he looked me in the eyes and shook his head.

"Go ahead, Pup. But I wouldn't if I were you." His expression stern, his eyes dark and dangerous, glimmering with a trace of amusement. He pressed his forehead to mine and sighed. "You and I could've had a lot of fun, Pup." He shook his head and for the first time I noticed the dark circles under his eyes and the redness of his eye lids.

He looked tired. And not the kind of tired you feel after a long day, but the kind of tired that lingers no matter how much sleep you get or how much coffee you ingest. The kind of tired that is less about rest and more about unrest.

I knew this because I was the same kind of tired.

He released me and stepped back. The second his intimidating presence was gone from my personal space I felt the coldness of his absence.

He grabbed the bottle from the nightstand and headed for the door.

I was still frozen to the wall. My jaw firmly affixed to the floor.

What the hell just happened?

"You're leaving?" I asked. My relief warring with some fucked-up misplaced sense of disappointment.

He cracked the door open and paused with his hand on the handle. The music filtered in through the opening, penetrating the silence, each heavy beat taking another footstep inside. "It's been a long fucking day and you've caught me at a really weird time. As much as the innocent thing you've got going on makes my cock hard, I don't do gentle, so you should be happy I'm walking away." He took a swig from the bottle and cast one last confused glance toward me, taking in my body that was still pressed up against the wall. "Three years ago I would have fucked you into the middle of next week without thinking twice."

Then he was gone.

What the fuck did that mean?

My stomach interrupted my thought by growling loudly. The twisting pain threatening to topple me over. I hugged myself in an attempt to soothe the ache. I'd looked around for some sort of food when I'd first arrived, but all the tables downstairs were covered with beer and liquor bottles. The coffee table had nothing on it but a mirror and a mound of blow, which was being cut into lines with a credit card by a man who looked old enough to be a grandfather.

A knock at the window made me jump. "Let me in, bitch!" Came a high-pitched voice from outside.

Nikki.

I scrambled over to the window to lift the latch. Nikki leapt up and stumbled into the room, falling onto the floor. Her greasy red hair was plastered to her forehead with sweat, her old faux-fur shawl that may have once been white, but was now an off gray color, was draped haphazardly over one shoulder.

"How did you know where I was?" I asked. I hadn't seen Nikki since she took off on me hours ago when we first got to the party.

"That Bear guy told me. I totally wanted to sit on his face but he just took off on his bike with some Tyra Banks looking chick."

There goes that option.

I helped Nikki up off the floor. "So how was it? How was he? I saw him downstairs earlier and holy hot man." She adjusted the strap of her bag across her shoulder. "Did you do that thing with your tongue I told you to do?" She asked me with the same excitement as if she was asking if I rode the Ferris wheel at the carnival. "Did you make him come? Did he make you come? Tell me everything."

I sighed, both defeated and relieved. "No. No one made anyone do anything. He just...left."

Nikki looked me up and down, her expression turned from elation to annoyance. "No wonder he left. Have you seen what the fuck you look like? I should've never let you come up here looking like that."

I looked down at the plain gray tank top that I'd tied in the back to make it appear more form fitting and the tattered, sequined skirt that was missing most of the sequins. I knew I didn't look great, but I didn't have the resources to look great.

Or even good.

Nikki shook her head, gesturing wildly with her hands up and down at my body. "You look like a kid fresh off the playground who's been playing with her mama's old clothes."

She sniffled and adjusted her own denim skirt that barely covered her ass cheeks. Her green tank top had a bleach stain over her right boob.

"It doesn't matter now. He's gone," I said bitterly. "Let's get out of here." I had to clear my head and come up with a new plan.

Which included getting away from Nikki.

"Not so fast, little one. What's your hurry?" Nikki took a turn around the room and when she reached the door she turned the lock. "Let's see what we can find in here," she said playfully, opening the drawers of a dresser one by one, searching the contents, pushing aside socks and t-shirts.

"What the hell are you doing?" I asked. "We need to leave and leave now. You didn't see the look on the guys face before, because if you did we would already be halfway across the state by now."

"Oh shush, you're so fucking dramatic. What's your hurry? Besides, this place has air conditioning," Nikki said, fanning her pits. She picked up a photo with a thin plastic frame and turned it to me. "Sweet looking kid huh?" She ran her fingers over the picture of a little blond girl with curls smiling into the camera. For the first time since I'd met Nikki I saw her smile, although there was a lingering sadness behind it. She shook her head, set down the picture, and opened the bottom drawer, shuffling through some paperwork.

"Motherfucking BINGO!" She shouted. When she lifted her hand from the drawer, she produced a huge stack of bills tied together with purple bands.

She waved it in the air and my stomach flipped at the sight. That money could buy a lot of food.

It could buy the start of a whole new life.

The thought went out just as fast as it had come in, because there was no fucking way I was about to steal it.

There is no way I am stealing from HIM.

I was desperate, not suicidal.

There was a loud bang followed by the rattling of the doorknob. "What the fuck?" A voice on the other end of the door shouted. "Why is this locked?"

"We gotta go!" I shouted. Nikki grabbed another stack of bills from the drawer and darted for the window, shoving me aside before I could offer for her to go first, losing a few bills along the way.

Nikki barely had one leg out the window when the door flew off its hinges, sending the door frame splintering into a million little wooden pieces throughout the room. Bear, the man who'd sent me up here, stood in the doorway. We locked eyes for a split-second before he noticed the empty drawer, the loose bills on the floor, and the open window where Nikki was already halfway out.

Bear took one step into the room. Nikki reached into her purse and produced a small handgun I didn't know she had.

"Stay where you are!" she shouted, aiming the gun at his chest. He stopped, raising an eyebrow at Nikki.

"Are you sure you want to do that?" he asked with no sign of fear in his voice, if anything he sounded like he was taunting her. Teasing her. He made it seem as if it was old hat to him to have a gun pointed directly at him.

The green-eyed shadow man appeared in the doorway and instantly my heart restricted in my chest. When he saw Nikki and the state of the room his lip curled up on one side. He took slow confident steps toward her, passing Bear. "Don't fucking move, or I'll fucking shoot!" Her voice wavered as he approached.

"So shoot," he dared, each step toward her a challenge.

Nikki turned toward me, the gun shaking in her hand, an unreadable emotion flashing in her teary eyes. "I'm so sorry," she said.

She squeezed the trigger.

There was a loud echoing crack in my left ear, like a pik being hammered into a block of ice, followed by a disorienting ringing sensation.

I don't know how I ended up on the ground, but I found myself lying on the carpet on my side, holding my knees up to my chest. My eyes closed. My hands covered my ears, and I just laid their willing the ringing to stop. Just as it had started to subside, strong hands flipped me flat onto my back. My head thunked against the ground like a dead weight.

"Redhead's gone," Bear said, tapping the screen of his phone with his thumb. "I sent Cash and Tank to find her and put the word out to the locals. Town's too small for her to get too far without someone noticing. We'll catch up to her sooner or later."

The green-eyed man glowered down at me from only inches above my face. A vein pulsed in his neck. "Seems I was wrong. You are a whore. A thieving little whore," He must have taken my confused look for not being able to hear because he ripped my hands away from my ears. "Listen you little cunt bitch..." He paused mid-sentence and looked down to where his hands held mine, and my gaze followed. Sticky red coated my palms. He grabbed my chin, turning my head one way and then the other. When he touched a spot over my ear, pain sliced down my neck, and I cried out.

"Fuck," he said, his fingers were now coated in the same red as my hand. *Is that blood?*

Bear stood off to the side with his arms folded across his chest. I opened my mouth to ask him what had happened, but nothing came out.

The two men exchanged some words I couldn't make sense of. A black halo formed around the room and its contents, and as the seconds ticked by everything faded further and further into the expanding dark tunnel. My fear of the dark caused my pulse to race, but a sudden eerie sense of calm took over and I concentrated on the beautiful face of the angry man hovering above me.

"I don't even know your name," I whispered.

I managed to stay conscious long enough to hear his answer.

"They call me King."

Then the blackness surrounded me and swallowed me whole.

chapter
five

King

I'D NEVER BEEN SO ANGRY IN MY ENTIRE FUCKING LIFE. AND IN THE PAST TWENTY-seven years I'd been alive more than a few people had felt the wrath of Brantley King.

Few had lived to tell about it.

How old was this girl anyway? Seventeen? Eighteen?

I didn't know her long enough to hate her, yet I had the overwhelming urge to wrap my hands around her throat and strangle her. Better yet I wanted to unravel one of the belts from my forearm and tighten it around her neck. I wanted her to feel every bit of my fury as I squeezed the life from her bony body.

I wanted to take out all of my frustration on her, but it wasn't just her I was angry with. I was also pissed-off at myself.

I've always been nothing short of meticulous about security, but I'd hap-hazardly tossed the stack of cash Preppy had given me that day into a drawer.

A fucking drawer.

The old me from three years ago would've placed it in my attic safe and changed the combination three times already.

How did I go from being overly careful to dangerously careless?

I should've had security guarding the doors. I had enemies going into prison, and I came out with a few more. Instead, I forgot all my past protocol and left a girl I didn't know shit about, alone in my fucking room, when I should've tossed her out on her ass the second I decided I wasn't going to fuck her.

Which wasn't me either.

I didn't fuck her because she was afraid of me? Because she seemed inno-cent and naive? Not to say that she didn't get my dick hard, because she did. I nearly came in my pants when her hands shook as she undid my belt. I told myself that I couldn't go through with it because what I needed was a girl who could work me like a pro so I could rid myself of the pent-up aggression that was turning me stupid.

But that was a lie.

Something inside me, something I could almost mistake for a con-science, told me not to take advantage of the situation. No, it told me not to take advantage of *her*. Walking away while her cheeks were still flushed from fear, embarrassment, anger, and if I was reading her right, a little bit of desire, was torture on my straining cock. It took a lot of control not to march back and take her up against that wall.

But that was before. Any feelings of doing right by her flew out the window with her friend and my money. The six grand the redhead managed to steal wasn't enough to scratch the surface on the amount I would need for a payoff, but the amount didn't matter. Two fucking cents would have been too much.

One way or another, the girl passed out in my bed was going to pay.

I sat down on the mattress and peeled back the covers. Her skirt, which was much too large for her little frame was rolled up at the waistband so it wouldn't fall off her hips. The material, which was missing most of the sparkly things hanging off of it, had ridden up to her waist in her sleep, her white cotton panties exposed to me. I trailed my fingertips up the outside of her leg from her ankles to her thighs. The simple contact caused my body to shudder and my dick twitched to life.

She was too skinny. Her cheeks were sunken. She had dark circles under her huge eyes. Her elbows were sharp and her ribs reminded me of how Preppy looked when I first met him. She wasn't the usual kind of girl I went for. I liked tits, ass. Something to play with while my cock took care of business.

So why couldn't I stop myself from touching her?

I peeled off her tank top and tossed it to the floor.

No Bra.

Small but perfectly round tits. Tits that made me wonder how much more perfect they would be with some meat on her bones. Tits I wanted to watch bounce in my face while she rode me.

The girl sighed heavily but didn't wake. When her breathing had again leveled out I traced lazy circles onto the smooth skin of her stomach, around her belly button and then around her little pink nipples. It took a fuck of a lot of restraint not to lean over and suck them into my mouth. I wanted to bite them until I drew blood. I wanted to lick the blood off of her pale white skin.

I'd never both hated and wanted something so much in my entire life.

A quick hate fuck might wipe away the unfamiliar sentimental feelings rolling around in my twisted brain, but the girl was injured and passed out in my bed.

Technically, you can say that I was caring for her.

Technically, I wanted to face fuck her until she gagged.

My conflicted feelings were giving me a fucking migraine.

I had to get out of there. There was no good that could come of me touching her while she slept, but I couldn't bring myself to get off the bed.

Then she stirred. Just a little, just enough to remind me that I was crossing into Preppy territory. But I couldn't leave just yet. What if she woke up and tried to escape? Then, I would really never know where the redhead went with my money.

I ignored the fact that it was impossible for her to escape, especially since I had her handcuffed to my headboard. Instead of getting up and walking out the fucking door like I should have, I stripped down to my boxer-briefs and got in bed beside her. Hauling her back against my chest, I covered us both with the blanket.

It was a first for me. I'd never been underneath the covers in my bed with a woman before. I'd never let anyone stay long enough to sleep before.

I splayed out a hand on her concave stomach, the heat from her core radiating onto my thigh making my dick even harder. I propped my head up on my elbow and found myself fascinated at the contrast between us, her pale and perfect, to my tanned and heavily tattooed.

Now I was painfully hard.

The thought of tearing off those innocent little school girl panties and defiling her pussy with my cock right then and there sent spasms up my spine. The only reason I came back to the room earlier was because I'd changed my mind. As innocent as she appeared, she was the one who'd offered herself to me, and who the fuck was I to say no to that?

Maybe prison had changed me, but I wasn't ready to accept that change. I had been downstairs for only ten minutes when I turned on my heel and headed back upstairs to strip her down, bend her over, and show her what the fuck she'd gotten herself into.

I twisted a lock of her white-blonde hair in my fingers. Over and over again, I reminded myself that the girl was a thief and a whore and that I had every right to take payment for what she stole from me and then some.

I owned this bitch.

She was mine to take.

Only as much as I wanted to roll on top of her and sink deep down inside, I couldn't bring myself to do it.

There was more to this girl's story than what was obvious on the outside. Her friend was obviously a junkie with her humungous pupils and shiny red nose. This girl didn't act like a junkie, but her clothes and rail thin frame had me thinking that dope could be the only reason she'd be hanging around with Bear and his crew.

I was going to pry her story from her when she woke up. Then I was going to decide what my plans were for her which would preferably consist of naked and on her knees.

She let out a deep sigh, and I stilled, fearing she might wake before I had the chance to get out of bed, but oddly enough her entire body relaxed back into me. Her ass pressed against my straining erection.

I stifled a groan.

Only my boxers and her panties separated us. I wanted to rock against her, alleviate the pressure building in my balls, but I stopped myself and just as quickly as I'd gotten into bed, I got back out.

I picked my jeans up from the floor. Before I left the room I glanced back at the girl sleeping in my bed. The moonlight shone through the window making her blonde hair appear even lighter, her skin even paler.

More haunted.

I didn't know whether I wanted to kill her or fuck her.

Maybe both, but one thing was for sure.

One way or another, I was going to make her scream.

I was finally starting to feel like my old self again.

chapter
six

Doe

I AWOKE GROGGY AND CONFUSED. MY SKULL FELT LIKE IT WAS GOING TO CRACK open against the pressure of my aching head. The mattress underneath me was soft, the sheets cool against my skin. A much better alternative to the park benches or pavement where I usually made my bed.

I stretched out my legs one by one, then raised my arms to do the same. Except my left arm wouldn't cooperate, it was stuck. My eyes sprang open when I heard a rattling. My wrist was bound to the headboard.

By handcuffs.

Fuck.

I sat up quickly and glanced around in a panic. Sharp scratching pain assaulted the side of my head when my shoulder brushed my ear. Feeling around, I realized my left ear had been covered in some sort of bandage. Then, I remembered the events of the night before.

I'd been shot.

Nikki had shot me.

I was in the same room as the previous night, but in the light of morning the details that the darkness had hid were now on full display. At the foot of the bed a wooden dresser that was splintering at the corners sat below a huge flat screen TV. A bi-fold closet took up the entire wall on the right side. The room was only large enough to fit one nightstand beside the bed. It wasn't huge, but it was comfortable with a plush navy-blue comforter and simple wrought iron headboard—the one I was cuffed to.

Where are my clothes?

I was completely naked from the waist up, but thankfully, my panties remained.

I had to get the fuck out of here.

My stomach twisted. I let out an agonized moan and clenched my hands over my belly. The door opened, and the man from the night before appeared.

They call me King

He stepped into the room like he was stepping out of the gates of hell and onto earth where the very presence of us mere mortals pissed him off. He held my gaze with a steady glare that shook me to my very core.

"Name," he demanded, closing the door behind him, stopping at foot of the bed. He folded his muscular arms over his chest. On the right side of his neck a vein pulsed beneath the ink of his tattoos.

His eyes darted down to my chest and I crossed my free arm over my breasts the best I could to cover myself.

"What's it to you?" I quipped. King wore the same dark clothes as the night before, same belts around his forearms. The only difference was the addition of a dark grey skullcap. In the light of day I noticed that the tattoos I'd caught a glimpse of the night before were very intricate. If you took the scary out of the equation, King was drop dead gorgeous. His eyes were so dark green they almost looked black. His lips were full and slightly pink.

"I figured we might start with your fucking name and then move on to you telling me where the fuck that bitch went with my money." He seethed.

He was the most terrifyingly beautiful thing I'd ever laid eyes on. With my fear of the dark, things always seemed scarier at night when my mind tended to exaggerate the situation. But in the daylight King was more everything. More intimidating, more scary, more angry…more beautiful.

"You stole from me, Pup. This is your one and only chance to tell me where the redheaded bitch went. You will pay one way or another, but if you tell me right now, you might just get out of paying with your life."

My head was fuzzy and starting to spin. My life was on the line, but I could only seem to focus on trivial things. "Where are my clothes?" I asked.

"You stole six fucking grand from me, your fucking clothes should be the least of your concern."

Holy shit! Six grand?

Fucking Nikki.

"Don't play with me girl." King wrapped his hands around my ankles and yanked, sliding me forward until I landed flat on my back. My arm stretched as far as it could without tearing out of the socket, held captive by the handcuffs. My other hand was braced on the bed, my breasts were again exposed. "Are you worried I copped a feel while you slept? Maybe I did. Because what you are going to learn is that I can do whatever I want with you, whenever I want. Because right now, I fucking own you."

In all the time I'd been living on the streets, I've had some close calls, some serious gut check moments. I've seen things that have made my skin crawl and my heart race. I was very familiar with feeling afraid.

Fear had nothing on King.

"Don't keep trying to cover those pretty tits of yours. Last night, you were about to wrap those pretty lips around my cock, so don't suddenly feel the need to cover up now. Even though, those little girl panties of yours have kept me hard since I stripped you down." King leaned forward, bracing a knee on the mattress on each side of my hips. He cupped my cheek in his hands. I tried to turn away from him and he dug his fingers into my jaw and yanked me back to face him. "Do you want to know what exactly it is that I do to people who steal from me, who take what's mine?"

"No," I panted. And I didn't want to know.

"I'd refer you to someone who could tell you firsthand, little girl, but none of them are breathing right now."

Shit.

"I don't know where she is, I swear. Please, just let me go," I pled as I squirmed underneath him. I didn't want to die because of Nikki's stupidity. "We can work something out," I said. I have no idea what exactly I meant by that, but I would've said anything to get the hell out of those cuffs and out of that house.

King looked me up and down. "I'm not interested. That ship has sailed," he said, coming close enough to me to run a finger along my protruding collarbone. "You may be pretty, Pup, and those eyes of yours get my cock hard, but you're all skin and bones. Besides, I don't fuck junkies."

"I'm not a fucking junkie!" I screamed wildly. Being called a junkie when in the time I'd been living on the street I hadn't touched a single drug, set me off like a lighter to a fuse.

"Bullshit! There is no other reason you could possibly be stupid enough to steal from me besides needing a fix. And I know you're not from around here, because if you were you wouldn't have even thought about taking what's mine." His voice grew louder, his glare ice cold. He thought I was just like Nikki. A junkie. He expected me to cower.

He expected wrong.

"I don't give a fuck who you are, asshole," I seethed. "And you're not as smart as you seem to think you are. Tell me something, who exactly was it who appointed you judge of all people?"

I thought my words would start an all-out war but instead King didn't look angrier, he looked only mildly amused. "Well you are partially right. Because when it comes to me and mine, I am the judge. I am the jury. And if need be, I am the motherfucking executioner."

His words hadn't yet had the chance to marinate in my brain when my stomach took the opportunity to interrupt by growling loudly. King's gaze followed the sound to where I hugged myself with my free arm around my mid-section in an effort to steady the ever-growing ache. The dizziness again threatened to take me under, but I fought it back.

King was still sitting upright on his knees, straddling me. I sat up as far as the handcuffs would allow until my face was only inches from his. "Nikki is the junkie. I'm just hungry you fucking asshole!" I spat.

King's fists clenched at his sides. He raised his hand. I ducked and covered my face the best I could, bracing myself for the strike.

But it never came.

After a moment I opened my eyes. King was staring down at me, his hand raised, but not in anger, he was rubbing his palm over his short hair. His eyebrows furrowed in confusion.

I was bound in his bed with no way out and no way of knowing what was going to happen to me. It was a bad time for my foot-in-mouth syndrome to be acting up. "I'm sorry. I didn't mean it. I mean, I just—"

"Shut up," He said with a new calm control.

"I don't do drugs. I never have. I mean, not that I know of. You see, the thing is—"

"Shut up."

My stomach growled again, it twisted so hard I saw stars in front of my eyes. I needed to eat. I needed to escape. I needed to be anywhere else, but in his bed. "I swear I didn't take your money. It wasn't me. That wasn't the plan. I was just supposed to get a biker to—"

"Shut the fuck up!" he roared, his explosive rage effectively silencing my scrambled monologue.

My stomach twisted and turned again. This time I closed my eyes until the pain passed. I tried to wet my cracked lips with my tongue, but it was also dry and hung heavy in my mouth. King reached down and touched my cheek with the pad of his thumb. I was so involved in trying not to pass out that I barely registered that he was touching me. After a few moments with nothing but the sound of my heart beating in my ears, King abruptly stood up and walked out, slamming the door behind him.

I was his prisoner.

I was either going to die of hunger, fear, or at the hands of King. But the how wasn't important. It was the when I was waiting for, because I was certain I wasn't ever going to leave that house again.

At least not alive.

chapter
s e v e n

Doe

I WAS DRIFTING SOMEWHERE BETWEEN AWAKE AND UNCONSCIOUS WHEN THE DOOR opened and heavy footsteps approached the bed. Something metal was set on the nightstand, clanking and rattling as it settled. It was the smell that brought me back to the land of the living as abruptly as if smelling salts had been waved under my nose.

Food.

The metal of the cuffs bit into my wrist as I lunged for the tray that was set just beyond my reach. I let out a frustrated shrill-sounding scream.

"Easy now, killer," a voice said. I hadn't noticed the guy leaning on the dresser at the foot of the bed, his arms and legs crossed in front of him. I recognized him from the party the night before. Only when his eyes traveled down to my bare breasts, I remembered that I was still nude from the waist up. I quickly covered myself by balling up as small as I could, huddling close to the metal headboard.

He smiled and slowly approached me.

"No!" I shouted when he got close enough to extend his hand out to me.

"No?" he asked. "So you don't want this?" He picked up the tray and set it on the bed in front of me.

"No, no, I do. I do want it," I assured him. I sat up again and winced when my injured ear accidentally rubbed against the metal headboard. If it was food he was offering, my modesty was going to have to wait until after my belly was full. I removed my arm from my breasts and reached out to slide the tray closer to me. When I saw what was on it, I paused.

What the hell?

There were two plates. One held a sandwich of some sort, wrapped in white paper, a sticker with the name of the deli held the wrapping together. The other plate was not really a plate but a mirror. On it, white powder, cut into three lines along with a rolled-up dollar bill. Next to it was a plastic Ziploc bag containing a needle, spoon, lighter, and another smaller baggie filled with another type of darker looking powder.

"What is all this?" I asked.

"Breakfast," he said straight-faced. "You get to choose one item from the tray and one only." He sat down across from me on the bed.

"Is this a joke?" Who the hell would choose drugs for breakfast?

Nikki, I thought.

"Choose wisely, girl." He pointed to the tray.

I grabbed the sandwich and tore off the wrapper before he could finish his sentence. I took a monster bite that contained both sandwich and paper.

"Slow down," he warned. I detected amusement in his warning. I ignored him, choking when I tried to swallow down half-chewed bites, but the feeling of chewing and swallowing was euphoric. I kept going until the sandwich was completely in my stomach.

I didn't need drugs. I was high on food.

I wiped at the mess I made on my face and licked my fingers clean. He handed me a glass of water, and I downed it in three big gulps. I sat back on the bed and patted my bare stomach, no longer caring that I was practically naked in front of this stranger. I opened my mouth to speak when a sudden wave of nausea washed over me. I sat up and held a hand over my mouth.

"What's wrong?" he asked, as I frantically looked around for something I could throw up in. I didn't see anything within arm's reach, but it only took him a second to realize what it was I needed. He leapt up and grabbed a metal wastebasket from the corner of the room and ran back, just in time for me to empty the entire breakfast into the basket. Every little bit of barely-chewed, undigested sandwich came back up in waves until once again my stomach was completely empty.

"I told you to slow the fuck down." He walked to the far side of the room and opened the window, tossing the entire basket out. "I'll hose that out later."

I never cried when I woke up in the hospital and couldn't even recall my name. I didn't cry when I was told I might never regain my memory. I didn't cry when I was thrown into a group home full of perverts. I didn't cry when I ran away and had to live on the streets. I didn't cry when I came to the realization that using my body was the only way I was going to be able to survive. I didn't cry when a bullet grazed my ear. I didn't cry when I was handcuffed to a bed by a tattooed psychopath who I was certain was going to kill me.

But losing the first full stomach I had in weeks?

I cried.

Not just a few little tears. I sobbed. Loud and long. Shoulders shaking. No end in sight.

Ugly cry.

Hope. It's something I hadn't yet given up, but right then and there, I was ready to throw in the towel. I didn't care if I stayed attached to that bed until I died and the skin rotted away from my bones.

I was done.

I'd been dealt all I could handle, and I was more than fucking over it.

Over being afraid. Over being hungry. Over redheaded hookers. Over being shot at.

Over this sorry excuse for a life.

I sat back on the bed and rested my head against my arm, which hung at an awkward angle. I let my body go limp. Looking out the window, I noticed the sun was out. I didn't even know what time it was. I didn't care.

No one looked for me when I might have been someone, so no one would be looking for me now that I was absolutely no one.

It's ironic really. I'd been wishing for a bed and a roof over my head and in a really fucked up way, for however long they kept me alive, I had it.

The guy whose name I didn't know left the room but left the tray on the bed. How much of that stuff did I have to take for it to be lethal? Half? All of it? Maybe, King's plan was to inject me with the drugs himself. Or maybe he was a coward and would order his friend to do his dirty work for him.

Maybe, if I was lucky, my death would be quick. Just a nice bullet to the head.

Either way, it didn't matter how I was going to go. I just knew it was the end, and oddly enough, it was comforting to come to terms with it instead of spending my remaining hours fighting it.

I was beyond exhausted.

Maybe, King thought I would make things easy on him and off myself with the drugs. I huffed. I wasn't about to give him that satisfaction. If he wanted me dead, he was going to man-up and do it himself. I used every ounce of strength I had and kicked the tray off the bed. The mirror bounced off the carpet. The coke billowed into the air in a white cloud of fine powder.

And I laughed.

I laughed so hard my entire body shook and tears ran down my face. I laughed so hard that the sound of my laughter got caught in my throat. There I was. Half-naked. Handcuffed to a bed. Puke on my face. A tray of drugs scattered on the floor.

Maniacally laughing like a schizophrenic who'd skipped out on her meds.

The door opened again and in walked the same guy from earlier. I didn't acknowledge him, just continued to stare out the window as the sun began to set.

"Do you know how much that shit is worth?" he asked with his eyes wide.

"Nope. And don't know why you would bother bringing it to me since I already told your friend that I'm no fucking junkie." I rolled onto my side, turning my back to him. "Why don't you just kill me, and get it over with."

"It was a test," he said, rounding the bed. He propped himself up next to me, his back against the headboard, a steaming ceramic bowl in his hands. "You passed."

"A what? What the hell does that mean?"

"King. He wanted to know if you were telling the truth, so he tested you. A junkie would've said 'fuck the food' and dove nose-first into the dope." He extended the bowl out to me. "Here. I'm Preppy, by the way."

Odd name for an odd guy. He looked like a cross between a thug, a teacher, and a surfer.

I'd seen him briefly the night before, but I didn't take the time to really look at him. Preppy was close to six feet tall. He wore light jeans and a short sleeved yellow collared shirt with a white bow tie. His sandy blonde hair was tied back into a wild ponytail on the top of his head, but beneath it his head was shaved clean on both sides above his ears, revealing intricate vine tattoos that started at his temples and circled around his head. His arms, hands, and knuckles were also covered with ink. He had a dark beard that didn't match his hair color. At first glance, you'd think he was much older than he was, but it was his eyes that gave away his youth.

"What is it?" I asked, staring into the steaming bowl.

"Chicken broth. Drink it slowly so you can keep it down. How long has it been since you ate?" He crossed his legs at the ankles and rested his hands behind his head.

"Not sure." I don't know why but saying the words out loud made me feel ashamed in a way I hadn't thought about before. "Days, I think."

Hesitantly, I took the bowl from his hands. It was warm on my palms and instantly made the ache in my weak hands subside. I lifted it to my mouth slowly, relishing the feeling of the steam against my cheeks and the warmth of the liquid as it spread down my throat.

"Why are you even bothering with feeding me?"

"You say you're not a junkie, but your fucking ribs are practically poking through your skin, and I could sharpen my knife on that collarbone of yours. King's not the kind of guy who starves someone to death."

"So, he's not going to kill me?" I asked, hopefully.

"Didn't say that. Just said he wouldn't starve you to death. Bears crew has a lead on the redhead. If we catch up to her and we find out you weren't in on it, he might let you go."

"Might?"

"He's not the most predictable guy, and he's been away for a few years. Hasn't been acting like himself, so there's no telling what's running through his head right now."

"Years?" That's when I remembered that the party last night was supposed to be a coming home party. "Where was he?"

"State."

"College?"

"Prison."

Prison made much more sense than college.

"What did he do?" I was pushing my luck by even asking. But I thought that maybe, if I knew more about King—knew what made him tick—I would have more of a chance of convincing him to let me go.

"You sure ask a lot of questions, little girl. Why do you want to know?"

I shrugged and sipped more of my broth. "Just curious, I guess."

"He killed someone, got caught," he said casually. I swallowed a huge mouthful of broth in one tight gulp.

"Who?" My curiosity made my mouth run faster than the speed of my usual word vomit.

Preppy smiled. His dark brown eyes glistened with excitement. I knew then that there was a lot more to him than what I saw on the surface. Something sinister was lying just beneath the tattoos and bow tie.

Something that made the hair on my arms stand on end.

Preppy leaned forward, resting his chin on the back of his folded hands.

chapter
eight

Doe

THERE WAS NO DOUBT IN MY MIND THAT KING WAS CAPABLE OF THE KIND OF things most normal people couldn't fathom, but what kind of person kills their own mother?

Preppy asked me the same questions King had about who I was, and I told him my story. The difference between Preppy and King is that Preppy actually listened to me.

I gave him the short version.

No memory.

Group home.

Living on the streets.

Nikki.

Attempting to sell myself for protection and shelter.

Also unlike King, Preppy seemed to actually believe me.

I drank every last bit of broth, and Preppy changed the bandage on my ear. It was already starting to itch as it scabbed over.

"Why don't you let me go?" I asked, bunching the waistband of the sweatpants he'd given me to wear in my hand so they wouldn't fall down. "You can just tell King that I escaped."

Preppy shook his head from side to side. "That's not going to happen," he scoffed, like there was something wrong with my question, not the fact that his friend had a girl handcuffed to his bed against her will.

Preppy uncuffed me. Temporarily, he made sure to tell me, and led me to one of the doors in the room I'd assumed was a closet but turned out to be a small but clean bathroom.

I hadn't realized how bad I had to pee before then. I let the sweatpants fall to the floor and was about to push down my underwear when I noticed the door still stood open and Preppy watched my every move.

"Can you please close the door?"

"Sure." Preppy took a step inside and shut the door behind him.

"Not exactly what I meant."

"Sorry, kid. Boss-man told me not to let you out of my sight."

"Do you always do what he tells you to?" I asked, bitterly.

"For the most part." Unable to wait a second longer, I pushed down my underwear and sat on the toilet.

Nothing came out.

"Don't have to go anymore?" He asked.

"I do, but I can't pee with you staring at me like that. Just turn around. It's not like I'm going anywhere. This room doesn't even have a window."

"I'm sorry. I wasn't aware that your highness had stage fright," Preppy said sarcastically, rolling his eyes.

He opened the bathroom door again and this time he turned his back to me. The second I knew he wasn't looking; my body was able to relax and let go. The relief felt so amazing I moaned out loud.

"I may appear nice, kid, but don't get it twisted. King and I are cut from the same cloth."

"If he asked you to kill me, would you do it?" I asked, needing to know if he would be the one to possibly end my life.

"Yes," he answered. No hesitation.

When I was done, Preppy led me back to the bed and secured my cuff around my wrist. This time, he connected it to a lower rung on the headboard so I wouldn't have to sit with my arm raised above my head.

"Prep," King's deep voice boomed from the doorway, startling me. He motioned to Preppy with a lift of his chin. Preppy tightened the cuff around my wrist and left the room. King glanced at me for a brief second, then followed Preppy out, closing the door behind them.

Did they find Nikki? Did she tell them I didn't have anything to do with stealing from him? Or maybe, she turned on me and told them it was all my idea. Nikki was oddly overprotective of me when she was sober, but when she was high she was unpredictable, and if her life or her drugs were on the line, there was no doubt in my mind that she would throw me to the wolves.

I heard a door slam, and then their muffled voices rose up to the window from outside. I strained my neck and peered out. King and Preppy were on the lawn, just beyond the deck. The sun was just setting; the sky glowed orange.

I stretched out my leg and slid the window open a crack with my bare foot.

"Found the redhead," King said. He lit a cigarette.

"Where?" Preppy asked.

"Andrews' place up the highway. That old motel with the pool in the parking lot."

"You get the cash?" Preppy asked. He leaned back against the railing and crossed his arms over his chest.

King shook his head and blew out the smoke.

"I think she's telling the truth, man," Preppy said, gesturing up to my window with his hands. I ducked in reaction although from that angle there was no way they could see me. "I think you know I'm pretty good at detect-ing a liar, and this girl doesn't scream thief to me. What did the redhead say about her?"

"She didn't say shit."

"How come?"

"'Cause she's fucking dead."

⌀

Nikki was dead.

I couldn't catch my breath.

My head spun.

King had said that anyone who stole from him would have to pay a price, and Nikki had paid it.

With her life.

There was no doubt, that without King being able to ask Nikki about my involvement, that I was next.

Thunderclouds clapped overhead. King and Preppy walked back toward the house, but I could no longer make out what they were saying. I closed the window and propped myself on the bed just as they'd left me.

The first chance I got I was going to make a run for it. There was no time to wait and plan. This was going to have to be quick and on-the-fly.

After a few minutes, Preppy came back into the room and uncuffed me. "Let's go," he said. Yanking me into an upright position, he dragged me to-ward the door.

"Where are we going?" I asked frantically. Then, it came to me. This was King's house. His bedroom. He wouldn't carry out killing me in his own home, so it was very likely they would take me somewhere else first. This was my only shot, and I was going to have to take it.

"Not far," Preppy said.

It was getting dark, and it was about to storm. Couldn't they at least wait until morning? I could think better when I wasn't being choked by my own fear of the dark.

"Why?"

"Come on. You'll see."

We walked down the narrow hallway and down the stairs to the main living area of the house. King was nowhere in sight. Figures he would ask Preppy to do his dirty work for him. A part of me wanted King to do it.

I wanted him to see the look in my eyes as he killed an innocent person.

But it didn't look like I was going to get that chance.

Preppy led me out onto the balcony, and I stopped short when we reached the stairs. Preppy was already a few steps below me, his grip on my wrist still tight. He turned around when he felt me come to a stop. This was my only chance to escape with my life. I didn't think. I just acted.

I reared my foot back and kicked him in the balls. HARD. He released my wrist to grab his crotch and I shoved on his shoulders with all my might, sending him tumbling backwards down the steep staircase.

I ran down the steps and jumped over Preppy who was curled up at the bottom of the stairs groaning obscenities face-first into the grass.

I took off as fast as my bare feet and weak legs would take me. Clutching the sweats with one hand, I ran down the dirt driveway, but when I reached the road, there was nothing but more trees in every direction. I didn't remember which way we'd come from the night before, and there was nothing telling me which way would bring me toward people.

Toward help.

A door slammed somewhere behind me. Heavy boots against the wooden deck echoed over my head. The wind carried the shouts of a very deep and very unhappy voice.

Shit.

The sun had almost fully sunk into the horizon. Although I couldn't see in the dark, I had to get off the open road where I was a sitting duck.

I took off across the road. Pushing some brush aside, I jumped through the opening I created, stumbling over twisting roots and cypress knees. Finding my footing on the soft wet ground was almost impossible.

So was running straight.

Vines and brush blocked my every move. Spider webs stretched over my face as I tried to clear a path. Just a little further in, and I would be able to hide within the thick brush.

My foot landed on something sharp and I hissed, tumbling forward onto a narrow path. I leapt across the mud and used all my weight to flatten a bush. I'd just lifted my leg as high as it could go so I could step over it when I was tackled from behind, landing hard on my side. The wind left my lungs with a whooshing sound.

No matter how hard I tried to suck air back in, I couldn't. Over and over again, I opened my mouth to breathe, and over and over again, my lungs failed me.

I was still gasping for air when strong arms flipped me onto my back. Massive, hard thighs held me like a vice on each side of my ribcage, threatening to snap them with one twist of his knees.

King leaned over me, his grip tight on my wrists, which he held together and raised above my head. I tried to gain control of my lungs. When I was finally able to pull in some air, my chest rose and fell in quick pants. My breasts brushed up against King's hard chest.

The wind howled. The sky answered with a thunderclap that I felt in my bones. The rain started slow. Icy drops caused my skin to prickle. I was suddenly hyper-aware of the man lying on top of me. The rain quickly turned from drops to sheets. Water poured down King's face and into his dark demon-like eyes, but he didn't look possessed.

He looked like the devil himself.

"I thought I made it clear that I owned you," he growled. His nostrils flared. "Your debt has yet to be paid, Pup."

"So, kill me already, and get it over with," I said hoarsely, in the loudest voice I could muster, which was barely a whisper. "Either let me go, or just fucking kill me!"

King scoffed. "That would be too easy."

"What then? What do you want from me? I heard you. Nikki's dead. Your money is gone, and I can't pay you back. I don't have anything you want." I struggled to throw him off, but I was as effective as a gnat to a tiger.

"Oh, but I think you can pay me back, Pup. You do have something I want," he said, running his fingers up my arm to my shoulder. He grabbed hold of my throat in his large palm and squeezed with calloused fingers, not enough to choke me, but just enough to remind me he could.

"Please, just let me go! I'm nothing! I'm no one! You don't want me. Last night, you walked out of that room because you didn't want me. Remember? So just let me go. Please. I'm begging you."

I'd stopped struggling because it was pointless, the only thing I had that could possibly get to him were my words.

And I was failing miserably.

"But that's where you're wrong. Last night, I thought you were a scared little girl, unable to handle what I want, what I can do, what I need. But that doesn't matter anymore. Because now you're my property, and I can do what the fuck I want with what's mine." He emphasized this by squeezing harder on my throat.

I opened my mouth to protest, to tell him that I wasn't his and never would be when suddenly King's lips came crashing down over mine with such force that the back of my head was pushed down further into the mud. There was nowhere for me to go, nowhere to get away. His full lips were soft, but his kiss was anything but. He sucked my lower lip into his mouth and licked at the seam of my lips with his tongue.

King was hard and scary as hell, so was his kiss. And if his words weren't getting his point across, his kiss told me that he owned me. It made me forget for just a second that the man behind those lips was a raging psychopath.

The rain continued to assault us. For once it wasn't my mouth speaking before my brain. It was my body. Because as much as I told myself that I didn't want his kiss, my body was very much saying that it wanted it. Wanted him.

I opened my mouth to protest, but the second I did, his tongue touched mine, and he groaned. The contact produced a spark, an energy that radiated through my entire body, pooling between my legs.

King used a knee to spread my legs apart, then settled between them. Not once did he take his lips from mine as he rocked his erection against my core. My body hummed at the friction, and I moaned into his mouth. His hands flew to the back of my neck, pressing me up against him as he kissed me until I was dizzy.

It was an entirely new type of hunger.

With a deep, throaty growl, King abruptly ended the kiss. Sitting back on his knees, he reached down and ran the pad of his thumb across my cheek. He looked down at me as if he were seeing me for the very first time. His expression soft. His lips swollen from our kiss.

My chest heaved as I again tried to catch my breath. Without King lying on top of me to shield me from the cold rain, a chill ran down my body. My teeth began to chatter. His eyes drank me in as they skimmed over my face, then down the rest of my body. I could swear that it felt as if he were actually touching me, not just looking at me.

"Go," King snapped, jumping to his feet like he'd been electrocuted.

"What?" I asked. I somehow managed to get to my knees, still holding up the now wet and heavy sweatpants, the drawstring already pulled as tight as it would go.

"Just fucking go!" he roared, standing up fully.

He took a menacing step toward me. His sudden proximity forced me backwards. I stumbled over a rock and fell back onto my ass.

"That path will take you to the highway," he said, pointing to the ground behind me. I turned and found the path, but when I turned back around, he was gone. The crunch of the brush under his boots faded quickly, swallowed by the sounds of the storm.

I was free.

But I was also truly alone. In the dark. And that clouded over the elation I should have felt.

My chest grew tight. I pressed my hands against my heart to try and physically tame it from leaping out of my body. Faster and faster it beat until I thought it would come to a screeching halt. Again, I couldn't catch my breath.

Panic set in.

My vision blurred. The forest around me spun and spun until the foliage blended together into one big green and brown vortex, like staring up into the eye of a tornado.

I'd felt safer minutes earlier, staring into King's hate-filled eyes.

I tried to get up. I sat up on my knees, but I slipped in the mud and fell forward onto my forearms. Unable to find the courage to try again, I turned onto my side and pressed my cheek into the mud, holding a hand over my exposed ear.

I needed to be invisible. I needed to disappear into the dark, and then just maybe the dark would disappear around me. I hugged my knees to my chest.

Twenty-four hours ago, I thought I would be set up in some biker's bed by now, basking in the comfort of a roof over my head and food in my stomach. I wouldn't have my dignity, but I hadn't had the luxury of dignity since I woke up in the hospital. Instead, I was barefoot and cold in the middle of the woods. And as the moon disappeared behind dark storm clouds, I was enveloped in complete blackness.

I tucked my bare feet as close to my body as I could to keep the chill off my toes. My chattering teeth turned into a full body shake as the rain pummeled me. Each icy drop felt like a pin-prick into my skin.

Why the hell did he kiss me? Why the hell did I let him?

I was mad at myself. For not fighting him off, for liking it.

I'd done a lot of fucked up things in the last few months. Eating out of dumpsters. Sleeping in abandoned cars. But nothing I'd done left me more disgusted with myself then yielding to his kiss.

What was even more fucked up was, that more than anything, I'd hoped at any second the tall grass would rustle and he'd appear out of the brush to rescue me from the dark.

King wasn't the rescuing type, I reminded myself.

He was the killing type.

My body shuddered. Still angry. Still scared. Still really fucking cold.

Still turned on.

In the light of day, it was easy to push things aside with the distraction of survival to keep me busy. But alone with only my own thoughts in the dark, I became more aware that without memories of the past, lessons lived and learned, I was a mere shell of a person.

I was a stranger to myself.

I was an alien, invading the body of a girl I didn't know. I stole it from her, entirely by accident, a byproduct of a tragic event that wiped her from the earth and set me up in her place.

On nights like these, when the panic threatened to consume me, I talked to her out loud.

I know it's weird but in an odd way, I miss you. I know I tell you this all the time, but I'm so sorry. I'm sorry if what I'm doing isn't what you would do. I wish you were here and that I wasn't, because starving on the streets isn't a life I want for you or for me. I am so sorry that I'm failing you.

I hope every day that when I wake up that you will be back. And I'm so sorry about earlier, about trying to sell my body for protection. It was a moment of weakness, but I'm over it now. I can do this on my own. I can protect myself. And I'm sorry about what just happened with King. I don't know how far I was going to take it, but I promise I wasn't going to let him fuck me.

Or fuck you. Fuck us both?

Weirdest fucking threesome ever.

I laughed manically into the mud, accidentally sucking some into my mouth. I coughed and gagged until it dislodged from my throat, spitting onto the ground.

I'll try harder. I promise. I can survive…for you.

chapter
nine

Doe

THE MOMENT THE SUN MADE AN APPEARANCE, I STARTED WALKING.
I made my way to a road with more potholes than asphalt, and for hours and hours I trudged on, covered in dirt that grew tight around my skin as the sun baked it onto my body and it hardened like clay.

Each step through the hot grass lining the side of the road was nothing short of complete agony. They call them *blades* of grass for a reason, as each one felt like a tiny knife against my already bare, bloodied, and battered feet.

I was limping my way to nowhere when I finally came across the first sign of civilization: a one-story apartment complex.

I needed to get to a phone, or a police station, or a church. Anyone who could help me, but I didn't have the energy to look any further and needed a place to sit and regain my wits because my mind was a cloud of confusion, exhaustion, and dehydration.

Why did King let me go?

There was something unsettling about his indecision that nipped at my nerves. I half-expected him to pull up along the side of the road at any second and drag me into the car. Maybe, it was the kiss that changed his mind. He thought he could use me for whatever perversion he had in mind, but when he kissed me, he must have realized he'd only be disappointed. So, he'd let me go.

That had to be it. But why, if he killed Nikki, wasn't I dead as well? Why did he spare me and not her?

Nothing made any fucking sense.

After thinking I was seconds away from death more than once in the past thirty-six hours, freedom was something I never thought I'd have again.

But being back on the streets was a captivity of another sort. Freedom meant you had choices.

I still had none.

I stumbled into the apartment complex. Old and unkempt, the building had about ten units and a dark shaker style roof. Half the shingles had been replaced with mismatched plywood. Knee-high weeds grew through cracks in the concrete walkways.

Unable to take another step, I collapsed against the wall of the breezeway and slid down until my butt hit the sidewalk. Finally sheltered from the blistering sun that still felt as if it were searing into my scalp through the center part in my hair.

I just needed to sit a while, catch my breath, and collect my thoughts.

"You can't stay here, girl. Move along." A husky man appeared, wearing a t-shirt three sizes too small that depicted a unicorn jumping over a rainbow. He stood over me and folded his arms across his chest. "You some kind of deaf, girl? You can't stay here. I can't be having the riff-raff lingering' about." He nudged my thigh with his sneaker like he was trying to rouse a lazy dog. "Move along, now."

"Please. I just need to use your phone. Please?" I begged, my voice dry and scratchy. I didn't even care about the fact that when I called the police they would probably throw me into another group home.

I thought about one thing and one thing only.

I had a murder to report. Nikki may have been a whore and a thief, but she didn't deserve to die for it. Somedays, I didn't think she even liked me all that much, but she was all I had.

If there was such a thing.

The man sighed, clearly annoyed. "What you need it for?" He dug into the party-sized bag of Cheetos he'd been holding. After shoving a handful into his mouth, he sucked his fingers clean of orange powder.

"Please. You have to help me. I'd been kidnapped. I was locked in a room, handcuffed to a bed. I escaped and I spent the night in the woods. I've been walking all day. I'm thirsty and sunburnt and tired, and this is the first place I came across. Please, I have to call the police. My friend, my friend Nikki was murdered by the same man who held me captive."

He shoved another handful of Cheetos in his mouth and wiped his hand across the unicorn. "Oh yeah? Well, you're in luck, I'm the deputy in these parts. Name's Crestor. So, you can report it to me." He lifted the fat of his stomach and pointed to a previously hidden badge attached to his belt. Cheese sprayed from his mouth when he spoke. "And who is it that you're thinking' killed your friend?"

"I don't think he killed her. I know he did. I heard him confess. And I don't know his full name, or even if it's his name at all. I only know what they call him."

"And what would that be?" He leaned up against the wall, focusing on a light bulb in the ceiling that turned off and on every few seconds on its own, completely disinterested in my story.

"They call him King."

His eyes went wide and his fingers loosened around the bag. He dropped the Cheetos to the ground.

Within a second, he'd bent over and grabbed me under my arms, yanking me to my feet. "Wait, what are you doing?" I asked as he shoved me toward the parking lot. My right foot twisted when I stepped on an uneven section of pavement, and I fell forward onto the road, skinning my hands and wrists.

"Go on and get! And don't you ever fucking come back here!" he shouted. With his hands on his head, he spun around and waved his arms in the air in frustration. "I don't need that kind of trouble here. Go, girl! If I see you again, next time it'll be my shot gun escorting you out."

He left me on the road and hustled back to the building, his back fat bouncing up and down as he disappeared behind a door with a window marked OFFICE. He drew the shade the instant he stepped inside.

I stood on shaky legs and wiped gravel from the wounds on my hands onto my t-shirt. The bottoms of my feet stung. My twisted ankle sent sharp pains through my shin with each step. My already bad limp became much more severe.

King apparently had reach. But how far? If I had any chance of seeking help for myself, or for Nikki, I had to get the hell out of Logan's Beach, but I didn't even know if I was going the right way.

My foot dragged behind me as if it were no longer attached to my body, but hanging on, like cans tied to the bumper of a car.

Hours passed, and although I'd been walking the entire time, I don't think I'd gone very far. I could still see the apartment complex in the distance behind me.

Not a single car had passed me all day. My stomach was again protesting its emptiness, twisting and groaning. My face and ears were hot to the touch. The soles of my feet were thick and swollen, thankfully becoming numb to the constant scraping.

I trudged on.

For every inch the sun sank into the horizon, my anxiety increased. A brutally sunny day was again about to be cloaked in the darkness of night.

I came upon an old, abandoned bank with boarded up windows just as thunder rolled in the distance. The sky flashed as lightning jumped from cloud to cloud. I smelled the rain before I felt the first drop splatter on the tip of my nose.

I hobbled toward the covered awning of the drive-through, but I didn't make it. The sky poured itself over me before I could reach shelter. By the time I took cover, I was sopping wet from head to toe, the blacktop underneath me turning brown as the water rinsed off the mud from the night before. I settled against the out of order ATM machine and sat down on the curb, resting my forehead against my knees.

I felt defeated. And somewhere in the back of my mind, I wished for one of the bolts of lightning to jump from the clouds and reach under the awning to strike me dead. Dead was better than unwanted.

Dead had to be better than this.

"Why hello there." A voice said from out of nowhere.

Chills spread from my spine to my neck. Goosebumps broke out on my forearms. I looked up to find a man with a dirty grey beard standing over me. The wrinkles around his eyes spread over to his cheeks. Some of his front teeth were missing, and his chin was covered in red sores.

"You lost or something?" He smelled of rotten milk, his clothes were torn and tattered.

"Or something," I muttered.

"I'm Ed," he said, extending a hand. His fingernails each about an inch long and yellowed.

Realizing I wasn't going to take his hand, he kneeled down to me, and my heart sped. Ed reached out a filthy hand and attempted to run a knuckle down my cheek. I shuddered and pulled away, jumping to my feet. I swayed unsteadily. Spots danced in front of my eyes. I grabbed the ATM on the wall to steady myself.

"Now don't be rude to ole Ed. What's your name?" he asked, licking his lips and adjusting the stained crotch of his once khaki pants.

"Um...nice meeting you, Ed," I said as confidently as I could. "But I gotta go." I tried to sidestep him, but he stepped in front of me, blocking my only exit.

"Why don't you stay here and dry off for a while." His eyes roamed down my body. His toothless smile grew bolder. "Although I like a woman who's all wet." He clucked his tongue against the roof of his mouth.

"Um, no thanks. I'm just waiting for my friend to pick me up," I lied, wishing it were true. I made a move to side-step him again, but this time he grabbed my arm. I tried to shake him loose, but even a child was stronger than me at that point. "Get off me!"

"Now, you listen here. You came into my house. Now, you're going to stay and see how hospitable I can be."

Ed yanked my wrist, turning me around until my back was flush up against him. He held my hands captive in front of me. His cock twitched against my thigh, and I gagged. If I'd had anything in my stomach, it would have come up right there.

I stomped on Ed's booted foot with my bare one, sharp pain exploding in from my foot to my hip, hurting me more than him, but it was just enough to momentarily stun him. I broke free from his grip.

I'd only made it a few steps when I was yanked backwards by my hair, sending me flying onto my back, smashing the back of my head into the concrete. For the second time in twenty-four hours, the wind was knocked out of me. My windpipe wouldn't open. My lungs struggled inside of my body, painfully asking for air. My vision became hazier and hazier.

This was the very reason why I was seeking protection from a biker. At that moment I wished that Bear had just taken me to his place instead of sending me to King.

But then, I remembered my renewed promise to her.

I had to protect her. At all costs.

And I wasn't going down without one hell of a fight.

When Ed tried to drag my legs down and pry them apart, I kicked out wildly until my foot connected with his face. Blood spurted from his nose, and the heel of my foot felt like it was on fire.

"You're gonna pay for that, bitch!" Ed hissed.

Rearing back, he punched me square in the jaw. My head twisted to the side and fell onto the concrete with a thud. My mouth filled with warm coppery liquid.

Ed held something cold and sharp at the base of my throat. "Try to fight me, cunt, and I'll slit your fucking throat," he warned through tight lips.

With an unsteady hand holding the knife, he ripped down my sweats and panties in one forceful yank. Each of my gasps elicited another sting from his knife.

I closed my eyes. This is what happens when you wish for death, right?

Sometimes, wishes come true.

I only hoped that he would kill me when he was done so I didn't have to relive this moment for the rest of my life.

Not even a day had passed since I made my promise to protect her and I'd already failed.

Ed shuffled around with his pants, and I braced myself, coming to terms with the fact that I was going to die under a bank awning in a little town in the middle of nowhere.

As no one.

Then, Ed was gone. His weight suddenly disappeared.

There was a shuffle, then a loud explosion that echoed through my ears. A familiar sound.

I wanted to lift my head to see what was happening, but my neck wouldn't cooperate, and my head felt like it weighed a thousand pounds.

Strong arms reached around my back and under my knees, lifting me effortlessly into the air, cradling me against a hard chest. I tried to fight off whoever it was, but I couldn't manage anything more than a wiggle.

"I've got you," a familiar deep voice murmured into my hair.

King.

"I thought you were letting me go," I said, my thoughts all swimming around each other in my head, smashing into one another.

"I changed my mind." King's muscles barely tensed under my weight. He covered me with a leather jacket and wasn't the least bit strained when he walked out into the rain.

The world around me grew fuzzy. "I thought my life was supposed to flash in front of my eyes?"

"Why would you think that?" he asked. In my weakened state, I didn't know if the concern in his voice was genuine or something I was making up.

"Because that's what happens when you're dying," I answered.

"You're not dying."

"Oh, good. Because I don't have a life to flash in front of my eyes. I thought whatever higher power exists up there was just showing me you instead."

"Why would you see me if you were dying?" he asked. When I didn't answer immediately King shook me and said something about trying to stay awake, but I couldn't listen. I believe what I said next was very similar to, "'Cause you might be all angry and stuff, but you're really pretty to look at." I yawned. "Why did you come back for me?"

I used all the energy I had left to open an eye and glance around King's shoulder. Ed was slumped against the ATM, staring blankly ahead.

A bullet hole between his eyes.

King held me tighter and lowered his mouth to my ear.

"Because you're mine."

chapter
ten

Doe

I AWOKE SUBMERGED IN WARM WATER. EVERY ACHE AND BRUISE AND SORE THROBBED in the healing heat. When I opened my eyes, King was hovering over the edge of the tub, washcloth in hand.

I gasped and sat up quickly, sloshing water over the side and onto the floor. I scooted to the far edge, crossing my arms over my breasts. King forcefully grabbed my wrist and pulled, removing the only protection I had against his gaze. With his other hand, he trailed his calloused fingertips from my collarbone to my breast. When he made it to my nipple, he pinched.

HARD.

I yelped.

"I've already seen them, Pup. No need to hide them from me now." King was shirtless, his ab muscles rippled and his tattoos became animated with his every movement.

"You killed Ed," I blurted out. The events from the night before tumbled over each other into my mind, one horrific detail after another.

"Ed?" King asked, cocking an eyebrow.

"The guy last night," I clarified. "The one you…"

"Killed," King finished. "I didn't realize you two had gotten to know one another." King raised the washcloth. I flinched. "I'm just wiping off the mud."

"You don't sound very remorseful. You seem fully convinced that you have the right to be judge, jury, and executioner," I said.

"A simple 'Thank you, King, for saving my life.' would do," King said. "But what you should know, and what Ed found out, is that if you fuck with me and what's mine then yes, I am the judge. I am the jury. And sometimes, when the situation calls for it, I am the motherfucking executioner." My stomach flipped.

"But why do you give a shit if he hurt me or not?"

"Because you're mine."

"Why do you keep saying that?"

"Because it's true."

"I never agreed to be yours, whatever that means."

"It's not something you need to agree to. This isn't a negotiation. Would you rather I'd let Ed do whatever it is he planned to do to you?"

"No, that's not what I'm saying." Even in the warm water, my skin turned to gooseflesh when I thought of what would have happened if King hadn't saved me.

I would be dead.

Was I upset that Ed was dead? No. It was a him or me situation, and I was glad I'd come out on the other side with my life.

"This is why I needed a biker," I mumbled.

"What was that?" King asked.

"Nothing," I said. Not realizing I'd said that last part out loud.

"No, you said that's why you needed a biker. What the fuck exactly does that mean?"

"For protection!" I snapped. "You don't know what it's like out there on the streets. There is an Ed on every fucking corner just waiting for you to fall asleep or not pay attention or wander into the wrong alleyway. It's not like it was my first choice, but I didn't know what else to do. Nikki said there would be bikers at your party. That if one liked me that he could protect me."

"You came to the party to whore yourself out to a biker?" He sounded angry and disappointed and for some stupid reason, I really hated the idea that I'd somehow disappointed him. Almost as much as I hated the fact that I'd disappointed myself.

Or *her*.

"Yes," I answered honestly. "At least for a little while. But I realize now how stupid that idea was. That's not what I want anymore." I didn't realize how embarrassed I was until I spoke the words out loud.

"At least, it all makes a lot more sense now. Here lean back," King ordered.

I tilted my chin back and he supported my neck with one hand. He grabbed a cup off the floor and scooped up water, slowly pouring it over my hair.

"You killed your mom," I whispered. As nice as the bath was, I was still completely unable to get a hold of my mouth and stop the words before they poured out like water from King's cup.

"Fucking Preppy." King shook his head. "He shouldn't have said anything. It's none of your fucking business," he spat. I'd hit a nerve. "It's none of anyone's fucking business." After a moment or two of silence, his breathing again evened out and the vein in his neck stopped pulsing. He finished rinsing my hair. "You know I was in prison then, yeah?"

"Yeah."

"Do you know how long I was locked up for?"

"Three years," I said, recalling what Preppy had told me.

"Yeah, three years. You know anyone that gets three years for murder?"

I don't know why I didn't think of it before. It didn't make any sense. I shook my head.

"There's a lot more to that story. But, I'm not in a storytelling mood tonight."

"But you killed Nikki," I cursed myself for not being able to keep my trap shut. Much to my surprise, King laughed. An actual laugh as if I told a joke. I didn't think the man was capable.

"No," he countered. "I didn't."

"Yes, you did," I argued. "I heard you tell Preppy you killed her. Why would you deny it?"

"Think about it. Did you actually hear me say that I killed her?"

He was right. I didn't hear him say the actual words.

"I only said she was dead. I'm sorry, Pup, but she is. I found her with a needle in her arm in a shitty motel a town over."

King wiped a wayward tear from under my eye with the pad of his thumb.

"She shot you. Does she really deserve that tear?" He surprised me by sucking it off his thumb.

"She didn't shoot me," I defended. "She was trying to escape. She shot me by accident. She was aiming at you. She was desperate. We both were. Desperate people do desperate things."

It was then I realized that I missed her. As fucked up as our relationship was, she was all I had.

And now she was gone.

"Pup, on purpose or not, the bitch shot you. To be honest, if I'd found her alive and she drew that gun again, she'd be dead now anyway."

"My life seems to be a bunch of questions piled on top of a bunch of questions, and frankly, I'm ready to add some fucking answers into the mix before my brain explodes and leaks out of my ears."

"How...graphic of you."

"I'm serious. Why did you look for me? Why did you even bother bringing me back here?"

"When I let you go, it was a momentary lapse in judgment. The reason why I let you go doesn't matter. The fact is that your friend is dead, and you still owe me. You're my property, and you will be mine until I decide otherwise."

He ran the washcloth down my legs and brushed over the wound on my foot. I cried out, and he scowled. "You're pretty banged up."

"I guess that's what happens when you're left in the woods to rot and then walk miles barefoot in the blazing sun," I spat. I expected him to argue with me, fight with me, but he surprised me.

"I'm sorry about that. As I said, momentary lapse in judgment."

"Did you just apologize to me?"

"No, I said I was sorry about having a momentary lapse in judgment. I didn't say I was sorry to you."

"How exactly am I supposed to pay you?" I asked hesitantly. "We've been through this. I don't have anything to give you," I sighed. "I don't have anything at all."

"In whatever way I want, Pup."

"What if I don't want to be yours?"

King didn't hesitate. "Then, I'll let Preppy have his way with you. He may seem nice, but you'll learn that kid is a sick fuck who will smash your back door in without warning. He likes it when they scream. He likes it when they're passed out. He likes it even better when they say no. Or maybe, I'll loan you out to Bear's crew. I hear Harris and Mono have a fetish for knife play."

There was no humor in his voice.

"But if you cooperate, you'll be mine and mine alone. You'll be under my protection. When I'm tired of you and I feel your debt has been paid, you will be free to go."

"Protection," I repeated. The very thing I'd been looking for. "What happens if you don't get tired of me?"

King chuckled. "Oh, it will happen. Always does. But until then, you'll do what I say. You'll live in my house." His eyes narrowed to the space between my legs. "You'll sleep in my bed."

"You're going to rape me?" My heart hammered in my chest. "Because it's one thing to sell myself. It's another thing entirely to have the decision taken from me. If that's your plan, you can just shove my head under the water and get this over with now."

"You may be weak in body, but it doesn't seem that mouth of yours got the message." Adrenaline sprung to life inside me, coursing through my veins, readying my body for another fight for my life.

I stood up, splashing more water onto the tile floor, my nakedness on full display. I didn't bother to cover myself.

King surprised me by standing up and stepping into the tub, soaking his jeans up to his shins. I held my clenched fists out in front of me like I was going to box him. He laughed and wrapped both arms around my waist, hauling me into his colorful, bare chest.

"You'll find out that I'm a lot of things, but I'm no fucking rapist. Before I fuck you—and I will fuck you, Pup—you'll be begging me for it," he whispered against my neck.

I clenched my thighs together to try and ease the ache he created there. The adrenaline surge I was ready to use for combat changed into something else entirely. I was still ready for him. Only in a completely different way.

Traitorous body.

"But first, you need to heal. Your feet are all sliced up and your ear is bleeding again." King stepped from the tub and lifted me out with him, setting me onto the cold tile my teeth started to chatter. He opened the cabinet under the sink and wrapped me in a soft towel large enough to double as a blanket. "And there are a few other things I need you to tell me."

"Like what?"

"Preppy told me what you'd told him, what happened to you. But how is it that someone like you is missing in the world?"

"Someone like me?"

"There has got to be someone out there who misses these beautiful eyes." He locked his fingers into my wet hair and tilted my head back.

"I tried to find someone who knows me," I said with my teeth still clacking together. King dried me with the towel, treading carefully over my injuries. "The police tried, too, but there was no missing person's report that matched my description. My fingerprints aren't on file anywhere. No paper-trail."

King unbuttoned his jeans and stripped them off, hanging the wet fabric off of the shower rod to dry. All that was left of his clothes were his black boxer briefs, his enormous erection straining against the stretchy fabric. He noticed me looking and made no move to make an excuse for his arousal. He didn't make any move to cover himself. He smiled out of the corner of his mouth, took a few steps toward me. He lifted me up into his arms as if he were cradling a baby and carried me out into his bedroom where he set me on the bed.

The cuffs from the night before still hung from the headboard.

"So that's it? I'm your prisoner? You're just going to keep me cuffed to the bed?"

King shook his head. "No, Pup. You're not my prisoner. I don't think we need these anymore." He gestured to the cuffs. His well-built, highly-tattooed, muscular physique gleamed under the light of the moon shining through the window. My mouth went dry, and I again had to press my thighs together to quell the building ache that was starting to overshadow my other injuries.

He may have been the devil, but his body was sculpted like a god.

I scrambled to form my question. "Then, what am I?" I whispered. My exhaustion beginning to take hold.

"I told you before." King leaned in close stripped the towel away, letting his gaze linger on my body before covering me with the bed sheets. With one knee on the mattress, King leaned over and sucked my bottom lip into his mouth. A tingling sensation started in my belly. He released my lip with a pop. "You're not my prisoner. You're mine."

chapter
eleven

King

GAINST MY BETTER JUDGMENT, I'D BROUGHT HER BACK TO MY HOUSE. I FED her. I bathed her. I put her to bed, and she didn't bother to fight me off when I climbed in beside her and held her close while she cried herself to sleep. She was here against her will and I was one fucked up motherfucker.

Because I'd never been happier.

It was the kiss that fucked everything up. I hadn't meant to kiss her in the woods, but I couldn't ignore the overwhelming urge to take her mouth. At first, I thought it was just a sick part of me that needed to kiss a girl who was struggling underneath me. But then, she opened her mouth to me, and all the sense I'd ever had was lost in that kiss.

Her taste, her tongue, the pull I'd felt toward her when she was first in my bed had exploded into something I couldn't reign in. I lost myself in her for a good minute before I came to my senses. Stopping was the hardest thing I'd ever done even though the idea of taking my revenge out on her body made every part of me turn rock hard.

I wasn't going to go after her. But the entire night I lay awake and stared at the ceiling fan. I didn't even fucking know the girl and I was worried about her. What was she doing? Did she make it out of the woods? Then, I spent hours hoping she went in the right direction, because if she went toward Coral Pines, she wouldn't find any sort of civilization for over ten miles.

I wrestled with the idea of going after her all day. Then, Preppy had filled me in on what she'd told him about not having a memory.

So I did something. Something that made the decision to go after her an easy one. A decision that would forever change the lives of everyone around me.

Some for the good.

Some for the bad.

Some for the dead.

I found out who Doe really was.

chapter
twelve

Doe

A LTHOUGH MY EYES ARE OPEN, THERE IS A DARKNESS SURROUNDING ME THAT IS ABOUT to open the flood gates of my panic. A pair of heavily-lidded chestnut brown eyes loom over me and remind me I'm not alone, and my fear is momentarily suppressed. The look of raw desire reflected in his gaze sends a flush of wetness between my legs. The heat of his naked chest radiates against mine, and I am lost in sensations of skin against skin.

Slowly, he drags his fingers up my thigh, touching every part of my body except the one place burning for his touch, aching and pulsing with a need I'd never known. His touch is soft but nervous, like he doesn't know where to place his hands next. I shift in an effort to send him where I crave his touch the most.

"Ssshhhh," a deep voice whispers into my neck, causing the hair on my arms to stand on end and my stomach to flip flop with anticipation. "Is this where you need me to touch you?"

His hand comes to rest on my breast, rolling my already sensitive nipple between his fingers. I arch my back and groan from deep within my throat.

"No," I say. It comes out as barely a breath. I need him lower. Much lower.

He releases my nipple and a soft hand cups my breast and squeezes lightly. "Is this where you need me?" the voice asks, teasing me with his words as well as his touch.

"No," I moan again, the agonizing torture of waiting for him to make contact is too much to bear.

I kick out my legs impatiently.

"Ssssshhhhh. Behave, and you'll get what you want," the voice whispers, trailing his tongue down the side of my neck at the same time working his hands between my legs. Slowly, two fingers brush over my clit, lingering there without any movement. An almost touch.

His body stills.

I writhe beneath him, seeking the release he is denying me. "Please," I beg.

No answer.

"Please," I say again.

Still no answer.

I look up into the eyes that held the promise of pleasure just a moment before, but they are slowly fading away. I reach for him, but I grasp only the night air. Even though I can still feel the places where he touched me as if he'd burned my skin, I can no longer feel him on me.

Then, he is gone altogether, and I am left alone in the dark.

Before I can panic, what I'd felt on top of me is now behind me, but the feeling isn't quite the same. The person isn't the same. This body is warmer, harder, and much, much larger. The hand rubbing my thigh isn't soft and gentle; it's rough and callused. The erection prodding against my lower back is thick and long, rubbing against the slit in my ass, into my wet folds and back again.

"Please," I beg. Release. There must be some sort of release at the end of all this. I craved it, needed it, and I knew he could give it to me.

These new fingers don't linger, and I almost fall apart when they find the wetness between my legs, spreading it over my clit until I am writhing against the thickness behind me, begging for it with my body, needing to be filled with it until the pure pleasure of it all splits me in two.

Two fingers penetrated me.

My eyes flew open. It was then that I realized I was no longer dreaming. I lay on my side, facing the wall. In a bed.

In King's bed.

WITH KING.

It was his fingers filling me, stretching me. He curled them inside me, and they brushed against a spot that caused me to buck up against him and arch my back. I gasped and tried to tear away when King tucked me under his forearm, wrapping it tightly across my chest, holding me against him.

"I've got you, Pup," he growled, his breath teasing a spot behind my ear, sending shivers down my spine.

I knew I should argue, or at the very least push him away, but I couldn't think. Right or wrong and good or bad escaped me because his fingers started pumping while the pad of his thumb circled my clit, faster and faster until I was panting into the pillow, throwing myself back against his hard body, chasing the release that I craved more than my next breath.

"I've got you," King said again. His voice was strained and thick. I lost myself in a fog of sensation.

"What are you—" I started to ask, but I couldn't form the words because my body clamped down on King's fingers, causing me to gasp.

"I'm going to make you come, Pup. I'm going to make you come real hard," he promised. When it felt like I was reaching the edge, King held me tighter and pressed down on my clit. I hung on, afraid to fall from the heights he'd brought me to.

"It's okay, baby. I want to make you feel good. Don't be afraid to come for me."

With one final stroke of his fingers, I saw stars. Then, I plummeted, crashing down in the most amazing free-fall I never knew existed, off of a place that I never wanted to leave. Screaming into the pillow, fisting it into my hands, my orgasm tore through me from my chest to my toes and back again. My core continued to pulse around King's fingers as I fluttered back down to earth.

"You're gonna fucking kill me, Pup," King groaned. He removed his fingers and then sucked them into his mouth. "Ahhhh fuck."

What the hell had just happened?

King sat up against the headboard. As much as I wanted to move, I was frozen to the mattress. "Something you need to know right now. Next time you're having dreams that make you moan and touch yourself in my bed, I'm not going to be responsible for what happens. That's on you. Because next time, I'm not going to be a nice guy and use my fingers to solve your little problem."

"Who said I needed you to solve anything? I don't remember asking for your help," I snapped. Blood rushed to my cheeks, burning me with embarrassment.

"Shit, anyone within ten miles knew what you wanted, but next time, you're going to wake up with something much larger than my fingers inside that pussy of yours. And when that happens, you're going to come so fucking hard you'll think what you had tonight was nothing more than a fucking hiccup. And I'll remind you that this is my bed. This is where I sleep, and now it's where you sleep. So, tread carefully."

"I..."

"And I don't need you dreaming about some guy while you're sleeping next to me in MY FUCKING BED." The sudden anger lacing his voice confused me.

And pissed me off.

"One, I don't see why, what or who I dream about is ANY of your fucking business, and secondly—" I held up two fingers. "I don't want to sleep in bed with you. It's you who carried me here. And three, how do you know it WASN'T you I was dreaming about?" I'd hoped to take some of the embarrassment off of me, but with every word I spoke, it built and built until I felt everything from my eyelids to my ear lobes burning red hot.

"You weren't dreaming about me," he said confidently, crossing his arms. Suddenly, I was aware of something.

"Did I call out someone's name? Whose name?"

"No, Pup. You didn't call out anyone's name. Although I can't wait until I'm making you call out mine."

"You weren't in my head so there is NO WAY you could know who or what I was dreaming about," I argued, my voice getting louder with each sentence. Disappointed that I'd gotten my hopes up over a name. Angry with myself for enjoying the mind-blowing orgasm he'd given me.

"Pup, do you want to know how it is I knew you weren't dreaming about me when you were about to come in your sleep?"

"Yes," I whispered.

The anger faded from his eyes for a brief moment. He fixed a cocky smile on his perfect lips and rolled over on top of me, forcing me to lie back against the pillows as he caged me in. He lowered his face to mine, his breath cool against my heated skin.

"Cause, baby, if it were me you were dreaming about, you'd been scream-ing a fuck of a lot louder than that," King growled.

"You cocky son of a fucking bitch!" I shouted, but he'd already leapt off the bed and left the room. My shouts reaching no one but the already closed door.

As much as my body responded to him, as great as I knew he could make me feel—and I had no doubt he could fulfill every promise he made about making me come—I had to stay away from him and keep my renewed prom-ise to *her.*

Which was going to be very hard, since I was going to be sleeping in his bed.

The dream I was having before King interrupted me was too real, too vivid. I had an underlying sense that it was more than just a dream. Maybe, if I was lucky, it was a glimpse into my past.

The chestnut brown eyes just might be the key to unlocking the truth about who I really was and what had happened to me.

I went back to sleep that night dreaming that the boy with the chestnut colored eyes came and rescued me, taking me back to a life filled with family and friends, and everything that had happened in the past few days was nothing more than a quickly forgotten nightmare. I dreamed there were really people out there who were sick with worry, who wouldn't rest until they found me.

I ran this scenario through my mind over and over again until I almost believed it.

Almost.

King was smart, calculating, and cunning. Worst of all, he had the power to make my knees both tremble in fear and weak with desire. He was someone I had to stay away from, but according to him, that wasn't about to happen.

I didn't dream about him; he was right about that. Because King wasn't a dream.

He was a nightmare.

chapter
thirteen

Doe

KING NEVER CAME BACK TO BED, AND I WAS RELIEVED. AS MUCH AS I DIDN'T want to be the property of someone who ran hot and cold faster than a faucet, I decided to focus on what was in front of me. Or rather, what was under me.

And over me.

And around me.

And inside me.

A bed. A roof. Walls. Food.

The sun beamed through the windows. I stretched out my arms and legs and took a deep breath. My situation may not be as good as I'd hoped it would be, but it certainly had some perks.

At least, my hands weren't cuffed.

"Rise and Shine!" Preppy shouted, flinging open the door and tossing some clothes on top of my head. "We've got shit to do, and I hate fucking waiting, especially for chicks."

I pulled the clothes away from my face and onto my lap. "Why are you so chipper? Don't you hate me for what I did to you?" I asked, referring to the not so pleasant kick to the nuts that sent him down a flight of steps.

"Nah, I was kind of impressed, actually. Don't get me wrong. It was fucking stupid. You should have seen the look on boss-man's face. He looked like he was about to bust an artery or something. And if Little Preppy and the boys weren't working properly, you would be singing a different tune, but thankfully the boys know how to take a hit. Sometimes, they like it. But they're good, so no foul. Now, let's fucking go!"

"Where are we going?" I pulled the shirt on over my head. Preppy jumped on top of the bed and bounced up and down like a little kid. I couldn't help but react to his infectious enthusiasm.

"Holy shit, she smiles!" Preppy beamed, jumping harder until I had no choice but to get off the bed or end up on my ass on the floor. "It's a nice smile. Doesn't make you look like such a crack-head."

"Excuse me?"

"Crack. Head," Preppy said, enunciating each word like I hadn't heard him.

"I know what you said. Is that really what I look like?" Suddenly self-conscious of my waif-thin frame, crazy bed head and raspberry colored sunburnt skin.

"No?" Preppy asked, smiling awkwardly. I eyed him skeptically and crossed my arms protectively over my chest. He jumped down from the bed and clasped my elbows in his hands. "We can fix that. Don't you worry. We can fatten you up and put some tits and ass on that boney body of yours in no time."

I suddenly remembered what King had said about Preppy, the things he liked to do with women. I tore my elbows from his grip and took a step back. If King wasn't around, would Preppy hurt me? I swallowed hard, and the look on my face must have given away my thoughts.

"Ah, I see. Boss-man threatened you with me, didn't he?"

I nodded reluctantly. "Is it true?"

Preppy took a step toward me and again grabbed me. This time, he yanked me forward until I had to tilt my head up to look him in the eyes.

"Yes, it's true."

He tucked a strand of hair behind my ear. Surprisingly, his touch didn't make me shudder. The man standing in front of me was capable of the same brutality as King and did things that made my skin crawl, but Preppy himself didn't. I felt oddly comfortable in his presence.

"I'm not sorry for it, either. I've had some shit happen to me you don't want to ever fucking know about. I'm not making excuses. Shit is the way it is. I am the way I am. That's all there is to it. That's all there is to me. However, I'm concerned why King felt he had to threaten little ole' you, with crazy ole' me."

"Maybe, he's losing his touch," I whispered.

"Ah, she makes jokes, too." He smiled. "What is it about you?" Cupping my face in his hands, he searched my eyes as if he was looking for an answer my words couldn't provide. He pursed his lips and raised his eyebrows.

"I keep asking myself the very same thing."

Preppy suddenly took a step back and shook his head as if he was clearing his thoughts. He smiled again, this time a full toothed, ear-to-ear smile. I was fast becoming familiar with this being his patented look. He clapped his hands together and rested his chin on the backs of his interlocked fingers.

For some reason, Preppy started talking in a fake Spanish accent. "Boss-man has informed me that you are now our slave, and since he's got important shit to do today, I am to take you with me on my run. So, get fucking dressed, slave, and let's get this fucking show on de road!"

Preppy pointed a finger into the air and snapped his heels together.

"Those should fit," Preppy said, pointing to the clothes on the bed. "Put them on, and let's roll. Time's a motherfucking wasting."

"We're going somewhere? Whose clothes are those? Where are we going?" I asked without stopping to take a breath between questions.

"I know you said you lost your memory, kid, but is your short-term still intact? Because I'd hate to have to repeat myself like this all the fucking time." He spoke mockingly slow. "Yes. *We* are going somewhere. Clothes are on the bed. Get dressed. Meet me in the kitchen in five minutes." He resumed normal conversational speed. "And stop asking so many fucking questions, or it's going to be a long, *looooong* day."

"You're leaving me alone?" I picked up the clothes and held them to my chest. "The other day you had to watch me pee, and today you are just leaving me?"

"You would rather I watch?" Preppy said with a wink. "'Cause we can make that happen, although I'm under strict orders—and I quote—'not to fucking touch you'." He punctuated each of his words while making air quotes with his fingers.

"No, I'm just confused is all. About Nikki. About King. About you. About everything." I bit my lip.

"Me, too, kid. Me, too, but I'm just following boss-man's orders," Preppy said. "But let's just fucking roll with it, and maybe, we can have some fun in the meantime—the boring PG kind—that is, when King isn't around to be the fun police. Now, hurry the fuck up!"

Preppy left the room without closing the door, whistling as he walked down the hall. The whistle faded, along with his footsteps, as he got further and further away, disappearing altogether when he turned and bounced down the stairs.

The clothes Preppy had given me were simple. A pair of jeans, a black tank top, and flat black sandals. The sandals fit like they were made for me. The clothes were all two sizes too big, but soft and comfortable. He'd also left me a new toothbrush and a pair of bright red lace panties with the tag still on it. I spent four out of the five minutes it took me to get dressed on just brushing my teeth.

I'd gone to bed with my hair wet from the bath, so it was a bit crinkly, I did the best I could taming it with a brush I'd found in the bathroom.

I was wearing real clothes and real shoes.

It was heavenly.

The bath had done wonders for my wounds. I found what I needed in the bathroom and changed the bandages on my ear and foot. Then I applied aloe onto my sun burnt skin, which looked a lot less red than it had the day before.

When I found my way downstairs and to the kitchen, I stopped dead in my tracks. In the middle of a small yellow kitchen with avocado green appliances was an old, faded table completely covered from top to legs with carvings and little drawings. People's names, pictures of penises, quotes, and a lot of INSERT NAME was here's. But that wasn't what caught my attention. It was what was in the center of the table that had me drooling.

Pancakes.

Stacks upon stacks of mouthwatering, buttery, perfectly round pancakes.

Preppy stood at the stove with a spatula in hand, flipping pancakes on a griddle pan. He wore a lacy red apron over his red short-sleeved dress shirt and faded jeans. His yellow checkered bow tie peeked over the top. His white sneakers were scuff-free and matched his white suspenders.

But *pancakes*.

Before he was done telling me to help myself, I'd already shoved two so far in my throat I might choke, but I didn't care. They could be fucking poisoned, I didn't care. If I died with a mouthful of pancakes while the poison ate out my insides, it would be a fate I'd surrender to willingly.

Because *pancakes*.

Preppy turned the burner off and flopped another stack down on the plate in the center of the table.

"Slow. Remember?" he reminded me. He poured me some orange juice into a red plastic cup, and I managed to swallow down the pancake that was threatening my life. After that, I made a half-assed attempt to take smaller bites and chew slower.

"So, what exactly are we doing today?" I asked.

"Errands," Preppy answered vaguely. "Business."

"Why can't I just stay here?"

"Oh you can, but I would have to cuff you to the bed again. I'll be a while. So eating, peeing, or anything other than laying there is kind of off the table."

I rolled my shoulder, which was still sore from being tethered to the bed. "Business it is then. What kind of business?"

As with most of my words lately, as soon as they were out, I wished I could suck them back in.

Something you probably shouldn't be asking about, you idiot.

Preppy didn't seem to mind my stupid question, but he didn't answer. "Shut up and finish your food, so we can get out the door this fucking century."

Preppy had a way of talking that was different than anyone else. His demeanor was light, but his words and language were crude.

But then I shut up, and I did what I was told.

Because *pancakes*.

I followed Preppy out to a large garage on the back corner of the property. I moved slow and still limped. Although my feet were much better than they were the previous day, each step was still more painful than the next.

I'd never really seen King and Preppy's house during the daytime. Now, I took a good long look around.

It sat directly on the back bay. The house itself was huge, and so was the property, at least an acre. Parts of it looked like it had been under renovation at one point, but whoever was doing it had given up. Rusted scaffolding lined one entire side of the house. Blue siding sat under plastic at the bottom, covered in dirt. Weeds had grown around it on all sides. Rusted buckets of paint and miscellaneous tools lay, strewn around in the grass. The back of the house was partially painted a dove gray. THE KING OF THE CAUSEWAY was written in graffiti onto a high peak of the house with black spray paint. It looked as if someone had tried to paint over it at some point, but the bold lettering was still clearly visible through the thin attempt.

"Are you my babysitter now?" I asked as we rounded the house.

"I guess I am," Preppy said. "I've done a lot of shit for King, but this is kind of new for me. I've never taken anyone on a run before. But he's also never taken in a stray either."

"Stray?"

"Well, you're kind of like a stray dog, without the mange. Cute, but too skinny, and kinds of scraggly."

"Okay, I guess, but I wasn't taken in. I'm here against my will," I corrected.

"When King saved you from that bum the other night, was that against your will?"

"No, that guy was going to kill me."

"Okay. So here is another question: you got somewhere else to be?"

I shook my head.

"See? He took you in. Just like a stray."

That was the first time I considered being there as anything other than a violation of my free will, and Preppy made me see that.

"I mean, yeah, he saved me," I conceded. "But on the other hand, he also expects me to pay off a debt that isn't mine by bending to his psychotic will."

"There are two sides to every argument. Two ways to be wrong. Two ways to be right," he sang as we passed the fire pit in the back yard. It wasn't just a hole in the ground as I'd previously thought, but a large brick circle built a few feet off the ground. Beyond the pit, at the end of the huge yard, was a wooden dock with mangroves threatening to swallow it on either side. From the dock was the mirror calm waters of the bay surrounded by nothing but nature.

No other houses. No other docks.

A bird took off from a nearby tree, shaking the branches. It hovered just inches above the glassy water. A small black snake dangled from its beak.

This place was as confusing as King. Hard edges, unfinished and unrefined, yet mysterious and beautiful in its own way.

A tattered frat house in some ways and a complete paradise in others.

"Who else lives here?" I asked as we entered a side door to the detached garage. Tarps at different stages of fading covered rows of what I assumed were cars and bikes. They hung thick with dust, like everything was wrapped a dirty fog. Specks of debris came alive in the one ray of sun that invaded the otherwise dark garage, through the corner of a broken window.

"It's just the two of us in the main house," Preppy said, lifting the tarp off of a shiny black sedan that looked like something right out of a movie from the fifties. "But Bear keeps an apartment here in the garage. He crashes here when he doesn't feel like being at the clubhouse, which is a lot lately." He gestured to the door at the far end of the wall that was covered from top to bottom with random bumper stickers.

Preppy started the car then ran to open the garage door. He drove the car out of the garage and put it in park so he could repeat the garage door routine except this time he closed it.

He rolled us down the driveway at an extremely slow pace. "Don't want to kick mud up onto Busty Betty," Preppy informed me, lightly smacking the steering wheel.

"You named your car?"

"Um...yeah, of course. Everything important should have a name."

"Isn't that the truth," I said, no longer referring to the car.

"Oh come on. You are important. And you do have a name. We just don't know it yet. Maybe, your name totally sucks. Like it could be Petunia Peoplebeater or something. You should be grateful that you are possibly avoiding a total name tragedy," Preppy joked.

"I guess Doe is better than Petunia Peoplebeater," I agreed with a laugh.

"Damn right it is." Preppy accelerated once we reached the end of the driveway and turned onto the road.

The only town I'd been to before Logan's Beach was Harper's Ridge. Along with being a much more populated area further inland, it also held the dubious distinction of being where I had first woken up in that alley. Where Nikki had first befriended me, if you could call it that.

Fucking Nikki.

Something tugged at me from deep inside when I thought about her. A part of me wanted to mourn her loss like I'd known her all my life, instead of a few weeks. A piece of me wanted to cry for her, but I shook those thoughts away because she didn't deserve my tears. She'd abandoned me.

The bitch *shot* me.

Preppy gave me a tour as he drove. When we crossed over a steep bridge, I learned that it was 'The Causeway' referred to by the graffiti on the side of the house.

I found myself sticking my head out the window like a dog. When I opened my mouth, I could taste the salty air on my tongue.

I could be back on the street at any minute, so I decided to enjoy the time I had free of the burden of my immediate survival.

Our first stop was at a tiny well-kept home with white siding. Preppy put the car in park. "Stay here," he ordered, before getting out and slamming the door.

I leaned back in the seat, preparing to wait for him when he startled me by suddenly appearing at my window.

"I want to be your friend, kid," he told me. "I feel real fucking sorry for what you've been through. I know what it's like to go through shit and end up on the other side of it. I'm a nice guy, for the most part. But just because I'm nice doesn't mean you should take advantage. You did that once, and I let that shit go. I just hope you're not fucking stupid enough to do it again. So, this shouldn't need to be said, but I feel like I need to say it anyway. Don't go anywhere, okay? Don't try and run away. 'Cause it doesn't matter that you're my friend. I'll slit your fucking throat and leave you to rot somewhere no one would ever find you, mmmmkay?"

He tapped the tip of my nose and jogged up the driveway. Leaving me stunned in the passenger seat.

The front door partially opened as Preppy stepped up onto the porch, like the person on the other side had been waiting for him. Preppy shuffled sideways and disappeared into the house.

I sat back against the cushy leather seat. Thankfully, he'd left the car running and the A/C blasting. Although there was a breeze on top of the causeway, here on flat land the air was stagnant, the humidity so thick I could see it rising from the grass.

I rolled my jeans up to above the knee in order to keep cool.

Preppy's warning, although freaky as shit, wasn't necessary. There was nowhere for me to go.

I'll protect you, King had said.

And sometime over Preppy's pancakes, I'd resolved to stay. King said he wouldn't force himself on me, so all I had to do was enjoy the free room and board and not give into King.

You're going to beg for it.

Yeah, right. He could keep on believing that while I kept on eating pancakes.

It was forty-five minutes before the front door opened. An older woman walked out onto the porch with Preppy and brought him in for an extended hug. She held his face in her hands and spoke to him intimately, her forehead almost touching his. Preppy gave her a kiss on the cheek and waved to her as he got back in the car.

"You okay?" he asked, turning the car back onto the road.

"Yeah. Why? Are you surprised I'm still here?"

"Nah, but there is just no cloud cover today. The sun is fucking BRUTAL even with the A/C on high, and that took a lot longer than usual. Gladys, she's a talker." He gestured to my rolled-up jeans. "But it looks like you worked it out."

"I'm fine. Is Gladys your grandmother?" I asked.

"Not exactly," Preppy said with a devious grin on his face. "She's business."

"Business? What kind of business do you have that includes spending forty-five minutes in an older woman's home?"

Then, it hit me. Preppy must have seen the recognition cross my face.

"What?" he asked.

"Did you have sex with her?"

"Oh my god, you think I'm a hooker!" Preppy pounded his fist against the steering wheel. He pulled over to the side of the road and wiped the tears from his eyes as he laughed himself into an uncontrollable fit.

"It's not *that* funny," I muttered, crossing my arms over my chest.

"Yes, yes it is, kid. What exactly did King tell you about me? Did somehow mention I got a thing for old ladies? Because if he did, I'm gonna kick his fucking ass, cause it ain't true."

"No, he didn't say that, but you were in there for a while, and she seemed to like you. A lot. If she wasn't your grandmother, then I just thought…"

"Go ahead and say it. You thought I was a hooker, pleasuring her with my man meat and getting paid for it." He turned toward me and leaned back against the driver's side door.

"Well, yeah, but now that you say it that way, it sounds ridiculous."

"That's because it *is* ridiculous," Preppy said, plucking a pack of cigarettes from the center console. He cranked down his window and lit one, turning his head from me to blow the smoke outside the car. He put the car back in drive and pulled onto the road. "I think I'll like being your babysitter after all."

I felt my face redden, "You don't have to make fun of me. I may not have much of a memory, but I do have feelings, so can we please just pretend like this never happened?"

"Yes ma'am, I'll forget all about it," Preppy said, although the amused look on his face said that was never going to happen. Preppy pulled up in front of another house that looked almost identical to the first one, except this one was blue instead of white. "I'll tell you what, kid. Why don't you come inside and see for yourself what it is that I do?"

"No, thank you. I'll just stay here and melt into the seat," I huffed, sounding very much like the brat I was being.

"Nope. My reputation is on the line here. You're coming in," Preppy said,

474 | T.M. FRAZIER

turning the engine off. With that, the A/C let out a hiss as it expressed the last bit of cold air through the vents.

"I thought you were going to forget all about it."

"Oh, I totally lied," he said, rounding the car and opening my door. "After you my dear."

I walked to the front door with Preppy following close behind. He rang the bell, and another woman around the same age as the one before opened it and waved us inside.

"Arlene, this is Doe. She's a friend. Okay if she comes in? Gets awful hot waitin' in the car." Preppy's slight southern accent was suddenly a full out drawl.

"Why, of course my dear. On a day like today, nobody should be made to sit in the car. Shame on you, Samuel, if you've already made her wait for you." She playfully swatted his shoulder as she stepped aside and shuffled us into her living room. "Sit, sit. I have tea all ready. Let me just grab another setting."

Preppy sat on an overstuffed couched draped with lace doilies and motioned for me to sit next to him. A silver tea set that looked as if it had just been recently polished sat on the glass coffee table. Next to it was a three-tiered serving tray filled with cookies and crackers.

"Help yourself, dear," Arlene said, coming back into the room with another saucer and plate set. She handed it to me and filled my cup. I looked over at Preppy who was stuffing cookies into his mouth at an alarming rate.

"Arlene makes the best cookies," he said through a mouthful of food. Crumbs shot out of his mouth.

Arlene put a cookie on my plate, and I took a small bite. It was warm and soft and the chocolate melted on my tongue. Now, I saw why Preppy was shoveling them. I finished the rest in one bite and tried not to lunge for the remaining ones before he could get to them. Instead, I sat back and crossed my legs, sipping my tea while secretly hoping Preppy would choke and die so that I could finish them off.

It was a bit dramatic, but the cookies were that good.

"See, Samuel. This one has manners. You might learn a thing or two from her," Arlene said over the brim of her teacup. "So, is this your new lady?"

"No ma'am, just a friend who's helping out today." I noticed that when Preppy spoke to Arlene he didn't swear.

"That's wonderful, dear. Friends are fantastic. Well, just the other day in bridge club…" Arlene went off on a tangent about friends that began with her bridge club, and lost me somewhere around the time when she abruptly veered off into talking about being a nurse in the war. Which war I wasn't quite sure. I smiled politely and nodded while Preppy inhaled the treats she'd set out for him.

He looked ridiculous in her living room. His tattoos and suspenders stood out amongst the lace and tea cozies.

Okay, so he wasn't a hooker, but maybe Preppy was some sort of granny nanny? Maybe, like a rent-a-friend?

I thought when he'd said I would be helping him on his errands for the day that we would be going to a bunch of dark alleys and seedy places where he would slyly exchange drugs for money with a carefully choreographed handshake.

I certainly didn't expect to be smack dab in the living room of a house that could belong to anyone's grandma.

"Oh, I don't mean to keep you. I know you have other stops. Janine just phoned before you got here, and I know she is looking forward to your visit as well. She made you a cherry pie," Arlene said.

"You ladies are going to make me fat." Preppy leaned back and patted his flat stomach.

Arlene stood up. "Samuel, you do what you need to do. I'll be out in the garden. Come say good-bye before you leave." Arlene set down her teacup, picked up a wide brimmed hat and a pair of gardening gloves, and disappeared through the front door.

"Let's do the damn thing," Preppy said. He stood and walked down the hall, pausing at a door furthest down the small hallway. "Are you coming or do you think this is where I keep all my old lady bondage gear? Because I'm not wearing the ball-gag again, totally hurts my jaw."

"Ha ha very funny." At this point, there could be a three-ring circus behind that door, and I wouldn't have been surprised. "We've already established that you're not getting paid to be a man-whore."

"Nope. Just a man-whore for fun."

"So enlighten me. Why exactly are we here?"

"We're gardening." Preppy opened the door and stepped aside, allowing me to enter first. What I came face to face with was far more surprising than a three-ring circus. Rows upon rows of leafy green plants filled the small space. High tech machinery lined the walls. A ventilation system hung from the ceiling. A mister chirped out a puff of vapor every few seconds. Preppy pushed his way past me and set his backpack down on the floor. He opened it and took out some tools. Walking through the rows of plants he inspected each one. Occasionally he used magnifying glass to closely inspect the leaves.

"You're growing pot?"

"BINGO."

"In an old lady's house, you're growing pot. Why?"

"If you had to guess what it was I was doing here would this have ever entered your mind as a possibility?"

"No."

"That's why."

"So Gladys, too?"

"And several others around town. We pay their mortgages or other bills, or just give them cash if that's what they want, and in return they let us use a room in their house to grow our plants."

"So, you aren't a granny nanny?"

"Was that your second guess? Well, I suppose that's better than hooker, but no, I'm not a fucking granny nanny. Although I do make it a point to be friendly with all of our greenhouse contributors. Keeps them happy. Keeps them wanting to do business with us. Keeps the law off our backs."

"I think I liked it better when I thought you were a hooker."

Preppy opened his arms wide and looked around the room with pride. "Kid, welcome to my brain-child. Welcome to Granny Growhouse."

"So, that's what you call your operation? Granny Growhouse?" We were back in the car after another three stops, and Preppy just announced that Betty had been our last stop for the day.

"That's what I call it. King hates the name, but he hasn't been back long enough to meet all the ladies and get a feel for it. He'll come around."

"You did this while King was in prison?"

"Yeah, kept getting fucked over by our main supplier who only wanted to deal with King, so I phased them out and started Granny Growhouse. It was how we earned while the big man was away."

"Have you thought of getting a job?"

"What would you call this?" he asked.

"No, like a real job."

"Fuck no. Never had a real job a day in my life. Don't plan on it either. Fuck the man."

"I don't know if you are completely odd or oddly brilliant."

"I can't decide if you are always this blunt or just have a bad case of can't-shut-the-fuck-ups," he countered.

"It's an always kind of thing," I said honestly.

"King sort of has a real job with the tattooing. It's how he stays under the radar. But he loves it, too. You should see some of his art. It's fucking amazing. He's been doing it since we were kids, using me as his human test dummy."

It wasn't until we arrived back at the house, car parked in the garage that I began to dread the reality that awaited me.

All six foot three of him.

Preppy saw me staring up at the house. "I know he's a little rough on the surface, but he's the best guy I've ever met."

"Oh yeah? You must not know a lot of people."

"She's got jokes!" Preppy said as he pulled down the garage door. "But seriously, he's not all bad."

We started to walk toward the house when a large shadow passed over the far window on the second floor, sending shivers down my spine. "You should probably tell him that."

chapter
fourteen

Doe

PREPPY MADE DINNER, A DELICIOUS PASTA WITH SAUSAGE DISH. I THINK THE OLD ladies were starting to rub off on him because we ate our meals on the living room recliners off of folding TV trays.

After dinner, Preppy disappeared into his room and since I was a glutton for punishment, I went upstairs to look for King. Or maybe, I just wanted to find him before he found me. It wasn't exactly the upper hand, but it was something.

A buzzing sound caught my attention. It was coming from the same room where I'd walked in on King with a girl.

The door was partially open. Inside was a girl with long, straight red hair straddling a low-backed chair. King sat behind her, but it was nothing like the scene from last time. King was perched on a stool, wearing black gloves. He held a buzzing tattoo gun that every so often, he would dip into a small plastic container before continuing on with his work.

A man with sandy-blonde hair that fell to his chin and bright blue eyes sat in the corner, reading a GUNS AND AMMO magazine. The redhead's eyes were closed, and King lightly tapped his foot to the Lynyrd Skynyrd song playing over the speakers.

Not knowing how King would feel about me watching him work, I turned to leave, but he stopped me. "Pup, I need more paper towels."

I turned back around. The blonde's eyes were on me immediately. The red head took out her ear buds, but King hadn't looked up.

"Me?" I asked, unsure if King was talking to me or if he called everyone *Pup*.

"Yes, you. Unless I'm calling Jake *pup* now, and something tells me he wouldn't like it all that much."

The man in the corner stared at me straight-faced with no readable emotion. The girl offered me a knowing look before putting her ear buds back in and closing her eyes.

"On the counter," King added impatiently.

I looked over to the corner of the room and spied the roll of paper towels. I grabbed them and walked over to King, setting them on the small table next to him. I was about to walk back out of the room when he spoke again.

"Stay," he ordered. Unfolding a piece of towel, he sprayed the girl's back with the liquid from a plastic water bottle and then wiped at the tattoo until he seemed satisfied. "I'm done here." He wiped something from a jar onto her back then taped the edges of the plastic with gauze tape. King tapped on the girl's shoulders and she again removed her ear buds. "You can take the plastic off tomorrow. Keep it clean."

"Always do," she said.

I hadn't seen Jake stand up, but suddenly, he was next to the redhead, helping her up off the chair.

"My feet always fall asleep when I'm getting tattooed," she explained to me. She leaned forward onto the blond man for a few moments until she was able to stand up on her own.

I got a brief glimpse of the new ink on her back. It was a tree, a delicate yet bold orange tree at sunset. The leaves spelled out *Georgia* through the middle. The tattoo looked as if it were in motion, like oranges were falling from the branches.

It was heart-breakingly beautiful.

They both wore wedding bands, so I assumed Jake was her husband. When he saw me staring at her new artwork, he reached behind her and released the clip that held up her shirt, rearranging it until she was covered.

"What do I owe you, brother?" he asked King.

"A favor," King said. "Keep your phone on."

"Done." Jake held his wife close as they made their way to the door.

When they passed me, she turned to me. "Hi I'm Ab—"

"We were just leaving," her husband interrupted, looking down at her as if to remind her of something she'd forgotten.

She nodded, and then flashed me a small smile before they left the room. I'd only been around them for ten minutes, but the guy seemed to be two different people. He sent out vibes of being antisocial and an asshole, but he looked at her like she was his most prized possession. But he didn't own her. That much was obvious.

She owned *him*.

"Who was that?" I asked. I watched from the window as the couple climbed onto a shiny black motorcycle. Her husband helped her with her helmet before they rode off down the drive, disappearing under the trees.

"If they wanted you to know, they would've told you."

"They're in love."

"I sure as shit hope so. They're married. Got a kid, too."

King took off his gloves and tossed them into a stainless-steel bin beside his worktable. He stood and joined me at the window. I could feel the heat from his body radiating onto my back. He leaned over me, his cheek brushing up against my temple. I closed my eyes and tried not to allow his nearness to affect me.

I'm stronger than this.

"There are plenty of married people in the world, but it doesn't mean all of them are in love. Not like that, anyway."

"No," King agreed. "It doesn't." He stepped away, leaving nothing but cold air in his place. I let out a breath I didn't know I was holding.

"Do you want me to leave?" I asked, turning from the window. King was sitting on the couch with his phone in his hands.

"No, I have a lot of people coming tonight. You can help me."

"You're really talented," I offered.

"You don't have to say that," King said, tapping away at the screen.

"I'm not trying to be nice. It's true. Her tattoo was seriously amazing."

"Hhmpf," he grunted, not looking up from his phone.

"You know, it's customary to say thank you when someone compliments you."

"Thanks for the heads up."

A car door slammed below, and two girls about my age giggled as they approached the door. The bell rang.

"Bring them up," he ordered.

My job over the next several hours consisted of shuffling the music when King needed a change of pace, running downstairs to get him Red Bulls, and sitting around doing nothing. At one point, I stood up, told King that I was just taking up space, and that I should get out of his way. He glared at me and nodded back to the couch.

"Why do you do this when you do…other things?" I asked him between clients while I was washing out paint containers in the small sink. "And why don't you have a real shop instead of doing this out of your house?"

"You ask a lot of fucking questions," King pointed out.

"Two."

"What?"

"You said I ask a lot of questions. I only asked two."

King folded his arms over his chest, accentuating his toned biceps. "If you must know, I do this because I've always done it. Art was the only class I liked as a kid. And I do this in my house because the places around here that are any sort of decent are on the other side of the causeway, and the rent wouldn't make the business worth having. Happy?"

"So you do this because art was the only class you were good at in school?"

"More fucking questions," King sighed. "And you don't listen. I did well in school. Very well, actually. I said art was the only class I liked, not the only class I was good at."

"Oh," I said, feeling stupid that I'd jumped to that conclusion. "I'm sorry. I just thought…"

"I'm a bad guy, Pup, not a dumb guy."

"I didn't say you were dumb."

"Look in that drawer over there." He pointed at a tool box. I opened the drawer. In it was a framed degree from the University of South Florida. Under it was a gun.

"Why do you keep this in here? Why don't you hang it up?"

"Because I earned the degree online."

"That's not a big…"

"While in prison," King interrupted. "And I'm glad I did it. I like having it, but putting it on the wall would mean I was proud of it. My feelings are a lot more mixed than that. Besides, Grace says you should always have a drawer that reminds you that who you are and what you do aren't always the same thing."

"Who's Grace?"

"You'll find out."

"Well, why don't you just start your own business?"

King laughed.

"What's so funny?"

"You are, Pup."

"Why is that?"

"Because you just asked me why I didn't start my own business."

"And?"

"And, it's funny, because…" King gestured to the gun. His face went serious. "I did."

A knock at the door interrupted us. I quickly returned the frame to the drawer and shut it just as Preppy let in King's next client.

A woman, older than me, strutted through the door wearing a tight tube top and shorts so short the bottom of her ass cheeks hung out. She set herself up on the table like she owned the place, popping her gum as she explained to King, in detail, the Orchid tattoo she wanted on her left ass cheek.

King told me what he needed set up, and I started gathering his supplies.

"Who's she?" the girl asked, casting me a sideways glare.

"She's none of your business."

"Can't she step out? I'm really shy," she whined, even as she pushed her shorts off in a suggestive manner. Leaving on her heels she crawled onto the table and stuck her thong-clad ass into the air.

"No, she can't," King said. Grabbing a marker, he freehanded the outline of an orchid onto her butt.

The girl made a pouting noise but didn't push the issue. After an hour, she asked if I could go get her something to drink. King nodded to me, and I went downstairs to grab beers from the fridge.

When I came back up, I paused at the door.

"Come on, baby. You don't remember me? You should. Your work is right here." The girl turned around and sat up on her elbows, spreading her legs, she revealed tattooed butterfly wings on both sides of her inner thighs.

"I remember the work. I don't remember you," King said stiffly. "Do you want me to finish this fucking tattoo or not?"

"Yes, but I want your big cock first," she cooed.

"That's not gonna fucking happen."

"Is it because of that ugly skinny bitch? She doesn't even have any fucking tits!"

There was a commotion, and before I could figure out what exactly was going on, King had thrown the girl's shorts out into the hallway and was pushing her out the door by her elbow.

"You can get that shit finished by someone else. We're fucking done here."

She grabbed her shorts off the floor and stomped past me. "Fucking ugly bitch. Fucking asshole," she muttered as she practically tripped in her rush to get to the stairs.

King stood in the doorway. "And if I hear you ever talk shit about her again, I'll find you and take that butterfly tattoo back."

"Oh yeah?" she shouted, stopping on the landing. "How the fuck are you going to do that?"

King was in the doorway one second and an inch from her face the next. "I'll tell you how," he seethed. "I'm going to find you, and then I'm going to take my time carving those fucking butterfly wings from that nasty pussy of yours with my knife. Sleep on that before you decide to open that good for nothing dick-sucker of yours again."

Her eyes went wide with fear. She couldn't move fast enough as she rushed out of the house, slamming the door behind her. The gravel spun under the tires of her car as she sped down the driveway.

"Clean up," King ordered. He grabbed one of the beers from my arms as he passed me in the hallway and went back into his studio. I stood with my mouth open for a full minute before following him.

"What the hell was that?" I asked, putting the rest of the drinks into the cooler by the door.

"It was nothing. Clean up. We aren't done yet." King chugged the beer, crushed the can in his hands and tossed it into the trash bin.

The clock above the door read three am.

The next client was a man named Neil who King had been working on a full sleeve for before he went to prison. Neil had waited three years for King to be released so he could finish it. He said he just didn't trust anyone else to do it right.

I sat on the leather couch and watched King as he scrunched his face up in concentration. How could someone so talented also be so menacing?

You already know how talented his hands are.

I bit my lip and remembered the way his fingers felt inside me. My face flushed.

"I can feel you staring at me," King said, snapping me out of my day-dream. Neil had a huge set of red headphones on with his eyes closed. He was either engrossed in the music or fast asleep.

"I'm kind of bored," I admitted, embarrassed I'd been caught staring.

King stood and removed a glove. He opened another drawer on the tool-box and removed something, tossing it over to me. A sketchbook landed next to me on the couch, followed by a box of colored pencils.

"Maybe, this will help you stop fucking fidgeting," he said. "It always helped me."

Then, he turned up the volume on the iPod docking station before pick-ing up his tattoo gun and diving back into his work.

I opened the sketchbook, which wasn't blank. The first few sketches were variations of the orange tree tattoo I'd seen King tattoo on the redhead earlier. Each one better than the next until I got to the one he used as a template for her tattoo.

Several pages of stunning artwork later, a beautiful dragon, a skull made completely of flowers, and a pin-up girl dressed as a nurse, and I was finally at a blank page. Doodling, I quickly found, was a much better way to pass the time than wondering about the man who made my head spin, and other parts of me throb.

I drew happy faces and stick figures at first. But then I started shading and one of the stick figures started to look like a person. I wasn't actually drawing. It felt more like I could already see the completed design in my mind and was just filling in what was already on the page.

When I finished, I was staring into the chestnut eyes from my dream. I looked up at King, who was still engrossed in his work. I quietly tore the page from the book and folded it up, shoving it deep between the cushions of the couch. Part of me was hiding it so I could come back to it later and maybe add to it. Another part of me wanted to keep this one thing that I knew was some-how connected to my past to myself.

I then decided to sketch the bird I saw earlier flying over the water. I visu-alized it just as I had with the eyes I'd just drawn. Before I knew it, my pencil was flying over the page. I wasn't just drawing. I was shading, smudging, and contouring.

When I was done, it wasn't exactly the bird I'd seen earlier, but a more exotic version of it. Dark. Fierce. Its feathers were ruffled wildly, and the snake dangling from his beak had its mouth open with its fangs exposed. I created smoke billowing out of the small nostrils on the bird's beak, as if he could breathe fire. But then I decided that he looked too harsh, too intimidating, so I gave the bird a broken wing, and in the reflection of his eye, I drew the snake before he'd killed it, swallowing a mouse. The final product was both brilliant beauty and vulnerability. Tears formed in my eyes, and I wiped them away before they could spill onto my cheek.

I can draw.

Not only could I draw, but I could draw well. It came as naturally as breathing.

The second thing connecting me to *her.*

When I put the book down, I looked up, and King's client was gone. King sat on his stool alone, watching me. "You were in the zone," he said. "You looked so fucking cute sitting there concentrating."

I swallowed hard, "I…uuuhhh…got caught up."

His words took me by surprise. I visualized stalking over to him and climbing onto his lap. His big strong hands coming around my back and resting underneath my shirt on my bare skin. I thought about what it would be like to let him do more than what he'd done before.

What would it be like if he used more than his fingers?

I shuddered.

"Bring it here," King said, holding out his hand, snapping me out of my own imagination where I was naked and writhing underneath him.

"No, you don't want to see it. I was just messing around. I'll just put it back in the drawer and clean up now." I walked over to the sink with the book under my arm. King reached out and snatched it away from me, flipping the pages in search of my sketch.

"Holy Go-go-Gadget arms," I quipped. I'd clearly underestimated King's reach.

"How do you know that?" he asked.

"What do you mean? How do I know what?" I asked.

"The 'Go-go gadget' thing. That's a reference to a cartoon. Have you ever even seen it?"

"Um…I think so. It's this guy who wears a trench coat and has a billion little gadgets all over the place that usually don't work the way he wants them to."

"I know who it is. What I want to know is have you watched it since you lost your memory?"

"No, I haven't watched any TV until earlier tonight when Preppy put on something called American Ninja Warrior." I stepped back and leaned against the counter. "What are you trying to get at? I thought you believed me."

"That's not it. I'm just trying to figure it out. Help me understand." King leaned forward and rested his elbows on his knees. "If you haven't watched it, then it's something that carries over from before. How exactly does that work?"

"I'm not really sure. When I was living in the group home, I saw a psychologist or a psychiatrist or one of those. He told me that memory loss works differently for everyone. For me, it wiped out all personal information. Names, faces, memories. But I can still walk and talk, so I retained all my functions. I also know facts. Like, I know who the president is, and I can sing to you the jingle for Harry's House of Falafel's commercial. I just don't know HOW I know those things."

King nodded. I bit my lip.

"You know, you're the only person besides the psychologist guy who's even asked me about it," I added.

King turned a page in the book and found my sketch. He studied it for several minutes. Time seemed to tick by slower and slower. I grew restless wondering what he thought of it. He was probably trying to figure out how to tell me it was complete crap. But then again I didn't take him for someone who would go out of his way in order to avoid offending anyone.

So, what the hell was he staring at for so long?

And why the hell did I need his approval so badly?

"Are you done for the night?" I asked, trying to draw his attention away from the sketch. If he hated it, I'd rather just not talk about it at all. He lifted his eyes from my sketch just long enough to give my body a slow once over, like he was looking at me for the very first time. His gaze ignited my skin as if he'd actually touched me.

"Am I done?" he repeated my question. King ran the underside of his tongue across his bottom lip, leaving a sheen where he'd made it wet. "I'm not sure. I'm thinking I could just be getting started."

Holy Shit.

The familiar redness burned its way up my neck and my ears grew hot.

The clock read 4:45am, and although I should have been tired due to the time, I was more alert than ever. The caffeine and sugar from the four Red Bulls I'd drunk felt like it could keep me awake for days, but I needed to get away from King because I felt myself starting to forget all the reasons why letting him strip me down and have his way with me would be a bad idea.

"What does that mean, exactly?"

"It means that I'm done with clients. But it also means that I'm not done with *you*." King grabbed my wrist and dragged me onto his lap, the very place I'd just fantasized about being.

I gasped.

The hard muscles of his thighs rippled under mine. His smell—a light mixture of soap and sweat—was intoxicating. He fisted a handful of my hair and yanked my head sideways, exposing my neck to him. He breathed me in, running his nose along my neck, followed by a long leisurely lick from my collarbone to the sensitive spot on the back of my ear. I moaned, and he chuckled. I could feel it vibrate through his body and into mine. "Oh, Pup. How much fun this is going to be."

Just like that, he released my hair and pushed me off his lap. My shaky knees almost gave way, and I had to hold onto the counter to avoid falling forward onto the floor.

"We've got one more," King said.

"I thought you just said no more clients tonight," I said, breathlessly.

King proceeded to set up three small containers of black ink. "Here." He handed me a thin-tipped black marker.

"What do you want me to do with this?" I asked.

"I want you to draw your sketch again. The same one. Hold it up for reference."

"Draw it on what?"

"On the back of my hand, it's a much smaller canvas than your sketch so you'll have to downsize a bit, but it's one of the few spaces of blank canvas I have left.

"Why?"

"Why do you always ask so many fucking questions?"

"Don't you have a machine that does this? You can copy this picture and just stick it on there if that's what you really want."

King sighed with frustration. "Yes, I do. But it's not the point. I want you to draw it on me. I want you to put that pen to my skin and recreate your sketch. I don't care if it's crooked. I don't care if it's not perfect, just fucking draw it!" he shouted, standing up. He took a few steps toward me until I was backed up against the counter, clutching the sketch book to my chest. "Please?"

A 'please' from the man who didn't say 'please'.

"Okay," I agreed. "But why?"

"Because I looked over at you while you were drawing this, and you looked all cute, biting your lip, your face flushed, the back of the pencil pressed against those pink lips. Then, when you showed me what you drew, I saw it right away."

"Saw what?"

"Me. The bird. You drew me." I opened my mouth to argue that it was just a bird, but I couldn't. He was right.

Dark and dangerous.

Hard but beautiful, taking what he wanted from the world.

It *was* him.

King propped the sketchbook on the table so I could reference my drawing. I did the best I could to create a smaller version of it onto the back of his hand. I worked even harder trying to ignore the electricity humming between us. King never took his eyes off of me.

It took me twice as long to complete than the sketch, but when I was finally done, I put the marker down and sat back.

"Okay?" I asked.

King held his hand up and examined my work. "It will work," he confirmed. "Now, go get me a coffee."

"No Red Bull?" I asked, standing up from the table.

"It's after 5am. After 5am calls for coffee."

"Okay, coffee then," I said, making my way down to the kitchen. By the time I figured out the single cup coffee machine thing they had—the only modern appliance in the kitchen—and got back to the studio, King was hunched over his hand with his tattoo gun buzzing.

"What the hell are you doing?"

Silence.

"So what? You're ignoring me now?"

He lifted the gun from his skin. "Yes, because if I talk to you, I'll be giving this bird a dick in his mouth instead of a snake," King said.

"I will get back to the fact that you sort of made a joke later, something which I didn't think you were capable of doing, but right now, the only thing I can concentrate on is that you are tattooing my sketch onto your hand!" I shouted.

"What did you think I was going to do with it?" King dipped his gun into the ink.

"I don't know, but not that!"

"Pup?" King asked softly.

"Yeah?"

"Enough with the questions. You're distracting me. Go the fuck to bed."

"But—" I started to argue.

"Pup?"

"Yeah?"

"Bed. Now. Or you can choose to stay, but I'm warning you, if that's the decision you make and you are still here when I'm done, I'm bending you over that couch and fucking you into next week."

Shit.

I scurried out of the room as fast as I could, not stopping to catch my breath, I could still hear him laughing as I closed the door and sank to the floor.

I was totally and utterly, for lack of a better word, FUCKED.

King

YOU LOOKED SO FUCKING CUTE, SITTING THERE CONCENTRATING. WHERE THE FUCK did that come from? I hadn't even realized I'd said it out loud until I saw the redness rise in her cheeks. On the other hand, flirting with her and making her uncomfortable was by far becoming my newest and most favorite source of entertainment.

Since she started eating Preppy's cooking, it only took a couple of days for Pup to pack on some weight. The additional few pounds had done amazing things for her figure. Her sunken cheeks were a little fuller and somehow made her appear even more innocent and cherub-like. Her tits and ass were rounder and begging to be touched even more so than before. She had the body of a woman and the face of an angel and I was constantly walking around like a thirteen-year-old who had to keep adjusting himself to hide his raging hard-on.

The truth was I didn't bother her while she was sketching because I didn't want her to move, and I was perfectly content to just sit and stare at her all night. But then, she would cross and uncross her legs while biting her lip, and all I could think about was how I wanted to be the one to bite that lip. How wet I could make her between those legs.

I didn't get up from my stool after Neil left because I was afraid she'd look up from her sketch and see my cock standing at attention through my jeans. If she were any other chick, I would draw her attention to it, but I didn't want to send her running into the other room. I already felt her fighting off whatever attraction she had for me. The horrible truth of the matter is that I didn't want to scare her away.

Because I actually liked having her around.

Somewhere, somehow, my anger toward her had turned to some sort of fucked-up affection.

Which I had to put a stop to right a fucking away, because any sort of feelings for her other than contention and lust would only get in the way of the plans I had for her.

She was afraid of me. That much was obvious, but there was a fire there, too, and the more she fought it, the more it turned me on.

The way her body reacted to me told me that there was only so long she could resist the inevitable. The inevitable being me fucking her until she couldn't remember her own name.

It's not like she knew it anyway.

But I did.

An unfamiliar nagging feeling tugged at my gut.

Guilt maybe?

I brushed it off. There wasn't time to entertain any feelings of guilt. A better opportunity to get Max back was not going to just fall into my lap like this again. And in the meantime, I was going to spend my time with her as I pleased. In her case, that meant doing everything I had to make her warm, wet, and willing.

"Boss-man!" Preppy shouted, bounding into my studio with his pupils dilated, forgetting to blink like he'd just snorted blow by the fucking truck full.

"What's up, Prep?" I asked, putting the finishing touches on the tattoo Pup had sketched for me. After I saw it, I needed it on my skin, immediately and permanently and for the life of me I didn't know why. But after it was done, I felt like a weight was lifted.

"What the fuck is that?" Preppy asked, pointing to the back of my hand. I wiped off the excess ink and blood and held it up so he could see.

"It's a tattoo, dumb-ass. Or did you forget what it is I do in this room?"

"I know it's a tattoo, fucker. I just wanted to know why you were tattoo-ing yourself right now."

"You've seen me do it a hundred times so what's the fucking big deal?" I barked, not liking Preppy's third degree.

"What exactly is it?" he asked, leaning over my shoulder as I put a layer of plastic wrap over the top.

"It's nothing. Pup drew it. What exactly is it you wanted?" I hated being short with him, but I wasn't about to answer questions I myself didn't exactly know the answers to.

"I came to tell you two things actually. One is that Bear called, and he overheard his dad talking. Isaac's coming to town. He's not sure when, just knows he's coming. Got eyes on him though. He hasn't left Dallas yet." The MC had a long-standing relationship with our former primary source of weed.

"And?"

"AND I'm pretty sure he's probably a little pissed the fuck off that we cut him out as our supplier."

"I was locked up, and he didn't want to deal with anyone but me. If he expected us to just do nothing until I got out, that was his mistake. We saw opportunity. We seized it. End of story."

"Yeah man, that's the way you and I see it. But Bear overheard his dad saying that Isaac sees it more like a kick to his balls that he wants to pay back to us a thousand times over."

"I'm not hiding from Isaac, or anyone else. If he wants to talk to me, he knows where the fuck I live. Now, what's the other thing you wanted to tell me?" I snapped.

"Dude, you're so fucking moody since you got out. You're like a bitch on the rag twenty-four hours a day. The second thing I wanted to tell you is that I'm going to take Doe out on a date Saturday night."

"You're going to fucking WHAT?" I suddenly wished my tattoo gun was a real one because with that one sentence, Preppy was walking into dangerous fucking territory.

"She's cool as shit, so I'm going to take her out. Maybe, a movie or something. The drive-in is playing some scary paranormal thing, and chicks fucking love that shit. Makes 'em all cuddly," Preppy said, hugging himself with his arms.

"Like fuck you are." Not only was he not taking her out, I got the impression that scary wasn't exactly Doe's favorite genre. The girl's been scared enough in real life.

"Dude, I'm not going to fuck her. Unless that's cool with you. In which case, I will most *definitely* fuck her."

I stood from my stool. It rolled back and crashed against the wall. "Not. A. Fucking. Chance." The thought of his hands on her made my stomach twist.

"You don't even like her," he barked. "Besides, you don't know anything about her. And that's your fault because she may not know a lot about herself, but the little she does know you haven't even bothered to ask her about."

He had a point, but Preppy didn't know that there was a reason for that, and I planned to keep that reason to myself for the time being.

"What exactly would you like for me to talk to her about? Because the *where do you come from, what's your name,* thing doesn't exactly apply in her case."

Preppy huffed and linked his fingers together behind his neck. "I don't know. You could ask her something simple, like maybe, how she likes her sandwiches or something."

"Sandwiches. You want me to ask her about sandwiches?"

"Why the fuck not? Everyone likes a delicious sandwich, and talking about them is better than talking about the heavy shit you seem to be carrying around these days."

This is why Preppy was my best friend. He saw right through me.

"I know Max is important. I know we need to get her back, but until then, you still have a life to live, man. And talking to the girl, who for all intents and purposes is living in our house, isn't going to get in the way of that."

That's what you think.

"Have you even fucked her yet? I mean, the chick sleeps in your bed and shit. What the fuck is that all about?"

"That's none of your fucking business," I warned. He was crossing a line.

He rolled his eyes. "I'll take that as a no. Maybe, that's why you've been so fucking grumpy since you got out. Maybe you just need to get some ass. Get laid. Get all up in there before your dick shrivels up and falls the fuck off."

"I've gotten laid since I've gotten out, so shut the fuck up about it. This isn't about liking her or about fucking her. This is about me saying NO and you listening to me for once!"

"King, you've been my best friend since the dinosaurs roamed the earth, so listen to me when I tell you that you look at her like you want to fuck her brains out, but you treat her like she's garbage under your shoe. It's not cool, man. You're the one who decided to keep her here, which wasn't the brightest idea to begin with, so let me have a little fun with her for fuck's sake."

"This is about a debt that needs to be paid," I said, unconvincingly.

"Oh come on! We both know she didn't take anything. And since when is it up to you to dole out life lessons on who needs to pay for what? You some kind of life coach now? Besides, she's not your property. She's a person, not a fucking car."

"That's rich coming from you." I've witnessed Preppy doing things that made even my skin crawl, but if he was going to throw my shit in my face, then I was going to throw his shit in his.

"Seriously, she isn't yours. You can't just take her."

"Yes, she *is* mine, and I *did* just take her. She sleeps in my bed, doesn't she? Next to me. I may not have fucked her, but it was me she turned to when she wanted to get off the other night, and me who gave her what she needed. So no, I haven't fucked her, *yet*. But the answer is still no, you can't fucking take her out," I said through gritted teeth, I could feel my veins tighten as my blood pressure sky-rocketed.

Preppy cocked his head to the side and smiled. A recognition of some sort settled over his face. "Well, she's not my property. She's my friend. So, if I can't take her out, then you have to take her. I'm not doing this for me. I'm doing it for her. She's been through some shit, and we both know what that's like. The kid deserves a break. A little fucking fun."

"Fuck no. I'm not going to fucking date her. And this isn't up for debate. No date. No nothing. Just fucking drop it." For the first time in my life, I felt like punching Preppy. He's never coaxed that kind of anger from me before.

"Man, get your fucking head out of your ass. She's just a confused kid. Either you take her, or you let me take her. I may call you Boss-Man, but we're friends, and that doesn't mean you can make all my decisions for me. You may call the shots, but I'm still my own person. I'm not asking you here. I'm telling you."

"Fine!" I shouted. Throwing my arms up in the air. "Take her out on a fucking date. What the fuck do I care anyway? Go! Have a fucking blast!"

I sat back down on my stool and pretended to fiddle with my equipment. Why the fuck I was getting so riled up to begin with was beyond me.

Maybe, I'd just forgotten how to interact with people who weren't wearing orange jumpsuits or correctional officer uniforms.

"Awesome!" Preppy hopped from one foot to the other. "I'm going to go iron my good bow tie."

"Prep?"

"Yeah, Boss-Man?"

"It's six in the fucking morning."

"And?"

"You want to take her out on Saturday right?"

"Yeah."

"It's Monday."

"Ah."

"So how about you go wipe the fucking blow from under your nose and get some fucking sleep. Iron your good bow tie tomorrow." Preppy may not have to listen to me, but the need to tell him what to do would never go away.

I'd forgotten while I was away that Preppy was one hell of a partier.

We both were.

Or, I used to be.

Before Max.

Before prison.

Before *her.*

Preppy wiped the powder from under his nostrils and rubbed it onto his gums.

"Yes, sir," Preppy said with a mock salute. He turned to leave.

"And Prep?" I called out.

"Yeah, Boss?" he asked, stopping mid-stride.

"You're taking her out as her friend only. You've got that?"

"I've got that."

"Good. Because if you so much as touch her, I'll fucking kill you."

chapter
sixteen

Doe

"WHAT IS ALL THIS?" I ASKED, STARING DOWN AT THE PLATE UPON PLATE of sliced meats and cheese.

"Sandwich stuff." King said, tossing me a roll.

"Yes, I can see that. But why are we making sandwiches on the dock?"

I wandered what his ulterior motive was. King didn't seem like the type to picnic on the dock, no matter what the situation. Plus, in the entire time I'd been staying with King, he'd never once made a meal for me.

Or even eaten a meal with me.

"Because it's a nice day to be outside, and because who the fuck doesn't like sandwiches?" King sat on one of the plastic chairs surrounding wooden table that was screwed to the dock so it wouldn't fly away during a storm. "And Preppy said…I don't fucking know, just go with it." King loaded his roll with salami and cheese and dug out a huge scoop of mayo from the jar with a spatula.

"That's enough mayo to choke a horse," I said, carefully selecting turkey and bacon for my own sandwich.

"Have you actually seen a horse choke from ingesting too much mayo?" he asked.

"I very well could have. I just don't remember." I grabbed a handful of Cheetos from the bag and smashed them into the top slice of bread with both hands. King pulled the other chair up alongside his until the arms were touching and motioned for me to sit down.

And then OUR arms were touching.

"So what's it like?" King asked, popping the top off a beer and handing it to me.

"What's what like?" I asked, setting my paper plate in my lap.

"Not remembering anything. I keep thinking about what that would be like and I can't imagine it."

"It's…" I searched my brain for the words but only one popped into my mind over and over, "…empty."

"You're a lot of things, Pup, but empty isn't one of them." King tucked an unruly strand of hair behind my ear.

"Oh yeah? Then, you tell me what I am, because I can't think of anything that doesn't have to do with me losing my memory." I took a bite of my lunch that was so big I could barely close my mouth around it.

King laughed. "Well, for starters...you're kind of quirky."

"Quirky?"

"Pup, did you or did you not just put Cheetos on your sandwich?"

"Duly noted. Okay, quirky. I can handle that. Keep going. What else do you think you know about me?"

"Well, you're bold. Brave. I would even go as far as to say that you're irritatingly feisty. You speak about three hours before you think. You ask way too many goddamn questions. You have this dimple on your left cheek that comes out when you're smiling, but it also shows up, along with the one on the right cheek, when you're pissed off." Embarrassment burned my neck as if I was standing too close to a fire. "Your neck and your face get red when you're embarrassed. It starts at your neck. Right here." King lightly wrapped the palm of his hand around my throat. "Then, it jumps up to your cheeks." He brushed his thumb over my cheekbone. "Then, it travels all the way up to these ears."

He leaned in and sucked my earlobe into his mouth, trailing his tongue along the delicate flesh of my ears sending sparks of pleasure down my body. My nipples hardened and pressed up against my shirt.

King chuckled and pulled back. "So don't say that you're empty, Pup, because you are anything but." There was a mischievous glimmer in his eyes. Something I hadn't seen before. "I think you are, by far, the most interesting person I've ever met."

"Thank you," I said. "But stop trying to imagine what it would be like without your memory. You're lucky you know who you are and where you belong."

King pulled at the label on his beer and sighed. "Sometimes, I wish I didn't."

"What do you mean?"

"If I could choose to wake up tomorrow and not remember who I am, the shit I've done, the people I would be leaving behind, I would do it. I could just start over. Be someone else."

"I don't want you to be anyone else," I blurted, interrupting his confession.

"You should hate me," King said, taking my plate from my lap and setting it on the table. "If I were you, I would hate me."

"I thought I did."

"And now? What do you think of me now?" King asked, leaning in closer.

"I think you are the most stubborn, overbearing, anger inducing, obnoxious, complicated, and beautiful man that has ever lived."

"I think you are beautiful, too," King breathed. In one graceful movement, he had me out of my chair and onto his lap.

His hands had just slid into my hair when a loud crash sounded from the other side of the mangroves.

"Stay the fuck here," King ordered. He stood and tossed me off his lap. I crouched behind the cement retaining wall that separated the dock from the yard. King leapt over it effortlessly and ran in the direction of the garage, toward where the sound had come from.

It seemed like I was there for hours, waiting for King to come back or for something to happen.

Nothing.

My stomach growled, and I was reminded that I had barely started my lunch. I scooted down to my ass and stretched out my leg in an effort to drag the chair that held my plate toward me. I hooked my foot around the leg of the chair and slowly pulled. It made a horrible scraping noise against the wood planks of the dock. I paused and waited.

Nothing.

So, I continued. Slowly, inch my inch, I dragged my lunch closer to me until my Cheetos smashed sandwich was within my reach. I pulled my plate off the seat and picked up my sandwich. I opened my mouth and was about to chomp down on victory when someone cleared their throat.

With my sandwich still in launch-into-my-mouth position, I looked up from behind the bread to see both King and Bear standing on the top of the seawall, peering down at me.

Bear looked just a good as he did the night I met him, but now, he looked even better. Because he was shirtless. His ab muscles glistened with sweat. I thought King had a lot of tattoos, but Bear didn't have a single inch of available real estate left on his skin.

King spoke first. "Oh no, don't worry about me. I'm fine. Just went to check out what that bomb like noise was, but you go ahead and finish your sandwich. We'll wait." He was smiling out of the corner of his mouth.

Bear crouched down. "Oh shit. Check you out. Didn't think you'd still be alive."

I put my plate down and stood up. "If you two are done mocking me, can one of you tell me what the fuck that noise was?"

"Oh shit. Sorry, that was all me. This girl came over, and she's got this old Volkswagen Bug. One thing led to another…"

"I don't want to know," I interrupted.

Bear continued, "All I was going to say is that while her lips were wrapped around my cock, I vaguely remembered promising to fix her bug for her. What you heard was that very car backfiring. For what I'm thinking was the very last time, because it's dead. Like super dead. Like there is no coming back from that dead. Which totally blows cause the girl could suck the—"

King held up a hand. "Okay, Bear, cut the bullshit, you can tell her what really happened."

Bear nodded and his phone rang. He pulled it out of his back pocket and clicked a button on the screen. "Yeah." He scratched his beard. "Fuck. Okay. Yeah. Yeah, I'll tell him." He clicked the phone again and put in back in his pocket.

"Isaac is on the move. Jimmy and BJ spotted him and his boys in Coral Pines this morning. Looks like they've got business there. BJ spoke to a guy in Isaac's crew. They'll be riding into our corner of the world in a week or so."

"Shit," King cursed.

"I told you to fucking get out of town, dude. You knew he was coming."

"Yeah, and when you told me that, I didn't care if he came right up to my front door, guns-a-fucking-blazing."

"But now?" Bear asked.

King nodded to me.

"Ah. I see. What do you want to do, man? Your call. You know I'm behind you no matter what." Bear lit a cigarette.

"I think we go on the offense," King said.

"Wait, what does all this mean? Who is Isaac?"

King ignored me. "I'll get her to Grace's before then," he told Bear.

"King, who the fuck is Isaac? Who the fuck is Grace?" I shouted, jumping up and down to make my presence in the conversation known.

"Pup, when Preppy took you out with him, did he tell you that when he and I started the granny operation, we cut out our main supplier?"

"Yeah. He did."

"Well, Isaac, was that supplier."

"Shit," I said.

Bear took a long drag of his cigarette and blew out the smoke through his nose, looking very much like the bird recently tattooed on King's hand. "Yeah, that about sums it up."

"What you heard was a warning," King said.

"What kind of warning?" I asked.

Bear stubbed out his cigarette into the concrete of the retaining wall. "The kind that goes boom."

"What was blown up?"

Preppy's wail broke through the air like another explosion.

"WHAT THE FUCK HAPPENED TO MY MOTHERFUCKING CAR?"

chapter
seventeen

Doe

ANY SIGN OF THE PLAYFUL VERSION OF KING FROM LUNCH WERE GONE. He gave me ten minutes to get ready and *get my ass in the fucking truck.* I didn't know where we were going, and something about the way he'd barked it at me made it clear he didn't exactly want me to ask.

We traveled together in a silence so heavy it had its own presence in the truck. Like an uninvited guest, it awkwardly sat between us on the bench seat. We turned down a narrow, dirt road. My curiosity piqued when King pulled over to the side of the road next to the gate of a yellow ranch style home with a short, white picket fence lining the front yard.

"Let's go," King said.

Getting out of the truck, he unlatched the gate and started up the cement walkway. I followed behind him, jogging to catch up to him and match his long strides. Several pinwheel lawn ornaments spun as we passed them, our motion creating the only breeze in the stagnant heat of the day. I thought that maybe King was making a pickup for Preppy, and that this was another one of their Granny Growhouses that I had not yet seen.

When we reached the door, King didn't knock, just shoved it open and walked inside. For a split second, my heart skipped a beat because I thought that maybe he was robbing the place, but I quickly squashed that idea when I heard him call out, "Grace?"

Grace. I recognized the name from earlier.

I followed him into the house and closed the door behind me. When I turned back around, I came face to face with a thousand tiny eyes staring back at me. The small living room was covered with them. From the plant shelves to the buffet style table in the entryway to the coffee table and on top of the old TV, ceramic rabbits of all shapes and sizes were everywhere.

King didn't pay them any attention as he strode through the living room to the sliding glass doors on the back of the eat-in kitchen where large stuffed rabbits occupied all six chairs of the table like they were about to enjoy a meal together.

I guess Grace likes rabbits.

"Out here!" shouted a high-pitched, yet scratchy voice.

King held the sliding glass doors open so I could pass, but he didn't step aside. I had to brush against his chest to get through. In my attempt to touch him as little as possible, I stumbled outside onto a wooden deck where a little woman with pixie–style, gray hair sat in a plush navy-blue deck chair. Her feet were resting on top of the table, crossed at the ankles. She drank out of a tall glass with light green liquid. A leaf floated on the top of the ice.

Instead of asking me who I was, she stood up and brought me in for a hug. She was easily in her seventies, and wore a denim-colored sweater, matching pants, and white orthopedic shoes.

"I'm Grace," she said, pushing me far enough away that she could study my face, but keeping her hands on my elbows.

"Hi." I wasn't sure what the protocol was about introducing myself to her, but King solved that problem for me.

"This is Doe."

"What an unusual name. What does it mean?"

I looked to King, and he nodded. "Doe as in Jane Doe," I told her.

"Are your parents into true crime novels, or are they hippies who fried their brains on too much acid? Lots of them peculiar types around here. Although I've never met you before, so I don't believe you're from Logan's Beach."

"I'm not sure what my parents are into, ma'am."

Grace looked at me quizzically and then over to King, who was still standing in the doorway. He shrugged.

"You're letting all the bought air out over there," Grace scolded King. "Come out here. Sit. Have a drink."

Grace waved King over and tugged me to a chair. She poured us both a glass of the green liquid from the glass pitcher on the table.

"I hope you like mojitos!" she exclaimed, finishing her drink and pouring herself another.

I took a sip. The ice clinked against my front teeth. The drink was both sweet and bitter, but under the heat of the noon sun, it tasted heavenly.

Thankfully, my sunburn was fully healed, and I no longer needed to hide in the shade. Nor did I resemble a ripe tomato.

King took the seat next to me and across from Grace.

"What you got for me?" Grace asked King.

He laughed and shifted in his seat. He removed a small black plastic bag from his pocket and slid it across the table.

"Thank you, sweet boy," Grace said, hugging the bag to her chest. She set it down on the table and turned to me. "So, how did you two kids meet? Tell me everything."

"Um…" I had no idea how to answer her, so I started with the truth. As I spoke, it became like word vomit of epic proportions, and I couldn't stop it from barreling out of my mouth. "Well Grace, we met on the night I decided to sell myself for a hot meal and a place to sleep. I was about to suck this guy's dick when he realized I was being skittish about the whole thing and threw me out. Then, my friend, who was a hooker, stole some money from him. Then, she shot me, or grazed me, or whatever. Then, he found my only friend dead in a hotel room with a needle in her arm, but that was before I escaped. Then, he killed my would-be rapist and brought me back to his house for a bath and a conversation about how I was now his possession and didn't have a choice about it."

I stopped and looked up at Grace whose glass was paused mid-air.

King cleared his throat. "She came to my coming home party." It was the truth, but he was leaving out all the cringe-worthy details I'd just laid out for her. Grace set her glass down and threw her head back in laughter.

"I don't think you two could be any cuter together," she said, ignoring everything I'd just told her. "I'm so glad you found someone, dear boy. I'd missed you so much while you were gone, and I prayed every single day that you would find someone who made you as happy as my Edmund made me." Grace turned a small silver band on her ring finger.

"We're not—" I started, but King put his arm over my chair and tugged me into him.

"I wanted you to meet her," he said, running his thumb against the side of my neck in an unexpected sign of affection.

Show or not, my skin came alive under his seemingly innocent touch, and I'm pretty sure I gasped out loud because King's shoulders shook with silent laughter. Grace stood and rounded the table. Pausing above King, she kissed him on the top of the head.

"You've made this old woman very happy," Grace said, wiping a tear from under her eye. She sniffled and clasped her hands together. "I'm going to start dinner. Doe, darling, would you like to help me?"

"Sure," I said, standing up from the table.

I still wasn't entirely sure why we were there, but I liked Grace, and having someone else besides the three tattooed amigos around was a nice change. She had a grandmotherly thing going on that set you at ease the moment she opened her mouth. I was going to enjoy it while I could until I had to go back to the house with Mr. Mood Swings.

"I've got stuff in the truck," King said, hopping down off the deck and disappearing around the side of the house. Grace led me into the kitchen and took out ingredients for pasta with meatballs. She moved one of the stuffed rabbits so I could sit at the table and chop vegetables while she used her hands to mix together all the ingredients for the meatballs.

"How do you know King?" I asked, chopping green peppers onto a cutting board. I used the knife to wipe them into a bowl and started on the onions.

"He didn't tell you?"

"He doesn't say much," I admitted.

"Man of few words, that one," Grace said warmly. "I've known Brantley since he was a snot-nosed middle schooler. He tried to steal from my garden one day. He wasn't a day over twelve."

"Brantley?"

"He really doesn't tell you anything, does he?" Grace cast me a sideways glance.

"What did you do when you caught him?" I was curious about how King forged a relationship with a lady three times his own age.

"I got a switch off the tree, just like my mama would have done, ripped his jeans down past his little, white butt, and whipped some sense into him," Grace said, casually as she rinsed a tomato under the tap and dried it with a paper towel.

"No, you didn't!" I said, half in disbelief and half because I couldn't imagine this little sprig of woman giving King a spanking.

"Yes, I sure did. Then, Edmund called Brantley's mom while I made dinner, but she didn't answer. Edmund left a message, but his mom never came. So, he stayed for dinner. Then, he stayed the night. He's come over every Sunday since. Well, every Sunday he hasn't been mixed up in something or sitting in prison. In that case, we went to him."

"You knew he was in prison?"

"Of course. Visited him every week. And when my Edmund died, that little boy came to his funeral wearing a green tuxedo he bought from the thrift shop that was three sizes too big. I've offered to let him live here a thousand times, but that boy was never one who could be contained. He chose to stay out there, do what he does, and he comes to take care of me and the house in between."

"So, you know...everything?"

Grace nodded. "Not the nitty gritty details but I'm no dimwitted woman. I know my boy isn't exactly walking on the right side of the law. But I know that I love him like a son, and he loves me like his mama so that's all that matters to me." Grace didn't pause when she continued. "Love is what you would do for the other person, not what you do in general. There is no doubt in my mind that he would throw his life down for me. I would do the same without hesitation." She opened the refrigerator and pulled out a bowl of green peppers. "I also know that everything you said out there, about how you two met, is true."

"Why didn't you say something?" I asked.

Grace sighed and looked away, deep in thought. "There was this movie I watched as a little girl. This black and white picture about a cowboy who robbed trains. I'll never forget the ending. You see, the cowboy turns to the woman he loves, after she just found out that he was the train robber, and he tells her that although he did horrible things, he stole from people, killed people, it didn't mean he loved her any less or that he wasn't capable of love."

Grace motioned for me to pick up the salad bowl and follow her out onto the deck. I set the bowl on the table, and Grace arranged the plates and forks. When she was done, she guided me to the railing and nodded over to where King stood on a ladder, replacing a light bulb on a small shed in the corner of the yard.

"What I'm trying to say, dear, and what I think the cowboy was trying to say to his love in that movie, is that there is a difference between being bad and being evil. Just because he was a very bad boy, that doesn't mean he couldn't be a truly great man." I was rolling her words around in my brain when she added, "And God help me, little one, you break his heart, and I will cut you where you stand. If I'm long gone when that happens, be assured that death will not stop me from bringing you down." Grace smiled like she hadn't just threatened my life and brought me in for another hug. "Now, let's go get the meatballs."

Grace may have been a little thing, and she definitely had the wrong idea about what was going on between myself and King, but I had no doubt that if I crossed her, she would carry through on her threat without blinking an eye.

King ducked inside the bathroom to wash his hands and then joined us out on the deck. The sun had just started to set when I noticed the strands of lights crisscrossing over our heads. As the sun sank lower, the lights got brighter until they looked like thousands of tiny stars shining over our meal.

We ate, and Grace did most of the talking. She frequently refilled my mojito, and at one point rushed inside to make another pitcher. She was curious about me and asked a lot of questions. In between shoveling meatballs into my mouth, I filled her in on my story.

"It's a good thing you have each other." She pointed out.

"She's not my girlfriend, Grace," King said, his lips compressed in a thin, straight line.

Grace shrugged and took another sip of her drink. "Edmund and I had an arranged marriage, you know. His mother and mine conspired together since we were still on the tit. The first few years we were together, I couldn't stand the man, but after a while, I learned to love him. Then, I fell in love with him and felt that way up until the day he died. Things don't always start out the way we want them to. It's how they end that's important. I may not have loved Ed in the beginning, but he grew to be the love of my life."

Grace had the most optimistic, if not bordering on warped, perception of relationships. But what did I expect? The woman was a walking, talking contradiction. A tiny little thing that drank like a fish and swore like a sailor. Not to mention that her house looked like an episode of HOARDERS: RABBIT EDITION.

"It didn't hurt that the sex was off the charts fantastic," Grace said, staring up into the lights.

I spit out a mouthful of mojito. Half of it splattered against King's shirt. I braced myself for his anger, slowly lifting my eyes to his, but there was none. His shoulders shook as he chuckled. Grace was downright howling.

I helped Grace clean up while King disappeared down the hall. I heard the bathtub running and thought maybe he was wringing the mojito out of his shirt.

"Grace, what's with the rabbits?" I asked her, needing to know. She smiled and closed the dishwasher. She turned the dial, and it sounded like Preppy's car exploding all over again.

"Ed used to bring me home a ceramic rabbit after every business trip." She looked around at the table. "I know it's odd, and I know they've taken over the house. But each one was a moment my husband wasn't with me, but was still thinking about me." Grace looked as if she was getting tired. My heart seized. I wasn't expecting the reason to be so sentimental, and I hated that I ever thought that she might have been just a crazy rabbit lady.

"I'll finish this up, Grace. Why don't you go lie down?"

She nodded and wiped her hands on the dishcloth hanging off her shoulder. Setting it around the faucet, she brought me in for another hug. "Thank you. Take care of my boy, will you? He's been having a hard time since he got out. I worry about him."

I didn't know how to respond, so I took the coward's way out and went with what I knew she wanted to hear. "Of course."

Grace made her way down the hall where I heard a door open and then shut. I finished the dishes and sat at the kitchen table for a good hour. It was getting late. Grace obviously needed to go to bed.

Where was King?

I padded down the hall and paused outside a door when I heard voices speaking in hushed tones. The door wasn't latched, so I pushed it open a little, hoping it wouldn't creak. Peering through the crack, I caught a glimpse of King and Grace in the mirror of a large ornate walnut dresser that took up most of the small room. Grace sat on the side of the bed in bright orange button-up pajamas with matching slippers. Her feet didn't touch the floor. King crouched in front of her and held up what looked like some sort of glass pipe.

"Like this," he said, lighting the pipe he took a hit and held it in his lungs before blowing out the smoke. Then, he passed the pipe over to Grace who did the same, looking to King for reassurance. When she exhaled, she started having a coughing fit. King held her arm while she laughed and coughed at the same time.

"Will I do that every time?" she asked when she was finally able to manage a sentence.

"No, just the first few times." King assured her with a small smile.

"Good. I hate coughing," Grace said.

"Are you sure there isn't anything else you need?" He asked.

"I'm an old lady, and a dying one at that, and you still come over to fix my house and take care of me like I'm still going to be around in six months. You do too much already."

"Don't talk like that," King scolded, pinching the bridge of his nose. Grace reached out, took King's hands in her own, and held them on her lap.

"You are the closest thing to a son I ever had," she confessed.

King looked to the floor. "You've always been more of a mother to me than...*her*."

Grace's face grew serious. "I'm only sorry I didn't kill that bitch myself."

It was on those words that I lost my footing and came tumbling forward into the room, landing on my hands and knees in front of the bed.

"Is she always this graceful?" Grace asked.

King kissed Grace on the top of her head and turned off the lights. I gave her a sad little wave as he ushered me from the room, closing the door behind us. He turned off all the lights in the house and locked the back-sliding door. Just as we reached the front of the house, King stopped and reached into his pocket, then placed something on the edge of the table on the hall. I fell a few steps behind so I could inspect what it was he'd left for Grace. When I saw it, my breath caught in my throat.

It was a tiny white ceramic rabbit.

Doe

"WE HAVE ANOTHER STOP TO MAKE," KING DECLARED, PUNCHING OUT a text on his phone with his thumb as we got back into the truck.

I looked at him, really looked at him as if I were seeing him for the first time. What I saw was a man who when you stripped away the intimidation and constant mood swings was someone who was taking care of a woman he loved in her final days. The man who I'd started out believing was a monster was capable of love.

"Why were you showing Grace how to smoke pot?" I asked.

"She puts up a good front, but Grace is in a lot of pain." King winced. "All the medications they give her are a bunch of bullshit. It's all supposed to make her comfortable, but she gets really sick from most of it."

"What does she have?"

"Some fucking bullshit aggressive cancer." King's hands tightened around the wheel until his knuckles turned white.

"Does she really only have six months?"

King looked uncomfortable, but, I felt like after meeting Grace and bonding with her I needed to know more about her condition.

He propped his elbow up on the ledge of the open driver's side window, thoughtfully resting his jaw on the back of his hand. "They say six months, but I've been told to take that and divide it in half because they usually exaggerate when they tell you how much time you have left."

"Who told you that?"

"Her doctor."

"Oh."

We spent nearly twenty minutes in silence as we rode to our next stop, which was another residential neighborhood. This time when King parked and I grabbed the door handle, he stopped me with his forearm across my chest.

"What?" I asked.

"We aren't getting out."

Killing the engine, he leaned back in his seat. I opened my mouth to ask why, but the dark look in his eyes said that he wasn't up for conversation. I folded my arms over my chest, waiting for the reason why we were there to produce itself.

After a few minutes, there it was. A light. Not from the house we were parked in front of but the one behind it. From where we sat, we had a perfect view of the back of the house and the illuminated sunroom. A tall woman with short black hair was sorting through some toys on the ground, when a small blonde girl came bounding into the sunroom.

King sat up straight.

We may have been a hundred feet or so away from the house, but I instantly recognized the girl prancing around in her PJ's.

"That's the girl from your picture, right? Is she your sister? Do you want to go say hi? I'll wait here if you want me to."

King remained silent, staring intently at the little girl until the woman found what she was looking for and ushered her back into the house, switching off the light. King looked into the darkness long after they were out of sight.

"I can't go see her. I have no rights. I'm her only family. She needs me, but to the courts, I'm just another felon. I don't even have visitation. I did everything I could in prison, hired every lawyer I could, but there's nothing they could do to help. I had to bribe a clerk to give me the address of her foster home. It's the only way I know where she is."

"I'm sorry." I said, and I meant it. King knew who and where his family was and they still couldn't be together. "She really is beautiful."

"She is," he agreed. He turned the key and started up the truck. "Max."

"What?" I asked.

"Max. Her name is Max."

"Short for Maxine?"

King smiled and shook his head, turning back onto the main road. "Like Maximillian."

"For a girl?" I wrinkled my nose.

"Yeah, and shut the fuck up. It's the best fucking name ever," King said, still smiling. There was a hint of pride in his tone that I didn't want to step on. "A strong name for a strong girl."

"It's a great name," I said softly.

"Yeah, it is."

"Why did you bring me here? And to see Grace?" I asked, using the small moment of vulnerability to my advantage.

"Because I don't know what the fuck I'm doing with you, Pup," King confessed. "You make me fucking crazy and I feel shit that I can't—" He paused. "Prison fucked me up, made me rethink things, but you've managed to fuck me up more than prison ever did. For some reason, I want you around. And since I'm shit with words, I figured the best way for you to get to know me, the real me, was for you to meet the two most important girls in my life."

"Oh." I bit my lip. I don't know what kind of answer I expected from him, if any answer at all, but what he said took me by complete surprise.

He WANTS me around?

"I've been in a maximum-security prison. I've been around the worst of the worst. I've had to sleep with one eye open, thinking my next breath could be my last."

"Why are you telling me all this?"

He turned toward me and our eyes locked. He reached out and ran the back of his pointer finger along my cheek. "Because I want you to know that none of those motherfuckers ever scared me as much as you do."

King's phone buzzed from the cup holder in the console, and he answered it, leaving me with my mouth open in shock.

"Yeah," King said, holding the phone up to his ear. "Motherfucker! No, I've got it. You stay where you are, and I'll come get you in a bit. Yes, I know. I'm sure. I got this."

King tossed the phone into my lap and turned the wheel of the truck so hard I swear we were up on two wheels.

"What's going on?"

"One last stop," King said through gritted teeth. Whoever it was on the other end had told him something he obviously didn't want to hear.

After a few minutes, we pulled up in front of a small dive bar with a neon green sign that flashed the name HANSEN'S with a symbol of a ship below it. There were only a few scattered cars in the gravel parking lot. King threw the truck in park and jumped out.

"Stay here," he ordered. He leaned into the bed of the truck and grabbed something out of it before making his way into the bar. King had to duck to pass through the low doorway.

I'd seen three sides of him in one day. The dark crazy scary shit. The sexy as hell shit that made my knees quake with the smallest look. And the side that I didn't think he had, the side that genuinely cared for someone other than himself. It was nice to know he wasn't a misogynist after all.

There was a commotion inside. The door to the bar swung open. A woman's screams followed King as his massive shadow emerged from the bar.

Less than an hour ago, he was pining for life where he could have his sister in it. Shortly before that, he was helping his elderly friend find relief during her last days.

Now, he walked back to the truck in long strides, an explosively angry look in his dark and dangerous eyes. It wasn't until he was within ten feet of me, standing under the buzzing street light, that I was able to take a good look at him.

King clutched a wooden baseball bat tightly in his grip. Dark spots were splattered across both him and the bat, droplets splattered across his chest and face. When he turned to put the bat back into the bed of the truck, he stepped fully into the light, and my breath hitched.

Both King and the baseball bat were covered in blood.

King tore out of the parking lot. When we hit the highway, he pulled off on the first exit and parked the truck under an overpass that was under construction. My heart was beating in my chest, quick and heavy.

Thud. Thud.

Thud. Thud.

The light of the moon shone through the front window, making the dried blood on his forehead look like it was shimmering.

"What the fuck just happened?" I shrieked, unbuckling my seat belt.

"Business," King said with no discernable emotion.

"You're covered in blood! Did you kill…whoever it was?"

"No, I didn't, but he'll think twice about fucking with my shit again."

"Who was that?"

"Someone who used to roll with Isaac. Preppy found out he was the narc who told Isaac about our granny operation. He needed to learn a lesson. He doesn't need to be running his mouth when he doesn't know shit about shit." King ran his hand over his head. "About starting wars that don't need to be started."

"Is that what's going to happen? A war?" I asked. "What are we going to do?"

"There won't be a war if I can help it. I've reached out to Isaac's people, asked for a meet. I want to get in front of this thing before it gets any worse." King turned to me. "You're not going to do anything. I've got this handled. And you should not be worried about any of this. I promise that nothing will happen to you. I told you I'd protect you, and I meant it."

"You think I'm worried about myself? Preppy's car got literally blown up. Bear lives in the garage ten feet away. You've got a guy, a dangerous guy by the sound of it, after you, and you think it's ME I'm worried about!?" I huffed. "How fucking selfish do you think I am?"

"You're worried about me, Pup?" King teased, cocking an eyebrow.

"No! I mean yes. Why are you so fucking irritating?" I yelled. King cut the engine. "And why are we parked under a—"

King interrupted my tirade by grabbing my hips and roughly sliding me down until the back of my head landed on the bench seat.

"I love that you worry about me," he said, covering my body with his, his mouth crashing down against mine. His were lips soft and full, but hard and needy at the same time. "Your lips are so fucking sexy. I've imagined them wrapped around my cock a thousand times." He slid a hand underneath my shirt, cupping my breast, kneading it with his palm. "I love your perfect fucking tits." His knee parted my legs, and he settled between them. His hard cock rested against an area that was already hot and wet with need. "I can't wait to be inside you." He trailed his lips to my neck where he licked and sucked and teased while he rolled my nipple between his fingers and rocked against me.

I arched my back off the seat. His every touch sent shock waves of need rippling through me, crippling every thought of resistance that ever floated around in my head.

"Tell me you want this, Pup. Tell me you want this as much as I do," he panted against my neck. With one flick of his fingers, he opened the button on my jeans and pushed his hand down the front until he found what he was looking for. I moaned when he reached the spot already humming from the friction of his erection. "You're so fucking wet. You want this. I can feel it." He used my own wetness to rub circles against my clit. "You're so ready for me. Tell me you want me to fuck you. Let me hear you say it."

I threw my head back, unable to form the words. He was right. He was so fucking right. I wanted him. I wanted this.

Maybe, Grace was right when she said that he could be both a bad boy and a good man. That one didn't necessarily dictate the other.

My brain may not have been on board with the idea, but my body reacted to his every touch like it was made to be pleasured by him, like it couldn't get enough. Like I was going to wither away and die without him inside me. I liked him on top of me. Touching me. Wanting me.

No. I didn't like it. I *loved* it.

I loved sleeping with his big body next to me. I loved the way he made me feel so small. I loved the way his nostrils flared when he was about to kiss me, and then when he did, I loved that he kissed me like he was mad at me. Like it was my fault I was so desirable that he just had to put his lips to mine, his hands on me.

King sat up, and I had to hold my thighs together to stave off the ache that started building the second he'd touched me. King reached behind him, pulling his shirt up and over his head. He tossed it on the floor.

My hands went to his chest because there was no way they couldn't go there. It was glistening with his sweat, heaving with his labored breaths, and covered in the most fantastic art. I leaned up and licked his nipple.

He groaned and fisted my hair, forcing my head back roughly. His lips came back to mine. His tongue slid in and out of my mouth, moving in sync with my own. He rocked against me, and I no longer felt like my body was my own.

"I need to hear you say it, Pup. Say you want this, and it's yours. Tell me you want me," King panted.

He pushed my jeans and panties down over my ass. He'd only gotten them to my knees when he leaned down and dove in, flattening his tongue against my clit. I almost leapt out of the truck at the sensation, but finally settled when he held me down by my thighs. Over and over again, he licked me and sucked on my folds. His tongue pushed inside me. If it wasn't for him holding me down, I would've crushed his head with my legs.

He wasn't just licking me to make me come.

He was kissing me down there just like he was kissing my lips, my mouth. He was making out with my pussy.

A pressure started to build in my lower stomach, and I writhed under him, seeking the release I needed.

King mumbled something that I couldn't quite make out as I neared the edge. I was about to jump off into the most amazing life-changing orgasm when suddenly he was gone, and the cool night air brushed against all the parts of me that he'd made sopping wet.

Suddenly all too aware that I was lying there with my legs spread, my nakedness fully exposed to him. My cheeks flushed.

"What's wrong?" I asked, breathless like I'd just run a marathon.

King leaned back in his seat. Other than his raging hard-on straining against the front of his jeans, he looked completely unaffected by what we'd almost done.

"I'm not going to take you unless you tell me you want me. If you can't say the words while I've got my tongue in your pussy, then it's not something you really want. I told you before, when I fuck you, it's going to be because you want it so bad you'll be begging for it."

"When you touched me," I said slowly, "did it not seem like I wanted it? Did it not seem like I wanted you?"

King shook his head.

"Your body wants me. Just like my body wants you. But if you can't say the words, there's an underlying problem. What's got you so wrapped up that you can't tell me you want me when you're obviously about to come apart around me?" King leaned in, tucking a strand of hair behind my ears. "Are you still afraid of me?"

My eyes shot up to his. Is that what he thought? Sure, he was scary as shit, and at one point, I'd feared what he might do to me. But, he hasn't hurt me. He hasn't done anything but give me a place to stay and food to eat.

Because of him, I found a friend in Preppy.

Because of him, I was living in a state of the female equivalent of blue balls.

"No," I answered honestly. "I was. I mean, you can be a lot to take in."

"Yes, that I am." He glanced down at his erection.

I licked my lips wondering what he would taste like in my mouth.

"No," he groaned. "Don't you go looking at me like that. We need to have this conversation. If you keep looking at me like that, any resolve I have to stop is going to disappear, and I will bend you over the hood of this truck and pound you into oblivion." His words sent a spasm to the area still throbbing with want. I almost came right there in the truck without him even touching me. "So what is it? What is holding you back if it isn't me?"

I squeezed my eyes shut. "It's not you. It's me."

"Said in every cheesy break-up movie ever."

"No, you don't understand. I'm not just making decisions for myself. I have to think about her, too."

"Pup, I like a good threesome as much as the next guy, but I don't see anyone else in the truck with us. Who, exactly, are you referring to?"

"You know I don't remember anything before the summer, before I woke up, feeling like I'd just been put through a meat grinder."

King nodded, dragging me closer so that our thighs touched. I closed my eyes and focused on what I was trying to tell him instead of the rock-hard thigh making my spine tingle.

"Go on," he urged, softly kissing my jaw, trailing his lips behind my ear.

"I'm not going to be able to talk if you keep doing that."

"Yes, you are. Keep going. I'm listening."

My insides clenched, and I spat out the rest of my story while being pummeled with the sensation of King's lips on me.

"Well, I refer to the person I was before, when I had a memory, as HER. Someone else entirely, because that's who I was. A different person."

"Get to the fucking point. Because if you don't have one in the next minute, I'm putting my cock in you. Before I do that, though, I'm going to let you take me in your mouth and give you a taste because I know that's what you were thinking about just now."

Again, I closed my eyes and attempted to concentrate as King lifted me by the hips and sat me on his lap so that I was straddling him with my back to the steering wheel. In this intimate position, there was nowhere for me to hide. Although his hard cock was rocking against me, I had to push aside thoughts of him sinking into me in order to finish my story.

"The point is that I can't do anything that could potentially be life-changing because it isn't just my life I have to think about. I have to consider that one day all my memories, everything I am and everything I was, will come back to me. It may never happen, but I can't take the risk. Because the possibility that it might happen is out there. That day, when and if I become HER again, I will have to deal with all the things I did when I didn't know who I was. That's why even though I think your artwork is beyond amazing and I've imagined you creating something for me since I saw you tattoo for the very first time, I just can't do that to her. What if she hates it? What if she is morally against tattoos and I've left her with something she can't get rid of? That's why although my body wants you, and I want you, it doesn't matter. Because the person you see in front of you is just temporary." King pulled back and was now staring into my eyes as I spoke. "I can't help but melt into you when you touch me, but I can't do this to her. What if she has a boyfriend, a fiancé? What if being with you means ruining her?"

I sniffled. Tears welled up and were about to spill from my eyes. King forced me toward him with a hand on the back of my neck, and just as I thought he was going to kiss me again, he turned my face and licked my cheek, wiping my tears away with his tongue.

"What if she's a virgin?" I whispered.

King slowly shifted me off his lap and set me back on the passenger seat.

"I hadn't thought of that," he said softly. "And while I am both appalled and incredibly turned on by the idea of being the first one inside that pretty pussy of yours, I feel it necessary to point out the holes in your little theory about the person you were, before you came stumbling into my life."

"What would those holes be?" I asked.

"First, your virginity theory. Who the fuck cares? If your memory comes back and you go back to a life where I'm not around, at least you'll have enough amazing memories to last you through faking the orgasms with whatever schmuck you're with."

"Why is he a schmuck?"

"Trust me. A guy who let you wander far away and hasn't found you by now, if he's even looking for you at all, is a fucking schmuck. I didn't even like you at first. In fact, I downright fucking hated you, and I still didn't want you more than ten feet from me. Neither did my cock."

I shuddered. "And the next hole in my theory?" My voice was strained.

"Tattoos. Anyone who doesn't like my art can kick rocks."

"It's that simple?"

"Yes, it's that simple," he stated flatly. Then, his face grew serious. "It's that simple, but not because of some guy who may or may not be out there pining for you or the fear that you will regret letting me fuck you or tattoo you." King traced a line from the back of my hand to the top of my shoulder like he was creating an imaginary tattoo. "It's that simple because you can't live your life for someone you *might* be. So what if your memories come back and the person you were before comes with them? She will just have to fucking deal with the fact that you were here when she wasn't. Make your mark while you still can, Pup."

"You make it sound so easy."

"It is."

"It's not. I just…I can't," I breathed. I wouldn't be able to live with myself knowing that I wasn't protecting her.

"You made a promise that you would protect me. Well, I made a promise that I would protect her," I said, my voice barely a whisper.

"Have you even thought that who you are now is exactly the person you're supposed to be? That maybe with the slate wiped clean of bullshit outside influences that you are now more yourself than ever before?" he asked, with each point he was trying to make he grew louder.

"No." I hadn't thought of that. King had a point. "But living life thinking that was the truth was a gamble I'm not willing to take." I looked down to the floor and wished it would open up and suck me down into it.

"So, let me get this straight. You were willing to fuck random bikers, but you can't be with me?" There was a hint of cruelty in his voice. If his intentions were to sting, they worked.

"That's a low blow."

But King continued on as if I hadn't just interrupted. "So I'm just like them to you? Just like a biker you don't want to fuck and end up regretting?"

King turned the key and started the truck, pulling back onto the highway.

"No, you're not like them at all," I whispered, unsure if he heard me.

"How is it that you can see me as worse than them when I know you want me? I can feel it. Don't fucking deny it. Because it's bullshit, and you know it." King looked straight ahead at the road. He turned up the radio until Johnny Cash was singing so loud it rattled my eardrums. The tears in my eyes spilled over onto my cheeks.

I leaned against the window and hugged my arms to my chest. The lights from businesses and signs blurred together as we passed into streams of colored lights.

"You're right. You're much worse than them," I whispered, knowing full well that King couldn't hear me over the music. "Because with them, it wouldn't hurt this much."

Doe

KING HADN'T COME TO BED IN DAYS. I STILL HELPED HIM AT NIGHT IN HIS studio but our conversation never escalated to anything more than him barking orders at me.

On Saturday morning I'd found a box on the kitchen counter with a note addressed to me. The card read:

FOR OUR DATE. BE ON THE PORCH AT EIGHT-PREPPY

Our date? Why would we go out on a date? Inside the box was a short black strapless dress and a pair of matching heels.

Preppy had made sure I had a bunch of jeans and tank tops to wear on a daily basis. He even stopped at a store and let me pick out some underwear and bath stuff one day, but I didn't have anything like this.

The clock on the stove read only ten am. I was disappointed I'd have to wait so long to put it on.

At eight o'clock sharp, I stood by the steps and fidgeted with the hem of my new dress. I'd spent hours showering, shaving, and blow-drying my hair. I was beyond ready, thrilled to be doing something new and grateful for the distraction.

I had no clue what Preppy had up his tattooed sleeves.

"You ready, Doe?" he asked, bounding out from the door under the stairs.

He draped an arm over my shoulder and ushered me toward King's truck, which was already parked in front. "I wish I could take you in my car. But you know, it fucking blew up and shit," he said bitterly.

His usual short-sleeved dress shirt had been swapped out for a dark blue long-sleeved button down that he wore untucked over a pair of dark boot-cut jeans. His usual bow tie carefully in place. He smelled like he'd just gotten out of the shower. Like soap and shaving cream.

"Did you shave?" I asked. His beard looked just as long as it had that morning.

"Huh?" he asked, looking down at me.

"You smell like shaving cream, but you still have your beard."

"It's a date, baby girl. I manscaped in case I get lucky."

I laughed. "You're not getting lucky."

"I know. King would kill me, and I rather like my life. So, I think we'll leave that off the table. For now." He winked. "Besides, you may not let me get my cock wet, but maybe someone else will take pity on me when the night's over and let me get it in."

I laughed at Preppy, his smile taking the edge off his crude words.

"You look nice," I said. If I didn't know any better, I would say that Preppy actually blushed.

"Thanks. But tonight, I'm not Preppy."

"You're not?" I asked. "Then, who are you exactly?"

"Nope, this is a date. So tonight, you can call me Samuel. I would say that you look nice, too, but you look way more than nice. I would say..."

Preppy took a step back and slid his hand down my arm, to lock his fingers around my wrist. He, then, lifted my arm and twirled me around slowly to appraise me. My face flushed with embarrassment when I noticed he was staring at my ass.

"Hot. You look HOT, baby girl. Pancakes do a body good. Real fucking good."

"Thanks." I felt my cheeks redden. "I wish you could call me by my real name, too, but I don't know—"

The roar of a motorcycle drowned out my words. We both turned toward the noise. King pulled up the gravel drive and parked a shiny black bike next to one of the house pilings. It was the first time I'd seen him drive anything other than his beat-up old truck. He swung off his bike and ripped his helmet off his head, tossing it to the ground as he stomped toward us with furious steps. His brows furrowed, and his fists clenched at his sides. His eyes firmly locked on me as he approached, looking me up and down and then to where Preppy was still holding my hand.

My heart beat in a quick, uneven rhythm as he approached. My palms began to sweat. I plastered a fake smile on my face.

"Where the fuck did you get THAT thing?" King roared, pointing to my dress. His gaze darted back and forth from me to Preppy.

Preppy smiled and released my hand. Once again draping his arm over my shoulders, he tugged me into his side.

King's eyes widened at the gesture, and I thought for sure he was going to punch one or both of us. Preppy, however, seemed unaffected by King's mood.

"We're gonna paint the town red, Boss-Man," Preppy answered coolly. "How do we look?"

Something in the way he asked made me think he was goading King.

"He bought me the dress," I added, slightly embarrassed that King obviously didn't like it. It was strapless and form-fitting. Showing off the curves I'd developed in the days I'd been stuffing my face.

"Fuck no, you're not. I've changed my mind," King said, staring Preppy dead in the eyes. "You're gonna get your fucking ass back in the house before I put a fucking bullet in your skull. That's what you're going to fucking do."

"Why not?" I heard myself ask before I had time to register the fact that I had also shook off Preppy and stepped to King. He came forward, too. Our feet touched at the toes. Since I was much shorter than him, I had to look up to meet his disapproving gaze.

"Cause I fucking said so, Pup," King growled, his nostrils flaring.

His usual green eyes were now shining black pools of anger. There was a hardness to his features that suggested this was a fight I'd never be able to win.

That didn't mean I wasn't going to try.

"I'm here because I don't have any other options! I get that you're fucking mad at me, or that you fucking hate me. I do. But I just wanted to pretend for one fucking night that I'm a normal girl on a normal date in a normal place!"

Just as I turned to head back into the house, King grabbed my elbow and spun me around, he tipped my chin up.

"Stay. Here," he ordered, his face still hard and angry. "You." King pointed to Preppy. "A fucking word. *Now.*"

He gestured with his chin to the house, releasing me as he stormed up the steps and slammed the front door behind him. Preppy looked amused, although I'm not sure how he could've been with King steaming in such close proximity.

"Sorry, babe," Preppy said with a knowing smile. "Maybe, another time?" He bounded up the steps, taking them two at a time. I thought about following them in, but I didn't want to provoke King further.

I spent the next ten minutes stewing on the porch, wondering if they'd killed each other because I hadn't heard anything inside. The sun had long since set over the trees, so I stayed under the safety of the light of the porch. I soon got tired of standing. My ass had barely touched the bottom step when the front door swung open, and King came bounding out. I jumped up and held onto the railing to keep from falling onto the walkway.

"Let's go," King said, holding out a hand to me. Anger still lingered on his face, along with a bit of confusion.

"Go? Go where?" I asked.

"On a date thing." His brows furrowed again like my question confused him.

"With you?"

King nodded. Since his hand was still extended out to me and I'd made no move to take it, he reached over and grabbed my hand. That's when I looked at him, I mean *really* looked at him.

He was freshly showered and smelled like he'd just put on cologne. He wore his usual dark jeans and a tight black t-shirt. His stubble was still there but neatly trimmed. It's amazing what he'd done in the ten minutes he'd left me outside.

"With me," he confirmed, slowly raking his eyes over my body. His gaze burned into me.

"What happened to Preppy?" King stiffened.

"He's no longer available," King spat, obviously put off by the question.

"Oh," I said, looking down at my feet.

"Fuck. Just forget it. It was a fucking stupid idea anyway."

"What? No, I just... this was all Preppy's idea anyway."

"Shut up," he said, silencing my rant. King tugged on my hand and led me over to his bike. He handed me a helmet and straddled the seat. He turned the key and it came roaring to life. He turned and gestured to the space behind him.

I shouted over the engine, "I'm wearing a dress!"

King grabbed my hand and tugged me toward him. "I think we know by now that you know how to straddle, so get the fuck on." I pressed my thighs together, willing the memory of the night in his truck away.

"Why can't we just take the truck, or we can walk," I suggested.

King stared me down. "Pup?"

"Yeah?"

"Get on the fucking bike."

"You really are a fucking asshole, you know that?." I punctuated my words by digging my pointer finger into his chest. King smiled obnoxiously. I didn't want a smile. I wanted a fight. I was beginning to think it was long overdue.

"Took you long enough," he said, grabbing hold of my finger.

"Long enough for what?"

"To figure out I'm an asshole. Now, get on the fucking bike."

"Fuck you," I spat.

King got off the bike and stalked toward me. He snatched the helmet out of my hands and roughly shoved it onto my head. My hair was trapped over my eyes and I was momentarily disoriented. King took advantage of that, by picking me up and setting me on the bike.

I shrieked into my helmet, and before I could protest and jump off, we were in motion. My options were then limited to holding onto King or flying off the back of his bike.

Reluctantly, I wrapped my arms around his waist.

What I really wanted was to wrap my hands around his throat.

We drove for what seemed like only a few minutes but in reality it was more like a half of an hour. The normally stagnant and wet Florida night air blew cool all around us as the bike pressed forward into the night.

My jaw dropped, and my heart sped when the neon lights came into view.

A carnival.

King had brought me to a carnival.

The Ferris wheel overhead appeared so close I thought that if I reached my hands up into the air I might be able to touch one of the swaying carts.

When King brought the bike to a stop in the grass parking lot, my body was still humming from the vibrations of the engine. In my excitement at being at a real live carnival, I jumped off the bike quickly, grazing my calf on one of the hot pipes.

"Shit, shit, *shit!*" I shouted, bouncing around on one leg.

King set his helmet down and came around to where I was hopping around and wincing in pain. "Come here," he said.

I was still angry, the twenty-minute ride doing nothing to take the edge off wanting to do him physical harm. I ignored his request and bent down to inspect the damage on my leg.

King shook his head and walked over to me, picking me up under my shoulders and setting me on top of a nearby picnic table. "You need to learn to do what you're told," he said, lifting my leg to inspect the burn.

I huffed. "Picking me up and tossing me around is unnecessary, you know."

King leaned down and gently blew across the burn, sending hot chills up my spine. I was all too aware that the dress I wore had ridden up my thighs when he'd picked me up. I caught him glancing at the exposed white fabric between my legs.

"Then, do what you're fucking told the first time." He then proceeded to inspect me thoroughly. "It's not a bad burn," he said, but I could barely hear him over the memory of his breath against my skin.

"I thought you didn't do gentle," I teased.

King helped me set my foot back on the ground and reached for my hand.

"I don't." He turned to the gate, roughly yanking me behind him as to prove his point.

King paid for our tickets, and we entered through a turnstile. Once inside, my inner child sprang to life, and my anger was temporarily forgotten. Neon lights, carnival music, corn dog and cotton candy stands.

It was everything I ever wanted in a first date. Well, except maybe for a date who actually wanted to be there. I yanked my hand out of King's grip, but he grabbed me again and held my hand tighter, pulling me closer into his side.

"What do you want to do first, Pup?"

"Everything. I want to do absolutely everything!" I craned my neck to get a better look at the giant Ferris wheel.

"The Ferris wheel is last," King said, pushing me toward the row of games.

As we moved deeper and deeper into the crowd, the noise level around us increased tenfold. A group of kids whizzed by us, leaving bursts of laughter in their wake.

The carnival workers shouted the names of their games and advertised how easy it was to win one of the big stuffed animal prizes they held up.

King stopped at a game where the goal was to shoot water from a gun into a hippo's mouth in order to move the baby hippo up the ladder. Whoever shot their gun the steadiest and moved their baby hippo to the top the fastest was the winner.

"You in?"

"I'm so in," I answered, barely able to contain my excitement. I bounced up on the balls of my feet.

"Two," King said He removed a money clip from his pocket and plucked out a few bills, handing it to the man controlling the game. King took a seat on one of the ripped leather stools, and I took a seat a few stools down.

"Afraid to sit next to me?" King asked.

"No, but you're huge and these stools are small. I don't want to bump into your arm and lose just because you haven't missed a workout in three years." I closed one eye and readied my water gun.

King shook his head, "That mouth of yours," he said. There are several ways I could have taken that statement, but I didn't have time to think about it because I had a game to win.

"I'm warning you. I'm really good at this game," King said to me.

Was he being playful?

"Competitive, are we?" I asked, keeping my focus straight ahead at the bulls-eye.

"Oh, Pup. You have no idea."

The bell rang, and the carnie shouted, "GO!"

I squeezed the trigger. Water sprayed out of my gun and directly onto the target. My little hippo shot up the ladder, and just as quickly as it had started, the game was over. I looked over to King who was sitting back smiling. What was he smiling over? I was the one who won.

"Winner! Winner!" the Carny shouted He unclipped a huge stuffed deer from the top of the tent and handed it to King, who received the prize and then started to walk away.

He'd won? How was that possible?

"Hey!" I shouted, chasing after him. "Why did you get the prize? I won. My hippo was so far ahead of yours that I didn't even see yours move." King stopped.

"Pup, you didn't see my hippo move because I was done before you even began." He was smiling. A genuine, real–life, swoon-worthy smile that reached his eyes. It was a good look on him.

No, it was a GREAT look on him.

"You've got to be kidding me!" I shouted.

"Competitive, are we?" King asked, mocking me. "I told you I was good at that game."

King seemed like any other young man who was taking a girl out on a date. Well, any other six-foot-something tattooed wall of muscle who looked like he could be an underwear model.

I liked playful King.

I liked him a lot.

"You must have played that game before," I pouted. "Unfair advantage."

"Yeah, I'll give you that. This carnival has come here every year since I was a kid. Preppy and I used to sneak in the back. Over there." King pointed toward a gate in a chain-link fence with a huge padlock keeping it shut. "We'd steal corn dogs from the food stands, right out of the fryer. Although the padlock happened only after they found out how we were getting in."

I knew Preppy and King were best friends, but this was the first time I'd ever heard any stories from their childhood together.

"I tell you what," King started. "Since this is a date and all, and guys usually give their dates their prizes, I will let you have my deer." He held out the stuffed animal.

I didn't know if he was toying with me. If I didn't know how to handle ornery King, I certainly didn't know how to handle nice and playful King.

I snatched it out of his hands like he was going to reconsider his offer, and I tucked it tightly under my arm. King laughed.

"What's so funny now?" I asked.

"Doe...holding a doe." Okay, he'd got me on that one. I held my hand over my mouth to contain my laughter.

For the next few hours, we played every single game the place had to offer. I won none of them.

King made a point of handing me each of his prizes. Soon, I ran out of arm space to carry them all.

"I don't think we can play anymore," I told him, gesturing to the huge stack of cheap toys up to my chin.

The bell sounded for one of the games, and I was just about to walk away when King stopped me. "No, wait a sec."

We watched as a tiny boy tried three times to win a prize against two much older teenagers. After a minute the boy's dad pulled him aside. "That's enough, Sam. We can try again another time."

"But I wanted the stuffed alligator," the boy complained.

"You'll get it. Maybe, next year when you're a little bit bigger." The dad smiled.

King plucked a stuffed penguin from my arms and approached the boy and his father who were walking away from the game, the boy's bottom lip set in a pout. Tears welling up in his eyes.

"Excuse me," King said, getting their attention. The father looked alarmed and pulled his son into his leg.

King ignored the dad's reaction and bent down to the boy, holding out the penguin. "I know it's not an alligator, but penguins are just as cool. As a matter of fact, they're cooler. They live in the snow, and they're the only bird that doesn't fly. Did you know that?"

"No, I didn't know that," the boy said, with a thumb in his mouth.

"They also slide around on their bellies on the ice."

"Cooool," the boy said, staring at the penguin.

"Now, you take good care of him, okay?" The boy nodded and took the penguin.

"Thank you." The boy's dad mouthed to King.

He nodded, and they disappeared into the crowd.

King made his way back to me. "You're up next," he said as he approached.

We stood behind the games and gave out my prizes to kids who lost their games one by one until all I had left was the deer King had given me first.

We ate cotton candy. We ate corn dogs. We ate fried Oreos. We laughed like kids. We rode a gravity ride that locked you to the sides as it spun, and for ten minutes afterwards, I thought all the food was going to come back up.

"Here," King said, pushing a cup in front of me. "Grace says that a ginger ale is the best cure for an upset stomach."

I slowly sipped the bubbly drink, and I started to feel better almost instantly. King grabbed my cup and walked a few steps to toss it in the trash when I noticed a nearby woman ogling him.

I looked around, and it seemed like every woman at the fair, whether she was with a man or not, was undressing King with her eyes.

"Do they all have to do that?" I muttered under my breath.

"Does all who have to do what?" King asked.

"Do all the women have to look at you like they want to jump your bones?" I scoffed.

King put an arm around me. His lips brushed my ear when he whispered, "Unlike some people, they aren't hiding what they want." I opened my mouth to say something, but I couldn't find the words. "It's cute that you're jealous though."

"I'm not—"

"Time for the Ferris wheel," King announced. It was getting late, and the crowd had thinned.

"Why did we save it for last?" I asked.

"Because it's the best part," King said. "You always save the best for last."

King helped me into the squeaky cart while the carnival worker closed the little door to the bucket. There was barely enough room on the seat for the two of us. When I shoved my deer between us, King picked it up and handed it to the carnie, along with a bill from his pocket. "Take care of this for me until we get down will ya?"

"Sure thing, man!" He set the deer on the chair next to the ride's control panel.

King rested his arm on the back of the seat over my shoulder.

Then, we were lifting up into the air. Higher and higher we rose, stopping every so often to allow for other riders to board. Once we were almost at the top, we started to move more fluidly. Round and round we went, watching the city lights beneath us flicker and glow.

"Wow," I said, watching the people scurry around below. "They all look like ants from up here." I glanced over at King but he wasn't looking at the lights of the city or at the crowd.

He was looking at me.

The depth of his stare pinned me to the seat. "Pup, what I learned from being in prison is that we're all just a bunch of ants."

"How do you mean?"

"I mean we're all scurrying around, doing insignificant bullshit. We get this one life. ONE. And we spend too much time doing shit we don't want to do. I don't want to do that anymore."

"What do you mean?"

"I don't want to be remembered as the notorious Brantley King."

"Then, how do you want to be remembered?"

"I don't. I want to be forgotten."

"You can't mean that."

"I do. I used to want to go out in a blaze of glory. Now, I just want to live in my house, fish on a weekday, and tattoo when the mood strikes. And when it's my time to go, I want to fade out like the ending of a movie and be quickly forgotten."

"That sounds lonely."

"Not if you're with me, it won't be."

"Please, you already told me that I'm gone the second you get tired of me." I laughed.

King wasn't laughing. "I'm serious. What if I said I changed my mind? What if I wanted you to stay for real?"

I shook my head. "I wouldn't know what to say to that. I don't even know if you mean that or not." I sighed. "It's just not that simple. You know that I have to look out for her."

"Fuck that. Fuck *HER*," King said, raising his voice. "As I said, we get this one life. One. As of right this fucking second, I'm no longer going to spend it doing anything other than what I want to do. I don't want to grow old and look back and realize that I may have had a life, but I forgot to live it." King brushed his lips against mine. "Are you with me, Pup?"

"What are you doing?" I asked, my breath shallow and quick. King leaned into me and kissed the spot behind my ear, his lips igniting my skin. I felt the kiss to my very core, and I trembled.

"After everything, you still have no idea. Do you?"

"No idea of what?" I panted.

No sooner were the words out of my mouth than his lips crashed onto mine. His kiss was harsh and demanding. His tongue parted my lips, gaining entrance into my mouth, licking and dancing with my own. I moaned into him.

I was on fire. King's hand slipped up under my dress and found the place where I was already wet and ready for him. He groaned and pressed a finger into me, his thick cock nudged my thigh. He ran a hand up my neck and fisted a handful of my hair, turning me up to him so he could gain better access to my mouth while his fingers pushed in and out of me. I clenched around him, my orgasm building, when he suddenly pulled away.

"Why did you stop?" I asked, flustered, my legs still parted for him.

"Because, Pup, the ride's over."

I hadn't even noticed that we were at the bottom. The carnival worker came over and let us out of the bucket. I adjusted my dress and stood on shaky legs while King retrieved my deer.

We walked to the parking lot in complete silence.

We passed some sort of tool shed on our way to the bike. King suddenly grabbed me and dragged me into the shadows, pinning me hard against the wall of the shed.

"This is the last time I'm going to ask you this, Pup. Do you want me?" King asked, his lips finding mine again, asking the same question with his demanding kiss. My skin came alive and danced with anticipation. "I can't stay away from you anymore. I tried, and I can't do it. I want you. I need you to tell me all that hesitation bullshit is over and that I can have you. Stop being alive, and start living." He pulled a hair's breadth away and sought the answer in my face.

"Yes," I answered breathlessly. Because it was true. Every part of me wanted him. I'd been fighting it for too long for reasons that the longer I was around him seemed less and less important. "I want to be alive."

"I want you so fucking bad," King said, pinning me to the wall with his hips pressed against mine. His erection hard and ready against my core. My dress was up around my waist. Only his jeans and my panties separated us.

"Why do you call me *pup?*" I asked breathlessly while he lifted the sides of my dress so his hands could dip into the back of my panties. He dug his fingers into my ass cheeks and I gasped.

"Because when I first saw these wide, innocent eyes, you looked like a lost puppy dog."

I was disappointed with the comparison to a puppy, especially after Preppy had called me a stray.

"And," he continued, "I knew at that very moment when you stood in my doorway, that I wanted to keep you."

He emphasized his statement with a thrust of his hips. I let out a guttural moan, and he laughed softly into my ear, his tongue licking and sucking along my jawline and back to my mouth.

"Not here" he said, pulling away from me and adjusting my dress back down to cover my ass.

He led me back to his bike, making quick work of putting on my helmet. When I hopped on behind him and wrapped my arms around him, I felt him shudder under my touch. I let my hands slip just under his belt onto the bare flesh of his abs, and I heard him groan over the roar of the engine.

He wanted *me.*

Whoever that was.

And I wanted *him.*

As crazy as that was.

At least for the night, I wasn't going to think about what the girl with the memories would do, the girl who I tried to please on a daily basis. I was going to be selfish, and I was only going to think about what I wanted.

Who I wanted.

I made the decision to *live.*

chapter
twenty

Doe

WHEN WE PULLED UP TO THE HOUSE, I DIDN'T EXPECT TO SEE A PARTY IN full swing. Bikes lined the street, blocking our entrance to the property. King drove past them and turned onto another small dirt path I hadn't noticed before that led us right up to the garage.

King parked the bike and cut the engine. I took my helmet off and passed it to him so he could set it on the seat.

"What's going on?" I asked.

"It seems my hospitality is being taken advantage of," he muttered. King dragged me into the house by my hand and up the stairs to the main floor. In the living room, we passed a bunch of bikers standing around, watching an older, dark-skinned woman bounce up and down naked on the lap of a boy who looked younger than me, his pants around his feet. The patch on his vest read PROSPECT. His face was turned up to the ceiling, his eyes hooded in ecstasy, his mouth partially open.

"King!" Bear shouted, motioning to him. "Come over here, and watch this. Billy's just popped his cherry."

"What the fuck, Bear! What is all this?" King growled. His fist was clenched at his side, and the hand that held mine grew tighter and tighter. I could feel his pulse racing in his wrist.

Bear smiled and held out his arms. "Dude, it's a party. It's Saturday. We used to throw ten of these in a seven-day week. Didn't think you'd mind."

"Don't go anywhere. I'm coming back down. You and I need to talk." King pointed at Bear then dragged me upstairs to his room.

"I need you to stay in here while I talk to Bear. I'll be right back." For once, he wasn't barking orders at me. It sounded more like a plea. "Close the door. Keep it locked."

"Okay," I said, stepping into the room and shutting the door. It was the first time he'd told me to do something that I didn't feel the overwhelming need to argue with him.

Three hours later, there was still no sign of King, and the music seemed to be getting louder and louder. I'd read for a bit, clicked through some channels, and done my best to distract myself, but my curiosity was getting the best of me.

I didn't want to disobey him, but maybe, I could at least change locations.

I figured going into the tattoo studio in the next room wouldn't be disobeying his orders too much. Besides, King's sketchbook was in there, and it could help occupy me until he came back.

I crept out of the room. The party downstairs still raged although none of the party-goers had made their way upstairs like last time. I pushed open the door and stepped inside.

I wasn't prepared for what I found.

My jaw fell to the floor along with my heart and any faith I had in King and his promises. My heart disintegrated in my chest.

It was dark in the room except for the neon lights beating in time with the bass of the Nine Inch Nails song playing on the iPod dock. King was perched on his chair with his eyes closed, a joint at his lips. His jeans were down around his ankles. A topless brunette was down on her knees in front of him, reaching for the waistband of his boxers.

"What the fuck," I gasped. I was going to be sick. The asshole was just toying with me the entire time. He hadn't meant a word. Maybe, that was the revenge he'd been wanting since Nikki stole from him. Maybe, that was his game the entire time and now that I was humiliated my debt had officially been paid.

King's eyes opened suddenly, and I half-expected an apology for walking in and catching him in the act. At least, I expected an attempt at pulling up his pants. But it was my fault for thinking that way. Somewhere between the tattoos, the sandwiches on the dock, Grace's house, and the carnival, I'd forgotten who I was dealing with.

This was the man who held me against my will. Handcuffed me to his bed. Threatened my life.

Killed his own mother.

He was the fucking devil himself. And all it took was a slutty brunette on her knees to remind me of that.

"Get out," he barked. He took a long drag from the joint, then tugged on the brunette's hair, tipping her head back. He leaned over until his lips were almost touching hers and made a show of blowing the smoke directly into her mouth.

I slammed the door and ran down the hall. I grabbed a bottle of something off of the kitchen table and headed outside to the dock, ignoring catcalls from some of the bikers I left in my wake.

I walked past the raging bonfire and toward the water.

I sat down on the end of the small pier and dangled my legs over the edge. I tore the cap off the bottle and tossed it into the water. I held up the bottom of the bottle and chugged a few mouthfuls of the amber liquid. It tasted like pure gasoline mixed with pine-cleaner, burning my throat and stomach on its way down. I took a breath and kept on drinking, swallowing one horrible tasting mouthful after another. I didn't stop until I felt the hazy warmth begin to spread through me.

I wiped my mouth with my wrist and looked out onto the water.

I may not have known who I was in the past, but I knew who I didn't want to be, and who I didn't want to be was someone weak.

I'd fallen for it. His words. His body.

I'd fallen for him.

I may have set out to be a whore, but I sure as shit wasn't going to allow myself to be treated like one.

He may have been the notorious Brantley King to everyone back in that house and everyone in that town, but to me, he just became the asshole. The asshole who just minutes before had broken my fucking heart.

Things were so much easier when I hated him.

"This seat taken?" A deep voice asked. I shrugged. Bear sat down next to me and lit a cigarette. "Something bothering you, pretty girl?"

"Nope," I lied.

"I may not know shit about shit, but I can tell you that when a girl goes running from a party with only a bottle of whiskey for company, something is most definitely bothering her. In my experience, that something usually has a cock attached to it." Bear exhaled the smoke.

"Well, you're not completely wrong," I admitted. Turning up the bottle again, the liquid no longer burned when I swallowed.

"Easy, girl," Bear said, grabbing the bottle from me. He took a swig. "What's going on between you and King, anyway? You his now? Cause he sure looks at you like you are. And seeing as he didn't kill you and all, I'm thinking what he feels for you might be pretty fucking serious."

I shook my head. "Right now, he's in his studio, belonging to a brunette with fake tits." My eyes welled up with tears, but I refused to cry at my own stupidity.

"Ah, I see," Bear said, passing me back the bottle. "The kid doesn't appreciate what's right in front of him."

"He's not exactly a kid, Bear. Actually, I'm pretty sure he's older than you, and it's not that he doesn't see what's in front of him. It's that he just doesn't give a shit." I was more than tipsy, working my way to more than drunk. My words grew bolder in my mouth before I spat them out. Any filter I ever had was completely gone. "What do you see when you look at me?"

Bear looked out on the water and scratched his beard. "I see a very, very fucking beautiful girl who shouldn't be hanging out with the likes of anyone up in that house. Or anyone sitting next to her, for that matter. We're bad seeds, little girl. You're a good seed. I can tell. Shit, anyone within a hundred miles of here can tell. You don't belong here. That much is obvious."

"I don't belong anywhere," I admitted. A fog started to settle over the water, emerging from the trees on the other side of the bay, traveling toward, and brushing my ankles as it spread under the pier.

"Sure you do. First, you have to figure out where that someplace is. Then, you just have to want to belong there."

I'm not sure if Bear knew my entire story, but what he said was way too simplified of an answer, especially in my case.

I laughed. "Oh yeah? Well, I'm leaving here tonight, and I have nowhere to go. I don't want to live on the streets again, but that's where I'm going to be. It takes a lot more than wanting to belong somewhere, or not belong, or whatever," I said, my words slurring together.

"I remember talking to you that first night. Do you remember what I told you about coming back to the clubhouse with me?" Bear asked.

"Yes."

"I should've never sent you up to King. I should have dragged you away right then and there and made you mine that night before King had his way with you."

"King has never had his way with me," I slurred. "His way or the highway, maybe."

"No shit? Well that changes everything, baby," Bear said. His smile reached all the way to his eyes which were shockingly bright and beautiful. I was pretty sure his beard hid even more of his good looks, and a very drunk part of me wanted to pull on it to see if it would come off.

"It changes nothing, Bear. I'm still leaving. He's still with the brunette girl with the…" I cupped my hands in front of my chest. Bear laughed out loud, revealing a perfectly straight line of pearly white teeth.

"It changes everything, actually. Our bro code only goes so far. Seeing as how he's not claimed you as his, as stupid as that is, my offer is still good. What's fair is fair," Bear said, again taking the bottle from my hands.

I looked over at him and half-expected to find him laughing at his own joke, but his lips were in a straight line.

He was dead serious.

He also wasn't bad to look at. That night was the first time I'd seen his blonde hair pulled into a high bun on the back of his head.

"Listen," Bear said. "King's been my friend almost my entire life, but he knows the rules I live by. In my world, you're fair game, and I would love to put you on your back in my bed."

"You're just saying that. The truth is that you're not gonna want me when you find out that I don't know what I'm doing when it comes to—" I darted my eyes to the bulge in his jeans. "—that."

"Fuck," Bear swore, biting his bottom lip. "Darlin', I believe I want you even more now."

"You've got freckles under your eyes," I said, leaning toward him. He grabbed onto my shoulders before I fell forward.

"Yeah, kid. So I've been told." He laughed. He also had a dimple on his left cheek, which was on its own a ridiculous contradiction when it came to the big biker man sitting next to me.

"Why did you send me to him?" I asked. "I would've gone with you. You're nice. I needed a place to stay, and you've got freckles under your eyes, and I would've been a good biker whore for you."

Bear's eyebrows shot up. "Oh yeah?" he asked, a crooked smirk on his face. "I don't really see you as the biker whore type. But I can definitely see you on the back of my bike."

"But you said I don't belong here. That I shouldn't hang out with you. Or any of those—" I waved the bottle around behind me, missing Bear's jaw by only an inch or two. "—people up there in the stupid house. Stupid people in the stupid house on stupid stilts." My shoulders slumped. "Bear, my heart was just getting warm. Now, it's all cold again."

Bear grabbed the bottle from my hand and set it down on the dock.

"I said you didn't belong here. I said you were too good to hang out with me. I didn't say that I wouldn't hang out with you. You may be too good for me, but I'm the kind of guy who can live with that." Bear placed a hand against my cheek. I could see why they called him Bear. He was strong and warm and his hands were so big they reminded me of giant paws. I closed my eyes and swayed into him. He leaned in close, his lips only a breath away from mine.

"Will you come with me, baby girl? I don't know if I can warm your heart, but I sure as shit can warm your body. I know for a fact that you can warm my bed. Then, maybe, we'll work on that cold heart of yours. We'll take it one day at a time." He assured me.

Bear sounded sincere, and what he was offering was exactly what I was looking for weeks earlier.

It seemed like a lifetime ago.

A lifetime ago when King wasn't in my life.

"I don't know," I answered honestly.

I couldn't stay with King anymore; that much I was certain of. And all the liquid courage in the world wouldn't be enough for me to convince myself that I could survive out on the streets again, scrounging for food and shelter.

Bear's offer was all I had, but I couldn't bring myself to say yes. Saying yes meant closing the door on King altogether. Was that something I was ready to do? I looked back up at the house. The light was now off in King's studio.

I may not have been ready to close that door, but just as I'd thought he'd opened it, he'd slammed it in my face.

It was time for me to do the same.

"I guess I'm going to have to do a little more to convince you." Bear wrapped his arms around me and pulled me into his big warm body. Right before his lips touched mine, I felt it.

Or rather, I felt *him*.

"Get the fuck away from her, Bear," King seethed. A clicking sound grabbed my attention, and I whipped my head around to where King stood behind us on the dock, his gun cocked and aimed at Bear.

"Done already?" I asked, all too aware of Bear's arms still wrapped around my waist. I made no move to push him away. "She must be disappointed that the almighty Brantley King, The King of the stupid Causeway, couldn't last longer."

Bear chuckled.

I've spent so much time trying not to make King angry, and it's never worked. I was tired of walking on eggshells around him. I wanted to make him angry. I wanted to fight with him more than I wanted anything. I wanted to scream.

I wanted to claw his fucking eyes out.

I wanted to hurt him the way he hurt me.

"Get the fuck away from her, Bear," King repeated.

"We're just talking man," Bear said, no sign of fear in his voice. If anything, he was amused.

"Looks like you're doing more than that. Get your fucking hands off her, and go fucking talk to someone else," King warned. "She's. Mine."

"Oh yeah? Well, you may want to tell her that because you ain't got her thinking the same thing."

"The only reason you don't have a bullet in your fucking skull is because we've got history. But in two fucking seconds, if you don't get your dirty fucking hands off my girl, I will say fuck-all to our history and blow your mother fucking head off," King said angrily through gritted teeth.

"Ain't gotta get your pretty panties all up in a twist, brother." Bear got up and brushed off his jeans. "Sorry darlin'. Maybe, some other time." He winked at me and whispered, "Offer still stands. You need me, you come find me."

I could feel the anger radiating off King when Bear walked past him, nudging his shoulder. "You might want to put your claim on that before the boys get wind that you haven't," Bear told him. "She's fair game to the bikers in these parts, including me, so you best do it and do it soon. That is, if she still wants your dumb ass."

Bear was one brave soul to talk to King while the look on his face screamed nothing but murderous rage. I half-expected King to go ape shit and make good on his promise to shoot Bear but the second he'd disappeared into the shadows, King stepped onto the dock.

"I hate the way you make me feel. Well, most of the time," I spat. I was tired of dancing around the truth. "I hate the confusion you bring into my already confused life. I need this back and forth shit to end." I took a deep breath. "I can't take it anymore. You like me. You hate me. You like me. You want to kill me. You want to fuck me. You want me to stay. You want me to *live*. My head is fucking spinning over here."

My buzz faded faster than the setting sun.

"You should leave. I don't want you here," I added.

"I know. I don't care," King said.

"Oh, I'm fully aware that you don't care. That I know."

"You don't know shit, Pup," King barked.

"Oh yeah? So you didn't just spend the entire night at the carnival all over me, saying sweet shit to me, making me feel like this stupid thing between us is something more than just a stupid thing, only to whip out your dick with someone else the very first chance you got? Go back to the fucking house, King. Go back to that girl. I hope she's everything you wanted."

"I can't," King said evenly.

"Why not? Seemed easy for you before."

"Because, Pup, I don't want to. No matter how hard I try to fight this, I'm drawn to you. You think I like this back and forth shit? You think you're the only one who's fucking confused here?" He shook his head like he couldn't believe the words that were coming out of his mouth. "I'm drawn to you," he repeated turning my chin up to him.

"What do you expect? Am I supposed to fall at your feet and thank you for being 'drawn to me'?" Not only was he confusing, he was fucking infuriating. "Drawn to me? You're drawn to me! Well, let me just take off my fucking panties then, and let's do this shit. Yeah, you were really drawn to me. Tell me something, *KING*. Do most first dates end with the guy getting sucked off by another girl? I mean, I've never been on one, so you tell me. I could be wrong here. Because if the answer is yes, then this date has gone fucking swimmingly!"

"I'm...FUCK! You think you know everything, but you don't. All you do is run those pretty lips of yours and expect me to be able to just give into you!" King threw his hands up in the air. "You make me fucking crazy, you know that!" he shouted.

"I make YOU crazy? How the fuck do you think I feel? Most of the time I don't know if you want to kill me or fuck me!" I screamed, every single word he spoke ignited my anger until it wasn't something I could even begin to hold back.

King had the audacity to actually smile. He leaned forward and whispered seductively against my cheek, "Can't I want both, Pup?"

I pulled back and stood up.

"NO! You can't! And stop calling me, Pup. It's a stupid fucking name. I'm not your fucking pet!"

I paced the dock. My rage was at a boiling point I couldn't turn off. This was his fault. He'd made me into this lunatic.

King stood and grabbed my face with both hands, forcing me to look at him. "Yes, you are," he said, as he lowered his lips and brushed them softly against mine in a move so gentle, so unlike him, it took me a few seconds before I registered what was happening.

Then, my anger returned, in full force. Using both my hands, I pushed against his chest until he had no choice but to release me.

"Fuck you! You don't want to keep me!" I shouted over my shoulder as I made my way to the front of the house and started down the gravel driveway. "Do you think I'm stupid? You wouldn't be getting your jollies while I'm in the next room if it was me you wanted."

A large hand grabbed my shoulder and spun me around.

"Let go of me!" I shouted.

"Listen, Pup. I've tried it your way. I tried gentle just now, but you didn't listen. Now, we're going to do it my way, and you're going to fucking listen. Don't make me have to cuff you again," he warned.

King's tone was all anger and confidence. I didn't doubt for a moment that he would make good on his threat. He wrapped his arms around my waist and held my hands together behind my back, locking my struggling body against his.

"I did that to push you away," he admitted. "I wanted you to see it."

"Congratulations, it worked," I spat. "You should be fucking happy."

"You and that tongue of yours." King shook his head. "No, I'm not happy. I'm far from fucking happy. I've been far from fucking happy since I got out of prison. If I think back, I wasn't exactly happy before prison either, and it's your fucking fault!"

"How the fuck is that my fault?" Now, he'd gone too far, blaming me for his life years before I was even in it.

"Because you are the one who made me realize I was fucking unhappy. Because with you, I think I can actually BE happy!" He shook me when he spoke, like he wanted to shake the words into my brain to make me understand what it was he was saying.

I needed it all to be over. It was too much. The mind fuck was more torture than I could take. I wanted him. I wanted to believe him. But words were just words, and coming from King, they were probably just another method to keep torturing me.

I just wanted to be left alone. It was time for me to go. "I'm leaving. Just let me go," I begged, softly.

King shook his head. "No. You're not going anywhere."

"You can't keep me here," I stated.

"See, that's where you're wrong. I think I've proven that I can," King argued. "Besides, where would you go? Back out on streets?"

"Maybe. What do you care, anyway?" I bit back.

"You seem to forget what it's like out there on your own. Or maybe we can dig up Ed, and he can tell you how he planned to dispose of your body when he was done raping you," King spat.

"I'd rather take chances with my life out there—" My chest constricted. "—than take chances with my heart here."

"No," King argued.

"What the hell do you want from me?" I asked. My anger battled against the heartbreaking thought of leaving and never seeing King again. "Why don't you just gut me, and get it over with? Do whatever it is you want to do to me. Hit me. Fuck me. Fucking *KILL* me. Just. Stop. *HURTING*. Me."

Sobs emerged from my throat, and I fell limp into his arms.

"Baby," King said, holding me tighter so that I wouldn't drop to the ground. It was the first time he'd ever called me that, and when I tried to register the endearment, it fell flat. "I'm so sorry. I didn't fuck that girl. I couldn't do it. She didn't touch me. I stopped the second you shut the door. I swear. I'm so sorry. You're the last person I want to hurt. I just don't know how to fucking do this."

"Do what?" I asked him. A tear fell from my cheek and onto his arm. As much as I didn't want to, I buried my face into his shirt and clenched the fabric in my fists.

His voice cracked when he whispered, "I don't know. Any of it. I don't even fucking know what this is."

"That's not good enough," I said, not really sure what part I was talking about. Maybe, his apology. Maybe his actions. Maybe, his uncertainty. Maybe, all of it.

"I think that's the problem," King said. "You deserve so much more than an ex-con who has nothing to offer you. You deserve so much more than me. It was easy to keep you when you were just my mine, my property. It's hard to keep you as my girl. I don't know when it all shifted, but it did. And that's what I want, but it's something I've never wanted before. I'd never even taken a girl out on a date before tonight. I want you in my life more than anything, but it's so much more complicated than just wanting it. So much more than you know."

"If you're going to let me go, let me go. If you're going to let me in, let me in. But, you have to pick one. You can't hold me close at night and push me away every morning when the sun comes out." I pushed off of his chest again and turned to walk away, but he pulled me back.

King kissed the top of my head. "I know, baby. I know."

"You don't know shit!"

Breaking free, I headed to the front of the house, away from the party, and away from King. I needed to be alone. I needed to think. King caught up with me easily, each one of his strides accounting for at least three of my own.

"I'm done with nice, Pup," King shouted from close behind me. I continued marching away, trying to put some space between us.

"You're done being nice?" I called back over my shoulder. "You've never been nice. You've lied to me and toyed with me, and that is not *nice*."

King caught me from behind just as I approached the first pillar under the house. He pushed me up against it and pressed himself to my back, his erection prodding the seam of my ass.

"Bear is nice," I said with my cheek pressed sideways against the pillar. "Bear offered to take me in. He wanted me to stay with him at the clubhouse. He wants me to keep his bed warm, fuck his brains out. Told me he wanted me on the back of his bike."

"What the fuck did you just say to me?" King hissed into my neck, his teeth against my skin. I didn't let that stop me from raining down my wrath on him. He deserved every last bit of it. I spun myself around in his arms, but he was too fast. Before I could bolt, he had me pegged against the pillar, my back to his front. His eyes darkened. A vein pulsed in his neck. His jaw was set on a hard line.

"You heard me," I said. "I was going to say yes, too. I was going to go with him and let him put his hands on me. You saw us. He was about to kiss me. I was going to let him." I was wild with power, crazed with lust, and completely reckless of the consequences of my actions.

I was free.

I gave zero fucks.

It was fucking amazing.

"What the fuck have I been telling you?" King roared pushing his knee between my legs, spreading them apart until I was straddling his thigh.

"Nothing. You've been telling me nothing but some fucking bullshit about being yours for weeks now."

"Newsflash, little girl. You were mine from the first moment you walked in on me fucking that girl on my table. You were mine then, and you're mine now." King looked as if any control he had was gone. He'd snapped.

I didn't care.

"You're a fucking liar," I spat.

"I've never lied about that. You. Are. Mine."

"Fuck you. I don't belong to you or anyone else!" I yelled. King pressed his forehead against mine.

"I'm only going to say this once more. You." He thrust up against me, his erection against my core, and I gasped. "Are." He did it again. This time, I had to put my arms on his shoulders to prevent myself from falling. "Mine," he said, hammering in his point with another thrust of his hips.

I pulled back and looked him dead in the eye. "Fucking prove it," I challenged.

King growled and pushed his hands up my dress, forcefully ripping my panties down my legs. We were in the shadows, but anyone walking by the side of the house could see us. The instant he touched me, I was too lost in sensation to care.

Zero fucks.

King kissed me. An all-encompassing kiss. A possession. He wasn't kissing my mouth. He was claiming me as his, and I was going to leave my mark on him in every way I could.

My entire body ignited into the flame he'd been stoking inside of me for weeks. He kneaded my breasts through my dress and attacked my neck with his lips. He lifted me up and wrapped my thighs around his waist. I grunted in frustration, gyrating against his erection. I couldn't get close enough. I couldn't find the friction I needed.

"You a virgin, Pup?" King asked wickedly.

"You know I don't know that," I panted.

"Cause I'm letting you know right now that there won't be a question if you are after tonight. I'm going to be buried so deep inside your sweet pussy you won't ever again forget who owns it."

He pushed down my dress, exposing my breasts, then yanked up the bottom until I was naked except for a scrap of fabric lingering around my midsection.

"Fuck yes," he hissed through his teeth.

After that, we were all hands and mouths. Touching, exploring, needing, biting. Teeth clacking together in an effort to get closer to one another. It was sloppy and wet and wonderful, and it wasn't enough. King reached down between us, released his belt, and pushed down the front of his jeans. His erection sprang free. Smooth, soft, and hard as stone prodded up against warm and wet, seeking entrance.

"Yes," I breathed. I was ready. I needed him inside me more than I needed to breathe.

King lined up his cock with his hand, and in one long thrust, he was inside of me. He groaned as he pushed his way into my tightness, stretching and filling me until I thought I was going to fall apart from the inside out. It hurt, but it was a pleasurable kind of pain, caused by the unfamiliar feeling of being so full.

The pain he caused was a pleasure all its own.

"Fuck yes," King moaned, now fully seated inside me.

I groaned loudly, not caring who heard me. King thrust up inside me, and my insides clenched around him. Every time he pulled out, he rubbed against that spot inside that made me see stars before thrusting angrily back in.

Again and again.

"I told you," he said. "I told you you're mine. This pussy. This pussy is mine. Don't fucking forget that shit again."

He thrust hard and angry. I took him. All of him. His cock. His anger. His possession. I let him claim me with his kiss, his cock, his words.

We were fighting with our sex.

A back and forth.

A give and take.

With our sex, we told each other *I hate you* and *I want you* and *I don't want you to leave.*

"Fuck, Pup. Fuck. I knew it. I knew it would be like this," King said breathlessly.

A pressure was building inside of me that was ten times more powerful than when King had made me come on his fingers. Growing with each stroke. Faster and faster he plunged into my depths until he didn't just give me an orgasm; he ripped it from my body.

I shouted out my release as I came and held onto King for dear life, tightening my thighs around him, digging the heels of my feet into his ass as he furiously pumped into me. I saw stars, bright and vivid, dancing in front of my eyes until I thought that I might pass out and die right there in his arms. Maybe, I did choose King being inside of me over breathing, because I couldn't seem to catch my breath.

"Look at me," King ordered, his voice deep and raspy like he was trying to hold onto his control. I was too lost in coming down from my orgasm high to pay any attention to what he was saying. "Look at me!"

This time he emphasized his words with a thrust of his hips. I moaned and opened my eyes.

"Don't look away," he ordered, holding my gaze as his cock hardened and twitched. He groaned as he came inside of me, spilling his wet warmth into my depths.

We'd said all the things with our bodies that our mouths had failed to communicate over and over again. He'd told me that I was his before, that I belonged to him. But before that night, I hadn't believed him.

It was what his body told me that took me by surprise and shook me to my very core.

He was mine.

chapter
twenty-one

Doe

"COME WITH ME," KING SAID. RIGHTING MY CLOTHES, HE TOOK MY hand and led me back to the pier. When we passed the bonfire, we were greeted with a lot of whistling and applause.

They'd obviously heard us.

I didn't care.

We sat on the dock with our legs dangling over the side. The fog had lifted off the water. The full moon cast our shadows over the glass-like bay, making it appear like black ice.

King held my hand in his, and when I tried to pry it away, he tightened his grip.

"King," I started.

"Brantley," he corrected. "Call me by my first name."

"Brantley," I said, testing his name out.

"I hated it growing up, but for good or for worse, it's the only thing my mama ever gave me. Grace is the only other person who uses it." He paused, then added, "I like the way it sounds when you say it." His serious tone and soft eyes made me question where he was going with this, but then, it hit me.

He was letting me in.

"Okay, Brantley, what else you got?" I nudged his shoulder. He took a deep breath.

"You know about Max?"

I nodded. The girl we went to see, the one from the picture. "Your sister."

"Pup, Max isn't my sister," King admitted.

"Then, who is she to you?" I asked. If she wasn't family, then why did he have so much interest in her?

"She's my daughter."

Holy. Shit.

"Your daughter?" I asked, my throat tightening.

"Yeah, Max is my daughter. She's the real reason why I went to prison, and only Preppy and Bear know the truth about her." He squeezed my hand tighter. Looking out over the water, he seemed pained to be recalling memories associated with Max. "Do you want to know the story? Because you asked me if I wanted to let you go or keep you, and I want to let you in. I want to keep you, but it's a hard story for me to tell. I've never told it to anyone. The only people who know were there in some way."

"I want to know."

"Do you know why I was in prison?"

"Because of your mom."

"Yeah," he agreed. "I don't make apologies for the things I've needed to do for the sake of business. Preppy and I had shit lives growing up. We did everything we could to turn it around for ourselves, most of those things were far outside the law, but we did it. Shit was amazing for a while. But my anger would get the best of me, and I would almost always be the one who ended up in jail here and there, usually just overnight. Sometimes, for thirty or sixty day stretches, depending on the charges. The other players in the game we play know the rules. They also know that when you step out of line, things happen. Things that make you dead. But this wasn't one of those times. I didn't pull a trigger, or use a knife, or send someone after her."

"Your mom?" I asked.

He nodded, then told me his story.

By the time I was fifteen, Me, Prep, and Bear were our own little crew. Just three young shitheads who just wanted to have a good time, get laid, and make some fucking money. Surprisingly, we did make money. Enough for me to buy the house.

The three of us were on top of the world for a while. I'm not gonna lie. It was the best fucking time of my entire life.

But then, I got pinched. It wasn't the first time, and it wasn't for anything I should've actually gotten pinched for. A stupid bar fight in an upscale place Preppy wanted to check out across the river in Coral Pines. Some shitty tourist spot.

I was talking to a girl when some pink sweater-tied-around-his-shoulders douche-bag stepped to me for talking to her. We got into it, broke some shit in the bar, chairs, glasses, tables.

I'm covered in tattoos, and I have a record. He's got a pink fucking sweater tied around his shoulders. It was easy to figure out which one of us was going to jail when the sheriff showed up.

I got ninety days because of my priors. When I was in County, this girl I used to screw around with showed up for visitation. She was as big as a fucking house. I thought that she was going to give birth right there in the visitors' room. She told me the baby was mine, said that she wanted to raise it with me when I got out.

I didn't think much of the girl, but she was nice enough, and after I got over the initial shock of it all, I was really excited to be a dad. I made a plan, made promises to myself that I was going to be a good dad, especially since I could only narrow down who my father was to every man in town except Mr. Wong who ran the corner store, for obvious reasons.

I wrote the baby letters from prison, though Tricia didn't know then if it was a boy or a girl. She'd said they tried to find out on the ultrasound but he or she was moving around too much. It was exactly what I needed. And then it was what I wanted.

Sure I had money, but the baby gave me a reason to want more out of life.

Purpose.

The morning I got out of county, Tricia was supposed to pick me up but never showed. I walked to a payphone to call her, and when she answered, she told me she'd had the baby the week before.

A girl.

She'd named her Max, the girl name we picked out when she was still pregnant.

I asked her where the baby was, and she mumbled something about it being too hard and that she couldn't handle it. That the whole motherhood thing wasn't for her. She said she wasn't coming back. There was a lot of noise in the background, glasses clinking, music. It sounded like she was at a bar. She was shouting into the phone.

Where the fuck is she? I kept asking her over and over again. For a second, I thought she was going to say I gave her up or something, and I was already thinking about who the fuck I was going to have to kill to get her back when Tricia said something that surprised me and turned my stomach.

I LEFT HER WITH YOUR MOTHER

Before that day, I hadn't seen my mom but a handful of times in years, and none of those times were on purpose. Most of the time, when I ran into her, she didn't know who I was. The very last time I'd seen her, she called me Travis and asked me how Bermuda was.

As soon as Tricia told me where the baby was, I hung up and called my mom, but the phone line was dead, and I didn't know if she had a cell.

I took a cab to Mom's and called Preppy to meet me there.

I got there before he did.

I knew walking up to the door that something was wrong. I could feel it in my gut.

I banged on the door of her apartment until my knuckles bled, but there wasn't any answer. I could hear the static from a TV inside. I screamed out for my mom, but there was no response. I was about to turn around and walk away, check with some of the neighbors to see if she even still lived there, but then I heard it.

I heard her.

My Baby.

Crying.

My baby was crying.

Not just a little cry or a cranky cry, but a strangled cry straight from the gut, the kind that says that shit ain't right.

It's like she knew I was there, and she was calling out to me.

I kicked in the front door. The living room was dark except for the TV. When I took a step, trash got stuck on my shoes, fast food wrappers, cigarette butts. The counter was littered with garbage. The trash can was overflowing. Flies circled the kitchen sink which was piled high with dirty dishes.

I heard her cry again. It was coming from the back of the apartment.

I ran into one of the spare rooms and turned on the switch, but nothing came on. It took a second for my eyes to adjust to the dark, but when they did, I saw this little baby, this beautiful, scared, skinny, little baby, no bigger than half my forearm, covered in shit from head to fucking toe. Her eyes were red and crusted over from crying. She wasn't in a crib. She was lying on a dirty sheet on the floor. No bottle. No blanket. No lights. No nothing.

I gently scooped her up in my arms, and she weighed practically nothing. Even though she was visibly hurting and I was hurting for her, I remember that first feeling of holding her. Before she was even born, she became the most important thing in the world to me, but holding her sealed the deal. There was nothing I wouldn't do for her. Nothing.

I would hurt anyone and everyone who ever made my baby cry like that again. I would burn down cities for her.

I fell to the ground with my back against the wall and rocked her until she calmed. I told her about all the things I was going to buy for her. I told her that daddy was here, that she was safe. I got up and found the cleanest towel I could and wrapped her up in it. She settled against my chest and fell asleep.

I was fighting mad. Deeply disturbed. And completely in love. All at the same time.

I was leaving with Max in my arms when the light from the TV flashed, and I saw a shadow in the La-Z-Boy.. Sure enough, it was my Mom. Next to her was an empty bottle of some cheap fucking whiskey and an ashtray full of little bags of leftover crystal.

She didn't take care of my newborn baby because she was too fucking busy getting drunk and high.

Max would've died if I hadn't gotten to her in time.

It was that thought that set me off. It still pisses me off to this day, and it makes remembering what happened next a whole lot easier to digest when I recall the memory.

Rage consumed me. The kind that makes you want to rip out someone's throat with your bare fucking hands.

A lit cigarette hung from her bottom lip, an open newspaper on her lap. Her face was covered in pock marks and her skin was draping off of it like it was melting. As much as I wanted to hurt her, it was like the fucking karma cosmos or whatever aligned, because the lit cigarette fell from her mouth, and the newspaper ignited.

I stood there and watched it happen.

I was happy. It couldn't have gone better if I lit the fire myself. It was a horrible way to die, but knowing what could have happened to Max, I really didn't give a shit if it was the most horrible death imaginable. To me, in that moment, she deserved it.

I still feel that way.

Mom's chest rose and fell, so I knew she was alive, but she was so far gone into whatever high she'd been chasing that not even a fire on her lap disturbed her.

When the paper fell to the ground, the carpet caught fire. The light from the flames allowed me to get a good look at the place. There wasn't a section of the floor that wasn't covered in filth and rusty syringes poked out of the couch like it was a pin-cushion.

When the flames got higher, I made the decision.

I turned around and left.

I felt the heat behind me as I walked away. I was halfway across the street when the windows exploded and the glass shattered.

I bought diapers, bottles, and formula from the nearby convenient store and hosed Max off in the restroom the best I could. It took me ten minutes to figure out how to put on the diaper.

Preppy saw the flames from my mom's trailer and pulled up behind the gas station.

He took us home.

He sang to her made up, profanity laced, lullabies.

Max gulped down a bottle so quick she would pause to choke, and my heart skipped out of my chest every time she did it, but then she would keep going.

I was so nervous. I was a single guy in my early twenties who'd never so much as been in the same room as a newborn before. I'd never even spent more than a couple of hours with the same woman.

And suddenly, I had this baby girl to raise. It was the first time in my life that I can say I was truly terrified.

I talked to her again and hummed some Zeppelin to her until she fell asleep on my chest.

I covered us both up with a blanket and watched the fan spin around until I saw lights flashing through my front windows.

Blue and red.

"It turns out the convenient store had some pretty decent surveillance. Since I walked away without seeking help and I made no attempt to douse the fire or save my mom, they arrested me. Charged me with manslaughter and put me away.

Max got sent to foster care right away since they couldn't find Tricia. They wouldn't release the baby to Preppy because he was a felon himself, not to mention he didn't have a legit job on record, anyway. Grace was in Georgia, getting treatment for her first fight with her cancer at the time.

"Do you know what ever happened to Tricia?"

"No, but if she's smart, she'll never show her fucking face in this town again." King sighed. "They took her from me. I was her dad for only three hours, and they were the three best hours of my fucking life. And they fucking took her from me."

"You're still her dad," I offered.

"Yeah, I've been trying to be," King said. "While I was away, I did everything I could. Filed papers. Hired lawyers. But it got me nowhere."

"Is there anything else you can do?" I asked. "There has to be. This can't be it."

"There are two options left, at least two that I know of. The first one is a long shot." King flashed a sad smile. "But there's this guy, a big shot judge. A dirty fucking politician. Bear has ties to him through the MC. The senator thinks he can make him see things my way and rule for custody in my favor."

"So what are you waiting for? Do that!" I shouted excitedly.

"It will cost me about a mil," King said flatly, killing my growing enthusiasm.

"Shit," I cursed. "A mil? As in a million dollars?"

King laughed. "Yes, Pup, as in one million green-backed American fucking dollars."

"Do you have that kind of money?" I asked.

"I did," King said. "I don't anymore. We sunk everything into getting the granny operation going. Even if I sold the house, it needs work, and that costs even more money. And the market sucks right now, so even if I sold it I wouldn't be able to come up with even half that."

"And if you do get custody, you need a home to bring her to," I added.

"Yeah, I've imagined building her a tree house in the big oak by the garage and turning my studio into her room, move my tattoo shit into the garage apartment."

"Then, where would Bear go?" I asked.

"Home! Bear has a room at his pop's place and a room at the clubhouse. He just likes to take up all the rent-free space he can." King laughed.

"I am so, so sorry, about all of it," I said, tears spilling out onto my cheeks. He wiped them away with the pad of his thumb.

"Don't be sorry, Pup. I'll never be the good guy in the story. I let my mom burn to death. I lost my daughter because of who I am and the things I've done. That shit's on me. That's my cross to carry."

The deep need to help reunite King with his daughter dictated my decision-making. I took a deep breath and grabbed his hands, folding them onto my lap.

"What do we need to do next?"

"We?"

"Yeah." I let the word sink in. "We."

"WE don't need to do anything. I'll figure something out."

"But wait. You said there was a second option."

King shook his head. "It's a worst-case scenario, and honestly, it's going to be bad whether I decide to do it or not. I can't win either way."

"Tell me what exactly is it you'd have to do."

"It's a dark road to travel down, and I'm not sure it's one I could ever come back from." It was the lingering sadness in his voice that made my heart break for him and made me not want to press him further. "But it's a worst-case scenario, so I'll cross that bridge when and if it comes down to it." King looked at me thoughtfully. "For now, I'm going to kick the granny thing in high gear and see what we can come up with."

"Let me know if you need my help. I'll do anything."

"I'll remember you said that," King said, pulling me onto his lap.

"I mean it."

"So did I," King replied, squeezing me tighter. He buried his nose in my neck. "I might need you to stay with Grace a while."

"Why, is she okay? I mean…you know." I stammered.

"Grace is fine for now, but we might have some shit going down here soon, and I need you far away from it."

"The Isaac thing?" I asked.

"Yeah, the Isaac thing. But don't worry about it. Just know that when I say you need to go to Grace's that's where you need to be. No questions asked. No arguing bullshit. You got me?"

"I got you."

"Can we talk more later, Pup? I feel like a fucking chick right now, spilling my guts to you." King laughed.

"Yeah, we can talk more later," I said.

I wrapped my arms around King's neck and looked over the water. The bird that was the inspiration for my sketch sat on top of a crab trap buoy in the middle of the bay. His beak was down, searching in the water for his next meal.

"So what now?" I asked, turning back to King.

"Now? Now, we need to go upstairs, and I need to get you in my bed because I'm not even fucking close to being done with you tonight."

chapter

twenty-two

Doe

"GET UP," KING SAID.

He took me by the hand and lifted me off the mattress. I was still half asleep. Knocked into a sex coma after King proved that when he said he wasn't nearly done with me, he wasn't lying.

Heat coursed from his hand into mine and shot directly into my erratically beating heart, causing my breath to hitch in my throat.

"Where are we going?" I managed to squeak out as I pulled on a tank top and my underwear.

Looking down into my eyes, King slowly tucked an unruly strand of hair behind my ear, allowing the very tips of his fingers to brush against my skin.

"Pup," he said, his voice almost hoarse, "it's time for you to stop living for who you might've been and start living for who you are now."

"I thought that's what I was doing," I said with a yawn. King's grip tightened around my palm. He dragged me down the hall into his tattoo studio and switched on the light.

"Sit," he commanded, releasing my hand and gesturing to the chair in the middle of the room.

"Why?" I asked becoming more aware as I slowly woke up.

My palms started to sweat. "You want me in THAT chair?" I asked.

King walked over to the iPod docking station, and with his back to me, he flipped through the songs. After a few minutes, the sounds of Florida Georgia Line's STAY filled the room.

When King turned back around and noticed I was still standing by the door, he narrowed his gaze and again pointed to the chair. "Sit, or I will come over there, pick you up, and toss you onto it."

His tone did not imply that I had another option. I reluctantly moved over to the chair and tentatively perched myself on the edge.

"Take off your shirt." His voice so suddenly strained, he had to clear his throat. King sat down on his rolling stool and opened the bottom drawer of his tool box. He started sorting out materials just as if he were getting ready to tattoo a client, just like I'd seen him do many times over the past few weeks.

"What? Why? What are you doing?" I asked, unable to hide the panic in my voice.

"Because, Pup, it will be very hard to do this fucking tattoo with your shirt on. So, take the goddamn thing off, yeah?" King was demanding, but his tone hinted at a softness that wasn't there when I'd first met him.

"I already told you. I can't," I said. "You just don't get it. I may want one, but I just can't. I've told you this." Then, another thought crossed my mind.

He wouldn't tattoo me against my will, would he?

King stood from his stool and slowly approached. A menacing look in his eyes. He pushed my knees apart and settled his large frame between my thighs. He rested his forehead against mine in a gesture that was both intimate and new.

"How many times do I need to tell you? You need to learn to do what you are told, Pup," he growled, his cool breath floating across the skin on my cheek and neck.

In one fluid movement, he yanked my tank top over my head and tossed it onto his toolbox. "You're mine now. In every way. And I need you to know that if you regain your memory and remember who you are, you're still going to be mine. If you have a boyfriend out there waiting for you? You're still mine." He paused. "And if you *ever* leave me to go back to your old life, just know that no matter who you are with, every inch of this beautiful body of yours will always belong to me."

Braless and feeling very exposed in every way, I made a move to cover my breasts with my hand. I looked down to the floor to avoid eye contact. I could feel his gaze on my body. The hair on my arms stood on end. My nipples hardened.

King's lips curled upward in a wicked smile. He leaned back into me and placed his hands over mine, removing them from my breasts, fully exposing me to his hungry gaze. He blew out a long-held breath. His tongue darted out, licking his bottom lip before sucking it into his mouth. After what seemed like a lifetime, he shook his head and lightly chuckled.

"This isn't about me right now," he said. I got the feeling he was talking to himself rather than to me. "Lay on your stomach." He snapped on a pair of black latex gloves.

"You can't. I can't," I argued.

He sat down on his stool and rolled it toward me with his feet. "You said you wanted a tattoo, right?"

"Yes, I did, and I do. But I can't. I can't because what if—"

"No. Let me guess, you can't because it may be what you want, but it may not be what SHE wants?" He didn't wait for me to answer. Probably because he knew that was exactly what I was going to say. "But what you aren't understanding is that you are her!" King roared, standing up so abruptly his stool slid back and hit wall behind him. "Don't you see? You can't second guess everything you want because you are afraid of remembering another life!"

He paced the room and wrung out his hands, cracking his knuckles.

"Fuck who you were!" King screamed, the veins in his neck pulsing with each of his ragged breaths. "Be you, this fantastic, amazing, fucking beautiful…" His tone softened, and he stopped pacing, lifting his eyes to meet mine. "We're not just going to have a life, remember? We're going to live."

He slowly approached me. Again, he moved my hands away from my breasts. He pressed his chest into mine. His hands circled around my lower back, his hardness to my softness.

"I fucking love who you are, Pup, and it's about damn time you learned to love her, too," he said, placing a soft kiss on the edge of my mouth, igniting a sensation deep within that caused my entire body to shake.

LOVE?

I started to protest again, but the fog of desire wouldn't lift, and instead, I just sat there with my mouth open, waiting for King to make the next move.

Much to my disappointment, he sat back onto his stool and opened another drawer of his toolbox. He took out a sheet of paper that was almost see-through with colorful lines already drawn onto the page.

"Here." He passed me the paper, averting his gaze to the floor. "I made this for you."

I reached for the paper. It took me a minute to figure out what it was. The lines were all colorful, deep purples, pinks, and blues. The design was ornate, and at first, it just looked like beautiful vine work, but when you looked closely, hidden in the design was…me.

Concealed in the design was a book opened to the middle with wings protruding out the sides as it perched upon a pink pair of brass knuckles. Further down and off to the side was a quote woven into vines, 'I don't want to repeat my innocence. I want the pleasure of losing it all over again.'

My breath hitched in my throat, and I couldn't form the words. It was completely me.

I had to have it.

Suddenly, nothing mattered anymore because this man knew exactly who I was. Not who I used to be, not some girl I was waiting for to return while putting my current life on hold in the process.

I was tired of standing still. I wanted to move forward. All that mattered was what I wanted now, and what I wanted was right in front of me.

"Where?" I asked, unable to tear my eyes away from it.

"Do you trust me?" King asked.

"Yes," I said without hesitation. Because it was true.

"Good. Then, lay down." King took the paper from me, and with one hand on my shoulder, he pressed me down onto the table, placing his knee on the outside of my thigh. His face hovered just inches above mine. "Now, be a good girl," he whispered on my neck, "and roll the fuck over." A crooked smile on his lips.

"Yes, sir," I said, no longer able to contain my own smile, my belly doing flips as I thought back to where those beautiful lips had been not long before.

"Good girl. Now, you're learning," King praised me, sealing his compliment with a smack on my ass as I did what I was told and rolled over.

He shuffled around, preparing his tools. The tattoo needle started to hum, and shortly after he applied the template, I felt the first sharp sting on my skin, followed by a scratching sensation.

It didn't hurt as bad as I thought it would. In an odd way, I welcomed the pain. I closed my eyes and lost myself in the sensation of the needle across my skin.

The sensation of taking over my life and making it my own.

The needle stung and scraped its way across my back and shoulders. At the same time, I said a silent goodbye to the girl I'd been protecting for months.

I wasn't going to miss her.

As King branded my skin, I embraced the girl whose life was just beginning. I embraced life.

My life.

King filled me so completely. Not just my body. My heart. My soul. My life. I didn't give a shit if I ever got my memory back.

Because with King, I knew exactly who I was.

I was his.

chapter
twenty-three

King

TATTOOING DOE WAS THE SINGLE MOST EROTIC MOMENT OF MY LIFE. MARKING her perfect, pale skin with a tattoo I'd designed for her made me so fucking hard I had to adjust myself every thirty seconds in order to concentrate on my work.

When I was done, I handed her the hand mirror, and she walked over to the full-sized mirror that hung on the back of the door, like she'd seen dozens of my other clients do before. When she held up the hand mirror, she gasped.

"What?" I asked in a panic, hoping she didn't already see what I'd hidden in the tattoo. I was an asshole for putting it there. I was an asshole for tattooing her in the first place.

I was just an asshole.

But I couldn't help myself. My name needed to be on her. It wasn't enough just to call her mine. I needed to mark her as well. So hidden in the vine work under the quote I found that I thought was perfect for her, was my name.

KING was woven into the design. In order to see it you had to tilt your head or otherwise you wouldn't notice it. But it was there.

I would tell her eventually, of course, but I wanted it to be my secret for a while. She'd stopped being my possession a while ago, a lot longer before I cared to admit it, but I still felt the need to mark her as mine.

I still liked the idea of owning her.

Only now, she owned me, too.

She didn't notice the name. Tears filled her eyes. She stood there staring at the hand mirror in just her panties. Little cheeky ones where her ass hung out of the bottoms. Her tits were only inches from my face. Her tears of happiness made my dick twitch. Although her sad tears evoked the same response.

My dick wasn't partial to which kind of tears he liked.

I took the mirror from her hand and lifted her up onto the counter. "You like it?" I asked, pushing her panties down her legs.

"I love it," she panted, wrapping her legs around me, drawing me close. Her wetness soaking my boxers. I pushed them down with one hand. I'd been hard for three hours, the entire time I'd been working on her, and couldn't wait any longer. I pushed inside her tight, wet heat.

We both moaned at the contact.

"You love it?" I asked, needing to hear her say it again.

"Yes, I love it!" she said as I thrust up into her, hard. "I love it. So much. I love you."

I froze when I heard the words, and when I did, her eyes flung open.

"I didn't mean—"

"Shut the fuck up."

"Oh my god, I have that word vomit thing. I'm sorry. Shit, I just meant that—"

"Shut the fuck up!" I demanded, thrusting hard to get her attention. She closed her eyes, and her head fell back. "That's fucking better. Now, keep that pretty mouth of yours shut while I fuck you."

"Okay," she whispered, breathless.

"Shut up," I said again, and she closed her mouth. "Shut up so I can fuck you…and show you how much I love you."

She nodded and although her eyes stayed shut, a tear rolled down her cheek. I sucked it off her chin before it could fall to the floor.

Then, I fucked her.

Hard.

I showed her how much I loved her until I couldn't tell where I started and she began. Until all that was in that room was me and her and the thing between us that kept pulling us together like magnets. Until we were lost in sensations and orgasms.

And in each other.

I fucked her until we were one person, and in a way we were, because I'd lost myself along the way, and I found myself again in the most unlikely place.

I'd found myself again in the haunted eyes of a girl who was just as lost as I was.

Or maybe, we didn't find each other at all.

Maybe, we just decided to be lost together.

chapter
twenty-four

King

DOE AND I WERE LYING IN BED ON A SATURDAY AFTERNOON, WATCHING Demolition Man. Her idea. Not mine. Out of all the DVDs in my collection, that was the one she's watched the most in the past few days. She also liked Disney movies, but every time she watched them, I thought about Max and a pain formed in my chest thinking that she might never be around to watch them with us.

Or Max might be around, and Doe might be gone.

I was going to do everything I could to get them both under one roof with me. Although as the days went by, the reality of putting together the money for the payoff seemed less and less likely.

Disney princess movies may have just been a bunch of fairy tales, but the idea of the three of us together—four if you count Preppy—was my idea of happily ever after.

"All restaurants are now Taco Bell," Doe said in sync with Sandra Bullock's character. She knew every line. It was downright adorable. Besides, we were naked, and I had one hand on her tit and the other was cupping her pussy, so I had no complaints. "Why is the house half-painted?" She turned to me abruptly, propping her head on my chest.

"Cause when Preppy and I first moved in, it was already an old house, but we kind of trashed it with all the parties and didn't think much of fixing it up. Then, I asked Preppy to fix it up a bit because I expected to bring Tricia and Max here.

"But why did he stop?"

"Because I went to prison, and the house being painted didn't seem to matter to either of us anymore. There wasn't a chance in hell they'd let me have her at that point. Besides, Preppy may be able to cook, and he's a killer mechanic, but he's a shit handyman. So, the place kind of went to hell while I was gone."

"Well," she said, stretching her arms over her head. Her perky tits bounced as she yawned and hooked her leg over my thigh. "You better get to painting again because we're going to get the money, and she's going to come home."

"Yeah, baby. We're going to get her back." I was unsure if I was speaking to her or trying to convince myself. The truth was that each and every day that passed by, Max was slipping further and further away.

550 | T.M. FRAZIER

Preppy opened the door, and Doe sat up quickly, pulling the sheet over her bare chest.

"Dude, fucking knock much?" I asked.

Preppy ignored me and hopped up onto the bed, settling himself between me and Doe. He slung an arm around each of us.

"I just love you guys," he said, squeezing the three of us together like we were one big, fat, odd-as-fuck family.

"Is there a purpose to this love fest?" Doe asked, giggling as Preppy leaned in to tickle her.

It should've pissed me off that he was even touching her, but there was nothing sexual about their connection. Although I often found myself jealous of their easy friendship. I had to work my ass off to get Pup to like me, and even then, I was shit at it.

But, Preppy wore both his crazy and his heart on his sleeve, and I was always a little envious of how easy it was to be around him.

All of us together just made sense. Doe could read bedtime stories to Max as she fell asleep at night. Uncle Preppy could teach her how to make pancakes. Those were the kind of images that made it all come together for me. It was clear. I had to do whatever it was going to take to make this shit work.

Max had to come home.

Pup had to stay.

I'd told her I was a selfish prick, and I'd meant it. I just didn't think she realized how true that statement really was. I guarantee that she had no clue that I was hiding the truth about her past from her.

I didn't plan to fall for her, but I did. Now, she wasn't just a pawn I was going to use to get Max back. Now, she was a part of my life.

A part I wasn't willing to give back.

Even if that means keeping the truth about who she really is a secret until I'm rotting in the ground.

"As a matter of fact, there is a point. So glad you asked!" Preppy turned to me, and his face went serious. "Bear wants us to come to the compound tonight. They're having a party since daddy over here got pissed when he threw the last one and grounded him for a month."

"Cut the sarcasm, Prep," I said, I had no patience for Preppy's humor because all I wanted was for him to leave so I could be alone again with my girl.

"Yes, a par-tay with the bikers and the four B's."

"Four B's?" Doe asked.

"Yep. Beer. Booze. Blow. Babes." Preppy looked between us. "Well, maybe not the babes since you two seem to be an exclusive thing. Are you an exclusive thing? Should I be getting out the fine china and calling the preacher?" Preppy turned to Doe. "Are you with child?"

"What?" she asked. "No! I'm not." She laughed while Preppy pretended to pass out on the mattress.

"But we are exclusive," I chimed in. I'm not sure why I felt the need to say it, but I did. I needed Preppy to get the message loud and clear. It may be an innocent friendship between them, but the warning to your fellow horn-ball friends about your woman could never be too obvious or too loud.

"Ahhhhh, so what do you say, my friends? Par-tay with Preppy tonight?" He rubbed his hands together like an evil warlock casting a spell.

"Do you want to go?" I asked Doe who was all smiles.

"Really?" She asked.

"Really." I replied. If going to a party was all it took to coax that kind of smile from her, I'd take her to one every fucking night if she wanted.

"Yipeeeee motherfuckers! Get dressed, lovers. We're going to the club-house." Preppy stood up on the bed, jumping up and down until his head hit a spinning blade of the ceiling fan. He dropped back down to his ass, clutching his forehead. "That's gonna leave a mark."

Doe leaned over Preppy and pushed his hand off his head to inspect his injury. She'd let the sheet fall from her chest, her bare breasts swayed in front of Preppy's face.

Preppy was no longer concerned about his wound. He openly stared at her nipples and licked his lips.

I might not have been mad that they were friends, but my best friend was about to take a fist to the face for ogling my girl like that.

I grabbed her waist and dragged her back to me, covering her chest with the sheet. She blushed.

If she thought my homecoming party was wild, she would be shocked to see what went on over at the Beach Bastards' compound. "Shit, I forgot about those fucking bikers," I said.

"Oh stop it," Preppy said. "Bear's people are harmless now. You've staked your claim, flagged your territory, put your sausage in the onion ring. That's all they care about. That's bible to them. She won't be fucked with. Besides, I'll be there, and so will Bear, and so will you."

"I'm not all that trusting of Bear these days," I said. "It wasn't a week ago that he was asking my girl to be his old lady."

"But as I said, you gots it in. It's all good, play playyyyyyy."

"Preppy, how much coffee have you had this morning?" Doe asked.

"Not much, six, seven cups. Why?" He twitched his fingers like he was playing an imaginary piano.

"We can go, but you're not to leave my fucking sight," I told Doe. "I mean it. Either me or Preppy are with you at all times, got it? Worst case scenario, go to Bear, but I swear to god if he lays a hand on you, I will chop it the fuck off."

It came out harsher than I intended, but I wasn't fucking around. The reality of what could happen to her if she wandered off on her own was what was really harsh.

Not a motherfucker in that place would survive if they touched her. Just remembering what Ed had almost done made me want to kill that piece of shit all over again.

"Got it," Doe said, recognizing the seriousness in my tone. She placed a hand on my shoulder. "I won't go anywhere unless you or Preppy are with me."

"Good." I let out a breath I didn't know I was holding.

"So, what are we watching?" Preppy asked, leaning back on his elbows and crossing his feet at the ankles. "Ooh, Demolition Man. This is my jayum."

"Get the fuck out," I said, shoving him off the bed.

"You guys are no fucking fun," Preppy pouted, picking himself up off the carpet. "You are all in lovers' land and forgot all about ole Preppy over here." He stuck out his lower lip and drooped his shoulders.

"Have the car ready in twenty," I barked, throwing a pillow at his head.

"You mean the truck. My classic caddy is in a million little pieces, and 'death by bomb' isn't covered by insurance," Preppy said, dodging the pillow.

"You don't fucking have insurance," I said. Preppy didn't believe in anything that kept him on the grid, no matter how illegal it was.

"But if I did, it wouldn't cover it," he said, waving us off and leaving the room.

"Remind me to get a deadbolt for that door," I said.

"Oh, stop. Preppy's great, just highly caffeinated," Doe said in his defense.

"You can back out now if you've changed your mind. We can stay here and stay naked and watch whatever stupid movie you want, as long as we are naked while watching it. We don't have to go to Bear's party if you don't think you will feel comfortable."

"I want to get to know your friends better. I want to get out of the house for a while. I want it all." Doe smiled. "And I want it with you."

I wanted to puff out my chest and beat on it like a gorilla. Her words were empowering. She wanted it all.

With me.

I felt so good about where we were and where we were heading that I almost felt okay about living the rest of my life lying to her.

Almost.

chapter
twenty-five

King

BEAR'S CLUBHOUSE WAS AN OLD TWO-STORY APARTMENT COMPLEX WITH A courtyard in the center and a small, kidney-shaped pool that had been graffitied a million times over.

Plastic patio chairs with gaping holes in the seats and backs, some missing legs, were scattered everywhere. A few were floating upside down in the deep end the pool in a foot of green sludgy water. There was no sophisticated speaker system. An ancient boom box sat on top of a small round table blaring Johnny Cash. Its cord ran into the shallow water of the pool and across the courtyard where it was plugged into a wall outlet inside one of the rooms.

Scantily clad women were everywhere, and bikers of all ages, shapes, and sizes lingered about in various states of drunkenness. Two muscle heads wearing their cuts with nothing but their bare chests underneath, arm-wrestled in the corner on top of an overturned laundry basket.

Two women with matching bleach blonde hair, both topless, were making out on the second-floor balcony against the railing, while a skinny prospect stood close by looking on with heavily lidded lust filled eyes, with a hard-on he wasn't even trying to hide, straining against his jeans.

Bear was the first person to greet us. "King, you motherfucker!" he shouted, standing in the open doorway of one of the motel rooms, his arm draped around the neck of a girl with innocent chubby looking cheeks, but a very weary look in her eyes. "In here!" He waved us over and practically shoved the girl out of the room. She would have landed face-first on the concrete if Preppy hadn't caught her and set her back on her feet.

"Thanks," she said, looking up at Preppy. Preppy scrunched his nose as if he was confused by her thanks, then stepped around her. She looked back at him as she walked away.

"What the fuck was that?" I asked.

"No fucking clue," Preppy said seriously, his usual humor nowhere in sight. "Let's get this party started."

"Doe, baby! You're here!" Bear exclaimed, pulling Doe into a hug that lasted a beat too long. I clenched my fists. Bear didn't seem to notice, and if he did, he didn't seem to care. "Bump, get my friends a drink!"

A freckle-faced redheaded prospect I'd seen a few times before, filled three red cups from the keg and handed them to us.

"Got anything in a bottle for the lady?" I asked, emptying my cup in just a few swallows.

I needed something to take the edge off, but I wouldn't put it past one of these little prospect fuckers to try and slip Doe something. We were friends of the club, but some of these newbies may not know the extent of which we weren't to be fucked with. I was about to explode out of my skin. Why did we come here again? Oh yeah, because Doe wanted to.

I was turning into such a fucking pussy over this girl.

"You heard the man. A bottle for the lady," Bear ordered, taking the cup from Doe's hands before she had a chance to lift it to her lips.

Bear chugged the contents of her cup while Bump handed her an unopened bottle of beer. I discarded my cup and used the buckle on one of the belts around my forearms to pop off the cap for her. "Overreacting much, buddy? Wouldn't let anything happen to her. Not on my watch. Not at my place. You should know that."

I shrugged, and Preppy chimed in before I could say anything. "Don't get all fucking butt hurt about it, Bear. King doesn't even trust me around her, and I only wanted to take her out on a date, and maybe put the tip in a little, but noooooo."

It was a lie. I hope Preppy knew that. I trusted him with my life, and I knew he wouldn't do anything with Doe that meant upsetting me. But that didn't mean I didn't want to slit his throat every time he smiled at her. Especially when every single day since the day I decided I needed her in my life, I'd felt like my every move had to be thought out around her so I wouldn't send her running scared.

Or worse, accidentally tell her the truth.

"You wanna get this shit started?" Bear asked, holding out his hand he pointed to an old nightstand where several lines of white powder were already cut. I shook my head. I hadn't touched anything but alcohol and weed since I got out, but Preppy stepped up and did two lines. He knew me better than anyone, and he knew that a bump was the last thing I needed with all the adrenaline already coursing through my veins. But he also knew that doing coke with the bikers, especially Bear, was like their version of bringing a nice bottle of wine to a dinner party. A show of respect. Biker etiquette, if that makes any sense. I lit a cigarette and glanced over at Doe, who was looking around the place like she was discovering the lost city of Atlantis.

Another one of Bear's crew popped his head into the room. I recognized him right away as a guy named Harris, who'd been voted in just before I went away. "Bear, your old man's here. He wants to see you and said to bring King and his crew so he can say hi. He's back in the office."

Bear chugged his beer and let out a long belch. He threw his now empty cup at Bump. It bounced off his head and landed on the ground.

"Clean that shit up," Bear ordered, leading us from the room. "Come on, kids. Let's say hi to my old man and get it over with."

Bear's dad was the president of the Beach Bastards. One day, he would take the gavel from him and become the man in charge.

When we walked into the office, the door closed behind us and a clicking noise echoed in the room. Preppy turned back to the door and turned the handle, but it was already locked.

Shit. Bear swore.

Behind the desk, on the far side of the room, a chair sat, facing away from us. It slowly turned, and where I'd expected to see Bear's dad, was Isaac.

"Motherfucker," Preppy swore.

Isaac's feet were propped up on the top of the desk. He was caressing his long-braided beard. A toothpick hung haphazardly from his bottom lip. His eyes immediately narrowed in on Doe.

Fuck.

His eyes darted from me to Doe as he spoke. "And who is this?"

I felt my face getting hot with rage. If I ever saw that cocksucker Harris again I was going to tear him limb from chubby limb.

It was at that moment I realized how stupid bringing Doe to the party really was. Isaac was a dangerous man, and although I thought I had time before he rolled into town, I'd known him being around was a possibility. I'd planned to send Doe to Grace's house in a couple of days, at least until this all blew over.

Obviously, it wasn't soon enough.

It was a complete lapse in judgment on my part. My brain had been put on hold because all the blood had been in my cock, which for the better part of a week had been deeply lodged inside Doe's tight as fuck pussy.

"She's with me," I answered, keeping my voice as casual as possible. Trying not to let my words scream SHE'S WITH ME, IN A FOREVER KIND OF WAY SO BACK THE FUCK OFF OF HER, ASSHOLE. Instead, I kept my face hard and unemotional. "They with you?"

I gestured to the two blondes with sketchy looking matching pink BITCH tattoos on their biceps. They were making a show of touching each other's huge fake tits.

"I guess they are," Isaac said with a laugh. He clasped his hands together and gestured to the chair in front of him. "Have a seat, Mr. King."

I sat and pulled Doe down onto my lap where I kept a hand possessively around the back of her neck. It was a gesture that said she was with me, but it was disrespectful enough to Doe to tell Isaac that she wasn't all that important. She let out a surprised little yelp, and I rubbed the back of her neck with the pad of my thumb to comfort her. Her pulse raced in her neck.

Isaac's gaze roamed up her calves and settled between her legs where I was sure he'd caught a glimpse of her panties. I wanted to cross her legs or throw her off of my lap so that he'd stop looking at my girl like he wanted to eat her, but that would show him that she was my weakness. Instead, I slightly parted her knees with my hands to show Isaac more of her. He licked his bottom lip, and his gaze met mine.

"It's been a long time, KING," he said, his eyes glimmered with amusement. I pushed Doe's legs back together.

The way Isaac said my name sent chills up my spine. Doe went along with what I was doing. She trusted me and thank god for that, but the way her body tensed, I knew she was horrified over what I'd just done.

So was I.

"It has. I hear you recently lost your nephew in a tragic construction accident. My condolences," I offered.

Isaac smirked. "It was tragic, Mr. King, but it was no fucking accident. Wolfert was stealing from me. Simple as that. So, I had his throat slit and buried under three feet of concrete. The only real tragedy of it was that I was stupid enough to give him a chance at all, and that his mother calls me weeping three fucking times a day." Isaac lit a cigarette and scratched his head. "I've learned my lesson, Mr. King, and I won't be that stupid again. The number one rule in this business is to make sure that the people who fuck you over get fucked right back, or get dead real quick."

Doe stiffened.

Isaac waved to the blondes who brought over a bottle of expensive whiskey. One of them poured while the other passed around shot glasses. When she got to me, she made a show of brushing her fake tits up against my hand. I was about to tell her to get the fuck away from me when out of the corner of my eye I noticed Isaac watching my every move.

I grabbed the shot glass from the blonde and set it in the other blonde's cleavage. I made a show of licking the salt off her breast before dipping my head between her tits to bite the glass with my teeth. I threw back the shot all while holding Doe tightly to my side. I waved my hand dismissively when I was done, tossing her my empty glass and then redirecting my attention toward Isaac, who for the meantime, seemed satisfied.

Preppy and Bear stood in the back of the room. I had an uneasy feeling about the situation, and obviously so did they because they were in position to where if the shit hit the fan, they would be able to shoot their way out.

"Let's not sit in here and hash this shit out right now," Preppy said. "Let's party tonight and schedule a formal meet for tomorrow, when we've all had a chance to get drunk and get some pussy."

I could sense Preppy's wariness. I was able to read him better than anyone, and what he was really saying was *let's get the fuck out of here.*

Bear chimed in as well, "Yeah man, let's go out to the courtyard. Strippers should be here by now. Bump and the boys are setting up mud wrestling out back. Let's get loaded, and get our dicks wet before all the serious talk goes down."

"Sounds good." I stood and started toward the door, dragging Doe with me.

Right when we reached the door, two of Isaac's men stepped into the room and closed it, blocking our exit, raising their guns.

When we turned around, three more of Isaac's men emerged from the room right behind the desk. Their pistols drawn and aimed.

"That's it? You fuck me over and expect that I would just party with you and forget all about it?" Isaac asked. He stood and walked in front of the desk. "You can't just shit all over a business I'd spent decades running. I'm not your whore. You can't choose to get in bed with me when it best suits you then leave me hanging after you have thoroughly fucked me."

"I was locked up," I argued, knowing that wouldn't be a good enough reason for Isaac. "You wouldn't deal with Prep. We needed to earn. We didn't cut you out. We made a business decision. A *temporary* one. I've been trying to reach you since my release, but you've had your balls in a knot. I'm not your girlfriend, Isaac. I didn't mean to hurt your feelings. Now, let's move the fuck on, and if you want to talk, we'll talk. But let them get back to the party." I waved my hands at my friends and Doe. "That way, they, at least, can enjoy themselves tonight."

"You think it's that fucking easy do you? This county may belong to you, but this is my coast. Anytime one of you little trailer trash bastards wants to so much as take a shit, you need my fucking permission!" Isaac spat, pounding a fist onto the desk. His face reddened. He turned his head to the side and passed the heel of his hand against his face, cracking his jaw from side to side.

Bear went for his pistol but he wasn't fast enough. One of the men who blocked the door pressed his gun to the back of Bear's neck.

"Don't even fucking think about it," he warned.

Preppy spoke up, "What the fuck do you want, Isaac? You want us to make it up to you? You want money? Fine, we'll up your cut. Make you richer than you already are. I honestly didn't think you'd care. We're small-time compared to your other operations. King was locked up. The idea was all mine. This entire thing is on me." His voice grew louder as he got bolder. "You want someone to blame? Blame me." He wasn't cursing, and his tone was serious. That worried me more than the guns to our heads.

Preppy was being reckless.

And he was doing it for us. So he could take all the blame and all the punishment.

I couldn't allow him to take all the blame, and I couldn't' allow this motherfucker to shit all over us like he ran the world. I wasn't a fucking drug lord, but I wasn't someone you could point a gun at and not pay for it with your life. I held Doe's hand and gave it a squeeze, trying my best to reassure her that I would protect her.

I very well intended to.

"But once I knew about it, I didn't stop it," I chimed in. "The Money was good, man. But we're ready to go big time. Need your help to take us there." I tried appealing to Isaac's sense of business. But there was a reason Isaac was successful. He cut down everyone who'd ever stood in his way like an angry lumberjack.

Even his family.

Isaac bent over and cackled like a possessed witch. The girls on the sofa scooted to the far edge in an effort to escape. "Stay right the fuck there, ladies!" Isaac warned. His laughter vanished instantly. Deep lines etched themselves into his forehead. His lips pursed. "This won't take very long."

"This ain't on them," Bear said, nodding to the girls and then to Doe. "Let all three of the bitches leave, and we'll handle this in any way it needs to be handled. Don't forget this is my house, my people. I don't know what you think is gonna go down, but it ain't going down without a fight. I got a few dozen of my brothers out there that don't sit idle when they hear gun shots."

Isaac strutted toward us. I instinctively shoved Doe behind me. Bad idea, because with that move, I showed Isaac she was more important to me than myself. It was instinct to protect her, but in that situation, instinct wasn't doing me any favors.

He smiled as he approached.

"King of the Causeway," Isaac said, quoting the air with his fingers around the label that had been given to me when I'd started to make a name for myself in Logan's Beach. "You ain't King of shit! The only King around here is me, and if you fuck with what's mine, the only way I see it is that I need to fuck with what's yours." He turned toward Doe. "Or fuck what's yours."

"You're not going to fucking touch her!" I roared, stopping just short of taking Isaac down when I felt the barrel of a gun at my back and Issacs's knife at my throat. My gun was still lodged behind my belt buckle in the waistband of my jeans.

There was no way of getting to it without getting us all killed.

Isaac waved to his one of his men. "Bring her to the back room."

The man stepped up and grabbed Doe, pushing her forward. She stumbled in her heels and fell onto her knees. The shoes fell off her feet and clattered against the floor.

With just a little fall, all my baser instincts screamed at me to go help her, protect her. But I was surrounded, and I couldn't do shit.

I'd never felt so weak in my entire life.

Isaac's man yanked Doe up by her arm and threw her forward. She landed with a smack, her cheek against the door. I growled. He opened the door and pushed her inside. Isaac followed her in and turned back to where I stood surrounded by guns aimed at my fucking head.

"Fuck," Preppy swore. We were utterly helpless.

"Like I said, KING. You fuck me. I fuck you. And since I'm not into cock, your girl here is going to have to do."

He shut the door.

chapter
twenty-six

Doe

A MAN CAME UP BEHIND ME AND GRABBED ME BY THE ARM, SHOVING ME FORWARD into a dark room, slamming the door shut behind me.

A small cot sat in the middle of high walls lined with empty shelving. I peered around Isaac, who entered the room after me and spotted King who mouthed IM SORRY as the door slammed shut.

Then, we were alone.

Dark and alone was my worst fear.

This was worse.

My only family in the world stood in the other room with guns pointed at them.

How fucking ironic was that? Because on the way to the party both Preppy and King were so concerned with my safety, they made me recite their rules to them several times over.

#1 Don't go off on my own.

#2 Make sure one of them was with me at all times.

#3 Don't take drinks from anyone but them.

We hadn't even been there an hour, and what they thought was the worst thing that could happen to me was in no way as bad as what was really happening.

They were worried about me being drugged and date raped.

What happened was so much worse.

Isaac wanted revenge on King, and it was obvious he'd planned it all out before we'd showed up at the party with the help of someone in Bear's MC.

King and Preppy could be killed.

They could've already been dead.

I couldn't feel my limbs, but I could hear the blood rushing to my head.

Maybe, it was all for show. I silently hoped that Isaac just wanted to prove a point and that his intentions weren't as bad as he'd let on.

No. They weren't as bad. They were worse.

Much worse.

Because the second the door closed behind me, the reality set in. I looked around for a weapon, something I could use to ward him off, but it was too late. I was on my back on the cot with Isaac's hand wrapped around my neck, silencing the guttural scream I didn't even know was coming from deep within my throat.

With one hand trapping my wrists, he straddled me, his thighs caging me in. He released my throat to roughly tug down my dress, exposing my breasts. I let out another scream, which was rewarded with his fist cocking back then landing square on my jaw. My brain rattled around in my head. I saw stars and my vision blurred. My insides were in full defense mode.

Every bit of adrenaline I had was being used to fight him off. But being dazed from the blow to the face, my efforts weren't enough because he released one hand from my wrists and fumbled with his pants, his fat, little limp cock rested on my thigh as I tried to buck him off with all I had.

He wasn't as big as King, but he was big enough to do whatever it was he had planned for me without much trouble. Fighting back with all my strength was nothing more to him than a slight amusement and minor annoyance.

I wasn't about to give up. There was no way King would be able to rescue me, this time. I was on my own and was going to survive this, even if that meant I had to rip his dick off with my fucking teeth.

In the meantime, I bit at any body part of his that came near me, my mouth landing on his wrist bone, rattling my teeth and barely piercing his tanned and tough skin. Immediately, I felt something cold against my forehead.

"I will fucking blow your brains all over this room if you don't stop biting me, bitch. Then, I'm going to have my men shoot your boys out there in the head and dump them in the fucking swamp. Is that what you fucking want?" he breathed, pushing the gun harder against my head.

"No," I gasped.

"That's what I thought. King needs to learn his place. He needs to know that when he gets in bed with me I'm the one who calls the fucking shots, and what's his is mine. These are my streets, my product. This is my fucking clubhouse. These are my fucking tits." He snaked his cold, wet tongue around one of my nipples, and I had to swallow down the bile rising in my throat. "That's why I'm going to fuck you right now. I'm going to fuck you without a rubber and send you back out there with my cum dripping down your leg so he can learn that he is the King of *nothing*."

He slid his hand up my leg and grabbed a hold of my panties. When I screamed, he again he covered my mouth and straddled me with a knee on each side of my rib cage, squeezing his legs together so tightly I heard my rib crack at the same time I felt the explosion of pain in my chest. With his free hand, Isaac reached into his boot and produced a long hunting knife. He raised it into the air, and then brought it down into my thigh until I felt it hit bone.

Twice.

When he pulled the serrated blade out, he took chunks of my flesh with it. "I told you not to fucking scream, you fucking cunt."

Pain coursed through my leg and spread to every nerve ending in my body until it felt like my entire leg had been stabbed, not just my thigh. Tears poured out of my eyes as I struggled to see past the pain-induced blurry vision.

Isaac's hands were back up my dress, yanking my panties down, the cool air blew over my newly exposed parts, letting me know that Isaac had successfully removed them.

He settled himself between my legs and reached down to position his cock at my entrance. "You fight me, and they're fucking dead," he said, looking me in the eyes.

There was nothing about his demeanor that would make me believe that he wasn't the kind of guy who didn't follow through with his threats. He meant every word. If I screamed, if I fought him off, the only people in the world who I loved would be dead.

King would be dead.

"That a girl," he hissed as I dropped my knees to the sides. With a whole lot of effort, Isaac managed to push himself inside of me. He was struggling. My body was so dry it was like it was fighting its own fight to keep him out. He spit on his hand and reached between us.

I closed my eyes tight. Maybe, if I didn't see it, it wasn't really happening.

But it was. Because although I couldn't see it, I could feel it.

He entered me, fully violating the body I'd finally taken possession over as my own. It wasn't just a violation of my body. It was an invasion of my soul.

Pop Pop Pop Pop.

The sound cracked through the air from the other room.

"What the fuck?" Isaac roared, lifting off of me just in time to turn his head toward whoever had just opened the door.

Pop.

Isaac's head exploded above me like a sledge hammer to a watermelon. My face became coated in thick, warm, red. The full weight of his limp body fell onto me, knocking the wind from my chest. Shrapnel of flesh and bone that used to be Isaac's head, landed in my open mouth, and I immediately turned my head and heaved into the floor.

King suddenly appeared beside me, gun in hand. He rolled Isaac off of me pushing his lifeless body to the floor, finally freeing me from his penetration.

King had lost his shirt and was only wearing a black wife-beater. Every inch of available skin on his arms and neck was covered with blood as if he just slaughtered a cow.

Or people.

King's eyes went wide when he looked down to my state of undress. Then even wider when he noticed the blood pumping from my leg.

"Fuck!" King aimed his gun at Isaac and fired twice, his lifeless body jumping when each bullet made contact. "Motherfucker," King muttered. "I am so sorry, baby. I am so fucking sorry."

"What the fuck is going on?" I asked. I was losing blood fast and getting more lightheaded by the second. King lifted me up into his arms. "Where's Preppy? Where's Bear?"

"Cover your eyes, Pup," King ordered.

"Why?"

"Because you may think differently of me if you keep them open," he whispered, carrying me into the other room. "It's not a pretty sight out here."

I knew I should have listened to him, but a part of me, a very stupid part of me, needed to see. But no matter how much I warned myself what was on the other side of the door, it wasn't nearly enough to fully prepare for the reality of what was in front of me.

Bodies.

Bodies. Everywhere.

Slumped over one another on couches, chairs, the floor. The white linoleum was covered in sludgy, dark red footprints.

Preppy sat in the doorway looking pale, clutching his side with one hand, blood saturating the area of his shirt his hand was trying to cover. Bear stood over him with his hands on his knees trying to catch his breath. Preppy looked up as we approached and scratched his head with the barrel of his gun. He flashed us a pained smile. That was so Preppy. Smiling while seriously injured in a room full of dead bodies.

"So…you guys ready to party now?" he asked, his usual loud and chipper voice was raspy, his breathing shallow.

He turned ghost white in a matter of seconds. The blood drained from his face at an alarming rate. His smile faded as his eyes rolled back in his head until his pupils were replaced with only the whites of his eyes. Bear lunged to catch him as he fell face-forward onto the cement.

Preppy exhaled on a strangled moan.

I would have given anything in the world for that smile and that breath, to have not been his very last.

chapter
twenty-seven

King
Fifteen years old

"FUCK NO! I AIN'T GONNA BE NOBODY'S BITCH," PREPPY SLURRED AT BEAR. He took another giant swig from the bottle of cheap tequila we were passing around. The three of us sat on overturned milk crates on the floor of the living room of the shitty apartment Preppy and I had just moved into. The crates were the only furniture we had. "That cut is cool as fucking shit, but you ain't gonna see me announcing to the world that I'm a criminal. I keep my shit on the DL."

The place was a complete shit hole. Two bedrooms, one bathroom, and a kitchen that consisted of a hot plate and a sink that sat on top of two cabinets in the corner of the square living room. One strip of black and white linoleum squares marked off the 'kitchen' area.

It was dirty. There was an ant mound growing under one of the baseboards, flies stuck to traps hanging from the ceiling. A fan with two broken blades that didn't turn on hung uselessly from the living room ceiling. The only window in the main living area was nailed shut so it couldn't be opened.

It was the greatest fucking place ever.

"Nah man, it's totally cool. Cops don't fuck with us cause they're scared of us. Besides, the MC parties all the fucking time. Pussy and blow everywhere, as far as the eye can fucking see, man." Bear swayed to one side and kept himself from falling off his milk crate by straightening one of his legs and anchoring the heel of his boot to the floor. "It's totally tits, man. You gotta join up. Prospect it out like me. Once I'm in, I'll vouch for you guys. Then after a year, it's fucking smooth sailing on the SS Tits and Ass. Besides, you'll love the clubhouse. It has a pool table *and* a fucking bar."

Bear had first told us he was going to turn Prospect for his dad's MC, The Beach Bastards, when he started buying weed from us in the eighth grade. He'd known what his future held for him since the day he was born. Since he spent most of his time with either the MC or us, he'd been trying to get us to Prospect with him since the day he decided that we were all going to be friends.

"Not for us, man. We're like our own MC of two. We're like the non-MC, MC," I said. I'd moved on from the tequila and was lighting the two-foot tall purple glass bong that sat in the middle of the living room on yet another overturned milk crate, this one acting as our coffee table.

"You gotta kill people and shit?" Preppy asked in a lowered voice, like someone was listening in and he didn't want them to hear. He reached over to take the bottle back from Bear, stretching out his too-long-for-his-body arm.

Where I was fifteen and taller and more built than most adults, looking several years older than I was, Preppy was smack dab in the middle of an awkward phase that made his arms and legs look like a stretched-out Gumby and his face looked as if he'd had a chronic case of the chicken pox.

"Only people that need killing," Bear answered like he was reciting something he'd heard a million times before, and no doubt he had. "No women or kids, nothing like that. Just people who know the score and understand the consequences, or people who fuck with the MC and us earning." Bear looked up at Preppy through his messy white hair and brushed it out of his eyes. "Why? You got someone who needs killing?"

He sounded very much like his father, President of The Beach Bastards. Bear's father was a psychopathic killer, who dealt in drugs and women, but Bear still managed to have the most stable upbringing between the three of us.

"Nah, man," Preppy said, waving his hand dismissively like the question was ridiculous, but I knew he was lying. I saw it in his eyes. "Just curious is all."

I also had a very good idea of who he thought 'needed killin'.

Bear looked around and leaned in close, waving for us to lean in bring it in as well. "We got these guys, specially trained. Pops calls them 'the janitors.' You know what their job is?" he asked pausing dramatically, waiting for Preppy and me to urge him on.

"What?" Preppy asked, totally enthralled. "What do they do?"

Bear smiled, elated that Preppy had taken the bait. "When people need killin', or get killed, they sweep in and make it so it never happened."

He made a wiping motion with his hands in the air, extending them out to his sides. He sat back, looking pleased that he could share with us something about the MC. It wasn't until he turned prospect that he'd finally gotten a glimpse of the inner workings of The Beach Bastards, and he was always excited to tell us more about the club he was raised in but didn't necessarily know a lot about before he was given a PROSPECT cut.

The kid was a born biker, but as much as he tried to get us to join, it wasn't for us.

Preppy and I never strayed from our plan.

Ever.

"You guys ever need a cleaning up, you call me. I can put a word in. Problem is, you'd owe us a favor. That's how it works. No matter when we call in that favor or no matter what that favor is, you gotta do it." Bear lit a cigarette and waved the smoke away from his face. "Nuff of that shit, boys. Preppy, you got the goods or what?"

"Goods?" I asked. I wasn't aware that we were selling to Bear today, or any other day for that matter. Since he turned Prospect, he bought his weed from the MC.

Preppy hopped up and walked over to the hall closet. He came back holding something covered with a ripped sheet. "What the fuck is that?" I asked.

"This—" Preppy waved his hand over the sheet. "—is your birthday gift, you ungrateful fuck." He set it on the floor and grabbed the sheet in the middle, lifting it off like a magician. "Voila!" He stepped back, and my eyes focused on what was in front of me. It was a cardboard box and inside of it were bits and pieces of something.

Not just something. It was a tattoo gun.

"Happy birthday, you fucking fuck! Now, let's figure out how to put this thing together, because Bear and I already picked out which tattoos we want from your sketchbook." I stared at the equipment in front of me, not believing my eyes.

"If you take any longer to get started putting it together, I'm going to request mine be put on my taint," Bear said, knocking me out of my stunned state.

"Thanks, boys." I lifted the box onto my lap and started tinkering with the parts. "And Bear?"

"Yeah, Man?"

"There is no fucking way in hell I'm ever going anywhere near your taint."

"Noted."

That day, I tattooed for the very first time. I didn't do the ones the boys had picked from my sketchbook. They were too elaborate and although I could draw, I'd never used a tattoo gun before so the full back piece Bear wanted with intertwining snakes, The Beach Bastards logo, would have to wait until I knew what the fuck I was doing.

Instead, Bear got a small shamrock behind his ear, although I'm not quite sure if he was any sort of Irish. Preppy settled for PREP on his knuckles. The lettering was thin and crooked. They were the worst tattoos in the world. Blown out edges, a bloody fucking mess. But the boys loved them, and I couldn't wait to practice on them some more.

"I'm so gangsta." Preppy said, admiring his newly tatted up knuckles.

"You're about as gangsta as my ninety-year-old Grandma," Bear said.

"Bear, doesn't your grandma have a full chest tattoo and purple hair?" I asked.

"Sure does," he replied.

"Then, I actually think she's way more gangsta then ole Preppy here," I said.

"You guys laugh now, but you'll see. King here is gonna tattoo my neck next. I'm gonna look real mean."

"Are you still gonna still wear button down shirts, bow ties and suspenders?" I asked.

"Fuck yeah. Always. That's my style."

Bear chuckled. "You may not look tough, or mean, but you might confuse the fuck out of people."

"Fuck this shit man," Preppy said, standing up. "I gotta go get the last of my shit from my stepdad's. I'll be back. Feel free to laugh at my fucking expense while I'm gone, shitheads."

"You want me to go with you?" I asked.

"Nah, I got this shit. It's past nine. Fucker's either at the bar or passed out on the couch. I'll be back in an hour."

Preppy never talked about it, but I was sure that his stepdad was still beating him up until the day he moved out. He was always slightly limping or clutching his ribs. When I asked him if he was okay, he usually told me he was working out. "Nah man, did chest today, hurts like a bitch when you do it right." He was a shit liar, but his pride was all he had besides me and Bear. Although we joked around with him, the last thing we wanted was for Preppy to be hurting at the hands of some drunken asshole.

When I hadn't heard from Preppy for two hours, I got on my bike and peddled over to the trailer park his stepdad wasted his life away in. As soon as I parked my bike, I heard a commotion inside.

"Prep?" I called out. No response.

"FUCK YOU!" I heard Prep roar from inside. His high-pitched voice cracking with his strained scream. With one kick, I knocked in the flimsy door.

What I saw beyond it would haunt my dreams for years to come.

His stepdad, Tim, had Prep bent over the end of the old corduroy couch, thrusting furiously into him while holding a pistol to his temple. When I sent the door flying into the room, he turned his attention my way, along with his pistol. Preppy turned and knocked him on his side, the gun slid across the floor. Preppy lunged for it but his jeans, which were still wrapped around his ankles, caused him to trip and fall forward against the wall.

"Get the fuck out of here, boy. You two think you're better than this place? Well, you're fucking wrong. I was teaching Samuel here a lesson. He belongs here. He ain't no better than me and needs to know it."

I kicked over empty beer cans and made my way to the gun. It was the first time in my life I remember seeing red. Seeing red isn't just a saying, I found out. My vision was tinted the color of the rage boiling inside my veins. I flexed my fingers. My joints itched with the need to release the pressure building within my bones. I wanted to hurt him, but the want was secondary to the *need* to hurt him.

"What, are you gonna do? Fucking shoot me?" Tim asked, sitting up against the kitchen cabinets. Pushing off the floor, he went to stand, but before he could, I raised the gun and knocked him in the temple with the butt. Tim went flying across the tiny kitchen, landing head first into the door of the refrigerator.

"Fucking shoot him!" Preppy called out, righting his jeans. Blood dripped from his nose. His cheek was already yellow and purple. Apparently, he'd taken one hell of a beating before Tim decided that anal rape was a more appropriate way to teach the kid a lesson.

"So, you're gonna beat me, kid? Is that it? Gonna teach me a lesson now, boy?" Tim looked up at me from the floor.

"No," I said, an eerie calm washing over me. The rage took a kind of precision-like control over my actions. "I'm not going to teach you shit."

Fear registered in Tim's beady little eyes.

"Then what, boy? You gonna call the cops? Cause I know the cops round here. They ain't gonna do shit!"

"No," I said, taking a step toward him, the gun in my still hand pointed toward the floor.

"Then, what the fuck, boy? You gonna kill me?" Tim laughed nervously until he saw the affirmative look in my face.

I raised the gun, aimed it at Tim's forehead, and fired.

"Yes."

chapter
twenty-eight

Doe

THE ONLY TIME KING SPOKE TO ME IN THE DAYS FOLLOWING PREPPY'S DEATH was to ask me to go into Preppy's room to find something I thought he would like to be buried in. At least, that is what I took from the grunting and nodding that he'd been using in place of actual words. King was hurting, and I couldn't do anything to make it go away.

I'd never been in Preppy's room before, and when I opened the door, I noticed that his room was huge, much bigger than King's. Preppy had the master bedroom. The room was neat and tidy but full of random things. Shelves of books, video games, action figures, and knickknacks of all kinds.

On his dresser was a single picture. A selfie of the three of us. He'd taken it one morning when he rushed into King's room and bounced on the bed to wake us up, which he did frequently. King and I were on either side of him, tangled hair and half–asleep. King was covering his eyes.

He'd never wake us up like that again.

Preppy's closet was a large walk-in, overflowing with clothes of all kinds. One wall was lined with storage bins that were all neatly labeled. One bin was partially opened. The label read *Shit random chicks leave in my room* and was filled with women's clothing. I guess that solves the mystery as to where Preppy was getting all my clothes from.

I chose a yellow shirt and the loudest bow tie Preppy owned, a multi-colored checkered pattern, from a bin labeled *Awesome Fucking Bow Ties*.

Suddenly, holding his clothes in my hands, the final clothes he would be wearing at his funeral, it all became too much. I crumpled to the floor and held his jacket to my chest. My heart felt a million times its size. I couldn't breathe. I couldn't do much of anything except silently cry, holding onto a little piece of the only true friend I'd ever known.

I don't know how long I was down there, but I must have cried myself to sleep, because I woke with dried tears on my cheeks and Preppy's suit wrapped around me in a crumpled mess. I stood up and rehung the jacket onto a hanger and just as I was about to hang it on the back of the closet door in an attempt to de-wrinkle it, I saw something taped to the back of the closet door. A small white envelope. And in Preppy's messy handwriting the words:

OPEN ME MOTHERFUCKERS

∽⌒∾

King insisted on taking his bike to the funeral in what I think was his way of continuing to avoid any sort of conversation. When we pulled up, there were already several bikes parked along the road that wound through the lush grounds of the cemetery as well as Gladys's old Buick.

We were the last ones to arrive. Bear and a handful of bikers, Grace, and six of the 'Growhouse Granny's' were already seated under the portable canopy covering the rectangular hole in the ground that Preppy's shiny black casket hovered above. All were dressed in black. Some of the grannies wore matching black floppy hats. King wore a black collared shirt and jeans.

I threw caution to the wind and wore a yellow sun dress. I think Preppy would have liked it.

As we took our seats on the damp plastic chairs in the front row, King grabbed my hand and set it on his lap, intertwining our fingers, bringing me as close as he could bring me without sitting me in his lap.

The preacher nodded to King, then started speaking about life and death. He even tried to say a few words about Preppy, although the two had never met. I had to stifle a laugh when he referred to him as a wholesome and well-respected member of the community. For a fraction of a second, King's stoic face gave way to reveal a hint of a smile, while Bear downright let out a blast of laughter from where he stood against one of the canopy poles. The preacher paused to collect his thoughts, then continued.

"Who has words for our dearly departed today?" His voice was mechanical, like he was reciting a manual.

I felt for the envelope in my pocket to make sure it was still there. When Bear started walking to the front of the small crowd, I stood and cut him off. King shot me a look of confusion, and Bear stopped in his tracks.

"Hi," I said, realizing my voice wasn't loud enough for everyone to hear when some of the grannies put hands to their ears to amplify the sound. I tried again, speaking a little louder this time.

"My name is Doe, and although I didn't know Preppy, er, Samuel, very long, he was my friend. A great friend. My best friend. As much as I want to say a few words about him and how much he meant to me, in typical Preppy form, he's already beat us to it."

I took the envelope from my pocket and unfolded the notebook pages with small scribbly handwriting. I'd already read it, and I didn't want to cry, so I tried to zone out while I read the final words my friend wanted his friends to hear before we laid him to rest. "So, just a warning, I know we have some… mature folks in the crowd. Because this is coming right from Preppy, it contains some, um…colorful, language."

I glanced apologetically at the preacher whose attention was already down at his cell phone, his thumb raced across the keys.

Friends and MoFo's,

Like you thought I would let you have the last fucking word.

Fuck that. I'm way too OCD to have you try to come up with some nice things to say about me, so I came up with them myself. I've updated this weekly since I was ten years old, thinking that because of the situation I was living in that I wasn't going to make it to see twelve and that my family, if you could bother to call them that, wouldn't expend the effort to say anything at my funeral. And the thought of that, the thought of silence when they put me into the dirt was worse than the thought of dying to me. After that, it became kind of a habit, so I kept doing it.

So in the event of my untimely death, this is what I need all you fuckers to hear.

If you're reading this to a crowd of people dressed in their funeral finest, then I've achieved a longevity I never thought I would reach. I've made it to the ripe old age of twenty-six and it's been one hell of a fucking ride.

By now, I'm dead and will soon be rotting in the fucking ground, being eaten by worms and other random bugs and shit. But don't worry about me because I died a happy fucking man. Looking back, I never thought I would live a life where the word happy could describe it, but I did and it was all because when I was eleven years old, this big fucking brute of a man-child rescued me from a bully who shall not be named, and then he became my friend. Oh fuck that, the bully's name was Tyler Nightingale and the pussy still lives with his fucking mom and works the night shift at the Stop-N-Go. Fucking twat. Go egg his fucking car on the way home.

Anyways, I motherfucking digress.

The man-child became more than my friend. He became the best fucking friend anyone could ever ask for. He became my only family. Our childhoods were complete shit, but because of him, we were able to live our lives by our own set of rules. He didn't have to befriend a skinny kid with bruises all over his body and a foul fucking mouth. He could have looked the other way. He could have ignored me when I pestered him to no end. There are a lot of things he could have done. But he chose me to be his family, and I chose him to be mine.

Although there were bumps in the road, a little juvie, a little jail, and whole lotta shit I can't talk about here. I don't look back at those things as poor choices. I see them as part of the highlight reel of the most epic fucking journey of my life. A journey I never thought I would see. Shit, I never thought I would live past the age of 14, and if it wasn't for my best friend, and him saving my ass one night, I wouldn't have.

I want to send a shout out to Bear. Big-ups to you, you big fucking animal. Go travel. Go do you. Go do all the shit you want to do before that club of yours swallows you whole and you can't see where your ideas start and their ideas end.

No shit. At first, I thought you were just an annoying hanger-on, but it turns out that I was capable of having more than one friend after all, and I'm fucking glad it was you, man.

Bear, you need to look out for King and Doe. Lord fucking knows those two will need all the help they can get. I mean, they fucking love each other, but both are too fucking stupid to see past their own crap long enough to keep their shit together.

I see major fuck ups in their future. Be there for them. Help them see past their ridiculous issues and preach to them about the joys of honesty and anal sex.

Continuing on.

I've done shit I'm not proud of. Thanks to all of you for not judging me. Thanks to all of you for being my friends in spite of it. Thanks for giving me a life that was worth dying for. I would do it all over again if I fucking could. So don't fucking cry for me, be happy for me. Be happy that I had friends like all of you who I loved more than fucking family, who I loved more than myself, and we all know how crazy I am about me. Be happy that I was happy and that all you fuckers were a part of that.

Doe, if King doesn't get his head out of his ass and marry you and impregnate you with millions of his little man-children, he is a dumb fuck and I promise I will rise from the grave to take his place. It may take me a while to figure out how, but if anyone can do it, it's gonna be me.

King, my brother, thanks for taking a chance on a skinny geek all those years ago. Thanks for fucking saving my ass, but you did more than that. You saved my life. You gave me a life.

I love you, man.

Be happy kids.

I gotta go be dead now. No after funeral bullshit. I fucking hate that shit.

Go get laid. That will make me happy.

Fuck. Party. Make merry. And know that I fucking loved all of you.

-Prep

PS-I have also written my own obituary which I would like published in all the local papers. I'm serious about this. I will haunt you if this doesn't happen.

"Ummm, I don't know if I should read this next part out loud."

"Do it!" Bear cheered me on. Even from the other side of the tent, I could see the tears in his eyes, but now there was a smile on his face. "Let's fucking hear it!"

The crowd joined in, and I was left with no choice.

"Oh, fine," I said, taking a deep breath and speed reading through Preppy's autobiographical obituary.

Samuel Clearwater
26 years old
Badass MoFo
Went out like a boss
Leaves behind the family he chose: King, Doe, Bear, and the GG bitches.

May God rest his soul...and his ten-inch cock.

The entire group of mourners burst out laughing. Not just a few chuckles, but knee-slapping, belly laughter. As I put the note away and took my seat next to King, I realized what Preppy had done. He was the kind of guy who couldn't bear the thought of us crying over him, so he did what Preppy always did.

He made us laugh.

I looked over to King, who wasn't smiling at all. I tugged on his hand, but instead of getting his attention, he stood up.

Before the preacher said his final words, King was already long gone.

chapter
twenty-nine

King

MY GIRL HAD BEEN RAPED, AND IT HAD BEEN A WEEK SINCE WE PUT MY BEST friend into the ground. In that time, I didn't know where to place my anger at the person I hated most in the world.

No, not Isaac. I killed that motherfucker. Splattered his head wide open with a bullet at close range.

The person I hated most in the world was me.

After everything Doe had done for me, after everything we'd been through, she deserved better than to live a life in fear of being raped or shot. As much as I wanted out of the life, it wasn't something I could just jump out of in an instant. I needed to do something for her, but no matter what came to mind, it wasn't big enough to make this huge wrong, right again.

Then, it came to me.

There was one thing I could do for her.

One fucking reverse GOOGLE image search. That's all it took to find out who Doe really was. I'd uploaded a photo of her I took from my phone the first night she'd slept in my bed and pressed search and there she was, staring into the camera like she was looking right into my eyes. I wished I'd never done the search. I wished I'd never known who she really was.

I'd used the fact that I knew who she was and what that could do for me as an excuse to bring her back to me. Even though it was her I wanted since the very first moment I saw her.

I'd planned to keep her forever, and her secret even longer if need be.

Until now.

Seventeen-year-old Ramie Elizabeth Price.

Either the police were really shitty at their jobs, or they never really tried to find out who she was to begin with, because for the second time after searching her image, less than a second after pressing search, I was staring at multiple images of the girl I'd fallen in love with on my laptop.

There were no articles about her going missing, just pictures of her from various events. Balls, galas, fundraisers. It was her in the pictures, but it wasn't. The gowns, the makeup, the fake smile, if there was any smile at all.

The last picture of her I found was taken almost a year ago. She had a blank look on her face. Her eyes were vacant.

I knew that look. I'd regrettably put it on her face myself. It was a look that broke my fucking heart.

Indifference.

She was holding the hand of a boy who looked a little older than her, who was smiling from ear to ear.

I wanted to reach through the computer and break his fucking hand and then break every single one of his pearly white teeth.

Senator Westmore Bigelow Price, with daughter Ramie Elizabeth and long-time beau Tanner Preston Redmond at the Heart Ball Gala to raise money for pediatric cancer.

Even though it was my second time scanning the pictures, my blood boiled. I don't know what made me madder. The boy who was touching my girl. Or the man they listed as her father.

A senator running for president. A man who would want to avoid scandal at all cost. That's probably why they didn't even try to find their missing daughter.

Fucking asshole.

I stood from the kitchen table and threw the laptop across the room. It smashed against a cabinet and fell to the floor in a million pieces.

Bear came storming into the kitchen. "What the fuck?" he asked, looked over at the broken laptop. "You on the rag man?"

"We have to take a trip," I said, staring down at the now broken laptop as though the image of Doe or Ramie, or whatever the fuck her name was and her boyfriend were still up on the broken screen that was flashing from blue to black over and over again.

"Where we going?"

"Tell me something, Bear, and be honest. What are the chances of us getting the kind of money we need for the payoff to the senator for Max?"

My eyes met his for the first time since he came into the kitchen.

"Slim to fucking none, man" he answered honestly.

"Then, get the fucking truck. I'll drive."

"But you still haven't said why I'm getting the truck."

"Because, my friend, there is a deal with the devil that needs to be made." I looked down the hall at the closed door of my bedroom, where the girl I'd fallen in love with slept peacefully in my bed. She was mine, and I would always think of her that way. But she deserved a better life than the one I could give her, which seemed to only hurt her at every turn.

After Preppy's funeral I was thinking about giving her the truth.

Now, I was just going to give her away.

"And who is the devil in this scenario?" Bear asked, shrugging on his cut.

I was going to see the senator and offer Doe in exchange for him making sure that I had signed custody papers for Max.

The only family I had left.

I stared out the kitchen window, but couldn't see a thing. It was like I was staring into a white abyss, a place I was about to go, that I wasn't ever going to be able to come back from.

"Me."

King

WHEN YOU FALL IN LOVE, YOU KNOW IT'S THE REAL DEAL BECAUSE YOU COME to the realization you would take a bullet for that person. And when you become a parent, you realize that you would not only use your own body but the body of the person you love as a human shield to protect your child.

That is the place where I existed.

The Senator had a daughter who had a life, a boyfriend. I wasn't doing Doe any favors by keeping her with me, involved in shit she shouldn't be involved in. It got Preppy dead. I wasn't doing my daughter any favors by leaving her hanging out there in the world without protection. She needed her father. She needed her family.

She needed me.

I was going to give it all up for her. I couldn't manage the payoff, but if the senator accepted my offer of a trade, then I could keep what money I did have and that was enough to sell the house, and disappear off the radar to somewhere where nobody knew who we were.

Me and Max.

I was going to be a good father to her. A good influence. A good role model. I would get us a house in a good neighborhood and send her to a good school. I would read to her at bedtime. I would make this fucking work because it *had* to fucking work. I was going to disappear because my life was going to reappear.

I lost my best friend, and that made me realize that sooner or later I was going to lose my girl, too. Because as soon as she learned that I'd known who she was from the very beginning, she would hate me forever.

I needed Max because she was all I had left, and I was bound and determined not to fuck that up. I prayed to any god who listened that if I could just be with her, I would make things right. I would give her my all.

My love.

My heart.

My daughter.

My everything.

I made a decision that broke my fucking heart and made it sing all at the same time. So what if I felt like a piece of me would always be missing? Fuck it. I would have my daughter.

And she was my heart.

In exchange for Max, I was going to give Doe, or Ramie, or Pup, or whatever you want to call her, back to her father.

By not telling Doe about what was going to happen, I wasn't giving her an option. But there was no doubt in my mind that when she found out what I'd been hiding all along that she was going to look at me like the monster I am.

But then again, she might be grateful to me for giving her life back.

Maybe, not.

I pretended not to care all the way to the senator's office.

I was going to have to be prepared to pretend for the rest of my life.

"Do you have an appointment?" the receptionist with curly black hair and dark freckles across her nose asked, without looking up from her computer.

"My name is Brantley King, and I don't need a fucking appointment. Let him know I'm waiting. Give him this. He'll want to see me."

I placed the folded-up picture on his desk, one I took of Doe this morning while she was sleeping. I didn't wait for her to answer. I took a seat in the waiting area in a plastic chair that faced her desk. When she finally looked up from her computer, her jaw dropped. She'd probably never seen someone who looked like me waiting to see the senator. I didn't have the patience to be inconspicuous. I needed to make shit happen and make it happen before I changed my fucking mind.

The receptionist stood and walked down the hall. She emerged a few moments later and dialed a number on her phone. She held her hand up over her mouth as she whispered into the receiver.

"Senator Price will see you now," she said, with a fake smile, setting the phone back on its cradle.

She stood, and I followed her down the hall until we came to an office with a double-door entry. She opened it and stood aside to let me through. When I stepped inside, she shut it behind me. There was another click, which I'm sure meant that she locked it as well.

"I know who you are, Mr. King, and the only reason I'm even letting you in this office is because I know you had to pass through the metal detectors. So, I know you're not armed," the Senator said, standing up from behind his oversized mahogany desk, holding the picture I'd given his receptionist in his hand. He was trying to even the playing field, but he didn't seem to understand that I was the one holding all the cards.

"That's where you would be wrong, Senator." I lifted up the front of my shirt and removed the pistol from the front of my pants. I was wearing my big metal junior rodeo belt buckle trophy. The one I got for looping a sheep at the fair. "Crazy thing about those metal belt-buckles. They make the alarms go off every single fucking time."

The senator sat back down and folded his hands on the desk, gesturing to the chair in front of him. "Let's cut the shit then, shall we?"

A picture on a shelf beside his desk caught my eye. It was my Pup, several years younger than she was now, on some sort of beach, her smile bigger and brighter than I'd ever seen. She'd been happy once, and it was seeing that bit of happy that made it easier to propose my deal.

"I have your daughter. You have ten-seconds to tell me why you don't know where she is and why you aren't looking for her. The truth. Not some bullshit lie either," I warned.

The senator's eyes grew wide. "You better not have harmed my daughter so help me…" He stood abruptly, his chair tipped backwards and crashed onto the floor. "What do you know?"

"Calm the fuck down. What I know is that she has big blue eyes and a tendency to talk too much when she's nervous." And then just for fun I added, "I know how her heart beats faster when she's turned on."

"What the fuck did you do to my daughter?"

"Oh, no. That's not how this works. You need to answer me first. Why haven't you reported her missing? Why haven't you looked for her?"

"Why do you think we haven't been looking?" the senator asked, settling back into his seat, nervously wringing his hands.

"Because if the senator's daughter went missing, you would think it would be kind of a big deal. All over the news and whatnot. And it isn't."

Senator Price picked his chair up off the floor and sat down, rubbing his hands over his eyes.

"We've been telling people she's studying abroad in Paris. But as you already know, that's not the truth," he admitted. "We didn't report her missing because Ramie is a troubled child. She started hanging with the wrong crowd. Disappearing for weeks at a time. This time, it's been months, and she hasn't so much as used my credit card. Her mother and I thought she was rebelling, teaching us some sort of lesson. We'd gotten into a huge fight before she stormed out. We haven't seen her since."

"So, you didn't report her missing, because she was a troubled child? Or because you were up for reelection and you were afraid the story would taint your oh-so-perfect political image?"

"Did you see what happened to Sarah Palin when they found out she had a sixteen-year-old who was unwed and pregnant? It killed her! I couldn't do that to my party, and I knew Ramie wasn't really missing. She'd just run away like she'd had so many times before. So I made up excuses, lies. I told people what they wanted to hear, and her mother and I prayed every day she would at least call." He looked distraught. "Tell me she's okay."

"Yeah. She's fine."

The senator let out a relieved breath.

"Why did she never come home? Does she really hate us that much?" he asked, his fingers pressed to his temples.

"She doesn't remember. She was in some sort of accident. She woke up with no memory. She doesn't even know her own name."

"What?" He stood up again. "Take me to her. Now! I need to see her!" he demanded.

"Not so fast." I held up a hand. "Sit the fuck back down, Senator. It seems we have a little trade we need to work out."

He sat back down. "Yes, of course. What are your terms?"

"No bullshit. No money. What I'm offering is a flat trade. Ramie for Max. My daughter. Here is her information." I placed a receipt on his desk. "On the back is my daughter's name, social security number, and the address of the foster home she's been living in, as well as all my information. Be at my place. Tomorrow at noon. Bring Max and all the custody papers, giving me full rights to my daughter and then and only then, you'll get yours back." The words hurt coming out of my mouth, but they needed to be said because the trade needed to be done.

"That can be arranged, but I'll need more than a day," the senator said, nervously shuffling his thumbs one over the other over and over again. I stood and walked to the door.

"Tomorrow at noon. If you're not there, if you don't bring Max—" I turned and faced him one last time. "I'll slit your girl's throat. No hesitation. If I can't have my daughter, I won't let you have yours. I don't give a shit what happens to me after that."

I waited until I was in the car and Bear was driving out of the parking lot to exhale.

"How did it go?" Bear asked.

I sighed.

"That bad?"

"It went about as good as it could have gone. It's what I did that I'm sighing about."

"What exactly is it that you did in there?"

"I just traded, Doe."

"For what?" he shouted.

"Who," I corrected.

"Okay, for who?"

"Max. I just traded Doe for Max."

"Oh. My. Fuck."

"Yeah, that about sums it up," I said, running my hand over my head.

If I wasn't sure whether I'd ever sold my soul before, I was positive I had now.

chapter
thirty-one

King

I WAS IN BED WITH DOE. IT WAS ALMOST MIDNIGHT, AND I WAS ALREADY COUNTING down the hours to noon. Noon was when I would see Max for the first time since I held her in my arms the night I let my mom burn in the fire.

Noon was also the last time I would ever see my girl.

Doe was going to become the person she was supposed to be, the person she was born as, Ramie Price. She probably wouldn't bother glancing back at me in the rearview mirror after realizing the life of luxury she was heading back to. I was never good enough for her to begin with, and this was going to be both the most selfish and selfless thing I'd ever done when it came to her.

I was giving her back.

I was getting my daughter back.

I'd never been so miserable, and excited at the same time. A few months ago, I didn't think that if I got Max back I would be doing it all alone. I thought at least I'd have Preppy. Then, I thought Doe would be in the picture.

Now, it was down to just me.

I lifted my leg over hers. I couldn't get close enough. I'd convinced her to let go of the person she was to be with me, but unlike Preppy, her past life had risen from the grave and had been haunting me since I hit the search button.

I was tossing her back like a fish that wasn't worth keeping.

But she WAS worth keeping.

She was worth fucking everything.

Everything I couldn't give her.

There was no doubt in my mind if something like soulmates did exist that Doe was mine. The problem was that Ramie wasn't. Ramie had a boyfriend. Ramie had money. Ramie had a future that didn't include a felon with tattoos and a penchant for violence. Ramie wasn't going to have to put herself in danger, risk getting shot, or ever have to worry that either one of us was going to get hurt or end up dead.

I wanted more for her. I wanted to break her heart and mine and get it over with so we could both heal.

Her with her family.

Me with mine.

I turned her onto her back and rolled on top of her. Spreading her legs, I lowered myself until I could taste her sweetness one last time. I slowly lapped at her folds as she woke with a moan on her tongue. Water welled up in my eyes. I'd licked her into her first orgasm by the time the first tear fell. I was glad her eyes were closed when I entered her and began thrusting fiercely into not just the greatest pussy I've ever had, and the greatest girl I'd ever known, but the greatest love I knew I'd ever have.

The only love.

If things were different, I'd put a ring on her finger. A baby in her belly. We'd have Max. We'd have Preppy. We'd be the family I always wanted but never knew could exist.

Because it didn't exist.

Preppy was fucking dead, and my girl was about to return to the life of privilege she was born into.

I told her I loved her with each thrust of my hips. I told her I was sorry. I told her that I wanted her to stay forever. I told her I wished she would have my child. I told her everything with sex that I dared not speak out loud. I told her that if things were different that we would be together forever.

Forever.

I'd never spoken the word in my life, but looking down at Doe, still half-asleep as I brought her to the brink of another orgasm, I saw what forever would look like.

And it was fucking beautiful.

A wayward tear dripped from my chin. I reached out and caught it in the palm of my hand before it had a chance to wake Doe from the state of sleepy ecstasy she was currently in.

Before she could find out how I really felt.

Before she was gone.

Forever.

The next morning, for the first time in my life, I made love to a woman. I didn't fuck. I didn't have sex.

I kissed her the entire time. I held her as close as two people could be. I told her she was beautiful. That I loved everything about her.

I waited until she was in the throes of her orgasm to whisper, "I love you." I don't know if she heard me, but I was saying it more for me than for her.

I needed to say those words while I still had the chance.

I think a part of me loved Doe from the first moment my eyes landed on hers. Haunted, beautiful, scared. I wanted her, body and soul.

I would only have her for a few more hours, and I was going to spend every second of that time, inside my girl.

While she still was my girl.

chapter
thirty-two

Doe

EVERY TIME I WOKE DURING THE NIGHT, KING WAS TOUCHING ME. IT WAS LIKE no matter how close we were, it wasn't close enough.

I dreamt that he told me he loved me. Once before, after finishing my tattoo, he'd told me to *shut up and let me love you*. But what I heard in my dream was the real deal.

There was something wrong. I felt it in my bones. I'd asked him what was bothering him, but he brushed me off and just kept making love to me.

For hours.

Maybe, he was lost in thoughts of Preppy, and just needed me to be there for him.

So, I was.

Our time together that morning was so unlike anything I'd experienced with him before.

I told him over again that I was okay after Isaac forced himself on me. It was a moment in life, a horrible one. But I know I'd be okay. As long as I had King, I would be okay.

It would all be okay.

I was helplessly, passionately, in love with the complicated man who touched me like I was a thin square of glass, and he was afraid I was going to shatter.

He whispered to me how gorgeous I was as he dragged his cock against my clit. He pulled out of me and rubbed against my sensitive bundle of nerves when he thrust back in.

I was alive with sensation, and full of questions.

He whispered how much he loved being inside me. How much he wished he wasn't so much of an asshole. How I deserved the world. How he wasn't good enough for me.

And then it hit me like a fucking freight train with no brakes, and my heart seized inside my chest.

King was saying goodbye.

✑

The sun was already high in the sky by the time I woke up and got dressed. At any second, I expected King to burst through the door and tell me he wanted me gone. It was a horrible thing to be waiting for. I was going to pack, but there was nothing there that was truly ever mine.

I threw on some clothes and headed outside to find King. Rather than waiting around with my neck stretched out on the block, I went in search of the executioner. I found him outside, rocking in the swing I'd recently convinced him was the only thing missing from the porch.

"What's going on?" I asked him. "Something's wrong. Tell me." He buried his face in his hands.

"Everything, baby. Everything is wrong," King said, looking up over the porch railing.

I walked over to him and he ran his hands up and down my arms. I sat on his lap and draped my arms around his neck. He burrowed his nose into my chest.

"Tell me. Please," I begged. "I can help."

"You can't. Nobody can."

"You're scaring me. You need to tell me what's wrong."

"My fucking heart is broken," he said, raising his raspy voice.

"Why? Who broke it?" I asked.

"You did," he said, looking up at me with tears in his eyes.

I was taken aback. What did I do to break it? Did I even have that kind of power over him?

The sound of an approaching car turned both of our heads to the driveway. A black town car with dark tinted windows pulled up in front of the house.

"Will you remember something for me?" King asked, snapping my head back around from the car to him.

"Anything," I answered. And it was true. I would do anything for him.

"Remember that I love you," he whispered.

He had said it. I didn't just imagine it.

"Why are you telling me this now?" I asked, finding it odd that King wasn't even acknowledging the approaching vehicle.

I wanted him to love me, especially because I'd known I'd been in love with him for so long, but the way he said it, and what had transpired that morning told me there was a lot more to what was going on.

"Tell me what the fuck is going on!" I leapt from his lap.

"Baby," he said, reaching for me.

"No! Don't *baby* me! Tell me what the fuck is going on!"

King finally looked toward the town car. The driver got out and walked around, opening the door of the back seat.

A boy a little older than me, with dark blonde curls stepped out of the back seat. He wore black Chucks, grey shorts, and a red batman t-shirt.

It wasn't until he looked up at me when I recognized him. Or at least, his eyes.

Chestnut brown.

The eyes from my dream.

I was stunned into silence, frozen on the porch as the boy approached.

"Ray? Ray is that really you?" he asked, looking right at me.

I looked up at King whose expression had completely changed from troubled and weary to angry and vengeful. He was staring daggers at the boy. His jaw tensed so hard I swear I could hear his teeth grinding.

"Who is Ray?" I asked King.

"Don't fucking do this," Bear snapped from the doorway.

"Go the fuck back inside," King barked.

"Fine. It's your fucking life. Fuck it up more than it already is. Preppy would've kicked your fucking ass for this. I'm going to visit my sister. I can't stick around and witness this shit." Bear stepped out onto the porch and pecked me on the cheek. "Love you, pretty girl," he said before disappearing around the side of the house. A moment later, his bike whizzed by, kicking up dust in its wake.

"You," King finally answered. "You are Ramie Price."

"Ray, don't you remember me?" the boy asked. "I'm Tanner. Don't you know who I am?"

I turned to King. "What is this? Who is he? Why is he here?"

"He's your...boyfriend." He forced the words off his tongue like they were stabbing him in his mouth.

"My what?" I didn't wait for him to answer. "You knew he was coming?" Then, it hit me, and I sucked in a strangled breath. "You knew who I was?"

King didn't say anything, but most importantly, he didn't deny it.

"How long have you known?" I whispered.

King looked down at his shoes.

"How long have you fucking known?" I shouted.

"Since the very beginning," he admitted. "Since before I came for you again after you escaped."

"Escaped?" Tanner asked, reminding me of his presence.

"The entire time?" I asked, feeling as if he just stabbed me in my chest. "You knew who I was this entire *fucking* time?"

"What the fuck do you want me to say? I'm a shit person, and I do shitty things. You knew that. I fucking told you that, but you went and fell for me anyway." He ran his hand over his head in frustration. "Well, it's over now. Welcome to your new life. Or I should say your *old* life," King spat.

He lowered his eyes. "You deserve better than all this shit anyway." He waved his hand toward the house. "You deserve better than me. You've got a family. Go be with them, and forget I exist."

His eyes darted down to Tanner who stood in the front yard with confusion marring his face. He glanced back and forth between me and King.

"What's going—" Tanner started to ask.

"Shut the fuck up," King snapped, effectively silencing the boy.

"That is NOT your decision to make," I told him. "You don't get to say where I go or who I go with."

"Actually, it is," King argued.

"What the fuck does that mean? What the fuck did you do?"

"Ray!" the boy shouted over our argument.

King looked down at him as if he were going to leap down the steps and crush his skull with his hands.

"Come down here," Tanner said in a gentle voice. "Just for a second. I just want to see you. Talk to you."

I looked back at King, and it dawned on me. It wasn't my decision to make because he was giving me away.

That's what last night and this morning were all about. He was saying his goodbyes.

King nodded to me as if to say I had his approval to go talk to Tanner. I rolled my eyes at him. I didn't need his fucking approval.

I tentatively descended the stairs one at a time. When I got to the bottom, I sat on the bottom step. "Do you know who I am?" Tanner asked, crouching down and resting his hands on his knees.

I shook my head. "I recognize your eyes, but nothing else," I admitted.

"As I said, my name is Tanner. We've known each other our entire lives. We were homecoming king and queen all four years of high school," he said with a chuckle. Then his face grew serious. "I love you. You love me. Always have." Tanner blushed and rocked back on his heels. "It feels weird to introduce myself to you when we've known each other since we were in diapers."

"Who am I?" I asked hesitantly.

Tanner took a seat on the step next to me, careful to keep some distance between us. I didn't need to look back at King to know he was watching Tanner's every move. I felt his gaze on my back as if they were rays of the sun singing my skin. Tanner smelled like the beach. His unruly hair fell into his eyes. He brushed it out of the way as he spoke. A huge smile spread across his face, revealing a dimple in his left cheek.

"You are the lovely Ramie Elizabeth Price. Daughter of Dr. Margot Price and Senator Bigelow Price. You live in East Palm Cove, about an hour from here. You were enrolled in art school, and you were supposed to start in the fall. You and I were going to backpack around Europe for the summer first, but then you disappeared."

I had a name.

Ramie. Ramie. Ramie.

"Ramie," I whispered, testing the name out on my tongue.

Still nothing.

"I went to the police. They said no one was looking for me. No missing person's report. Why didn't you look for me if I was missing?" I asked.

Tanner shook his head. "I didn't want to have to be the one to tell you this, but you had this friend, and she was going through some bad stuff. She got in trouble a lot. You left a note, said you were running away. They didn't look for you because they didn't think you wanted to be found. You had just turned eighteen. You were an adult. There was no missing person's report because you weren't missing. You were just gone."

"I left?" I asked.

"Yes."

"I left you?"

"Yeah," he admitted. "You left me. And your mom. And your dad. Everyone."

I had a mom.

"Why isn't my mom here?" I asked.

"We didn't want to overwhelm you. Your mom is at home, waiting for you to arrive, but your dad is in the car." Tanner said, pointing to the town car with the blacked-out windows, still running on the driveway.

"I still don't remember. I thought I would remember if I saw someone from my past, if they told me who I was, but I don't." My head spun. If I didn't remember him face to face, would I ever remember him?

Would I ever remember anyone?

"You will, but it will take time. You just need to get back into the groove of things for a while. Your normal routine. It will come back to you. We won't rush it. Your mom's got the best doctors already on call. Specialists. You'll be back to your old self in no time," he said, nudging my shoulder.

King had already told them everything. At least enough for my mom to already have doctors at the ready.

The girl who I'd given up on might be back after all.

The back door of the car opened again, and out stepped a tall man in a sharp black suit and a solid red tie.

"Who is that?" I asked Tanner.

"Your dad," he told me. "The senator."

"Ramie," the man said. "Your mother is worried sick. Let's go. Get in the car," he said sternly, buttoning the bottom button of his suit jacket.

It was ninety degrees outside, and there wasn't one drop of sweat on his forehead. No redness on his cheeks. It's like he was too important to be affected by the heat.

From above me, King leaned forward over the railing. With the light of the sun directly overhead, his massive frame cast a shadow onto the ground.

He really did look like a King. A force to be reckoned with. Zeus, on his perch above the world.

The senator stepped out of King's shadow as if he were too good to be standing in it. This irked me.

He wasn't better than King.

No one was.

King was a bad guy, but he was my bad guy. He was more than that. He was my world. My heart. These people may have known who I was before, but I knew who I was now, and the two versions of me were going to have to figure out how to merge before I uprooted what I had with King in search of something unknown.

"Senator," King acknowledged the man.

"Mr. King," the senator greeted, shielding his eyes from the sun with his hand.

"Where's Max?" King asked, bitterly.

"Soon, she'll be here soon. There is another car on its way here with her in it."

"Trade means trade." King said. "She isn't going anywhere until Max gets here."

Then, it hit me. King had said I didn't have a choice, and now, I knew why.

If I stayed, King wouldn't get his daughter back. The trade he mentioned was me for Max.

"There she is now," the senator said as another town car pulled up into the driveway. King bounded down the steps jumping over me as he made his way over to the car. The second it stopped, King opened the back door.

"Max?" he shouted into the car.

The driver rounded the vehicle and produced something from his jacket pocket. He slapped a metal cuff around King's wrist.

"She's not in there," King shouted, pulling at the cuff. "What the fuck is this? Where is she?"

The man I thought was the driver twisted King's other arm forward and secured the cuffs in front of him.

"What are you doing?" I shouted, running up to King. "Let him go!" A pair of strong arms grabbed me from behind and stopped me from getting any closer. "What the fuck is going on? I need to go to him!"

I kicked my feet in the air as the man I was told was my father lifted me up off the ground. King's nostrils flared as the man who'd just put King in cuffs, wrestled him into the back seat of the car.

"Mr. King, this is Detective Lyons. You're being arrested for the abduction of my daughter," the senator said, all the while maintaining his hold on me.

"But he didn't kidnap me! He didn't do anything. He saved me. He SAVED me!" I shouted, biting at his arm as I tried to break free of his grip.

And I meant it. King had saved me. In every way. He'd saved me from myself, from a life of standing still. Because of him, I was moving forward.

I wanted to move forward with him.

"You motherfucker!" King shouted. Detective Lyons closed the car door, and I lost sight of King behind the heavy tint of the windows.

"No!" I called out. The car took off and disappeared under the trees. "Let me fucking go!"

The senator turned me around to face him and grabbed me roughly by the shoulders. "Calm down, Ramie, or you're going to scare him," he warned.

"Who? What the fuck are you talking about?"

Tanner walked over to the car and opened the door. A little boy with curls like Tanner's and hair as white as mine tumbled out of the back seat.

The little boy saw me and opened his arms. He came bounding up to me and crashed into my thigh.

The senator released his hold on me. The little boy nuzzled his face into my leg.

I looked down at him, puzzled.

Because it wasn't the way his eyes were as icy-blue as mine, or how the dimple on his chin matched mine that alarmed me the most.

It was what he shouted that made my heart stop.

"Mommy!"

King & Doe's story is continued in TYRANT.
Available Now.

acknowledgments

Thank you first and foremost to my readers for your patience. I love you all so very much. Thank you for making this dream of mine more wonderful than I could have ever imagined and thank you for sticking with me.

Thank you to Karla Nellenbach for making my words look pretty AND make some sort of sense.

Special thanks to Aurora Rose Reynolds for all of your encouragement and for taking the time to be an early reader for KING. I am honored to call you my friend.

To the blogs both big and small who have supported me since day one, thank you so very very much. I don't know where I would be without you. Aestas, TRSoR, LitSlave, and so many many more.

Special thanks to Milasy, my book soulmate. So much filth to read, so little time.

Thank you to Joanna Wylde for offering to help me and for all of your wisdom. I am forever grateful for your advice.

Thank you to my agent, Kimberly Brower, for believing in me and for being patient.

Thank you so much to Andree Katic for being a phenomenal King and cover model, and to Chocolate-Eye Photography for taking such a wonderful picture.

Thank you to my wonderful husband and beautiful baby girl. I couldn't do any of this without you and I wouldn't want to.

also by
T.M. FRAZIER

THE PERVERSION TRILOGY
PERVERSION (Book 1)
POSSESSION (Book 2)
PERMISSION (Book 3)

THE OUTSKIRTS DUET
THE OUTSKIRTS (Book 1)
THE OUTLIERS (Book 2)

THE KING SERIES
LISTED IN RECOMMENDED READING ORDER

Jake & Abby's Story (Standalone)
The Dark Light of Day (Prequel)

King & Doe's Story (Duet)
KING (Book 1)
TYRANT (Book 2)

Bear & Thia's Story (Duet)
LAWLESS (Book 3)
SOULLESS (Book 4)

Rage & Nolan's Story (Standalone)
ALL THE RAGE (Spinoff)

Preppy & Dre's Story (Triplet)
PREPPY PART ONE (Book 5)
PREPPY PART TWO (Book 6)
PREPPY PART THREE (Book 7)

Smoke & Frankie's Story (Standalone)
UP IN SMOKE (Spinoff)

Nine & Lenny's Story
NINE, THE TALE OF KEVIN CLEARWATER

King & Doe's Novella
King of the Causeway

Pike's Story (Duet)
Pike (Book 1)
Pawn (Book 2)

about the author

T.M. Frazier never imagined that a single person would ever read a word she wrote when she published her first book, *The Dark Light of Day*.

Now, she's a *USA Today* bestselling author several times over. Her books have been translated into numerous languages and published all around the world.

T.M. enjoys writing what she calls 'wrong side of the tracks' romance with sexy, morally corrupt anti-heroes and ballsy heroines.

Her books have been described as raw, dark and gritty. Basically, while some authors are great at describing a flower as it blooms, T.M. is better at describing it in the final stages of decay.

She loves meeting her readers, but if you see her at an event please don't pinch her because she's not ready to wake up from this amazing dream.

For more information please visit her website www.tmfrazierbooks.com

FACEBOOK:
facebook.com/tmfrazierbooks

TWITTER
twitter.com/tm_frazier

INSTAGRAM
instagram.com/t.m.frazier

JOIN MY FACEBOOK GROUP, FRAZIERLAND
www.facebook.com/groups/tmfrazierland

bad
penny

STACI HART

chapter
one

Dick Lips

"**D**ID YOU KNOW THAT A MAN'S LIPS ARE THE SAME COLOR AS THE HEAD of his dick?"

I took a long lick of my ice cream to punctuate the question. Ramona choked on hers, and Veronica, our other roommate, laughed openly and a little too loudly for a public place. A few people in the ice cream parlor turned to look.

"I'm serious," I said. "It's a real thing. I can vouch for it. I've seen a lot of dicks."

Veronica snorted. *"Oh my God. Stop it."*

Ramona couldn't stop giggling. The three of us sat at a small table on the patio of our favorite ice cream joint, which was conveniently located around the corner from our apartment. It was *hot*. June in New York is no joke—though nothing compared to August—and that day was particularly humid without a cloud in the sky to give us reprieve from the blazing sun. Hence, the ice cream, shorty shorts, and tanks we all wore.

Curse of getting ready to go anywhere with your roommates. Everyone matched.

It happened more than I'd admit to openly. But we were attached at the hips: we lived together, worked together at Tonic—a tattoo parlor— and boy hunted together. Well, I hunted boys, Ramona played with her engagement ring, and Veronica rejected all potential suitors. The only difference in our appearance was the color of our messy buns: Veronica's was pitch-black, Ramona's was platinum-blonde, and mine was a silvery shade of lavender that I'd stuck with for three whole months. It was nearly a record.

"Like take this guy for example," I started, nodding into the ice cream parlor where a group of guys sat just inside the rolled up garage doors.

We all looked, not even pretending to be inconspicuous. Everyone knows no one can tell if you were looking at them when you have sunglasses on.

Two of their backs were to us, but the third faced our direction, and, boy, was he a looker. He was in a sort of muscle shirt, which sounds horribly douchey, but he pulled it off well enough that I wished he'd pull it off. He was tan and dirty blond with biceps that had curves like a rollercoaster and a tattoo on his shoulder that I couldn't make out from the distance. Black

Wayfarers sat on his nose, and when he laughed at something one of his friends had said, I swear his smile blew a circuit in my brain.

"Wait, which one are we looking at?" Veronica asked.

"Blondie. With the arm porn," I answered. His lips were wide and full, a dusty shade of pink that sent a little tingle between my legs. "So, check his lips out—they're like the perfect pink. Like not *too* pink. You just want a nice, neutral shade, nothing extreme. Don't want any surprises when he unleashes the beast."

Ramona snickered. "*That* is a neat trick, Pen. I swear to God, I can picture it now. I bet it's pretty," she said dreamily before licking her ice cream.

My bottom lip slipped between my teeth. "Mmm, I bet it is too. Shaped like a pretty little mushroom with veins in all the right places."

Veronica groaned with her mouth full of ice cream. "You are so gross."

I made a face at her. "It's not my fault you don't appreciate the finer things in life. Like a gorgeous dick."

A laugh burst out of her, and I smiled. She could pretend she thought dicks were gross, but I knew it was a boldfaced lie. I'd heard her calling for Jesus behind the wall we shared—though it was rare enough that I found myself constantly on a mission to get her laid.

Blondie glanced over and caught all three of us looking. A slow smile lifted one corner of his lips, and I found myself mirroring him.

The girls and I didn't look away because we were utterly shameless. And with him looking at me like that, I did what any woman with a pulse would do: I held his gaze and did something blatantly sexual to my ice cream.

His eyes were on my lips. I was pretty sure at least—he had on sunglasses too, so he could have been watching the granny who sat behind me. But I knew I had him when his smile faltered, his brows rising just a hair, and a little shock worked through me, a rush that set my heart ticking a little faster.

Veronica hit me, effectively knocking my elbow out from underneath me and sending the tip of my nose into my cone.

"Hey!" I said with a simultaneous pout and scowl.

She only laughed and picked up a napkin to wipe my nose off for me.

"You are so fucking boy crazy," she said with a laugh. "Get serious."

"Never." I let her wipe off my nose. I'd earned that. "And what's wrong with being boy crazy?"

"Nothing," Ramona answered for Veronica and in my defense. "You're happy chasing all that dick, and it's super entertaining to watch."

"Thank you," I said gratefully and stuck my tongue out at Veronica.

"You're welcome. If we were on *The Golden Girls*, you'd be Blanche."

A laugh shot out of me. "Duh, she's my spirit guide. A different beau every episode. A drawer full of crotchless panties. A lot of dramatic flailing." I licked my cone with my eyes on Blondie, who was still watching me too. "And Veronica would be Dorothy. Forever single and an absolute killjoy."

Veronica rolled her eyes. I heard it from behind her sunglasses.

"Who would I be?" Ramona asked.

"Sophia, except taller. Or Rose but with less anecdotes about cows."

We broke into more giggling. Maybe the heat was making us punchy.

"Anyway, the dick-lip thing works for women too."

Veronica chuffed. "Oh? You can tell the color of our dicks?"

"I wonder if it would apply to a clit." I hummed thoughtfully. "But no, our lips are the same color as our nipples."

Ramona froze, her red lips dropping open in a little O. "Oh my God, it's true."

"I know it is." Eyes locked on Blondie, I stuck out my tongue to swirl around the top of my cone. I closed my lips over the top of it real slow, making a show of it.

He gripped the edge of the table.

Ramona shook her head. "I'm never leaving the house without lipstick on again."

Veronica snorted.

"Isn't it weird?" I asked. "It's like nature was like, *This is your mouth. It's for eating and putting genitals in. Let me color-code that into your brain, so you don't forget that lips are for food and fucking.*"

Ramona chuckled. "Only you, Penny."

I put up one hand and shook my head. "Blame nature, not me. Lips are so sexual. Why do you think women wear lipstick? We want men—or women, if you swing that way—to notice our mouths, but we don't really give their lips the consideration they deserve. Blondie's lips are soft and smooth, and I bet his dick is too. I bet he kisses like a god and fucks like a porn star."

Veronica laughed and stood. "All right, that's enough out of you. Let's go. If we stay any longer, you're going to face-rape that poor, unsuspecting man you've been taunting with your sexual salted caramel."

"Sexual a-salt." As she pulled me out of my chair, I licked my lips, my eyes still on Blondie. "I wonder what he'd look like under a little salted caramel."

Ramona playfully pushed me in the shoulder, and I followed the girls, twiddling my fingers at Blondie as we walked away from the shop, laughing.

Her hips swung as she walked away, and I sat there like an idiot with ice cream dripping down my hand.

"Dude." My twin brother, Jude, slapped me in the arm, sending my cone teetering.

I scowled at him. "What the fuck, man?"

"You weren't even listening."

"You're right. I was too busy watching one of the hottest girls I've ever seen lick her ice cream like it was her job."

He looked around. "Where?"

"She's gone."

"Man, why didn't you tell me?"

I smirked. "Because I saw her first."

Phil rolled his eyes from across the table. "You guys argue like sisters."

"That's what happens when you share a womb for nine months." I took a bite of my waffle cone, still thinking about her.

Her hair was a soft shade of purple, tied up in a bun, and her face was framed by a blue bandana, tied on top. She looked like a pinup girl, and when she'd stood and walked away, I'd caught sight of the sweetest heart-shaped ass. I couldn't help but imagine my hands around it and my face buried in her—

Jude slapped my arm again. "You're drooling, asshole."

I punched him in the bicep. "Lay off."

He rubbed the spot where I'd hit him and frowned.

Phil shook his head and propped his skinny forearms on the table. "I miss the days when you guys were more worried about your *Magic: The Gathering* deck and binging on Snickers bars than girls."

Jude smirked. "Ah, the great sexual drought of our teenage years."

Phil made a face and pushed his glasses up his long nose. "Easy, guys. Some of us never outgrow that curse."

"Aw, come on, Phil. You've got Angie."

"True, and I love her. And, beyond all reason, she loves me too. Fortunately, Ang doesn't give a shit that I'll never be a blond, buff Bobbsey twin."

I shook my head. "You should have gotten into surfing with us, Philly."

He gave me a flat look. "First off, there's no real surfing in Berkeley. Second, sharks."

Jude laughed. "I get it, man. If Dad hadn't guilted us into learning before we left for college, we wouldn't have either. But even if we hadn't, you don't live in Santa Monica without becoming a surfer."

I nodded. "It's true. I mean, I hated surfing the pier, but the sound of panties hitting the ground when we came in from a session made it all worthwhile."

Jude sighed. "Ah, the good old days. It was so easy to get chicks. But I swear, when we started surfing, I thought I was gonna die. I could barely even paddle out past the breaks without having a coronary."

"Too many donuts." I took another bite of my cone.

"I think I lost thirty pounds in two months. And then came the girls," Jude said, his eyes all dreamy.

"So many girls," I added.

Phil made a face. "I hate this story."

"If you'd gotten into USC, you could have paddled through pussy with us," Jude said matter-of-factly.

"Please, UCLA would have been better," I shot.

"Whatever, dicks. Berkeley is better on all counts."

"Anyway," Jude started, "New York is a totally different game. In LA, if you have a BMW and surf, you can bag pretty much anybody on the West side. Here, the bar is high. New York chicks don't give a shit about any of that."

I frowned. "Sounds like a lot of work."

"Yeah, but it's worth it," Jude said with a smile. "You'll see tonight. We'll hit a couple of bars, see what there is to see. I'm so ready to get back into the game after wasting all that time with Julie."

He sounded flippant, but I knew just how much she'd hurt him. They'd moved out here together years ago, and just before I'd moved from LA a week ago, she'd dumped him.

I clapped him on the shoulder, hoping he could find a distraction at whatever bar we were going to that night. "Tonight, you get in where you fit in."

He smiled. "Hell yeah. And you'll see what New York is really like. We need a break. We've been locked up in the loft coding ever since you got here."

I shrugged. "We've been talking about this game since we were in middle school, and now that we have the tools and the degrees and we're in the same place, it's been good. We've been coding it for eight fucking years, and now we can really do it instead of just dicking around with it in our spare time."

Phil nodded. "Thank God you lost your job."

"Thank God for my severance and savings," I added. "And that your parents are Silicon Valley yuppies and pay for the loft."

He laughed at that. "Otherwise, us quitting to go all in on the game wouldn't have been an option."

"No pressure, right?" I joked, skirting the magnitude of the situation by pretending the risk we were taking wasn't a big deal.

Jude's face softened until he looked all sappy and sentimental. "Really, man, I'm glad you're here. I don't like being split up. It's been a shitty four years without you."

"It has," I agreed. "But we're back together now. And even though I hate being stuck in the city with the beach an hour away and no surf to be had—"

Jude's sappy face turned into a frown.

"—I'm glad I'm here. Now, show me this high-class ass before I head back to the land of a thousand bikinis."

After we finished our ice cream, we headed back to the loft, and I found myself thinking about the pinup girl, wondering if I'd ever see her again. I'd been a fool for not chasing after her, stunned stupid by her blatancy, knocked out by the boldness of her. She'd seemed like a girl who knew what she wanted, and that confidence, that forwardness of her actions, had lit a fire in me that no amount of mint chocolate could cool down.

chapter
two
Sideshow

COURTNEY LOVE WAILED ABOUT WAKING UP IN HER MAKEUP AS I SAT WITH MY roommates in front of the long mirror hanging on my bedroom wall. I'd hung it sideways a couple of years before, low enough on the wall that we could sit at it, and framed it with lights, just like I'd seen on Pinterest, and I'd even used a drill, and nearly drilling a hole in my leg was so worth it. No one put makeup on anywhere else in the apartment.

The light was perfect, the music was perfect, and the company was perfect. I sat between Veronica and Ramona, singing along with Courtney, as I uncapped my lipstick, a dark red matte called *Heartbreaker*. It couldn't have been more accurate of a shade for me and not just because of my skin tone.

See, I didn't do serious or permanent, not with my hair color and not with my boys.

I'd been lollipop pink and shamrock green. I'd been fiery orange and cotton-candy blue. In fact, I hadn't really seen my actual hair color past a half-inch of roots since high school back in California. I hadn't had a serious boyfriend since then either.

Why choose one when you could have them all?

Veronica called me boy crazy like it was an insult, and I was. Every time I met a new guy, I would fall into easy infatuation, a giddy affair with a time limit. I wanted zero commitment. I wanted the fun and the thrill and to call it before things got messy. Sticky. I always skipped out the door before those pesky old feelings got involved and wrecked the whole train. I wasn't into napalm. I was more of a rainbows-and-ponies kind of girl—I wanted feelings, but only the good ones. And good feelings didn't last past three dates. After three dates, somebody inevitably wanted more. Usually, it was them. Every once in a while, it was me.

At that point, I didn't skip out the door. I ran like my hair was on fire.

You'd think it wouldn't be so hard to find guys who were cool with no strings, but this was shockingly untrue.

They would *say* they were fine with it, but I swear to God, at least a third of the time, we would hit that three-date mark, and they would profess their love. Date one would be easy, fun, always the best. Date two, I could feel those strings looming, hanging over me like a goddamn raincloud, but I'd just pop open my rainbow-striped umbrella and keep on skipping until date three when I'd get some variation of, *I think I'm in love with you.*

The last one was a perfect example.

As I had been getting dressed, he'd sat up in bed with eyes like the saddest beagle ever and said, *I feel like you're using me.*

I'd smiled and kissed him on the forehead and told him I'd call him.

I never called him.

I know, I know, trust me. I wish I could let myself fall helplessly in love, but I'd done that once, and when it had ended and I had been left alone to put myself back together, I'd known without a doubt that love wasn't for me. The reason: He had driven me crazy. And not the cute kind of crazy. The kind of crazy that earned you a restraining order.

Not that I was butthurt about what had happened—hanging on to things just wasn't my style. I looked forward, not back. Forward was easy. Forward was fun.

No point in lamenting all the things I couldn't change. Instead, I'd learned my lesson and kept myself blissfully unattached.

Once my lips were red and plump, my skin creamy and white, and my liner black and winged, I felt ready, getting up to inspect my reflection. My favorite black-and-white-striped bustier set off the tattoos across my chest with its sweetheart neckline, and I'd paired it with high-waisted black shorts with sailor buttons on the front.

I smoothed a hand over the wide finger waves in my purple hair as Ramona belted the last verse of the song, and I joined in with an air-guitar accompaniment that would make Lady Love proud.

Veronica swiped at the corner of her lips with the pad of her finger, inspecting her makeup. "Courtney Love was a badass. I don't care what anybody says about her."

"I mean, she was a hot-ass mess, but she got to bang Kurt Cobain on the regular. I miss him." I sighed and sat on the edge of my bed to put on my red wedges. "They were like the '90s version of Sid and Nancy. Totally, terrifyingly romantic. That's what love is. All-consuming, self-destructive, and absolutely not something I'm interested in experiencing."

Ramona laughed. "You're so dramatic. Shep and I aren't like that, and you see us all the time, so I know you know better."

I shifted my boobs around in the bustier to maximize my rack. "Yeah, but that's not how I love. You know me. Do you really think I'm capable of doing halfway on anything? I mean, need I remind you about Rodney? I would have gone toe-to-toe with Satan himself to hang on to that boy in high school. This is the same guy who wouldn't let me speak when that commercial with Paris Hilton eating a hamburger came on. Like he would clap his hand over my mouth and force me to be quiet until it was over. He was a psycho, and for two years, I let him torment me."

"Ugh, fuck that guy," Veronica said. "Even if he is a rock star."

"Don't remind me." My face was flat. "If he hadn't dumped me, I probably would have hung onto him like a barnacle. A screaming, psychotic barnacle. Can you imagine me on tour? I really would have been like Courtney—lipstick smeared and mascara running down my face when I ran onstage and shoved him because he'd banged a groupie. But at least the three-date rule came from the whole mess."

Veronica rolled her eyes. "First of all, it's three bangs, not three dates."

My brow quirked. "Who doesn't bang on a date?"

She ignored me. "And second, that rule is so stupid. And I say that with love. Think of how many relationships you've missed out on."

"You say that like it's a bad thing. Listen, a multitude of things can happen after the three-date zone, and I don't want to deal with any of them. Either I'm bored or I try to climb up their b-holes like an enema. Either they blow up my cell phone or get stalky. Or they propose marriage, like Clay." I gave Ramona a pointed look.

"What? He flew here all the way from Italy to ask you to marry him. What was I supposed to do? Leave him in the hallway with two dozen roses and that look on his face?"

"No, you *should* have called the cops. The last thing I expected was him sitting naked on my bed looking like he'd delivered me everything I'd ever wanted via Lufthansa Airlines. I had to fake a headache and let him cuddle me, pretend all the next day that things were cool. I couldn't break up with the psycho until he left for the airport."

Veronica laughed. "Oh, which one was the baby-talk one?"

I groaned. "Derek. My God, he drove me nuts. We would get tacos, and he knew I liked the chips that were like three chips wrapped up together, so he'd dig through the basket, hand them to me, and watch me eat them."

They laughed, and I kept going, always happier with an audience.

"The baby talk though, that was the worst. *I wuv you a yacht. I wuv you a whole FLEET of yachts! Aw, schmoopsie-poo. Are you a sheep or awake?*"

Ramona waved her hand with the other on her stomach as she laughed so hard that she was barely making noise. "Oh my God!"

"Seriously. But he was so hot. I mean, how could I resist a firefighter? With that ass? And that smile? I was willing to overlook a lot for bunker gear and smelling like a campfire." I sighed. "But I mean, those guys are so much easier to deal with. The real kicker is when *I* go bonkers. Like when I was five dates in with Tony. Remember him?"

Veronica sighed wistfully. "The one who could cook."

"Right? Dude made his own pasta. Fucking dream guy. But, I swear, I was begging to meet his mother by date five—*after* I told him no strings, and he was so about it. He slowly backed toward the door, said he'd call me, and I never heard from him again. There's a chance he died in a gutter somewhere, but I'm pretty sure it was from his phone exploding from the eighty-four-thousand text messages I'd sent him. And that was just a mild case of stalking—I've crossed the line so many times, I'm surprised I've never had the cops called on me."

"You're too cute for jail," Veronica said with a laugh.

"Not when my crazy eyes get going." I crossed my eyes and drew a circle in the air around my ear. "Rodney trained me to trust no man, so ninety percent of the time, I convince myself they're lying to me about where they are, what they're doing, how they feel. I go clinger. I'd rather be clung to."

"I dunno. See, I disagree with Veronica," Ramona said. "I think the rule makes sense. Penny, you're larger than life. I've been friends with you for eight years, and I've seen how guys treat you. Every hetero man in the room notices you when you walk in. It's like every curve on your body is sending a signal directly to them. They want to know you, and some, like Rodney, want to control you. This is a way for you to protect yourself against the whole thing. You break hearts so yours doesn't get broken. And who knows? Maybe someday you'll meet somebody who changes your mind."

I laughed. "God, I hope not."

She smiled like she knew better than me. "How long have you been on the three-date wagon now?" Ramona asked.

"Two whole years," I answered, proud of myself. "Two years of normal dates with no crazy on either side of the line. Everything has been perfectly smooth ever since I really decided to stick to the rule. This is better for all parties involved, trust me. I'd rather not put my heart through the meat grinder again, thank you very much."

Veronica snickered. "She said to her friend whose wedding is in two weeks."

"Oh, stop it. That's what I'm saying—Ramona and Shep are perfectly perfect. I'm just a mess, like Courtney Love but with tidier makeup."

But Ramona's face had fallen into a sad expression. "Two weeks. That's all we have left for this."

Veronica looked the same. "Less than that. You're moving next week."

Ramona's eyes misted up. "What am I going to do without you guys?"

I knelt down between them. "You'll start your life with Shep, and it's going to be everything you ever wanted. We'll see each other at the tattoo parlor every day. And Ronnie and I will be here, doing our makeup and trolling for boys at *least* three times a week, so you can come with us anytime. Be our wing woman."

She laughed and rubbed her nose. "Ha. As if you need help."

I smirked. "I wasn't talking about me."

Veronica rolled her eyes. "Oh, ha-ha. You're a fucking riot, Penny."

I shrugged innocently. "I mean, if you weren't so picky, you'd be able to find a guy—at least for a night."

She made a face at me. "Maybe not all of us want a guy just for a night?"

"That's fair. But not even sometimes? I'd love to be your wingwoman, but it's exhausting, and I've got goals of my own."

"Yeah, to eat every dick in Manhattan," she shot, eyes twinkling and lips in a smile.

My mouth popped open, and I laughed. "You bitch. I don't have to eat them all, but having them in or around my vagina would be fine. You know, as an alternative."

"So slutty!" Veronica shook her head.

"Thank you," I said sweetly. "I love being slutty. I don't make any promises, and I know exactly what I want. What the hell is everyone's problem with that anyway? Who cares who I sleep with? Does it affect anyone but me and the guy involved? Answer: No. And I tell all the guys I *whatever* with what my expectations are, and they agree. It's not my fault if they catch feelings." I shuddered. "It's like the emotional equivalent of gonorrhea—the clap, but for your heart!"

Veronica laughed. "I mean, with that endorsement, why wouldn't you want a boyfriend?"

"Precisely my point. And anyway, it's such a fucking double standard. Guys are allowed to fuck whoever they want, and other dudes are like, *Way to go, bro,* and slap them five. Girls are supposed to be all demure and pure and rely solely on their vibrators if they're not in a committed, monogamous relationship. Fucking patriarchy."

"Fuck the patriarchy!" Ramona crowed as she held up her hand for a slap. I obliged.

I rapped the chorus of "I'm not a player" like Big Pun. "Ronnie, you need to crush a lot. I'd even settle for a little crushing. You're too hot not to crush as much as humanly possible."

Veronica laughed. "Maybe tonight. Wing me."

My mouth popped open. "Oh my God, seriously?"

She nodded, closed lips smiling. "You won me over with your slut speech."

"Finally. I've been working on you for years. I can't believe I've seen the day. And I'm not even in Depends!"

She laughed and pushed me over, and I couldn't even be mad about it.

$\backsim\!\!\!\!\infty\!\!\!\!\sim$

A half an hour later, we were walking into a bar on Broadway called Circus that had popped up a few months before. The thing about themed bars was that they were hit or miss. That was mostly because, in an attempt to be cute, the bars would end up overdone, and within a few months of the novelty wearing off, the bar would close and a new one would take its place.

Not Circus.

A circular bar stood in the center of the room, and it was made out of a small version of a carousel. It looked like someone had plucked the top off a carousel and hung it from the ceiling. Around the top, Edison bulbs lined the panels of alternating mirrors and vintage paintings of circus scenes, and long white bar lights spoked from underneath the center, like a wheel. Red-and-white striped fabric draped from the peaked top of the carousel and out into the darkness of the edges of the ceiling, and the barstools were all saddles.

Everything in the bar had a circus feel—from creepy-cool oddity art to brushed brass fixtures on everything. The bartenders were dressed up like ringmasters, complete with handlebar mustaches and red tails, and the cocktail waitresses were all dressed in tails too. Rather than shirttails, they wore black bras, and rather than pants, they wore high-waisted shorts and fishnets. They even had little top hats on.

I swear to God, if I hadn't had my dream job as a tattoo artist, I'd have dropped everything and joined the *Circus*.

I led the charge through the crowd and to the bar with my roommates behind me, squeezing in between two gigantic guys to lean on the bar.

They looked down at me.

"Hey, fellas."

They smiled.

The closest bartender set a drink in front of a girl down from me, and the second he saw me, he headed straight over, effectively skipping everyone ahead of me.

It might have been the fact that I'd hopped up a little, caging my rack in my arms to put it on display. Oldest trick in the book.

I told you—I was absolutely shameless.

With drinks in hand, I gave the bartender a smile, and the girls and I headed away from the fray to look for a table. A group was just getting up, and we swooped in like birds of prey just ahead of a pack of bitter chicks wearing painful-looking shoes.

I sipped on my tequila—it was chilled: I'm not that hard—looking around at the mass of people, soaking it all in, as "Pretty in Pink" by *The Psychedelic Furs* played.

And then time stopped, and the crowd parted like the universe wanted to point right at him.

It was Blondie from the ice cream parlor.

The music stretched out, people slowing under the red and white striped fabric, the naked bulbs of the carousel painting him in golden light. He stood right there like he'd been placed in that spot just for me, tall and beautiful, his skin tan and smile bright as he laughed at something his twin had said.

I almost fell out of my chair. There were two of them. My insides turned into raspberry jelly at the thought of what kind of damage they could do to a woman.

But my eyes found Blondie again—his twin was wrong somehow, which was bizarre in itself because they were identical. From where I sat, they were night and day. There was something about Blondie, some vibe that hit me even more now than it had at the ice cream parlor. He felt … *familiar.* Something about him I couldn't quite place caught me, something in the line of his profile and the curve of his lips. But I was certain I'd never seen him before—I remembered all of the Adonises I'd met and arduously logged them in my mental bank of spank.

He was tall and jacked with a smile like a lightbulb and hair like spun gold. It was a little long, curling around his ears, and I wondered if it was soft, wondered what it would feel like between my fingers as I rode his face like a pony.

I didn't realize I had slipped off my stool and was walking toward him—I had locked onto him like a goddamn target—until he met my eyes, froze for a split second, and then walked toward me like he was caught up just as much as I was.

I should have known right then that I was in big Blondie-sized trouble. But I couldn't seem to find a single fuck to give.

The pinup girl from the ice cream shop had the reddest lips curled into an irresistible smile, and my feet, which had been moving entirely of their own accord, didn't stop until we met in the middle.

I knew her somehow, but I couldn't place her and wondered if it was just that I'd been thinking about her since I saw her a few hours before.

Shock and awe, man. She was standing there in front of me like a dream, but up close and personal where I could see her. In a split second, I'd catalogued everything about her—her gold septum ring, the black gauges with tiny cat ears, the curve of her plump red lips, the shine of her hair, and the tattoos across her chest, her shoulders, her arms, her thighs. I wondered where else she was tattooed and found myself smiling down at her, imagining the answer.

"Heya, Blondie," she said slyly. "Fancy meeting you here."

610 | STACI HART

"If I didn't know better, I'd think you were following me."

One dark brow rose with one corner of her lips. "Who says you know better?"

I chuckled as my eyes combed over her face like it was the first face I'd ever seen. She was so familiar to me, but I'd have remembered the purple hair, the piercings, the tattoos. That smile.

I blinked.

I knew that smile.

"I'm Penny," she said, extending her free hand.

I took it, my smile spreading. "Bodie."

She showed no recognition at my name—when she had known me, I'd gone by a nickname. Her eyes were on my lips, and I realized fully that she had no idea who I was. I wondered if I'd really changed that much from when she'd seen me last, realizing I had. Sometimes I'd look in the mirror and barely recognize myself. And earlier she'd had on big sunglasses, on top of being far enough away that I couldn't tell it was her. Eight years had changed her too, but only the colors of her feathers. Everything else seemed exactly the same.

I considered telling her, but dismissed the thought. Because there was really only one thing to do: fuck with her until she figured it out.

"Good to see you again," I said ambiguously.

"You too, but I'm surprised. I mean, after going down on a waffle cone for you earlier, I figured you would have had plenty of me to last."

A laugh burst out of me. "Oh, I have a feeling your kind of ice cream is the kind you can't get enough of."

She shrugged and brought her drink to her lips. "It's been said." She watched me for a second again. "So what's your story, Bodie?"

"I just moved here from LA."

"For a job?"

"You could say that. I'm a software engineer."

She laughed. "Wow, not what I would have guessed."

"Oh?"

Penny dramatically looked me up and down. "Hmm. I'd say ... personal trainer. No, no. That hunky moving company I always see commercials for."

"Manly Movers?"

She lit up and snapped. "Yes! You definitely look like the Manly Mover type. All those muscles."

I chuckled. "That's super sexist."

"Male model. That would have done too."

I couldn't stop smiling, and I hated thinking that my dimple was on display. "I guess I should be flattered that you think I'm hot enough to be a male model."

Her eyes twinkled. "Oh, you definitely are."

"How about you? What do you do? Where are you from?" I asked, baiting her.

"I'm a tattoo artist," she offered but didn't elaborate, and I sensed a story there. "I've lived in New York since I graduated high school, but I grew up in Santa Cruz."

"Me too."

Her eyes widened, and she smiled. "No way. I went to Loma Vista. What a small world."

She still hadn't figured it out, and I found myself grinning like an idiot, wondering how long it would take her to put it together.

"Ever surf?" I asked.

She laughed. "No way. Sharks."

"That's what my buddy Phil says too."

She glanced behind me, twiddling her fingers, presumably at Jude and Phil. "So, you're a twin, huh?"

I nodded and took a sip of my Maker's as "Rock the Casbah" kicked off, and everyone around us started bouncing and dancing. "Since birth."

She laughed. "What a win for the universe that there would be two of you."

"Double your pleasure, double your fun."

That caught her off guard, and her bottom lip slipped between her teeth as a flush rose on her cheeks.

Just like that, I had one objective, and it began and ended with her lips.

"Although I should tell you now," I stepped closer, slipping into her space, and her eyes widened, pupils dilating as she leaned into me, "I don't like to share."

The tip of her pink tongue darted out to wet her lips, and her eyes were locked on to my mouth.

"Are you thinking about kissing me?" I asked.

She shook her head, though her eyes didn't stray. "No, I'm thinking about what your dick looks like."

I laughed from way down deep in my belly, shocked in the best way and turned on in the worst. And as the ocean of people waved around us, she rose up on her tiptoes, grabbed a handful of my T-shirt, and pulled.

I caught the smallest breath—a surprised, satisfied gasp—just before our lips met, and fireworks exploded in my brain. The kiss wasn't soft or sweet; it was strong and determined, those red, red lips pressing against mine, opening to let me into her hot mouth, her tongue finding mine like she'd been looking for it her whole life.

The surprise left me as quickly as it had hit, and I leaned into her, my free arm winding around her back to press her body against mine. There wasn't an inch of space between us, and all the while, our mouths worked each other's in a long dance that left my heart chugging like a freight train in my chest.

She pulled away, her lips swollen and eyes lust-drunk as they met mine and held them while she kicked back her drink and grabbed my hand.

"Let's get the fuck out of here," she said.

And I smirked, breathless. "Your place or mine?"

chapter
three
Mr. Diddle

FOR THE RECORD, I HAD EVERY INTENTION OF TELLING HER WHO I WAS.
It was just that I was so caught up in her as we hurried back to my apartment that my brain had short-circuited, thinking only from my raging hard-on in my pants. I didn't have time to consider what it meant or what would happen, and I didn't have the will to break whatever trance I'd found myself in.

I should have been surprised to have her by my side. I should have been confused about how I'd ended up with Penny's hand in mine. But wondering felt like the absolute first and last thing I should be doing, so I didn't. And as I towed her toward my apartment, I was unable to consider anything other than the feeling of her fingers twined in mine and the sight of her smiling up at me, eyes shining and hot.

The loft felt like it was on Mars for as long as it was taking to get there.

I took the opportunity to kiss her as we waited for a stoplight to change, slipping my fingers into her purple hair, closing my lips over hers, and she tipped her chin and gave me her mouth, her tongue, with her hands clutching my shirt, pulling me into her like she was starving and I was a porterhouse.

My keys were in my hand before we hit the elevator—another opportunity to kiss her, my fingerips brushing her bare collarbone, down the curve of her breast, around her waist to her ass. I squeezed, pulling her into my cock, pleased with the whimper against my lips.

We practically ran down the hallway. She panted behind me as I unlocked the door, and we tumbled inside.

I closed it behind her and turned. "Hang on, there's something I need to—"

She launched herself at me, and I caught her, my back hitting the door with a thump, as she wrapped her arms around my neck. Her feet dangled off the ground, and I held her around the waist, kissing her deep.

In that moment, there was no point in stopping to tell her I was the chubby, nerdy kid with glasses she went to high school with. If she even remembered me.

But I remembered her. I'd imagined kissing her a thousand times, but never in my life had I thought I'd ever get the chance. Until now.

I turned her around, the decision made and my mission singular, and pressed her against the door. She pulled my lip between her teeth, and I growled, moving down her neck, nipping and sucking a trail past her collarbone and across the tattoos marking the soft skin of her breasts.

I wanted her naked. I wanted to see every tattoo, every inch of skin. I wanted her in my mouth. I wanted inside of her.

But first, this.

I dropped to my knees, my fingers working the buttons of her shorts. There were four—two on each side of a panel—and my heart thudded in my chest as I dropped that panel to reveal a rectangle of skin covered in tattoos. Flowers framed two pistols just inside her hip bones, barrels angled in a V, pointing down. I slipped my hands into her shorts and around her naked hips, pushing them down her legs, and as she stepped out of them, my eyes caught on the gold barbells above and below the hood of her clit.

"Oh, fuck, Penny," I whispered, my hands gripping her hips, my lips already on a track for it.

I closed my eyes and buried my face in the sweetness of her.

She braced herself with her hands on my shoulders, murmuring something I couldn't make out and didn't try. My tongue rolled against the bottom ball that rested right over her clit, circling until her nails dug into my skin through my shirt.

When I broke away and glanced up, she was looking down, her eyes half-shut and those red fucking lips hanging open in pleasure.

I smirked and lifted one of her legs, hitching it over my shoulder to spread her open. I trailed my hand down, framing her piercing in the V of two fingers, and when I squeezed gently and shifted in a circle, her eyes rolled back in her head that rested against the door, stretching her long white neck out.

For a second, I wished I could be everywhere at once, licking her neck, sucking her lip, my face in her pussy—everywhere. I wanted to devour her. So I started with what I had at my fingertips.

I moved my hand down to cup her, my fingers shifting against the slick line of her core.

"God, you're soaking fucking wet." My voice was ragged, my body coiled.

She whispered a plea, begging me with a single word, *"Please."*

I happily obliged, licking my lips, bringing them just close enough to her hood that they touched only infinitesimally, waiting for a stretched out second before I slipped my fingers inside at the exact moment I closed my lips over her clit.

"Oh God," she whispered, bucking against me, closing around my fingers as they slid in, out, in, reaching for the rough spot inside.

Her fingers slipped into my hair and twisted, and mine matched the pace of my tongue.

She clenched around my fingers, pinning me between her thighs as I moved faster, harder, and then …

Then, she came with a cry to a higher power and a burst that I'd be thinking about on my death bed.

As she came down, I slowed, softly kissing and licking her, every flick of my tongue sending another pulse through her pussy around my fingers.

"Jesus fucking Christ," she breathed. "Where the fuck did you come from?"

I closed my lips, reverently kissing her once more before looking up at her with a smile. "Santa Cruz. Loma Vista, Class of 2009."

Her eyes went wide, and she blinked. "But there wasn't anyone named Bodie in my class."

"There was. You just knew me as Diddle."

Her mouth hung open, and a shocked laugh escaped her. "No way. No fucking way. Diddle was …"

I moved her leg, putting her foot back on the ground, but she still hung on to my shoulders. "Chubby? Glasses? Into Dungeons and Dragons? With an equally dorky twin? Friends with Rodney Parker since the second grade when he moved in next to us and gave me that stupid nickname?"

I rose, and her hands on my shoulders stayed put until I was standing before her with my hands on her hips, feeling ashamed of myself for not telling her sooner. She stood there, stunned and still blinking at me.

"Are you mad I didn't tell you?"

At that, a smile spread across her lips. "How could I be mad at a guy who just ate my pussy like it was his last meal?" And she laughed, pulling me down to kiss her, running her tongue across my lips to taste herself.

When she broke away, she looked up at me with the devil in her eyes. "Now, if you don't fuck me and show me what the rest of you can do, I might actually die."

I laughed and bent to sling her over my shoulder, smacking her bare ass once I had her where I wanted her.

Everything was upside down—his apartment, his ass I was clinging to, my insides after the orgasm I'd just had.

I'd been diddled by Diddle.

I giggled at the thought of that and the fact that I was slung over his bohunk shoulder as he carried me down a hallway and into what I assumed was his bedroom.

He kicked the door closed behind us, and with his big arms wrapped around my legs, he tilted, dumping me on the bed with a bounce.

I watched him walk around the room, clicking on a couple of lights, as I stared at his face, looking for the kid I had known in high school. Rodney was my ex-boyfriend—the *last* boyfriend. And Diddle—Bodie—and his brother, Dee Dee, were always hanging around Rodney's band practices or at his house. I couldn't connect the dots that they were the same person.

When he reached back to grab a handful of his shirt and yank it off, I quit caring.

He had muscles on top of muscles, his arms touched with ink here and there. I itched to get a closer look. But that could wait. There were other things I needed a closer look at first.

I sat up as he walked to the bed, and I moved to the edge, parting my legs. My eyes were on his—his were between my legs.

His cock was right in front of me, tethered by his jeans, though I could see the bulging outline of it like a beast. I bit my lip and unfastened his belt with a clink, unbuttoned his pants with a soft pop, and dropped his zipper with a buzz I felt all the way up to my elbow.

He wasn't wearing underwear.

The sight of the tight skin so low on his stomach, the V of his hips, the shape of his cock still tucked into his pants—all of it hit me with a shock that hit me straight between the legs, so I reached out and freed him, leaving my fist closed around his base.

The head was the same dusty pink as his luscious lips, and I smiled, my pulse picking up and tongue sweeping my bottom lip, as I leaned forward and placed the silky-soft crown in my mouth.

Bodie hissed, his hands slipping through my hair as I grabbed his ass, pulling him to me as I leaned into him, taking him as deep as I could, which was deep. Perks of not having a gag reflex.

"Fuck, Penny," he whispered, his fingers tightening, pulling my hair just enough to sting.

I let his base go so I could grab his ass with both hands, guiding him, and he matched the rhythm with his hands in my hair, pushing me farther as my throat relaxed, his cock rock hard in my mouth.

He pulled out with a pop, and before I knew what was going on, his hands were on my face, his lips against mine, his tongue deep in my mouth, like he was trying to taste where he'd been.

"When I come," he whispered against my lips, "it's going to be inside you. Now, take your clothes off, Penny."

My heart thudded against my ribs as he backed away. I didn't have much on, just the bustier and my wedges, so I stood, smiling as I turned my back to him and folded over at the waist, unbuckling one shoe, then the other. When I peeked at him through my hair, his jeans were hanging off his hips, his hand was rolling a condom onto his cock, and his lips were pinned between his teeth, the line of his jaw hard and his eyes locked between my legs.

I turned around to face him and unhooked the corseted bustier one blessed hook at a time before letting it fall to the floor.

His eyes raked over my body for a long moment before he rushed me, grabbing me around the waist, and we tumbled into bed together as our lips connected. He nestled between my legs, and my arms wound around his neck, my legs around his waist. And when he shifted his hips, I felt the tip of him press against the center of me.

"Oh God, Bodie," I breathed. "Get your fucking pants off."

I scrabbled for his jeans that hung half off his ass, sliding them down enough to hook my foot in the crotch to push them the rest of the way until he was blissfully naked and lying on top of me.

He hummed against my neck, teasing me, as he moved down my body to my breasts. For a long minute, he cupped one, closing his lips over my tight nipple, sliding the barbell back and forth with his tongue, the sensation sending a pulse directly to my aching clit.

"Fuck, Bodie. Please."

He ran his teeth across the tip of my nipple, sending another shock down my spine as he brought his body to mine. And, when he pressed his wide crown against me, my breath froze in my lungs.

He propped himself up, his lids heavy. And when he moved, when he filled me up until he couldn't get any deeper, I thought I'd died and gone to heaven.

His hips rolled like he knew my body, rocking against my piercing exactly where I needed, pressing against my clit, hitting me in the perfect spot, inside and out, with every pump of his hips. He stayed propped up, somehow maintaining his cool while I wriggled underneath him like my body wasn't my own.

With every slow wave of his body, I lost my mind a little more with no idea what to do with myself. The whole thing happened in bursts—his hand on my breast, kneading and toying with my nipple ring; his thighs pushing my legs open wider so he could get deeper; his lips on mine, not that I could kiss him back. Because I felt the orgasm building, the heat of it deep inside me, spreading through me, and when he took my nipple between his teeth and hummed, my body didn't know what else to do but explode. My heart, my legs, my arms, my pussy—everything flew apart and back together, pulsing and squeezing as I breathed his name on a loop.

I barely registered him coming—I was too high from what he'd done to me—but I could feel his fingers in my hair, the sting as he pulled, exposing my neck, making a space to bury his head as his body rocked, slamming into me with a guttural noise that made what was left of my insides turn into mush.

All I could hear was my panting and the thundering of my heart in my ears, a steady *da-dum* that matched the feeling of Bodie's heartbeat against my breasts. I was surrounded by him—his arms bracketing my head, his face in the curve of my neck, his fingers threading into my hair, his body pressing me into the bed—and it was absolutely and utterly glorious.

It was the feeling I lived for, everything I wanted. Who needed love when you could just have the good? The rush, the easy rightness of being together without demand? Love only complicated things, weighing down the good until the high was gone. I never wanted the high to end.

After a little while, he shifted his face to kiss my neck, sending a warm tingle up to my ear and down to my nipple like some sort of sorcery. I smiled out of sheer instinct from the sensation, bending my neck to press my cheek to his head.

"Mmm," he rumbled.

I clenched around him, still inside of me, and he twitched in answer.

"Seriously, where have you been hiding?" My voice was rough and lazy against his ear.

Bodie kissed my skin again. "LA. I've only been here a week."

He twisted, rolling us onto our sides so he could pull out, leaving me empty. I didn't like it, not one bit.

"What brought you?" I asked, propping my head on my hand to admire his back as he turned away.

He sat on the edge of the bed and cleaned himself up. "I got laid off."

"Oh God. I'm sorry."

He smiled over his shoulder at me. "Don't be. That just made the move about a hundred times more worthwhile."

I smirked as he lay back down next to me, mirroring my posture. "So, what did you do?"

"I was a software engineer for a start-up that was bought out. They canned all of us and replaced us with their own people."

I chuckled, my eyes raking over his gorgeous face, his massive body. "You don't look like a computer geek."

He laughed at that. "Maybe not now, but back in my Diddle days, you wouldn't have thought twice."

"True. I still can't get over it. I can't even see Diddle in there."

"You sure?"

He leaned a little closer, smiling that brilliant smile of his that forced the sexiest dimple I'd ever seen. I didn't even know dimples could *be* sexy.

It was his eyes, electric blue and sparking with intelligence—that was where I saw the boy I used to know.

Just like that, I was taken back years to the boy who would pick up my pen when it rolled off my desk, the boy who would share his notes with me and give me rides home when Rodney had left me somewhere. His braces were gone, and the softness of his face had filled out into hard lines and full lips. I was left wondering just how I'd missed it, how I'd missed *him*.

My smile stretched wider along with my heart. "Oh, there you are." I cupped his cheek and laid a little kiss on his lips.

But then his hand found my naked hip and pulled, bringing me closer, and the kiss wasn't so little anymore.

I broke away after a moment, breathless. "Jesus, Bodie. I don't even know if I could have another orgasm."

"Is that a challenge? Because I really, really love to win."

His hand trailed to the back of my thigh and pulled, slinging my leg over his hip—his cock was already hard again against me.

"I didn't get to take my time," he said, his eyes darkening as his pupils shot open.

So I did the only thing I could with him looking at me like that, with the hard length of him shifting against my piercing—I let him.

An hour later, I found myself trying to catch my breath, lying flat on my back with a sweaty Penny splayed across my sweaty chest.

"I can't feel my legs," she panted, her voice gruff.

I couldn't wipe the smile off my face to even pretend to be cool. "Then my work here is done."

She laughed, and all I could think about was the feeling of her nipple rings against my skin.

Get a fucking grip, man.

Of course, then I imagined her gripping me, which didn't help me stave off another boner. I wasn't even sure how it was physiologically possible, yet there it was.

She noticed and propped herself up to look at me, incredulous and amused. "I don't think my vagina can take any more tonight, Bodie."

I smirked. "I can't either, but it's got a mind of its own."

She laughed as she slid off me—literally, we were soaked—and starfished out next to me on her back. "God, that was good. Can we do it again?"

I chuckled. "Anytime you want."

Penny turned her head to look at me, and I did the same, resting my hand on my chest.

"I have to warn you though …"

One of my brows rose. "You come with a warning label?"

"No, I come with your face between my legs."

A laugh burst out of me.

She smiled. "I don't date, Bodie. It's not just for me—I haven't been serious with anyone in a long time, and … well, that's not what I'm looking for. I need you to know and agree to it before we go any further."

I watched her for a second before answering. Her purple hair was fanned out all around her, her naked, tattooed body stretched out next to me, and right then, I knew I was in trouble.

The first problem: I'd been crushing on her since I was sixteen.

The second problem: I was officially obsessed with every inch of her body.

The third problem: There was no way I would walk away from her after that. Not without putting up a fight.

But the biggest problem of all was this: I couldn't put up a fight, or I'd spook her.

I knew Penny well enough from high school to know that I was playing with fire. And I knew I'd probably get burned if I fell for her, but if I could hang on to her? Well, it'd be worth the risk. Because I wanted more Penny. I wanted more of her smiles. I wanted to know where she'd been and what she wanted out of life. I wanted her in my bed and in my shower and anywhere I could get her. All I had to do was convince her that she wanted the same.

So I made up my mind and stepped into the lion's cage with a chair in one hand and a whip in the other.

"I'm in. No strings."

That ruby-red smile widened. "Good. And if you catch feelings, I need to know."

"Deal," I lied, "and you do the same."

She laughed at that, a sound that hit me right in the chub. "Oh, I don't catch feelings. On account of my black heart and all."

By the way she was looking at me, I didn't believe her for a second. But if that was what she thought … well, like I'd said, I loved to win.

four

What Would Blanche Do?

I SKIPPED DOWN THE STAIRS OF OUR BUILDING THE NEXT MORNING, WHISTLING "Yankee Doodle" with Veronica and Ramona in my wake.

"'Yankee Doodle'? Really?" Ramona called after me.

I jumped off the last step and spun around, making a whistle show of calling it macaroni, complete with jazz hands.

Veronica laughed. "I still don't get why Yankee Doodle would call the feather in his hat pasta."

They caught up, and we started down the sidewalk, heading for Tonic—the tattoo parlor a couple of blocks away where we all worked.

"Well," I said like the know-it-all I was, "that's because macaroni used to be a term for fashionable."

"How do you know shit like this?" Veronica asked.

I shrugged. "I just remember useless stuff like that. I hear it once and *bam.*" I tapped my temple. "Steel trap. Problem is, it doesn't actually hold important information. Or numbers. Don't make me try to remember numbers, or math. I cannot math."

"We know, honey." Ramona smiled and patted my arm. "We've all seen you try to split a check."

I rolled my eyes.

She didn't wait for further response. "So, are you going to tell us what happened last night? If I hadn't woken up late, I would have alarm-clocked you so hard. I need answers."

"I can't say I'm bummed to have missed you jumping on my bed to harass me before I had to be up."

Bodie crossed my mind—flashes of his hands and lips and smile and *God*, I was about him. I smiled to myself.

I'd left his house sore in all the right places and knees about as stable as quicksand. Once I'd floated home, I'd sunk into my bed and slept like I was dead—no dreams, nothing. I didn't even think I'd rolled over once.

I hadn't been nailed that well in a good long while. And when I'd woken, he had been on my mind.

I was infatuated. Smitten. Giddy and grinning and gone.

"Earth to Penny. Anybody in there?" Veronica pinched my arm.

"Ow!" I rubbed the spot and stuck my tongue out at her.

"You deserve that. So much for a wingwoman. Your ass barely hit the seat before you disappeared with Blondie."

I wrinkled my nose, but I was smiling. "Yeah, sorry. And you're never going to believe this; I fucking know him."

Ramona's brow quirked. "Well, I mean, that was the guy from the ice cream shop yesterday, wasn't it?"

"Yes, but also, we went to high school together. I didn't even recognize him—he looks completely different."

"I'd imagine so if you didn't recognize him," Veronica said. "No way Blondie wouldn't have made it onto your radar."

"Right? The guy went from Chris Pratt in *Parks and Rec,* dumping Skittles into his mouth, to Chris Pratt in *Guardians of the Galaxy,* shirtless and ripped and orange and all mad because they stole his Walkman. Except it's even less obvious than that. Like, he had glasses and braces and … I don't even know, man. He was hidden inside of there that whole time. I remembered his eyes the most. Is that weird?"

"Not at all," Ramona answered. "When did you figure it out?"

"When his face was between my legs."

They both busted out laughing.

"Just kidding. It was actually post-face-between-the-legs."

Ramona frowned a little. "He wasn't, like … stalking you or anything, right?"

"I don't think so," I said, considering it again. "No, I mean, he seemed just as surprised to see me as I was to see him. But, man, let me tell you, the dude went downtown like it was his only purpose in life."

Veronica sighed. "I need to find a boyfriend."

"No, you *need* to find a fuck boy," I corrected. "Anyway, his name is Bodie, and he has a twin brother named Jude. Maybe his pussy-eating is a genetic trait." I waggled my brows.

She laughed and shoved me in the arm. "Ugh, you."

I just smiled.

"Are you going to see him again?" Ramona asked hopefully.

"I want to." I felt high, my body still humming and purring his name. "Guys, he kinda blew my mind. I can't believe I went to high school with him."

"So, what's the story?" Veronica stuffed her hands into the pockets of her black romper, her heels clicking on the sidewalk. Hair in a French twist, high on top, she looked totally elegant and gorgeous and classic, offset by full sleeves, a septum ring, and gauges like mine. I swear, she was the most badass of us all and the least emotionally available.

"Well, he was friends with Rodney—"

A collective groan passed over the peanut gallery of two.

"Just hear me out, for chrissake," I huffed. "*As* I was saying, he lived next door to Rodney, and I guess they'd been friends since the second grade or something. But when we hit high school, Rodney turned into a fox and started his band, and Bodie and Jude … well, I guess they were late bloomers. They were always so cute—you know, in that, like, puppy sort of way where you go *Aww.* But I didn't even know their real names. I knew them by Diddle and Dee Dee."

Veronica's mouth popped open. "Those nicknames are fucking awful."

I chuckled. "I know, trust me. I meant to ask him the story there, but I was way too busy with his dick."

They giggled.

"Guys," I said on a laugh, "I got diddled by Diddle."

I got a solid cackle for that one.

I shook my head, smiling. "I guess Rodney gave them the nicknames. That's not altogether surprising. Rodney was a cockjuggler."

"So are you," Ramona teased.

"It's true, and I don't judge a fellow juggler of cocks for their extracurriculars," I said with a hand out. "He was always kind of shitty to them." My tone softened a little, the edge all gone as I thought back, wishing I'd seen Bodie back then, wishing he hadn't just disappeared into my periphery. "They were around a lot—hanging at practice, sometimes at the parties. I just don't know why they hung around when Rodney was such an asshole to them. He was always teasing them about something, but he was so slick about it, you know? Most of the time, I didn't know if he was complimenting or cutting me down. Bodie had so much more in common back then than I realized."

I hated Rodney for what he'd done to all of us and found myself scowling at the memory of him, but I brushed it off and bucked up, smiling again with a shrug.

"Anyway, his loss. And now I find out that Diddle grew up to be Bodie, the super-hot surfer hunk. I would have bet a million dildos that I'd never see him again and been wrong, and I've never been so glad to be wrong in my life. He was incredible. Life-changing. He's real smart too. I mean, he was always a brainiac in high school, and now he does … something in computers, I think."

I got a look from Veronica. "You don't know what he does for a living?"

I made a noise like an air leak. "You are such a judgy whore, Ronnie. One of these days, the tables are gonna be turned, but instead of being all *Oh, look at me. I'm so perfect and smart and do everything right,*" I mocked, "I'll be like, *Way to go, bitch!* and buy you a really big, whorey penis cake."

She laughed.

"I'm gonna tell the erotic baker to make it spurt vanilla icing. I'll have them make licorice pubes and everything. Dick cake. It's genius really—two of my favorite things. And *that's* what you have to look forward to—no judgment."

Veronica shook her head, though she looked entirely amused. "You are so bad, Penny."

"I am. And I'm just like a bad penny too. I always turn up. There's no getting rid of me."

"Wouldn't want it any other way." She slung an arm over my shoulder. "You're a good friend—"

"Thank you," I said sweetly.

"Even if you're disgusting."

I leaned into her as we walked up to Tonic's door. "Aw, I love you too."

Ramona pulled open the door, and Veronica and I walked in, still canoodling. "Precious" by The Pretenders played over the speakers.

"Look, Ronnie—it's your song!"

She laughed, slapping me on the ass when we parted.

Ramona beelined for the counter where Shep waited, smiling from behind his thick beard. I swear to God, he and his brother, Joel, had the most virile hair of any men I'd ever seen.

She practically jumped into his big, meaty arms. Ramona was a tiny blonde thing covered in tattoos, and he was a big, hairy beast with a smile only for her.

I found myself smiling too, watching how gross they were. They almost made me wish I wanted to fall in love.

The thought actually made me laugh out loud.

I made my way to my station in the back and stepped into my little cube to get myself situated.

Tonic was one of the premier tattoo parlors in Manhattan, so good that most of us were booked out for months. Joel and Shep had opened it forever ago and had curated some of the best talent in the city—so much talent that they got attention in the way of awards, magazine features, and even a deal with a TV studio.

About a year before, we'd started filming a reality show in the shop, which basically turned the place into a telenovela. Drama city. But man, was it fun, and everyone had seemed to get it all out of their systems in the first season. Season two would start filming soon, kicking off with Ramona and Shep's wedding.

I sat at my desk, humming along to Stone Temple Pilots, pulling out my sketchbook to work on a piece for that afternoon, and in a snap, the day was nearly gone. My thoughts had been on Bodie the whole time.

I wondered all sorts of things—what was he doing? Where had he been all those years? Where the fuck did he learn to bang like that? What had happened to the kid I knew so long ago?

I'd always liked Diddle. I remembered him making me laugh, even when I was sad, the snark in him appealing to the snark in me. I never thought about him like I had been since running into him, and now it bothered me a little that

I'd been so shallow back then. Of course, I was sixteen and had been obsessed with a complete and utter dickhole. I'd had no sense. None. If I had, I'd have dumped Rodney and found somebody who at least had a little respect for me and wouldn't give Anna Dorf *rides home from school*, which I'd later learned was code for *blow jobs*.

One time, we had all at a bonfire on the beach for a kegger, and Rodney just left me there. One minute he was there, the next, *poof*, I had been stranded at the beach with no ride home.

I'd been sitting away from the crowd, drunk and crying and dejected, and Bodie had sat next to me with his drink. He hadn't asked me what was wrong or pointed out that I was crying. He hadn't mentioned Rodney at all. He'd just sat there with me until my tears ran dry, and then he'd asked me if I'd ever seen *Donnie Darko*. And for the next hour, we'd talked about a hundred other things—movies and music, our teachers and school gossip—and by the end of the night, I'd felt like I was going to be okay after all. He'd asked me if I needed a ride home and delivered me safely at my doorstep like a white knight.

It was maybe one of the nicest things a guy had ever done for me without expectation on how they'd be repaid. Bodie had given exactly what I needed in the moment without me having to ask. He'd just known.

And now ... now Diddle had gone and grown up, and boy, had he grown up right.

I couldn't help but smile, my heart all flippy and fluttery and ooey and gooey. I thought about all the things he'd done to me and thought about how many more I wanted him to do. I imagined his body, so strong and hard, his smile, so bright and gorgeous, and then smiled even wider at the knowledge that those braces that had helped disguise him back then had granted me that smile.

I thought about his lips and how they were the exact same shade as the head of his cock, just like I'd figured. And then I was thinking about his cock and clenching the saddle stool between my thighs to relieve the pressure. Three shifts of my hips, and I probably would have had an orgasm. That was just how ridiculously hot I was for him.

I didn't even know why he was any different from the other dudes I'd dated. I'd been with plenty of guys—hot guys, funny guys, smart guys, dumb guys. Rich guys, poor guys, and more. But Bodie was like the best of all of them, rolled into one. If I could have hand picked a guy, with the brains, looks, attitude, and wang skills I wished for, it would be him.

And now I couldn't stop thinking about him, couldn't stop wondering when I'd see him again. And I wanted to see him again as soon as possible even if it was too soon.

Maybe it was just because I'd known him so long ago. Maybe it was because he'd nailed me into oblivion. Maybe I was just infatuated, which was my primary function.

All I knew was this: I was so very impressed, and it was so very hard to impress me.

Once, I'd heard Patrick, one of the other tattoo artists, joking about a chick being dicknotized. And the word hit me as my needle buzzed in my hand, working on an elaborate henna design on a girl's thigh.

I was dicknotized.

I laughed way louder than was appropriate, thankful for having the foresight to have moved my gun, since the girl in my chair jumped a mile.

"Sorry," I said through my giggling as I got back to work. "So, I have to warn you. I'm a verbal processor, and there's something I've gotta talk out. Can I ask you a question?"

"Sure."

"Have you ever had dick so good that you can't ever forget it? Like, you're obsessed with it?"

"I'm a lesbian."

I rolled my eyes and traced the purple lines of the transfer on her thigh. "Oh, come on, killjoy. Voodoo pussy. Ever have one?"

She sighed wistfully. "Yeah. Her name was Brandie."

"Ha! Mine's Bodie. Maybe they're gender twins. So, what's the story with Brandie? Did you get over her VP? Ever forget it?"

"Nope. Never."

I frowned. "Well, the problem for me is that my dick is temporary."

"How come? Is he, like, from Austria or something?"

One of my brows rose. "That's really specific, but no. He isn't leaving the country."

"So, what? Is he not into you?"

I laughed. "Oh, I'm pretty sure he's into me. Like, *all the way* in, if you catch my drift."

"Yeah, I think I get it," she deadpanned. "So, what's the problem? He married?"

"No, not married either. Just ... I don't know. I'm not really the settle-down type. I've dated more guys than I have lipstick, and I have a metric fuck-ton of lipstick. As in like a grand total of twenty-thousand-Sephora-points fuck-ton."

She snickered.

"I wonder if a couple more hook-ups might get him out of my system?"

She shook her head at me like she felt sorry for me.

"What? That's a valid, reasonable question. And entirely possible. Maybe he'll be super stinky or gross next time. Or maybe he never flosses."

"No one flosses."

I gave her a look. "Seriously, do you even know how to have fun?"

She gave me a look back.

"I like you," I said with a smile. "And I predict that in two more meetings with his magnificent hammerhead, I will have had it all fucked out of my system."

"Why two more?"

"Because, by the end of date three, it always goes south. Usually it's about them turning into crazies or coming on too strong. It's just like on *The Golden Girls*. Dudes propose to Blanche like she's the last woman on earth, and within a week of meeting her. She always turns them down though, that sassy bitch. She's my guru. When I don't know what to do, I just ask myself, *What would Blanche do?*"

"So, what would Blanche do?"

I thought about it. "Well, she'd bang him until it got weird and then kiss him goodbye, wiggling out the door, twiddling her fingers at him."

"Why not do that?"

"Ugh, I hate the thought of it getting weird, that's why. It's easier to just bolt before it happens. I've gotten so good at dipping out of the third-date situation."

"Mmm," she said noncommittally. "When will you see him for date two?"

I frowned. "I don't know. Date one was last night, and I'm still recovering. Physically. You know, because he nailed me so hard."

"Naturally."

"I have two whole bangs left, so I've gotta make the most of it. I need to maximize my bang-to-date ratio. But, if I could do whatever I wanted, I'd see him tonight. Or now. You don't mind if I just go, do you?"

She laughed. "Sure, and this is free, right?"

"Obviously."

I sighed, gun buzzing up my arm as I kept working. "He's exactly what I need right now."

"So are you going to call him?"

I frowned. "It hasn't even been twenty-four hours."

"Hold up," Ramona said from the wall of my booth, startling me.

"Jesus," I said, heart jumping. "I've got a tattoo gun in my hand, asshole. Give a warning cough or something."

"Sorry. I was eavesdropping and have unsolicited thoughts to share."

"Well, by all means, do tell." I gestured for her to go ahead.

"Since when do you follow rules? If you want to bang, call him and bang."

I nodded my head as I considered it. "I approve of your logic."

"I mean, what are you afraid of? That he'll think you're coming on too strong?"

We both laughed real loud at that. As if I knew another way to come on.

"Seriously though," Ramona said, "if you want to call him, call him."

I really wanted to, but the rule had been so deeply ingrained in my brain that I struggled to override it.

"Penny, if he called you right now and asked you over, what would you do?"

"Pretend I got diarrhea so I could leave," I answered without hesitation.

Ramona nodded. "That's what I thought. Also, someday you're going to try that line and it's not going to work."

I waved her off with a laugh. "Please. No one questions diarrhea." I turned to the girl in my chair for the final word. "What do you think? Honest answer, no bullshit."

She smirked. "I say, go get that dick."

So I laughed and decided to do just that.

I was so deep in the code on my screen that afternoon that I almost missed my phone buzzing on the desk. And that would have been a goddamn shame because it was a one-worded text from Penny.

Question.

Insta-smile happened as I picked up my phone, sat back in my chair, and typed.

Answer.

Little dots bounced.

Would you think I was needy if I wanted to see you again tonight?

It would be a little hypocritical of me to judge.

More dots as she typed, and I stared at my phone with a healthy helping of disbelief.

It hadn't even been a day, and here she was, asking to see me—the girl who didn't date. And maybe it was nothing. All I knew was that I'd gone to bed with a smile on my lips and her face in my thoughts, and I'd woken up exactly the same way. My mind had been rolling her around like a fine wine, appreciating every second I'd had with her over and over again. And if I had a chance to see her again, I'd take it, and I'd use it.

So, sounds like we're both needy then. What to do, what to do?

I typed back, my smile stretching. *I could think of a thing or two. Or three. If you come over later, I can show you. I'll have visual aids.*

Tell me there will be graphs. I love a good graph.

I laughed out loud, garnering looks from Phil and Jude, who flanked me at their monitors.

Girl, I've got graphs like you've never seen. Big, long graphs, packed with data I compiled all by myself.

Fuck, I love it when you talk dirty to me. I'm off at 8. Be there around 8:30?

Good. And make sure you don't have panties on.

Too late.

I set my phone down and leaned back in my chair, sighing, knowing I looked like a sap. My saving grace was that I was thinking about all the places I'd fuck Penny in my apartment in a few hours.

"Was that her?" Jude asked, looking like a hyperactive puppy.

"Yeah. She's coming over tonight."

Jude shook his head. "Man, I cannot believe you bagged *Penny*. After all this time. I guess your high school voodoo shrine in your closet didn't completely go to waste."

My face went flat. "I didn't have a shrine."

Phil snorted. "You kept a gum wrapper from a stick of Wrigley's she gave you junior year."

"Fuck you. It had her number on it."

"Sure it did, buddy. What about that broken bracelet you kept of hers?"

I rolled my eyes and chuffed. "She asked me to fix it."

"But you didn't," Jude shot.

"Because it was too broken," I volleyed.

"Then why didn't you give it back to her?"

"Because it was fucking broken, and I didn't want to admit it to her, dick."

Jude gave me a look. "You wanted to keep it."

"Jesus, I'm not arguing with you about this, Jude." He was right. I'd never tell him. "She's coming over tonight at eight-thirty, so I need you guys to … you know. Leave."

Phil frowned. "Man, we were supposed to work tonight."

"Yep, and now you two are going to work at Angie's."

Phil pouted. "I won't get any work done, though. I can't be with Angie and not hang out with her."

"You'll find a way."

Jude perked up. "Philly, ask her to make those blondie things she makes. Or brownies. Or, like, she can bake anything because I want to eat her sweets."

Phil's face hardened. "You're not eating my girlfriend's sweets. Those sweets are *mine*."

Jude put his hands up. "Easy there. I'm talking about the baked goods, not the baker."

Phil was still pouting. "I can't believe we're getting kicked out so you can nail Penny. No," he said with a shake of his head, "I can't believe you're actually nailing Penny. Is she the same as she was in high school?"

I thought about it. "Yes and no. She's just … *more* now. People love to say they don't give a fuck, but Penny actually means it. She's got her own gravity, and it's so hard not to want to know her, want to orbit her, even if just for a minute. When she walks in a room, everyone turns to look. But she was always that way. It was why Rod picked her out to torture in high school; he wanted to rein the brightest star and treat her like his pet."

"Ugh, that dick." Jude folded his arms. "Penny was so gone for him, and he didn't give a single shit about her. While she was gushing over their six-month anniversary, he was bragging about the laundry list of girls he'd fucked behind the bleachers. And she had no idea, not for two full years. She was stupid for him."

I sighed. "Well, seems Penny has flipped. She *doesn't do* dating. Ever, apparently."

Phil pushed his glasses up his nose. "Do you think it's because of Roddy?"

"I don't know." I rubbed the back of my neck. "I guess it's possible. I don't know how many times I found her abandoned at a party or crying after one of their fights. It was like I had a sixth sense for her. I'd just stumble onto her and know how to make her feel better." I sighed. "All I know is that she says she doesn't do feelings and wants no strings, which is fine. For now."

Jude jacked a brow at me. "For now?"

I shrugged. "If I make myself indispensable, maybe I can hang onto her. I've got a shot, and I'll be damned if I'm gonna waste it."

"You sure that's wise?" he asked. "I mean, aside from the fact that she told you she didn't want anything serious."

"I'm not saying I want anything serious. I'm saying I have a feeling what she means is she doesn't want anything *complicated*."

"So you think you're an exception to the rule."

"Maybe."

"You want to be."

I smirked. "Maybe."

Jude snorted. "Well, you've only been fantasizing about her for ten years."

Phil warily watched me. "So, what are you going to do?"

"Whatever I can, Philly. Whatever I can. Keep things easy and simple. I don't want to own her."

Jude opened his mouth to speak, but I cut him off, "I mean I want to own her with my dick—" he looked satisfied at that, "but I'm not trying to put her in a cage, ever. I want to show her that it doesn't have to be messy or hard. It can be easy and fun. I just have to respect her space."

Jude laughed. "Oh, man, you should tell her that while you're nailing her. *I just respect you so much, Penny,*" he teased in a girlie voice.

"You are such a dick, dude."

He kept laughing. "I know."

"I didn't think I'd hear from her so soon, but I'm not complaining. Last night wasn't enough. Tonight won't be either. Hopefully she's just as into me, and we can keep this going. Easy."

Phil still wasn't convinced. "Doesn't sound easy. Relationships need three things to be successful." He held up his fingers and ticked them off. "Respect, communication, and trust. If any one of those things breaks down, you're in deep shit."

"Thanks, Dr. Phil." Jude started laughing all over again.

Phil looked wounded. "Angie told me that, and it's fucking true. I'm just saying—if you're not communicating about where you're at, your shit's gonna fall apart. Kablooey."

I tried not to overthink it. "Don't worry, Philly. I'll talk to her about it when the time comes."

"And in the meantime?" he asked.

I smirked. "In the meantime, you leave so I can woo her."

"With your dick," Jude said.

The fucker popped out of his chair and ran off before I could deck him.

five

Dicknotized

I WET MY SMILING LIPS AS I KNOCKED ON BODIE'S DOOR, TRYING TO IGNORE MY banging heart, hyperaware of the soft fabric of my skirt against my bare ass and the point where my thighs met, warm and naked and sizzling at the thought of him.

Dicknotized. I'd been completely and utterly dicknotized.

The door swung open, revealing Bodie, tall and blond and beautiful, smiling that megawatt smile at me.

"Hi," I said stupidly, smiling back like an idiot.

"Hey. Come on in."

He moved aside so I could pass, and I swayed my hips, hoping he'd catch the motion of my black skater skirt to remind him that I wasn't wearing panties.

When I looked over my shoulder at him, it was obvious my nefarious, self-serving plan to convince him to ravage me had worked. His eyes were on my upper thighs, and his lips were pinned between his teeth.

I decided to prolong the inevitable, stretching out the tease for as long as I could with the desire to rip each other's clothes off crackling between us.

I set my bag next to the couch and looked around the apartment with my heart beating well above the normal resting rate. "I didn't really get a good look at your place last night. I love it." The loft was open, with exposed bricks and warehouse windows, simple, modern furniture, and tidy, considering three dudes lived there.

"Thanks. Phil and Jude have been here for a few years now."

I shook my head, still looking around. "Man, they must have great jobs."

"They did," he said as he approached from behind. "Phil is a software engineer, and Jude is in digital design. They quit so we could work on our video game together."

I started wandering just before he reached me, heading toward their office space. "Really? You're designing a video game?"

"Mmhmm." He was still behind me where I'd left him.

"Which desk is yours?" I asked, standing in front of the three, which were all side by side, facing the windows. Six monitors sat on top, two for each desk.

"This one," he said against my neck, surprising me.

I hadn't heard him approach. One hand slipped around my waist while the other pointed at the desk in the middle.

"And what do you do here?" I leaned back into him, my plan largely forgotten when he pressed himself against my ass.

"Mmm, lots of math."

His hands moved from my hips to the bend at my thighs, his fingers reaching between my legs, and I arched my back to shift my ass against the length of him.

"Not really up for conversation?" I asked breathlessly.

"I am," he whispered against my neck.

His hot, wet tongue for only the briefest of moments.

"But first, I want to fuck you like I've been daydreaming about all day."

I swear to God, my pussy flexed like he was speaking directly to it.

His fingers clenched, gathering my skirt up with them until his glorious hands were on me.

First, he found my piercing and stroked it, circling with no hurry at all, teasing me. Then lower, dragging the pad of his finger up the line at my center, so slow, so light that he had my hips shifting, my core aching.

I whimpered, and his finger clenched at the sound.

"Don't tease me," I begged. "Fuck me."

"Oh, don't worry, Penny," he said calmly and quietly and with authority I hadn't realized I'd granted. "I'm going to."

My brain had already exploded, and my awareness was focused on every place we touched, so when he disappeared for a second, the loss was a cold shock against my hot skin. But then he grabbed my hand, pulling me over to the couch. When he sat, he pulled me down to sit next to him, my heart pounding as I tried to kiss him. He had other plans, stopping me by cupping my cheek. His thumb slipped into my mouth, and I closed my lips over it, telling him with my eyes that I wished something else were in its place entirely.

"Lie down," he ordered gruffly, guiding me to stretch across his lap with my ass up and my knees and elbows on the couch.

His cock was rock hard against the space between my belly button and clit, and I found myself wriggling against him, shifting slowly, my pulse frantic. I felt crazy. He was actually driving me mad, and he'd barely even touched me.

Dicknotized. If I were a cartoon, my eyes would be pinwheels with dicks in the middle, spinning around and around.

I was already panting, partly because I had no idea what he was going to do to me.

Where are his hands? Why aren't they on me? Why aren't they in me? I need them to touch me.

Part of me just wanted him to flip me over and fuck me senseless. The rest of me wanted him to tease me forever.

I looked back at him, but he wasn't looking at me. His eyes were on my ass—my skirt didn't fully cover it, lying down like I was.

"Cross your ankles." His hand found my ass cheek and squeezed, kneading it as his thumb slid under the hem of my skirt.

I did as I had been told, my heart hammering.

His hands were reverent as they lifted up my skirt, flipping it so my entire backside was on display. His face was reverent too, as if he'd found some secret of the universe under my skirt.

Bodie grabbed my ass again, groaning softly, his cock flexing under me. His thumb slipped between my ass and gripped, spreading me open, and I arched, lifting it into the air.

"That's right," he breathed, voice deep. "Open up for me." His hands moved—one kept me exposed, the other explored.

First were his fingers running down the line and to my clit for a split second of glorious pressure before trailing back up. Then down they went with more pressure as he passed through the slickness of my core, wetting his fingers even more. The third time, his fingers nestled between the length of my lips, the tips capturing the ball of my piercing, and my hips bucked in answer. When he shifted them laterally, the sensation across the entire length of me coupled with my piercing circling my clit was too much.

I gasped, heart slamming, nails scrabbling for purchase against the leather couch cushion, my face buried between my clenching hands.

"Please," I groaned. "Fuck, Bodie. Please. *Please.*"

He said nothing, and I couldn't look, not with starbursts flashing behind my pinched lids.

I felt his wet fingers move up and then his thumb, now somehow wet too.

It was so slick, so smooth, that it didn't even give me pause when he circled the tight hole I rarely let anyone near.

His thumb gently ran across me, his fingers stroking my pussy at the same speed, same pace, the pressure increasing until he flexed his fingers and slid into me, both holes at once.

I raised off his lap, my mouth hanging open, my breath frozen in my lungs, but he didn't stop. He stroked me, played my body, pushed every button, even buttons I hadn't known I had. His fingers performed some exquisite gymnastics that I'd be thinking about for a decade, though in the moment I didn't care how he was doing it, only that he didn't stop. Ever. His pinkie rocked against my clit as the rest of his hand fucked me with tender determination.

The deeper he went, the harder he went, the less control I had. Part of me wondered if I'd ever had any at all.

I couldn't even move, just laid there on his lap with my ass in the air. My hands moved to his leg under me, gripping his jeans, bracing myself.

"Come on, Penny," he said roughly, begging. "Come, so I can fuck you."

His hand flexed again, and three pressure points that he pressed screamed.

"That's right. Come on. Come for me."

Another flex. My heart strained against my ribs.

"F-f-fuck," I groaned as my body orgasmed, not a single thing in my control. "Fuck, fuck, fuck," I whispered against the leather of the couch cushion with every pulse of my body, full in every possible way and nowhere near full enough.

"Thank God," he breathed. A flurry of motion, he moved my limp body off his lap, put my knees on the ground, and moved behind me, kneeling between my legs.

I barely possessed any awareness of my surroundings, not until he grabbed my hips and slipped into me from behind, hitting my G-spot like he fucking had radar for it.

"*Fuck!*" I cried, sliding my hands into the back of the cushion to hang on as the orgasm I'd thought was gone got a second wind.

"Jesus fucking Christ, Penny," he growled as he pounded me.

His hand twisted in my hair and pulled. My orgasm thundered back to life with every pump of his hips. I didn't even know how—it just wouldn't stop, rolling through me like it would never end. My body was on fire, writhing and wriggling and flexing and contracting as he slammed into me over and over again, finally coming with a moan, a cry, a shudder, and jackhammering hips that hit the end of me so hard that I couldn't breathe.

I don't even know how we came down or how long it took or what happened after that—I blacked out from bliss.

When I regained a fraction of my senses, I found myself lying on the rug, tucked into Bodie's side, both of us still fully clothed other than his unbuckled pants, condom still on.

I didn't even remember him putting it on, and the fact that it hadn't even crossed my mind when he was nailing me from behind freaked me out. But only for a second. Lucky for me, he was a trustworthy guy, and he had been since high school. Maybe it hadn't crossed my mind because I *did* trust him.

That foreign thought freaked me out too.

I didn't have too long to contemplate it before Bodie seemed to reconnect his wires, turning to look down at me with a smile.

"So," I started, the word lazy, "if you tell me you earned your nickname by fucking girls like that in high school, I'm really going to be burned about missing that shot."

He chuckled and ran his hand down my arm. "Trust me—that was not the case. Roddy started it. First I was D, and Jude was Judie. Then D evolved into Diddle and Judie to Dee Dee. The nickname had nothing to do with anything other than him trying to humiliate me. I didn't see a vagina in real life until college."

"Really?" I asked wondrously, nestling into his side a little more.

"Yeah, really. I mean, you saw me. When it came to my friends, I had a mouth and confidence to beat their asses at literally anything, but I didn't have the courage to *really* talk to girls. You and I were around each other enough that I could have. I should have."

"We talked," I offered.

"Yeah, but not like that. I just didn't think I had a chance. Not then."

My heart sank. I wanted to tell him that he was wrong, but at sixteen, I had been looking for guys like Rodney—fast car, fast hands. Hell, I didn't know how different I was now. The thought made me feel even worse.

So instead of arguing, I curled deeper into his side.

His arm flexed in answer.

"College was … fun then?"

"You could say that." I could hear him smiling as he continued, "It probably wouldn't have been, if not for surfing."

"Yeah, what's the story with that? I don't remember you surfing in high school."

"That's because I didn't. My dad tried to get me and Jude to surf with him from the minute we could swim, and we did a little when we were kids, but once we hit junior high, we were more interested in playing D&D in the basement than sports. I blame the whole reject-what-your-parents-want idea. They're total hippies. I mean, they supplied weed to half the high school like it was fucking milk and cookies."

I laughed. "Your mom made a mean edible. She'd put her *vegan* cookies in those little sandwich baggies with a ribbon on it and smile and pat your cheek when she gave it to you. Half the time, she wouldn't even let us pay."

"It's funny now, but I was so embarrassed. How I didn't turn out to be a burnout is beyond me." He was still smiling, fingertips tracing circles on my back. "Anyway, before we left for college, Dad finally convinced us to surf with him for the summer, and Jude and I figured it was the old man's last chance to hang with us before we were gone. We fell in love with it and went at least once a day in college. We were those crazy fuckers, freezing our asses off at five a.m. so we could get a good session in before class."

"I love that," I said, imagining Bodie running into the ocean in slo-mo with a board under his arm. "And then came the girls?"

"If I'd realized just how many girls, I'd have picked up surfing way sooner. Maybe then I could have stolen you away from Rod—that dick."

"Ugh, he really was. Is?"

"Is. We're still friends on social media. His Snapchat makes me want to fucking vomit."

I felt squirmy at the mention of Rodney. We weren't friends anywhere, not after he'd stretched my heart out to the point that it lost its shape.

I changed the subject. "Hey, I hate to ask, but I was so antsy to get over here that I didn't eat after work. Do you have anything? I'm not picky. Popcorn will do. Cold cuts. Hot Pockets. Whatever you've got."

"Yeah. We've got some frozen pizzas, I think."

"Mmm. Totino's?" I asked as we got up.

"Red Baron."

"I'll take what I can get, I guess."

He laughed and headed back toward the bathroom, fooling around between his legs as he walked. "Gimme one second."

"Take your time," I said, my eyes on his ass, the top of which was exposed from his unfastened pants.

He disappeared into the bathroom, and I sat down at the island in the middle of the kitchen, leaning on the counter, musing.

My body purred like a kitten, thanks to him, and I found myself fluttery and smiley and absolutely happy. Bodie was good and he was fun and he was perfect. And I knew I was going to miss him when he was gone.

One more date, max.

I loathed the notion. I loathed it so deeply that I felt sick at the thought of not seeing him again.

He walked back in before I could think twice about it, smiling that goddamn smile that made my vagina spell his name in Morse code. I pushed my feelings away. I'd live in the moment. It was what I did best.

Bodie opened up the freezer and moved things around for a minute. "Bad news. No pizza."

I frowned. "What have you got?"

More shuffling.

"A bag of peas, a half a bag of crinkle fries, and some popsicles with freezer burn."

My frown deepened.

He closed the door and turned to lean on the other side of the island. "We could order one?"

"That'll take forever and I'm starving. What are the odds of a PB and J?"

He smirked. "Pretty good. Just depends on your jelly preference."

"Grape or strawberry?" I asked. This was a test.

He narrowed his eyes, recognizing the challenge. "Strawberry."

"Good. If you'd said grape, the whole deal would have been off."

He laughed and moved around the kitchen, gathering supplies.

"Wait, it's smooth peanut butter, right?"

He shot me a look over his shoulder from the pantry. "Of course. We're not animals, Penny."

"Thank God. Proper PB and J has universal rules that must be honored."

He laid everything out on the island between us. "So, how did you get into the tattoo business?"

"Well, I was always into art, you remember?"

He nodded as he set four slices of bread out on a cutting board.

"After graduation and Rodney dumping me, I just had to get out of Santa Cruz. My aunt lived here in Manhattan, so I crashed with her. She was tatted up like crazy. I went with her to get a few at Joel's shop, and when I was waiting for her one time, sketching, Joel asked if he could take a look. I'd never considered the profession until he asked me if I'd be interested."

Bodie smiled. "Kismet."

I folded my hands on the countertop. "It kinda was. He gave me my first tattoo. This one." I turned to show him the piece on my shoulder and upper arm. "Joel ... he's like a big brother to everyone at the shop, and he brought most of us in as apprentices and taught us everything he knows, which is a lot."

"Like a big brother ... not a big boyfriend?" Bodie asked, still smiling.

I laughed. "Oh, definitely not. He's not my type, and plus, he's engaged to the producer of our reality show, Annika."

His hand stilled, peanut butter knife hanging midair. "Reality show?"

Another laugh. "I thought you might have known. Don't watch much TV?"

He shook his head. "You're on TV?"

"I am. It's a reality show—*Tonic,* named after the shop where we work. Real original, I know. We're about to start filming season two."

His head was still shaking. "That's crazy. What's that like?"

I shrugged. "It's fun. Kind of weird having cameras in your face all the time, but I don't mind. Last season was drama though—Annika was kind of a bitch. She lied to Joel before she made it up to him, and he ended up putting a ring on it. I wanted to rip her face off for doing him wrong, but she's like nine feet tall and Russian, so I'm pretty sure she'd beat my ass. I've got a real big bark though."

He slathered on the peanut butter and opened the jelly jar. "I remember that bark very well."

I laughed. "Yeah, I guess the Rodney breakup wasn't super private."

"I'm pretty sure every parent and student in the audience heard what you had to say about him dumping you at graduation."

I felt myself blush. "Well, he deserved every word."

"No arguments here. You guys used to fight like crazy."

"Because he drove me crazy. Like, on purpose. I swear, he kept me just close enough to keep me coming back for more and far enough away that I never felt like he was really mine."

Bodie didn't speak for a second as he spread strawberry jelly over the peanut butter, all the way to the edges, like a good boy.

"Think he's why you don't date?" he asked, his face still.

I chuffed. "I don't think. I know." I thought about it, feeling my willpower turn into steel at the thought of Rodney. "Here's the thing, Bodie. When I love, I don't do it halfway. I go all the way into the fire until it burns me up. It's obsessive. I lost myself once to someone else, and I'm not doing it again."

He nodded and closed one sandwich, then the other. "You sure it wasn't just Rod?"

I shrugged. "Not really interested in finding out."

"So you've never felt the urge to stick with a guy, even without commitment?" He sliced our dinner into triangles and plated them.

I squirmed, and he saw it.

"I'm not asking for myself, Penny. I'm just curious."

I sighed. "If I'm being honest? No. I used to, and I've tried to, which only reinforced my belief that relationships aren't for me. It's just fun, and I don't need any more commitment than that. I'm committed to my job. I have my girlfriends, and they wouldn't hurt me. I don't need a man to be happy. I just need a man for my vagina to be happy, but that bitch doesn't run my life."

He laughed at that and handed my plate over. "Want something to drink?"

"Just water, thanks."

"I've really only done flings too," he said as he made his way around the kitchen. "I mean, there were a few girls I dated for a while, but nothing serious. Just never turned into more. Know what I mean?"

"Yeah, I do. It's so hard when you're different people or you have different expectations. But sometimes there's just no connection. Like when they don't get your jokes—that's the worst. Or they just go straight to stage five clinger."

He chuckled and set our glasses in front of us. "It was so weird when I first started dating because I had no idea what I was doing. Like, I had no experience, so I thought I was supposed to woo, date, and fall in love with every woman I was interested in, so I tried. But then I realized that chicks were like guys sometimes too. That dating is not about wooing and love. It's all about expectations, you know? Like some girls really do want full commitment with a ring in the future, or it's nothing. But that's such a weird thing to expect when you're nineteen."

I picked up one triangle of my sandwich. "I mean, seriously. People don't know how to live in the now. Why do we all have to have some five-year plan that won't even be possible to follow? Life doesn't work that way. Everything is fluid."

I took a bite and moaned as my eyes rolled back in my head. "I don't know if it's because I haven't had one of these in forever or because I'm starving, but this is incredible."

He smiled at me as he chewed and swallowed. "It's the peanut-butter-to-jelly ratio."

"You and your math," I said with a shake of my head and a smile on my lips, wondering why he had to be so funny and smart and hot and amazing. It wasn't even fair. "The only time I love math is when it's coming out of your mouth."

His smile climbed on one side. "What's sixty-nine plus sixty-nine?"

I narrowed my eyes, trying to sort it out.

"Dinner for four."

I laughed and took another bite.

"I'm like pi—really long and I go on forever."

More laughing, lips closed, chasing it with a sip of water so I wouldn't choke.

He leaned on the counter, still smirking at me. "I'm not obtuse; you're acute chick."

"Okay, that one was bad." I kept stuffing my face now that the hunger switch had been flipped.

"What do math and my dick have in common?"

My brow rose as I swallowed.

"They're both hard for you."

That time, I laughed hard enough that I snorted.

Bodie set down his sandwich and dusted off his hands. The look in his eyes made me take one more bite, a big one that I chewed hastily, figuring dinner might be over.

"Can I plug my solution into your equation?" he asked, voice low and smile crooked as he rounded the island.

"I dunno. Can you?"

"Maybe I can be your math tutor for the night." He spun me around on the stool. "Add a bed." His hands slipped up my thighs, opening them. "Subtract your clothes." His hands moved higher until they rested in the bend of my hips. "Divide your legs." He nestled between my legs, angling for my lips. "And multiply."

I wanted to laugh, but when he kissed me, I forgot what was so funny.

❧

Obsessed— that was what I was.

Obsessed with her salty, sweet lips against mine.

Obsessed with her milky-white thighs around my waist.

Obsessed with her silky purple hair between my fingers.

Obsessed with *her.*

I'd been kissing her for long enough that she was panting, and my heart was thundering like a racehorse.

She was perfect—other than the fact that she didn't want to date me. Yet.

I broke away, leaving her sitting on the stool with her eyes still shut and her lips parted like they were waiting for me.

"I want you naked," I growled as I reached behind me to pull off my shirt.

When I looked down at her, her eyes were half open as she fumbled with the zipper on her skirt.

I dropped my pants and stepped out of them, grabbed her by the waist to lift her up and set her down hard enough that her ass slapped against the surface of the counter with a pop and a yelp.

My hands moved up her waist and under her Ramones shirt, pushing it up and over her head. Her lavender hair spilled out of the neck like a waterfall, and I tossed the shirt behind me. She reached for my face, pulling me to her for another kiss, and I lost myself in her hot mouth for a long moment—until she shifted, pressing her wet pussy against my shaft.

I groaned into her mouth with one hand clutching the back of her head to keep her mouth against mine while the other roamed to her breast, kneading and squeezing, my thumb playing with the barbell in her nipple until she whimpered.

That sound connected straight to my cock. I wanted to record it. I wanted to hear it on a loop. I wanted to touch her until she moaned and called my name.

I broke away. "Naked. Now."

She reached behind her back, panting, and she unhooked her bra as I swept an arm on the island behind her to clear it, sending utensils clattering to the floor. She was shimmying out of her skirt when I lost all patience and pulled it down her legs to toss it.

"Lie down," I ordered.

Penny rested back on her elbows, her body stretched out in offering, illuminated by the overhead lights.

She was a fucking dream, a fantasy, with her legs spread open and eyes hot, locked on mine, as I grabbed a condom from the pocket of my jeans. When I ripped open the packet, she shifted her gaze to watch my hands grip my cock and roll it on. Her lip slipped between her teeth, and I stroked.

"What do you want, Penny?"

"I want your cock," she breathed, opening her legs wider. "I've wanted it since I walked in the door. What do you want, Bodie?"

I stepped to her, one hand still pumping my shaft, the other grabbing her ankle to pull her to the edge of the counter.

"I want to bury myself in you until I can't get any deeper. I want to fill you up so much, you'll feel empty when I'm gone." I rested the tip of my cock against her piercing, pressing it into her with my thumb on my shaft. "I want to fuck you so hard, you'll never forget me."

She writhed and whispered, "I won't if you won't."

I ran my cock down the line, and when I hit the dip, I flexed my hips, filling her agonizingly slow, my eyes on the seam where I disappeared into her.

"*Fuck*," she whispered.

When I glanced up, her head was hanging back, her neck stretched out, her long white fingers circling her taut, rosy nipple.

"Jesus," I breathed, my thighs trembling as I pulled out slow and eased back in.

My hands slipped under her thighs and brought them up parallel with my body, her calves tucked between my ribs and arms. I felt her feet stretch out to a point as I pulled out and slammed in.

She lay down flat, chest heaving as one hand worked her nipple and the other founding the piercing between her legs, rubbing a circle in time with my hips.

She felt like heaven, soft and wet and tight, and as I watched her touching herself, I was too close, too soon. I wanted to fuck her all night, all day tomorrow, all week. For a year. For as long as she'd have me.

I slowed my pace and pulled out, eliciting another whimper from her—this time, in mourning—but I ignored it, grabbing her thighs to scoot her back until her hair hung over the edge, giving me room to crawl up with her. I pushed her thighs apart with my knees, and she lifted her legs, opening them up, hooking them around my hips as I positioned myself to slide into her again.

"Come on," she said hotly. "Fill me up."

So I did, not at all gently that time, not stopping until there was no space between us.

I caught sight of the jelly jar and smiled, slowing my hips so I could reach for it. She peeled her eyes open and looked over, wickedly smiling back.

"Still hungry?" I asked.

She nodded.

I dipped my thumb into the jelly and brought it to her lips, parted and so full, smearing it across the bottom one. Her pink tongue slid out to lick it clean, and I cupped her jaw, slipping my thumb into the heat of her mouth. She closed her lips and sucked, wrapping her wet tongue around it.

I hooked the digit and forced her mouth open so I could take it with my own, wanting her tongue against mine.

My hips took control, rocking and pumping and fucking her, unaware of anything before or after, only that moment, only her body.

She bent her legs wound around my hips to force me to get as deep as possible, holding me there as she twisted at the waist to guide me onto my back. I did, not caring that I was lying on a sandwich, not caring about anything outside of the feeling of being buried in Penny.

She sat up and rested her hands on my chest, her eyes down and lips parted, and when she moved, when she shifted her hips and moaned, my head kicked back, my hands gripping her tattooed thighs like she'd fly away if I didn't hang on to her.

"Bodie," she called.

I found myself enough to open my eyes and sit up, wrapping my arms around her to crush her against me, to bury my face in her neck, to twist her hair in my hands as she rocked against me making the sweetest noises I'd ever heard.

"I'm gonna come," she whispered, her hips moving faster with every rotation.

I let her go, leaning back enough that I could watch her with my hands on her hips, guiding her as she ground and bounced harder against me, the slap of her ass against my thighs speeding my pulse, speeding time. And when she came, breasts jostling, a cry on her lips, eyes pinched shut, I kept her hips going as I came so hard, I thought my chest was going to explode from the force.

The sight of her coming would be burned into the back of my eyelids for the rest of my life.

She collapsed on top of me, and I lay back, taking her with me. She pulsed around my cock, slowing with each heartbeat, and I pumped inside of her lazily in answer.

"Hey, Penny?" I asked, my voice low and rough.

"Hmm?" she hummed against my chest.

"Are you the square root of negative one? Because you can't be real."

She laughed, nestling a little deeper into my chest, and I tried to pretend like she wasn't already finding her way into my heart.

chapter
SIX

Fuck you, Brad

PENNY HAD LEFT THAT NIGHT WITH A LONG GOODBYE KISS AND A SMILE FULL OF promise, and since we'd seen each other twice in twenty-four hours, I figured I'd hear from her soon.

Wrong.

The first day hadn't been so bad although I ended up in the gym twice to try to get my mind off of her. The second day, I'd tried to satiate my thoughts by watching her show. I'd avoided it because I thought it might be creepy, and when I'd turned it on, it was with the intention of watching a single episode. Eight hours later, I'd made it almost through the season and had Cheetos dust all over my T-shirt. And I'd felt a zillion times worse. I'd even picked up my phone to text her enough times that I threw the fucking thing in my nightstand drawer so I'd stop thinking about it. That had lasted a solid hour before I'd caved and retrieved it and commenced staring.

I was on day three, and I wasn't happy about it.

Three days. Three agonizing days of pounding away at my keyboard instead of her ass. Three days without a single sexual pun that hadn't come from my brother. Three nights of my hand on my jock, thinking about her spread eagle on my counter. Three long days without my hands in places they tingled at the thought of. Places where my tongue should be, like deep in her—

"Dude, did you hear me?"

I turned to Jude, frowning. "Huh?"

He rolled his eyes. "God, you're so fucking sad. Just text her."

I scowled. "Don't you think I would if I could?"

"What's the matter? Fingers broken? Didn't pay your phone bill?"

"Fuck you, Jude."

"You act like she's some delicate fucking flower."

My eyes narrowed. "She's more delicate than you think. I can't just text her, man. That's not how this works."

He shook his head. "Your big plan to woo Penny is to not talk to her? It's to let her ghost you?"

"She hasn't ghosted me, asshole."

"Maybe she has, dickwad. You haven't heard anything in three days and have been walking around here like a goddamn rottweiler who had his bone stolen."

My scowl deepened.

"Get it? Your *bone*?"

"I hate you," I muttered as I turned back to my screen.

"Liar. You know I'm right."

I turned in my chair to face him again. "No, you're fucking not. My big plan is to leave the ball in her court so I don't come off as needy. The last thing a chick who wants no strings needs is a guy up her ass."

"Maybe she *does* need a guy up her ass," he joked with his eyebrows waggling.

"Fucking cretin."

"I'm just saying, what rule states you can't even text her after three days?"

"Oh my God," I groaned with a roll of my eyes. "All of them, dipshit. You had a girlfriend way too long."

"And you might have cocked it all up by acting like you're not interested."

I huffed. "I've gotta play this smart, Jude. She's going to come back around. I know it."

"And if she doesn't?"

"Then I'll figure it out." My hope sank like the Titanic, slowly and with a chill. He wasn't wrong, but he wasn't right. There was no way of knowing, not until she texted me. I checked my phone, just like I had about four billion times in the last three days.

Nothing.

I ran a hand through my hair.

Jude watched me. "You should take a walk. Get out of the apartment. We've been cooped up here for three days, working and binge-watching TV, and I think you need some vitamin D, since you're not giving any."

I made a face. "Hilarious, jackhole. And I would have already *seen* her show if you'd fucking told me about it when you found out."

"I *did* tell you, bro."

"Dude, there's no way I would forget you telling me that *Penny* was on TV. Literally no fucking way."

"Well, there's no fucking way I *wouldn't* have told you because I knew you'd had a boner for her for a decade."

I chuffed, opening my mouth to argue, but he cut me off.

"I'm serious. Why don't you get us ice cream? It's, like, a thousand degrees out, and you're miserable. No one can be miserable after ice cream. It's scientifically impossible."

I sighed and stood, sticking a finger in his face. "Fine. But only if you promise to keep your fucking mouth shut about Penny. It's hard enough without your nagging."

"Yeah, I bet it is."

He tried to flick me in the nuts, but I jumped back and countered with a solid slap upside the back of his head.

"Get me some cherry chunk," he called after me.

I flipped him off over my shoulder as I walked to the door, opened it, and slammed it behind me.

Frustrated was a good word to use—sexually, emotionally, generally. I'd had a little taste of something that had consumed me like wildfire, and now that I was deprived of it, I felt wild. Feral. Like I'd crawl out of my skin if I couldn't see her, smell her, touch her.

Even the thought of touching her had my johnson reacting.

Maddening, that was what it was.

I stepped out into the blazing summer afternoon, and my mood spoiled like rotten milk in the heat. I mean, why hadn't she called? We'd spent an hour in the shower the last time I saw her and another hour in my room, in my bed, touching, talking, kissing. She'd made me feel so good, and I thought the feeling was mutual.

Maybe I was wrong. Maybe she was playing me.

Maybe I was just a fuck boy, someone whose body she could use.

The thought made me feel cheap. Cheaper still when I wondered how many guys out there had felt just like I did.

Maybe Jude was right and I needed a new plan. At what point should I stop waiting? At what point should I take action, and what could I do? Because one thing was perfectly clear.

I wanted to be with Penny in any context she would let me have her. But to be with her, I had to play by her rules even if I bent them to get my way. I wanted to win, and I wanted to win *her*.

There wasn't much I could do besides texting, not without crossing the line. Showing up at her work would *definitely* be crossing the line. I could send her flowers at the tattoo parlor, but that would be way too big, too serious. I imagined her getting flowers from me and her eyes bugging out like I was psycho. Or worse—I imagined her laughing.

No. Definitely no flowers.

I huffed, running my fingers through my hair again, annoyed with myself for being so annoying. But I felt like an addict with no dealer, cracked out and irrational and driven to the point of desperation.

At that thought, I took a breath and told myself to ease up. The plan was to wait, so I'd wait.

She'd come around. My hope glimmered, revived by the thought. And when she did, I'd take advantage of every single second I had with her.

The bell over the shop's door rang, and Ramona laughed.

"Penny, delivery."

I glanced up from my desk in my booth to find a delivery guy looking around the room with a vase of flowers in his hand.

My heart shot into my throat.

Bodie!

Yeah, his name had an exclamation point in my head because I hadn't stopped thinking about him for three full days and nights, and I was mildly—extremely—annoyed that he hadn't texted me. Of course, I hadn't texted him either.

The third date loomed, and I wanted to stave it off for as long as possible. I mean, until I couldn't even stand it anymore. I was probably almost there because the thought of those flowers being from him made my vagina do stuff. Squeezy, clenchy stuff.

I hopped out of my seat and bounded to the delivery guy. "Are those for me?" I asked, grinning like a goddamn fool.

"If you're Penny, yes, they are."

I squealed and bounced on the balls of my feet. Every one of my co-workers watched me like I'd been possessed.

I had been. By Bodie's dick and math jokes.

The delivery guy had me sign his little doohickey and handed me the flowers, which I promptly skipped over to the desk with, and Ramona and Veronica appeared by my side, eyeballing me.

"This is literally the first time I've ever seen you excited about getting flowers," Ramona said incredulously.

Veronica watched me like my body had been snatched by an alien.

"They have to be from Bodie," I said, digging through the rose blooms for a card. "He hasn't even texted."

"We know. You've only mentioned it every hour, on the hour, for three days." Ramona patted my arm.

I found the card and plucked it out of the bouquet with an, *Aha!*, opening it with frantic fingers.

My stomach fell into my shoes with my smile.

"To Penny. Miss you. Consider my offer. Love, Brad," I read aloud.

Veronica groaned. "Ugh, fuck you, Brad!"

I read it again, sure there was some mistake. "Brad? I haven't even fucking seen that shithead in weeks, not since he asked me to move in with him. The curse of date three." I picked up the bouquet by the vase and dropped it in the tall trash can behind the desk.

Ramona eyed them, torn. "Do you have any idea how expensive those are?"

I pointed at her. "Don't you touch those. Those flowers are tainted by freaknut *Brad* and his inability to take a hint. Those flowers are from the wrong guy."

I was whining, and I didn't even care. I was way too butthurt to care.

"It's not fair," I said, bobbling a little.

Joel frowned at me from his station in the front of the shop before glancing at Veronica. "What's the matter with her?"

She took my shoulders gently, angling me to him as I pouted. "Bodie hasn't called her."

"New fuckbuddy?" he asked.

"Doesn't he like me?" I asked, my voice squeaky.

"I'm sure he does, honey," Veronica cajoled. "Maybe you should just text him. You obviously want to see him again."

I groaned. "I know, but it's date three! And instead of turning into a pumpkin, he's gonna turn into *Brad*." I tossed a hand at the trashcan as if those flowers explained everything.

Joel sighed. "You like the guy, right?"

I nodded.

"Then fucking text him, you weirdo."

"But what if—"

"Who cares? You want to see him, so see him. If it falls apart, deal with it."

I was still pouting. "Why do you make everything seem so simple?"

"Because it is." He rested his meaty, tattooed forearms on his knees and leaned toward me. "Listen, your afternoon job canceled, right?"

"Yeah," I answered begrudgingly.

"It's too hot in here, and your booth is the hottest in the shop. Go cool off. Cold shower. Ice cream. Something."

"But what about the walk-ins?"

"Max is here for walk-ins. You just get outta here." He jabbed a finger at the door with authority.

I sighed. "Fine. But only because you said ice cream, and that's my weakness." I could already taste the cold salted caramel on my tongue. This also made me a little sad—it reminded me of Bodie.

Who even ARE you right now?

I walked back over to my station to grab my bag, stopping by Veronica's station next to Ramona, who leaned on the short wall.

"Just text him, Pen," Ramona said. "You'll feel better."

I nibbled my bottom lip. "Even if he gets clingy? Even if he bugs out?"

She laughed and kissed me on the cheek on my way out. "Better him than you."

I sighed and headed into the sweltering sun, slipping on my sunglasses.

My problem was this: I was obsessing.

I was so predictable, I could have been a fucking atomic clock. I'd always been this way, and it was one of the many reasons why I didn't date. I didn't like how I felt, which reaffirmed that the three-date rule was just as much for myself as it was for them. And here I was, after only *two* dates, already all itchy over Bodie. He was just so dreamy and funny and smart, and I couldn't stop thinking about him.

All of this was dangerous.

Of course, it was entirely possible that I'd gotten weird simply because I was holding out. Maybe if I just ripped off the Band-Aid and saw him again, it would take care of itself. Once he got all gooey on me, I'd probably lose interest anyway.

That placating and naive thought put a little spring in my Chucks and a smile on my lips.

We could have our last hurah and let the chips fall where they may. Let fate take its course. Which, in my experience, meant I'd be absolutely over him and ready for whatever was next.

My heart folded in on itself at the fleeting thought that it might be *me* who'd be gooey over *him*. But I waved my thoughts away like bumblebees after the honey pot and resolved to text him when I got home.

But when I pulled open the door of the ice cream parlor, I stopped dead in my tracks as a smile spread across my face like peanut butter on toast.

I didn't have to text him after all because he was standing right in front of me.

His broad back was to me as he waited in line, peering into the cooler at the flavors on display.

I swear to God, my heart did a roundoff back handspring and stuck the landing as I walked up to him.

"If I went binary, you'd be the one for me," I said as I brushed against his arm, my knuckles grazing his.

He whipped his head around, blue eyes bright. And when they connected with mine, his smile could have lit up midnight.

He let out a laugh. "That was a good one. I didn't know you spoke nerd."

I shrugged, smiling. "I don't. I speak Google."

"What are you doing here?" he asked, sounding surprised.

"Getting ice cream. Isn't it obvious?"

Another laugh as the attendant asked him what he wanted.

Bodie turned to me. "Want to join me?"

"I'd love to."

"Know what you want?"

"A scoop of salted caramel in a waffle cone, please."

The attendant nodded and looked to Bodie.

"Mint chocolate, one scoop in a waffle cone too. Thanks."

We stepped over to the register, and Bodie pulled out his wallet to pay.

"How've you been?" he asked, the question tight from hiding another—*Why haven't I heard from you?*

But I smiled. He was still interested, and that right there was proof.

"I've been good, just working a lot. You?"

"Same. Jude kicked me out since I hadn't seen daylight in days. It's too hot to go outside without the promise of the ocean or ice cream."

We were handed our ice cream cones and turned to find the inside of the shop packed.

I frowned. "Way too hot, but outside we go."

He followed me to a table for two on the patio, and we took seats across from each other.

I grinned. I couldn't help it. I swear he'd gotten hotter in three days—his eyes were bluer, his hair blonder, his smile brighter as he grinned right back and put on his sunglasses.

Either that or my imagination was a sad, sad substitute for the real thing.

"Highway to Hell" came on the overhead speakers as I took a long lick of my ice cream and moaned.

Pretty sure Bodie was staring at my mouth from behind his shades.

"I've been thinking about you," I started, sticking out my tongue to run my ice cream across it.

He wet his lips and smirked. "Me too."

When he licked his ice cream and flicked his tongue at the top, I felt warm all over, and it had nothing to do with the ninety-five degree weather.

I crossed my legs, my mouth undeterred as I licked that ice cream like my future depended on it.

"It was *so hard* not to text you." I closed my lips over the top of my scoop.

"How hard?" he teased me back.

I just kept watching that creamy ice cream on his tongue, squeezing my thighs together like a goddamn vise.

"It just kept getting harder and harder with no hope of release. Cruel really."

"So why didn't you text me?"

I shrugged, playing coy. "Didn't want you to think I was easy."

We both laughed for a minute.

"So how much did you think of me?" I asked innocently, fondling my cone.

"Oh, only about every minute of every day." His feet sandwiched my foot on the ground and squeezed, shifting his sneakers up and down in slow, opposite strokes, just an inch or two's distance.

Somehow, it drove me completely insane.

"You?" he asked.

"A time or two. Once when I was in the shower."

"Mmm," he hummed with his cone in his mouth.

"Another time when I was lying in bed, wishing you'd texted me. I thought about you a *lot* that night. Three times. Every time, I would think I'd gotten you out of my head and *whoops*—you'd pop up again."

"Well, I can't help popping up. Not when I remember you eat ice cream like that."

I smiled and dragged my tongue around the diameter of the scoop.

"All that thinking and no doing," he said. "I really feel like we should be *doing* a whole lot more than we have the last couple of days."

I nodded. "Why didn't you text me?" I tried to keep the uncertainty out of my voice.

If he'd heard it, he didn't react.

He shrugged and echoed my words, "Didn't want you to think I was easy."

I laughed. "Maybe I like easy."

"Well then, you're in luck. Because when it comes to you, I'm so easy."

Bodie's elbows were on the table and so were mine, the two of us leaning toward each other.

"What do you say we get out of here?" he asked.

And I smiled back. "I thought you'd never fucking ask."

chapter
seven
Commando

WE HURRIED DOWN THE SIDEWALK, STILL HOLDING OUR ICE CREAM, OUR free hands threaded together, fingers shifting and stroking each other's. Only Penny could make holding hands feel dirty.

She lived just around the corner—we didn't even have to stop for a light—and when we reached the building, we ran up the stairs, both of us laughing, bursting into her quiet apartment.

I closed the door, and our laughter faded to soft smiles as we watched each other, breathless, from across the room.

Penny took off her sunglasses and set them on the kitchen table, licking her ice cream as she kicked off her shoes.

I kicked mine off too, my eyes on her.

She wasn't wearing a bra—her nipples were hard, the barbells of her piercing straining against the fabric of her T-shirt as my cock fought the confines of my shorts.

Her fingers trailed down her sternum, and my eyes locked on them as they hooked under the hem of her shirt. And then she pulled, dragging it up until it rested just above her breasts, exposing her tattooed torso to me. Large etched and watercolor flowers climbed up her ribs, stopping under the curves of her breasts, meeting between them in a point, like a corset, and the artwork above framed them with perfect symmetry.

She stuck out her tongue and put it to the scoop, spinning the cone to coat it, but she didn't swallow. She left her tongue out, dripping creamy ice cream down her chin as she took her cone and dragged the scoop between her breasts and down to her belly button.

I tossed my ice cream toward the sink without looking, thankful to hear the thunk as it hit its target. There was no way in hell anything was going to stop me from getting to her.

I rushed her, closing my mouth over hers, sucking the sticky sweetness from her tongue as she moaned. It had been too long without her, too long since *this*. Her arms wrapped around my neck, and I stood, lifting her off the ground, her body pressed against mine like I'd been dreaming of.

"Bedroom?" I panted.

She jerked her head toward a room behind her. "That way," she breathed.

"Don't you dare leave that ice cream."

She smiled and kissed me, wrapping her legs around my waist as I blindly carried her through the apartment, bumping into furniture along the way.

I lowered her onto the bed and moved down her body, sucking on her skin where she'd left a trail to the promised land, cupping her breast in my hand.

I missed you, I thought, saying nothing with words and everything with the long caress of my tongue on her body.

When I reached her shorts, I looked up while I unfastened them—she lay there, head propped up by pillows, watching me as she ate the fucking ice cream cone that might be the death of me.

I pulled off her shorts and threw them before gripping her naked hips, my thumbs stroking that soft skin in the crease of her thighs.

"Do you ever wear panties?" I asked.

"Never. Can't stand them."

I laughed and pulled my shirt off, tossing it, and then my shorts, tossing them too.

One of her brows rose. "Do you?"

I smirked as I climbed up to meet her, nestling between her legs. "Nope, I never wear panties either."

A little laugh passed her lips before I kissed her silent.

Her shirt was still hitched up to her collarbone, giving me all the room to touch her that I wanted, so I did, my lips against hers as I squeezed and cupped, thumbed and twisted until her hips were rocking under me.

Her arms were around my neck, the ice cream dripping down my back from the cone still in her hand, and after a minute, she broke away and smiled.

"Roll over."

I smiled back and did what she'd asked, stretching out in her bed, vulnerable, waiting for her to do what she wanted.

Our eyes were locked as she straddled me, though she didn't lower her hips—she hovered above me, and I looked over every inch of her body that I could see.

She was a work of art—pale, pale skin covered in ink, purple hair and piercings, winged black liner that made her look like a cat, full, pouty lips that parted like she wanted to taste the world, starting with me.

Penny ran that ice cream across her collarbone—I touched her thighs: I had to touch her—and down her breast to circle her nipple. Then around the curve of her breast—God, I was so rock hard it hurt—down her ribs, and then lower still, dragging it over the hood of her clit.

I wanted to move, wanted to lick every part of her until she came, but before I could, she took that ice cream and dragged it up the length of my cock.

I hissed, the pleasure of touch and the icy-cold shock a mixture of sensations I hadn't been ready for.

She brought the cone up to her smiling lips and bit off a chunk before hinging at the waist, angling for my cock. And without any more pretense, she wrapped her hand around my base, lifted me up, and slid me into her mouth, dropping down until I hit the back of her throat.

I drew a shuddering breath with one hand on her shoulder and the other cupping the back of her head as her hot tongue dragged a lump of freezing cold ice cream up my shaft and down. And then, she bobbed her head again, sliding back down.

My fingers tightened in her hair—I wanted to slam into her mouth until I came, but I closed my eyes, trying to breathe.

Closing my eyes made it worse.

Over and over again she took the length of me, humming and sighing through her nose, eyes closed, long lashes against her cheeks, purple hair in my hands, her body rolling and shifting like its only mission was to make me come.

My cock flexed in her mouth, and I squeezed her shoulder in warning.

She let me go and crawled up my body—apparently she didn't want me to come yet either.

I sat up to meet her halfway, and my hands holding her jaw, tilting her head so I could get deep into her mouth, wanting to take her. I twisted to guide her onto her back, and when I broke away, her mouth hung open like it didn't know I was gone.

I reached off the edge of the bed for my jeans and growled, "Take your shirt off, Penny."

She opened her eyes lazily, ice cream cone somehow still in her hand, and half-reached for the nightstand. "Condom," she murmured.

"I've got it. Now take your fucking shirt off." I ripped the packet open and slipped that fucker on so fast it was a blur of hands and motion before she was shirtless, the ice cream had disappeared, and I was between her legs again, resting at the tip of her heat for a moment as we stared at each other.

"Oh God. Do it," she begged.

I flexed with a moan, and her head lolled to the side. I pulled out and flexed again, slipping in even easier as my lips found trails of ice cream on her body and licked her clean. Then again my hips pumped, and I hit the end with a jolt that ran up her thigh, jerking her leg. I grabbed that leg and pushed it open wider, spreading my own legs to get low, and when I slammed into her, her breasts jostled.

She gasped, head kicking back into the bed.

"God, Penny," I huffed. "I could fuck you all day. All night."

"Yes," she breathed. "Do that thing—" Another gasp as I ground against her piercing. "Oh, fuck. Yes, please. That. Oh God. That."

I didn't stop the motion once I knew what she wanted, only pressed harder, moved faster until her brows drew together, her lips parting, and she came all around me like thunder.

That face, her face. I couldn't stop myself, no matter how bad I wanted to. Three pumps of my hips and I came with her hands in my hair and my name on her lips like a prayer.

When I pressed my forehead to hers, when she trailed the tip of her small nose up the bridge of mine, I caught a glimpse of just how deep the deep end was.

And I had no idea how to swim.

It took me all of about two minutes to come down from my orgasm with Bodie in my arms and the glorious weight of him pressing me into the bed before I freaked the fuck out.

I liked him.

I wasn't supposed to like him.

And now it had to end. All the fun. All the happy. All the Bodie. All that glorious D and laughing and excitement. Over. Poof. My three dates were up, and now my carriage was gonna turn into a pumpkin.

I had to walk away.

I didn't want to walk away.

Fuck.

My heart hammered, and I clawed my way through my thoughts. How could I tell him it was over? Did I even have to? Could I let him leave and just let the whole thing die?

I told myself I could. I also told myself I was a liar.

He propped himself up, holding my face in his hands as he smiled at me, and my insides trembled and fluttered in response. I was smiling back, betraying my freak-out so easily, I almost got whiplash. Or dicklash.

What is happening to me?

"I'm glad to see you, Penny," he said, his eyes on my lips.

"I can tell."

He kissed my nose and rolled away.

I sat up in bed and leaned against my pillows, pulling the covers over me as I watched him walk out of my room, stark naked. He turned the wrong way for the bathroom, and I forgot all about my anxiety, laughing when he passed the doorway again, pointing in the other direction.

God, I was in the deepest of shit. All the way up the creek of shit with no paddle.

Screwed.

Fucked.

And only partly in the literal sense.

I sat there, panicking over what to do. I should have been ready to tell him goodbye, but I wasn't. But I had to. It had to end.

Didn't it?

Maybe if he bugged out on me, everything would be easy. I would probably follow the old pattern, and I'd be turned off so fast, I could wave *sayonara* without question. There was still time—his dick was barely out of me, which was something I was really, really missing already.

But then again, maybe he won't bug out at all. Maybe he doesn't actually like you, a little voice in my head said.

I'd named the owner of that voice Peggy about eight years ago (thanks, Rodney!). My psychotic alter ego smoked Pall Malls and whispered around her cigarette, shuffling around me in her bathrobe with rollers in her hair, reminding me that I was a good lay and that was it. Because that was what I was good for—sex and tattoos. The good-time girl.

He's probably got another girl or two in his rotation, one who's less of a mess. Once he leaves, I doubt he'll ever speak to you again, she said, which was a point that should have given me a modicum of comfort but gave me absolutely none.

That sick feeling in my stomach was back. I fucking hated Peggy. She ashed on my soul and existed solely to make me miserable.

Peggy was why I wasn't allowed to have feelings.

I stole her imaginary cigarette and put it out, which shut her up long enough to light another one. It was the only thing that worked to keep her quiet—making sure she was stocked with beer and cigarettes and all the dick she could eat.

And when she was finally quiet, I wondered if *I* would be the one to bug out.

That thought sent my heart chugging so fast, it hurt.

He came back a second later with a cool, wet washcloth for me, which he handed over with a smile that panicked me even more.

Bodie made his way around the room, gathering his clothes—first his shorts, which I mourned as his ass disappeared into them, and then his shirt, another sorrowful moment of my day. And then he climbed back in bed with me, flopping down on his stomach at my side.

"I've got to get back to work."

"Okay," I said, waiting for him to profess his undying love or pledge to cherish me forever or admit that banging me was nice but he really thought we should call it.

But instead, he smirked. "Do me a favor and hit me up sooner rather than later next time, okay?"

I laughed, surprised and relieved and filled with traitorous hope. "That's it?"

His smile fell. "What do you mean?"

"I mean ..." I paused, not sure what to say. "You don't want ... *more?*"

His brow quirked. "You said no strings. This is what no strings looks like. Penny, you don't owe me anything."

I watched him, unsure if it was a trap. "You really mean that?"

He laughed at that. "Yeah, I really mean that." He crawled half into my lap, his arms on either side of my thighs as he looked up at me. "It doesn't have to be complicated. It doesn't have to be hard. It can be easy. And I'm around. Whenever."

As I sat there in my bed with the most beautiful man I'd ever known smiling up at me, I believed every word he'd said. I heard Veronica's voice in the back of my mind, telling me the three-date rule was stupid, and in that moment, it was.

Bodie had said it could be easy, and being with him was fun. Being with him made me happy. Being with him was like a balm to my blistering crazy.

But was that enough to throw my rule out the window and risk the consequences?

There were so many reasons to say yes, including:

1. That smile.

2. The warmth nestled in the middle of my ribcage.

3. That wonderful wang that had dicknotized me.

In fact, I'd been dicknotized so hard, that list was all it took to punt my rule into the end zone and do a victory dance. It was stupid and irresponsible and I didn't give a single shit. I wanted to be with him, and I foolishly believed I was safe and strong enough to know my limits.

So I answered him with a kiss full of relief and thanks and absolute pleasure.

When I broke away, he was smiling again.

"Hit me up, Penny."

"I will," I said.

And as he left, I reassured myself that I could have fun and keep seeing Bodie with no strings.

I couldn't even blame him for the fact that I was already falling for him, and I was so naive that I didn't even realize it.

chapter
eight

Easy Peasy

I HIT THE BED WITH A THUMP AND A BOUNCE, NAKED AND OUT OF BREATH AND grinning from ear to ear.

The bed jostled as Bodie flopped down next to me, smiling just as wide as I was, looking just as sated as I felt.

It had been four days of nothing but work and Bodie. Somehow I'd found myself at his place every night, plus once during my lunch break. Ramona had moved out, a tear-filled, horrible day that I ended in Bodie's bed. The void of her moving had been filled by Bodie and his smile and his jock and his big, muscly arms.

He was absolutely perfect.

There were no strings, not a single longing gaze, not one second where I felt the itch to ditch.

It was a goddamn miracle. I'd found the unicorn of men—a smart, snarky, magical sex creature who made me want to stay put for a minute—and I didn't think I'd been so happy in my whole life. I didn't feel crazy, and neither did he. It was easy, just like he'd said.

I hadn't laughed so much in ages. I hadn't felt so *good* in ages.

Bodie let me lead under the promise that I wouldn't wait too long between us seeing each other. As if I could stop. I was addicted. A-dick-ted.

I giggled stupidly to myself at the thought, and he somehow smiled wider, deepening his dimple.

We rolled to face each other at the same time, and I curled into his chest, his arms wrapping around me as our legs scissored.

"You sure are something else," I mused.

He chuckled, the sound rumbling through his chest and into me.

My smile falling as I thought about leaving. "Ugh. I wish I could stay for a while."

"Well, you can hang here as long as you want."

I frowned—in part because the thought of staying didn't bother me at all, which bothered me, and in part because I couldn't actually stay.

"I've got to head back to the shop to film an interview."

"I thought you weren't filming until the wedding?"

I snuggled deeper into his chest and smelled him shamelessly. "We aren't, but we have these interview things we have to do for a recap on what's been going on since the break. They're going to film a little for a montage at our dress fittings in a couple days."

"Is it weird being on TV?"

"Not really. I mean, every once in a while someone will know who I am, which is really strange. Like, they feel like they know you because they watch you on TV, and they know all this stuff about you, but you have zero context for who they are. Mostly I just smile and listen and take the occasional picture with them."

He laughed again. "You have fans."

"I do. So strange," I said with an echoing laugh. "Otherwise though, it's kind of fun. I like to show people what it's like in the shop, and our show is different from the other parlor reality shows—we don't focus too much on our personal lives. Sometimes it's unavoidable though. Like when Annika and Joel started banging on the sly. They had this huge blowup on film. Like, Joel ripped a camera out of a guy's hands and threw it across the shop."

He sucked in a breath through his teeth. "I saw that episode. I bet that wasn't cheap."

My mouth popped open. "You watched it?"

He nodded, smiling with his lips together. "I did. Is that weird?"

"Not at all. What'd you think?"

"Well, I binge-watched it in a day, so I guess you could say I liked it all right."

I chuckled as my cheeks warmed up.

"I liked seeing you work. And I liked your pink hair, too. But I think I like the purple better." He ran a strand through his fingers.

I sighed, smiling like a fool. But it was gone in a poof when I remembered I had to leave. "What time is it?"

He shifted to look, not letting me go. "Four thirty."

I groaned. "I've really got to go. I'm sorry."

He laughed, kissing my forehead before he let me go. "What are you sorry for?"

I peeled myself off the bed and moved around the room, putting on my clothes and gathering my things as I spoke. "Bailing so soon. I really do wish I could stay."

"Penny, you can come over for a quickie anytime you want."

He was propped up in bed, smiling back at me in a way that made me want to jump right back into bed with him.

In fact, once I was dressed—somehow in my mind, clothes could actually stop us from having sex again—I did climb back in bed to lie on my stomach next to him with a smile on my face and a secret in my hand.

"I got you something," I said mysteriously.

One of his brows rose with one corner of his lips. "Oh?"

I nodded and extended my hand, opening it to reveal a calculator watch.

He busted out laughing and took it, holding it up for inspection. "Where did you get this?"

"Chinatown. I was there buying hair dye and thought of you."

"I love it." He chuckled and leaned forward to kiss me. "What color hair dye did you get? Thinking about switching things up?"

"Oh, I think I'm happy where I'm at for now." I raised my feet into the air and crossed my ankles behind me. "I'm off tomorrow. Maybe we can see each other?" My eyes trailed over the tattoo on his arm and shoulder, which flickered as he put the watch on.

It capped his shoulder and ended mid-bicep, an octopus drawn to look like a Victorian-era etching, framed by swirling waves in the same style. He had a few other smaller pieces, but this one was my favorite.

"Yeah, I'll be around."

I touched his arm, tracing the artwork. "You got these done in LA, I'm guessing?"

"Venice Beach. Do you approve?"

"Mmhmm," I hummed, admiring it.

"Good. I'd hate to think I got ripped off."

I chuckled. "Does it mean anything in particular?"

He shifted to look at it. "I've always thought octopuses were interesting. They're the smartest creatures I've ever come in contact with. My dad caught one once and put it in our tank at home—he was always bringing home starfish and sea cucumbers and fish to add to the tank. I named him Stephen, and he was an escape artist. I'm pretty sure he was a whiz at game theory too."

I laughed, and he trailed a finger down my arm. "How about yours?"

"Mostly they have stories, but some are just pretty, like the flowers on my stomach. Ramona, Veronica, and I all have tiny tacos here." I pointed at the little line drawing of a taco about the size of a dime on the front of my shoulder. "Because what says friendship more than tacos?"

He let out a little laugh through his nose.

"This one is for my aunt." I ran my fingers over the two elephants that wound around my forearm, the smaller one holding the bigger one's tail. "She collected elephant things. After she died, I sketched this up, and Ronnie tattooed me. Now I can carry her around all the time. Elephants don't forget."

His smile fell. "I'm sorry, Pen."

"It's okay. Cancer fucking sucks," I said with a small smile, not wanting to get into it. "This one is self-explanatory." I held up my arm to expose the inside of my bicep where it said, *Oh yes I can.*

"What about this one?" He touched the Latin running down the back of my other arm.

"*Veni, vidi, amavi.* We came, we saw, we loved."

His smile was back, and it sent a slow burn through my chest—it was the smallest of things, a firing of a few muscles that shot a hint of understanding at me and hit me deep. So of course I changed the subject again.

"Thinking about getting more?" I asked.

"I actually had another one on the books, but then I lost my job and moved out here before I could get it done."

I perked up at that. "Really? What of?"

"A Japanese woodcut design of a wave, here." He gestured to his bicep and shoulder that wasn't inked.

"With the wave curling around your shoulder?"

He smirked. "Yeah."

"Still have the design?"

"I do. Why?"

"Because I can do it for you," I said, chipper and grinning. "Tomorrow. I'm off, remember?"

He laughed, and his cheeks flushed a little. "Yeah, but I can't ask you to do that for me, and not on your day off."

"You didn't ask. I want to." The thought of making my mark on his body sent a tingle through me I couldn't ignore. I silently did the math to see if I had time to jump him again before I had to go. I didn't.

He didn't look convinced, staring at me like I was a quantum physics equation.

"I mean it. And I want to see you tomorrow. Meet me at the shop, and we'll do your piece. Can I have it?"

"Are you sure, Penny?"

I shrugged. "Why not?"

He shook his head and swung his legs off the bed, making his way to his closet. I watched his butt like a creep without a single fuck to give. Then I watched his dick as he walked back.

What? It was a very pretty dick.

He handed the artwork over, his eyes twinkling.

"Thank you." I stood, stepping into him until I was pressed against his chest. "Let me know what time works for you tomorrow, and I'll be there."

I wrapped my arms around his neck, and his wound around my waist.

"I'll see you then." And with that little sentence, he kissed me like he was trying to make sure I never forgot him.

As if.

I was all warm and tingly again when he pulled away. He slapped my ass with a pop and stepped into Jersey pants before walking me to the door, leaving my body singing his name as it did every time we were together.

I felt like my feet were barely touching the ground as I walked the few blocks to the shop, daydreaming about Bodie's body and his smile and his dimple.

He was right; things didn't have to be complicated. I didn't have to answer to him, and Ididn't expect him to answer to me. Although I did find myself telling him where I'd be or what I'd be doing, and he seemed to do the same. It was just so *easy*, just the two of us.

Of course, we'd spent every minute we could together, though it didn't feel unreasonable. We'd never spent the night together, but we'd spent late nights and full afternoons all tangled up with each other. I knew the amazing noises he made, knew what he liked, what he wanted from my body. I knew his laugh and his smile, knew his hands, knew every inch of his body. I'd spent over a week exploring it, and what a glorious week it had been.

I was struck for a moment that I hadn't even considered being with anyone besides him since I met him. But the thought didn't freak me out—how could I want something other than absolute perfection? What could possibly lure me away?

I was struck again when it crossed my mind that he could be seeing someone else, so struck that I nearly tripped over my own feet and hit the sidewalk.

Surely he felt like I did. I mean, we hadn't discussed our relationship or defined anything. He'd said I didn't owe him anything, including exclusivity.

The thought made me irrationally angry, so irrationally angry that I fantasized about hunting down an imaginary bitch who had tried to touch him and scratching her eyes out.

I frowned as I crossed the street.

It had been a very long time since I was jealous, particularly of a made-up thieving man-stealer.

This confused me on levels I wasn't ready to admit existed.

So instead of admitting anything, I reminded myself that he had been with me daily. We'd had so much sex that there was no physical way he'd be able to have *more*.

At least I had that. The thought cheered me up.

I bounced into the coffee shop to grab goodies for everyone before heading to Tonic. I made the rounds once I got there, passing out everyone's usual drinks along with a few lemon bars—they were the best in the city, I swear—stopping at Joel's booth last. The Clash was playing over the speakers, and I smiled, thinking about kissing Bodie as a hundred people sang along with "Rock the Casbah" all around us.

Joel eyed me, smirking a little from behind his dark beard. "You okay?"

I smiled and leaned on the wall around his booth. "Peachy keen, jelly bean. I'm here for my interview with Annika."

His eyes sparked at the mention of her name. "She's upstairs in the control room getting everything ready."

"You excited to start filming again?"

He shrugged. "You know how I feel about all that. But I'm glad Annika has something to do. Without an objective, she comes unglued. I think she reorganized every book I own, color-coded my closet, and rearranged my sock drawer twice. And that was just in the first week."

I laughed. "Well, I'm glad she has a sweater to knit now, something to keep her busy."

"Me too."

"Hey, I wanted to run something by you. I was going to do some work on a friend of mine tomorrow, if it's okay. You don't need my booth, right?"

He shook his head. "You're good. Who's the friend?"

I couldn't even play it cool; I found myself grinning. "Bodie."

One of his brows rose. "The guy who was supposed to send you flowers but didn't?"

I waved a hand, dismissing him. "No, I didn't want him to send flowers, but if I get flowers, yes, I'd like them to be from him."

He narrowed his eyes in concentration. "It's like you're trying to tell me something."

I laughed. "Yes, that's the guy."

"Hmm," he hummed, watching me.

"What?"

He shrugged and rearranged things on his desk. "Nothing. It's just you've never brought a flowers-not-flowers guy around."

"It's no big deal. He was supposed to have work done in LA and moved here before he could. I'm not even drawing it."

He chuckled. "Yeah, I mean, that makes it completely impersonal."

I rolled my eyes. "Ugh, Joel. You're such a drama queen."

He laughed extra loud at that.

I pushed off the counter and winked at him. "I'll tell Annika you said hi."

"You do that."

The bell dinged as I left and turned into the door right next to the shop, climbing two flights to get to the control room. Joel and Annika's apartment was on the second floor, and the third was rented out by the network to set up as an on-site base of operations. The door was unlocked, and I walked through the monitor room, which was usually bustling with PAs and producers, but it was relatively empty since we hadn't really started rolling yet.

Annika was back in the green screen room, waiting for me with a cameraman. She slipped off her director's chair and glided over to me, smiling.

I swear to God, she was the most beautiful woman I'd ever seen. If Joel were a dark, grumbly bear, Annika was like a porcelain doll—all icy-blue eyes and ruby-red lips and long legs, her hair blonde and skin like milk.

"Penny," she said, cheerily—at least for her. She wasn't overly emotive.

"Hey, Annika," I answered. "Look at you, working that skirt."

I gestured to her black and white business clothes, which sounded nerdier than it was. Her clothes were immaculately cut, the lines clean and simple and modern and flattering. She looked straight off a runway.

She laughed. "I learned this summer that casual wear and free time don't suit me."

"I swear, I almost passed out when you came into the shop in leggings a couple of weeks ago."

"If a pipe hadn't burst, you'd never have seen it."

I chuckled and took my seat across from hers as a PA entered the room and miked me.

Annika sat and flipped through the sheets on her clipboard. "So, we're pretty basic today, just a little bit of catch-up. What have you been working on, how's the shop, how's life—that sort of stuff."

"Cool," I said, settling back into my seat as the camera started rolling.

Annika smiled. "All right, let's start easy. What's the weirdest tattoo you've done since we saw you last?"

"Well, weird's relative, right? Like, you'd think it was super crazy to get a tattoo of a gun, but I have two on my stomach, pointing down to my I-can't-say-that-on-network-television."

She laughed. "That's true. That's the whole point of a tattoo, right? That it means something to you. Lessons I learned from your boss."

"He's a smart dude. But to answer your question, I did a Care Bear tattoo on the back of a girl's calf that made me salute her bravery. Everybody has their thing," I said with a shrug.

"Okay, favorite piece you did?"

I thought about it and crossed my legs. "Damn, that's a hard one. But I did one on Veronica's arm that's two skeletons embracing, like one is clutching the other to its chest. I love being able to work with nothing but black ink, no color, just that ink and the negative space of skin to tell a story."

Annika was still smiling, her lips wide and red and perfect. "I love to hear you guys talk about your work. Sometimes I just listen to Joel geek out about art and tattoos with my head propped on my hand and my heart all fluttery." She sighed and glanced down at her clipboard. "So, what have you been up to this summer?"

"Nothing much. We've mostly been working on Ramona's wedding, but everything's been done for a few weeks, so now it's just a matter of waiting."

"What's left to come?"

I ticked everything off on my fingers. "Dress fittings tomorrow. Bachelorette party in a few days. Then it's time to get the lovebirds hitched."

"You make it sound so easy." She looked a little skeptical.

I chuckled. "Yep, and you're next. But you were built for wedding planning. I bet you have spreadsheets out the wang. Color-coded. With, like, fourteen tabs."

"At least I'm consistent enough to be predictable," she said on a laugh. "So tell me about the bachelorette party."

"Oh, that's not fit for censored television. Let's just say, there will be debauchery and plastic penis accoutrements."

She wrinkled her nose.

I pointed at her. "You're participating. No pussing out, dude."

Annika dodged the implication and smiled. "Have a date for the wedding?"

I waved a hand. "Nah, I'll just go stag."

Her smile fell. "You don't have anyone to bring? You always seem to have guys on your heel. Surely one of them looks good in a suit. Your taste in men is impeccable."

"Thank you," I said with a nod of my head, but I squirmed a little. "I dunno. Weddings are a big deal. Like, I'll have pictures from this wedding on my fridge until I've got tennis balls on the feet of my walker. Plus, there's love in the air at those things. I wouldn't want to catch something."

She laughed. "So you're not seeing anyone?"

I shrugged, still feeling squirmy. "I'm always seeing someone," I answered lightly.

"Who's the current guy?"

That stupid smile crept onto my face again. "Oh, just a guy," I lied, not wanting to talk about him on camera.

When things fell apart, I'd have to look back on any admissions without regrets. My stomach sank at the thought, but I put a lifejacket on that motherfucker, and it perked back up.

"Favorite thing about the guy?"

"His dick," I said without hesitation, knowing she'd have to cut the whole segment.

She burst out laughing, which was especially funny for her—she was a self-contained creature. But when she let loose, it was like a unicorn galloping across a rainbow.

"Well, I hope you change your mind about inviting Mr. Dick Guy to the wedding."

I laughed. "Oh my God. That's going to be my new name for him. Mr. Richard Guy."

"I'd love to meet the man who has you so into him that you won't kiss and tell." One of her brows was up, teasing me.

"Oh, come on. I don't always kiss and tell."

She gave me a look.

"Fine," I sighed, rolling my eyes. "I just want to keep this one to myself for a minute. Is that so wrong?"

"Not at all. I'm intrigued, that's all."

At that, I smiled. "You and me both."

nine

Operation: Penny Jar

THE NEXT AFTERNOON, I WALKED DOWN THE SIDEWALK TOWARD THE TATTOO parlor where Penny worked, the sun shining on my skin, the birds chirping in my ears, and the same smile plastered on my face that had been there for a week.

Operation: Penny Jar had been a success. So far at least.

I'd seen her every day since we ran into each other at the ice cream shop. She'd knocked me out then, and just when I'd thought it couldn't get better with her, she'd proven me wrong.

I was right after all; Penny didn't want complicated. So I didn't complicate things. It wasn't hard—being with her was so easy and so fun that there wasn't a need to talk about more. Every second with her was perfect to the point of disbelief. A crush realized. A fantasy in physical form.

I'd shown her that I meant what I'd said, even if my heart betrayed it all. Because the pretense hung in the air between us—the pretense she'd asked for and I'd agreed to.

For her, this was temporary.

For me, it wasn't.

Not that I was looking for a commitment. I wasn't. But I knew I didn't want it to end until we'd run our course. Thing was, I didn't know how long the tracks were, and I had a feeling mine were longer than hers.

My plan was still in place: be so fucking awesome that I became essential, necessary to her. Of course, in doing that, I'd also found that she was indispensable to me.

Catch-22.

In any event, I was taking advantage of every second with her. Including today.

She'd surprised me when she'd offered to do my tattoo—it felt like a *relationshippy* thing to do. Personal. Intimate. She was going to mark me with ink that would stain my skin for my whole life. Of course, she'd marked hundreds of people, maybe even thousands over her career.

It was as small and impersonal as it was huge and meaningful. But I locked my focus on the end of the spectrum labeled *Not a Big Deal* just as I approached the parlor.

The word *Tonic* was printed in a font that looked like an old Victorian apothecary label with gold leaf and line work above and below, framing the word. When I pulled open the door, the sounds of Nirvana hit my ears as the sights the shop had to offer washed over me.

Everything looked vintage with a Victorian flair. Old velvet couches lined the full waiting area, and the walls were covered in macabre paintings in elaborate frames. Booths lined the long wall, all with counter-high walls to mark each space. Each booth contained a retro black tattoo chair, an antique desk, and cabinets for inks and supplies, I assumed. The electric buzz of tattoo guns hummed in an undercurrent to Kurt Cobain as he sang about heart-shaped boxes, and I scanned the room, looking for the flash of purple that would tell me where Penny was.

She bounded out from a hallway leading to the back, smiling and practically skipping to me as everyone in the shop watched her—her coworkers curious, the people in the waiting room practically salivating.

I had no idea the protocol for such a public greeting, so I stood there smiling, waiting for her to make a move that would tell me where the boundary was.

The thought was moot. She practically jumped into my arms, hooking hers around my neck as she kissed me hello with enough gusto that I felt it all the way down to my shoes.

She broke away, smiling at me with twinkling eyes. "Hey," she said, the sweet scent of bubble gum on her breath.

"Hey," I echoed, setting her feet on the ground.

She grabbed my hand and pulled. "Come on, let me introduce you to everybody."

I already knew who everyone was from watching the show, which was really weird. So I played dumb, following her into the shop a bit, walking up the line of booths to start at the front where a gigantic dude with an intense beard and the thickest head of hair I'd ever seen was tattooing a girl's back. She was stretched out on her stomach, back bare, and he moved his machine, stopping the buzzing by removing his foot from the pedal.

"This," Penny said, extending a hand toward him, "is Joel, the owner of the shop."

Joel smiled, but his eyes sized me up. "Good to meet you."

"You too." I tried to smile in a way that was amiable but also as masculine as possible, feeling the alpha roll off of him. He was most definitely the boss.

"And this," she said, guiding me to the next booth back, "is Tricky. Patrick if he's in trouble."

Patrick stood and extended a tattooed hand for a shake. The guy looked like a male model with a sharp jaw and deep, dark eyes, every inch of his skin tattooed, except for his face.

"Hey, man," he said with a sideways smile. "Heard a lot about you."

I took his hand and pumped it. "Thanks," I said lamely, wishing I had something to offer other than, *Cool tattoos, bro.*

Next down was a dark-haired, leggy brunette with lined eyes and red lips.

"So, you didn't officially meet the other night, but this is one of my roommates, Veronica."

Veronica smiled and waved. "Glad to finally meet you, Bodie."

"And this," she said as she dragged me across the room to the counter where a blonde stood, smiling, "is Ramona, my best friend and our piercer."

"Need your dick pierced?" she asked brazenly.

I couldn't help but laugh. "I'm good today, but thanks."

She shrugged. "Let me know if you change your mind. I've heard good things." She looked down and jerked a chin toward my waistline.

The girls cracked up laughing, and I shook my head, not even embarrassed. I took the fact that they had talked about my dick as a good sign.

A couple of guys were laughing in the booth behind Veronica's, which was our next stop.

"These knuckleheads are Eli and Max."

"Hey," they said at the same time. One punched the other in the arm.

I waved a hand, and she pulled me back to her booth.

It was very Penny. The artwork on her walls was everything from comic-style to detailed portraits. The largest heavy-framed painting was of a woman with a starburst crown, holding a flaming heart in one hand and a rosary in the other. And in the center of the smaller pieces on her wall was a gilded mirror, speckled and veined with age.

She smirked at me and patted the seat of her tattoo chair. "Come on. I don't bite."

"That's a lie, and I have the marks to prove it."

She giggled, her cheeks high and flushed and pretty.

I took a seat, and she moved to her desk to get the transfer she'd printed. "Shirt off, please."

I waited until she turned around to face me before reaching back between my shoulder blades and grabbing a handful of T-shirt, pulling it over my head.

Her lip was between her teeth. She was wearing the same high-waisted shorts she'd had on that first night with the buttons on the front with a T-shirt that said, *Feed Me Tacos and Tell Me I'm Pretty,* in red iron-on letters that matched her lipstick. But the best part was that she had on tall black wedges, her legs long and knees together, toes pointed in. She looked like a goddamn calendar girl, and the way she was eye-fucking me had me wishing the booth had four walls and a door.

She blinked and walked over, hips swaying, lips smiling. "Is this too big?" she asked, holding up the transfer.

I opened my legs a little wider. "No such thing."

Penny laughed at that and held it over my arm, inspecting it. "I *do* like it when it's extra big."

She stood at the arm of the chair, and I slid my hand up the outside of her thigh.

"Oh, I know all about that."

She was unfazed other than shifting to lean into me as best she could with an armrest in the way. "I think it'll work. Let me put it on, and we can look at it."

She went to work, arranging the transfer before wetting it down with a paper towel. When she smiled down at me, a little jolt shot through me.

"You ready for this?"

"Always," I answered.

She peeled the transfer off and blotted my skin dry, inspecting it all the while. It was like she had flipped a switch and was all business and then flipped it again, all pleasure.

"Okay. Take a look."

I stood and checked out the placement. It started just above my elbow and moved up and around my bicep and the cap of my shoulder—it was bigger than I'd imagined but exactly what it should be.

"I like it," I said.

"Good. Me too." She nodded to her chair. "Go ahead and have a seat."

Her station seemed to already be set up, and she took a seat on a saddle stool with wheels, straddling it before rolling over to me, pulling on black rubber gloves.

Several reactions hit me. The sight of her rolling over to me with her legs open, snapping those rubber gloves, hit me below the belt. The realization that she was about to take a needle to me sent adrenaline shooting through my veins in a cold burst. And the look in her eyes got me right in the rib cage.

"All right," she said as she poured black ink into a little cup. "So here's the deal. This is way too big to do all at once if you want color. But I kinda think it'll look better all black, just the outline. We've got to do that first anyway, so if you want to have it filled in later, you totally can."

"How long until I can have more done?"

"A couple of months is usually wise." She loaded her gun, wrapping a rubber band around the base of it. When she hit the pedal to test it, she smiled. "But anybody can do it. The line work is the hard part. You don't have to come back to me to get it filled in."

My heart deflated just a bit, just enough. Penny was putting space between us, telling me we wouldn't be together in a few months, giving me permission to have it finished somewhere else.

She rolled her tray where she wanted it, scooting close to me with her eyes on my arm.

"Here we go." She pressed that buzzing needle into my skin.

The thing about tattoos is that when it starts, you think it's not so bad. Four hours in, and you feel like you've been carved like a turkey. So I enjoyed the burn before it consumed me.

Hearts worked the same way, I figured.

"You okay?" she asked after a moment, her eyes darting to mine for a solid second before looking back to my arm.

"I'm good."

I watched her work, admiring the sureness of her hand, competence radiating from her. She was confident, so certain, completely capable. Penny could take over the world if she wanted to. She could take me over.

She kind of already had.

I looked over the shop and realized I'd met all the important people in her life—her family. I was in her chair as a customer, but it was more than that. There was an intimacy to the act and intimacy to her bringing me to the place that meant so much to her. Not that she'd made a big deal about it, but I knew by how she talked about everyone I'd met that they were her *people*. And that filled me with hope and pleasure at the connection to her.

Of course, that connection scared me too. Because I knew deep down that I didn't have as much control as I'd thought I did over the situation. Every single day, she'd marked me in more ways than one, and I couldn't turn back any more from my heart than I could from the needle in her hand.

"So, Bodie," Ramona started from the wall of Penny's booth.

When I glanced over, she was leaning on the wall from the other side, next to Veronica. They were both smiling unabashedly, their eyes never quite reaching mine—they were too busy scanning my chest.

"What is it you do again?" Ramona asked.

"I'm a software engineer. My buddies and I are working on a video game."

They nodded their appreciation.

"What kind of game?" Veronica leaned in, shoulder to shoulder with Ramona.

"It's an open world role-playing game. Steampunk, story-driven."

Their faces were blank.

"Ah, like … think Victorian era, airships, like blimps. Treasure hunting, like Indiana Jones meets Han Solo but British."

They lit up at that, including Penny, and I found myself feeling pleased.

"What's it called?" Ramona asked.

"Nighthawk. It's the name of the ship."

Penny bounced a little in her seat. "Oh my God, that makes me want to draw stuff. This is seriously genius, Bodie. Who's doing your artwork?"

"Jude. He's a graphic artist and handles all of our 3D renderings. Phil and I are the code jockeys. Jude is the art."

Penny waggled her brows at Veronica, who rolled her eyes.

"So how does that work?" Ramona asked. "Like, what do you do with it when it's done?"

I took a breath and let it out as Penny carved a line in my skin and wiped it with a paper towel. "The first real step is to get a gameplay demo ready so we can pitch it to a big developer. The idea is that they pay us for the concept and bring us on as part of the development team. But we've been working on the demo for seven years," I said with a laugh.

"Man, that's intense," Penny said as she dipped her needle in the ink and got back to work.

"It's moving a lot faster now that we've been working on it full-time, but yeah. It's been a long time coming. I mean, we came up with the idea in junior high and have been working toward this ever since. Phil's focused on our outreach, networking through college and career buddies to see if we can get a meeting. There's this one development company that's at the top of the list. If we can get in with them, it's a guarantee that the game would be everything we could possibly dream of. They've got the chops and the cash to throw at it."

"What's the company called?" Veronica asked.

"Avalanche," I said, unable to keep the excitement out of my voice. "The games they produce are off the charts. But that's the pie-in-the-sky kind of dream. We'll probably get it picked up by a smaller company—I just hope they'll let us do the work to make it what we want."

Another gigantic hairy dude walked out of the hallway and into the shop, eyeing me in the chair, then he smirked at Ramona. He slapped her on the ass, and she yelped, laughing when she saw him.

"Hey, Shep," Penny chirped. "This is Bodie. Bodie, this is Shep, Ramona's fiancé and Joel's brother."

I jerked a chin at him in greeting. "How's it going?"

"Not too bad," Shep said, every word loaded, "other than the fact that my future wife is salivating over Penny's guy."

Everyone laughed but me. I was a hundred and ten percent sure that he could wreck my face without breaking a sweat.

"Come on, girls," Shep said. "Leave Penny alone so she can do her job without an audience."

They grumbled about it, but he effectively shooed them off, leaving Penny and me as alone as we could be in a tattoo parlor full of people.

Penny was engrossed in her work, and I watched her, smirking.

God, she was so beautiful, so talented, so strong and wild and free. A force of nature. I couldn't imagine ever changing her, couldn't imagine ever taking what made her *her* away. To lose those qualities would be tragic, a loss to everyone who knew and loved her. The thought that Rodney had tried to pin her down all those years ago, that he hadn't been happy until he'd stripped it all away, made me hate him all the more.

"Something about you with that gun in your hand is almost too much for me, Penny."

Her eyes caught mine and moved back to her work, though she was smiling. "You shirtless in my chair is almost too much for me, Bodie."

I chuckled. "Tell me you're free tonight."

Her smile fell at that. "I wish I were. I promised Ronnie and Ramona that we'd go out. You know, since last time we tried to go out, I bailed on them."

"Worth it."

She laughed. "So worth it." She shot up in her seat, eyes wide and smile big. "Oh my God, I have an idea. We should all go out together. Like, you should come with us and bring your brother. Make a group thing out of it. I want to hook Veronica up with Jude—she needs to get laid so bad. And then Ramona can bring Shep, and maybe Joel and Annika can come too."

"I doubt Veronica has trouble with that on her own."

"You'd be surprised."

"Well, I'm sure Jude would be down to help out," I joked.

She lit up like a floodlight, her red lips smiling wide. "It's perfect. This way I can see you, and Veronica can get the grump nailed out of her. Everybody wins."

I shook my head, smiling at her. "Schemer."

She shrugged and got back to work. "I get what I want."

"I'm sure you do."

As she worked, I considered the fact that she'd just asked me on a date. A group date, sure, but we would be going out with her friends, the important people in her life. In public. Not just getting together to hook up. No, we'd be hanging out all night, and *then* we'd hook up.

If that wasn't a date, I didn't know what was.

As she traced the lines of the ocean on my skin, I wondered if she realized it. I wondered if she knew. Or maybe things were just the same for her as they ever were. Maybe this was all just for fun, all for the thrill.

But I told myself not to overthink it. Because if I did, I might lose the glimmer of shine I'd found on Penny.

My eyes scanned the thick crowd at Circus, looking for Bodie. We stood clustered next to a gigantic painting of Siamese twins in an ornate gilded frame. Ramona and Shep laughed with Joel and Annika, leaving Veronica and me on the edge of the circle, a little isolated. I considered canoodling with her, but she seemed as edgy as I was. Setups weren't her thing. Waiting wasn't mine.

Not that Veronica wasn't great company, but after having my hands on a half-naked Bodie all day and not doing anything about it, I was anxious to see him. And by anxious, I meant I felt like my insides were trying to get outside.

I should have gone home with him like he'd asked me to after his tattoo. But I wanted to see him tonight even more than just the afternoon, and I was afraid to overdo it with both. In hindsight, I should have just committed. God knew I couldn't get my fill of him, so it wasn't like I had to save myself.

I laughed to myself at the thought. The most he'd gotten out of me in a day was six orgasms. *Six.* The last one had taken him a full hour, but Christ almighty, was it a ringer.

My phone buzzed in my hand, since I was holding it like a needy girl in preparation of him getting there, and when I saw it was him, I fired off a response, navigating him to us.

I caught sight of him and hopped over, my heart doing all the warm and squeezy things in my chest. I slipped my hand into his much larger one and popped up onto my toes to kiss him for a brief, fluttering second.

"Come on!" I yelled over the music. "This way."

I led him, Jude, Phil, and Angie over to the group, standing between the tightrope walker in pasties with a sparkly thong and a platform for two hoop dancers who might have been naked—they were covered in body paint and glitter and sparkles.

Veronica perked up as we approached, and I smirked.

I doled out introductions where necessary, saving Veronica for last.

"Jude," I said, grabbing him by the arm and pushing him toward her with my free hand, "this is my friend Veronica."

She smiled. He smiled.

"I dunno. I'd say you were more of a Betty." One of his brows rose salaciously.

Her smile flattened faster than you could say *douchebag*. So did mine—that look meant he didn't have a chance in hell.

"Hey, Jude. Don't make it bad," Veronica snarked, throwing the *Never heard that before* back at him.

A girl in a top hat and red tails mercifully interrupted the awkwardness to take drink orders before disappearing into the ocean of people, and I leaned into Bodie, smelling him like a weirdo. I couldn't help it. The smell of his soap and whatever other products he used made me think of my face buried in his neck or his pillows or his chest. Other places too, places where I'd like to be buried in at that moment.

He wrapped his arm around me and pulled me closer, pressing a kiss to the top of my head.

"How's your arm?" I asked, sliding my hand around his middle.

"Still works," he answered with a flex.

I giggled like a dum-dum and leaned away, though I kept my arm around his waist, my fingers fiddling with the top of his pants.

"Thanks again for today," he said. "I wish you'd let me pay you."

"I'll tell you what—you can pay me back later."

He angled toward me, pressing his lips against my ear. "Oh, I plan to," he whispered straight to my vagina.

A shiver rolled down my back. "Can't we just leave now?"

"We could, but I'd rather tease you for the next couple of hours first."

I laughed as his hand slipped down to my ass and gave it a squeeze. "Ugh, I hate waiting."

"I know. That's why I love to make you wait."

Within a few minutes, everyone had moved around and mixed up, talking with each other, and I smiled to myself as I floated from group to group, happy that the odd collection of friends jelled. Joel and Phil were deep in a conversation about sci-fi that I understood zero of. Angie, who was the sweetest little bookish thing with big brown eyes and a giggle that instinctively made everyone in her radius giggle with her, had been talking with Ramona and Veronica about baking. Shep and Jude laughed together, swapping stories with Bodie, who smiled at me when I walked up.

Everything felt so *good*. All of us hanging out and talking and laughing. Bodie hanging his arm on my shoulder and kissing my temple and touching my hand, reminding me over and over again how much I enjoyed being around him. *He* made me feel good, and I wanted to make him feel good too.

The group shuffled around a few times, and a little while later, I found myself watching them all from the outside with Ramona, who bumped my arm.

"Have I told you that you've ruined my life?"

I frowned. "What? Why?"

"I went to the grocery store yesterday, and I couldn't stop thinking about the little old checkout lady's nipples when I noticed how pale her lips were."

I burst out laughing. Ramona looked pleased.

"Bodie's great, Pen."

I smiled. "He is, isn't he?"

She nodded, smirking. "I never thought I'd live to see you on a real date."

I frowned. "This isn't a date. This is a preamble to naked cartwheels and an attempt to get Ronnie laid."

That earned a laugh. "First, this is totally a date. And you guys have been all over each other in the cutest way."

My frowned deepened. "Yeah, because we're hot for each other."

"Oh my God, Penny. It's a date. Open your eyes."

I blinked, watching Bodie from across the room. "I mean, I guess *technically* it is, but that's not what we're doing. I'm not his *girlfriend*." I said it like it was a filthy word.

Ramona laughed, shaking her head at me. "You know that being a girlfriend doesn't mean you're chained up in somebody's basement, right?"

"If you say so." I took a sip of my tequila.

She let it go, thankfully. I was starting to feel itchy.

Ramona nodded to the group. "So Jude and Veronica went over about as well as lead frisbee."

I sighed. "Man, I'm so disappointed. They had to go and open their mouths and ruin my plans."

She chuckled. "They didn't even make it two sentences into a conversation. But look at them eyeballing each other."

"I think they're trying to explode each other."

They really were—the two of them were staring across the room with narrowed eyes, and I wondered what else had been said. It must have been seriously infuriating, and I wished I'd heard every word.

"Well," Ramona started, "even if the Ronnie trap failed, the Bodie trap is still fully in place and ready to blow."

I snickered. "Yeah, it is."

She smiled at me. "I'm happy for you, Penny. I really like him."

I sighed wistfully. "He's perfect for me right now. I had no idea that guys like him existed in the dating wild."

She opened her mouth like she had something to say but stopped herself, smiling instead. "Speak of the devil."

When I followed her eyeline, I found Bodie walking over, his eyes on mine in a way that made my knees go weak, though there was nothing lewd or suggestive about it. It was just *pervasive*, slipping into me, through me, spreading all over me in a way that set me on fire.

"Hey," he said with a smile.

"Hi." I smiled back like the fool that I was.

Ramona touched my arm. "I'm gonna go make sure Shep's not telling any stories he shouldn't. You know how chatty he gets."

I laughed. "Oh, man. Hopefully not the dick sock story again."

"Oh, he's well past that. We're into koala bear territory."

I waved her away. "Go. Run."

And with that, she headed back to the group, leaving me and Bodie alone.

"Having fun?" I asked.

"I am. I like your friends."

"I like yours too."

"Too bad about Veronica and Jude though."

I pouted. "I know. We were just talking about that. Honestly, I've met your brother, and I can't believe I thought it was a good idea. Pretty much the only thing they have in common is that they're single."

"Not true. They're both artists, and they have smart-ass mouths."

I laughed and stepped into him, resting my hand on his chest. "So, I was thinking about you surfing the other day."

"Oh, were you?" He pulled me closer.

"Mmhmm. And I was thinking about what a badass you are."

He laughed. "Said the badass."

"When you guys go, can I come with?"

One of his brows rose. "Any chance I might get you on a board? Because that would fulfill so many fantasies."

I drew a little circle on his chest with the pad of my finger. "Only if you promise to surf shirtless. I think it might be worth getting eaten by a shark to see that once before I die."

When he chuckled and kissed me, I thought I might melt right there in his arms.

"Have we waited long enough?" I asked when he broke the kiss like a tyrant.

"That was the question I came over here to ask. Are you ready to go?"

My heart thumped, and my lips smiled. "Only since you got here."

We said our goodbyes and headed out, hand in hand, then with our arms around each other as we walked to his apartment.

I thought about what Ramona had said, thought about Bodie and how easy it was to be with him. Even having been with him all night, he was never needy, always independent. In fact, I had been the needy one, seeking him out to touch him, kiss him.

I had no idea what had gotten into me, but when I actually thought about it, it freaked me out.

Were we dating? Was I his *girlfriend*? I couldn't even say the word in my head without my insides shriveling up.

But when I thought about how I felt about Bodie, those shriveled up insides bloomed and filled up again. He'd told me it could be easy, and now … well, now I was on a date with him, one I'd set up without even realizing I was doing it.

If that wasn't going with the flow, I couldn't imagine what was.

He hadn't put any demands on me, hadn't pushed the boundaries of what I was comfortable with. He hadn't done anything but let me breathe, let me be, and somehow that was exactly what I needed. And he knew it.

We'd been on a date, and I hadn't felt trapped or uncomfortable or cagey at all. I felt good. I felt happy.

So I took that as a sign that I was on the right track. And if we could keep on being easy, then I could stay put—for a little while at least. Ride the wave. Enjoy the scenery. Get high off of Bodie.

I did my best not to think about what would happen when I came down.

chapter
ten
Steak at Stake

THE NEXT AFTERNOON, I TOOK A SIP OF MY CHAMPAGNE, FACING THE MIRRORS in the bridal shop, but I turned as Ramona came out from the dressing room, cheeks pink and eyes shining.

She looked stunning and stunned and absolutely gorgeous.

She was a rustling of lace and silk chiffon as she spanned the room and stepped up onto the platform, pressing her palm to her stomach.

The dress itself was simple and beautiful with beadwork that looked Edwardian—structured and flowing all at once in draping designs. Her waist was waspish from the corset underneath the soft fabric, and the sweeping neckline cut the slightest V between her breasts, framing her chest and neck tattoos like they had been made for each other.

"It's happening. This is it," she whispered with a shaky breath. "I … for a long time, I didn't think it would. He never asked, you know? He couldn't leave Joel, but Joel finding Annika changed everything. I should buy that woman an island."

Veronica and I laughed and moved to her side, turning to look at our trio in the wide-angled mirrors. But Ramona was looking down at us, smiling and crying.

"Thank you. Both of you. I couldn't do this without you, and I wouldn't want anyone else to share this with me the way you two have."

Tears filled my eyes too, and Veronica and I stepped up onto the platform to hug. The three of us hung onto each other for a long moment.

When we turned back to the mirror, I looked us over. "Damn, we look good."

We laughed. It was our final fitting, and everything was perfect. Our bridesmaid dresses were dove-gray chiffon, soft and flowing and long, each a little different. Mine tied around the waist with a deep V and flowing skirt that made me feel like a goddess. Veronica's was strapless, the top corseted and the skirt the same as mine.

I reached for the small table next to the platform where Ramona's champagne stood, bubbling and waiting for her, raising my glass as I placed hers in her hand.

"To your next beginning," I said simply.

And we touched our champagne flutes together with the sweetest of tings before taking a sip.

I'd barely noticed the camera crew until they began to pack up. One of the cameramen nodded to me with a smile as they disappeared.

Another thing to thank Annika for—she'd made sure we were bothered as little as possible. In fact, I bet she'd cut the emotional stuff altogether. After having her own personal life thrown all over network television last season, she'd made it her mission to preserve the privacy of our lives as much as she could.

The shop girls materialized to inspect Ramona's dress, and Veronica and I moved out of the way so they could work, still sipping our champagne. I felt a little bubbly in the head—I was on my third glass.

Ramona eyed me. "So, I hate to ask this."

"Uh-oh." My mood was instantly not so bubbly.

"Well, I put you down for a plus-one for the wedding, so I need to know if you're bringing someone."

I squirmed.

"I paid for an extra steak, Pen."

Veronica rolled her eyes lovingly, if that's a thing. "Just ask Bodie. You're seeing him. And I bet he looks good in a suit. I mean, unless he's a vegetarian because then what will Ramona do with his steak?"

I snorted. "Ugh, I don't know, guys."

Ramona and Veronica shared a look.

"She doesn't think last night was a date," Ramona said like I wasn't in the room.

"Ah," Veronica said back, equally traitorous.

"Listen, I realize it was a date."

Ramona perked up and cupped her ear. "What's that? You said I was right?"

I rolled my eyes. "Yes, you were right. He's just … I don't know. Easy. He's like a heart ninja." I made a karate chop with my hand.

"So why don't you ask him to the wedding?" Veronica asked.

"Hey, you don't have a date either."

Veronica's lips flattened. "We're not talking about me."

"You could always ask Jude," I offered.

She balked at that. "I wouldn't want to slit any throats at my best friend's wedding. There will be steak knives there."

I laughed. "Oh, come on. He's not that bad."

"He's the douchiest douche to ever douche, Pen. He is so into himself, and his jokes are fucking terrible. It doesn't even matter that he's hot and muscly."

"What? That's basically all that matters," I said. "Just tell him not to talk when he goes down on you, and you guys will be fine."

Ramona cackled and took a sip of champagne.

"I don't want to sleep with somebody I don't like," Veronica stated plainly as if I couldn't get her drift.

I shrugged. "Beggars can't be choosers, Ronnie."

She wrinkled her nose at me. "Anyway, we're not talking about me. We're talking about you. Just ask Bodie."

I wrinkled my nose back at her. "That's so much pressure. I mean, I can barely admit that we went on one pseudodate and you want me to ask him to a *wedding*? I don't even know if we could have dinner alone without me climbing out the bathroom window."

Ramona considered that. "I mean, a wedding is almost safer. You don't even have to be alone. He already knows Joel, Shep, and Annika. And us. It'll be fun, just like last night."

My face was still all pinched up.

Veronica smiled and cocked an eyebrow. "Just think of the after-wedding sex. You'll both be all dressed up. So many clothes to take off."

I bobbed my head in consideration. "Okay, now you're speaking my language."

"There will be dancing and drinking and eating," she added. "Bodie in a suit—just think about that. Those broad shoulders, his thick neck in that tie. Maybe he'll tie you up with it after."

I bit my bottom lip, imagining it. "Mmm," I hummed.

"It won't be a big deal," Veronica said.

And like the dumbass I was, I believed her.

"Okay, I'll do it."

They cheered, and we giggled and jumped up and down, careful of our champagne, which was what I blamed the giggle-bouncing on.

"Text him!" Ramona begged.

I rolled my eyes. "I'm not texting him to ask him to a wedding. I'll ask him tonight."

"What's tonight?" Veronica asked before taking a sip of her drink.

"Nothing, yet." I turned to the velvet chair where we'd set our purses and dug through mine for my phone.

"Did you see that lingerie shop across the street?" Ramona dropped the question like she was sneaky or something.

"Of course I did. Why? Think I should get a little something?"

She shrugged. "Couldn't hurt."

I champagne-giggled some more and texted Bodie.

Busy tonight? I've got a little surprise for you.

He started typing before I even set my phone down, and I tried to pretend like that didn't make my heart skydive in my chest.

I'm free, and I've got news about the video game. Want to celebrate?

I shot off an answer as quick as I could. *Yes, please. My apartment okay? We'll have the place to ourselves.*

I'll be there. Text me when you're home.

I will. <3

I grinned. "He's in. Or he's not in yet, but he's about to be *so* in. All the way in."

Veronica laughed. "Yeah, yeah. We get it."

And just like that, I'd talked myself into asking Bodie to a wedding.

Heart ninja. I was helpless to fight him. He was just too sneaky.

I bolted out the door the second I got the text that Penny was home, barely waving goodbye to my brother and Phil. Her name cycled through my brain with every footfall.

I had news—big news—and there was only one person in the world I found myself wanting to tell.

Penny.

I should have been scared out of my mind at the fact that she'd already become the person I told everything, especially since we'd been dancing around what we meant to each other for two weeks. But I wasn't. I was too happy to be afraid, which was so beyond stupid that I thought I might have made it back around to smart again.

My heart banged from taking her stairs two at a time. Seconds after knocking, the door swung open, and there she was.

Just when I thought my heart couldn't beat any harder, it proved me wrong.

She stood there in the doorway in nothing but lingerie.

No, I couldn't even call it lingerie. It was like an elaborate necklace; from the collar hung dozens of silver chains that flowed around her naked breasts and torso, swaying with every breath, connected to a ring a few inches below her belly button. More chains hung down from there, draping over the perfect curve of her hips and upper thighs, and from the center of the ring was a chain tassel that brushed against her piercing.

Something about the swing and shine of it, the peekaboo of the tattoos covering her milky-white skin, the way the chains moved on either side of her breasts, her nipples pink and taut, framed by barbells—all of it overloaded my senses, and I found myself standing stupidly in the hallway, staring in wonder.

She laughed and reached out just enough to grab my shirt to pull me into the apartment, closing the door behind me.

I palmed her breast as she stepped into me, and I finally got a good look at the rest of her. Her hair was a brighter purple than it had been yesterday, and her lips were blood red and smiling at me. She wore a headband of some sort, but it ran across her forehead with hundreds of tiny chains hanging down, shielding her eyes just enough to drive me crazy.

"You like it?" she asked as she wrapped her arms around my neck.

All I could do was nod and kiss her.

God, she felt so good pressed up against me, her bare ass in my hands, her tongue against mine as I tasted her like it was the first time.

She broke away and smiled, taking my hand before turning for her bedroom.

The back of the contraption she had on was almost bare with another ring just over her ass where another little tassel swung with the sway of her hips, and more draping chains followed the curve of her backside.

"Where the fuck did you get this thing?" I breathed in appreciation.

She shot me a smile over her shoulder. "The store."

I shook my head as we stepped into her room. "I need to check out the stores where you shop."

She laughed at that and closed the door. The lights were low, just a few small lamps to bathe the room in a golden light, and her portable speaker played a slow, sexy sort of electronic music. Her hips moved to the beat just a little, sending the chains swinging and my cock straining.

I pulled off my shirt and dropped it by the door, kicking off my shoes as she closed her eyes, her body moving in a wave to the music like I wasn't in the room. I took the hint, dropping my pants and stepping out of them before moving in her direction.

She didn't want me to stop her—she would have looked at me if she had—so I climbed onto her bed and sat propped up against the pillows, watching her.

With every roll of her hips, my pulse ticked faster, and my eyes drank her in—her hair, her shrouded eyes, the light catching the metal hanging on her. Her lily-white hands moved down her body and across her breasts, her fingers grazing her nipples.

I gripped my cock—it was so hard it hurt—stroking myself to ease the ache, wishing it were her around me, but I wouldn't have stopped her if you'd paid me.

She spun around, sending the chains arching around her, her hips still shifting, her torso rolling, just like it did when she rode me. Her lips parted as she looked down, her neck and shoulders rocking opposite her hips, and when her hands moved down her body and between her legs, when her long white finger disappeared into herself, my cock throbbed in my fist.

I moaned a curse, and she looked up at me, slivers of her eyes burning hot through the curtain of chains, and I couldn't take it anymore. I moved to the end of the bed, rising up onto my knees to tower over her, slipping my hand into her silvery-purple hair so I could kiss her. Her mouth opened up, and her tongue slid past my lips as mine did the same, teasing each other. My hands were in her hair, our mouths open wide, our breath coming heavy, our bodies determined to find release, so determined that we were barely in control.

But I was never really in control. Not when it came to Penny.

She took my cock with both hands and pumped, and I groaned into her mouth, which did nothing but spur her on.

My control slipped even further away. I flexed into her fists, fucking her hands with my cock, fucking her mouth with my tongue. But it wasn't enough. I wanted more, and I always would. Anytime I said different, I was a fucking liar.

When I broke away, I sat on the end of the bed, setting my feet on the ground. I looked up at her, mesmerized by the shadows across her face as she looked down at me, her hands cupping my jaw.

She started dancing again.

Penny let me go and turned around—her ass was just under eye-level with that tassel swinging over places where I wanted my face. But before I could grab her and do just that, she rolled her hips in a figure eight and lowered her body until her ass was cradling my cock.

Up and down she went, stroking me with her body. My hands were on her hips, squeezing, but she didn't need me to guide her. She looked back over her shoulder and raised her hips, stopping when the tip of me rested against the center of her. And I wouldn't wait any longer, wouldn't be teased for another second—with a flex of my hips and a shift of my hands, I pulled her down onto me until I was so deep inside her, I never wanted to leave.

She sighed my name as I gently pushed her away by the hips to lift her, then pulled her down again, grinding against her every time I hit the end.

"Lie back," she breathed.

And I did with an aching chest and a racing pulse and the length of me buried in her.

Without separating us, she rolled her hips a few times, her hands on my knees, and I watched my cock disappear and reappear in the heat of her from the best possible angle, every part of her exposed and open and full of me.

She climbed backward onto the bed in a feat of skill, first one knee coming to rest outside of my matching thigh and then the other, leaving her straddling me with her feet tucked into my ribs and her ass in my hands.

Her body moved, needing no help from me as she rose and fell, and I was so focused on every inch of her that a nuclear bomb could have detonated and I'd never know—I'd have died a happy man. I cupped her ass low, so low that my thumbs grazed my cock with every up and down of her body until they were slick from her. And then I spread her open and ran my thumb around the rim of her tight ass. It clenched under my touch as I circled, and she sucked in a breath.

"Do it," she said, voice rough as she dropped down.

I smiled and pressed.

The warmth of her, the tightness of her around me in more than one place was almost too much. It was too much for her, her body working faster. Every moan and sigh out of her said she was close. And she wasn't alone.

One of her hands slid between my thighs, cupping my aching balls, and my eyes rolled back when her fingertips against the space just behind them.

My hand squeezed involuntarily, pressing my thumb deeper inside of her, and she gasped. The sound sent a shock through me, and my cock pulsed inside her.

"Fuck, Penny," I growled.

Her body moved faster, harder, her skin smacking against mine with every motion. "Say my name again," she breathed.

"Come on, Penny," I said, the words gruff and hard. My abs burned as I watched the lips of her pussy swallow me. "Come for me, Penny."

"Oh God. Fuck," she cried, her voice breaking as her body clenched around me like it wanted to keep me still.

But I knew better.

I sucked in a breath through my nose, pounding into her as I pulled her down onto me with a slap and a jolt. And when I came, it was with her name on my lips, her flesh in my hands, her body throbbing around me like a song I never wanted to end.

I lay back hard as our bodies slowed, our hips still connected, and I rocked her against me, savoring the feeling for a minute longer as we tried to catch our breaths unsuccessfully. My abs were on fire. So was the rest of me.

After a moment, she sighed and lifted herself off of me before stretching out with her back to the door, looking sated, smiling at me.

I ran my clean thumb across her bottom lip. "How come this never comes off?"

"I use a special lipstick that doesn't smudge if I think I might have a dick in my mouth."

I laughed. "Prepared for anything."

"A girl's gotta be."

I kissed her nose. "Be right back."

I climbed off the bed and made my way to her bathroom, unable to keep the smile off my face. It was the third time we'd gone bareback, having had the whole birth control/clean conversation after she practically begged me to fuck her bare. It'd been years since she had sex without a condom, and though I never asked, I wondered how it was possible that she hadn't been with anyone long enough to get to this point.

The thought made me feel like a king and a caretaker. It was a gift I had no intention of squandering. It showed her trust, told me she was letting me into more than her body.

I cleaned myself up and grabbed a washcloth for her, running it under the warm water before heading back to her bedroom. But I stopped mid stride at the sight of her.

She lay curled on her side with her back to me, purple hair spilling over the bed in waves, her head on her bicep as she toyed with her hair. My eyes followed the curve of her tattooed waist and hips, coming to rest at the center of her. My gaze hung on the silvery rivulets that streamed out of her, what I'd left inside her.

I was instantly ready to fuck her again. Needed to fuck her again. Wanted to fill her up with me, every part of me.

My eyes were still locked between her legs as I approached the bed and sat next to her, folding the washcloth before running it up the length of her, cleaning her tenderly, both hands fully occupied.

I never did anything halfway.

She sighed and rolled over onto her back, the chains flowing around her breasts and the curves of her stomach and hips, and I shifted until her legs were open and slung over my thighs. I kept cleaning, and she smiled up at me.

"Tell me your news," she said, her voice a little rough.

"We got a pitch meeting for the game." I was smiling, grinning even.

Penny popped up onto her elbows. "Oh my God! Bodie, that's ... that's amazing! When?"

"Two weeks," I said as I went back to work on her pussy, which was as clean as it was going to get. I just didn't want to stop touching it. "There's a lot to do, so I might be busy until it's finished."

She frowned a little at that, spreading her legs wider. "Well, just don't forget about me."

I laughed. "That's funny, Pen."

Her frown disappeared, turning into a smile as she watched my hands. "God, I'm so happy for you. You gave up everything to follow your dreams. I'd never be brave enough to take a risk like that. It's impressive. You impress me."

"The feeling is entirely mutual, believe me."

She smiled, lying back with a sigh. "Tell me more about the game."

"Well, there's a madame of a pleasure ship, Gemma."

"Oh, I love this already."

I smirked. "She's a smuggler, and so are her girls."

"Naturally."

"Then there's Nate— he's the airship pirate and a smuggler too. They go on this treasure hunt together and have to team up—he has the map, and she has the key. Of course, the bad guy is after them with an army of goons called Ravens. Basically, they wear these leather masks they wear with beaks and top hats."

"Ugh, that is so cool," she said as I ran the cloth over her piercing softly. "I want to draw all the things—airships and girls in leather with knives and pistols and chakrams. What color is her hair?"

"Fire-engine red."

"A woman after my own heart."

I smiled. "So, how was the dress fitting?"

"Good. Everything was perfect, and we went home with dresses. Ramona cried, which made me and Ronnie cry. I blame the champagne though."

I chuckled and ran the cloth over her.

"So, I wanted to ask you something," she started, seeming nervous.

I kept my eyes on my task, hoping it would give her room to say what she needed to say. "Ask away."

"Well," she flexed her thighs, bringing her hips closer to me, "Ramona put me down for a plus-one, but I don't have a plus-one."

I tossed the washcloth toward her closet where her hamper was, trying not to smile. "Oh?" My focus was on my hands as I rested them on either side of her hood and ran my thumbs up and down the line of her center, soaking them.

"Mmhmm," she buzzed with her lip between her teeth and eyes on my hands. "Wanna go?"

My heart leaped. This was beyond a date. This was a wedding.

This was big.

I stroked her, opening her up, pressing against the warm pink hole that led to Shangri-la. "Sure," I said simply, hoping I sounded cool. Because inside, I wasn't cool at all. Inside, I was fist-pumping and whooping and jumping around like a maniac.

She smiled and sighed again as I ran my thumbs up to her piercing, slicking it, rubbing it, teasing it. I didn't want to say anything else about the wedding. If I did, I wouldn't be able to pretend like it wasn't a big deal.

"Good," was the last thing she said, a soft sound that left her lips on a breath as I worked her body with my thumbs.

Instead of speaking, I decided to use my tongue for other things.

I hinged at the waist and kissed her piercing with an open mouth and a sweep of my tongue, but she was a little too close for it to be comfortable, so I hooked her thighs over my shoulders, gripped her waist, and sat up, taking her with me.

Her shoulders were still on the bed, and her hands wrapped around my legs, nails digging into my skin as she gasped with surprise, then pleasure.

I buried my face in her, running my tongue up the hot slit I'd been touching. The metallic tang of what I'd left inside her sent a jolt through me, and I delved deeper into her, looking for more.

She rocked against my face, which I moved from side to side, nestling deeper into her still. Her fingers moved to her piercing, rubbing that bottom ball against her clit as her thighs squeezed, hips bucking. And when I hummed long and deep, she came against my tongue with a warm rush and a pulsing flex. With her thighs clamped around my ears, I couldn't hear anything but her distant moaning, and I slowed, kissing her swollen, tender clit gently.

Her body relaxed, and I lowered her back to the bed, my biceps on fire.

Worth it.

Her cheeks were pink as she pulled herself up to sit and got on her knees to climbed onto my lap, not stopping until our lips were a seam and her arms were around my neck.

When she broke the kiss, she smiled wickedly and backed away, ending up on all fours in front of me.

"Get up on your knees," she ordered.

I did, my heart banging, my cock throbbing when she licked her lips and crawled to me.

Her hand found my base, and her lips opened, tongue extending to guide my head into her hot, wet mouth.

I slipped my fingers into her hair, tugging off the headband so I could see her eyes as she looked up at me, her body a wave as she took the length of me into her mouth.

She moaned.

I hissed.

Her eyelashes fluttered closed, and she got to work, chains swaying from the curve of her waist and hips, and my eyes traced every line from the tip of her nose to her heart-shaped ass.

Heaven existed inside Penny's mouth.

My hips moved on their own, and she matched my rhythm, her hands on the bed, my eyes drinking in the sight of her on all fours with my cock in her mouth, and too soon, I was close.

I pulsed in her mouth, my hand in her hair clenching in warning, and she backed away, letting me go with a pop.

My heart beat so hard it hurt, my breath burning my lungs as she stretched out on the bed and motioned for me to follow, her hands reaching for my aching cock. I crawled up her body, and she took me in her hands.

"Get up," she whispered.

I straddled her waist, leaning over to brace myself on the wall. Her hair was fanned out all over the pillow, her eyes hot as she gripped me with both hands and stroked.

I was still so wet from her mouth. Her hands, gentle and firm, pumped and stroked, and my pulse raced. My hips sped. And when I came, my heart stopped from the act, from the sight of Penny, eyes closed and neck out-stretched, hands around me, angling me to come in hot bursts all over her tattooed breasts, her collarbone, her neck, the chains.

"Jesus fucking Christ, Penny," I whispered, the words ragged, my brain on fire and body burning from her touch.

She opened her eyes and smiled, and I fought the urge to ask her if I could keep her forever.

chapter
eleven
Wait, What?

THINGS I WOULD NEVER IN MY LIFE FORGET: THE SIGHT OF RAMONA WEARING A penis crown and a greasy, gyrating bohunk in her lap, who held onto his cowboy hat and humped her to the tune of "Save a Horse (Ride a Cowboy)."

I was possibly going to die from laughing, and I had *definitely* snuck a photo.

Veronica and I were chanting, *Mona, Mona,* as we threw money on the stage, which was ridiculous since we'd already paid to have her pulled onstage for public humiliation.

When the song ended, we all cheered, and the banana-hammocked stripper offered a hand to help her stand and guided her to the stage stairs with a kiss on the cheek. She curtsied as she walked toward our group.

The night had been a good one—heels were high, laughs were from the belly, and the drinks were cold and ample.

Ramona was tanked.

All was as it should be.

We took our seats at the edge of the men's stage, and I reached over to straighten Ramona's tiny veil with bobbling dicks on springs around the tiara.

She smiled at me, her eyes glossy and wet. "I love you, Penny."

"I love you too," I said on a laugh. "Need another drink?"

She nodded, grinning now. "Jameson on the rocks."

"I know what you drink, pumpkin." I booped her nose.

"You always take care of me, even when I'm a drunk bitch," she said, motioning to herself.

"Well, you take care of me literally all the rest of the time, so we're even. I'm the lucky one. And I pay you back in the form of humping cowboys and Jameson!"

Ramona giggled. "He was so hot. But not as hot as Shep." She sighed. "How the fuck did I get so lucky?"

"Well, for starters, you're a fucking catch."

"So are you. And now you got caught by Bodie the fisherman with his giant pole." She pretended to cast a fishing line from her crotch.

I cackled, only a little freaked out by the thought. "You are so drunk. Let me get you even more drunker."

"More drunker!" she crowed.

I flagged our waitress, who had on the most epic studded bra, thong, and garter set I'd ever seen. Like, so epic that I'd asked her where she got it and *maybe* bought it on my phone.

Once I was settled back in my seat, the music changed as a new stripper came out dressed like a B-Boy. The song was by Machinedrum and totally obscure, which caught my ear and my eye. It was a sexy dubstep song I had on one of my playlists, and he immediately won points for originality.

He was hot as fuck, gliding across the stage, popping and locking in the sexiest striptease known to woman.

I sat at the edge of my seat, hands in the air as I danced in place, excitedly singing the words.

B-Boy Johnny locked onto me with his lip between his teeth. He made his way across the stage to stop right in front of me and pulled off his shirt, rolling his body as he tossed it.

And just like that, he was planking on the edge of the stage with his feet in the air and his face inches from mine.

I laughed and sang the words to him, hoping he was harmless and/or gay. He spun away and danced some more, but he kept coming back to me like I was the center point of the universe, like the dance was for me.

I didn't even have any dollars for him; I'd given them all to Ramona.

This fact did not deter him.

A few minutes in, I felt a little squirmy—he was definitely not harmless *or* gay—so I turned to Ramona to give her all my attention, hoping he would get the hint. Instead of ignoring me like I wanted, he flipped off the stage and landed right in front of me, dancing in my direction until he had me pushed all the way back in my seat and was straddling me. So I let the man give me a lap dance like a good girl, slipping a couple of bucks someone had shoved in my hand into the waist of his pants.

I mean, the guy had to eat, right?

He spent the final two minutes of the song in my lap, taking my hand to run it down his chiseled chest and abs, and we laughed at the brilliant awkwardness of it all.

A month ago, I probably would have gone home with him. But tonight? Tonight I wasn't interested at all, and I couldn't stop assessing him.

He was tall but not as tall as Bodie. And he had a great smile, but his bottom teeth were a little crooked where Bodie's were almost unnaturally straight, thanks to his orthodontist and those braces that had helped hide him from me years ago. Plus, B-Boy Johnny was missing that dimple that made me crazy. No way was he as funny as Bodie either. I knew almost without a doubt that Bodie ate better pussy.

So I endured that lap dance like a champ as well as a little kiss on the cheek he gave me before he gathered up his clothes and cash and disappeared behind the curtain.

Another guy came out, a gigantic, jacked motherfucker, who smirked and danced across the stage to R. Kelly, and I zoned out. Not my type. He was too … brunette.

I frowned.

He was too Not-Bodie.

I was instantly uncomfortable, which instantly surprised me.

Never in my life had I been with a man who no one could match up to. I'd never been with a man who was so easy to be with that I found myself on a date with him without even realizing it. I'd never been with a man so much over such a short period of time and not gone insane or driven someone else insane.

The whole thing was baffling and made me so uneasy that I needed to get up. To walk. To change the scenery.

So I leaned into Ramona and grabbed some of her singles. "I'm gonna go get a drink. Be back."

"Don't we have a waitress?" Her face quirked up like a cartoon character.

"Yes, but I forgot something. I'll be back. Just watch that." I pointed to the stage, and she smiled.

"Okay, hurry up!" she slurred, not taking her eyes off the stripper.

I nodded to Veronica to make sure she knew she was in charge before heading deeper into the club.

It was co-ed—really, most of the club was women with just a small stage for the wang. And as I walked through the club, I zeroed in on a girl with a superhuman bootie who was working her way up a side stage pole. When she did the splits with her crotch an inch from the ceiling and the pole wedged between her tits, my mouth hit the floor, and I cheered, hurrying over.

"Shut up and take my money!" I called, waving a stack of dollars as I took a seat on the edge of her stage.

The woman defied gravity. Her hair was long and curly, and she spun around that pole like it was easy, which I knew to be an absolute lie. I'd tried it once on a dare and had pole-burn for a week.

I had no idea how long I sat there, but let me tell you this; when she got down on her knees in front of me and booty-clapped to 2Pac's "Hail Mary," my life was forever changed. I swear to God, I found Jesus in her G-string.

Ramona materialized at my side. "What the fuck, Pen? What are you doing over here? You know I depend on you for supplementary entertainment at these things."

"Because, look." I grabbed her by the chin and turned it so she could see the Booty-Clap Queen speak the gospel.

Her eyes widened. "Oh my God. That is incredible," she said reverently.

"I know. Plus, those guys were just meh."

"Just meh?" she asked, turning to look back at me like I was nuts. "You're kidding, right? That breakdancer was hot enough to have made the cut for *Magic Mike*, and he wasn't even gay. I'm about ninety-six percent certain he wanted to impregnate you."

I laughed. "I mean, he was okay. But he wasn't like *this*." I gestured to my new hero as she spun down the pole like a goddamn sexual siren.

She giggled and grabbed my hand. "Come back over. It's almost time for Annika's lap dance, and you know the look on her face is going to be so fucking worth it."

I sighed and followed her back to the men's stage, but she'd let my hand go before we got close, so I hung back for a second, watching my friends from afar.

I felt so weird, so off. I was usually the one up at the edge of the stage, stuffing money in my bra so the only way the strippers would get paid was with their faces in my cleavage.

But tonight it seemed kind of boring.

In fact, I kept thinking about Bodie. I wondered if he could dance like any of these guys, and then I wondered if I could convince him to strip for me. I wondered if he would have liked my new mentor's galactic ass as much as I had. I wondered if he would have been jealous when B-Boy Johnny was all up in my grill.

I wondered if one of the ladystrippers had been on him, how I would have felt.

And then I imagined pulling a stripper out of Bodie's lap and shoving her, subsequently being escorted out of the club by security. It didn't make me feel better. I mean, shoving an imaginary stripper who had dared to touch Bodie made me feel better, but the reality was that I felt a little tingle in my chest that scared the shit out of me. Feelings. Real feelings.

Not-Bodie's Armani cologne hit me before I sensed someone standing next to me.

"Hey."

I turned to find B-Boy Johnny smirking at me, fully clothed, with his hat pulled down over his eyes.

I bet he's balding. Bodie's hair could stop traffic.

I smiled politely. "Hey. Good job out there."

"Thanks. I couldn't help but notice you."

I laughed patronizingly and pointed at my head. "Yeah, it's the hair. Kinda stands out."

"It's not just that," he said, slipping a hand around my waist. "You're ... I dunno. Different."

Johnny was apparently real wordy. And handsy.

I chuckled and put a hand on his chest as I twisted out of his grip, itching to get away. "You're sweet, but I have a boyfriend."

He was still smirking. "That's all right. It's just mind over matter, baby. If you don't mind, it don't matter."

I couldn't help but laugh again as I stored that one in my Come-On Lines folder. "I'm sorry. Have a good night," I said as I walked away.

My heart was banging. I had no idea what had gotten into me. In fact, I couldn't remember the last time I'd turned a guy down who was hot and could move his hips like a fucking snake.

But what nearly knocked me over was the fact that I'd called Bodie my boyfriend. I stopped dead in my tracks as that tingle in my chest worked down my spine.

Wait, what?

It wasn't like I'd never lied and said I had a boyfriend just to get away from a guy, but that wasn't what this was. When I'd said boyfriend, I'd meant *Bodie*. I had thought his name as clearly as if I'd spoken it. I had seen his dimple in my mind like my name was written in it. I'd felt his presence as if he were standing in the room with me.

I didn't want B-Boy Johnny because I wanted Bodie and no one but Bodie.

I was so freaked out that I barely got to enjoy Annika's lap dance by the hulkiest black man I'd ever seen outside of a Knicks game. He got so in her lap and in her face that I could barely see her around him. She was half-crying, half-laughing and wholly amused, though clearly uncomfortable. Her eyes were closed for a good portion of the show, which seemed to only egg him on.

I had a sneaking suspicion that it was her first encounter with a stripper, which made it that much better. And I was too busy wigging out to get any mileage out of the jokes I'd been saving up to embarrass her with.

Within an hour, we were stumbling out of the club, heading toward Shep and Ramona's new place, laughing and chatting along the way. We stopped on our way to get pizza from a window booth, which was the only reason Ramona wouldn't be puking her guts up all day the next day.

And all the while, my thoughts were on Bodie, just as they had been all night. I didn't think I'd said more than ten words since we left the strip club, and I used them all to order pizza.

Somehow, I'd found myself in some sort of relationship without even realizing it, and I had no idea what that meant.

Denial was a thing, and I was the queen of it.

For weeks I'd been seeing him, and I'd had no desire to look anywhere else. He was smart and hot. He knew how to work my body almost better than I did, knew how to make me laugh and make me swoon and make me *happy*.

Peggy was quiet. Probably too quiet.

But from the jump, I'd said no commitment. From the start, I'd said we should talk if we caught feelings.

Clearly, I'd caught feelings, and no amount of antibiotics would save me.

I wondered if that meant I had to tell him, and my stomach dropped at the thought. I couldn't—not yet. I mean, *yet* was such a dumb word to use because I didn't know if I could *ever*. If I admitted it, it would be real. If I admitted it, things would change. And I didn't want things to change.

The pizza was like cardboard in my mouth as I walked in the back of the laughing pack.

The real issue was that I didn't know for certain that he had feelings for me too. I didn't know if I made him feel as good as he made me feel. Whatever he felt—if anything—he kept on lock. He was totally blasé, super chill, reminding me over and over again that this was all for fun. Implying that it meant nothing.

Me calling him my boyfriend definitely wasn't nothing.

I wondered just how he felt, if he'd call me his girlfriend if a stripper hit on him. The thought of asking him made me gag, and I tossed my pizza in the next trash can I came across. I didn't want to know if he didn't feel the same. I didn't want whatever we had to end, not until it was inevitable. And the only way it would be inevitable was if I opened my big fucking mouth.

Things were too good to blow it all up. So I'd keep it to myself for now, maybe forever. Because I didn't want to lose him. Not yet, and definitely not tonight. Tonight I wanted to see him more than ever.

I grabbed my phone from my clutch and texted him.

Still up?

My heart skipped when I saw him typing. *I am. Working late. How was the strip club?*

Good. I had my mind blown by a stripper's ass. I mean it. My whole universe was shaken.

Learn any new tricks?

I smiled. *I don't have nearly enough junk in my trunk to do what she did. I don't have enough core strength either.*

Hahaha. What are you doing now?

Well, now that I know you're up, I'd like to be doing you.

What do you know? My schedule just cleared.

God, I was so into him, and I couldn't even be mad about it.

Be there in thirty.

And as I put my phone away, I felt lighter. Because denial was a sweet, sweet place to be, and I'd stay there until I was dragged out, kicking and screaming.

◦◦◦

I thought I'd be able to finish what I was working on before Penny came over, but there was no way. Instead, I bugged Jude and Phil while they worked, antsy out of nowhere.

Penny did that to me. Made me crazy. Made me want things I couldn't have. Every day it got harder to play it cool, harder to pretend. But until she was ready to talk about it, I'd keep it to myself.

She knocked on the door, and I walked over, trying not to hurry, throwing my chill on at the last possible second.

Penny looked incredible, as she always did. Tonight she was in the tightest black jeans I'd ever seen in my life, the waist high and her crop top short, exposing a slice of the flowers tattooed on her stomach and ribs. She wasn't wearing a bra again, and I tried not to think about how many men noticed the curve of her breasts, the peaks of her nipple, the bars on each side.

It wouldn't have bothered me so bad if I'd known she was mine.

She smiled and stepped into me, and I pushed the thought away as I pulled her into my chest and kissed her.

I closed the door, and we walked through the living room.

"Hey, guys," Penny said, wiggling her fingers at them.

They waved over the backs of their chairs, not turning around.

"Working hard?" she asked as we walked into my room.

I closed the door and reached for my phone to turn on music. "Always. We're in DEFCON One now that we have a meeting."

She smiled and sat down on my bed, reaching down to unbuckle her shoes. "It's so amazing, Bodie. I have a good feeling about this."

"Me too," I said as I stretched out in bed, propped up by my pillows. "So tell me about this stripper's ass."

She laughed and climbed up the bed, sitting next to me on her knees. "It was magnificent. It made me want to do a thousand squats because if I could badonk my donk like that, I could die knowing I'd accomplished something that made the universe a better place." She perked up and popped off the bed. "Oh! I brought you something."

When she bounded back over from her purse, she hopped up on the bed and bounced a little, holding something behind her.

"How'd you know you'd see me tonight?" I asked, smirking in an attempt to keep my eagerness hidden.

She shrugged. "I couldn't be around all that gyrating and not come see you after. Okay, now—you ready?"

"I dunno. Am I?"

She chuckled. "You are. *Voilà!*"

When Penny brought her hand out from behind her back, it held a small painting, about five-by-seven—an illustration of a girl in a leather bustier and leather garters with knives strapped to one thigh, red hair blowing in the wind, and an airship behind her. The word *Nighthawk* arched over the top of the watercolor drawing, framed by gears.

I took it reverently, my eyes raking over it in wonder. "Penny, this is gorgeous."

Her smile could have been a thousand watts. "You like it?"

"I love it," was all I could say.

"I told you it made me want to draw. Bodie, I'm just so happy for you. And I want you to know that I believe you can do this. I believe you can do just about anything."

I rested my hand on her thigh, and her face softened as she leaned into me, pressing a sweet kiss to my lips. When she backed away, I saw something new in her eyes, something different. Something good. Something more.

I felt the warmth of it spread through my chest.

I wanted to speak, but if I did, I'd admit things, and if I admitted what I wanted to admit, the feeling could be gone just as soon as I'd earned it. So instead, I cupped her cheek and slipped my fingers into her hair, bringing her closer to kiss her with more intention.

Penny communicated through sex and through ink, and maybe I could do the same. Maybe I could telegraph how i felt through my lips alone. Maybe she could feel my heart through the tips of my fingers.

I hoped she could. Because the game we'd been running was long, and I felt the end coming too soon. There would be a moment when we couldn't avoid it anymore, when the words wouldn't stay inside me any longer.

The chances of her feeling the same were slim, and I knew it. I'd known my odds when I stepped into the lion's cage and started this dance with her.

But that didn't stop me from hoping.

chapter
twelve
Wild Horses

"SO WHEN'S YOUR *BOYFRIEND* COMING?" RAMONA ASKED MY REFLECTION IN the massive mirrors of the bridal suite.

"Hopefully the second I can get my dress hitched up," I answered without missing a beat before sipping the champagne in my hand to punctuate the joke.

Ramona and Veronica laughed, and I shimmied my rack in my bridesmaid dress with one hand.

"Seriously, my boobs look amazing in this. Maybe he'll come before I can even get it pulled up." I turned to inspect my ass, which was on point. "Anyway, I'm not calling him that. I don't like that word."

Veronica raised one brow. "And what are you calling him?"

"My slam piece. 'Cause he's Sexy Like A Motherfucker, and he can slam me all night. Like, literally all night. My vagina has never been slammed on the Bodie level."

She snickered. "Slam piece? I mean, whatever helps you sleep at night."

"No wonder he somehow tricked you into being his *girlfriend*."

Ramona was baiting me. I was no dummy even if I was a sucker.

Oddly, the moniker didn't make me want to puke up my champagne and donuts like it had a couple of days ago.

"*Slam piece*," I said flatly. "You act like I've pledged my undying devotion to him. God, a girl can't even get steady dick anymore without everyone starting a pool on when she's going to get engaged."

Ramona laughed—she was cool as a cucumber, which was beyond all reason, considering she was an hour away from getting married. We stood in the middle of a regal room with a chandelier the size of Delaware and more French antiques than I'd ever seen in one place outside of a museum. She looked beautiful, blissfully happy, and without a single indicator of nervousness, which was impressive seeing as how she was about to walk down the aisle.

She touched my arm, her eyes and smile full of love. "I'm happy for you."

I smiled back, my heart so furry and warm and full that I didn't know if all the happiness would stay in my chest. "You too. Are you ready for this?"

She shrugged. "I've been waiting for this day forever, but I'm just … I don't know. Zen as fuck. I don't even care how things go—in an hour, I'll be his wife. And then we'll eat and drink and dance and fuck like rockstars in the Kennedy suite."

"Yeah, you will," I said, gyrating my hips.

"Everything is done and taken care of." She hooked her arm in mine and hung her other around Veronica's shoulders. "I have you two. I have Shep waiting for me at the end of an aisle to promise me forever. There's nothing else I could possibly wish for."

I misted up. "Ugh, you're so happy it's disgusting."

Ramona laughed. "I know. Isn't it amazing?"

I rested my head on her shoulder and took in the sight of the three of us in the mirror. "It's kinda the best thing in the whole world."

My phone buzzed in my pocket—my dress had pockets, guys; winning hard.—and I pulled away, reaching for it.

The photo displayed behind Bodie's name lit up my phone and my insides; I was nuzzled into his neck laughing, and he was laughing too, his dimple flashing.

Veronica laughed and pointed at my screen. "Oh my God. *Boyfriend.*"

I rolled my eyes and answered the phone, smiling. "Hey," I said as I stepped off the platform, passing the tornado that was Ramona's mom on my way out. I swear, I think she was shouldering all the nerves for both of them.

"Hey," he echoed, his voice rumbly and low and velvety.

My body reacted immediately to that one mundane syllable like it was a secret password.

I hadn't seen him in two days, since after the strip club. We'd been too busy with wedding stuff to have a free millisecond.

"Are you here?" I asked.

I could hear him smiling. "I am. Just got here."

"Meet me by the bar."

"Already there."

My grin stretched wide as I rushed to the door, calling over my shoulder that I'd be right back.

I hurried through the garden where people were milling around, waiting for the ceremony to start. The venue was gorgeous, an outdoor garden with a big tent for the reception and a gazebo in a hedge alcove that felt like a fairy land. There was a rope swing and a massive bar that had been imported from a pub in France, all brass and mahogany and gorgeous and elegant.

But not as gorgeous as the man standing in front of it.

His dirty-blond hair had been cut short on the sides, kept longer on a top, combed back and to the side in a gentle swoop, and I nearly stopped in my tracks at the transformation. The laid-back surfer in a muscle shirt and sneakers had been replaced by a clean-cut masterpiece of power. The gravity of the vision of him pulled me toward him like a tractor beam. He looked like he'd stepped off a magazine cover with tan skin and eyes shining a shade of sky blue that felt infinite. The suit he wore fit him perfectly—charcoal gray swathing every angle of his broad shoulders and chest, one button of his coat fastened, his shirt crisp and white, and tie thin and black. One hand rested in his pocket, his coat bunched up at the seam where his hand and hip were, and the other held a scotch.

I was nine hundred percent sure my uterus whispered his name when he smiled at me, popping that dimple and my ovaries with a simple flicker of cheek muscles.

I might have floated into his arms, slipping mine around his neck as I kissed him. There was quite literally nothing else I could have done when I saw him standing there, dressed like that.

His lips were so warm and familiar and soft and sweet. The two measly days we'd been apart felt like a month.

I pulled away, humming, but I didn't give him his neck back, just fiddled with the short hair at the nape, marveling over the soft bristling against my fingertips.

"Your hair," I whispered, smiling as my eyes scanned him in wonder.

"You like it?"

"I love it. If it wasn't combed, my fingers would be buried deep, deep in it."

He laughed softly, the sound rumbling through his chest and into me. "Later we'll bury all kinds of things in all kinds of places."

I answered with a laugh of my own. "What in the world possessed you to do it?"

Bodie shrugged. "I went in for a trim and decided to cut it. It matched the suit."

"True. But do you think you might grow it back out?"

"Why? Miss it already?" he asked with a smile, holding me tighter.

"Maybe. I do love your long hair, but this is so soft." I ran my fingers over it. "And I swear, somehow, your jaw looks a hundred times sharper. You've got a good looking head, boy. You could be a part-time model."

He laughed at that and kissed me again.

I smiled up at him feeling dreamy and light and unbelievably happy. "I missed you," I said without thinking.

His face held its shape, but something behind his eyes shifted, sending a jolt of uncertainty through me, cooling my mood. "I missed you too."

I swallowed and looked at his tie, running my hand down his chest. "Where the hell did you get this suit?"

His smile shifted sideways into a smirk. "Same place as you get your lingerie."

I laughed. "Oh, I very much doubt that."

Bodie chuckled, his hand on my hip, thumb shifting against the soft silk before he twisted the tie around his finger and held it up. "So tell me, what happens if I pull this?"

I pressed the length of my body against his and smiled, stretching on my tiptoes to get to his ear. "Boom, I'm naked."

His lips were at my ear too. "Good to know."

The man was magic. He could whisper anything in my ear—*My grandma makes a mean scone. I'm all out of peanut butter. I wish I had more time to climb trees*—and I'd forget that there was ever or would ever be anything to do besides him.

I sighed into his ear, and he held me a little closer. I found myself pouting because I couldn't stay right there like I wanted.

I pulled away and stepped back, though I slid my hand down his arm and to his hand to hold it. "You gonna be okay out here? It's about to start, so it shouldn't be long before I'm back to entertain you."

He held up his scotch, smiling. "I'll keep myself company." He paused, his eyes on mine in a way that I felt in the tips of my fingers and toes. "You look beautiful, Penny."

My cheeks flushed, and I smiled back. How could I not? Adonis in a suit was smiling at me with a scotch in his hand and a suit that made my vagina do an involuntary Kegel.

"You're not so bad yourself, handsome. I'll see you in a little bit."

"I'll be waiting," he said.

And the words worked their way through me like I'd been the one drinking scotch.

I watched Penny walk away as I took a sip of my drink, my eyes running over all the places I wished my hands were. The deep V of the back of her dress, framing her tattoos. The small circle of her waist, tied by that little sash that would strip her with a tug. The swing of her hips as she hurried away in the direction she'd come from.

A sigh rose and fell from the bottom of my lungs.

I hadn't seen her in two days, not since she came over after the bachelorette party. Things had been the same that night as they had always been—we'd spent an hour or so wrapped up in each other, an hour or so talking and laughing, and then she'd left. But something had shifted, something I didn't know how to place or what to do with. All I knew was that I could feel the depth of it in me and in her. And she hadn't run away.

We hadn't spoken about the status of our relationship since the ice cream parlor, and her shock that day—when I'd reaffirmed that I wouldn't ask for more than she was willing to give—was still fresh in my mind.

How could she have gone for so long without knowing this feeling? Without wanting more than just a fuck boy?

I wanted to know. But the last thing I wanted to do was ask.

Because the last thing I wanted was to lose her.

So as far as I knew—as far as she'd said—things were the same. But what she *did* didn't match up with what she *said*. She'd tattooed my arm. She'd spent almost every day with me for weeks. We'd been on a date, and tonight I was her date at a *wedding*.

It didn't feel like no strings, no commitment, no rules. It felt like she was mine, and I was hers. It felt like we were together. And that felt good—so good that I wasn't likely to rock the boat out of fear I'd sink it.

I drained my drink and set it on the surface of the bar, checking my calculator watch before following the signs to the gazebo.

Annika and I merged paths as we entered an arched tunnel covered in vines. In heels, she was almost as tall as me, her blonde hair in a loose bun at her nape and black dress sleek and simple.

She smiled, transforming her aloof runway model vibe, warming her up. "Hey, Bodie."

"Good to see you, Annika."

"You too. You're here with Penny?"

I didn't miss the mild surprise in her voice. I couldn't say I blamed her. I was probably more shocked than anyone.

"I am."

Her smiled widened. "Lucky you. Want to sit with me?"

I relaxed a little. "That'd be great. I don't know anyone who isn't in the wedding party but you."

She chuckled. "I only know the crew who were invited, but I'm just about the only one who's part of the production of the show who's here as a guest. The rest are filming."

I looked around once we exited the tunnel for the camera crew, finding them in little hidden alcoves, blending in like chameleons. I'd signed a waiver, and I still hadn't realized they were here.

"Huh. How about that?" I said half to myself, guiding her into a row of white wooden chairs.

"We want to film in the most unobtrusive way possible. It's not always easy, but thankfully, my boss is sympathetic to the cause." She wiggled the fingers of her left hand at me, flashing her engagement ring. When we were seated, she turned a little in her chair to face me, crossing her long legs in my direction. "So, how'd you land her?"

I wished I'd gotten another drink. "Well, I'm not sure I've landed her just yet."

"Oh, I am," Annika said on a chuckle.

I glanced at her, intrigued. "That so?"

She nodded. "As long as I've known her, she's never had a steady guy. She'll date one for a little bit and then flit off to the next, never getting attached, and I've *never* seen one of the guys, only heard the stories. She won't bring them around us like she has with you. And I've seen the way she looks at you, the way she talks to you. It's my job to read people, and I've been reading Penny for a year now. She likes you, and she's happy, happier than I've seen her. So I'm curious as to how you did it."

"I haven't done much but let her be who she is."

Annika's face softened. "Penny's like a wild pony; she's beautiful and untamed and completely free. Free from the tethers of judgment, free from being controlled, contained. She lives one day at a time, doing exactly what she wants, accepting her consequences without a single care for what anyone else thinks." Annika sighed at that. "She's the freest woman I've ever known or seen, and I have more respect for that than anything. I'm even a little envious."

I nodded, smiling at the truth of her words. "I know what you mean."

"But she loves to run. That's the trick, the catch I haven't seen anyone overcome." She shook her head. "None of this—you and her, I mean—is any of my business, and I don't mean to pry. I'm just so interested in how you snagged her. You're like the pony whisperer."

I laughed at that. If she'd replaced pony with pussy it might have been spot-on. "Honestly? I don't even know. She asked for no strings, so that's what I've given her. I let her lead. I respect her too, respect what she wants even if it's not what I want."

"And what do you want?" she asked. But before I could answer, she waved her hand as the color rose in her cheeks. "I'm sorry. My job has me trained to ask personal questions that I shouldn't. Please, don't answer that."

"No, it's okay," I said as the music started.

We turned in our seats.

From the green archway, Penny appeared on Patrick's arm, that dress sweeping the green grass at her feet like she was floating, and her eyes found mine and held them.

"I just want her," was my answer to Annika, to the universe. To myself.

The ceremony was simple and perfect. Ramona and Shep were married under the gazebo, staring into each other's eyes like no one else was there. When they said their vows, when they kissed, a lump formed in my throat, and Annika pressed her fingertips to her lips. We all stood and clapped and cheered and smiled as they walked down the aisle—this time, as husband and wife. And when Penny passed me and her eyes found mine, they were shining, her cheeks flushed. She told me a million things I somehow couldn't decipher; I could only feel them all and try to understand.

I offered my arm to Annika, and we made our way into the reception tent and to the head table where our dates would be joining us. We sat next to each other, chatting as everyone found their seats.

The DJ kicked off "I Believe in a Thing Called Love" by The Darkness, and Penny blew onto the dance floor with Patrick, inflatable guitars in hand, air-strumming. Penny actually hitched up her skirt and slid across the parquet, red bottom lip in her teeth and head banging in time to the beat.

The rest of the wedding party came out, and once they were present, they made an archway with their black guitars, and then Ramona and Shep ran through to finish the song to a standing ovation.

After the song, they headed over to us—Penny practically jumped into my arms, sending me off balance, and I swung us to keep us upright.

The sound of her laughter in my ears was the sweetest song.

I set her feet on the ground, sliding her down my body, and she cupped my cheek and kissed me gently, smiling softly. She looked at me like I was a king, and I felt like every bit of one with her on my arm.

We took our seats and ate our steaks, laughing and talking and high off the night, the moment. Toasts were given. Speeches were made. Tears were shed. And all the while, Penny's hand was in my lap, our fingers threaded together.

And then the party started.

The sun had gone down, and the dance floor was illuminated by naked bulbs strung in arcs from one end of the tent to the other. Shep and Ramona's first song was a spinning, swaying, brilliantly choreographed dance to "Never Tear Us Apart" by INXS. After that, Ramona, Penny, and Veronica did their own choreography to "Scream & Shout," and the guys surprised them by jumping in halfway through with their own moves.

Joel, Shep, and Patrick—aka two tattooed Sasquatches and a male model—throwing lassos and yelling *Britney, bitch* was the most hysterical thing I'd ever seen in my life.

And then Penny was in my arms for the rest of the night. First, we were bouncing around to New Order and Lady Gaga. Then, The Clash came on, and I kissed her in the middle of a sea of people jumping and singing to "Rock the Casbah," just like the first kiss, the kiss that I thought of so often.

I pulled her outside to get a drink and spotted a swing on a gargantuan old tree.

I tugged her in that direction, stopping just next to it. "Remember the park by the beach where we used to party in high school?"

My hand rested on her waist, and she smiled up at me, reaching for the rope of the swing.

"How could I forget?"

"You're just the same as you were, except now you're more *you* than you ever were. You're just as beautiful. You're just as brash and brilliant. But now, you're free."

She fiddled with my lapel with her free hand, and her eyes watched her fingers. "Oh, I don't know about that. I want to be. I try to be. But sometimes, my freedom is a cage." She seemed to shake the thought away and smiled, meeting my eyes again. "Your outsides have changed, but your insides are exactly the same. I wish … I wish I'd seen you then like I see you now. If I had, maybe things would have been different. Maybe I'd be different." Her words were soft, her eyes bright and shining.

"I wouldn't want you to be any different than you are right now, Pen." The words were quiet, solemn.

And for a moment, we stood in silence until I couldn't take it anymore. I couldn't let her say anymore, because if she did, the thin façade I'd built would crumble and blow away, exposing me, exposing her.

So I kissed her instead. She tasted of bourbon and cake, smelled of jasmine, felt like silk against my fingertips, against my lips.

When I let her go, I guided her to sit on the wide wooden plank, her long fingers wrapping around the ropes to hang on. And when I pulled her back by her waist and released her, the gray silk of her dress billow and her silvery hair fly with the sound of her laughter in my ears.

Too soon after, the night was nearly over. The DJ had brought the tempo down, and I found myself in the middle of the dance floor with Penny against my chest, The Cure singing "Pictures of You" as the two of us moved in small circles on the parquet.

It was strange, how I felt. Like I was dreaming. Like my heart had opened up and so had hers. That we were open to *each other*. I could feel the connection like a tether between us. That everything that I felt, she felt. That everything I wanted, she wanted.

I kissed the top of her head, and she shifted her face against my beating heart.

I had to tell her. I needed her to know that I wanted her, wanted more, felt more. I wanted to soothe her, ease her fears, promise her anything she asked for. Because I'd give her anything even if it meant giving her nothing. Even if it meant we kept going just how we were.

But if I told her, things wouldn't go on like this. Things would change.

I could lose her.

My heart skipped a beat against her cheek.

The war between trusting her with my feelings and giving her the space I knew she needed battled in my ribcage. When did the sacrifice of what I wanted become too much? How would I know she was ready, that I wouldn't scare her off?

I'd coaxed the wild pony out to eat from my hand, but putting a bridle on her was another thing altogether.

I couldn't tell her, not yet. I only hoped I had the resolve to hold on.

I could have stood there on the dance floor in Bodie's arms with The Cure on repeat for the rest of my life.

The night had been full of magic.

Every moment between us deepened my feelings, and I knew he felt what I felt. I didn't know how I knew, but I did. It was as if every second that ticked by whispered, *Yes*, as if we were caught in something we couldn't turn back from, swept away in each other. I didn't even want out. I could drown in him, and I should have been afraid.

But I wasn't.

I felt safe. Safe and warm and cared for. This was what trust felt like, *real* trust between someone who valued you as much as themselves—I realized it distantly, as if I were floating above the two of us swaying in each other's arms. I trusted him because he'd proven that his words were truth. He'd agreed to everything I'd asked for. He'd made me promises and held them, and I had no reason to doubt him.

But when I really held his actions and words up next to each other, they weren't quite the same. He'd said it was all copacetic, sure, but he felt more just as much as I did. He wanted more. I'd denied my feelings, but he'd known all along.

I knew it as suddenly and clearly as if I'd looked in a mirror for the first time.

He'd just been giving me what he knew I needed, just like he always had. He'd sacrificed what he'd wanted to make me happy.

I thought I'd want to cut and run at the realization, but I didn't. I couldn't, not only because he had done everything for me without asking for a single thing in return, even my heart, but I wanted to stay because he'd shown me how to trust again. He treated me with care and respect. He honored me without thought to himself.

I wanted to stay because I'd never been with anyone who didn't play games. And with Bodie, there was no power play, no control, no upper hand.

We were equals. And I'd had no idea something like this could even be real.

I had two gears—full-blown obsession and apathy. This gear that I was on was unknown, a lurch in my life that left me reeling, without any context or boundaries or rules.

That unknown brought a flicker of fear. But in the circle of his arms, with his heart beating under my cheek and his breath warm on my skin, I was safe. He was exactly what I needed, and he was everything right.

There was nowhere else I could have imagined being.

The DJ came on when the song ended, directing us to the front of the gardens so we could send Ramona and Shep off, and Bodie and I hurried over to the stairs. We each grabbed sparklers and lit them when we were told, holding them up so my best friend and her husband could run through. I'd sworn I wasn't going to cry, but there was no stopping it—the sight of them golden and beautiful and smiling and crying as they waved goodbye to all of us was too much.

When the door to the limo closed, I turned to Bodie, who smiled down at me as he captured my chin, and then he kissed me, stealing my breath, stealing my heart.

I was beginning to realize that I'd never stood a chance.

Worry sprang like a broken fire hydrant—I didn't know if I could keep my heart together. If I let myself go, if I opened that door, would I be able to maintain what we were?

The more I felt for him, the less rational I'd be. I'd scare him.

I'd lose him.

I needed more time.

So I turned the giant wrench on that spewing fire hydrant and shut the motherfucker down.

Tonight, I wasn't crazy. Tonight, I had Bodie.

Tonight, he was mine.

When the limo was gone and the guests dispersed, Veronica and I dashed off to gather our things from the bridal suite. She took all of Ramona's things, citing a trip by Ramona and Shep's new place to drop it all off. Something in her eyes said she was a goddamn liar about her plans, and I should have pressed her. But I was too anxious to get back to Bodie to care. She could go be a sneaky liar on her own time.

The cab ride was too long, but I spent the duration tucked into Bodie's side, the two of us recounting the night like we hadn't been together for all of it. And then we were walking down my silent hallway together, smiling at our shoes. And then we were inside, and I was closing my door.

I took him by the hand, and he followed without question into my bedroom and leaned against the door as I turned on one of my smaller lamps just so I could see him. Just so he could see me.

My heart thumped at the sight of him, so tall and easy, hands in his pockets, the line of his shoulders and arms and long legs speaking to the artist in me. Because he was art with a heartbeat. But what hit me, what nearly stopped me in my tracks was the expression on his face.

The playfulness and charm were gone, replaced by something deeper, something *more*. It was the tightness at the corners of his eyes, the depth of his irises, so blue. It was the shape of his lips, the crease of his lips where something waited for me, words he didn't want to speak. Words I wasn't ready to hear, and he knew it.

But that was what Bodie did. He anticipated what I required and gave it to me, even when the gift was his silence. He cared about me more than he'd said. But he still cared for me without demand, without expectation.

He was air and sun and soil, just existing around me to give me all I needed to grow. And all the while, I'd grown and blossomed and bloomed, not realizing that I needed him to keep me breathing.

I crossed the room, overwhelmed and overcome by the revelation, trying not to think of what it meant or what it would mean. Instead, I looked into his eyes and told him without a word what I felt for him. I told him with my fingers slipping under his coat that I wanted him. I told him with my lips pressed to his that he'd changed me and there would be no going back.

His body was hard against my palms as they roamed up his chest, and I leaned into him, the two of us angled against the door, me standing between his legs so I could reach his lips.

And that was the thing that struck me the most; he felt what I felt. He knew what my body told him just as much as I knew what his told me.

Never in my life had I felt this before. I'd had power sex. I'd had flirty sex. I'd had fun sex and serious sex. But in that moment, I became aware of a fact that that changed me, there in my room, kissing Bodie.

I had never been intimate.

I wasn't just hungry for his body. I was hungry for his heart and soul.

I wanted all of him. I just hoped I could hold onto him without it breaking me.

My tongue swept his lip, and he opened his mouth, turning my face with his hand, and I opened up in kind, leaning into his palm. He pulled me into him with his free hand—the length of him pressing against my belly sent a shock up my spine, to my lungs, springing them open as I sucked in a small breath.

He hooked his arm around my waist, keeping me flush against him as he pushed away from the door, leaving my feet dangling off the ground, even as I wished they were wound around his middle but my dress wouldn't allow it. And then gravity shifted as he lay me down in bed gently. But he didn't lower his body onto mine like I wanted, and I hung onto his neck like it could convince him to.

His hand ran up my arm and to my face, and he broke the kiss with a smile, his eyes laden with something that betrayed the levity of his lips.

"I'm not going anywhere, Penny," he whispered, coaxing me to let him go.

But the words meant more than that to me.

I relaxed my arms, and he stood, his eyes sliding up and down my body as he unbuttoned his coat and grabbed his lapels, pulling it open, exposing his broad chest, then shoulders, then arms. His big hands tugged the knot of his tie, slipping one piece from the other with a whisper of silk. And it seemed to take an hour for him to unbutton his shirt. I could have watched that in slow motion on a loop—the sliver of skin on his chest that grew wider with every button, his hands gripping both sides as he opened it just like he had his jacket. Except when that crisp white shirt was gone, all that was left was his beautiful naked chest, all shadows and angles and planes and the tattoo on his arm where I'd put it.

He could have undress and redress and undress again and again, and I would have laid there and watched, content and unhurried and perfectly satisfied.

His pants were next, his leather belt in his fist sending a burst of images through my head—his cock in his hand, the pop and sting of that leather belt against my ass. He snapped open his button with a flick of his fingers, lowering his zipper just as quickly, kicking off his shoes and dropping his pants in movement that felt deliberate and restrained.

And then he was naked before me, the man who'd snuck his way in without me even realizing.

I moved to sit, but he stopped me, laying me back with his hand on my cheek and thumb shifting against my skin. I turned my head to press a kiss into his palm, and he bent to kiss my lips, a kiss without demand but one that burned with smoke and fire and want and need.

He still wasn't in bed with me, and I reached for him, wanting him on me, around me, in me. Just wanting him. He was too far away, but he didn't give me what I was asking for, not this time. This time, he would do what he wanted.

Bodie walked to the end of the bed and slipped his hand over the bridge of my heeled foot and up my leg, pushing the hem of my dress up with it. I opened my legs, and one of his knees slid between my calves and then the other, his hand still on a track up my leg as he climbed onto the bed and knelt before me.

His hand moved from my thigh to the tie of my dress, a simple bow, and he slid the silk between his fingers, meeting my eyes as he pulled. The bow came undone and fell away, and my dress opened just enough to expose a slice of skin down to my belly.

He sighed, his eyes on his hands as he ran his fingers down my sternum, down my stomach, hooking under one side to expose my breast, leaving the chiffon pooling around the bend of my hip. But that sliver of me was naked, from my neck to the center of me, and his eyes drank me in like he was parched.

I spread my thighs, opening myself up to him. And he lowered his lips to my offering, closing his eyes as he kissed the hot line between my legs like he was confessing a secret.

My hands slipped into his hair, my hips rocking and breath shuddering, my pulse climbing as my body neared the edge, the blissful edge.

I called his name—a plea— my hands on his shoulders to tell him I needed more, that I wanted it all, I wanted everything, and he climbed up my body, his hand on my jaw, his fingertips in my hair, the tip of his crown at the slick center of me. And then he looked into my eyes and shifted his hips, filling me up, claiming me as his, giving himself to me, all in a breath.

His body moved, rolling and flexing, his eyes on mine, his lips parted and brows together, and he said my name. And that whisper on his lips was all it took to push me over that edge in a rush of heat and a burst of electricity down my spine, sending my back arching and lungs gasping and body pulsing. And at my release, he found his own, my name in a loop that followed every thrust of his hips as they slowed.

Our eyes were closed, his forehead against mine, his body pinning me down and our breaths mingling. And for some reason, I felt tears pricking the corners of my lids, my nose burning and a lump heavy in my throat.

I wrapped my arms around his neck and pulled him down to bury his face in my neck so I could hide from him. Because in that moment, for the first time, I'd found something real, something beyond me, even if I didn't know what to make of it. I only knew how it felt, and I felt it all the way through me, through every atom. And I made a vow never to forget it.

If I hadn't been addicted to him before, now there would be no hope. No amount of rehab would cure me.

We held each other like that for a long time before he rolled onto his side, pulling me with him and pulling out of me in one motion. He kissed me sweetly before rolling out of bed and heading to the bathroom, leaving me alone.

I lay there on my side with my back to the door and my heart full of shrapnel. It burned—my chest was shredded and smoldering and elated and aching. I didn't know what it meant. I didn't want to think about what it meant. I just wanted him back in bed with me. I wanted my name riding his breath and his arms around me and his lips against mine.

I wanted simple and easy. But we were past that.

He came back a minute later with a warm washcloth and cleaned me up like he always did but without the intention of more. Something in him was reserved, contained, like he was trying to separate from me.

The thought made me want to hang onto him more.

He stood and began to collect his clothes, and I felt my heart break.

"Stay," I said simply, holding my breath in the hopes that he would say yes, the word hanging in the air as he turned to me.

I had never intentionally spent the night with anyone—I'd never wanted to. But the last thing in the whole world I wanted was for Bodie to walk out that door.

His face was soft and cautious as he asked, "Are you sure?"

And when I smiled and nodded, relief washed over him, and he slipped into bed next to me, holding me in his arms, whispering my name as we drifted off to sleep.

chapter
thirteen

Bear Trap

I POURED A LADLE OF PANCAKE BATTER INTO THE PAN WITH A SIZZLE, SMILING AS IT spread into a perfect circle.

It was a little late for me—I had to get home to work, the impending meeting looming over me like a dark cloud—but still I'd crawled out of Penny's bed, wishing I could stay there all day.

There were a lot of things from the last eighteen hours I'd never forget, but Penny curled up in bed, swathed in fluffy white bedding in the morning sunshine, her tattoos and purple hair bright against the crispness of her sheets—that was almost at the top of the list. Dancing with her to The Cure and pushing her on the swing were up there too. But the very top? The number one?

Her eyes locked on mine when she'd given herself to me.

A jolt of happiness and pleasure and anxiety shot from my stomach to my throat at the thought. As much as I wanted to talk to her, that moment had been enough for me. She didn't need to say anything.

I just knew. I knew how she felt and what she wanted. That line of communication was so much deeper than words could ever express.

At the same time, I had to let her lead. So I'd tried to tell myself to go like I knew she always needed me too. And when she'd asked me to stay, it was all I could do not to confess my feelings on the spot. Instead, I'd slipped into bed with her and told her in all the other ways I could that I needed her.

I slid the spatula under the flapjack and flipped it just as her door opened.

She shuffled out, yawning, her hair in a purple bun on top of her head. And she was wearing my dress shirt, the hem cutting her mid thigh and only the tips of her fingers visible past the sleeve cuffs.

I could have died a happy man.

She smiled at me, her eyes blinking slowly as she sidled up next to me and wrapped her arms around my bare waist.

"You cook," she said in wonder.

I laughed and picked up the box of Bisquick. "No, I follow directions."

She laughed. "If I'd known I'd wake up to you making pancakes in dress pants and no shirt, I would have asked you to stay over a long time ago."

I wrapped an arm around her back. "If I'd have known you'd wear my button-down like a nightgown, I would have begged you to let me stay."

She nuzzled into me, but I felt the wall crumble a little, felt her uncertainty behind it in the small sigh that left her.

So I kissed her crown and changed the subject. "There's coffee."

She kissed my chest and slipped away. "You are just too good to be true."

The words held double meaning, and I knew it. But I kept my eyes on the task at hand, moving the pancake onto the stack I'd been building and poured another.

She poured her coffee in silence and took a seat at the table. When I snuck a glance at her, she was cradling her mug with both hands, bottom lip between her teeth and her brows together, sending my heart off a bridge.

I set down the spatula and strode over to the table. The worry in her eyes was so clear when she met mine, and I knelt next to her chair, grabbing the seat to turn her to me.

"Get out of your head, Pen."

She didn't say anything, only watched me with the question *Why?* shifting in her irises.

"Hey." I cupped her face with my heart hammering a warning. "It's okay. This can be easy," I soothed, smoothing my face, smiling gently with a handful of oats and Penny stamping her hooves in front of me. "Nothing has to change, okay? I ... I feel it too, but we don't have to name it or label it. Let's just do what we feel like doing, just like we have been. Call me when you want. I'll do the same. It can be easy, Penny."

She took a breath and touched my cheek. "Promise?"

And I sighed, the easy smile on my face now one hundred percent genuine from relief. "I promise." And I sealed the lie with a kiss.

She melted into me, winding her arms around my neck and squeezing to bring our bodies flush, her legs parting to make room for my waist. My hands traveled from her cheeks to her breasts to her ribs to her hips, and then I grabbed her ass and held her to me, using every muscle in my core and thighs to stand.

She wrapped her legs around me and hummed into my mouth as I turned for the bedroom.

Penny broke away, lips swollen. "What about the pancakes?"

"Fuck the pancakes," I whispered before pressing my lips to hers again.

I watched Bodie washing dishes in his white button-down and dress slacks as I sat at my kitchen table with my chin propped on my hand and a dippy smile on my face.

I didn't even know who I was anymore.

Bodie had spent the night, and I'd slept better than I had in my whole life.

He'd made me pancakes and fucked me senseless and danced with me and made me laugh and made me *happy*. And as freaked out as I was, I kept telling myself that it was going to be okay, just like he'd said.

He'd promised. And I believed him, which was probably naive. In the moment, I couldn't have cared less.

He turned with a smile, drying his hands on a dishtowel before striding over to kiss me gently.

My eyes were still closed for a second when he broke away, and he chuckled.

I sighed and pried my lids open, chin still on my hand. "I hate that you have to go. How much work do you have?"

His smile fell, and he looked a little tired at the thought. "A lot. Too much. I'm not even sure how we're going to get it done in time."

"You will. You're a mathmagician."

"Ha. If only I had a magic wand."

I waggled my brows. "Oh, but you do."

He leaned down to kiss me again before backing away, his blue eyes searching mine. "Hit me up, Pen." The words were soft and edgeless but with a hidden request in the shadows.

So I smiled, having heard him and understood, and said, "I will."

He pressed another small kiss to my temple and walked away, and I watched him until the door was closed.

The second it clicked shut, Veronica threw open her door with her eyes like a couple of fried eggs and her hair a mess, striding into the room.

She pointed at the door. "Oh my fucking God. Did Bodie spend the night?"

I smiled with my lips closed and nodded, making the bun on top of my head bob.

She squealed and did a little *Flashdance* before swooping into the chair next to me. "I thought I heard him, but I was afraid it was someone else. And if it was someone else, I was prepared to brain you with a frying pan."

I frowned, offended. "You thought I might have come home from the wedding with someone besides Bodie?"

She huffed and rolled her eyes. "You've done it before."

"Not true. I always go home with my dates, asshole. But yes, that was definitely Bodie. And he definitely spent the night. And he *definitely* made me pancakes this morning."

Her cheeks flushed, and she giggled. "God, he's such a fucking catch, Pen."

I eyed her. "Why are you so happy?" I scanned her face and body and lit up. "You got laid!"

Her blush deepened. "No, I didn't."

This time, I pointed. "Oh my God, you did! You got nailed! *Finally*. I was worried your junk was gonna dry up. All dust bunnies and mothballs and shit," I said, wagging my hand at her nethers.

Another eye roll. "You are such a drama queen. We're talking about you and Mr. Math. Penny, he spent the night. Like, what the fuck does that even mean?"

I shrugged and drew a little circle on the table with my finger. "It means I got pancakes and morning sex."

"Don't do that. I'm serious. This is a big deal."

"I know, but we're not ... I dunno. Calling it anything. We're just letting it be what it is," I said simply.

"And how long do you think that'll last?"

I chuffed, my emotions bubbling and steaming and hissing with uncertainty and anxiety. "God, why are you being such a dick about it? I don't know what it is. I just know that I like him. I like him a lot. I want to be around him all the time, and I want to tell him stuff and let him sleep in my bed. And the whole thing freaks me the fuck out *without* you on my ass, so maybe just lay off a little."

Her face softened. "I'm sorry. You're right. I just ... I want you to be happy and okay, and I'm a little scared for you."

I sighed and sagged in my chair. "Me too. Ronnie, I don't know how to do this. Like, I have no chill when I really like a guy."

"In fairness, the last guy you really, *really* liked was in high school."

"And he made me crazy. Courtney Love, rip-down-the-curtains, where-the-fuck-is-my-man crazy. For two years. And through the whole thing, he treated me like shit, and when I lost my mind, he'd just press his finger to my forehead, and I'd calm down and give him whatever the fuck he wanted." My chest ached at the memory.

She sighed. "But he was manipulating you."

"Fuck yeah, he was. You know, one time, he called me at two thirty in the morning just to say hi. I thought it was so cute and sweet that he was thinking about me, and I asked him where he was. And you know what he told me? That he was at Anna Dorf's house—that skank. Motherfucker *knew* I hated her—she had the biggest thing for Rodney and didn't even pretend to hide it— and he straight-up told me that was where he was. He told me to stop being crazy. So of course, I'm upset trying to figure out if he was fucking with me, and we're going back and forth, and he's getting meaner, and I'm getting more and more pissed. And then I heard him ask someone for syrup."

"Syrup?"

"Yeah, because he wasn't at Anna's house. He was somewhere getting breakfast food. So I hung up on him. I got dressed and got in my car. There were two places he could get pancakes at that time in Santa Cruz." I held up two fingers for dramatic effect. "IHOP, where he wasn't, and House of Pie, where he was. I marched into that motherfucker, stomped over to his table, stuck my finger in his face, and told him never to lie to me about where he was because I'd fucking find him. He looked at me like he was scared to death of me, and he was probably wise to be afraid because I was in a full-blown psychotic break. And just like that, he pulled me onto his lap and laughed and told me he was only joking and that he loved me. The worst part is that by the time he got to the apology or diversion or whatever it was, I wasn't even mad anymore."

Veronica blinked, surprised, and I felt ashamed.

"I told you. Crazy. Psycho. I don't want to go psycho on Bodie. I don't want to wig out and scare him off, but all of this is … it's *happening,* and I don't know if I can even stop it. I don't want to stop whatever's going on between us, but I'm scared."

The admission spilled out of me, and the truth of it dragged my high down to the bottom of the ocean.

But Veronica reached for my hand and squeezed it. "Pen, listen, that's Peggy talking."

"Ugh, fucking Peggy!" I groaned.

"Exactly. She's trying to sabotage you, but don't let her. Fuck that bitch."

I didn't respond—I was too busy feeling sorry for myself—so she kept going with more determination.

"You are the toughest chick I know, and the very last thing I expect from you is to let fear stop you from doing anything. Jump out of the plane, Pen. Because Bodie isn't Rodney—he's not going to manipulate you or hurt you, not on purpose. Plus, you aren't sixteen; you're twenty-six. You've lived and learned, and you can do this. Bodie's worth the risk even if you fail."

I dropped my eyes to the table.

"You *aren't* going to fail."

I still didn't say anything.

"Okay, how about this? Let's come up with a … safe word of sorts. If you feel the psycho coming on, you just text me the safe word, and I'll save you. I'll be your shot of whiskey. I'll be your fucking life jacket."

I perked up a little. "Maybe that'll work. Can I pick the safe word?"

She laughed. "Of course."

I smiled as filthy words rolled through my head, but it didn't feel like a Dirty Sanchez sort of a safe-word situation. "Hmm," I hummed, thinking. Then I snapped my fingers. "Bear trap."

Her eyebrows shifted; one went up, and one went down. "Bear trap?"

I sat up a little straighter in my seat. "Yeah, like I'm skipping through the forest, minding my own shit, and then—*wham*. Bear trap. Totally derailed, chew-my-own-foot-off crazy."

Veronica chuckled. "I like it. So you just say the word, and I'll spring the trap so you won't have to eat off an appendage."

I sighed, feeling relieved. "I like this plan. Plans are good."

"Plans are great. And you know what?"

"What?" I asked hopefully.

She smiled with knowledge and understanding, and I felt a zillion times better.

"You're going to be okay."

And I was dumb and desperate enough to actually believe her.

chapter
fourteen

#ThingsThatAreLies

P HIL SHOOK HIS HEAD AND PUSHED AWAY FROM HIS DESK. "I CAN'T FUCKING figure this out, man."

I rubbed my bleary eyes with the pads of my fingers and rolled over so I could see his monitor, scanning the code, looking for errors.

"Here." I tapped the screen. "You divided by zero, and it's terminating."

Phil groaned. "I'm so tired. We can't keep going on like this."

I nodded. "Look, we'll get caught up tonight if we can keep our shit together. And tomorrow, you can sleep all day."

Angie appeared behind him with a plate of brownies, her big brown eyes shining. "Sounds like it's time for a break."

"Oh, sweet," Jude said, leaning over to swipe one. "Man, I'm starving," he said with his mouth full.

"Maybe we could order another pizza," Phil offered.

I glanced around at our desks—a graveyard of plates, coffee cups, napkins, and empty cans of Red Bull. "We had pizza yesterday."

"And the day before," Jude added.

Angie lit up. "Let me make you guys dinner."

Phil rested a hand on her hip. "You don't have to do that, babe."

She shrugged and smiled. "Oh, I don't mind. I'll make something easy. How does spaghetti sound? I'll run down and grab a salad and some French bread too, and make it extra fancy with sausage instead of beef."

My mouth watered at the thought. "So much better than pizza. You're an angel, Angie."

She blushed and waved a hand, giggling; the sound was like tinkling bells. All three of us smiled back at her.

Jude jerked a chin at Phil. "You picked a good one, Philly."

Phil just smiled.

I ran a hand over my face as I yawned, hoping I could stay up for another eight to twelve hours so we could get back on schedule. We were less than a week from the meeting, and the demo was so close to being ready. We just needed to spend the next week spit-shining it and working out the kinks.

And honestly, Jude had the most work cut out for him, getting the graphics where we wanted them. Because graphics would be the first thing that would sell it. Then story, then usability. And we were ambitious enough to want all three to be of such quality, there would be no way they could tell us no.

My phone rang from my desk, and I picked it up, smiling at a photo of Penny and me, a selfie we had taken at the wedding.

I hadn't seen her since I burned her pancakes two days before. And I hated the eight to twelve hours that stood between us.

I answered and sat back in my chair. "Hey."

"Hey yourself," she said on a laugh. "How's it going in the cave?"

"None of us have showered in days, we've had pizza for the last three meals, including breakfast, and our coffeepot has had hot to warm coffee in it for forty-eight hours straight."

"So, productive?"

"Very. We're almost caught up."

"Thank God. I miss you."

"I miss you too," I said, warmth spreading through my chest.

Jude flapped his hands and made kissy faces at me. I turned my chair so he was behind me.

"What are you up to?" I asked.

"The usual—just working a lot, thinking about you. You know, normal stuff. Can I see you tonight?" She was nervous and hopeful and a little cagey, and it broke my heart.

"I wish I could. We're right on the edge of the deadline, and it'll take us until the middle of the night, I'm sure."

"Oh. Okay. I figured, just had to ask."

Her disappointment was almost too much—I nearly caved.

"Pen, I want to see you. Are you around tomorrow? All I need is a nap and a shower and I'll be as hot and ready as a Little Caesars pizza."

She laughed, the tension dissipating just a little. "Sounds good. Just let me know when you're free."

"How about you tell me when you're off, and I'll make time."

Angie walked through the living room, digging through her purse. "Any special requests?"

I held up an empty can of Red Bull and shook it, and she nodded.

"Angie's over?" Penny asked, something tinging her words with anxiety again. Jealousy? My brows dropped.

"Uh, yeah. She's feeding us so we don't overdose on caffeine and junk food."

"Cool. That's cool."

I frowned. It didn't sound like she thought it was cool. "You okay?"

"Yeah, no, for sure. I just figured you guys were all No Girls Allowed, like the *The Little Rascals*." She attempted to joke, but it fell flat.

720 | STACI HART

I tried to save it. "Just call me Spanky."

She laughed, but it sounded fake, and I got up and walked to the kitchen for a modicum of privacy.

"You sure you're okay?"

She sighed, a defeated noise and the first sign of honesty. "Yeah, I'm okay. I just really want to see you, that's all."

"I know. Me too. Tomorrow, okay? Anytime, you name it, and I'm all yours."

"All right, *Spanky*. I expect you to hold good on the nickname though."

"Deal. Text me later and let me know how your day is."

"I will," she said, and I could hear her smiling. That at least was a win. "Bye, Bodie."

"Bye," I echoed and hung up with a sigh of my own.

Penny was bugging out, and I wasn't sure what had happened or what I could do to ease her mind.

For two days, we'd barely talked—two days after a night that changed me, changed us. And now that the brazen, unapologetic, confident woman I'd come to care for had been exposed, her insecurities and uncertainties were apparent.

I didn't care past wanting to make it all right, make it better. Though part of me wondered if there was more to the shift in her.

I knew she cared, but maybe she didn't trust me after all. I sensed she felt I'd penned her in, and if I couldn't prove that I would take care of her heart, she could bust out of the fence and run for freedom. Maybe keeping her would drive her crazy. Maybe she just didn't know what to do with herself.

I shook my head and ran my hand through my hair, which still felt too short, as I stared at my phone, imagining her somewhere in the city staring at hers too.

Angie was still in the kitchen, jotting on a piece of paper. She smiled up at me. "Jude had a list."

I chuckled and leaned on the island. "Of course he did."

"Everything okay?" she asked, glancing at my phone.

"Yeah. I think so at least."

"How's it going with Penny?"

"I can't really tell. Things are getting a little ... complicated."

Angie raised a brow. "Oh?"

"I dunno. Maybe complicated isn't the right word. Like, everything between us is fine, great even. But I think we're both having feelings, and only one of us knows what to do with them."

"Hmm. What's going on?"

"She's just acting cagey, uncertain."

Angie frowned. "How come?"

I sighed and raked a hand through my hair again. "She doesn't want commitment, and we've sort of outgrown the idea that it's casual."

"Have you guys talked about whatever feelings you're having?"

I shook my head. "I'm afraid I'll scare her off. She gets all in her head, and it's like I can just see her snowballing away from me."

"Do you know why she's so …"

"Skittish? She dated this guy in high school, and he was horrible to her. He was fucking half the school and somehow kept it a secret from her until they broke up. Not only that, but he had her so under his thumb, and I don't know if she ever escaped. Asshole," I hissed to myself, hot anger churning in my chest at the thought. "He had no idea what he had. And when she got hurt, she decided not to let herself ever get hurt again. Which meant she won't get into anything serious."

Angie watched me for a second. "I think you need to talk to her."

I squirmed.

"I mean it. You know, I always say that a relationship needs three things—"

"Trust, communication, and respect?"

She smiled. "That's right. How many of those do you have?"

"Two out of three. I think the trust and respect are there, it's just the communication part that's not happening."

"I know you don't want to lose her, but you might anyway if you keep your mouth shut. If she doesn't know how you feel, how can she be okay? And if you don't know how she feels, how can you be okay? You should be honest, communicate. Then it'll be easier to make decisions on what comes next."

"And if she tells me she doesn't feel the same and bolts?"

Angie's big brown eyes softened. "Well, then you'll know you weren't in the same place."

I scrubbed a hand over my mouth. "I dunno, Ang. That's not how dating works. It's all about this game, this power struggle. And Penny doesn't just play the game. She practically invented it. I'm an anomaly for her, and I know she cares, but I don't know if she knows how to play it straight."

"You don't have to play the game, you know? You don't have to participate. Just tell her what you want and how you feel and see if she feels the same way."

"Maybe I will. I've just got to be careful."

"I know," she said gently. "But you're not going to break her."

I only wished I could have believed that were true.

⁒

722 | STACI HART

We're cool.

Everything's cool.

It was my mantra for the rest of the afternoon at work, like a goddamn record skipping in an anxiety loop in my brain. It wasn't like I hadn't known he was going to be busy. I had. He'd told me. I knew. I swear.

It wasn't me. He just had work to do, that was all. Which meant nothing was wrong and everything was cool and fine and perfect.

My guts twisted up at the lie.

The last two days had been nothing like the two days before the wedding. Those days had been busy with wedding stuff and happy lovey-dovey feelings about Bodie. And then, shit had to go and get all serious.

My mood had vacillated a thousand times in forty-eight hours, going from perfectly content to doomsday in a five-minute span. We'd texted and talked a few times, but he was working, and I was trying to respect that. It was just that my psycho brain wouldn't comply.

I tried to visualize the wedding. I thought about the sweetness of Bodie's arms around me, his lips against mine. Pictured him holding my face in my kitchen, telling me it was okay.

Of course, then I thought about what he was doing. I mean, Angie was over there, but I wasn't allowed to be. I told myself that I'd be a distraction, but then I thought maybe he could use a break. He'd been working so hard, and I missed him. I considered swinging by with donuts or ice cream or some offering. I imagined him being so happy to see me, imagined him ditching work for a bit for kissing and laughing and talking, just so we could be in each other's arms for a minute, so I could hold onto the feeling of him, to reassure myself that things were fine.

I could just stop by for a minute or two or whatever—I had an hour before my next job—and I smiled to myself, grabbing my bag and blowing out of the shop without a word to anyone, daydreaming about him being so happy to see me that he'd kiss me and ask me to stay.

I wanted to see him. I could make it happen. I would make it happen.

Even though he doesn't want you to come over.

I nearly skidded to a stop on the sidewalk at the thought.

Fucking Peggy.

With a smile that would make the Grinch cringe, she told me that he didn't want me there, that he didn't want to see me. He wanted me to wait until tomorrow because he didn't care to see me, or maybe he wanted to dump me. Either that or he was seeing someone else. Or just didn't really like me all that much. He wanted my body, wanted my flesh, not my heart, not my soul.

I took a deep breath as cold panic set in. In the span of five minutes, I'd disregarded what he needed, what he'd asked of me, for my own wants and needs. I'd pushed up against that line, and the shock of the realization hit me with a jolt.

This was everything I'd been trying to avoid, everything I didn't want.

I'd broken the three-date rule for what had become my favorite dick in the whole world, and this was the price I'd pay. I'd turn into a hot, steaming mess and ruin everything, self-destruct, sabotage my happiness, burn it all down.

But it was too late to go back. The floodgates were open, and the current was too strong to close them again.

Although maybe, just maybe, there was a way to slow things down.

The curse of him giving me what I wanted was that he still wasn't being honest with me. I had no idea how he really felt, and that fact had me betraying myself and his wishes too. So I'd take a little space to buy a little perspective. It was time to take back an iota of control over myself—the helplessness I felt was overwhelming. It wasn't fun anymore. It wasn't good and happy and easy. It was sticky like flypaper, and I was stuck in it, trapped, immobilized.

I couldn't deny I cared about Bodie. But maybe, if I took a minute to get myself right, I could come back to him fresh and ready and happy again.

Peggy whispered that I'd never go back because I was afraid. So I kicked her down the stairs and shut the cellar door. And then I picked up my phone, pulled up my messages, and texted Veronica two words.

BEAR TRAP.

chapter
fifteen

Savage

THE WORST FOUR WORDS IN THE ENGLISH LANGUAGE: *HIT ME UP, PENNY.*

When she blew me off the next day, I told myself she was just busy.

When she didn't call me for two days after that, I realized we had a much bigger problem.

My texts had been answered with single words and emojis. My calls had been sent to voice mail, followed by a one-off text that she was working, or out with Veronica or whatever the excuse *du jour* was. And the result was my absolute frustration.

So I kept busy with work and tried not to think about her. Which was, frankly, impossible.

That connection I'd come to depend on had been severed, and though I wanted to believe that she was just occupied, I knew she was putting space between us, separating from me. Leaving me. And I was alone and isolated and driving myself mad at the thought of losing her.

I tried to problem-solve, picking apart every interaction since the wedding to look for clues. If I'd done something wrong, I could fix it. If there was a way to salvage what we'd had, I would find it. Because I needed her, and I wasn't ready to walk away. I didn't think I'd ever be able to.

Three days in, I realized I might not have a choice.

My options were few.

I could try to reach out while attempting not to pressure her, but what with her lack of reciprocation over the last few days, I'd already exhausted that avenue.

I could wait her out, give her space, try not to worry, and hope she came back—this was where I found myself.

Or I could let her go. I could write her off. Close the door. Move on.

But being an honest man, there was no way I could pretend like that was even a remote possibility.

chapter
sixteen
Bring a Friend

THE SHOP HUMMED THAT AFTERNOON FROM THE DOZENS OF PEOPLE WAITING with *Siamese Dream* playing over the speakers and the buzzing of tattoo guns in the air.

I should have been happy. I should have been content and smiling and wonderful since I'd gotten everything I asked for in the form of sweet, quiet solitude.

I didn't know who the fuck I thought I was kidding. I was miserable. I hated being alone I'd realized, which shouldn't have surprised me, but there it was. I was never alone. Alone was when my crazy blossomed into full-blown insanity—the curse of being a talker. If I couldn't talk, I couldn't figure it out. Half the time I didn't even know how I felt until I said it out loud, and right now, I had no one. Ramona was on her honeymoon getting banged senseless. Veronica was busy doing God knew what.

Trust me, I knew I should have answered Bodie's texts, called him back, and it was exactly what I wanted to do. But I was working hard to spare us both from having to deal with my psychosis. My solitary confinement was an attempt to decontaminate, an attempt to get my bearings so I could find my way back to him.

Problem was, my grand plan had backfired—the distance had made the crazy worse.

I'd made up an excuse not to see him that next day, once I'd gathered my wits and stopped trying to force my way into his apartment. I'd decided to take one day to think and separate and unscramble my brain. So I'd stripped and dyed my hair—this time, a pastel blue. I'd painted my nails. I'd taken a bubble bath and read an *entire* book. I'd cleaned my room. And the whole time, the whole fucking time, I had thought about Bodie and how much I'd rather be with him than at home.

I'd been certain I'd wake up the next morning feeling right as rain.

No such luck.

And I'd found myself at a loss.

He'd texted me the day after, and I'd blown him off again, citing work, which wasn't a complete lie. He'd called me too, which I'd sent to voicemail like a coward. And then … then he quit messaging me altogether.

So I hadn't gotten in touch with him. But he hadn't gotten in touch with me either.

I tried to pretend like that didn't break my heart.

I didn't even know if we were good anymore. Maybe he didn't want to talk to me. Maybe I'd made him mad—I'd pushed him away, and if the tables were turned, I'd be pissed too. Or maybe he was just playing defense on whatever he thought I was playing with him.

What if I never heard from him again?

Part of me—a big part of me—almost called him at that question alone. But what would I say about the last few days? Should I say I'd been busy? Should I tell him I'd been feeling things and risk his reaction?

What if he didn't want me like I wanted him? And what if he did? Could I be with him in the real way? Could I give him what he wanted, what he deserved?

I didn't even know anymore, but I'd had a lot of time to think about it.

If it were any other guy at any other time in my life, I'd have called on my little black book for comfort, but I'd rather have shaved with a rusty razor and risked tetanus. The thought of being with anyone else, even *calling* anyone else, made me feel sticky and gross.

That was its own bad sign.

Of course, the problem wasn't even really a problem. I wanted to be Bodie's girlfriend, but (A) I was crazy, and (B) I couldn't seem to find a way to admit that out loud to him.

Space was supposed to make me feel better.

Wrong.

And now it was all topped by anxiety that I'd fucked up.

I'd blown my dream guy off. And why?

Peggy. That's why.

Ramona floated into the shop, tanned and glowing and smiling as she said hello to everyone. I practically shot across the room and scooped her into a hug.

"You're back!" I cheered, nuzzling her like a puppy. "I missed you."

She laughed. "I missed you too. Look at your hair!" she said when she leaned back.

I smoothed it, smiling. "You like it?"

"I do. Does that mean …"

My brow quirked. "It means it felt like it was time for a change."

"Right." Ramona didn't stop assessing me, but she changed the subject. I thought at least. "How's everything going?"

"Fine, who cares, whatever! Tell me about your honeymoon!"

She laughed. "You act like we haven't talked every day since I left."

"I can't help it; I'm codependent." I hooked my arm in hers to walk back to my station. "Did you let him stick it in your butt?"

That one got a cackle out of her. "It's like the one time I can't refuse."

"That, and his birthday."

"Fortunately, he's a gentle lover when it comes to ringing at the back door. Like maybe the *only* time he's gentle."

"Psh, lucky."

She squeezed me. "I missed you."

I squeezed her back. "You already said that."

"Well, it deserved saying twice. Now tell me what's been going on around here. You know all about Tahiti and honeymoon anal, so spill the deal."

"So," I said as we passed Veronica's station, "Ronnie is acting super weird. She's had *plans*."

Ramona's face quirked, and she looked around me to Veronica, who waved excitedly but was in the middle of a piece and couldn't get up.

"Weird," Ramona said quietly. "Maybe she's seeing someone."

"Maybe. I can't exactly blame her for not telling me either. I'd charbroil her for information. Fricasseed."

Ramona giggled, and we rounded my wall. She took a seat in my chair, and I sat on my saddle stool, so relieved to see her.

"So," Ramona started, "how's Bodie?"

My nose wrinkled. "We haven't really talked much since the wedding."

Her brows dropped. "Why not?"

I shifted to lean on my desk. "Because I'm a mess, and I ruin things."

She didn't answer, which forced me to keep talking. That asshole.

"I dunno, Ramona. I don't know what I'm doing. He got busy with work, so I didn't see him for a couple of days, and I bugged out. Like butthurt and needy and demented. I just figured a little space would do me good."

"Has it?"

I groaned. "No. I mean, yes. But no."

She sighed and gave me a loving look. "Just call him, Penny."

"But I'm unhinged! I don't do alone. I'm co-dependent and psychotic, and this is why I don't have boyfriends. *You know this!*"

"I know this. You've just got to get over it."

I laughed. "That's cute, Mona."

"I'm serious. You can't go dying your hair and then find a new guy every time things get hard."

I made a face at her. "That's not why I—"

"Liar! You wigged out, so you *wigged* out." She motioned to my hair. "Your hair is like a mood ring. Do you know how he feels?"

I inspected my cuticles. "Not really. I mean, I think I do, but I'm not sure."

"So talk to him, Pen. Be a grown up and call him and *talk to him*."

"Maybe I've already screwed it up."

"Or maybe you'll call him and everything will be fine. Because he's into you. I have a feeling he's wigging out too. Hopefully he didn't shave his head or something."

I laughed and ran a hand over my hair, feeling insecure about it now that I'd been called out. "Do you really think it's that easy?"

"I really do. I mean, even if he doesn't want to be with you, that would be better than this, right? Because then you could just try to get over it."

I sighed. "Yeah." And then I thought about calling him. I thought about seeing him smile. I thought about just *being* with him, like it had been before Peggy came around, blowing cigarette smoke in my face. "I don't know how to get back to the happy place, Ramona."

"Tell him how you feel, and let him tell you how he feels. Once you talk about that, you'll both feel better. And instead of having to text Ronnie *BEAR TRAP*, you can talk to *him* about it."

"Traitor!" I shouted at Veronica, who shrugged.

Ramona leaned forward, resting her elbows on her thighs. "Just call him. It's the only way to stop the crazy. I know you're afraid, but not talking to him is what made you crazy in the first place. The only power anyone has over you is what you give them."

I took a long, deep breath and let it out slowly. "Okay."

She watched me for a second. "Okay?"

I nodded and smiled, reaching for my phone. "Okay." But before I could even unlock the screen, it rang in my hand.

The number was from Santa Cruz. It was a number I recognized. It was the first number I programmed into my Razr when I was sixteen and the number I'd dialed from my mom's cordless phone.

Rodney fucking Parker was calling me.

I stared at my phone stupidly for a second before snapping out of it to answer. "Hello?"

"Pen?" His voice was familiar and velvety and full of swagger and ease.

My eyes were big and round, and my mouth was sticky and dry. "Rodney?"

Ramona's mouth popped open

He laughed. "Holy shit. I can't believe you kept the same number."

"What the hell, man?" I said lightly, shooting for breezy, which wasn't easy considering every nerve in my body fired in warning. "How are you?"

"Good, good. Damn, it's good to hear your voice."

I mouthed *Oh my God* at Ramona, who blinked at me. "You too. What's up?"

"You're in New York, right? I caught your show on TV. Couldn't believe it. You're just as hot as you always were."

I stood and paced out of the shop and into the steaming hot afternoon. "Uh, thanks."

"So I called my agent, and she called your agent to get your number. If I'd known it was the same, I would have called you yesterday," he said, smiling on the other end of the line. "Listen, I'm in town with the band—we're playing at Lucky's tonight, and I've got a couple of tickets for you. Tell me you'll come see me."

I felt sweaty and a little nauseous. "Yeah, okay," I said a little sarcastically. I had literally no intention of going to see that asshole anywhere.

"Good. I was prepared to beg."

Rodney. Begging me. For anything.

It was the stuff of my wildest dreams and my worst nightmares.

I laughed. I couldn't help it. I had to be dreaming or having a full psychotic break or a stroke or something.

"You okay?" he asked as I laughed like a hyena.

I pressed my fingers to my lips and tried to stop, succeeding after a second and a few heavy breaths. "Yeah. Yep. I'm good."

He chuckled, and I remembered all the nights with him, all the kisses at my locker, all the hours listening to the band practice. All the good. All the bad. All of it rushed back over me like a tsunami.

"All right," he said. "The tickets will be at Will Call under your name. And bring a friend."

"Sure, sure," I answered as I swallowed my laughter.

"Doors open at seven. Man, I can't wait to see you. It's been too long, babe."

"Oh, yeah. Cool. For sure."

I hung up without waiting for him to respond. And then I sat down on the dirty fucking curb and burst into hysterical laughter.

Rodney had called me. And invited me to a show. And asked me to bring a friend. And called me *babe*.

The universe had to be fucking with me.

The last time we'd actually spoken, he'd dumped me after graduation, and I'd unloaded two years of feelings on him with my volume level at twelve and an audience of at least two fifty. I'd seen him at a few parties after that, and both times, we'd ended up fucking in a bathroom and his car, respectively. There was no talking either time.

After that summer, I'd moved to New York, and I hadn't really thought about him much. I had thrown myself into my life, my goals, which in part included not ever getting serious with anyone. Which insured they always wanted to get serious with me.

And I know what you're thinking—*God, Penny, you're such a liar. You thought about him all the time.*

But I really hadn't. He'd affected me, but I'd closed the door and tried not to let it bother me otherwise. It was simply a sticking point, a reason why, devoid of general emotions on the matter.

I was an excellent suppressor of emotion on that particular matter.

Things I could thank Rodney for.

My abs hurt a little from laughing, and I wiped a stray tear from the corner of my eye.

Rodney had done so much to shape who I was, and Bodie had undone it all just by existing, just by caring for me.

I thought about Diddle, the boy I used to know. I thought about the man he'd grown up to be and how brilliant and determined and wonderful he was. I thought about how good he made me feel, how he cared for me, how I cared for him. I thought about how different Rodney was from Bodie, how one could be so cruel and one so kind. How one could seek to tear me down while the other lifted me up.

I thought about how Bodie was everything I wanted, and I thought about how wrong I'd done him.

I thought about how I could possibly make it right again.

And then I unlocked my phone, navigated to my favorites, and touched his name, hoping I still had a chance.

When my phone rang and I saw our picture on the screen, my heart stopped and started again with a jolt I felt down to my toes. I'd imagined the moment for days and had lost hope that it would happen, that I would hear from her. And now that my phone buzzed in my hand, I had no fucking clue what to say or do or feel.

So I went default.

"Hey, Penny," I answered, hoping I sounded cool.

She laughed nervously. "Bodie, oh my God. You won't believe who just called me."

A slow tingle climbed my neck. *Not what I thought she'd say.* "Who?"

"Rodney."

My insides liquified at that single word. "Really?"

She laughed, the nervousness slipping away until it edged on hysteria, her tone giddy and rushed. "Seriously! Get this: he had *his* agent call *my* agent." She laughed again, a burst of feverish giggling that made my blood boil.

I tried to chuckle, but it sounded a little like I was choking. "No shit. What did he want?"

"He's in town and has tickets to his show tonight at Lucky's."

More laughter—my pulse ticked up.

"He told me to *bring a friend.*"

"Great. I'm your friend. I'm coming with you."

Another round of giggling, this one hitting me in the heart, reminding me how much I wanted her for my own. It was a sound meant for me this time, a sound that said she wanted me with her.

All that was gleaned from a simple series of bursts of air from her lips.

"I didn't think you'd be interested," she said, half-joking.

If there was one thing I didn't joke about, it was Penny and Rodney in the same room together.

"Penny, I'm interested in all things related to you."

She paused for a second. "Listen, I don't really think—"

"I'm coming with you. What time's the show?"

Another pause.

"The doors open at seven, but I don't want to—"

"Pen," I said with finality, "I want to see you. I *need* to see you. And you're not going to Lucky's without me. So it's settled—I'm coming with you. I'll meet you there at seven."

"All right," she said quietly, tentatively. "How've you been?"

"Busy with work but good," I lied, suppressing a sigh, the pressure in my chest mounting. "You?"

"Oh, I've been okay. Just working a lot."

She lulled, and I grappled with what to say.

"I … I missed you."

My anxiety softened by the smallest degree. "Me too, Pen."

"Bodie, there's so much to say. I've been thinking about everything, about you and me, and—"

I heard someone call her name in the background, and she hissed a swear.

"I've got to go. Let's talk tonight, okay?"

"Okay," I answered with my heart drumming, and we said goodbye, disconnecting.

My palms were swampy as I slipped my phone into my back pocket and paced into the living room where Jude and Phil sat at their desks working.

I ran a hand through my hair as they turned to eye me.

"This is the worst possible thing that could fucking happen."

Jude's brow quirked. "What is?"

"Penny called." I turned to pace in the other direction.

"Wait, that's bad?" Phil asked.

I sighed. "Penny called to tell me that *Rod* fucking called her to ask her to go to his show tonight."

Jude's mouth popped open. "No shit."

"No shit," I echoed.

"Fuck," he said, running his hand over his lips. "This is bad."

"I'm so fucked. *Fucked.* Eight years later, and that asshole is coming back to throw a wrench in everything, and the timing sucks. We haven't talked, she's wigging out, and he's the one person who has the power to ruin everything. Nobody gets under her skin like he does."

Phil looked confused. "Why the hell would she agree to go?"

"Because," I huffed, walking back toward the door, "he's a fucking rock star, and he had her under his thumb for half of high school. Because she's *Penny*, and of course she wants to go. But I told her I'm going with her."

Jude laughed at that. "You *told* her?"

"Yeah, I fucking told her. You think I'd let her go without me? I mean, at least if I'm there, he can't get to her. Plus, there's too much unsaid that needs to be said once and for all."

"And you think Rod's concert is the right time? With him up on a stage, licking the microphone in a leather jacket?" Jude asked, shaking his head. "Bro."

I groaned and paced the room again, hand in my hair. "Fuck. Fuck! What the fuck am I gonna do?"

Phil sighed. "Cross your fingers and pray."

"Go to Lucky's and deck Roddy as a show of manhood and territorial superiority," Jude said helpfully.

I shook my head. "I've just got to survive. Show up. And hope to God I don't lose her for good."

chapter seventeen

You Can't Actually Be Serious

Y EMOTIONS WERE JUMBLED UP LIKE SCRABBLE TILES AS I WORKED through my day, trying to keep busy, which wasn't too hard. From the second I'd hung up the phone with Bodie, I'd had somebody in my chair, affording me plenty of time alone with my thoughts.

The last thing I wanted to do was go to the concert, and somehow I'd gotten roped into it. And Bodie had sounded hard and a little angry on the phone, and when he'd insisted we go to the show, I couldn't find a way to say no. I needed to see him as much as he'd said he needed to see me, and the prospect of seeing him, talking to him, was too much to argue. That on top of not wanting to make him any angrier.

The conversation had taken a hard left, and I'd found myself agreeing to go to my ex-boyfriend's rock concert with my current boyfriend-slash-slam-piece who I hadn't spoken to in days.

Basically, the whole thing was a fucking hot-ass mess.

The sound of Bodie's voice had made my insides squishy and warm. The thought of seeing him made it hard to breathe. I'd missed him so much that in hindsight, staying away seemed ridiculous and futile. I wanted to be with him; that hadn't changed. I was still scared; that hadn't changed either. All that had changed was my resolve to go after what I wanted instead of running away.

The problem was that I didn't know what to expect, and I dreaded meeting him at Lucky's.

I should have called it off. I should have told him to just meet me somewhere else, anywhere else. But the afternoon got away from me, and one thing after another went wrong. My last job, a massive back piece, ended up running over. Like, an hour over.

I texted Bodie the first chance I got, but by that point, he was already there. And the second I was finished, I blew out the door and caught a cab with my pulse speeding. I hadn't even had time to go home and change. I fussed over my clothes—my Misfits tee with the oversize neck, black mini-skirt, shredded up tights and combats. And as I touched up my makeup, nerves overwhelmed me, stoked by the anxiety of being late and not knowing what to expect from the night.

When the cab pulled up to the curb in front of Lucky's, I spotted Bodie

734 | STACI HART

leaning against the wall next to the box office, his eyes dark and brows low, hands in his pockets and ankles crossed.

He looked gorgeous.

Gorgeous and pissed.

I paid the cabbie and slipped out of the car into the sweltering heat, trotting across the sidewalk to him as he pushed away from the wall.

I found myself breathless, probably from jogging. Or from Bodie—broody and tense and pumping out testosterone and pheromones at me like tear gas.

"Hey," I breathed, wishing I could wrap myself around him like a boa constrictor. As much as I'd thought I'd missed him, it was nothing compared to standing there in front of him without permission to touch him. "I'm so sorry I'm late."

He attempted to relax with a deep breath that lowered his square shoulders just a touch. "It's all right, but can we get inside? I could use a drink."

I smiled, hoping it looked like I wasn't nervous as shit. "Yeah. Of course."

We headed over to the box office in heavy silence, and I picked up our tickets. And within a few minutes, we were stepping under the blasting air-conditioning and making our way to the bar.

It was already packed and loud, and within ten feet, the air-conditioning was a distant memory—the heat from the hundreds of bodies packed into the space had turned it into a sauna. We waited in line at the bar, trying to shout at each other over the noise with a thousand things we wanted to say pressing on us like the oppressive heat.

Lucky's was general admission only, and we wormed our way through the masses to get as close to the stage as we could. Every second, the crowd closed in a little tighter around us, and I slammed my double tequila almost as fast as he slammed his double whiskey.

Bodie leaned down to my ear. "I'm gonna get us another round."

I nodded and yelled, "I'll be here," which sounded way less cute in scream-speak.

He disappeared into the crowd, and I took a breath and let it out. As excited as I had been to see Bodie, he was angry and tense, and it was my fault. The combination of me going radio silent, him having to wait an hour for me in the hundred degree heat, and the fact that we hadn't talked about anything we wanted to—it was almost too much to bear in the span of a few minutes.

It all of a sudden felt like a kamikaze mission, and I clambered for a way to salvage the night.

A few minutes after he left, he was back with a fresh drink, looking a little more relaxed. He smiled and brought his lips to my ear. "I found another bar upstairs, it was empty."

I reached up on my tiptoes to get to his ear in return. "Good. Thank you."

He repeated the ridiculous motion to get to my ear, the frustrating lag in conversation pissing me off.

"You're welcome." He ran a strand of my blue hair through his fingers. "You changed your hair."

I nodded, our lips had found places, our cheeks almost pressed together so we didn't have to move. "You like it?"

"It's different," he answered enigmatically just as the crowd began to cheer.

I turned to find the opening band making their way onto the stage, raising their hands to the crowd as they picked up their instruments. And just like that, any shot we'd had to talk was blown.

We bounced around to the opening band, pounding drinks. By the time their set was finished, Bodie and I hadn't spoken, and we'd each had three doubles. This could have been a good thing, except for the fact that we were both drinking to ease our nerves. Or at least I was. Bodie seemed to be drinking so he could tolerate me.

He went to get us our fourth drink during the set change. And by the time he got back, the lights were dimming, and the crowd screamed and clapped as Rodney walked out from backstage.

It was then that I realized something very important—far too late for it to matter.

I'd had a lot of bad ideas in my life, but agreeing to meet Bodie at Lucky's that night was hands down the worst.

My breath was still, my eyes blinking as Rodney fucking Parker—my albatross and cross to bear—took the microphone in a leather jacket and skinny jeans, looking like a goddamn motherfucking god.

He wasn't a boy anymore. He was a man with a guitar and a voice and that hair and those hands. I was like a bug in a spiderweb with my eyes locked onto Rodney as I struggled to break free. For two years, I'd been obsessed with him even though he hurt me, and there he was, in the flesh, a grown man, resurrected. My past stood there before me, and my future stood next to me whole I stood in the middle, completely frozen from the unanticipated shock of it all.

If I'd been able to form a cognizant thought, I would have grabbed Bodie's hand and run out of that stuffy, steamy, loud room like it was on fire. But since my brain had ceased primary functions, I found myself stuck to the spot with my mouth open and my drink warming in my hand.

It was bad. So, so bad.

I found my wits somewhere near the end of the set, stiff drink in my hand and stiff Bodie next to me. I snuck a glance at him and found him some-how looking even more pissed than he had when I walked up an hour late.

Disaster. Complete fucking disaster.

I slammed my drink, teetering a little under the burn as the no-longer-chilled tequila made its way through my esophagus, and then there was only one thing to do—get the fuck out of there as quickly as possible.

I grabbed Bodie's hand and lifted my chin, tilting my head to indicate I wanted to talk to him, and he lowered his face so I could reach his ear.

"Let's go," I said hastily and with a little bit of a slur.

He nodded, everything about him softening with relief, but before we could even take a step, Rodney was on the mic, and I heard my name.

"Penny! Hey, guys," Rodney said, his voice rumbling at a trillion decibels from forty-eight-million speakers. "Check it out. See that girl there with the blue hair and the hips that could knock a motherfucker out?"

He pointed straight at me, and everyone turned around to gawk, except Bodie. Bodie stared at Rodney like he wanted to separate his head from his body.

"Come on up here, Pen."

I shook my head.

"Come on! Help me out, guys. *Pen-ny. Pen-ny. Pen-ny.*"

The entire fucking joint was chanting my name, and the next thing I knew, I was being pulled toward the stage by strangers, looking back over my shoulder at Bodie, begging for him to save me, begging for him to forgive whatever was about to happen.

I was lifted up and put on the stage, and before I could even protest, I was in Rodney's arms, pressed up against his chest as I angled away, scanning the crowd for Bodie, but I couldn't see shit. I didn't even know how Rodney had picked me out.

Stupid fucking hair. Dead giveaway.

"So, you might know Penny from her TV show, *Tonic.*"

The crowd cheered.

"Well, wouldn't you know it? Penny used to be my girlfriend a long, long time ago, but I was a stupid little prick back then." His tone was self-deprecating, and I didn't buy it at all. "I wrote some of your favorite songs for her because, let me tell you something—you don't forget a girl like Penny."

He turned to me, all smiles as he let me go and stepped back, slinging his guitar from back to front, calling the song to the guys, and the drummer kicked off the beat.

And I stood there on the fucking stage with a hundred lights on me, a screaming crowd—minus one pissed off Bodie—singing along as Rodney sere-naded me with their biggest hit. The song was a drug-and-addiction metaphor for love, all about this muse who had ruined him, left him hanging to dry, spent and tired and needing more.

I felt like he'd gotten his wires crossed about what had gone down between us.

I was shocked and stunned, locked to the spot to the side of the stage by the expectations of several hundred people. I couldn't walk off without causing a scene, and there were all those faces and eyes and lights—*so* many lights, blinding and sharp—pinning me down as a zillion thoughts zinged through my head.

I legitimately want to die.

Where did Bodie go?

God, there are so many people staring at me right now.

I should get an award for being so fucking dumb.

Fuck, it's so loud. This is ridiculous.

I should walk. But what if he stops the song? Then everyone is going to boo.

Do I even care?

Yes, yes, I care if three hundred people boo me.

Bodie's watching. He's got to be so pissed. I would be a raging psycho.

Why didn't we leave? We should have left.

What the fuck do I do with my hands?

I should have fucking called this off. Stupid, Penny. Stupid, stupid, stupid.

Am I supposed to smile? Dance? Sing along? I don't even know the damn words.

Seriously, death would be a welcome release. Any second now, I'll get struck by lightning and be put out of my misery.

And so on for approximately four minutes, while I stood there like a fucking idiot, wishing I could run like hell.

The song ended, mercifully, and Rodney made his way over, reaching for me for what I thought would be a kiss on the cheek.

Wrong again. So, so wrong.

His lips hit mine, soft and familiar, sending a rush of memories back to me, and I immediately turned my head, smiling awkwardly as I attempted to push him away. Discomfort covered me like a bucket of slime, and I pushed harder.

He finally stopped, but before he let me go, he nuzzled into my ear. "Come see me backstage after the show." His hand snaked down to my ass, and he squeezed it. "Fuck, you look good."

I pushed away from him hard, furious on the inside, laughing uncomfortably on the outside, with my cheeks flaming and all those people staring at me. When I turned, a security guy waited behind me with a hand extended to guide me down the stairs, and as I made my way down, I searched for Bodie in the crowd.

All I caught was a glimpse of the back of his head and the set of his shoulders as he wound his way through the crowd toward the door.

"*Fuck, shit, fuck,*" I hissed, a little wobbly from the tequila as I hurried as best as I could after him through the throng of people to the deafening sound of the band's final song.

I burst through the door and onto the sidewalk to find Bodie storming away.

"Bodie, wait!" I called after him.

He didn't stop.

My heart broke, and I trotted to catch up, laying a hand on his arm.

"Bodie, please," I said.

He whirled around so fast, I almost fell backward.

His eyes were hard, his jaw set and lips a thin line. I barely recognized him. "*What?*" he shot.

And the accusation in that single syllable cut through me.

"I … I—" I stammered with my mouth open like a trout, completely stunned by the shift in him, though not at all surprised. I deserved every bit of his anger and braced myself.

"Jesus, Penny. What the fuck am I supposed to do with you?"

I blinked, angling away from him a little. "What the fuck does that mean?"

He took a controlled breath, his eyes boring into me like icy blue drills. "I've done everything I know to do to try to make you happy, and the second things got real, you dropped me like a bad fucking habit. You didn't speak to me for days—*days*, after everything—and when you did call, you called to tell me *he* called you." He jabbed a single finger at the venue. "And then? Then we came here together—"

"Hang on, that was *your* idea! I didn't even want—" I tried to say over him, but he was a steamroller.

"—And the whole fucking time you were staring at him like he was God's fucking gift. He treated you like garbage, Penny. Fucking trash. And then you went up on that stage and you fucking kissed him and *I just can't with you, Penny.* I can't."

I fumed and stuck my own skinny finger in his broad chest. "I didn't kiss him, you asshole. He kissed me, and I *tried* to get away from him!"

He laughed, a sound as dry and hot as the desert. "Please. You laughed and smiled and *stood there* instead of walking away."

My heart stopped and started again with a painful kick. "What the hell was I supposed to do? Make a huge scene on the stage? Bodie, for fuck's sake, I came here with *you.*"

"You haven't spoken to me in days!" he raged, the muscles in his neck taut and red. "You left me hanging, blew me off, and I'm supposed to feel good about you kissing that prick in front of three hundred people? I mean, what the actual fuck, Pen?"

"Hey, Penny," Rodney said from behind me.

I looked back in horror to find him jogging up with a smile on his face.

"I thought you were coming backstage?"

One second, Bodie was standing there with his fists clenched, looking like a coil about to spring, and the next, his arm was pulled back, and he cold-cocked Rodney in the face.

I watched the whole thing happen in slow motion, accompanied by a series of noises—the smack of knuckles against flesh, my gasp, Rodney yelling *Son of a bitch!,* and Bodie's heavy breathing as he shook out his hand.

Rodney crumpled to the ground, and out of sheer, shocked instinct, I reached for him to help him sit up as he held his bleeding nose.

"What the fuck, man?" Rodney yelled but narrowed his eyes as he really got a good look at Bodie. "Wait … Diddle?"

But Bodie just shook his head and looked at me with eyes as cold and sharp as a switchblade. "You two deserve each other," he said. And then he turned and walked away.

Tears burned my eyes, my throat in a vise, my gaze on Bodie as he stormed down the sidewalk, taking all my hopes and wishes with him.

Ruined. I was ruined. My heart was ruined. And it had been ruined long before I let him in.

Rodney tried to make sense of what was going on, inspecting me. "You're dating Diddle?"

I sniffed, blinking to keep my tears at bay as I pulled Rodney to stand. "It's complicated."

Rodney wiped the blood from his nose and inspected his hand. "Well, he's gone now. Come on backstage."

He smiled around the gore on his face, the effect gruesome and sickening. Or maybe it was the tequila. Or the fact that Bodie had just dropkicked my heart.

I shook my head. "I just really want to go home."

His smile widened as he tried to put his arm around me. "I'll take you."

I turned to avoid his grip. "I can make it on my own. Thanks for the tickets, Rodney."

That smile of his fell, slipping into anger. "Hang on. You're not actually ditching me for *Diddle,* are you? That fucking loser never had a shot with you, not then and not now. He always had a thing for you. So fucking embarrassing."

I clenched my teeth, hot anger boiling in my ribs as the flip switched, illuminating everything I'd avoided, lighting up all the things that had been right in front of me the whole time, if only I hadn't been too blind to see.

"Fuck you, asshole," I fired. "He's fucking *incredible*. *You're* the loser. How dare you. How dare you call me up on that stage and embarrass me and kiss me without my permission in front of all those people. You son of a bitch—you *ruined* me, and now you think you can call me up and bring me to a show and fuck me like you used to?"

He shrugged and ran his tongue over his teeth, his hands slipping into his pockets and his body shifting into a position that was intended to dominate, intimidate. "Listen, Pen. You're a thing—you're on TV—and I'm in a band. We've got status, and we make sense, more now than ever. Why wouldn't I try to get back in with you? I mean, look at you. You and me on camera? On tour? I could fuck you like a rock star, just like before."

"Fuck you, Rodney," I said with a shaky breath.

I turned to go, but he grabbed my arm and said my name. And when I turned, it was with my tiny fist balled up and flying toward his eyeball.

The pop was the most satisfying sound I'd ever heard in my life.

Rodney yelled and doubled over, hands over his eye and ruined nose. "What the fuck, Penny? God, you always were such a fucking psycho," he said to his shoes.

So I did the only thing I could.

I put my hands on his shoulders and kneed him as hard as I could in the balls. And then I left that motherfucker next to the gutter where he belonged.

chapter
eighteen
Hair Of The Dog

WHEN I CRACKED MY EYELIDS THE NEXT MORNING, THE VERY FIRST IN MY list of regrets was the tequila.

I felt like I'd been hit by a smelly, greasy garbage truck driven by Macho Man, who happened to be high on cocaine.

My stomach rolled, and I shifted to lie on my back, hoping to calm the raging bile down as it crept up my esophagus. A long drag of air through my nose helped, and I swallowed, reaching for the glass of water on my nightstand.

Bad, wrong. Bad, wrong, was the song my heart screamed, my brain expanding and contracting in my skull with every masochistic beat.

Yeah, tequila was the mistake that demanded all my attention. But Bodie was the regret that had broken me in the first place.

The night came back to me, not in flashes but like a creeping fog, spreading over me in tendrils. Bodie, distant and hot and angry, so different from the sunshine I'd found in him before. Rodney calling me onstage. The cold dread I'd felt as I chased Bodie out. The hurt when he'd thrown my heart on the steaming pavement. The satisfying pain from punching Rodney in his stupid fucking eyeball.

I flexed my aching right hand at the memory, and pain shot across the bones up to my wrist.

"Fuck," I croaked, opening my bleary eyes just enough to inspect my swollen phalanges.

My knuckles were split and swollen, fingers bruised, especially where one of my rings had been. Thankfully I'd taken it off or I probably would have had to cut it off. On top of that, I'd broken a nail over that fucker.

Worth it.

Of course, in a few hours, I'd have to use that hand to tattoo people all day. And as I closed my fist, I realized just how bad that was going to suck.

Still wouldn't suck as badly as the fact that Bodie and I were through.

He was right, and he was wrong. I was right, and I was wrong. I should have gone after him. I should have called him or texted him. I should have known better than to go to that show at all, especially with Bodie.

I shouldn't have waited so long.

I should have talked to him about how I felt.

And now it was probably too late.

Tears pricked my eyes, and I took a deep, shaky breath again. I'd come home to an empty apartment, drunk and hurt and defeated. A long shower couldn't wash away my guilt or sadness or loss. It couldn't erase all the things Bodie had said. It couldn't wash the dirt off my heart after I picked it up and carried it home. So I dried off, threw on the first thing I could grab from my drawer—panties and an inside-out New Order T-shirt—and slipped into my sheets in the dark.

And then I cried.

I cried until my pillow was damp and the burning in my chest had died down to a smolder. I cried until my eyes were swollen and my nose was red. And when I finally caught my breath and the tears ran dry, I slipped into a fitful sleep.

My muddled dreams ran in circles, waking intermittently to open my eyes to find my room spinning, tequila metabolizing out of my mouth and back into my nose. I hadn't been smart enough to eat anything or take any-thing, and I felt that mistake too.

I reached for my phone to check the time, and a shot of adrenaline sent my tender stomach on a turn when I wondered if he'd called or texted.

He hadn't.

And I was about to be late for work.

"Shit," I hissed and sat up too fast, dimming my vision and sending me back into the spins, heart banging its warning as I pressed the heels of my palms into my eye sockets until it passed.

I expended a healthy amount of caution as I slipped out of bed and shuf-fled around my room, pulling on jeans and Chucks, taking my shirt off to put it on right side out. At that point, I stumbled back to my bed and sat, wondering if I was still drunk. But no. I was dehydrated and brokenhearted, but I wasn't drunk. So I drank the glass of water on my nightstand, took four ibuprofen to guarantee success, and got out of bed, praying to the Mexican devil Agave that I would survive the day.

No makeup happened, and I pulled my hair up into a messy bun to match my messy life, tying a red rolled up bandana around my thumping skull, knot-ting it at the top. I didn't even look in the mirror. That was how you know shit was real.

I put on my biggest, darkest shades and hurried as best I could out the door and into the humid, sticky summer day to head to Tonic. The walk felt forever long, and I felt beyond dead.

By the time I opened the door and stepped into the air conditioning, I was practically dragging myself. The shop was loud and buzzing, and I didn't take my sunglasses off as I headed straight for my station with the singular goal to sit the fuck down.

If the music had been a record, it would have screeched to a halt at my entrance. The entire crew stared at me like I might bite them, and I might have if they'd stopped me from getting into my chair.

I dropped my bag and climbed into my tattoo chair, sighing as the cold leather touched my overheated skin, and I closed my eyes, leaning the chair back without a single fuck to give about anything but trying not to puke.

"Rough night?" Ramona said from my elbow.

I cracked my eyes to see the dark shape of her through my glasses.

"You could say that." My voice was gravelly and deeper than usual from all the yelling and crying.

"Here's some water."

I smiled, lighting up as much as I could as I reached for the offered plastic bottle. "Bless you."

"What happened, Pen?"

The bottle was to my lips, and I drank half of it before I could bring myself to stop. My stomach gurgled a warning as it prepped itself. "It was bad. Really bad."

She frowned. "How bad?"

"Apocalyptic." I sighed, mouth dry and heart wrung out. I took another drink to buy time and to attempt to mend my busted up body. "I drank about ten shots of tequila on an empty stomach, kissed Rodney, and fought with Bodie."

Her eyes blew open like I'd electrocuted her. "You kissed Rodney?" she said way too loud.

I winced from the memory and the decibel. "Shhh! Fuck, you don't have to yell. Jesus."

Her face pinched in anger. "I cannot fucking believe you, Penny! How could you do that to Bodie? God, it's like I don't even fucking know you!"

My eyes squeezed shut as my head rang. "Seriously, you have to bring it down, or I'm gonna hurl. I didn't kiss him like that. Just calm down and let me explain."

She folded her arms across her chest, and I took a deep breath, taking another sip of water to fortify me, wishing it could bring my dried up soul back to life.

"We were at the show, and Bodie was acting all angry and weird and didn't seem to even want to be there. And at the end of the show, Rodney spotted me and called me up onstage to sing to me."

"He did not," she breathed, mouth open.

"He fucking did, that cockgobbler. He sang to me, and then *he* kissed *me*. Onstage. In front of everyone. Including Bodie."

She cupped her mouth with her hands.

"Yeah. So beyond fucked up. That stupid fucker with his stupid fucking hands on my ass, like he had any right to touch me. And what could I even do? A hundred phones were pointed at me, and frankly, I was stunned stupid. But the second I could get away, I chased Bodie out—because of course he'd left; I would have left me too—and we got into this huge fight. Then Rodney came out, and Bodie punched him in the nose."

She was blinking now, hands still over her mouth.

"And then he left us there, and Rodney was being *Rodney*, so I punched him in the eye."

"You didn't!" she said from behind her hands.

I held up my right hand, knuckles out, and rested my head against the headrest, closing my tired eyes.

"Get the fuck out of here. How are you going to work today?"

"I don't even know." All that water I'd had to drink hit my stomach and began to reverse direction. "Everything sucks. Literally everything. I just want to go home and die slowly, alone, in my bed."

"Are you gonna talk to Bodie?"

"I don't know, Ramona. I don't think he wants to see me again."

"You have to try. You can't just walk away. You can't just give up."

I shook my head, heartbroken and exhausted and worn down. "I don't want to talk about it, not right now."

"But—"

I held up a hand and burped with my lips closed. "Ramona. I need to get through today. And—" Bile raced up my throat, and I scrambled out of my chair. "I'm gonna puke."

I ran to the bathroom, hitting the john just in time for the volcano to blow, the mass quantities of alcohol I'd consumed leaving me in a burning rush. And the minute that hell was over, my stomach almost sighed, having exorcised the demon, leaving my body feeling frayed and threadbare but less like it was going to expire.

I only wished the same could be said for my heart.

It was after noon by the time I finally woke. I'd slept like I was dead, a deep, dreamless sleep. But I woke feeling like I hadn't slept at all.

My stiff body creaked and groaned to life, and when I rolled over and slid my hand under my pillow, pain shot up my forearm and into my heart.

I'd clocked Rodney.

I'd lost Penny.

I flipped onto my back and hooked my arm over my face, sending me into darkness. Images flashed behind my lids like a horror show. Penny watching

Rodney, her blue hair foreign, a change I'd known nothing about, a change that had felt like its intention was to isolate me, separating me from her. Penny up on that stage with Rodney's lips against hers, lips that were mine, lips that had been avoiding me. His hand on her ass and his face buried in her ear—that was the thought that hit me over and over. It had been the thought in my head when I put his face through the meat grinder.

I shouldn't have left her there with him on the sidewalk. I shouldn't have left her at all. I shouldn't have said what I had, but I didn't want to take it back either. I'd suppressed how I felt for so long that there was no holding it back, not after a fifth of whiskey and Rodney's hands all over her.

I was wounded, and I didn't know if I'd get over it.

The cold truth was that, over the span of the last week, since the wedding, I hadn't seen her. She'd blown me off, leaving my calls and texts largely unanswered, and then, when I'd finally seen her, it had been a nightmare.

The more I thought about it, the more my hope sank.

Penny hadn't said or done anything to admit that she cared for me, nothing concrete, nothing *real*. In fact, the way she'd been treating me over the last week only pointed to a simple, undeniable fact.

She just wasn't that into me.

Everything I'd thought I felt, I'd made up and imagined. I'd read too much into it, and here I was. If she wanted me, I'd know. There would be no cat and mouse, no games to play. No waiting to answer or avoiding each other. And at the end of the day, that had to be my answer.

Operation: Penny Jar was a massive failure after all. I'd knocked the jar off the shelf and it had shattered, leaving broken glass and shiny copper all over the floor of my heart. I was the asshole who had ended up getting hurt after all.

My heart hardened under my sternum, calcifying and shrinking at the realization that it was over. Maybe it had never gotten started. Maybe she'd never cared about me at all.

I flipped off my sheets and climbed out of bed, wanting to leave my thoughts on my pillow but they followed me around like a ghost.

Phil and Jude were already at their computers, and they turned when I shuffled in wearing nothing but sleep pants, rubbing my eyes.

"Morning, sunshine," Jude sang.

I humphed.

"How's your head?"

"Fine," I grumbled as I poured a cup of coffee. "I don't remember coming home." I took my mug with me to the island and sat on a stool, facing them, back against the cool counter.

Jude smirked. "You ate half of a cold pizza, drank a gallon of water, and ranted for two hours. I'd give you another high five for decking Roddy, but I don't want to hurt you."

I inspected my hand, bruised and cut up and aching, just like my heart. "Fuck that guy."

Phil watched me. "You gonna be okay?"

"Don't really have a choice, do I?" I took a sip of coffee when I should have let it cool off, and a scalding trail burned down my chest.

"I don't mean to be a dick," Phil started, which indicated he was about to be a dick, "but you've been gone, distracted, checked out, man. We're so close, but we need you to get to the end of this thing. I want you to be happy, but she's driving you crazy, and we don't have time for crazy right now."

I nodded, eyes down and heart sinking. "It's over. And I'm here. I'm ready. No more distractions. *This*—the game, you guys—*this* is my priority. I'm sorry I've been tied up with her." *Mistakes. Regret. It's over.* "She's out of my system," I lied and stood. "So let's do this."

They smiled, though their eyes were sad, and I headed back to my room to put on a shirt.

When I picked up my phone, I found myself looking for her name, for a text, a call. Anything. But I only found the time. And the time said to move on.

So I powered it down and tossed it into my nightstand where it could stay in the dark.

"Don't worry, Penny. Tacos will make everything better," Veronica said as she hooked her arm in mine.

This was untrue. Tacos could solve a lot of problems, but Bodie and I were not one of them.

The sun blazed down on the three of us, Ramona at my other side, as we headed toward a taco joint to pick up lunch for the shop, and I found myself frowning, eyes on the sidewalk in front of me, feeling like utter shit. Batshit, if I were being accurate, because my shit was crazy.

It had been three days, four texts, two phone calls, and a bottle of Patrón, and I found myself even further away from closure with Bodie than I had been on the night I last saw him.

His silence should have been enough to let me know how he felt. But instead, I'd been driven mad with a thousand questions that only he could answer.

"Have you heard from him?" Ramona asked, reading my mind.

"Nope." I popped the P as my mood sank a little deeper.

"Ugh," she groaned. "This just doesn't even feel like him, does it?"

"No, it doesn't. But I seriously fucked it up. I just can't help but wonder if that's really it. Is it over? If I apologized, would it be okay? He won't answer me though, so there's not really anything I can do. I just wish I knew. I wish I had a chance to find out."

Veronica frowned but said nothing.

I rambled on. "I'm so frustrated and butthurt and mental over it. I wonder if he's doing it on purpose? Freezing me out to punish me?"

Veronica squeezed my arm. "Bodie wouldn't do that. I'm sure he's just busy. Don't they have that video game thing coming up?"

"Yeah," I conceded. "The whole thing sucks. I wish I could go back and do everything over again."

Ramona nodded. "Have you thought about going over there?"

I jacked an eyebrow at her. "He's not answering my texts, so you think I should stalk him?"

"Not stalk, just … face him."

"Showing up over there would be crazy, which I realize I am, but that's, like, next-level crazy."

"Pen," Ramona said as she hooked her arm in my free one, "you're not crazy. You're a mess, but you're not crazy."

I chuckled. "Thanks?"

"I mean it. And Bodie's not going to think you're crazy, especially if you apologize. I think he'll give that to you. I've said from the jump that you need to just talk to him, and I think this might be your last chance."

My heart burst apart like it had been stuffed with a lit M-80. "You think?"

"I do, on all counts. Go over there and talk to him. Tell him you're sorry. Either he'll tell you thanks, but no thanks or he'll take you back. Either way, you'll know."

"So either I'll be happy or miserable. That sounds super promising and not at all terrifying."

Veronica chuckled. "Penny, you're not afraid of anything but this *one thing*. I'm with Ramona. I say you should try so you can put it behind you. You're miserable. It's weird and very Four Horsemen."

"I know," I said on a soft laugh. "I'm sorry."

"Don't apologize for how you feel." Ramona leaned into me as we walked up to Taco Town. "But don't be afraid to do something about your feelings either."

She pulled open the door, and the smell of tortilla chips and greasy meat hit me like a wall of savory deliverance. I wanted to be with Bodie. I wanted to beg and grovel and get him back. And this was my last chance to do it.

"Okay," I said, standing up a little straighter. "I'll do it."

Ramona smiled, big and genuine and relieved. "When?"

And I sighed against the mounting pressure in my chest. "No time like the present. I've got a few hours—I'll swing by now. And maybe I'll bring tacos as a peace offering. He can't be mad at me if I'm holding tacos. It's a physical law of the universe."

Veronica laughed, and I only wished tacos were a guarantee.

The game glitched. Again.

I huffed and raked a hand through my hair, opening the code to comb through it. Again.

I'd done nothing for three days but work, sleep, and eat. My phone had stayed in my nightstand where I left it, and though I was fully occupied with the game, a little piece of my mind was always on Penny.

I was grateful for the distraction work provided.

Sorting through how I felt was too hard.

Numbers were simple. They didn't play games or lie—it was fact. You couldn't argue with math. It was unfeeling and logical and right.

It was a shame hearts didn't work the same way. They were the exact opposite of facts and reason. Hearts wanted what they wanted, regardless of the truth. And mine wanted Penny.

The sensible part of me—my brain—told me to just let it go. For the most part, I had. And the truth was, even though I wanted Penny, I didn't know if I wanted to be with her. Not at the status quo.

And that left me straddling the fence of her corral with no idea which way to go.

In any event, I had no time to expend on the decision. And that lack of time was a blessing, a bridge to put space between us that I desperately needed. So instead of thinking of the fight or how I missed her or how she'd hurt me, I filled my brain with ones and zeroes, a buzzing hum of logic that comforted me.

Well, not at the moment. At the moment, I was wrestling with the same string of code I'd been fighting since I woke up.

A knock rapped at the door, and when Jude answered and I heard the voice on the other side of the threshold, I spun around in my chair, stood numbly, and walked toward the sound.

The first and last person I'd expected to find on my welcome mat that day was Penny.

She stood in the hallway, sneakers turned in, shoulders rounded, red bottom lip between her teeth and eyes uncertain. She looked beautiful, sweet and beautiful and dangerous, with a bag stamped with the name *Taco Town* clutched in her hands.

Jude and I exchanged places at the door, and rather than moving to let her in, I stepped out and closed the door, leaving us alone in the hallway.

Somehow, she shrank into herself even more.

"Hey," she said simply.

"Hey," I echoed.

And then we stood there in the hallway with a thousand words hanging in the air.

She broke the silence. "I brought you some tacos."

Penny held out the bag, and I took it, opening it to look inside, not knowing what else to do. Five minutes ago, I'd been starving. Now I didn't know if I'd ever eat again.

"Thanks." I rolled the bag back up. "What's up?"

Her eyes were down, and she slipped her hands into her back pockets. "I … I'm sorry to just show up like this, but I hadn't heard from you, and …" She took a deep breath and met my eyes. "I'm sorry, Bodie. For everything. For bailing on you. For taking you to that stupid show. For hurting you. I'm … I'm sorry, and I was wrong."

I pulled in a deep breath through my nose and let it go. "Thank you."

Everything else I wanted to say piled up in my throat.

"I didn't want to go to the show, and I tried to argue, but I … I just wanted to see you so badly, and I didn't want to upset you any worse than I already had, not until I had a chance to talk to you." She took a breath and looked down again. "I know I don't deserve you, and I don't deserve another shot, but I need to know if I have one. Is there a way to go back? To fix things?"

I ran my fingers across my lips and tried to put the words together the right way. "Penny, I've gotta be honest. Right now, I am just … I'm so done. You're right; you hurt me, but I can't even blame you. But this isn't about the other night. This is about *us*. I can't keep up with you like I thought I'd be able to. You were always honest—you told me from the jump what you wanted, but I didn't listen. I thought … I thought I could tame you, convince you I was worth keeping. But I didn't think about what it would cost me. Play with fire and get burned, right? And, Pen—you are fire."

She took a breath but didn't say anything, just worked her bottom lip between her teeth, chin flexed like she might cry.

Please, God, don't let her cry.

"But the bottom line is that I can't deal with this right now. I've put so much on hold for you, for us, but now … now I need to go all in with the game, with my dream. Our meeting is tomorrow, and we've got so much to do that I don't have the bandwidth to figure out you and me. This game, Jude and Phil—this is my life. This is everything I've been working for, and it's happening *right now*. And I can't handle anything besides that. I'm sorry."

She nodded, her breath shaky. I could see she was definitely about to cry, and I wanted to scoop her into my arms and hold her, tell her I wanted her and needed her. But what I'd said was true. Penny was a white-hot flame, and I was made of wax. Holding her would ruin me.

"I'm sorry too," she said, looking up at me again with a smile meant to be brave.

That smile broke my heart into a thousand pieces, scattered on the floor with the broken glass of the penny jar.

She took a breath with shining eyes and said, "Hit me up, Bodie, if things change."

And I nodded and watched her walk away.

I hurried away from Bodie with tears burning my throat and sneakers flying as I rushed down the stairs and outside, dragging in a breath so heavy with humidity and pain and regret that I felt like I was drowning.

It was over.

It was over, and it was my fault.

I wrapped my arms around my ribs and walked with no destination in mind, only desire to get as far away from my problems as humanly possible. Maybe I could find a cheap, last-minute flight to Tokyo. Or Budapest. Or Mars.

The exchange had been everything I'd feared, except somehow infinitely worse in reality than my imagination had been able to conjure. The look on his face, the resigned tone, the sadness in his eyes when he let me down gently.

But there was no amount of care that could have stopped me from breaking completely when I hit the ground.

The lump in my throat was sticky and hard, and I swallowed it down painfully only for it to bob back up.

Over, over, over. The word echoed with every footstep.

I'd come for closure and gotten it. I'd gotten it so hard, I might never get over it.

chapter
twenty
Avalanche

P HIL PACED ACROSS THE WAITING ROOM OF AVALANCHE'S HEADQUARTERS IN Midtown, and I stared at my hands clasped between my knees with steam under the collar of my tailored shirt.

Jude seemed completely calm. The subtle façade of not giving a fuck in action. It was for show, though. He was just as nervous as the rest of us were.

We'd presented our demo to a handful of execs, which was weird to say since they were wearing jeans. One guy even had a T-shirt on with a binary joke on it that made me think of Penny. Because even then, even during our presentation, she'd found a way into my head.

I'd done all the talking, and when they had gotten their hands on the controllers and started to play, I'd found hope. Every one of them had gone wide-eyed, and as I'd pitched the story to them, their smiles had brightened just enough to betray their attempts to keep their poker faces on.

It had gone well. Very well.

But I counted on nothing as we waited for them in the lobby of their office.

My palms were damp and nerves shot as our hopes and dreams hung in the balance of a few quiet minutes.

It won't be the end if they don't take us, I told myself.

There were dozens more companies we could pitch to if this didn't work out, especially now that the demo was finished. But this … this was the holy grail, the absolute, the top of the list. The dream. The fact that we'd even gotten a meeting was unreal. The hopes of it getting better than that felt too slim to count on.

The doors to the conference room opened, and we were invited back, so we filed in and took seats. I was so nervous, I thought I might combust. But outwardly, I tried to keep cool, scanning their faces for some hint as to what they'd say.

Paul, the CEO spoke first. "I'd like to start by saying that we don't make a habit of keeping designers here while we talk, but I have to say—we were impressed."

Hope sprang, putting out the fear with a sizzle.

"You've hit all the high notes. The story is epic, and the twist … the twist just makes the whole thing sweeter. We see a three-game series over the course of six years. Breakneck, I know, but with our team and your brains, I think it's feasible. That is, if you're still interested in a partnership with us."

I blinked, trying to remember to breathe. "Absolutely."

Paul smiled. "Great. We've got to get with our team to put together the numbers, but we'd like to offer you a deal. This is one of the best demos we've seen—the hard work you've put into it is the real reason we feel comfortable taking the step—so we want you all to come in on lead positions to help us get the game produced just how you want it. You'll retain a level of control over everything—story, content, gameplay, UI—though it'll ultimately need approval. But I give you my word; this is your story, your vision, and because we like what we see, we'll put our trust in you. What do you think?"

I glanced at Phil and Jude, who nodded their approval. And then I smiled back at Paul. "I think you've got yourself a deal."

We beamed as we all shook hands, and with another meeting on the books to discuss details, the three of us headed out of the office. When we made it outside, we broke into jumps and laughter and back-clapping and bro hugs, and I thought my heart might blow from sheer joy. Because we'd done it. The hard work had paid off.

We'd just landed jobs at one of the best game design companies in America.

Once we caught our breaths, Phil pulled out his phone to call Angie, and Jude got his phone out too, wandering off to talk to who knew who.

Before I knew it, my phone was in my hand and my thumb was hovering over Penny's name.

I'd been so caught up that I'd forgotten we weren't okay. I'd forgotten I couldn't just call her, not without answering questions I didn't have a response for. Not without making a move I didn't know I was ready to make.

I pictured her face as she'd stood before me on my doormat, the smallness of her in the expanse of the hallway. She was all of a sudden the only person in the world I wanted to talk to, and the last person who I could.

The worst part was that I wasn't even mad anymore. I was hurt and sad and exhausted by her, but I wasn't mad. And I missed her.

A sick, masochistic part of me—my heart—wanted to give it another shot, wanted to hear her out and try again. The rest of me—my brain—told me I'd already slammed my hand in the door once, making a point of reliving the pain in an attempt to convince me not to do it again.

In the end, I figured they were probably both wrong. Because either way I looked at it, I was damaged, and I didn't know how or when I'd recover.

chapter
twenty-one
Moby Fucking Dick

MY ROOM WAS DARK EVEN THOUGH IT WAS AFTER NOON. BETWEEN THE STORMY day and my drawn curtains, I found myself happily miserable, buried in my sheets and blankets, listening to my Sad Panda playlist on repeat. I'd done nothing but work and sleep for two days, and that morning, I'd woken up at seven, completely rested and still completely exhausted. I existed in that in-between—that state of mind where you couldn't physically sleep anymore, but you couldn't get out of bed either, folding in on yourself like origami until you disappeared. So I'd made plans to do absolutely nothing on my day off besides lie in bed and stare at my wall.

There was just so much to think about. I counted my mistakes and regrets in a loop like "99 Bottles of Beer on the Wall," though less cheery and somehow infinitely more depressing and obnoxious. I'd exhausted my tears. At least, I thought I had. Every time I'd said it, they'd find their way back again, pricking the corners of my eyes.

It was over. And it was all my fault.

I sighed and rolled over, pulling a pillow into my aching chest.

My bedroom door flew open, and Veronica stood in the frame, hands on her hips like an unamused Wonder Woman. "Why are you still in bed?" she asked like she didn't know the answer.

I frowned and sank a little deeper into my blanket burrito. "Leave me alone, Ronnie."

"Nope." In three steps, she was at the foot of my bed with my blankets in her fists. She pulled, effectively subjecting me to the cruel, cruel world.

I scrambled to catch the covers before they were gone, but they lay in a pile on the floor, and Ronnie's hands were back on her stupid traitorous hips.

"Come on, smelly. You've been locked in here listening to Mazzy Star for days. You need a shower and a drink and a new playlist."

I covered my face with my pillow and curled up in a ball like I could hide. "Go away."

"Nope! Get up!" The bed dipped as she climbed on, stood up, and started jumping.

"Ugh!"

I flung a pillow at her, and she laughed, catching it midair to toss it behind her.

"Whoops, you lost another place to hide." She put a little more force into her bouncing, sending me jostling.

I grabbed another pillow and threw it but was thwarted again. "I hate you."

"Liar."

She giggled and stopped jumping, lying down next to me. Her face softened, her smile cajoling. "Seriously, though, let's go do something."

I pouted, curling up even tighter. "I don't wanna."

She rolled her eyes. "Real mature."

"Everything sucks."

"*Everything* doesn't suck," she corrected. "Just one thing."

I groaned. "But that one thing really, really sucks. I don't think he's going to call me."

She didn't answer right away. "Maybe not. Maybe so. You just have to wait and see."

"Waiting sucks too. Time sucks. Breaking up sucks. Everything sucks. See?"

"It's only been two days, Pen," she said gently. "Give him a little more time."

"He had his meeting. I wonder how it went. I wonder if he's okay." I paused. "I should call him."

She gave me a look.

"Ugh, don't look at me like that. Are you gonna slap my phone out of my hand again if I try?"

"Maybe."

I groaned. "But I can't call him. You're right. I'm trying to respect his space." My face bent under the weight of my conflict. "God, can't you just go sleep with Jude to find out what's going on over there?"

"Ha, ha." She pulled my last pillow out from under my head and pressed it over my face like she was going to suffocate me.

We laughed for a second, and then I groaned again. "This *sucks.*"

"All right, you win. Everything sucks."

"Thank you."

"But this is ridiculous."

My face went flat. "Thanks."

"What? It is, and you know it. Seriously, if I hear 'Fade into You' one more time, I'm going to open a vein. So let's get you cleaned up and out of the house. Even if just for a minute. Even if just for tacos."

"I don't want tacos."

One of her brows rose. "Wow. You really *are* fucked up."

"Told you."

"Okay, then call him."

"Oh, so *now* you'll let me call him?" I huffed. "I can't, and you know it. I literally just said that."

"I know, and I take it back. I'm changing my tune since my old tune is worn out, and you clearly don't want to hear it. If you want to talk to him, call him."

"He said he didn't have time to 'deal' right now." I made air quotes with one hand.

"I mean, I guess you can't really blame him."

"I don't," I said sadly. "I don't blame him at all. I blame me. I'm the one who did this. He's right; I kept all my feelings to myself, and this was the result. I hurt him, Ronnie. I don't even know if I deserve to have him back. So I'm at an emotional impasse."

She watched me for a second. "All right, then how about going back?" Somewhere in her twinkling eyes, I thought she might be baiting me.

I frowned. "What do you mean?"

"Let's get Old Penny back. The girl who doesn't do relationships because of exactly *this*."

A tiny sliver of hope shone on me as she continued.

"You're like this about guys because you don't want to get hurt. You just lived through a self-fulfilling prophecy. So, why not adopt the old rule again? Revive it. Bring it back from the dead."

I smiled for the first time in days as I relit the pilot light in my heart. "Yes. Yes! Old Penny is fucking smart. Feelings are dumb and stupid and ruin lives. I was so much happier when I had the rule and boundaries. You're right. I can't believe you're actually right. We should mark the calendar."

She laughed and pinched me in the arm. "Okay, so let's go out and prove how smart Old Penny is. We can go to Diesel and see Cody. Remember Cody? He always puts you in a good mood."

I sighed dreamily. "How could I forget? That's no man. That's a god, covered in tattoos. And he has that hair."

"Gah, that hair. That hair should have its own Tumblr."

I laughed, feeling less like my heart was going to fall out of my chest.

"Come on. It'll be fun. You can get back on the horse. Or the Cody. Whatever."

I laughed, but my insides knotted up at the thought of riding anybody but Bodie. "Okay. Let's do it."

She smiled and booped my nose. "Atta girl. It's gonna be okay, Pen," she said so softly and sincerely that I actually believed her.

My liner was winged, my heels were high, my shorts were short, and my mood was about as sturdy as piecrust—a thin, golden buttery façade over the gooey, messy, blood-red cherry filling. But I found myself strutting into that bar on a mission that felt awfully real even if it was bullshit.

Diesel was packed wall-to-wall with people. Everything in the bar was metal and brick and leather, dark and inky. The light fixtures were made of machine parts with naked bulbs and glowing filaments, and the bar itself was black brushed metal and my destination from the second we walked in the door.

We wormed our way up to the bar with smiles and arm touches, parting the crowd like Moses. Veronica pushed me in front, and I squeezed in between a couple of guys to lean on the bar, rack on display.

I spotted Cody at the other end of the bar, and he glanced at me and away before looking back to me with a whip of his head that was so fast, he might have sprained something. A slow smile spread across his face, and he jerked his chin at me in greeting.

Cody was one of those gritty, dirty tattooed types with the irreverent beard and hair a little too long, pushed back from his face with ruts from his fingers. The gauges in his ears were just big enough to be big without being obscene, and he not only had his nostril and septum pierced, but he also had snakebites—two rings on his bottom lip where, if he were a rattlesnake, his fangs would rest.

I'd had a boner for Cody since the first time I ever laid eyes on him, but he'd always had a girlfriend. I might love me some dick, but I'd never knowingly hook up with a guy with a girlfriend, so we'd kept it to flirting, but he was the number one reason why we used to come to Diesel. And when he made his way over, my insides went ballistic because:

1. He was gorgeous.

2. His eyes pinned me to the spot.

3. He wasn't Bodie, and him even looking at me like he was made me feel nineteen ways to wrong.

Cody leaned on the bar right across from me, ignoring everyone around me who'd been waiting.

"Damn, it's good to see you, Penny. Where the hell have you been?"

The guy next to me huffed and slapped a hand on the bar. "What the fuck, man? We've all been waiting longer than her."

Cody's eyes went hard as he glared at the guy. "You don't let a girl like *this* stand at the bar without giving her your full attention. And if you want a drink the rest of the night, I suggest you shut the fuck up and wait until I address you."

The guy pointed at Cody. "This is fucked up. Fuck this place!" And with that eloquent goodbye, he turned around and left.

Cody turned back to me, his gaze smoldering again. "Double Patrón, chilled?"

I smiled as discomfort twisted around in my stomach like snakes. "You remembered."

"Psh. You're impossible to forget, Pen," he said with a smirk, leaning a little closer. "Lean over."

I did, against my better judgment, and when I was half-bent over the bar, he leaned in close, his lips brushing my ear.

"Alley-oop," he said softly as he grabbed me by the waist and pulled.

I took the cue and lifted myself as he helped me onto the bar. I spun around on my butt until my legs were on his side of the counter and my feet dangled just outside the shelves of liquor and glasses tucked under the bar top.

My heart thundered its warning as I hung onto the edge and crossed my legs, locking my elbows and straightening my back. I felt like a pinup girl, and was pretty sure every eyeball in the bar was on me. A month ago, I would have been in hog heaven. In that moment, I'd rather be in a pig pen.

Cody kept on smirking, pouring well more than two shots of Patrón into a shaker. "How've you been? It's been too long since you've been in."

"Oh, I've been good. Just surviving." Surviving *Bodie* was the rest of that sentence, but, color me crazy, it seemed like the wrong thing to say in the moment. "How about you?"

He shook up my drink with his eyes dragging a path from my heels to the hem of my shorts, which were regrettably short. Sitting on a bar might sound sexy and brash and cavalier, but the truth was that it was sticky as fuck. I just hoped there was no grenadine. All I needed was a cherry stain on my ass to end the week on a high note.

"I've been waiting for you to come in. Sheila and I broke up."

My mouth popped open, and I blinked, noticing that he was shaking that shaker at his waist like he was pumping his dick.

"You're kidding." I had no idea what else to say.

He shook his head, not looking sad in the slightest, probably because he had me sitting on the bar like a trophy. "It's been over for a long time. Plus, I've had my sights set somewhere else."

Cody popped the top of the shaker and poured my drink, hooking a lime on the edge of the glass before handing it over. I took a sip, hands on my drink as he bracketed my crossed legs with his arms.

I'd been waiting for this moment for months, and here it was. The filthy, hot, tattooed, pierced bartender of my dreams had literally picked me up and set me on the bar to tell me he wanted to bang me. A month ago, I would have climbed him like a jungle gym. But when he ran his hand down the curve of my calf, I laughed awkwardly and chased his hand with my own, redirecting it.

"Straight to the point, huh, Cody?" I said, hoping I sounded cool. And then I swiveled around on the bar and hopped down, praying for that millisecond I wasn't going to break my ankle. I didn't, thankfully. "I'll see you later," I said over my shoulder with a smile.

"I sure hope so," he called after me as the crowd swallowed me.

My smile fell faster than a GTO hits sixty, and I stomped my way around the bar, scanning for Veronica.

I found her at a table. She was on her phone, texting so intently that she didn't even see me stalk up.

"Well, this is a fucking disaster," I shot and took a heavy pull of tequila. Too heavy. My face pinched up, and I shook my head to set it back to rights.

"What happened?" She eyed me.

"He fucking hit on me, that's what happened."

Her eyes narrowed. "And that's ... bad?"

"Yes! I mean, no, but, yes! He and his girlfriend broke up, and he picked me up and set me on the bar and touched my leg and—ugh!"

That stupid look in her eye was back, the one that said she had me right where she wanted me. "You had the white whale in your clutches, and you didn't snag him?"

I took another drink, this time more moderate. "Yep. I had Moby Fucking Dick in my harpoon sights, and not only am I uninterested, but I'm ... what is this feeling?" My face fell. "Is this what it feels like to feel offended?"

She laughed—that asshole.

"Oh my God," I groaned as I plopped onto a stool next to her. "I'm broken. Bodie broke me, and now I'm ruined." My chest ached, and I slammed the rest of my tequila to burn the pain away. "I don't want to do this, Ronnie."

Veronica smiled at that, just a little, just enough. "Well, well. I'm not gonna lie. I kind of hoped this would happen."

I sucked in a tiny breath and gaped at her. "Did you fucking set me up?"

She shrugged. "I had a feeling you needed a push. I mean, you *definitely* needed a shower, so even if that was the only thing that came of tonight, I was going to call it a win."

I set my glass down with a clink and glared. "You dick."

But she reached for my arm, her eyes caring even if she was a douchebag. "Pen, you said you didn't want to do *this*, Cody, tonight, boy-hunt, whatever. So what other choice do you have? You want Bodie, right?"

"Yeah, I do." I didn't know why I wanted to cry, but I did. It had been at least ten hours. I was due.

"Then what are you gonna do about it?"

A tingle worked across my skin, either from the tequila or the realization of the truth.

I couldn't go back because Old Penny didn't exist anymore. Old Penny had lost her heart to Bodie.

He had changed me, rearranged me, and as I sat in that bar with an empty glass in my hand, I knew I'd never be the same. Even if I'd fucked it up, even if I'd lost him forever, I'd learned something very important.

I wanted to trust someone else with my heart.

Bodie had shown me what it was like to be with someone I trusted, someone who cherished me and whom I wanted to cherish. He'd taught me that letting someone in was a risk, but the reward was immeasurable. I'd let him in, and I'd gotten hurt because I'd fought the feeling. For a second there, I'd fallen into him and let myself go, and that second had been so glorious, so perfect, that all I wanted to do was get the feeling back. I wanted to get *him* back. I wanted to give him everything in the same way he'd given everything to me.

I loved the way he made me feel, loved his mind and body and soul, loved the way he cared for me, the way he'd let me breathe and given me exactly what I'd needed, even when it hurt him. Even when I hurt him.

The truth of the matter dawned on me like a ray of sunshine, illuminating what I'd known all along.

I didn't want to trust just anyone with my heart. I wanted to give my heart to Bodie.

It was already his.

Right then, I knew I would do whatever it took to get him back. Even if it didn't work and even if there was no way back to him, I had to try. I had to fight for him.

The sweet relief of decision knocked all the weight off my shoulders so I could breathe again, and that pilot light in my ribs fired up, igniting me with purpose. And as an idea came to me, I only hoped he would give me one last chance.

chapter
twenty-two
Bail

I DROPPED MY HANDS INTO THE OCEAN ON EITHER SIDE OF MY BOARD TO WET THEM and ran them through my drying hair. Jude and I had been waiting on a decent wave for long enough that I was ready to call it.

I sighed and glanced down the line of surfers—all sitting on their boards off Rockaway Beach looking bored—then at the beach, dotted with sunbathers. It was my first session in New York, and if things had gone differently, Penny would have been one of those dots on the beach. She would have been my dot on the beach.

I imagined her letting me teach her how to surf, imagined her on a board laughing, and my mood sank even further.

"Ugh, man. Quit being so fucking mopey."

"This sucks. Let's just go."

He rolled his eyes. "Quitter."

"Bro, this is bullshit. We rode the subway for an hour to get here with boards and wetsuits, and it's nothing but closeouts. I told you to check the fucking reports, man."

"I did," he said with a huff.

"Liar. Nobody's getting a decent ride today. It's not happening, so why the fuck are we still sitting here? I mean, I appreciate you trying to cheer me up and all, but the longer we sit here, the more pissed I am."

"You're just bitchy because of Penny."

I narrowed my eyes at him.

He held up his hands. "Look, I'm not judging. I'm just saying."

"I'm not calling her, dude," I said for the hundredth time.

"I don't see why not. We were busy before, but we did it. It's over, so now you can figure out what you want to do about her. It couldn't hurt to just talk to her."

I rested a hand on my thigh and turned to him, making a face. "Seriously? Because if I talk to her and she says the right thing, I'll be right back where I started."

"Why's that a bad thing?"

"Because I don't know if I can trust her. Don't you think I want to call her? Don't you think I want to go right back to the way things were? Because I do. I want to so bad, I can't even stand it. But the problem is that there *is* no going back, and I don't know if Penny's capable of going forward."

"What if she is and you just don't know it?"

I sighed and shook my head. "I dunno, man. I don't know if I'm ready to put myself through that again. I'm scared of her. I care too much *not* to be scared. Maybe I just need a little more time. Space."

"Yeah, because that's going so well for you."

He wasn't wrong. I'd been reserved and in my own head ever since the concert, even worse since she'd come over with tacos.

I ran a hand over the smattering of stubble across my jaw. "I almost call her every day. I just don't even know what to say or how to handle her. I don't know what she wants from me or if I can even give it to her anymore. Because if she wants to pretend like we don't care about each other, I'm out. I want her. I want her for keeps, and I'm through playing games."

"Then you need to tell her."

"Man, you don't fucking get it. I can't just tell her. I can't guide her through this; she's got to figure it out and let me know. If I tell her what I want, who's to say she won't agree without really understanding what I'm asking of her? I can be patient, but I can't teach her this. I can't tell her what to do or what she wants."

"Don't you think she deserves the chance? She's waiting on *you*."

"Yeah, well, she shouldn't," I said, my throat tight as I lay on my belly and paddled away, angling for a wave that wouldn't last more than six feet, but I didn't care. I didn't want to talk. I didn't want to participate. I just wanted it all to go away.

I popped up onto my feet and rode the wave until it folded in on itself. When the barrel disappeared, I bailed, diving off my board and into the ocean, opening my eyes underwater to watch the wave roll away from me upside down, taking my hope with it.

twenty-three

What Part Of $\sigma=\lambda(\nabla\cdot u)I+2\mu\varepsilon$ Don't You Understand?

THE WHISKEY IN MY HAND WAS COLD, BUT IT WENT DOWN WARM AS I WALKED around the party the following night, trying to have a good time and failing miserably.

Jude had the idea to throw a party to celebrate our dreams coming true, and maybe if I'd lived in New York for more than a month, I would have been having a better time. Maybe if I knew anyone in New York besides Jude, Phil, and Penny, I'd have someone to talk to. But Jude was busy working the crowd, Phil was busy with Angie, and Penny was, of course, not there.

I paced through the people scattered all over the roof of our building, a common space strung with lights and dotted with islands of chairs. Everyone seemed to be having a good time—we'd even sprung for a DJ who spun actual records and a bartender who we'd tipped extra to get everybody tanked.

I walked to the edge of the patio, looking toward Central Park, the strip of darkness cradled in the light of the city with Penny on my mind, as she always was.

Jude and I had come home from Rockaway the day before with almost complete silence between us. Well, Jude had talked a lot, and I'd listened and responded when I was supposed to. But the whole way, I had thought about what he'd said, and when I had been alone in my room, I'd held my phone in my hand for a long time, thinking about calling her.

Because he was right; she deserved the chance to tell me what she wanted, and I needed to know. I just didn't know if I was really ready to hear it if it wasn't what I wanted to hear.

And that was the real truth of it. It was easier to leave that door open and wonder than to hear that she didn't want me like I wanted her.

But Penny had bolted after all, and I couldn't make her stay. In the end, she'd bucked me off and left me stranded.

She was wild, and I should have known better than to try to hold on to her.

Of course, the other thing about loving something wild was how it changed you. And I'd found myself changed for the better—having held her for a moment—and for the worse—the wounds from my grip on her still fresh and tender.

A deep sigh did little to vent the pressure in my chest, and I turned to head inside, exhausted beyond measure.

Jude was striding toward me looking suspiciously subversive, and my eyes narrowed. He'd been barring me from going downstairs all night.

I held up a hand. "I'm going down. Don't try to stop me."

He smiled. "It's cool. I won't. You've fulfilled your obligations tonight, so go ahead and mope all by yourself while we party until dawn."

I shook my head and rolled my eyes. "That trick doesn't work on me."

Jude shrugged. "Had to try."

He clapped me on the shoulder, and I headed for the stairs, lost in my thoughts, grateful to be alone as I trotted down to our apartment.

Except when I walked inside, I wasn't alone at all. And when I saw her standing before me, time stopped.

Penny stood in front of our computers next to a blank chalkboard on wheels looking afraid and hopeful and absolutely beautiful. Her hair was purple again and spilling over her shoulders, her fingers toying with the short hem of her gauzy black dress that was sweet, almost demure, though she hung onto her edge with the deep V and strip of broad lace around her waist where her skin peeked through.

My heart jumped in my chest like it was reaching for her, and my throat closed up, jammed with a hundred things I felt and wished for and wanted. A question was on my lips, and I opened them to speak, but she took a breath and beat me to the punch.

"They call me Pi because I'm irrational and I don't know when to stop."

A single laugh burst out of me, and she smiled, relaxing just a little as she stepped closer to the chalkboard.

She drew a line with a shaky hand, then drew another perpendicular line in the center to make a right angle. "I'm not always *right*." She drew another line at about the one hundred twenty degree mark. "And I know I've been *obtuse*." Her final line was at around the forty-five degree point. "But luckily I'm *acute* psycho, which makes me a little easier to deal with."

I folded my arms and squeezed, heart thudding, smile on my lips, disbelieving as my eyes and ears sent signals to my brain that my heart had always known.

"It's all fun and games until someone divides by zero, which I did when I took you to that godforsaken concert and that zero came between us. But even before that, I should have told you something I was too afraid to admit," she said as she drew two right triangles, backed up to each other to make a whole. "You and I are so right."

She drew a box on the chalkboard underneath the triangles with an anatomical heart inside without a single mistake, like it was second nature.

"I can't let you go, not without telling you how I feel, but I had to think outside the quadrilateral parallelogram to figure out how. Bodie, you're like a math book; you solve all my problems. And like decimals, I have a point."

She turned and moved toward me with her eyes so full of questions and answers and secrets and love that it broke my heart and healed it. My hands fell to my sides, my breath shallow, when she stopped just in front of me.

"I'm sorry. I'm sorry I was afraid, and I'm sorry I hurt you. You're the best thing that has ever happened to me, and I want to return that gift. I want to be your everything if you'll take me back. Because there's no equation in my heart that doesn't put you and me together and end in infinity. I'm all in, Bodie. All three hundred sixty degrees of me."

I took a breath and stepped into her, bringing her into my arms as my lungs filled with air, filled with her.

"You are one well-defined function, Penny," I joked quietly, holding her against my beating heart, searching for words. "This was all I needed—to know how you felt. If we're going to work, you've got to tell me. You've got to trust me."

"I do," she said softly. "Does this mean …"

I gazed down at her, drunk on her, smiling. "You know," I said as I brushed her hair from her face, "they say the best angle to come at something is the *try*angle."

"Do they say that?" She smiled, her eyes shining as she leaned into me, her breaths short.

"They do," I answered, thumbing her cheek, searching her eyes. "I don't want to lose you either, Pen. So I'll take your three-sixty and give you mine. It was already yours," I said against her lips.

And with the smallest of shifts, we connected, breathing out relief and breathing each other into its place.

Her lips were so sweet, the feel of her in my arms so much better than I'd been daydreaming about since I'd held her last. And all my fears fell away. All except one.

Slowly, reluctantly, I broke away slowly.

"You changed your hair again," I said as I slipped a lock through my fingers.

She nodded, smiling lips together. "It was a complete science experiment of pink-to-blue ratios, but it worked out. I really like this color after all. I think I'm gonna stick with it for the long haul."

"Penny," I started, looking down at her, hoping this was it, that she was mine for good, "I need to know you're not going to run when it gets hard. Because it will get hard, and I … I can't hang around on the fence waiting to see which way you'll go."

She nodded. "God, I hate that I've done this to you, that you'd question it. So I'll tell you now, and I'll prove it as we go." She held my jaw in her hands and looked into my eyes. "I'm here to stay. I'm not going to run, and I know it'll get hard. And you're right; we can't pretend like everything's fine when it's not. I can't be afraid to tell you how I feel, and you can't either. I promise to be honest with you if you do the same."

"I promise. But that's not the only reason you bugged out."

She took a breath and looked down. "No, it wasn't the only reason. I've never felt like this before, Bodie. For so long, I've suppressed all of this, hid from it, stopped it before it started, and now that I'm letting go of that, it's like learning how to walk. And I want this. I want you. But I'm scared."

I cupped her cheeks and tilted her face up to meet my eyes. "I know," I said softly, gently. "But I'm not going to hurt you, Pen. I want to protect you. I want to love you." My chest tightened as the word passed my lips.

"I want to love you too," she said as the fear left her eyes, "and I know you won't hurt me. All you've ever done is try to make me happy. So now it's my turn."

And when she stretched onto her toes, when her lids closed and lashes cast shadows on her cheeks, when she pressed her lips to mine, I knew without a doubt that it was true.

She opened her mouth and opened her heart, and I slipped in, holding her against me. She held onto me like she never wanted to let me go, and I did the same. Her hands found their way into my hair, her tongue sliding past mine, her back arching her body into my chest, bringing us almost as close as we could be fully clothed.

She seemed to notice the same thing as she brought the kiss to a close and ran her hands down my chest, tilting her chin to watch them.

"I missed you," she said.

I pressed a kiss to her forehead. "I missed you too."

My heart chugged under her palm.

"Should we go to the party?" she asked.

I knew for a fact it was the last thing she wanted to do.

I smirked. "How'd you know about the party?"

She smiled back. "Jude. I had his number. He helped me set this all up."

"No wonder he wouldn't let me come down," I said with a laugh.

"He told me they want the game, that you did it. You got the job. You chased your dream down and caught it, and I'm so proud of you. I wish I could have been here for you."

I held her close, full of gratitude and reassurance and utter joy. "You're here now. That's all that matters."

She smiled. "We should go up and say hi."

But I bent to grab her around the waist, picking her up as I stood. "Not a chance."

She wrapped her legs around my waist and smiled, and I slid my hands up her thighs to her bare ass.

I groaned and squeezed. "Fuck, Penny."

And all she did was laugh and kiss me.

I made my way into my bedroom, lit only by a lamp next to my bed, kicking the door closed behind me before tipping her onto the bed to kiss her, to press her small body into the bed with mine. And for a long time, we lay together in my bed—my hands in her hair, on her face, reverently brushing her collarbone, and her hands in my hair, on my jaw, riding the backs of my fingers as they traced the curves I'd thought I'd never touch again.

I could have kissed Penny forever. If I was lucky, maybe I would.

But our hands and lips and bodies weren't content with that and moved on their own. Her hips rolled gently against mine, stroking her body against the hard length of my cock, and my hips flexed in answer, my lips harder, my hand roaming to cup her breast through the thin fabric of her dress. When I thumbed the peaked flesh of her nipple between her barbell, she cupped my neck and whimpered. And that was all it took to lose my patience.

I backed off of her, and kneeling at the foot of the bed, I tugged off my shirt and flung it, hands moving for my belt and eyes on Penny shifting on the bed, watching me.

I popped my button and lowered my zipper, hooking my thumbs in the waistband to push my jeans over my ass and down my thighs, shimmying out of them with the help of Penny's feet.

I nestled my hips against hers, the fabric between her clit and my cock thin enough that I could feel everything—the balls of her piercing, the soft, warm flesh waiting for me. But I left her dress where it was between our hips and kissed her again. I kissed the sweetness of her lips and silently told her I'd take care of her. I kissed her neck and promised her she was safe. I kissed the space between her breasts, her heart thumping against my lips, and vowed I'd never break it.

My fingers pushed the strap of her dress over the curve of her shoulder until her breast was bare, and I ran my hand over the sweet, supple flesh, pressing myself into her with an ache in my chest from the weight of all I wanted and wished for and held dear. And my lips found hers again as our bodies wound together, a knot of arms and legs and hands whose purpose was only to bring us as close as we could get.

Her hips moved with intention, inching her dress up until we were skin-to-skin. She sighed through her nose against my cheek, gave the smallest of hums against my tongue in her mouth, and I wrapped my arms around her and squeezed. She tilted her hips to press the slick center of her to the length of my cock, and it was my turn to hum.

It had been too long without her, without *this*. And now that I had her in my arms again, it was beyond what I'd dreamed of. Because now, she was mine.

With every flex, she angled for my crown until I gave her body what it asked of me, backing up until the tip of me rested just inside her. I waited for only a moment before I slipped into her slowly in a motion that pushed a breath from both our lungs with every aching millimeter.

I pulled out and slid in easier, faster than before but still slow, deliberate, as if I could prolong it. As if I could make it last forever. And when I hit the end of her, when our bodies were a seam, she lay underneath me, bracketed in my arms, lids heavy and eyes full of love, and I committed every sensation—mind, body, and soul—to memory.

And when I kissed her again, it was with more emotion than I knew what to do with.

I pushed the other strap of her dress over her shoulder, wanting her skin on mine, and she wiggled her arms out and pushed the dress down her ribs. Every stroke of ink on her chest was brushed by my fingertips. The feel of her metal barbells and the soft flesh between impressed themselves in my palm. Her hood piercing pressed into the skin just above my cock, giving me a target, and I ground against it with every pump of my hips until she muttered my name, hooking her legs around my waist to twist us.

I let her guide me onto my back, our bodies still connected, hers rocking as she reached across her body and grabbed her dress, pulling it off, leaving her naked. And then she braced herself on my chest and raised her ass, dropping down on me achingly slow, working my body with hers, hips rolling.

Every time I disappeared into her, my pulse raced faster until my heart hammered against my ribs, and I sat, reaching for her, winding my arms around her, burying my face in her breasts, my hands cupping her ass to lift and lower her.

She clenched around my cock once, gasped my name—the sound sweet and right and everything—and her body tensed as she squeezed me so tight, so hard that when she came, I did too with a growl and a moan and the nerves in my body so raw and connected to herthat I vibrated like a tuning fork.

My hands flexed, holding her against me, rocking her gently as the last flickers worked through us. She curled into me, arms tucked into her chest and head under my chin. I wrapped my arms around her, so small and right and mine.

She was mine. I was hers. And that was it.

My fingertips skated the length of her back while we came down, and when she sighed—a heavy, satisfied sound—I lay back, taking her with me, pulling out of her. And as we lay there on our sides together, wrapped up in each other, I found myself so content, so happy. I knew right then and there that I'd do anything to hang on to that, hang on to her. I cursed myself for ever walking away.

Of course, as I slid my hand into her hair and kissed her, I realized I couldn't have stayed away. Penny and I felt inevitable that way. I hadn't stopped thinking of her any more than she had of me. And even though I'd been hurt, I couldn't imagine ever *really* walking away. We would have found a way back to each other.

The alternative hurt too much to even think about—I'd have lost my chance at *this*. Because holding Penny, I knew I could spend a thousand nights like this and never get my fill.

She stirred against my chest and kissed my collarbone. I kissed her forehead in answer and whispered I'd be right back before climbing out of bed to dart across the empty hallway to the bathroom. And when I came back with a washcloth and a smile, it was met with hers. She was curled up in my bed like a cat, looking sated and content and just as happy as I was.

I crawled to her, kissing her bare hip before rolling her over onto her back to clean her up, and she watched me with a purple strand of hair between her fingers and her lip between her teeth.

"I missed you," she said, her voice husky. "I was a mess without you."

I chuckled. "You're a mess with me."

"That's true. But so, so much worse without."

I shook my head, marveling over the night. "I can't believe you did all this. Where'd you get all the math material?" I tossed the washcloth in the general direction of my closet.

"Mostly the internet, but I asked one of the girls on set who's a real math whiz."

She reached for the covers tucked under my pillow and slipped between the sheets, and I followed her in.

"And you memorized it and everything," I said, still smiling as I pulled her back into my chest and our legs scissored together. I wondered absently if I'd ever stop smiling.

"Mmhmm. Ronnie made flashcards."

I laughed at that.

"I just … I'm sorry I didn't try harder sooner. I'm sorry I didn't tell you how I felt from the start."

"It's all right," I said quietly.

"But it's not. Bodie, I know it's no excuse, but I've been this way for a long time and for a lot of reasons that seem really stupid now." She took a breath. "You remember how it was with me and Rodney in high school?"

My fingers dragged across her shoulder blades and back again. "I remember."

"He used to manipulate me, gaslight me to make me think I was crazy, which made me crazier. It was like a self-fulfilling prophecy. And even at that, I never left him."

"Penny, you aren't responsible for what he did to you. And plus, we were just kids then."

She backed away and propped herself up on her elbow. "But see, it changed me. I looked at what happened with him and knew I didn't want to feel that way anymore, ever again. And in my brain, that meant not letting myself care about anybody. So I conditioned myself over eight years. And everything went along shipshape, until I met you. You came along with your dimple and torpedo cock and sank my battleship."

A laugh burst out of me, and she smiled.

"But then I was drowning. Clearly, I do not know how to swim. It was cruel really," she teased.

"I'm not sorry I sank your battleship, and neither is my torpedo." I propped my head on my hand.

Penny giggled, her cheeks rosy and smile warm. "I ain't mad atcha. That ship was a bucket of bolts." She paused, perking up. "Oh, I meant to ask you how your hand was."

I showed her my knuckles, which were almost fully healed. "All better."

She held hers up with a smirk— they were a little scraped up. "Mine too."

My brow quirked, and I reached for her hand to inspect it. "What happened?"

"Well, I couldn't let you be the only one to get licks in on Rodney."

A surprised laugh shot out of me. "You're kidding."

She shook her head. "He called you a loser, and I punched him in the eye."

I laughed even more and kissed the back of her hand.

"And then he called me a psycho, and I kneed him in the balls."

That one earned her a kiss on the lips.

"God, I wish I'd seen that."

"There might be a YouTube video out there somewhere. Who knows?"

I chuckled. "Well, I have a confession to make since we're confessing things."

One of her brows rose. "Oh?"

"Mmhmm." I watched her, smiling. "I knew from the jump that I wanted to be with you, and I knew I'd have my work cut out for me when it came to convincing you to let me stick around longer than a few dates."

Her mouth opened in a red O that wasn't at all serious. "You fucking sneak! Heart-ninja sneak, with your heart-ninja stars that make girls fall for you. I've been tricked."

I chuckled and rested my hand on her hip under the blanket. "More like lion tamer than a ninja."

She lit up. "Ooh, do you have a whip?"

"No, but I can get one." I leaned forward to kiss her, laughing through my nose.

"I like it. I'm the lion. How are you gonna keep me from eating your face off?"

"Just gotta keep you well fed." I pulled her hips into mine to show her just what I could feed her.

She laughed. "That'll do."

I smiled at her for a minute. "Scared?"

"Fucking terrified."

"Trust me?"

And she leaned into me, cupping my jaw as she said against my lips, "Without a doubt."

chapter
twenty-four

Donut You Know?

T HE SUN BROKE IN THROUGH BODIE'S WINDOW, SHINING A RAY OF LIGHT across his nose and lips, illuminating them from behind and casting them in shadows in the same feat of physics.

I didn't know how long it had been since I'd woken—not overly long, I didn't think—but I didn't care to move. I didn't care if my phone had a bazillion texts or if the world was on fire. All I wanted to do was lie there next to Bodie.

I watched him sleep with a smile on my face. His hand rode his chest up and down as he breathed slow and deep, and his hair was mussed, his face soft and young and beautiful. And in that moment, I swear I was the luckiest girl on the whole planet.

Somehow, he'd taken me back. Somehow, we were going to be together, and as scary as that was, I had no fight-or-flight urge at all. I had the love-and-snuggle urges instead, which was far preferable.

He pulled in a loud breath and shifted as he woke, and I lay there, practically bouncing as I waited for him to open his eyes.

When he did, they found mine, and he smiled.

"Hey," he said sleepily.

"So, whatcha doing today?"

He chuckled and rolled over to grab me and pull me into him, nuzzling into my neck. "Hopefully, you."

"That's a guarantee. Wanna spend the day together?"

"Mmhmm." He kissed my neck, slipping his thigh between my legs. "I wanna take you on a date."

"Ooh, fancy." I wrapped my arms around his neck and hitched my leg onto his hip.

"Fancy date for my shiny Penny."

I smiled and pulled him even closer. "Can we go by my place and pick up some stuff?"

"Yep," he said against my skin as his hand roamed down my ribs to my ass, his fingertips grazing places that made my heart speed up and hips squirm against his very morning wood.

I hummed and slipped my fingers into his hair. "Good. And can I stay the night again?"

"Pen, you can stay as long as you want." He licked the skin of my neck and kissed the hollow behind my jaw.

"You won't get sick of me?"

"Not possible," he whispered in my ear.

"But maybe it is; you don't know," I said as he cupped my breast, thumbing my nipple while he kissed my neck as if it tasted like honey.

"You're probably right," he muttered between kisses, shifting his hips to angle for me. "I'm sure today will be awful. All that talking." *Kiss.* "Hanging out." *Kiss.* "Eating." *Kiss.* "Fucking," he said as he pressed his tip against my pussy and flexed, filling me up with a *kablam* that made fireworks go off behind my eyelids.

I had no words after that. My lips were too busy with his. My body was too busy processing the feeling of him sliding in and out of me, full and then empty, over and over. My mind was too busy with the realization of just how gone I was over him. And my heart was too busy opening up to let him in.

Bodie fucked me slow and sweet in the golden morning sunshine, and I wished for a hundred more mornings just like it. My whole life, I'd been missing this, missing him, and now that I had him, I wouldn't give him up so easily. Maybe not at all.

A few hours later, we were laughing and holding hands and walking back to his place from mine. I'd packed a bag and gotten nailed good and hard in the shower, and found myself starving, so we ducked into a donut shop to grab a dozen.

He assured me it wasn't our date.

Just saying—I would have given him an A-plus if it had been.

By the time we got back to his place, I'd convinced him through begging—whining—to let me play his video game demo. He actually had the nerve to ask me if I knew how to use the controller.

Fortunately, he had Mortal Kombat, and I blew his mind up with all the things he thought he'd knew about me but had no idea. Nobody fucked with Sub-Zero. Not even Bodie, video-game-genius-of-the-world-and-my-heart.

And then I played his game.

It was glorious. For twenty too-short minutes, I ran through a temple solving puzzles and watched cut scenes that looked almost like they were out of a movie. While eating donuts and getting cinnamon sugar all over everything. While Bodie watched me like I was a goddess.

He made me feel like a goddess.

It was in the small moments—him smiling down at me as he opened the door to the restaurant that night, holding my hand across the candlelit table while we ate, the look in his eyes when he told me how happy he was.

But Bodie made me feel like *more.* He made me feel loved and treasured.

And the best part was that I loved and treasured him too.

At the time, in the moment, I couldn't place the feeling, the whisper of premonition. I just knew that my life would never be the same. I knew I didn't want to be without him. I knew he'd take care of me, and I knew I'd take care of him too.

That night, we made love in the moonlight. That night, I lost my heart to him forever, and I never wanted it back.

I had his instead.

epilogue

I T WAS JUNE IN NEW YORK, WHICH MEANT IT WAS HOT AS FUCK, BUT THINGS WERE looking up. A double scoop of salted caramel was in my hand-slash-mouth, and Bodie was smiling at me from across the table of the ice cream shop where I'd seen him for the first time since high school.

I moaned as I took a long lick of my ice cream, eyes rolling back in my head, hand resting on my very pregnant belly.

"Jesus, fuck, that is *so good,*" I mumbled around a full mouth, not even swallowing before I went back for more. "I swear, everything tastes better when you're knocked up."

He chuckled and licked his ice cream. "Feel better?"

"Mmhmm." I swallowed. "I'm sorry I've been such a raging bitch. It's just so fucking hot and I'm so fucking fat and I'm so fucking hungry. But this ice cream is *so fucking good.*"

"You're not a bitch, Pen."

I barked out a single laugh. "That's funny. I nearly slit your throat this morning for leaving your shoes in the living room after I almost tripped and fell and broke my neck. You know I can't see anything past this." I gestured to my stomach. "I haven't seen my feet in a month. Who even knows what my bush looks like."

He laughed. "Trust me, it looks perfect."

"Psh, you say that now. Wait until I push your baby out of it. God, my vag is gonna look like a roast beef sandwich." I frowned, bummed out. And just like that, I thought I might cry.

"Penny," he said sternly, "your pussy is pink and perfect and mine and nothing will change that."

I sighed and reached for his hand. "I fucking love you."

He smiled. "I fucking love you too."

"Even though I've spent a small fortune on fancy stretch-mark lotions?"

"Yep."

"Even though I'm crazy?"

"Especially because you're crazy."

I sighed and licked my ice cream. "You're the best, babe. You're like a unicorn."

"A sex unicorn?"

"I dunno what that is but clearly, the answer is yes." I pointed to my stomach.

"Hmm, well, the sex unicorn is horny." He took a lick, eyes twinkling.

I laughed, and the baby shifted and stretched. My hand flew to the spot. "Whoops. I woke Coco up. Sorry, cupcake." I patted the spot that I thought might be her butt as I took a full-on bite of my ice cream. My teeth stung, and I couldn't even care—I moaned like I was in a porno.

Bodie laughed and took a bite of his cone.

"This is all your fault, you know," I said, motioning to my belly. "You and your super sperm. Only I would be in the zero-point-one percent of the population who gets pregnant on birth control."

"Psh, that was all you. And the stomach flu. You puked your pill up three days in a row."

I shook my head. "I'm going with super sperm. Lucky for me, you're a hottie. Our baby is gonna be so pretty."

"Rock the Casbah" played over the speakers, and I lit up. "It's our song!"

He smiled at that, and I saw a little secret behind his eyes.

"Know what today is?"

My brow quirked. "June something?"

"Two years ago today, we sat right over there while you ate your ice cream just like that. And that night, we went to—"

"Circus!" I grinned stupidly as my lovesick heart sprouted daisies and butterflies. "I didn't even know what day that was."

He shrugged and ate his ice cream like it was no big deal. "I remember stuff like that."

"I can't even remember what I had for breakfast this morning," I said in utter awe. Why a guy like him wanted anything to do with the likes of me, I'd never understand.

"Bagel with strawberry cream cheese, lightly toasted."

I shook my head, giggling. "You're my dream guy, you know that?"

"I'm glad you feel that way."

He pushed a black velvet box across the table at me, taking another lick of his ice cream like it was a totally normal day and he wasn't giving me one of *those* boxes with what I was pretty sure was one of *those* things in it.

"Bodie," I breathed, my eyes on the box and ice cream dripping onto my hand.

"Penny," he said softly, a lightness to his voice that betrayed the heaviness underneath.

When I looked up at him, his face was soft and beautiful and perfect and made my insides turn to goop.

"I love you, and I don't want to be without you. Not ever. I've wanted you to be mine every day for the last two years, and I want you to be mine for every day for the rest of my life. I've had this ring since we found out you were pregnant, but I figured it would be best to wait until you were so big and dependent on me for foot rubs that you couldn't say no."

I laughed through a sob.

His voice softened. "I've been waiting for the perfect day, and I found it. Open the box."

I shoved my ice cream at him and wiped my hands off before picking up the box with trembling fingers. And when I opened it, the most beautifully simple ring lay inside, shining with diamonds and gold and promises of forever.

"Marry me, Pen."

I breathed for just one second, one savored moment where the man I loved told me he wanted me always, when the life we'd created stretched inside me, when everything was right and perfect and an absolute dream.

And then, I jumped out of my seat and into his arms as best I could weighing a metric ton, and he caught me as best he could with his hands full of ice cream cones.

"Of course I'll marry you," I said with my throat tight and heart singing. "I might be crazy, but I'm not stupid."

He laughed, and it was only then that I realized I was crying, my cheeks soaked and warm and aching from smiling.

And when I kissed him, he tasted like mint chocolate and love and forever.

acknowledgements

No book is written without the help of a massive support system, and here are some acknowledgements to some of those who were a part of this story.

Jeff Brillhart—You are a king and a savior, and without your love and support, I just couldn't even get through it. I don't think I'd want to. Thank you for always providing inspiration for these books. You're the reason I believe in love.

Kandi Steiner—How much hand holding could a hand holder hold if a hand holder could hold hands? I think we found the answer. #Freakoutcentral. Hopefully everyone finds Penny as amusing as you and I do. I

Karla Sorensen—There has never in the history of the world been a better critique partner than you. You know exactly what I need to hear when I need to hear it. You know how to cheer me on and bark at me like a drill sergeant in a way that is always genuine, always just what I need to get motivated. When it's hard, you're there, and in a handful of rambling voice messages, we can solve pretty much anything. Maybe we should try our hand at world peace.

BB Easton—Beastie, you're my hero, my soul sister, my brain twin. I had more fun plotting this book with you than should be legal. Every day you're here for me to pet my hair and tell me I'm pretty, even when I'm a smelly, bloated sack of garbage. How I ever got so lucky to find you, I'll never know, but I'll never stop thanking the universe for you.

To my many, many beta readers—You are all so appreciated. Your feedback shaped this book, shaped these characters, and that influence is as much of a part of the story as my heart is.

Penny Reid and Sara Ney—Here's to writing characters people hate with our chins up and our hearts behind them. Your pep talks gave me the courage to put my sassy, irreverent character out into the world, and I can't thank you enough for that.

Marcus Diddle—Thank you for your moniker. I'm sending Janet a T-shirt that says "I got Diddled by Diddle." She'll probably use it to clean toilets, and I'm totally cool with that.

To my editors, Ellie McLove and Jovana Shirley—you've once again made my story as clean and perfect as humanly possible. Thank you for your hard work and dedication to your work and mine.

Lauren Perry—You are a magical unicorn who finds me magical unicorns and produces magical unicorn photos for my covers. If you ever stop doing cover shoots, I might actually die.

To the bloggers—You make the book world go around. I see you, I appreciate you, I love you, and I thank you for everything you do,

And to you, reader, thank you for your love, your support, and for reading my words. I wouldn't be where I am without you all, and I love you for picking this up, for following me, just for being.

also by
STACI HART

CONTEMPORARY STANDALONES

Bet The Farm: A small town enemies to lovers
romantic comedy, coming January 2021

Bright Young Things
Fool Me Once
Everyone wants to know who's throwing the lavish parties, even the police commissioner, and no one knows it's her … not even the reporter who's been sneaking in to the parties and her heart.

Hidden Gem
Preorder for May 2021

The Bennet Brothers:
A spin on Pride & Prejudice
Coming Up Roses
Everyone hates something about their job, and she hates Luke Bennet. Because if she doesn't,
she'll fall in love with him.

Gilded Lily
This pristine wedding planner meets her match in an opposites attract, enemies to lovers comedy.

Mum's the Word
A Bower's not allowed to fall in love with a Bennet, but these forbidden lovers might not have a choice.

The Austens
Wasted Words (Inspired by Emma)
She's just an adorkable, matchmaking book nerd who could never have a shot with her gorgeous best friend and roommate.

A Thousand Letters (Inspired by Persuasion)
Fate brings them together after seven years for a second chance they never thought they'd have in this lyrical story about love, loss, and moving on.

Love, Hannah (a spinoff of A Thousand Letters)
A story of finding love when all seems lost and finding home when you're far away from everything you've known.

Love Notes (Inspired by *Sense & Sensibility*)
Annie wants to live while she can, as fully as she can, not knowing how deeply her heart could break.

Pride and Papercuts (Inspired by *Pride and Prejudice*)
She can be civil and still hate Liam Darcy, but if she finds there's more to him than his exterior shows, she might stumble over that line between love and hate and fall right into his arms.

The Red Lipstick Coalition

Piece of Work
Her cocky boss is out to ruin her internship, and maybe her heart, too.

Player
He's just a player, so who better to teach her how to date? All she has to do is not fall in love with him.

Work in Progress
She never thought her first kiss would be on her wedding day. Rule number one: Don't fall in love with her fake husband.

Well Suited
She's convinced love is nothing more than brain chemicals, and her baby daddy's determined to prove her wrong.

Bad Habits

With a Twist (Bad Habits 1)
A ballerina living out her fantasies about her high school crush realizes real love is right in front of her in this slow-burn friends-to-lovers romantic comedy.

Chaser (Bad Habits 2)
He'd trade his entire fortune for a real chance with his best friend's little sister.

Last Call (Bad Habits 3)
All he's ever wanted was a second chance, but she'll resist him at every turn, no matter how much she misses him.

The Tonic Series
Tonic (Book 1)
The reality show she's filming in his tattoo parlor is the last thing he wants, but if he can have her, he'll be satisfied in this enemies-to-lovers-comedy.

Bad Penny (Book 2)
She knows she's boy crazy, which is why she follows strict rules, but this hot nerd will do his best to convince her to break every single one.

The Hardcore Serials
Read for FREE!
Hardcore: Complete Collection
A parkour thief gets herself into trouble when she falls for the man who forces her to choose between right and wrong.

HEARTS AND ARROWS
Greek mythology meets Gossip Girl in a contemporary paranormal series where love is the ultimate game and Aphrodite never loses.

Paper Fools (Book 1)
Shift (Book 2)
From Darkness (Book 3)

about the author

Staci has been a lot of things up to this point in her life: a graphic designer, an entrepreneur, a seamstress, a clothing and handbag designer, a waitress. Can't forget that. She's also been a mom to three little girls who are sure to grow up to break a number of hearts. She's been a wife, even though she's certainly not the cleanest, or the best cook. She's also super, duper fun at a party, especially if she's been drinking whiskey, and her favorite word starts with f, ends with k.

From roots in Houston, to a seven year stint in Southern California, Staci and her family ended up settling somewhere in between and equally north in Denver. When she's not writing, she's reading, gaming, or designing graphics.

www.stacihartnovels.com
staci@stacihartnovels.com